Finding our Way
Through the Dark

...an astrological companion to
Mysteries of the Dark Moon...

*its
Progressed
lunation
phases*

FINDING OUR WAY
THROUGH
THE DARK

The Astrology of the Dark Goddess Mysteries

DEMETRA GEORGE

International Standard Book Number 0-935127-36-4

Cover art by Molly Sullivan
Cover design by Daryl Fuller

Printed in the United States of America

Published by ACS Publications
5521 Ruffin Rd
San Diego, CA 92123-1314

First Printing, October 1995
Second Printing, December 1995

ACKNOWLEDGMENTS

I wish to acknowledge my mentors in the lunation cycle teachings from whose writings I've gleaned much of the information presented in this book: Dane Rudhyar, Marc Robertson, Joanne Wickenburg, and Leyla Rael; and to my first teacher Virginia Dayan who gave me my foundation in humanistic astrology.

I pay special tribute to Dane Rudhyar for bringing to light the ancient teachings on the phases of the moon and articulating them in contemporary psychological language.

Gratitude to my family and friends for their encouragement, support and patience: Daniel, Reina, Artie, Jimmy, Michelle, Jacob, Mary Lou, Jack & Jean, Larry & Barbara, and my circle of women students—Maggie, Cathy, Arlene, Mara, Avana, Susan, Sharon, Lala, AJ, Theresa, Scarlett, Wendy, Suzette, Joan.

Thanks to all the people who participated in the various Mysteries of the Dark Moon workshops over the last six years for helping to mid-wife this book, and to Vicki Noble and Barbara Morgan who sponsored many of them.

My appreciation to Chagdud Tulku and Tsering Everest for my understanding of Buddhism.

Once again, I am especially grateful to Douglas Bloch, whose editorial help in the final stages enabled this book to come into manifested form.

Demetra George
May 1994
Waldport, Oregon

Invocation

Hail! Goddess of the New Moon and God of the Rising Sun
Guardians of the East
Keepers of the Winds
Protectors of Birth and Beginnings
We honor your clarity, insight and wise luminosity
Kindly accept our offerings and songs of praise
Om Tare Tam So Ha
Please bestow upon us the Brilliant Clear Light.

Hail! Goddess of the Waxing Moon and God of the High Noon Sun
Guardians of the South
Keepers of the Fires
Protectors of Fertility and Growth
We honor your courage, creative will and wise generosity
Kindly accept our offerings and songs of praise
Om Tare Tam So Ha
Please bestow upon us the Radiant Gold and Amber Light.

Hail! Goddess of the Full Moon and God of the Setting Sun
Guardians of the West
Keepers of the Waters
Protectors of Fruition and Fulfillment
We honor your compassion, healing, and wise union
Kindly accept our offerings and songs of praise
Om Tare Tam So Ha
Please bestow upon us the Healing Lavender Rose Light.

Hail! Goddess of the Waning Moon and God of the Midnight Sun
Guardians of the North
Keepers of the Earth
Protectors of Completion and Release
We honor your silence, strength, and wise action
Kindly accept our offerings and songs of praise
Om Tare Tam So Ha
Please bestow upon us the Shadowy Silver Hued Light.

Hail! Goddess of the Black Moon and God of the Black Sun
Guardians of the Center
Keepers of the Void
Protectors of Death and Rebirth
We honor your utter, naked, honest truth-seeing
Kindly accept our offerings and songs of praise
Om Tare Tam So Ha
Please bestow upon us the Light That Shatters Delusion.

May All Beings Be Blessed.

Table of Contents

INTRODUCTION

Finding Our Way Through The Dark is the companion volume to *Mysteries of the Dark Moon: The Healing Power of the Dark Goddess* (Harper San Francisco, 1992). *Mysteries of the Dark Moon* explores the mystery, wisdom and healing power of the dark phase of the moon's cycle as a lunar-based model for moving through the dark times in our lives with understanding, consciousness, and faith in renewal. It offers a new vision of darkness, providing a psychological, mythical, and spiritual perspective on the shadowy, feminine symbolism of the dark moon, and furnishing ways of cultivating the darkness's regenerative powers.

Many of the ideas that I presented in *Mysteries of the Dark Moon* arose out of my practice as a counseling astrologer. While listening to the stories of several thousand clients and friends, I gradually began to see how important it is to give people a vision of how they can best pass through and better understand the deeper meaning of the many major changes and transitions, often in the guise of crises, that life presents to everyone.

Finding Our Way Through The Dark explains astrological techniques whereby you can apply the philosophical concepts presented in *Mysteries of the Dark Moon* to your own life. This book is written primarily for the astrological community. However, parts of it are also directed to non astrological persons in the hope that they can follow some of the simpler exercises and benefit from the information. Those of you who are new to astrology may want to first obtain a copy of *Astrology For Yourself: How to Understand and Interpret Your Birth Chart* (by Douglas Bloch and Demetra George, Wingbow Press, 1987) as a primer on the language of astrology.

> **In order to do the workbook sections you will need a
> copy of your natal birth chart and a lifetime lunar phase
> report. If you do not already have these, you will find
> information in Appendix C about obtaining them.**

The Nature of the Dark Moon Phase

The story that the moon tells is of birth, growth, fullness, decay,
and disappearance, followed by rebirth and another growth cycle.
The new, full, and dark phases of the moon are prototypes for the
emergence, fulfillment and completion of any life process. Like
the waxing and waning of the moon, all life unfolds in cycles. In
every cycle, there is a naturally occurring dark phase when the
life force seems to disappear for a period of time. The purpose of
the dark phase of cyclic process is for retreat, healing, transformation and preparation for renewal. It symbolizes a necessary
stage that involves the death of something old, and a descent into
the darkness out of which the birth of something new proceeds.
The ending of any life structure periodically moves all of us on
journeys through the darkness and back into the light.

The activation of the dark moon energies often corresponds to
times of change and transition when we experience a personal
loss and pass through a period of disruption and grief. This
can occur when we are immersed in the closure phase of a relationship, job, belief system, family responsibility, living
environment, or addiction. Whenever we face the loss of that form
which has given our life a structure and us a sense of identity, we
are caught in the chaos of formlessness, and we may experience
free-floating anxiety. What has been is no longer, and what is to
come has not yet appeared. We may feel overcome by an immobi-
lizing depression, locked into the grief and mourning of our loss,
or trapped in the madness of the uncertainty of our situation.

The dark moon phase spans the transition between the destruction of the old and the creation of the new. This process is
called transformation, a process that occurs whenever any life
form has fulfilled its purpose and used up its store of vital energy.
It then becomes necessary for that form to be broken up in order
to liberate the contained energy to be revitalized, recharged, and
made available again for infusion into a new life form.

The transformative process destroys old patterns of thought
and behavior that hold us back. Old concepts and their correspond-

ing life structures, which prevent growth or no longer serve a creative purpose, need to be eliminated. Much pain and agony may arise in the process of releasing our vital energy from useless forms or habitual nonproductive psychological patterns, but this is also the very energy that will nourish us and enable us to push onward toward new growth. The end result may not become apparent until we have clarified and enacted our new vision, and this often takes some time.

The Fear of the Dark

Because modern belief systems have lost or discarded the ancient teachings that death is a natural part of cyclic rebirth, we have been conditioned to fear and resist the great, dark unknown. Therefore when we encounter the inevitable endings and transitions in our lives, we experience them as terrifying because they threaten our known security with loss of love, abandonment, isolation and disintegration. We often react with terror, panic, chaos, or despair and therefore miss the inherent opportunities available in the dark phase of cyclic process for healing, inner wisdom and renewal.

The contents of the closure phase of the cyclic process have been labeled "dark," shrouded in mystery, perceived as threatening, and promoted as taboos. As the conscious ego rejects and denies the experiences of the dark phase, these contents grow to embody our worst fears and assume the frightening form of the demonic "shadow" in individuals and society. The societal attitudes toward people of color, female sexuality, menstruation, menopause, the occult, the unconscious, the psychic arts, the aged, and death itself are all manifestations of these fearful dark-moon projections.

Most of us do not realize we all have many dark-phase times in our lives, and that these are naturally occurring periods in any life cycle. We fail to understand that endings are the precursors to new beginnings; thus when our life rhythms move us into and through these dark phases, we are ignorant of what is actually happening. We find ourselves frozen in fear or panicking in desperation. We are afraid that henceforth chaos, uncertainty, and pain will be lifetime burdens, and this feeling engenders more fear and panic.

We experience the qualities of the dark of the moon at many times and in many ways. We periodically go through times lasting from several days, to weeks, months or even years during which the dark-moon, closure-phase energies are operative. These are the timings for death and renewal transitions in our lives. In the same way that we go to sleep each night in order to feel rejuvenated for another new day, there exist other periods of turning within that ask us to let go, pull inward, purify, distill wisdom essence, and wait in the still silence for renewal.

The opportunity for this inner work exists not only in the days preceding the new moon each month, but also every night in the last hours before dawn or awakening and, for women, every month when they menstruate and after menopause. Each year the dark phase energies are also prominent in the month before our birthday, in the shortest days of sunlight in the weeks before the Winter Solstice, and in the last frozen part of winter before spring thawing.

There exist generic periods when everyone experiences the dark phases at the same time or at similar ages. In addition, there exist specific individual dark-moon phase periods in our personal life cycles. Many esoteric traditions teach that it is possible through the ancient systems of astrology, tarot and numerology to predict and identify the timing and duration of these closure-phase, transitional periods in our lives. For example, in numerology, the dark moon phase corresponds to a nine year, and in the Tarot to a Hermit/Crone year.

To gain the wisdom and healing that dark moon periods bring us, our images of the dark must be revised. This is a courageous movement toward accepting the wholeness of our being that challenges our misogynic cultural conditioning of fearing the great, dark unknown. By revisioning the dark, we can come to know the dark phase of cyclic process as a place of healing and renewal rather than one of fear and dread.

The Structure of This Book

In astrological cycles the symbolism of the dark phase of cyclic process is expressed in many ways. Each month, the final dark phase of the moon's cycle occurs in the several days preceding the new moon. The astrological term for this dark phase is balsamic. While everyone experiences the energies of the balsamic moon phase for a few days each month, some people, approximately one-eighth of the population, are born during this phase. These individuals carry the dark moon energies as one of the basic thematic patterns that permeate their entire lives.

Because of one of the timing systems in astrology, referred to as progessions, everyone, no matter what their birth lunar phase is, goes through a progressed Balsamic phase for three and one-half years during recurring thirty-year cycles. The progressed Balsamic phase, which for some people occurs three times during their lives, is one of the major dark moon phase periods. The teachings concerning all of the natal lunation phases, the progressed lifetime lunation cycle, and the progressed Balsamic phase will comprise the first section of *Finding Our Way Through The Dark*.

Another important dark moon phase symbol in astrology is the twelfth house. The twelfth house is the final closure phase in the wheel of the houses and has to do with all that is hidden from the conscious awareness. The twelfth house is said to rule over karma, the unconscious, the collective, and the spiritual. The sign on the cusp of the twelfth house and its ruling planet, as well as planets and asteroids contained within the twelfth house, have much to say about how we relate to this hidden dimension of our lives. Those people who have a full or powerful (in both a constructive or problematic sense) twelfth house are impacted by the dark moon energies as part of their basic personality makeup.

However all of us experience the activation of our potential twelfth house energies for several days each month when the Moon by transit passes through this house, and for one month each year when the Sun by transit passes through our twelfth house. In fact whenever we have any planetary transits through the twelfth house, and especially the transits of the outer planets Jupiter, Saturn, Uranus, Neptune and Pluto, our unconscious life is stirred and disturbed. The teachings of the twelfth house, both natally and by transit, will comprise the second section of *Finding Our Way Through The Dark*.

In earlier cultures that worshipped the Moon as the Goddess, the dark phase of the lunar cycle was personified by various Dark Goddesses such as Lilith, Moira, Medusa, Hekate, and Persephone. In astrology, there exist asteroids, planetary bodies that orbit between Mars and Jupiter, that share the names of these Dark Goddesses. *Mysteries of the Dark Moon* relates the mythical biographies of these Dark Goddesses who in the modern psyche express today as the feminine shadow, the denied and rejected aspect of feminine wholeness. This aspect of the dark feminine needs to be reclaimed and honored in both women and men in order to heal our relationship to the two most powerful forces of our capacity to regenerate ourselves – death (endings) and sex.

Some people have the Dark Goddess asteroids in prominent places in their natal birth chart such as in a close aspect to the Sun, Moon or angles, or completing a major aspect pattern. These individuals carry the Dark Goddess energies as primary archetypes in the personality. For others, these goddesses become activated for certain time periods when they are transited by the outer planets. The third section of *Finding Our Way Through The Dark* will help us to identify how the Dark Goddess asteroids and the dark moons operate in our birth charts, both natally and by transit.

Other astrological indicators of the dark moon energies are the void of course moon periods, lunar eclipses, the South Node of the Moon, the planet Pluto, and the final year(s) of any planetary return cycle, such as the year before the Saturn return. These teachings will comprise the fourth section of this book.

Utilizing the understanding gained through the astrological techniques described in *Finding Our Way Through The Dark* can help us to confront and release our fears of the dark, of the unknown and of death itself. It can help us to access a part of our psyche that fear has shut down and denied and to release our negative images that create pain and suffering in our lives. Working through the exercises in this book will offer a healing perspective that can enable us to transform the pain around the dark times and dark issues in our lives, and empower us to welcome the periodic and natural dark phase times as openings into our inner wisdom. We must learn to revision the dark, know it as the journey of our renewal, and tap the secret healing and empowering wisdom inherent during the many dark moon times in our lives.

SELENE

Selene, Goddess of the Full Moon
Winged and crowned, she drives the lunar chariot
across the night sky.

CHAPTER 1

THE LUNATION CYCLE

Astrology is the study of cycles—the cycles of orbiting planets in relationship to themselves and to each other. Any two moving bodies orbiting around a common center have a cyclic relationship to each other. Periodically, they may align along the same radius as viewed from earth and then we say they are conjunct at the same degree of the zodiac. The faster planet gradually pulls away from the slower one until they are at the maximum possible distance away from each other. This is called their opposition point. The faster planet then begins to draw back, coming ever closer to the slower planet until they align and conjunct again. This constitutes one turning of their cycle together.

The flow of energy through a cycle has the qualities of both a circle and a spiral. As a circle, every cycle has a beginning, a middle and an ending that returns to the beginning. As a spiral, each new cycle makes a shift to another level where it both recapitulates the previous one and moves beyond it.

In *Mysteries of the Dark Moon,* I used the cycle of the sun and moon as metaphor for the nature of all cyclic processes. The sun and moon are the two brightest and most prominent astronomical bodies in the sky that surrounds us. And, we can easily see their ever-changing and moving relationship in the visual imagery of the phases of the moon.

Together the sun and moon embody the principle of polarity both in our physical world and in our psychological nature. In our daily lives, the alternating rhythms of the sun and moon regulate our day and night cycles. As the sun rules the daylight of consciousness and the outer objective world, the moon rules the night of the unconscious and our inner intuitive, instinctual life.

In astrology, the sun and moon are the two primary symbols of human personality, and each has a wide range of individual symbolic meanings. However when two planets are considered in terms of a cycle of relationship with each other, the slower planet and the faster planet each have a distinct function in the accomplishment of their mutual objective. The slower planet signifies the shaping or determining action, while the faster planet shows how this action will be carried out.

The *sun*, which is the slower of these two bodies, represents our conscious life purpose. It is a symbol of our power and will which seeks to actualize our life's purpose. The *moon*, the faster of the two, shows the manner of acting out our purpose in our daily activities. It corresponds to our personality as a vehicle through which to channel the radiant solar energy and transform it into a concrete manifestation of what we were born to be.

The moon's phases depict the moving and changing angular distances between the sun and moon in their monthly cycle of relationship with each other. From now on we will refer to the cycle of the moon's phases as the lunation cycle. The lunation cycle follows a pattern of the moon increasing and decreasing in light as she separates from the sun and then returns back to him.

In order to perceive the meaning of the moon's dark phase, it is first necessary to understand the entire cycle. The successive phases of this cycle describe the process by which any life form unfolds and continually renews itself. This life form can refer to the life cycle of a plant, of a person, or of a relationship, belief system, business, creative talent, etc.

The Dynamics of the Lunation cycle

The moon circles the earth every twenty-nine days, and each night reflects a different amount of the sun's light. We describe these changes as the phases of the moon. At the new moon conjunction each month the moon, poised between the earth and sun, is at the closest point to the sun (in the lunation cycle as viewed from earth) and we do not see any reflected light. As she pulls away she slowly grows from the sliver of the waxing crescent moon, increasing in light until totally illuminated at the full moon opposition. Then, as the moon wanes, she gradually decreases in light until the dark phase, when she is invisible and has returned to the sun. These varying amounts of light reflected during this cycle display her

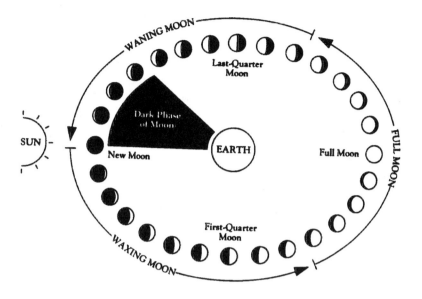

fluid and ever-changing relationship to the sun as it is experienced from Earth.

The teachings concerning the lunation cycle as a whole, including the dark phase, are not commonly studied and practiced by many astrologers today. Yet as far back as 35,000 years ago, the ancients used lunar phases to keep track of time on pieces of notched bone and stone[1]. These first calendars noted the correlation between the twenty-eight days of the moon's cycle and the twenty-eight days of a woman's menstrual cycle. Early peoples therefore concluded that the moon must be feminine and personified her as the Great Goddess, a symbol of the transformative power of feminine energy. Like much other evidence about matriarchal roots and women's roles in prehistory which has been forgotten, the significance of the moon's phases in contemporary astrology has not been given widespread attention.

As the ancients saw the rapidly moving moon change place, shape, and color, and disappear and reappear, the waxing and waning moon came to symbolize the cycle of change and transformation. As the Great Mother Goddess, the moon was perceived as the fertile matrix out of which all life is born and into which all life is reabsorbed. The story that the moon tells is of birth, growth, fullness, decay, disappearance, with rebirth and growth again.

The essential movement of all life is cyclic in nature, and all life forms have cycles of birth, growth, death and renewal which are mirrored in the progressive phases of the moon's cycle. The moon turns from new to full to dark, and likewise all living things resonate to her instinctual rhythm of emergence, fulfillment and completion. All that lives, all that is alive, resonates to the rhythmic beat of the moon and the sun, tapping out the reoccurring pattern of how life creates, fulfills, and destroys itself, only to be reborn anew.

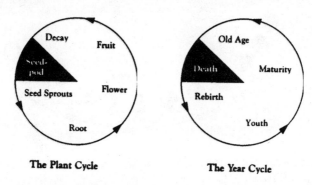

The Plant Cycle   **The Year Cycle**

And so, in Dane Rudhyar's words, we give homage to the Moon in her dance with the Sun.

"The relationship of the moon to the sun proceeds according to a wave pattern of increase and decrease in light, or separation from and return to the sun. The cycle begins at the new moon, when the moon is lost in the brilliancy of the sun. A day or so later, the thin crescent of the moon appears in the western sky after sunset. At "first quarter" the moon is half-full and elevated at the zenith while the sun sets. The zodiacal distance between the two Lights keeps increasing as the moon also increases in roundness and in light; until moonrise in the east coincides with sunset in the west. The rays of the setting sun run alongside the surface of the earth to become reflected in the lunar mirror. Because she is completely distant, yet face to face with the sun, the moon has become truly equal of the sun. She can release the fullness of the sun through the night to earth-creatures who can now receive the solar "seed-idea"

in its completeness—who can commune with the sun by assimilating the fullness of the lunar Eucharist.

Then, as if because of her gift to the earth, the moon, gradually depossessed of her light, seems to slow her motion in order to draw closer to the sun, yearning for his radiance. At the "last quarter" phase, she is seen at the zenith while the sun rises. Ever stronger, the pull toward the sun compels her to rise later and later in the night until, about three days before the cycle's end, she rises as dawn already begins to color the eastern sky. The following days she is seen no longer, lost as she is in the exalted light of the sun. She communes with the sun, to be filled once more with the potency of light—that she might be able to again to make of it a gift to earth-creatures ."

...Dane Rudhyar (2)

Dividing the Cycle into Phases

Each time a new cycle begins, something is born. This life form grows and develops because the need exists in the larger environment for what it can potentially become. When it has fulfilled the purpose for which it was born and used up its store of vital energy, the life form dissolves. As it disintegrates, it provides the fertile compost to nourish the next new life. Let us now look at how the phases of the moon illuminate the forces of life and death flowing through cyclic process.

In humanity's attempt to conceptualize the holistic meaning of the moon's cycle, various cultures have subdivided it in terms of two hemispheres, three phases, four quarters, eight cross-quarters, and twenty-eight mansions. Each lunation phase, or division of the cycle, represents a certain quality and kind of energy that is utilized at a particular stage in the growth and development of any organic form. Every time the cycle is further subdivided, each additional phase reveals a more subtle and refined meaning of the process.

The threefold division, based on the triangle, (the delta of a woman's body), consists of three phases: the new moon, the full moon, and the dark moon. We will discuss this threefold division of the moon's cycle as the ancient Triple Goddess in greater detail in our chapter on the Dark Goddess asteroids.

In the following discussion, we will look at the lunation cycle from the perspective of a twofold, fourfold, and eightfold process.

Dividing the Cycle by Two

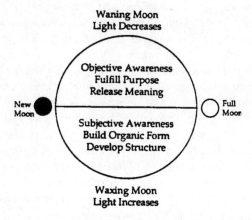

Dividing the cycle by two yields the waxing and waning hemispheres. Each hemicycle has a distinct function and purpose. During the first half of the cycle when the moon's light is waxing from the new to full moon, the life energy is increasing. The movement is to initiate a seed impulse and spontaneous growth, in response to a pre-existing need. The process operates in an instinctive and unself-consciousness manner, building structures that can contain and support the germinal intention. With ever more reflected light, awareness of what is happening and why, grows. At the full moon there can be an illumination of purpose.

The light, having reached its maximum, begins to wane as the moon starts her approach back to the sun. During the second half of the cycle, meaning is infused into the forms that were built during the first half of the cycle. The mind, rather than the instincts, now predominates, operating in a fully aware and conscious manner to fulfill the purpose.

Dividing the Cycle by Four
These two hemicycles, the waxing and waning phases, can be divided again into four quarters. In the lunation cycle, this quartering is displayed as the new moon, the first quarter moon, the full moon, and the last quarter moon. These four lunar quarter phases mirror the symbolic meanings of the four directions, and their corresponding seasons, elements and cardinal points.

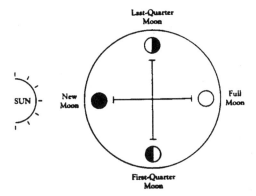

During the first phase of this four-fold sequence, from the *new moon to the first-quarter,* the impulse of the evolving life energy is to emerge and move forward. It is a time to initiate action toward new goals and aspirations. Awareness is subjective and movement is instinctual. This phase corresponds to the direction East, the season Spring, the element air and the rising sun with all of the implications of new beginnings.

The flow of energy during the second phase of the cycle from the *first-quarter to the full moon* seeks to build, stabilize and perfect the form that is being developed to contain the eventual meaning. It is a time of creative action, where struggle and challenge push the life entity toward growth. The energy is outgoing and vital. This phase corresponds to the direction South, the season Summer, the element fire, and the High Noon Sun. The attributes of power, strength, and will culminate during this part of the cycle.

It is in the period from the *full moon to the last-quarter moon* that the meaning is released into the form and the energy distributed. It is a time of fulfillment and accomplishment. The moon's maximum amount of reflected light brings objectivity and conscious awareness to both past and present actions. This third phase corresponds to the direction West, the season Autumn, the element Water, and the Setting Sun. The qualities of relatedness, emotions, and fulfillment infuse this part of the cycle.

Finally from the *last-quarter moon to the new* moon, the form is broken down and the meaning is assimilated into a new seed which is prepared during the dark moon. It is time for letting go of the old and preparing for the new cycle. Awareness turns inward, releasing the past and dreaming the future to be. This phase relates to the direction North, the season Winter, the element Earth, and the Midnight Sun. Silence, wisdom and renewal are the characteristics that are associated with this final phase.

Dividing the Cycle by Eight

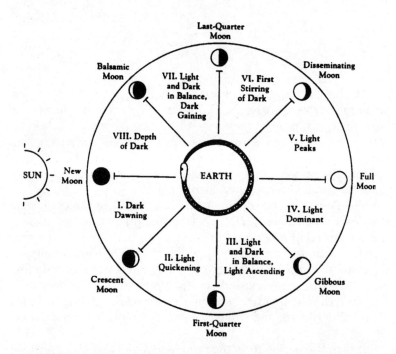

When the fourfold division of the moon's monthly cycle around the Earth is again halved, it yields eight distinct lunar phases. They are named the New, Crescent, First Quarter, Gibbous, Full, Disseminating, Last Quarter, and Balsamic. It is this eightfold phase cycle that will be explored in greater detail in the remainder of this work. We now will overlay the growth cycle of a plant upon the eight lunation phases to illustrate the successive stages of cyclic process by which life forms unfold, fulfill, complete, and renew themselves.

The process begins at the *new moon phase* when a seed, containing a new vision infused with an intention, germinates in the darkness. With the light of the waxing *crescent phase*, the first tender shoots of this vision have struggled to push themselves above the ground. During the *first-quarter phase* the life force of this vision takes root by establishing itself; its stem and leaf structure give shape to a strong, definite form.

The waxing *gibbous phase* corresponds to the development of the buds with the promise and expectation of the flower that blooms during the full moon phase. Now, halfway around the lunar cycle at the *full moon phase*, the vision is fully illuminated and infused with meaning and content. The waning gibbous phase, also known as the *disseminating phase*, corresponds to the fruition of the cycle, when the vision is acted on and lived out through the lives of humanity and thereby fulfills its purpose.

The *last-quarter phase* refers to reaping the harvest of the crop, when what has been realized throughout the cycle is ingested and assimilated. Whatever fruit is left on the vine begins to wither and decompose. The essence of the vision is then distilled into a seed capsule that is buried underground during the final *dark, or balsamic, phase* of the cycle, where it is nourished and prepared for rebirth. This germinal idea is subsequently released with the initiation of a new cycle.

The Lunation cycle and the Wheel of the year

This eight-fold cycle of transformation as seen in the increasing and decreasing light of the moon's monthly cycle is also evident in the increasing and decreasing light of the yearly solar seasonal cycle. Our seasonal cycle derives from the sun's apparent annual motion north and south of the equator. Ancient cultures charted this cycle, marking the solstice, equinox, and cross-quarter points, and then ritualized it through the agricultural mysteries that were celebrated in the Wheel of the Year.

These eight holy days, called Sabbats, were believed to be times of power when there existed a crack or opening between worlds. At these times the sacred energy of the cosmos could fully enter into the earth plane.

In the lunation cycle the new moon, which does not reflect any light, corresponds to the Winter Solstice (December 20-23), the shortest day of the year. The slim crescent moon slowly in-

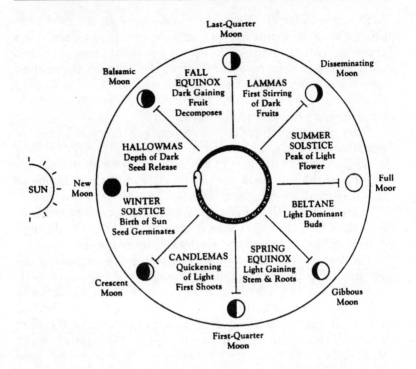

creasing in light corresponds to Candlemas on February 2nd when the days begin to lengthen. The first-quarter moon, which is half light/ half dark corresponds to the Spring Equinox (March 20-23) when days and nights are of equal length. The swelling gibbous moon corresponds to promise of longer days at Beltane (May 1). And the full moon, the time of the moon's maximum amount of reflected light, corresponds to the Summer Solstice (June 20-23), the longest day of the year. The gradually decreasing disseminating moon corresponds to Lammas on August 1st, with the first hint of lessening daylight hours. The waning last-quarter moon which again is half light/half dark corresponds to the Fall Equinox (September 20-23) when day and night are of equal length, but now the night force will predominate. The shrinking balsamic moon dissolving into darkness corresponds to Hallomas (October 31) and the shortest daylight hours of the year.

When the rhythm of the lunation cycle, with reference to the Moon as a feminine being, is reflected in the Wheel of the year, the Goddess is annually reborn at the Winter Solstice (new moon).

She is a fragile new hope at Candlemas (crescent), and a child at the Spring Equinox (first quarter). The maiden begins to menstruate and discover her sexuality at Beltane (gibbous), and becomes the mother of all life at the Summer Solstice (full moon). At Lammas (disseminating moon), she ripens into the maturing matron; reaches menopause at the Fall Equinox (last quarter); and completes her life cycle as the ancient crone preparing for death at Samhien (dark balsamic moon). (3)

In ancient cultures where the Wheel of the year was celebrated, the importance of both the female and the male principles was recognized. The fusion of male and female energies, resonating to the cyclical rhythms of birth, death and renewal, became incorporated into a body of ceremonies and rituals that were celebrated as the major transitions in the seasonal and lunar calendars. Sacred rituals developed depicting the annual solar cycle where the dying and resurrected young god, known in various cultures as Tammuz, Adonis, Damuzi, Baal, and Dionysus, also followed the Goddess's vegetative cycle.

In these traditions, the Wheel of the year symbolizes the story of the birth of the Son from the Great Moon Mother at the Winter Solstice (new moon), the emergence of the reawakened Goddess as daughter at Candlemas (crescent moon), and their growth together through the Spring Equinox (first-quarter) rebirthing the world. At Beltane (gibbous moon), the lovers celebrate the rituals of the Sacred Marriage, and consummate their union in the fertility of the earth at Summer Solstice (full moon). At Lammas (disseminating moon) the mature god dies and goes into the grain that is harvested at the Fall Equinox (last-quarter moon). By Hallowmas (dark balsamic moon), the dark phase of the solar cycle, the Moon Goddess mourns his sacrifice and she ages, but then she once again becomes pregnant with him. He is reborn along with the rebirth of the sun's light at the Winter Solstice.

For more information on the lunation cycle and ritual seasonal holidays as celebrated in the Pagan tradition, see *The Circle of Cosmic Muse* by Maria Kay Simms.

Whether this pattern of increasing and decreasing light is viewed through the lunar cycle or the solar cycle, both systems were used by early peoples to understand how life flows from birth to death and back to renewal.

Dividing the Circle by Twenty-Eight

Another way of looking at the phases of the moon was presented by the Irish poet William Butler Yeats in his revelatory book, *A Vision*. This book, partly channeled through Yeats' wife, outlined an elaborate metaphysical system relating variations of the human personality to the phases of the moon. Yeats described twenty eight archetypes which correlated to the twenty eight days that it takes the moon to revolve around the earth. This was not an astrological book, for Yeats did not assign his descriptions to the phase of the moon during which a person was born.

Then, in 1976, a book called *Phases of the Moon*, written by Marilyn Busteed, Richard Tiffany and Dorothy Wergen, took up the problem of assigning individual moon phases to specific portions of the lunar cycle. The book presented detailed and uncanny descriptions of twenty eight moon phases that correlated with the twenty eight archetypes in Yeats *A Vision*. In 1988, Martin Goldsmith published the book *Moon Phases: A Symbolic Key* in which he put forward his images and explanations of the twenty eight phases, also inspired by Yeats. If you are interested in exploring this system of phase division, please refer to the above sources.

The Vedic system in the astrology of India uses 27 *nakshatras*, or lunar mansions, each associated with a particular deity.

The Eight Lunation Phase Personality Types

As the sun and moon are individually such important factors in astrological interpretation, the relationship between them, depicted as the successive lunation phases, is equally significant. It was Dane Rudhyar who, in 1945, initially brought to light the ancient moon phase teachings. In *The Lunation cycle* (1961), he reframes and reinterprets this soli-lunar relationship in light of eight personality functions and types.

Each of us is born during a particular lunation phase, and we reflect the characteristics of that phase of cyclic process. Our lunation phase is determined by the angle of separation between the sun and moon at the time of our birth. Instructions on how to determine your own lunation phase can be found in the workbook section of this chapter on page 79.

The lunation phase at the time of our birth describes the core of our personality type and the nature of our ultimate life purpose. It is a major significator of personality because it describes the flow of energy between the two primary symbols of our being— our solar consciousness and lunar instinctive awareness. It indicates the kind of interactive energy that we can best utilize to express and actualize our life's purpose.

We experience the process of the eightfold lunation cycle on a monthly basis through moon transits, several times within our lives through moon progressions, as well as over the course of many lifetimes through cumulative cycles of death and rebirth.

Each month when the moon is in the same lunation phase as when we were born, we are more highly sensitized. Whatever we are feeling (Moon) tends to come closer to the surface of our conscious awareness (Sun), particularly concerning the relative meaning or lack of meaning in our lives (lunation phase). If we have a sense that we are 'on track' and flowing in our lives, we may feel especially happy and optimistic. On the other hand, if we are not sure of what we are doing or why, we may be overcome with depression or despair. Then the phase changes, and we often forget about that flash of insight until the following month when it surfaces again.

This phenomena of a brief period of acute sensitivity each month has a distinct biological correlation. Czechoslovakian researcher, Dr. Jonas, discovered that a woman can be fertile during her lunation phase each month, as well as midpoint in her menstrual cycle. Called the cosmic fertility period, there is the possibility of spontaneous ovulation at this time. This accounts for many unexpected pregnancies when women thought that they were carefully keeping track of the fertile midpoint days of their menstrual cycles. This sensitive period can also be used for the successful conception of a child or to help determine its sex and the viability of the fetus. (Astro Communications Services will calculate this fertility report for anyone who requests it.)

This is not only a biologically fertile time for women, but also a period of creative, mental, or spiritual fertility for both women and men. The reoccurrence of our birth lunation phase each month is our personal lunar power time when we can engage in any meaningful activity and get productive results. Whatever seeds we plant at this time can yield a rich harvest.

We are all born into one particular phase, and the major part of our awareness operates with this kind of energy. However life is not a static process. A timing system in astrology called secondary progression measures the movements of the planets in the

At the New Phase, the flow of the solar-lunar energy emerges, initiates and projects the seed impulse in an instinctive and subjective manner that will fulfill and complete a purpose as the remaining cycle unfolds. In the absence of light, the vision is felt, not seen. The symbolic seed germinates underground.

New
- Moon rises at dawn, sets at sunset
- Moon is 0-45 degrees ahead of the Sun
- up to 3^1/$_2$ days after official New Moon

DARK DAWNING

At the Crescent phase, the life impulse encounters a challenge as it must struggle away from the inertia of the past cycle, mobilize Its energy and resources and move forward. As the light Is stirring, first glimpses of the vision may be perceived. The symbolic seed breaks out of its seed casing and pushes its first shoots above ground.

Crescent
- Moon rises mid morning, sets after sunset in western sky
- Moon is 45-90 degrees ahead of the Sun
- between 3^1/$_2$ to 7 days after New Moon

LIGHT QUICKENING

At the First Quarter Phase, the life force must firmly establish itself in its environment and take direct action to build the organic structure that is to become the vehicle for the life purpose. With the light gaining, the structural outline of what is to be comes into form. The symbolic seed establishes its rout and stem structure.

First Quarter
- Moon rises at noon, sets at midnight
- Moon is 90-135 degrees ahead of the Sun
- between 7-10^1/$_2$ days after New Moon

LIGHT AND DARK IN BALANCE, LIGHT ASCENDING

The Gibbous Phase necessitates analyzing whatever was developed in the previous phase, and perfecting the form so that it can operate efficiently and effectively. As the light becomes dominant, there is a questing for revelation. The symbolic seed buds.

Gibbous
- Moon rises in mid afternoon, sets around 3 AM
- Moon is 135-180 degrees ahead of the Sun
- between 10^1/$_2$ - 14 days after New Moon

LIGHT DOMINANT

LIGHT PEAKS

Full
• Moon rises at sunset, sets at dawn
• Moon is 180-135 degrees behind the Sun
• 15 days after New Moon

The Full Phase is the flowering of the cycle when the meaning of the life purpose is revealed and must be infused into the structure built during the waxing half of the process. If the form is inadequate to contain the meaning, or the meaning is not worthy of the form, there can occur a breakdown, abortion or dissolution of the life impulse at this point. This is the peak of the light and total illumination of the vision is the promise of this phase. The symbolic seed flowers.

FIRST STIRRING OF DARK

Disseminating
• Moon rises at mid evening, sets at mid morning
• Moon is 135-90 degrees behind the Sun
• between 3½ to 7 days after Full Moon

The Disseminating phase corresponds to the fruition of the cycle. The seed germinated at the New Moon has now become what it was meant to be. The life impulse must fulfill its purpose by distributing the energy and disseminating the meaning. With the first stirrings of darkness, here becomes an urgency to live out and share the value of the meaning. The symbolic seed bears its fruits.

LIGHT AND DARK IN BALANCE, DARK GAINING

Last Quarter
• Moon rises at midnight and sets at noon
• Moon is 90-45 degrees behind the Sun
• between 7 and 10½ days after Full Moon

The Last Quarter Phase the life impulse has completed its mission, and now begins to reorient to a dimly intuited future. Rebellion against old patterns and break- down of old useless forms characterizes an inner revolt and crisis in consciousness. The dark becomes increasingly dominant as the life force turns away, diminishes and composts the old. The symbolic seed withers on the vine and decomposes.

DEPTH OF DARK

Balsamic
• Moon rises at 3 AM and sets at mid-afternoon
• Moon is 45-0 degrees behind the Sun
• between 10½ days after Full Moon up until the next New Moon

At the Balsamic phase, the life impulse distills and concentrates the wisdom of the entire cycle into a capsule of seed ideas for future visions. During the dark of the moon, the life force transforms the past into a mutation of the future and makes a commitment to seeding new concepts within old structures. The symbolic seed once again turns back into itself.

days after our birth, and it symbolizes the unfolding of our birth potential over time.

The progressed sun and the progressed moon move on after our birth, and via their changing angular relationship, called our progressed lunation phase, we also experience the qualities of each of the other phases as well in twenty-nine/thirty year cycles. Approximately every twenty-nine to thirty years the progressed Sun and progressed Moon come together at a conjunction point which astrologers call the progressed New moon phase. This occurs at different ages depending on the phase of the lunation cycle at a person's birth. We then initiate, fulfill and complete one entire turning of our life's unfolding meaning as we move sequentially through each of the lunation phases. Each progressed phase lasts for approximately three and one half to four years, and we respond to the prompting of each stage of cyclic process. We have the opportunity to utilize the various sun/moon energies at the critical periods of actualizing our life purpose.

When we place the events of our life against the backdrop of the progressed lunation cycle, two major shifts in consciousness can occur. The first shift occurs when what we had previously perceived as seemingly unrelated events take on a pattern of meaning within a larger whole. The second shift is a move away from a linear, sequential view of life as having a beginning, middle and end, with the end representing a final termination, toward a circular and spiraling perspective where each ending is seen as the preparation and prelude for the next beginning. Instructions for determining your own lifetime lunation phase cycles are contained in the workbook section of this chapter on page 54.

Finally, from a reincarnational point of view, it is suggested that we incarnate successively into each lunation phase during an eightfold sequence of lifetimes in the development of a certain experience or lesson. Our birth phase does not indicate how evolved or unevolved we are, but it does point to the stage of development within one particular cycle. We may be a new soul completing a final phase of experience, or an old soul initiating a new cycle of experience. In either case, our lunation phase suggests the particular lessons and qualities our evolving soul consciousness is being called upon to develop in this lifetime as it relates to a larger process and goal that will be realized over a series of lifetimes.

For those who do not include the doctrine of reincarnation in their belief system or conceptual framework, the lunation phase can describe the stage that our lifetime symbolically represents in the model of cyclic process.

In human personality there seems to be a direct correspondence between how much of the sun's light the moon reflected at the moment of birth, and the kind of awareness with which a person functions. With less light, an individual's awareness operates in an instinctive and subjective manner. With more light, the awareness operates with greater objectivity, fully conscious of what has gone before and how that relates to the present and future[4].

Let us now explore the eight lunation archetypes.

New moon phase
(Moon 0-45 degrees ahead of the Sun)
Keywords: Incarnate Emerge Project
The moon begins her dance with the sun at the New Moon conjunction. Astronomically, at this time there exists an alignment of the sun, moon and earth; the moon being between the sun and the earth. The moon's light side is facing the sun, and her dark side is turned toward the earth. At the new moon, we do not see any of her reflected light, and people born during this phase are symbolically coming out of the dark.

The keynote of New Moon activity is to germinate and emerge out of the seed capsule in order to begin an entire new cycle of activity. From a reincarnational perspective, it is suggested that New Moon people stand at the threshold of an eightfold cycle of incarnations where the evolving soul consciousness has an aspiration and intention to develop a new aspect of its growth, whether it be on the physical, intellectual, emotional or spiritual level. In this lifetime, the quest of the evolving consciousness is to inhabit a new body and to discover a new identity as vehicles through which to continue the unfoldment of one's larger meaning and purpose. New Moon people are not necessarily young souls; they may be old souls initiating another round of evolutionary development.

Because there is no visible light at the New Moon to reflect back to one's consciousness, the awareness of people born during this phase is purely subjective. New possibilities are just beginning to be intuited at deep inner levels, and as New Moon types venture forth, they function in an unself-conscious manner. It is their instincts coming from the natural wisdom of the body, rather than conscious mind, that moves them; and therefore their actions are often spontaneous and impulsive. They have difficulty in being aware of why they do things, and due to this are often regarded by others as being irrational in their reactions to situations.

In beginning a new cycle, New Moon people do not have a foundation of past experience to reflect or draw upon. Analyzing the past in order to act upon the present or decide the future does not have much meaning for New moon phase individuals. For them, the present is a unique moment, unlike anything that has ever occurred before, and it deserves to be responded to from that perspective. They do not function well according to others' predetermined plans, schedules or elaborate structures. They operate best when they can spontaneously plunge into new experiences without a logical reason or plan because they instinctively know the time is now and the place is here. New Moon people do not need to know in advance where they are going or how they will get there, as long as they can decide from moment to moment what to do next as new situations arise. Like space pilots exploring dark, uncharted territory for new worlds, New Moon people are here to fine-tune and hone their instinctual awareness as a guide to the unknown future.

Because this is the first phase of the cyclic process, there is a childlike innocent, open, and sometimes naive quality to many New Moon types as they encounter the myriad of life's experiences that open to them. They are not cynical and jaded like some of the later moon phase types who have symbolically been everywhere and done everything. The first phase of any cycle, like a newborn child, contains the maximum amount of vital life force. New Moon people demonstrate a fresh, energetic and enthusiastic approach as they project their nascent personalities into the world. They often have a star or charismatic quality to their personality as they radiate warmth, charm and vitality bursting forth with the need to be seen and noticed. New Moon personalities are strongly driven to project something new, but often do not consciously know just what that something is. Their vision of possibilities often involves an ideal, but it can be one's still confused and unformed ego that is instead impulsively erupting.

Many New Moon people feel dissociated; they sense they are in the world, but not of it. As the first phase of the cycle, one of the major challenges for new moon types is to fully enter into their bodies, gain a sense of their identity, and stamp this impression into their environment. An example to illustrate what this means comes from a Buddhist teaching about someone who has died, but who is not sure if he or she is really dead. The advice is to take a walk on the beach, and if there are no footprints left in the sand, this is a verification of death. Conversely, New Moon types need to leave those footprints in the sand to know that they have truly arrived in this incarnation.

Because they are unaccustomed to being in the world, New moon phase people may sometimes appear to be insubstantial, unreal, or overbearing. At one extreme of New Moon functioning, individuals may lack self-confidence because they do not know who they are. At the other extreme they may be obsessively self-absorbed, self-concerned or overbearing because they feel insecure about being acknowledged by others. These behaviors are the still young manifestations of the New Moon personality who is trying to become aware of his or her identity or aspiration.

While there is not yet enough light to fully see the shape of what is to happen and what the ultimate purpose may turn out to be, New Moon personalities are here to emerge, intuit some new possibility or potential, inhabit their bodies, project a strong image upon the screen of the outer world, and propel their movement forward in an instinctive manner.

Examples: Angela Davis, Queen Victoria, Sigmund Freud, Ringo Starr, Elvis Presley, Pablo Picasso, Florence Nightingale, Dalai Lama.

Crescent moon phase
(Moon 45-90 degrees ahead of Sun)

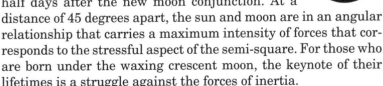

Keywords: Overcome Focus Move Forward
The Crescent phase begins about three and one-half days after the new moon conjunction. At a distance of 45 degrees apart, the sun and moon are in an angular relationship that carries a maximum intensity of forces that corresponds to the stressful aspect of the semi-square. For those who are born under the waxing crescent moon, the keynote of their lifetimes is a struggle against the forces of inertia.

In the plant cycle, the Crescent phase corresponds to the newly sprouted seedling, struggling against the force of gravity, to push its first tender shoots up through the thick dark soil. Likewise for the evolving soul, the urge to mobilize means that Crescent people must take charge of their new bodies, focus their energy, and relate to their dense, physical environment.

During this phase of cyclic process there is a dynamic tension between forces of the past and those of the future. As Crescent moon people begin to focus their vision and attempt to move forward toward actualizing this new possibility, all of their past patterns of resistance, inertia, and fear arise and refuse to budge. The backward pull of the past is embodied in the guise of crystallized habits which were carried over from the previous cycle of incarnations and now reside in the unconscious psyche as the karmic residue of the soul.

Crescent phase individuals may feel surrounded and overwhelmed by these "ghosts of the past"–their dependencies, unconscious patterns, habits, addictions, insecurities, and fears of the unknown. Their challenge is to break with the values, attitudes, or traditions of their culture or family of origin and develop a whole new social and economic identity for themselves. They instinctively realize that their very survival depends on their ability to do this. Yet they fear that if they are unable to do so, the outcome will be one of having to resign themselves to leading lives of quiet desperation, knowing their potential will never be realized. Imagine the situation of a person in his or her mid-thirties, still living with the parents in the room in which he or she grew up, and you can empathize with the fear that stands behind many Crescent phase individuals if they cannot pull away from the past conditions which seem to grip them. The resistance to moving forward in their growth is the essence of the resistance Crescents need to overcome in this lifetime.

However this is often a painful and difficult process because the feelings of Crescent people are so highly sensitized. Because they are susceptible to the emotional needs of loved ones, they are vulnerable to being emotionally manipulated and guilt-tripped by others. Also, their fledgling bodies are most secure in a known environment of safety, familiarity and comfort. It is this need for closeness and security that makes them so enmeshed in their past, whether it be the past of past lives, the past of childhood, or the past of last week. Because the Crescent life purpose is to impress the goal of some new intention into their psychological and emotional bodies, it calls for them to continually repolarize old habit patterns, relationships, or situations carried over from any previous experience which do not support expression of the goal and have no purpose or value for the future.

As Crescent people gradually overcome the resistance of old fears and insecurities, they begin to get excited with a sense of their new powers. However they may experience a shock as their imagined subjective possibilities clash with the realities of the outer world. They may become quite frustrated when their initial disillusionment contributes to the sense the vision will never work out, they just can't do it, or it may be more trouble than it's worth. On the other hand Crescent people can use these reality checks that take the form of obstacles and set-backs to test their growing strength and to nurture their increasing sense of capability. The flow of soli/lunar energy moves them to overcome the inertia of the past by pushing them to gather their resources and mobilize their energy toward actualizing their fledging identities, visions, and potentialities.

As Crescent literally means "growing one," the momentum of the cycle is increasing and these individuals feel the urge to move in the direction of fulfilling a goal that may still only be inwardly felt or subjectively understood. In order to do so, Crescent people need to make contact with the physicality of their environment and to discover the resources available to them. By developing their talents and skills and learning to express these new abilities in a tangible form, the Crescent types can build self-confidence in their ability to move forward. These people become strengthened as they successfully overcome obstacles and develop the qualities of self-reliance, faith in themselves, persistence and determination. As the Crescent moon types become more rooted in their new identity, their final challenge is to see and take advantage of the many opportunities in their environment that will open up for them, ones that can further their goal.

Examples: Indira Gandhi, Simone de Beauvoir, Vincent Van Gogh, John F. Kennedy, Dr. Benjamin Spock, Maria Montessori, H.P. Blavatsky.

First quarter phase
(Moon 90-135 degrees ahead of Sun)
Keywords: Decide Act Build

At the First-quarter phase the moon is half-full and steadily increasing in light. The moon has reached a 90 degree angle in relationship to the sun, their stance is one of squaring off each other. The first-quarter square generates a tremendous amount of tension. The momentum of the cycle is now strong and forceful.

In the New moon phase the evolving soul learns to inhabit its new body and follow the instincts. In the Crescent phase the cyclic movement is to focus the vision, overcome the inherent resistance, and develop skill to build self-confidence. Now in the First-quarter phase, the keynote is to take direct action towards firmly establishing the growing life force by building a structure that can support the actualization of the soul purpose. The plant, during this phase of growth, establishes its root system and puts forth its stem and leaf structure. The cycle must now become rooted in its new direction.

Like the racehorse chafing at the bit, First-Quarter people are ready to test their burgeoning strength. They want to reach out, shape, manage and control their environment. They are impatient with any limitations which restrict their movement and prevent further growth. If the new direction is to grow, any old patterns that were confronted and tentatively overcome in the crescent phase must be totally repudiated. Like pioneers settling new lands, these individuals must forcibly clear the way so that they can actively build new structures to contain their purpose.

First-Quarter phase people often encounter many crises in their physical world. On an inner level, the crisis, coming from the Greek word *crino*—to decide, comes from the necessity of circumstances forcing them to make a decision, to choose among alternatives, and to take action based on that decision. For many First-Quarters, an inability to decide is intertwined with fear, and perceived as lack of courage. Fear paralyzes the ability to take action, and any further growth is halted. First-Quarter people need to learn the importance of taking a stand and developing the maturity to actually do what they said they would do.

Another kind of crisis with which First-Quarter people must deal is the crisis that arises as a result of their taking direct forceful action to challenge the status quo or to manage their environment. First-Quarter people encounter antagonism and resistance from others who resent them for barging in, taking control, and redirecting the situation. But First-Quarter types have little tolerance for anything or anyone who tries to hold them back, restrain their expression, or prevent them from acting out what is trying to come to concrete manifestation through them. A strong will, courage, and confidence characterizes First quarter phase people, but a strong ego can easily become a dominating one and lead to ruthless and exploitive behavior.

Finally First-Quarter people seem to magnetize other people's crises as well in the course of their daily lives. They often live in a world filled with action, movement, crisis, conflict, and challenge. This is because First-quarter people are here to learn how to manage the huge amounts of energy that are released in all these crisis-producing situations. As old structures shatter and break apart, the First-Quarter challenge is to skillfully harness the released energy and refashion it into a new form that can support and facilitate whatever is trying to happen through them.

First-Quarter people can rise to the occasion when things fall apart. Because of their experience with meeting crisis after crisis, many have an instinctive sense of how to take control of the energy, manage, and redirect it so that the problem can be solved and business as usual can resume. Some First-Quarter types actually thrive on crisis as they become animated, energized, excited, and are able to shine at these times by becoming the heroes or heroines who save the day. They also experience an adrenaline rush released in response to this high-geared activity. For these reasons First-Quarters must become aware of the unconscious tendency to create unnecessary crises in their lives in order to be in the spotlight or to get their fix.

Those First-Quarter types who are still young and unskillful in their crisis-coping capabilities live in a world surrounded by an undercurrent of potential and actual chaos. They experience great tension, frustration, and anger as their potential supportive foundations collapse, pointing to their inability to build and maintain the structures that are necessary to support their evolving life purpose.

First-Quarter people feel the urge to move out from their known world, and it is through the structures that they build to

26 *Finding Our Way Through the Dark*

contain their life purpose that they establish their identity within a larger social context. The maturation of the First-Quarter type is demonstrated by commitment to taking deliberate action to develop workable and productive forms that can fulfill the need released at the New Moon, the beginning of the cycle.

Examples: Gloria Steinem, Shirley MacLaine, Joseph Stalin, Albert Schweitzer, Timothy Leary, James Hoffa, Alice Bailey

Gibbous Moon Phase
(Moon 135-180 degrees ahead of Sun)
Keywords: Evaluate Analyze Perfect
At the Gibbous phase, the moon is rapidly distancing herself from the sun and approaching her fullness at the full moon opposition point of the cycle. Mirroring the moon's increasing light, the evolving soul consciousness is becoming more aware that it is a separate self with a specific purpose to accomplish. Like the stage of the swollen buds in the plant cycle, there exists an air of anxious expectation that awaits the opening of the flower. As one is poised on the brink of this revelation, the keynote of the Gibbous moon phase is to improve and perfect the structures that were built during the first-quarter phase as worthy vehicles through which to express the life purpose.

The 135 degree sesqui-square aspect opens the Gibbous phase, and there is another confrontation of counter-forces related to those experienced at the 45 degree semi-square of the Crescent phase. Gibbous people experience a shock when they realize what is actually being asked of them, and all that this entails. They are confronted with a wall of resistance in the form of the physical world, and the reality of the environmental factors that need to be acknowledged and taken into account if they are to accomplish their goal. They are challenged to use the discordant forceful energy of the 135 degree aspect in a controlled and focused way to push through this resistance and overcome any obstacles that are slowing down the substantial growth that needs to occur during this phase of cyclic process.

In the First-quarter phase the life purpose was anchored and established through the form-building activity. Now during the Gibbous lifetime, people must live with the decisions made and structures built in the previous phase. However, the leap into Gibbous consciousness is the awareness that they can still improve upon these structures.

Symbolized by the 150 degree quincunx aspect between the moon and sun midway through the Gibbous phase, there is a kind of dissatisfaction that runs through many Gibbous people. They often perceive themselves and their life structures as falling short of their visions of perfection. However, the power of Gibbous phase people lies in their capacity to continually adjust and refine these structures, but they must develop the qualities of perseverance and flexibility in order to proceed. In this lifetime, Gibbous people are being tested in their commitment to their goal. Are they serious enough to persevere in the process of improving the forms which will facilitate the expression of their soul's purpose? And are they flexible enough to be able to adjust these forms to fit into everyday reality so they can be truly useful and effective for society?

The Gibbous dissatisfaction and drive for perfection of outer structures also manifests as a drive for inner self-improvement. This is what leads Gibbous people to continually analyze themselves, as well as others, and everything in their environment. They are trying to understand themselves in order to find better ways of operating and better techniques for doing things. They feel the urge to hone down to essentials, and eliminate whatever is superfluous and non-functional in their lives.

Steeped in analysis and questioning, their minds are sharp and keen. They are always asking the difficult questions of how and why things operate as they do, and what would happen if another method were used. They are at their best when they question the process of any operation, evaluate, analyze, adjust, refine, perfect, and then contribute new working patterns for more efficient functioning, whether it be on an inner or outer level. They can become obsessed with details, and need to remember that not everyone else has, or even should have, the same need for perfection.

The Gibbous desire is to become as skillful an artisan and technician as possible in their chosen field of vocation or expression. For this reason many Gibbous people go through periods of apprenticeship and training in order to master the skills, techniques, and methods that will enable them to contribute perfected forms that are of value to their society or group.

The light becomes dominant during this phase, and Gibbous phase people are involved in making the transition from subjective to objective awareness. There is now enough light for them to both sense and see that they are dealing with something larger than their own personal selfhood. They have developed the ability to link ideas to concepts which opens the possibility for illumination. Their instinctual senses are in a state of heightened expectancy, on the brink of clarity, that the why of what they are doing will soon be revealed.

Examples: Janis Joplin, Franklin D. Roosevelt, Sarah Bernhardt, Aleister Crowley, Hillary Clinton, Prince Charles, Barbara Walters.

The Full moon phase
(Moon 180-135 degrees behind Sun)
Keywords: Culminate Illumine Fulfill

At the Full moon phase the moon has drawn as far away from the sun as she will in their cycle together. At the opposition point, she shines in all her fullness. This completes the first half of the lunation cycle which began at the New Moon with a vision that was subjectively felt in response to a need. In the preceding phases, the evolving soul, guided by the instincts, built and perfected forms through which to express this vision. Now that the form-building process has been accomplished, in the second part of the cycle as the moon gradually moves back toward the sun, it is necessary for the evolving soul to progress from its instinctual body-oriented awareness into an awakened mental state. The next stage of the process is to develop the growth of one's consciousness and the ability to think before acting.

At this point, evolving Full Moon people must learn how to use their minds in order to be able to realize the meaning of their lives. They need to become conscious of the purpose for which the forms that have been built are intended, and then to infuse this meaning into their life structures. This is similar to the process of a carpenter building a house, which corresponds to the form. However it is not until the family moves into the house and transforms it into a home that the meaning of that structure is being fulfilled. The discovery of what it means to live a purposeful life with conscious intention is the crux of Full moon phase functioning.

Because the sun and moon are the two main keys to personality, Full Moon people who are born when the moon is directly opposite the sun can, in the brilliance of the reflected light, clearly see and experience the polarity between self and other. This is why the issues of relationship are so important to Full Moon people. Mirroring the stance of the sun and moon, at this point in cyclic process these people are called to integrate the polarities that exist within themselves. Until Full Moon people realize that this is an inner process, they may project their inner tensions outward onto their relationships. However, in either case, it is through the resolution of the inherent conflict with the *other* that Full Moon people develop objectivity and clear sightedness about the larger meaning of their life purpose.

The meaning of the opposition aspect speaks to two parts of the personality that are diametrically opposed, yet intimately related. When they function in unconscious ways, a person will experience them as an inner conflict—two parts of oneself pulling in opposite directions. And ultimately each one is prevented by the other from getting its needs fully met or operating at optimal capacity. The challenge of all planetary oppositions, but especially for Full Moon types whose sun and moon are the protagonists, is for each side to become aware of the existence, the nature, and the potential importance of the other. Through an understanding of the deeper issues around their struggle, the process is then to integrate the polarities by realizing, i.e. clearly seeing, some kind of larger structure in which the two can function meaningfully and consciously. Rudhyar says that, "successful polarization actualizes a person's latent capacity to bring to an objective manifestation a creative fullness of what is implied by two opposing functions." (5)

The birth of objective consciousness is the recognition of the other as separate from oneself. The movement of the evolution of consciousness is toward an openness to accepting, validating and including all differences within the larger whole.

As this process operates within the Full moon personality, the sun represents one's soul purpose and the moon signifies one's personality as the form, or vehicle, of that purpose. At the Full Moon, the sun is waiting for the moon to recognize him as being the essence of the purpose. The moon is waiting for the sun to recognize her as the means through which a purpose can be expressed and achieved. When the sun and moon can begin to operate together, integrating into a meaningful synthesis what had previously been separate, Full Moon people can enter into a conscious awareness of their life purpose.

Whatever has been developed up to this point in the cycle, for better or worse, is now fully seen in the light of the full moon. If the organic form is not adequate to contain the purpose, or if the purpose is not worthy of the form, Full Moon people can disintegrate and feel a deep-seated failure. They feel that they are like hollow empty shells, or that there is no meaning to their lives.

For Full Moon people this inner drama between their sun/moon polarity also manifests in their outer relationships. In the plant cycle, the flower opens at the Full moon phase. When women's blood cycles are synchronized to lunar rhythms, they will ovulate and likewise open sexually at this time. Inherent in this phase of cyclic process is the urge toward union and merging with the other in order to insure fertilization, the conception of the next seed, and the continuation of the life force.

Many Full Moon individuals conceptualize this search for meaningful union as the search for the ideal partner. We have all heard the lament, "If only I was with the perfect mate, then my life would have meaning and purpose." This search for meaning can become the search for the great love, the perfect partner, or the soulmate who is expected to make life worth living. Some Full Moon people's lives are often made or broken on the basis of how meaningful their relationships are. As ideal relationships are difficult to find and sustain, these individuals may also turn to a cause, belief system, great idea or guru/God/dess to provide the transcendent meaningful content with which to fill their life structures.

In the process of becoming conscious, the level of how well Full Moon people have integrated their inner polarities will be reflected in the quality of interaction in their outer relationships. Many Full Moon people cannot help but be drawn to relationships. But in order for their relationships to be meaningful, they must develop objectivity and clarity regarding how they relate to the other. As they clearly and fully see how their actions affect others, they must practice thinking before acting to make sure that their actions are considerate and meaningful.

Once Full Moon people have integrated their inner polarities, discovered their purpose, and consciously infused it into their life structures, they can then proceed to dynamically live out the meaning of their life within its larger context.

Examples: Elizabeth Barrett Browning, Gertrude Stein, Krishnamurti, Princess Diana.

The Disseminating Moon Phase
(Moon 135-90 degree behind sun)
Keywords: Distribute Disseminate Convey
The moon, most brilliant when at her farthest distance from the sun, now begins to long to return to him. The Disseminating phase unfolds about three and one half days after the full moon as the waning moon pulls in her light, hanging low in the night sky. In the plant cycle, the Disseminating phase corresponds to the ripened fruit that is ready to eat. For the evolving soul this lifetime is likewise the fruition of the seed vision that germinated five phases before. Having become aware of a life that can be lived with meaningful purpose in the Full phase, the keynote for Disseminating people is now to live out this purpose and spread the meaning.

Like the word disseminating, these people are here to spread out and communicate. The substance of their communication is the product of what has grown in them so far in the cycle. They are here to convey what they have found to be of value and meaning through their own experiences and what has deeply impressed them. This is a life of teaching what they have learned and sharing their wisdom. The form is now fulfilling the purpose for which it was intended, and Disseminating people need to display the fruits of their accomplishments.

Steadying their understanding and vision, Disseminating people focus on expressing themselves. For many, this communication takes place through talking, writing, networking, sharing, interacting, exchanging and working with others. As the life energy, mirrored by the waning moon, begins to collapse back in upon itself, Disseminating phase people take into themselves, assimilate, and embody what has been revealed to them. In the process, they integrate their values into a workable life philosophy. They can then communicate their vision, not only with words and activities, but also by living a conscious intentional life as a demonstration of their beliefs, or in the words of the Native American cultures, by "walking their talk."

When Disseminating people feel that they have an important message to share, an adequate vehicle with which to communicate it, and others who are interested and responsive, then they have a sense of their life being in the flow. By contrast, at those times when Disseminating people feel as if they don't believe in or care about anything, and no one is interested in hearing them anyway, they can be overwhelmed with a sense of the meaninglessness of life existence, "a tale told by an idiot signifying nothing." Self-validation for Disseminating people is based on their ability to express and share their understanding of something that is meaningful and which is consciously envisioned in a larger social context.

A potential difficulty that Disseminating people sometimes encounter is getting so caught up in their mission to imprint their message upon the world that they get lost in their causes, becoming fanatics. They cannot understand why other people don't accept the truth as they themselves see it. So they persist in relentlessly trying to convince others of the rightness of their own view, and fall into intolerant and narrow-minded attitudes and behaviors. Disseminating people need to realize that while it is imperative for them to spread their message, it is not necessary for everyone else to feel the same sense of urgency. Furthermore it is no indication of their failure if others do not take immediate action.

As Disseminating people move out to anchor their vision into a real world that is populated by others, they are drawn to group participation. Desiring to link with others, they become involved in collective efforts. Caught up in the swell of the group tide, they participate in advocating meaningful social action toward raising the consciousness of others in a particular area of life experiences. In the process, Disseminating people's minds become cross-pollinated through intermingling with others whose beliefs, ideas, and knowledge are different from their own.

The evolved consciousness of Disseminating phase people is one of being open, nonjudgmental and potentially inclusive of all views. Yet at the same time, this new material taken in from outside oneself inevitably leads them to question the assumptions and basis on which they previously acted. It is this confrontation between their former belief system, now having been expressed, and the new knowledge they've taken in during the process that precipitates the "crisis in consciousness" of the next lunation phase.

Examples: Jane Fonda, Helen Keller, Carl Jung, Ram Dass, Adolph Hitler, Bill Clinton.

Last Quarter Moon Phase
(Moon 90-45 degrees behind Sun)
Keywords: Reevaluate Turn Away Revise
The straight-edged moon at the Last Quarter phase is half-light, half-dark, and the light will now rapidly diminish. In the plant cycle the harvest is reaped, and whatever fruit is left on the vine withers and decomposes. In the previous Disseminating phase, the goal of the cycle has peaked and been accomplished. In cyclic process when the form has fulfilled the purpose for which it was intended and used up its store of vital energy, the movement is to let go of the obsolete dying form. The new seed that is forming must begin the process of severing itself from its parent plant. The keynote of the Last-quarter phase is that of reorientation away from what has already transpired toward some intimations of the future.

The second half of the lunation cycle is geared toward the realization of meaning, rather than the building of forms called for in the first half of cyclic process. Rudhyar called this phase a crisis in consciousness because the crisis that occurs at the Last-quarter phase is not one of action, but rather one of thought. Based on the exposure to different information encountered in the previous Disseminating phase, the evolving soul starts to question its previous beliefs and values. In light of this new understanding, it must then begin to discard old ways of thinking and behaving that no longer work and do not harmonize or fit into its developing consciousness. What had been built up must now be torn down.

Last-quarter phase people may experience this process as hearing those first grumblings of discontent that arise from within. Their lives are marked by a continual turning away from what they have accomplished. Disillusionment sets in as they are unable to continue a lifestyle that has become devoid of meaning. Last-Quarter people go through at least one major life-altering event where they are forced to probe deeply into the validity of their beliefs, philosophy, religion or values. This precipitates an inner psychological crisis where they must reevaluate all they've accepted as being true. They question, challenge, and often turn away from many of their taken-for-granted assumptions and values learned from their parents, society, and the collective. It is a lifetime marked by rebelling against the status quo and destroying old, limiting ideologies.

Last-quarter phase people must sever and let go of the conditioning into which they were born. If they cannot do so and instead try to meet their present life circumstances on the basis of an ideology that is no longer valid, many of the ways in which they go about living their lives will simply not work. Irritation and frustration over repeated failures can lead to anger and a sense of resignation about their inability to be effective in their jobs and relationships.

The crisis for many Last-Quarter people is one of trying to figure out how to disengage themselves from life circumstances that are based on a now-discarded belief system. Further adding to their growing tension is the fact that other people are often counting on them to continue and preserve some structure that they, in part, have been responsible for creating. Many Last-quarter phase people have difficulty in externalizing this process of inner change. The fermentation and decomposition of old belief systems generate much tumult and disturbance in their minds. They reject the old, but have not necessarily replaced it with anything else. They often maintain an aura of secrecy and protectiveness about themselves, not trusting that the outer world will accept their turning away. As a result, they tend to wear a mask of their old selves, acting and performing as expected, while on the inside there exists a state of total anarchy. When Last-Quarters are finally ready to reveal themselves, it may come as a great shock to others.

Rudhyar makes the astute observation that Last-Quarter people are being asked, for an ultimately constructive purpose, to be part of a destructive or destructuring process... which helps to break down whatever in oneself or one's community or society no longer positively contributes to evolutionary progress, but instead stands in the way.[6]

In the process of letting go, Last-Quarter people should not necessarily discard everything; there often remains something of the past that is of essential value and timeless meaning. This essence is their harvest of understanding from the cycle that they now need to infuse into the kernel of the next developing seed. Those people who were born while the waning moon is rushing to reconnect with the sun are called to reorganize their thought around some new source of creative potentialities. This image is as yet unformed; it may be only the vague outlines of something new intuited in the fading lunar light. In this way Last-Quarter people, through keen mental discrimination on an ideological level, participate in the formative visualization of the future-to-be.

The underlying pattern in the life of Last-Quarter types is the continual ninety-degree shift away from the attitudes and assumptions into which they were born toward the embodiment of an ideological system based on intimations of the future.

Examples: Isadora Duncan, Yoko Ono, Mick Jagger, Albert Einstein, Lenin, Annie Besant, Mohandes Gandhi, Anaïs Nin, Marc Edmund Jones.

The Balsamic Moon Phase
(Moon 0-45 degrees behind Sun)
Keywords: Distill Transform Envision

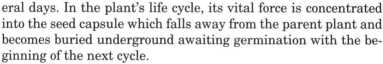

The thin slice of the inverted crescent moon now rapidly wanes, and it vanishes from sight for several days. In the plant's life cycle, its vital force is concentrated into the seed capsule which falls away from the parent plant and becomes buried underground awaiting germination with the beginning of the next cycle.

The Balsamic phase is the eighth and final phase of cyclic process. Since ancient times this "dark of the moon" was considered a mysterious and secret period, ranging from dangerous and unfortunate to one imbued with healing power and auspicious for magical rites. In the depth of the dark, the Moon Goddess rejoins the Sun God, and they perform their mysteries of transformation and renewal. The final phase of cyclic process bridges the death of the old and the birth of the new.

For the evolving consciousness, this is the closure-phase lifetime of the entire eightfold sequence of incarnations and therefore especially karmic in its implications. The evolving soul is called upon to distill the wisdom it has gained from this cycle of lifetimes and infuse this meaning into some new vision that will emerge in the future cycle. Those people born at the dark phase of cyclic process stand at the point where the old life force is being released, transformed, and prepared to be reborn at the New Moon. For this reason, Balsamic personalities are one of the most complex lunation types as they straddle both the past and future. Over the course of their lifetime they spend much time and energy desperately trying to tie up loose ends and bring to a conclusion multiple situations that always encumber them so that they might move forward into an unknown future that beckons them.

One major area where this phenomenon occurs is in their relationships. Balsamic people find themselves involved in many intense, but short-term relationships. These are not only romantic or mating liaisons, but also situations involving people they encounter at work, at school, in the community, and on vacation with whom they experience instant feelings of recognition and familiarity. An in-depth exchange soon occurs which is often felt on the soul level. Then, these people seem to leave the Balsamic person's life. This is not to say that Balsamic people don't have any long-term relationships; they can and they do. But simultaneously there exists a pattern of many brief, yet deep encounters.

In this lifetime Balsamic people are meeting many people from past lifetimes with whom they have unfinished karmic business. During this phase, they are given a chance to reconcile old differences, bring peace, and resolution, and heal broken hearts with those they have loved and hated over lifetimes. In this way Balsamic people have the opportunity to infuse kindness, decency, and acceptance into their relationship patterns that will bloom in future times.

Balsamic relationships are a means to something larger than the relationship itself; they serve a purpose in which patterns that have been working out over a longer span of time can be resolved and transformed. Once each relationship has been taken as far as it can within the context of this lifetime, it ends, and the Balsamic person moves on to another completion.

Born during the dark moon, Balsamic phase people are often the black sheep of their families. Life, as most other people live it, does not have much meaning for them. They rarely grow up to conform to their parents' expectations and aspirations, and at some critical point realize that how they are being raised will not prepare them for the demands of their future. Like the old plant decaying into compost, Balsamic people must often make a conscious break with or destroy some aspect of their past or identity. Thus Balsamic people are often specialists in endings, closures, terminations, and finalities of all kinds, knowing when something is over and it's time to move on.

Even as youngsters, Balsamic people know that there is something different, out-of-synch, about themselves. This sense shows up most poignantly during adolescence when these individuals discover that very few of their peers can relate to or understand what they are thinking and feeling. It may be only with older, or more serious people, that they have a sense of rapport. This is because Balsamic people are the visionaries of the zodiac and often are at least three to five years ahead of their time. It will take others a number of years to catch up to what they have already intuited on the cutting edge of the future. When Balsamic people realize that it is this prophetic visionary quality that sets them apart from others, they can begin to release much shame that has built up from trying to conceal the ways in which they are different in order to prevent being ridiculed or rejected.

While Balsamic people are a product of their past, their life purpose moves them toward identifying with a future that most other people cannot imagine or relate to. Ahead of their time and responding to the intimations of what is yet to be born, they are here to encode their visions into seed ideas they then scatter for future generations. The transformational experience of this lifetime which bridges two cycles involves a commitment to living out some new concept of the future within a framework of the present.

Many Balsamic people feel a sense of special destiny, an urgency that there is something important that they must do. They are challenged to effect a mutation in their consciousness by distilling the pith of their rich life experiences into a seed capsule that can be passed on to others, even if it is only to one person. This is done in the hope that the wisdom gained throughout the entire cycle can continue to be of use beyond the span of their own lifetime.

In some religious traditions when a master has fully embodied the precepts of his or her philosophy, it becomes essential to find a student to whom to pass on the teachings in order to keep the direct transmission alive. In a lesser way, destiny for Balsamic people is to serve as a vehicle or channel through which the wisdom of the past can become implanted in the consciousness of the future. Often aware that something larger than their personal selves is involved, they may accept sacrifice or martyrdom so that they can release seed ideas to assist the future, even if they themselves are forgotten.

Examples: Elizabeth Kubler-Ross, Abraham Lincoln, Bob Dylan, Thomas Paine, Karl Marx, Michaelangelo, Betty Freidan, Dave Rudhyar, George Gurdjieff.

The following diagram provides keywords for each of the eight lunation archetypes.

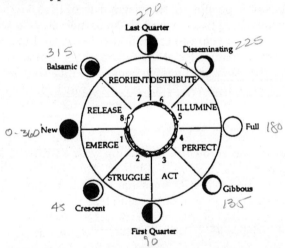

In conclusion, we can sum up the stages of cyclic process in terms of the evolving soul's journey in the development of consciousness over the span of a number of lifetimes.

At the New moon phase, the evolving soul initiates a new cycle of experience by incarnating into a body, allowing a subjective sense of new possibilities to surface, and projecting an identity into the world. At the Crescent phase, the evolving soul struggles to overcome the resistance of the past in order to move forward, gradually focuses its vision, and develops new talents and skills.

At the First-quarter phase, the evolving soul activates the personality and builds structures to anchor the vision and establish itself in the world. At the Gibbous phase, the evolving soul perfects itself and its structures as worthy vehicles of expression, integrating them into the reality of the environment so that they can be of use to others.

In the brilliant shining light of the Full Moon, the evolving soul becomes 'conscious,' objectively realizing the meaning of its life and infusing that meaning into the structures that were initiated, built and perfected during the first four incarnations. In the Disseminating phase, the evolving soul embodies this meaning and lives out its purpose, spreading what it has found to be of value.

In the Last-quarter phase, the evolving soul begins the de-structuring process as it turns away from old, limiting belief systems and reevaluates and reorganizes its ideology. In the Balsamic phase, the evolving soul distills the wisdom essence of the past and intuits the visions of the future, creating the seed that will germinate at the next New moon phase.

For the advanced reader

The late astrologer Marc Robertson suggested that certain planets and signs are associated with each lunation phase. The Sabian symbol of the planet associated with each phase, the house the planet occupies, and the house that the planet rules all give clues as to how an individual can recognize and anchor the goal of his or her lunation phase into daily life in order to then proceed on to the next stage of the cyclic process. In memory of Marc Robertson, I am including his material in the following paragraphs so that you may experiment with his insights.(7)

New Moon people are here to begin a new cycle of activity. The positions of the Sun and the sign Leo are important and often in some way significant in their charts. The Sabian symbol of the degree of the Sun points to the nature of the new goal of the incarnating consciousness. The house in which the Sun is located shows the kinds of activities that will initiate new moon people into this series of lifetimes. The house with Leo on the cusp indicates the area of life in which this goal must be established in order to embark on the next step in the cycle.

Crescent people must move away from old patterns which keep them tied to the past. The positions of the Moon and the sign Cancer are important and often in some way significant in their charts. The Sabian symbol of the degree of the Moon points to the habit patterns that Crescent people must repolarize. The house in which the Moon is located shows the kinds of activities which will have to be changed to make the cycle effective. The house with Cancer on the cusp indicates where the personality must eventually strongly manifest to prove that it has broken from the past and is allowing the new to proceed.

First-Quarter people must build structures that will serve to anchor their vision in society. The positions of the Jupiter and the sign Sagittarius are important and often in some way significant in their charts. The Sabian symbol of the degree of Jupiter points to the reasons that First-Quarter people need to establish themselves in society. The house in which Jupiter is located shows where one will make his or her most effective impression upon society in individual activities. The house with Sagittarius on the cusp indicates where, in activity, this social impression will eventually leave its strongest imprint.

Gibbous people must perfect themselves as a vehicle of expression. The positions of Saturn and the sign Capricorn are important and often in some way significant in their charts. The Sabian symbol of the degree of Saturn points to the motivation behind the personality's urge to perfect itself. The house in which Saturn is located shows what kind of activities need to be defined in order that they can become effective. The house with Capricorn on the cusp indicates in what area of life activities their perfected forms can be of real use to society.

Full Moon people must use their objective mind to realize the meaning of their lives. The positions of Mercury and the signs Gemini and Virgo are important and often in some way significant in their charts. The Sabian symbol of the degree of Mercury points to the purpose of awareness in this life. The house in which Mercury is located shows the experiences in life that will most bring about this awareness. The house with Gemini on the cusp indicates where, in life activities, the awareness can most effectively be applied in small matters and the house with Virgo on the cusp indicates where this awareness can be organized into a systematic approach to the world beyond small matters.

Disseminating people must live out their purpose and spread what they have found to be of value. The positions of Venus and the signs Taurus and Libra are important and often in some way significant in their charts. The Sabian symbol of the degree of Venus will point to the motivation behind the values the individual will adopt in this life to go about making living worthwhile. The house in which Venus is located will show the activities that can transform personal values to the task. The house with Taurus on the cusp indicates where personal love can be best utilized, and the house with Libra on the cusp indicates where social values will most strongly manifest if the incarnation is to be effective.

Last-Quarter people must tear down old, limiting belief systems and antiquated life structures which have fulfilled their purpose and have no further use in what is to come. The positions of Uranus and the sign of Aquarius are important and often in some way significant in their charts. The Sabian symbol of the degree of Uranus points to how one can make the transition from conditioned ego consciousness into the realm of greater transpersonal awareness by awakening the intuition. The house in which Uranus is located shows the activities which can best assist one in breaking out of society's belief systems. The house with Aquarius on the cusp indicates where the changed consciousness can be most effective in life activity.

Balsamic people are here to bridge the past and future by releasing seed ideas. The positions of Mars and the sign of Scorpio are important and often in some way significant in their charts. The Sabian symbol of the degree of Mars points to the experiences that can repolarize the physical and emotional energies so they can participate in envisioning the next step. The house in which Mars is located shows the activities that must be repolarized to harmonize with the future. The house with Scorpio on the cusp indicates the areas that will be transformed in their nature if this repolarization is effective in the life.

CHAPTER 2

THE LUNATION CYCLE
WORKBOOK AND JOURNAL

My Sun, Moon, and Lunation Phase

This workbook and journal section is designed to help you apply the concepts of the lunation cycle to your own life. You will need to know your lunation phase and have a copy of your birth chart in order to fill out the exercise on your sun, moon, and lunation phase. You will need a lifetime lunar phases report to complete the exercises on the progressed lunation phases in the second part of this workbook.

Instructions for assembling a lunation phase wheel and for determining your lunation phase can be found at the end of this chapter. An Astro Communications Services order form for computer birth charts and lifetime lunar phase reports is located in Appendix C. Or you can call them directly at 1-800-888-9983.

The key phrases for the signs and houses that you are asked to fill in can be found in Appendix A in the table entitled Keywords of the Astrological Alphabet. The key phrases for the lunation phases are summarized in The Lunation Phase Cycle Table which is located on the page following the exercise.

In the attempt to help nonastrologers complete this section, the technical astrology is kept to a minimum. However, the most important part of these exercises is composed of nontechnical questions and journal entries. The purpose of the astrological data is similar to a tuning fork—to stimulate your own process of association and insight. Whatever comes to you as you consider these questions is significant. Suspend your critical mind so as not to invalidate this flow of information.

In this section you will be answering only those questions that apply to your own birth lunation phase. However, you can deepen your understanding of the other phases by jotting down the names of your friends and family next to their lunation phases. Then, consider those questions in light of your knowledge of their behavior.

1. My Sun ☉

The **Sun** resides as the center or heart of our being, and is a symbol of our source of energy, power and will. The Sun illuminates new possibilities that lead toward the growth, realization, and expression of our life purpose.

• My Sun is in the sign of _____ .

My Sun sign describes *how,* the style in which, I use my will and power to illuminate new possibilities which help me to express my life purpose. I can best express this potential by fulfilling _____

(Fill in sign key phrase from Table 1, Appendix A)

•I do this in a _____ manner.
(Choose several sign keywords from Table 2, Appendix A)

• My Sun in is the _____ house.

My Sun's house position describes *where*, in what area of life activities, I am best able to grow and become aware of my life purpose. This potential is most easily realized in these areas of my life _____

(Fill in house keywords from Table 3, Appendix A)

2. My Moon ☽

The Moon is a symbol of all the memories and coping mechanisms that we have learned over the course of our lives, particularly in childhood, that inform us through our feelings which of the Sun's new experiences will be safe and meet our needs. We continually integrate this new knowledge, filtered through our emotions, into our personalities as we attempt to actualize and apply the Sun's purpose into everyday life.

• My Moon is in the sign of _____.

My Moon sign describes *how,* the style in which, I use my personality, born out of my safety and security needs, to bring my purpose into daily application. I can best express this potential by fulfilling _____

(Fill in sign key phrase from Table 1, Appendix A)

•I do this in a _____ manner.
(Choose several sign keywords from Table 2, Appendix A)

• My Moon is in the _____house.

My Moon's house position describes *where,* in what area of life activities, I can best use my personality to actualize my life purpose into everyday life. This potential is most easily realized in these areas of my life _____

(Fill in house keywords from Table 3, Appendix A)

3. My Lunation Phase ☉/☽

The Sun and Moon operate together each month, creating a flow of energy as the Moon distributes the light of the Sun to the earth in varying amounts each night, reflected as the phases of the moon. Each person is born during a specific phase of the moon's cycle, which astrologers call the eight lunation phases.

The Lunation Phase indicates the relationship (or angular distance) between the Sun and Moon at the time of our birth, and is a symbol of the kind of energy we can best use to express (Sun) and actualize (Moon) our life purpose. The lunation phase also points to what this purpose might be within a larger cyclic context.

The key phrases for the following exercise are summarized in table entitled The Lunation Phase Cycle Table on the following page.

• My Lunation (or Sun/Moon) Phase is _____.
(If you don't know your lunation phases, turn to the back of the chapter for instructions on how to determine it.)

My lunation phase indicates what my life purpose is within a larger cyclic context, as well as what kind of solar-lunar energy I can utilize to best express this purpose.

The Lunation Phase Cycle Table

Lunation Phase	A Incarnating Soul's Purpose Within a Larger Cyclic Context	B Flow of Solar- Lunar Energy
Phase 1 *New Moon*	Incarnate into My New Being: Emerge & Project	Projecting my personality into new experiences in spontaneous, impulsive and instinctive ways.
Phase 2 *Crescent Moon*	Claim Possession of my Body: Struggle & Move Forward	Struggling away from the inertia and dependencies of past conditions which to seem to hold onto me and mobilizing my resources so I can move in a forward direction.
Phase 3 *First-Quarter Moon*	Activate My Personality: Act & Build	Taking direct action to manage the energy released from the many crisis situations in my life. Clearing away old structures to move out to build new ones in order to create definite forms which can contain my life purpose.
Phase 4 *Gibbous Moon*	Evaluate My Expression: Analyze & Perfect	Analyzing self-expression in order to find better techniques for doing things or facilitating my personal growth. Introspection as I quest for meaning.
Phase 5 *Full Moon*	Clarify My Purpose: Illumine & Fulfill	Searching for the ideal and infusing that meaning and content into my life structures. Discovering objectivity and clarity about my life purpose through relationships.
Phase 6 *Disseminating Moon*	Distribute My Values: Disseminate & Convey	Living out and embodying my values. Sharing and communicating ideas that I have found to be meaningful.
Phase 7 *Last-Quarter Moon*	Revise My Thinking: Reorient & Turn Away	Going through internal crises as I turn away from old patterns of behavior and attitudes in order to allow something new to germinate inside. Difficulty in externalizing the process until the change is complete.
Phase 8 *Balsamic Moon*	Mutate My Consciousness: Distill & Transform	Feeling "out-of-synch" with the majority. Distilling wisdom gleaned from entire cycle as a legacy to pass on to others. Completing karma and committing to the future which brings transformation.

•A. This purpose is _____.
(Fill in "A" key phrases from the Lunation Cycle Table on the previous page)

•B. My lunation phase refers to the core of my personality type. The kinds of experiences I encounter as underlying themes in my life are:

_____

_____

(Fill in "B" key phrases from the Lunation Cycle Table on the previous page)

Now turn to and complete the journal questions on the following pages that refer to your own lunation phase.

I. My lunation phase is New Moon.

1. What kinds of new possibilities are trying to emerge from within me?

2. How do I project myself upon the outer world? Am I aware of my emotions or of why I do things?

3. To what extent do I operate on the basis of instinct and improvisation, without a thought-out plan? Is this a successful way of functioning for me?

II. My lunation phase is Crescent Moon.

1. Who or what are my "ghosts of the past"—(family of origin imprints, fears, insecurities, dependencies, addictions)?

2. How am I emotionally tied to the past and in what ways am I afraid to let go? How do I experience the struggle to make a break with whatever holds me back?

3. What ways are most effective for me to develop new talents in order to mobilize my resources so I can move forward?

III. My lunation phase is First-Quarter Moon.

1. To what extent do I live in a world of crisis and challenge? Do I thrive on this kind of intensity? How do I manage the energy released in these crisis situations?

2. What kinds of direct action do I take to clear away old structures and build new ones? To what extent do I experience resistance from others and ensuing conflict due to my assertiveness?

3. How do I expand my activities and establish myself in social terms?

IV. My lunation phase is Gibbous Moon.

1. Who or what do I analyze in an attempt to develop better techniques for doing things or understanding my part in relationships?

2. To what extent do I ask "why" and search for answers and revelations?

3. What is the nature of my apprenticeship? What am I here to perfect?

V. My lunation phase is Full Moon.

1. In what ways do I search for a larger meaning, purpose or reason for my life ?

2. To what extent do I seek fulfillment through others? How do I evaluate the quality of my life and reason for living on the basis of meaningful or unmeaningful relationships and affiliations?

3. To what extent do I think before I act, particularly in interactions with others? Am I willing to take responsibility for my actions towards others?

VI. My lunation phase is Disseminating.

1. What ideas do I share and spread? How do I convey and communicate them?

2. To what extent do I find life meaningless if I don't have a cause to believe in?

3. Do I get "lost in my causes" and become impatient with others for not readily accepting my views or taking action on my beliefs?

VII. My lunation phase is Last-Quarter Moon.

1. What kinds of old patterns, attitudes, and values of mine based on what other people think do I become disillusioned with and then turn away from? What meaning do I give to these internal mental crises?

2. To what extent do I experience patterns in my life as shifts or reorientations away from what I have already accomplished toward some new intimation of the future which may not be altogether clear?

3. Do I find it difficult to externalize my inner process of change until it is completed? How do I drop the mask of my old self when I am ready to live out my new approach? How does this affect my relationships with others?

VIII. My lunation phase is Balsamic Moon.

1. Have I had many intense, but short-term relationships in my life (friend, mate, business, sexual, etc.)? To what extent do I see the karmic connections and opportunities for resolution in all my relationships?

2. Am I "ahead of my time" and attuned to visions of the future. How do I try to live out these new concepts within old frame-works?

3. What is the nature of my wisdom that I distill and concentrate as my life work? How do I pass it on so that my insights can continue to have a life of their own beyond my personal lifetime. How does this relate to my feelings of destiny?

Lifetime Lunar Phases

The Progressed Lunation Cycle

As mentioned earlier in this book, we are born into one particular lunation phase, and this phase shows the core of our personality type and the kind of solar-lunar energy we best use to fulfill our ultimate purpose. However the lunation cycle is not static, but moving.

The astrological technique of secondary progressions measures the continuing movements of the Sun, Moon and planets in the sky after our birth. It is based on the formula that one day is equal to one year. This is a symbolic relationship, but one that has proven to be valid in astrological practice. What this implies is that the first ninety days after our birth correspond to, and in some way are a blueprint for, the first ninety years for our life. That is, the quality of the fifth day of our life is a seed encapsulation of the influences we experience in our fifth year of life, and so on.

Dane Rudhyar elucidates a most fascinating theory that attempts to explain a philosophical basis for why this technique works. It takes us here on earth one year to make a complete revolution around the Sun. The Sun represents the life principle, and the complete formation of a person, who is considered to be a microcosmic condensation of the forces active in the macrocosm, should likewise take one whole year. "As the embryonic development in the womb takes nine months, it would be natural to assume that the extra three months needed to complete the solar cycle would refer to the also embryonic unfoldment of a psychic organism..." (8). It is in these three months after birth that we derive the relationships between the progressed Sun and Moon as an archetypal blueprint for the growth of individual consciousness during the course of our lifetime.

The progressed moon moving in relation to the progressed sun takes approximately twenty-nine and one half years to make one complete progressed lunation cycle. During this time period, we experience the entire flow of the solar-lunar energy through each of the successive phases, each one lasting for about a three and one half years. If we live to be ninety years old, we will experience three progressed lunation cycles over the course of our lives. And the Triple Moon Goddess once again impresses her rhythm upon our beings.

Our progressed lunation phase allows us to utilize each of the eight particular lunation phase energies, challenges, and potentials as we seek to fulfill our growing purpose within a cyclic context. When we place the events of our life against the backdrop of the progressed lunation cycle, we can see seemingly unrelated experiences take on a pattern of meaning within the larger whole of our life purpose. What happens to us during a particular lunation phase period has the same significance in the larger meaning of our life as the phase has in the cycle.

The first entry in your Lifetime Lunar Phase report is the New Moon Before Birth. The zodiacal degree at which the Sun and Moon conjoined at the New Moon previous to your birth date is an important factor in understanding the progressed lunation process. This degree contains the symbolism describing the preexisting influences of karma and ancestral heritage into which you are born. This is the unseen background of the forces that shape your life in your early years. *The Astrological Mandala* by Dane Rudhyar contains symbolic descriptions for each of the 360 degrees of the zodiac. The description of the degree of your New Moon Before Birth can give you an image that points to the underlying qualities that become focused as the major issues of your life purpose, as well as the most significant factor during your first progressed lunation cycle.

If you were born early in the lunation cycle (New, Crescent, First-Quarter or Gibbous) you will experience your first progressed Full Moon Phase early in childhood, before you are fifteen years old. What culminates at the Full Moon is not so much a factor of your individual selfhood, as it is of preexisting karmic and ancestral influences depicted by the symbolism of your New Moon Before Birth degree. Your first progressed New Moon will come later in your life when your personality is deeply conditioned by these earlier patterns. It will require much will and strength to emerge with a true individuality at the progressed New Moon.

If you were born late in the lunation cycle (Full, Disseminating, Last-Quarter, or Balsamic), your first progressed New Moon will occur early in childhood, before 15 years of age. The influence and karma of the past is purified quickly and is not so strong a factor in early development. At a young age you are responding to new influences, and so the strong urge for a new kind of individuality may not occur until the second progressed New Moon during your thirties.

The lunation cycle repeats itself about every thirty years. If you live to a ripe old age, you can expect to experience up to three progressed lunation cycles over the course of your life. There exists a repetitive quality from one cycle to the next. The actual events of your life will be different during similar phases of successive cycles, but the meaning, issues, and challenges underlying these events are similar. Each successive cycle enables us to build upon the past, clarify the issues, and further develop the themes of our life purpose.

How To Determine Your Lifetime Lunar Phases

In order to determine the dates of your progressed lunation phases, turn now to your Lifetime Lunar Phases Report. In the printout you received from Astro-Communications Services you will be referring to the columns entitled "Progressed Date" and "phase" in order to fill out this exercise.

You have three Progressed Lunation Phase Wheel worksheets in this booklet, one for each complete progressed lunation cycle.

To make this process as simple as possible, we will first walk you through the method by referring to a sample Lifetime Lunation Phase Report and three sample Progressed Lunation Phase Wheel worksheets located on pages 59-61. Once you see how the process occurs with someone else's chart, you can then do it for yourself.

1. To begin, fill out the AGE WORKSHEET (on page 62) following the directions given. This will help you to determine the age you were when the progressed moon phase changes. In our sample, on page 57, we have filled it out for a person born in 1946.

2. Find the birth lunation phase on our sample Lifetime Lunar Phase report by looking to the right of the words "BIRTH PHASE." In our example, it is the Balsamic phase. (In the 2nd column from the left under hading progressed date.)

3. Next, on our sample report, look directly under the word BALSAMIC where you will encounter the words "NEW MOON." This means that the next progressed phase after Balsamic was the New Moon phase. Now look to the left to the date in the "Progressed Date" column. It reads July 17, 1949. This means that on July 17, 1949, the progressed Moon phase changed from Balsamic to New Moon.

4. Now look at the age worksheet opposite the year 1949 where you will find the number "3." Hence, this change happened when the person was 3 years old.

5. Now we can transfer this information onto the Progressed Lunation Phase Worksheet. Let's look at our first sample sheet. The birth phase is the BALSAMIC phase. The progressed phase ended on July, 1949 and covered the period from birth to three.

6. Now return to the Lifetime Lunar Phase report and look directly under the words NEW MOON in the phase column where you will find the word "CRESCENT." Hence the next progressed phase was the Crescent phase which began January 9, 1953. Under

the word crescent is FIRST-QUARTER. To the left is the date, December 2, 1956, signifying when the progressed First-Quarter phase began. If you continue down the Phase and Progressed Date columns, you can locate the dates on which the progressed Moon entered its succeeding phases—Gibbous, Full, Disseminating, etc.

7. As we did in step 5, we can to transfer this information onto the Progressed Lunation Phase Worksheet. For example, on the second worksheet page, we see that the progressed NEW MOON phase began on 7/49 and ended on 1/53. It covered the ages from 3 to 6 ½.

The progressed CRESCENT PHASE began on 1/53 and ended on 12/56, lasting from ages 6 ½ to 10.

This continues until the BALSAMIC MOON phase has been filled in, which represents the completion of one full progressed lunation cycle. Therefore, each time you complete the Balsamic phase entry, begin a new worksheet wheel at the New Moon Phase.

8. The lines under the various lunation phases provide you with a way of recording one or several significant life events you experienced during that time—major moves, travels, educational or career changes, births and deaths of family members, relationships, spiritual or philosophic shifts, etc. In our sample wheel worksheet, the person has written down some of the important events that occurred during each of her progressed moon phases. You can do the same for yourself.

Consider these events in the light of what you now understand about the lunation cycle. The meaning of the events during a specific progressed phase, with reference to your life cycles, will be similar to the meaning of that phase in the unfolding of cyclic process. The specific dates of the lunation phase changes are not as important as the general trends around this time period.

9. To help you assimilate this material, go now to the workbook and journal section for the Progressed Lunation Cycle which appears in a few pages. Additional commentary and questions are provided about the meaning of the progressed lunation phases for you to think about and answer.

SAMPLE AGE CHART

This chart will help you to determine your age at the various years since you were born. Find the year of your birth. Write down the month of your birth before it, and after it enter 0 years old. Then enter 1 for the following year, 2 in the year after that, and so on until you reach the current year and your current age.

	Year	Age	Year	Age
	1930		1966	20
	1931		1967	21
	1932		1968	22
	1933		1969	23
	1934		1970	24
	1935		1971	25
	1936		1972	26
	1937		1973	27
	1938		1974	28
	1939		1975	29
	1940		1976	30
	1941		1977	31
	1942		1978	32
	1943		1979	33
	1944		1980	34
	1945		1981	35
July	1946	0 born	1982	36
	1947	1	1983	37
	1948	2	1984	38
	1949	3	1985	39
	1950	4	1986	40
	1951	5	1987	41
	1952	6	1988	42
	1953	7	1989	43
	1954	8	1990	44
	1955	9	1991	45
	1956	10	1992	46
	1957	11	1993	47
	1958	12	1994	48
	1959	13	1995	49
	1960	14	1996	
	1961	15	1997	
	1962	16	1998	
	1963	17	1999	
	1964	18	2000	
	1965	19	2001	

LIFETIME LUNAR PHASES FOR Demetra George

EPHEMERIS DATE	PROGRESSED DATE	PHASE	KEYWORD	SUN POSITION	MOON POSITION
22:06 Jun 28, 1946	BEFORE BIRTH	NEW MOON		6 CA 49	6 CA 49
6:22 Jul 25, 1946	BIRTH PHASE	BALSAMIC	release	1 LE 56	21 GE 14
5:54 Jul 28, 1946	Jul 17, 1949	NEW MOON	emergence	4 LE 47	4 LE 47
17:29 Jul 31, 1946	Jan 9, 1953	CRESCENT	expansion	8 LE 7	23 VI 7
14:56 Aug 4, 1946	Dec 2, 1956	FIRST QUARTER	action	11 LE 51	11 SC 51
18:01 Aug 8, 1946	Jan 17, 1961	GIBBOUS	overcoming	15 LE 48	0 CP 48
16:26 Aug 12, 1946	Dec 24, 1964	FULL MOON	fulfillment	19 LE 35	19 AQ 35
7:51 Aug 16, 1946	Aug 16, 1968	DISSEMINATING	demonstration	23 LE 5	8 AR 5
19:17 Aug 19, 1946	Feb 7, 1972	LAST QUARTER	re-orientation	26 LE 25	26 TA 25
4:50 Aug 23, 1946	Jul 2, 1975	BALSAMIC	release	29 LE 42	14 CA 42
15:08 Aug 26, 1946	Dec 5, 1978	NEW MOON	emergence	3 VI 0	3 VI 0
7:34 Aug 30, 1946	Aug 12, 1982	CRESCENT	expansion	6 VI 34	21 LI 34
8:49 Sep 3, 1946	Aug 31, 1986	FIRST QUARTER	action	10 VI 29	10 SG 29
10:37 Sep 7, 1946	Sep 27, 1990	GIBBOUS	overcoming	14 VI 26	29 CP 26
4:00 Sep 11, 1946	Jun 19, 1994	FULL MOON	fulfillment	18 VI 3	18 PI 3
14:56 Sep 14, 1946	Dec 2, 1997	DISSEMINATING	demonstration	21 VI 25	6 TA 25
0:45 Sep 18, 1946	Apr 30, 2001	LAST QUARTER	re-orientation	24 VI 45	24 GE 45
12:02 Sep 21, 1946	Oct 18, 2004	BALSAMIC	release	28 VI 8	13 LE 8
2:46 Sep 25, 1946	May 30, 2008	NEW MOON	emergence	1 LI 41	1 LI 41
0:31 Sep 29, 1946	Apr 26, 2012	CRESCENT	expansion	5 LI 31	20 SC 31
3:54 Oct 3, 1946	Jun 17, 2016	FIRST QUARTER	action	9 LI 35	9 CP 35
2:21 Oct 7, 1946	May 24, 2020	GIBBOUS	overcoming	13 LI 28	28 AQ 28
14:41 Oct 10, 1946	Nov 28, 2023	FULL MOON	fulfillment	16 LI 56	16 AR 56
22:12 Oct 13, 1946	Mar 23, 2027	DISSEMINATING	demonstration	20 LI 13	5 GE 13
7:28 Oct 17, 1946	Aug 10, 2030	LAST QUARTER	re-orientation	23 LI 34	23 CA 34
21:35 Oct 20, 1946	Mar 13, 2034	BALSAMIC	release	27 LI 8	12 VI 8

LUNAR PHASES refer to the angle formed between the progressed Sun and progressed Moon positions. The former moves about one degree per year, while the latter moves about one degree per month. These positions are given in the two rightmost columns. The Information Special ILUNX discusses this option.

The Progressed Lunation Phase Wheel

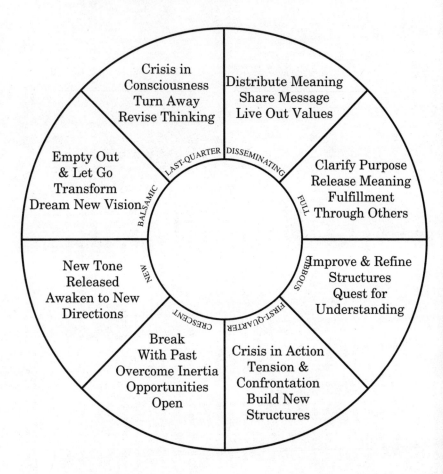

The Progressed Lunation Phase Wheel Worksheet

Progressed Last-Quarter:

Begins _____ Ends _____

From Age _____ to _____

_____

_____

_____

_____

Progressed Disseminating:

Begins _____ Ends _____

From Age _____ to _____

_____

_____

_____

_____

Progressed Balsamic:

Begins _7/46_ Ends _7/49_

From Age _0_ to _3_

• *Father diagnosed with cancer & hospitalized*

• *Raised by Greek-speaking Grandparents*

_____

(NOW GO TO NEXT PAGE)

Progressed Full:

Begins _____ Ends _____

From Age _____ to _____

_____

_____

_____

_____

Progressed New:

Begins _____ Ends _____

From Age _____ to _____

_____

_____

_____

_____

Progressed Gibbous:

Begins _____ Ends _____

From Age _____ to _____

_____

_____

_____

_____

Progressed Crescent :

Begins _____ Ends _____

From Age _____ to _____

_____

_____

_____

_____

Progressed First-Quarter:

Begins _____ Ends _____

From Age _____ to _____

_____

_____

_____

_____

New Moon before birth or Progressed New Moon of Current cycle

Sign and Degree _6 ♋ 49 = 7 Cancer_

Sabian Symbol ___*Two Nature Spirits Dancing Under the Moonlight*___

The play of invisible forces in all manifestations of life.

The Progressed Lunation Phase Wheel Worksheet

Progressed Last-Quarter:

Begins ___2/72___ Ends ___7/75___

From Age _25 1/2_ to ___29___

• *Jan. '72 - son Daniel born*
• *growing dissatisfaction with commune*
• *Sept. '73 - leave commune; take astrology*
  classes in Portland
• *Nov. '74 - daughter Reina born*

Progressed Balsamic:

Begins ___7/75___ Ends ___12/78___

From Age ___29___ to ___32___

• *June '75 - nuclear family moves to isolated*
  country farm
• *correspondence courses in astrology*
• *June '77 - end relationship & move to town*

(NOW GO TO NEXT PAGE)

Progressed New:

Begins ___7/49___ Ends ___1/53___

From Age ___3___ to ___6 1/2___

• *March '50 - Father dies*
• *move away from childhood neighborhood*
• *go to kindergarden, learn to speak English*
• *go to Greek Orthodox church everyday*

Progressed Crescent :

Begins ___1/53___ Ends ___12/56___

From Age ___6 1/2___ to ___10 1/2___

• *Aug. '52 - move to NYC to live with mother's*
  parents, try to forget sadness of the past
• *Nov. '54 - Mother remarries - new step-father*
• *May '55 - move to house on Long Island*
• *Mar '56 - sister Helen born*

Progressed Disseminating:

Begins ___8/68___ Ends ___2/72___

From Age ___22___ to ___25 1/2___

• *1969 - travel to Europe & Mid East*
• *Feb. '70 - live on commune in Oregon*
  "flower child living organic lifestyle"
• *2nd realtionship* • *discover astrology*

Progressed Full:

Begins ___12/64___ Ends ___8/68___

From Age _18 1/2_ to ___22___

• *Sept. '64 - leave for college*
• *1966 - 1st major relationship*
• *1966 - "looking for meaning" in philosophy*
  studies

Progressed Gibbous:

Begins ___1/61___ Ends ___12/64___

From Age _14 1/2_ to ___18 1/2___

• *attend high school*
• *study hard to get college scholarship*

Progressed First-Quarter:

Begins ___12/56___ Ends ___1/61___

From Age _10 1/2_ to ___14 1/2___

• *new school, new friends, new neighborhood,*
  establish foundations
• *Feb. '58 - sister Margie born*

New Moon before birth or Progressed New Moon of Current cycle

Sign and Degree ___4 ♌ 47 = 5 Leo___

Sabian Symbol ___Rock Formations Tower Over Deep Canyon___

The structural power of elemental forces during the long cycle of planetary evolution

The Progressed Lunation Phase Wheel Worksheet

Progressed Last-Quarter:

Begins _____ Ends _____

From Age _____ to _____

_____

_____

_____

_____

Progressed Disseminating:

Begins _____ Ends _____

From Age _____ to _____

_____

_____

_____

_____

Progressed Balsamic:

Begins _____ Ends _____

From Age _____ to _____

_____

_____

_____

_____

(NOW GO TO NEXT PAGE)

Progressed Full:

Begins __6/94__ Ends __12/97__

From Age __48__ to __51__

• *Sep. '94 – AFAN*

• *July '95 – make plans to return to*
  college, graduate school

• *important relationship*

Progressed New:

Begins __12/78__ Ends __8/82__

From Age __32 1/2__ to __36__

• *new identity as single woman, active social life*
• *Jan. '80 – begin doing readings and teach*
• *meet Douglas, talk about writing asteroid book*
• *Apr. '81 – begin Tibetan Buddhist practices*

Progressed Gibbous:

Begins __9/90__ Ends __6/94__

From Age __44__ to __48__

• *much more teaching, speaking & research*
• *Apr. '91 – OCCWS center*
• *Apr. '92 – publish Mysteries...*
• *May '94 – complete Finding Our Way...*

Progressed Crescent :

Begins __8/82__ Ends __8/86__

From Age __36__ to __40__

• *Sept. '82 – accept money from investors to*
  write Asteriod Goddesses – Struggle!
• *detach from distracting friends, learn*
  computer and writing skills
• *struggle as single mom to survive*

Progressed First-Quarter:

Begins __8/86__ Ends __9/90__

From Age __40__ to __44__

• *June '86 – publication of Asteroid*
  Goddesses
• *June '87 – publication of Astrology For*
  Yourself
• *invitations to lecture & speak*
• *Nov. '89 – 3rd major relationship*
• *contract for Mysteries of the Dark Moon*

New Moon before birth or Progressed New Moon of Current Cycle

Sign and Degree ___3 ♍ 0 = 3 Virgo___

Sabian Symbol ___*Two Guardian Angels*___

Invisible help and protection in times of crisis

SAMPLE AGE CHART

This chart will help you to determine your age at the various years since you were born. Find the year of your birth. Write down the month of your birth before it, and after it enter 0 years old. Then enter 1 for the following year, 2 in the year after that, and so on until you reach the current year and your current age.

Year	Age	Year	Age
1930		1966	17 12
1931		1967	18 13
1932		1968	19 14
1933		1969	20 15
1934		1970	21 16
1935		1971	22 17
1936		1972	23 18
1937		1973	24 19
1938		1974	25 20
1939		1975	26 21
1940		1976	27 22
1941		1977	28 23
1942		1978	29 24
1943		1979	30 25
1944		1980	31 26
1945		1981	32 24
1946		1982	33 28
1947		1983	34
1948		1984	35
Aug 1949	0	1985	36
1950	1	1986	37
1951	2	1987	38
1952	3	1988	39
1953	4	1989	40
1954	5 0	1990	41
1955	6 1	1991	42
1956	7 2	1992	43
1957	8 3	1993	44
1958	9 4	1994	45
1959	10 5	1995	46
1960	11 6	1996	47
1961	12 7	1997	48
1962	13 8	1998	49
1963	14 9	1999	50
1964	15 10	2000	51
1965	16 11	2001	52

The Progressed Lunation Phase Wheel Worksheet

Progressed Last-Quarter:

Begins _1/72_ Ends _8/75_

From Age _21_ to _26_

-interest in astrology - ocault
metaphysics -
1973 met Bruce - married
went back to Presbyterian
1974 - bought 1st house church

Progressed Balsamic:

Begins _8/75_ Ends _12/7/78_

From Age _26_ to _29_

-House in Fullerton
-1976 - Josh born - quit working
-1977 Bruce went into army
-Sold house - moved to Georgia
Then Oklahoma
(NOW GO TO NEXT PAGE) Jenny born

Progressed New:

Begins _8/2/49_ Ends _10/52_

From Age _0_ to _3_

Born in Glendale - moved
to Pacoima before Brother
was born in Feb 1952

Progressed Crescent :

Begins _10/30/52_ Ends _3/56_

From Age _3_ to _6_

1954 started school
lived - played - had a
idyllic childhood

Progressed Disseminating:

Begins _12/67_ Ends _1/72_

From Age _18_ to _21_

1968 medical assistant school - job
aug - got married
1971 got divorced - mucky
Jan - Feb 72 divorce final

Progressed Full:

Begins _11/63_ Ends _12/21/67_

From Age _14_ to _18_

1964 - graduated Jr High - moved to
Sepulveda - High School years
1967 - graduated HS, went to Pierce
got engaged
1966 worked at Savons

Progressed Gibbous:

Begins _11/59_ Ends _11/63_

From Age _10_ to _14_
61. - 64
junior high -
lost weight w/ doctor & diet
pills summer of 63.?

Progressed First-Quarter:

Begins _3/56_ Ends _11/59_

From Age _6_ to _10_

1957 sister born
1958 went to Iowa for summer
gained weight

New Moon before birth or Progressed New Moon of Current cycle

Sign and Degree _☽ ♍ 39'_

Sabian Symbol _In a portrait the best of man's traits are idealized_

The Progressed Lunation Phase Wheel Worksheet

9/97 Jenny to Ellensburg

Progressed Last-Quarter:
Begins 8/2001 Ends 2/05

From Age 52 to 55

10/01 - feeling unsatisfied as student (astrol)
Travel To Hawaii, explored idea
of moving to HI - work going
well - promotions

Progressed Balsamic:
Begins 2/05 Ends 4/22/08

From Age 55 to 58

remodeled house - Edith died
Rt knee + leg injury + healing. Molokai
Sally came to RSDU - Trouble
w/ Rick - lost 60#

(NOW GO TO NEXT PAGE)

Progressed New:
Begins 12/7/78 Ends 2-20-82

From Age 29 to 32

12/7/78 Jenny's Birthday
Idyllic time - kids little
life was generally good.
Josh had occasional problems
volunteered at Vet Clinic
volksmarching

Progressed Crescent :
Begins 2/82 Ends 8/6/85

From Age 32 to 35

Aug 1983 - moved to Baumholder
I loved Germany -
job at USO
volks marches - OWC
secy + treasurer

Progressed Disseminating:
Begins 9/97 Ends 8/2001

From Age 48 to 51

2/98 began at WSDOT 7/99 permanent
4/98 psychic fair - 9/98 astrology class
8/98 begin Shamanic journeys
8/99 Moved to Olympia - restoring old house
8/2001 1st trip to Hawaii - loved it!

Progressed Full:
Begins 7/53 Ends 9/97

From Age 43 to 48

11/93 Bruce out of Army moved to
Seattle.
9/94 - went to UW for MLA
9/95 Josh killed - met Carol
8/97 finished MLA
6/97 Jenny graduated HS

Progressed Gibbous:
Begins 6/89 Ends 7/93

From Age 39 to 43

9/89 Began CSULB - Josh in Jr High
6/91 graduated w/ BA in Geog ΦBK
8/91 moved to Heidelberg - worked
at High School
Lost 50 pounds
Josh started drinking

Progressed First-Quarter:
Begins 8/85 Ends 6/89

From Age 36 to 39

1985 moved to Babenhausen - depressed 1st yr
1986 - finally adjusted - friend
1987 moved to Calif - went to
college
1989 graduated from Orange
Coast College

New Moon before birth or Progressed New Moon of Current cycle

Sign and Degree 29° ♍ 09'

Sabian Symbol Having an urgent task to complete, a man doesn't
look to any distractions

The Progressed Lunation Phase Wheel Worksheet

Progressed Last-Quarter:

Begins 1/28/31 Ends 1/2/34

From Age _____ to _____

_____

_____

_____

_____

Progressed Disseminating:

Begins 4/28/27 Ends 1/28/31

From Age _____ to _____

_____

_____

_____

_____

Progressed Balsamic:

Begins 7/2/2034 Ends 9/23/2037

From Age _____ to _____

_____

_____

_____

_____

Progressed Full:

Begins 4/10/23 Ends 4/28/27

From Age _____ to _____

_____

_____

_____

_____

(NOW GO TO NEXT PAGE)

Progressed New:

Begins 4/22/08 Ends 7/18/11

From Age 58 to 62

Bob came to live with us. Jenny
married 7/09, Kyra born 5/10
trip to HL for Carol's wedding 6/10
promoted to RSDU manager during
reductions at WSDOT - L knee injury 8/10
walking before - exercises after - gained 30#

Progressed Gibbous:

Begins 2/20/19 Ends 4/20/23

From Age 68 to 72

_____

_____

_____

_____

Progressed Crescent :

Begins 7/18/2011 Ends 2/17/2015

From Age 62 to 65

_____

_____

_____

_____

Progressed First-Quarter:

Begins 2/18/2015 Ends 2/20/19

From Age 65 to 68

_____

_____

_____

_____

New Moon before birth or Progressed New Moon of Current cycle

Sign and Degree 28° ♍ 09'

Sabian Symbol Humanity seeking to bridge the span of Knowledge

The Progressed Lunation Phase Wheel Worksheet

Progressed Last-Quarter:

Begins _____ Ends _____

From Age _____ to _____

_____

_____

_____

_____

Progressed Disseminating:

Begins _____ Ends _____

From Age _____ to _____

_____

_____

_____

_____

Progressed Balsamic:

Begins _____ Ends _____

From Age _____ to _____

_____

_____

_____

_____

Progressed Full:

Begins _____ Ends _____

From Age _____ to _____

_____

_____

_____

_____

(NOW GO TO NEXT PAGE)

Progressed New:

Begins 9/23/2037 Ends 1/26/2041

From Age _____ to _____

_____

_____

_____

_____

Progressed Gibbous:

Begins 12/19/2048 Ends 1/19/2053

From Age _____ to _____

_____

_____

_____

_____

Progressed Crescent :

Begins 1/26/2041 Ends 10/31/44

From Age _____ to _____

_____

_____

_____

_____

Progressed First-Quarter:

Begins 10/31/44 Ends 12/19/2048

From Age _____ to _____

_____

_____

_____

_____

New Moon before birth or Progressed New Moon of Current cycle

Sign and Degree _____

Sabian Symbol _____

Lifetime Lunar Phases for Demetra George

The following text serves to amplify and expand on the notes that were recorded on the sample Progressed Lunar Phase Wheel Worksheets

I was born into a Balsamic moon phase, and within a year of my birth my father was diagnosed with cancer and shortly thereafter hospitalized. The first years of my life were overshadowed by his terminal illness and the grief of both my mother and my father's parents with whom we were living. My grandmother was my primary caretaker. My earliest memories of her were as a crone dressed entirely in black who took me with her every day to pray in the Greek Orthodox church for her many deceased children.

My progressed New Moon corresponded with the death of my father, and a move away from the comforting familiarity of my old neighborhood. I had to make the transition from speaking Greek to becoming fluent in English when I stated kindergarten and came into a sense of my own identity. As the new moon phase came to a close, my mother moved us from Chicago to New York City to live with her parents.

During the progressed Crescent phase which began at age 6 and 1/2, my mother and I tried to forget the sadness of the past and to get on with our lives. My mother remarried; I gained a new stepfather and we moved into a new house of our own on Long Island. My first sister was born.

With the progressed First-Quarter phase at age 10 and 1/2, I began to have a sense of strong foundations in my life. I was very busy and active with a new school, new friends, and new neighborhood. My second sister was born.

The progressed Gibbous phase corresponded with my high school years. I became totally immersed in my studies as I strived for perfect grades in the hopes of obtaining a college scholarship.

The progressed Full Moon phase saw me attending college, searching for the 'meaning of life' in my philosophy courses. This was also the time of my first major relationship, and the dawning awareness of the hippie revolution, student dissent, and drug cultures of the late 1960's that were to expand the consciousness of my generation and leave a lasting impression on the culture at large.

The progressed Disseminating phase marked the completion of college and movement into the larger world. I traveled throughout Europe and the Middle East where my real education began by seeing the diversity of many different belief systems and life-styles. Shortly after returning to the US, I went to live on a commune in Oregon where some of my college friends had migrated. For the next several years I was embodying my philosophy as a flower child living the organic lifestyle close to the land. Here I entered into my second major relationship with a person much older than myself, and discovered my passion for astrology. The overall feeling of this phase was of fully and exuberantly living my life in the here and now.

A month before my progressed Last-Quarter phase began, my first child, a son Daniel, was born. I became gradually disillusioned and increasingly dissatisfied with communal living. I attended my first astrological conference and met Eleanor Bach who gave me her new book on the asteroids. In the middle of this phase we left and moved briefly to Portland where I attended an astrology class. It closed with a move to Oregon Coast, and the birth of my daughter Reina.

Concurrent with the start of my progressed Balsamic phase, my partner and I with our two small children purchased 80 acres of land way out in the country. I suffered from terrible isolation and depression; my only solace was the correspondence course in astrology that I held onto as my lifeline. A year before the end of this phase, I left the relationship and moved to town.

Both of my progressed Balsamic phases carried the tone of isolation. In the first one, the seeds for my spirituality were incubated in the many hours of church. In the second one, it was this very isolation that gave me the time and focus to devote myself to my astrological studies which then became the germinal impulse of my next lunation cycle. In the first Balsamic phase, I lost my father, in the second one I separated from the man who had become like a father to me. The sense of being on my own (this was the first time in twelve years that I was not in a committed relationship) moved me into the next progressed New Moon phase.

Here I developed a new identity as a single woman, and became involved in an active social life. I began doing astrological readings and started to teach classes in my community. At the end of this phase I met Douglas Bloch who encouraged and offered to help me write a book about the asteroids. This mirrored the energies on my first progressed New phase where I had to develop language skills to communicate.

My first progressed New Moon phase saw me immersed in the religion of my ancestral heritage; in the second progressed New Moon phase I became deeply involved in another spiritual practice and tradition.

One month after my progressed Crescent phase began, I accepted money from some investors in order to write *Asteroid Goddesses*. It was a struggle to persevere and I kept on procrastinating. It became necessary to distance myself from the friends who had now become a major distraction to the writing effort. I learned computer skills which facilitated the process and enabled me to move forward into a rapidly changing technological world. The need to overcome the past in order to move into the future was evident in both progressed Crescent phases.

Two months after my progressed First-Quarter phase, *Asteroid Goddesses* was published! The following year saw the publication of *Astrology For Yourself*. Many invitations came to lecture and speak, and I began to build the foundations for my role in the larger astrological and women's spirituality groups. I started working on *Mysteries of the Dark Moon*. This was a busy and active time, and like the first progressed First-Quarter phase I rooted myself in my socially expanding world.

My progressed gibbous phase was full of much more teaching, traveling, writing, researching, counseling and generally refining my skills of expression and presentation. *Mysteries of the Dark Moon* was published, and I became the director of the Oregon Coast Center for Women's Studies. In the final month of this phase I am now completing *Finding Our Way Through the Dark*. Aiming toward achieving a standard of proficiency and excellence in my work was the overriding theme of both progressed Gibbous phases.

I am now anxiously awaiting the illumination of meaning and purpose that will be revealed over the next few years as I enter into my progressed Full Moon phase.

Now one year into my progressed Full Moon phase, I am making the final corrections on this manuscript. My election to the AFAN Steering Committee, chairing Grants and Scholarships, has opened an avenue of participation with and servive to my astrological community. I am also making plans to finish my college education that began during the previous Full Moon phase, and like the last time around, have begun an important relation-

ship during this time of opening up to allow something from oput-
side myself to enter into myself.

Progressed Lunation Phase
Workbook and Journal

Depending upon your age, you may have up to three progressed
lunation phase wheels that go up to your present age. However in
this journal, you are given just one set of questions for one cycle
to consider. In the spaces following the questions, you may want
to notate the dates and a significant event for each one of your
progressed cycles. You have the choice of responding to the questions in regards to just one cycle, or you can make notes about all
of them if it is applicable to you.

For example:

1st progressed New Moon phase: begins: <u>3/12/1948, Age 5; Birth of my sister Marie</u>
2nd progressed New Moon phase begins: <u>6/7/1978, Age 35; left my marriage</u>
3rd progressed New Moon phase begins: 6/25/2008, Age 65 _____

   After answering the journal questions, you may want to write
a narrative of your life, as I have done on the preceding pages,
making sense of the events in terms of the meanings of each phase
of cyclic process. In this way you can begin to see your life resonating to the rhythm of the phases of the moon in spiraling cycles
of emergence, fulfillment and completion, followed by renewal.

JOURNAL QUESTIONS

Progressed New Moon Phase

1st progressed New Moon phase: begins: _____ Age: ___ _____
2nd progressed New Moon phase begins: _____ Age: ___ _____
3rd progressed New Moon phase begins: _____ Age: ___ _____

   The progressed New Moon phase occurs approximately every
thirty years when the progressed Moon conjuncts the progressed
Sun in your birth chart. At this time there is often a clear demar-
cation between the ending of an old way of life and the beginning
of a major new cycle of activity that will take nearly three decades to unfold. The keynote of the progressed New moon phase
is the birth and emergence of some new possibility. A tone, aspiration, or intention is germinated from within you that calls for a
re-orientation to life and the world.

The nature of this new direction may not become clear for several years, slowly assuming a shape as the moon increases in light It is important to trust that this new energy has a purpose and to instinctively follow where it leads you. For some people this period may mark a definite break with the past, but for others it represents a time of feeling dissatisfied with old patterns that seem empty of meaning and a yearning for something different. The progressed New Moon phase often signifies a gradual awakening to creative new directions. It asks that you be open to what you have not experienced before.

1. What new changes in your life or identity were initiated during this time?

2. To what extent did you experience confusion or lack of clear direction about what was occurring?

3. In retrospect, can you now see the results, for better or worse, of what was initiated at this time?

Progressed Crescent phase

1st progressed Crescent phase: begins: _____ Age: ___ _____

2nd progressed Crescent phase begins: _____ Age: ___ _____

3rd progressed Crescent phase begins: _____ Age: ___ _____

As the Moon's light increases with the waxing Crescent phase, life events clarify the general direction of the cycle. The shape of your new direction begins to come into focus and take form. However as your fledging identity emerges, you may be overwhelmed with doubts concerning this new direction, feeling that it may take more effort and struggle than it is worth or wondering if you have enough willpower to see it through. You are challenged to assert yourself and to overcome your fears of the unknown, your insecurities and conditioned habits. In order to free yourself from the inertia of the past, it may be necessary to make a break with the patterns, situations or people in your life that either do not support you or try to prevent you from moving forward with your aspiration. As this phase unfolds, you are called to develop new talents and skills. Opportunities will open up that help to facilitate the expansion of your goal, and your final challenge is to take advantage of these opportunities by acting upon them.

1. What conditions did you feel were holding you back?

2. How did you respond to this confrontation between past patterns and future goals? What new skills and talents did you develop?

3. Were you able to take advantage of the opportunities available to you?

Progressed First-Quarter phase

1st progressed First-Quarter phase: begins: _____ Age: ___   _____

2nd progressed First-Quarter phase begins: _____ Age: ___   _____

3rd progressed First-Quarter phase begins: _____ Age: ___   _____

During the progressed First-Quarter phase, you often encounter a crisis or series of crises regarding your new direction as it's now time to actualize your aspiration. First you must clear away and repudiate anything that is still holding you back from pursuing your goal. As you move intentionally toward the future, you are challenged to make definite decisions and take forceful direct actions to build and firmly establish a structure for your goal. The tensions that arise from these confrontations, as well as fear of failure and its consequences, can lead to blocked psychological energy manifesting as frustration and anger. During this critical turning point in the progressed lunation cycle, you are called to exhibit a strong will backed by purposefully committed decisions and actions. It is helpful to cultivate the qualities of courage and confidence regarding your new direction.

1 What crises in the physical world did you encounter? Did you grow in courage and confidence?

2. What new structures did you build to more firmly establish your foundations? How did you move out into society?

3. How did you use the psychological or emotional tension in your life to force issues? If you were unable to confront your life issues, how did you handle your feelings of frustration and anger?

Progressed Gibbous Phase

1st progressed Gibbous phase: begins: _____ Age: ___   _____
2nd progressed Gibbous phase begins: _____ Age: ___   _____
3rd progressed Gibbous phase begins: _____ Age: ___   _____

During the progressed Gibbous phase you now see the concrete results of what you have built and must learn how to live with these structures. You are tested to persevere in your commitment to this new direction by integrating your daily actions into this structure, paying attention to details, learning how to function smoothly and efficiently in your everyday reality. In order to do this, you analyze and evaluate your growth so that you can perfect the techniques of the process that you have been developing since its inception at the progressed New Moon phase. This can be a time of intense productivity, but it requires that you make continual adjustments to improve and fine tune your operational vehicle, adapting it to the environment and the limitations of the real world.

1. What adjustments did you need to make to everyday reality, and what techniques did you try to perfect?

2. To what extent did you have to struggle to persevere on your path?

3. In what ways were you asking "why" and questing for some kind of revelation?

Progressed Full Phase

1st progressed Full phase: begins: _____ Age: ___   _____
2nd progressed Full phase begins: _____ Age: ___   _____
3rd progressed Full phase begins: _____ Age: ___   _____

During the progressed Full phase, the seed intention germinated at the progressed New Moon flowers, and whatever was born 14-15 years ago now reaches some kind of culmination. During the Full Moon phase, the Moon reflects the maximum amount of the Sun's light. Under this illumination you can clearly see both the successful and unsuccessful aspects of whatever you have been developing.

This is a time to look at your life situation objectively, to consider the meaning of what you are doing, to clarify your life purpose, personal desires, and goals, and to integrate any conflicting energies. This consciousness can allow you to release the creative meaning of what you have been developing onto a higher or deeper level and realize fulfillment in your life. But if you are not clear about the purpose of what you are doing, you may become disillusioned, depleted of vital energy, and your structures may begin to disintegrate. The progressed Full moon phase calls for you to infuse a sense of meaning into the structures you have built and perfected.

1. What situations or relationships reached a culmination?

2. How and where did I find meaning to infuse into my life? How did I respond to lack of real meaning?

3. What issues was I compelled to face consciously?

Progressed Disseminating phase

1st progressed Disseminating phase: begins: _____ Age: ___ _____

2nd progressed Disseminating phase begins: _____ Age: ___ _____

3rd progressed Disseminating phase begins: _____ Age: ___ _____

After you have focused your understanding in the Full phase, during the progressed Disseminating phase you move out into the world, link with others, and share the content of whatever was illuminated during the progressed Full Moon phase. This is the fruition phase of the cycle when your new moon seed impulse has ripened into the fruit. You are called to teach your truth as well as to allow yourself to be cross-pollinated by listening to the reactions, feedback, and ideas of others. It is a time to demonstrate what you have found to be important by living out your values and embodying your beliefs into a workable life philosophy. Without a value system, you may experience aimlessness and the sense that life has gone by and missed you, that nothing really matters.

1. In what ways did I live out my values?

2. What messages did I try to convey?

3. How did I link with others in order to make my efforts more meaningful within a social context?

Progressed Last-Quarter Phase

1st progressed Last-Quarter phase: begins: _____ Age: ___ _____
2nd progressed Last-Quarter phase begins: _____ Age: ___ _____
3rd progressed Last-Quarter phase begins: _____ Age: ___ _____

During this phase when the moon's light is sharply waning, mental and emotional tensions build and you may experience a crisis in consciousness. You may feel restless and discontent as you realize your beliefs and life structures are no longer working for you. During the progressed Disseminating phase you accomplished the purpose of the progressed New Moon intention; it is now time to turn away from what has already been done and gradually prepare for something new to begin at the next progressed New Moon.

As you assimilate and digest the awareness gained throughout the cycle, you begin to question and reject what is no longer valid in both your philosophy and activities. As you tear down life structures that have become obsolete, you turn inward to uncover new ideas that will become the foundation underlying the coming new cycle. Your tension is compounded as it is often difficult to externalize and share with those closest to you your inner process of disillusionment, agitation, and rebellion as you begin to reevaluate and reorient your life.

1. What old forms did I turn away from and repudiate?

2. In what ways did I conceal from others the process of my inner revolt and reorientation until I was able to externalize my changed perceptions?

3. What new concepts formed the foundation of my ideological beliefs based on intimations of the future?

Progressed Balsamic phase

1st progressed Balsamic phase: begins: _____ Age: ___ _____

2nd progressed Balsamic phase begins: _____ Age: ___ _____

3rd progressed Balsamic phase begins: _____ Age: ___ _____

The progressed Balsamic phase is the dark moon phase of the lunation cycle. It is the bridge between the ending of one cycle of activity and the beginning of the next one. During this time you are summing up and completing all that you have been involved with for the previous twenty-seven years. It is a time of letting go, purifying, healing, and preparing for renewal.

You may experience the loss of what has previously given you your sense of identity and purpose. Relationships end, loved ones die, children leave home, jobs terminate, cherished homes are lost. Some people become ill or become the caretakers for others who are suffering. Some people make discoveries about their past that shatter their taken-for-granted assumptions, and some move to isolated settings. It is not unusual to feel lonely, depressed, suicidal, crazy, chaotic, alienated, and without direction. Tremendous grief may come up at this time as you mourn your losses.

The message is to release whatever has ended for you. It has served its purpose and has no further value in what is to come. Like the snake shedding its skin, an old part of you is truly dying. Allow the old to be destroyed. This is a period of retreat, emptying out, and the final letting go. You need to make room for the birth which is to follow at the next progressed New Moon.

Individuals from the past with whom there exists unfinished karmic business may reappear in your life, or you may get involved in relationships with those who trigger your old unresolved issues. You may hit rock bottom with your addictions, and circumstances may force you to enter into recovery programs. This is a time of healing old wounds.

During this time you may need more rest in order to facilitate a healing process that wants to happen. It is a time to become quiet, introspective, and receptive. You will benefit more from entering into a state of being rather than one of doing.

As you withdraw from your previous life structures and outer activities, it is time to develop a deeper relationship with your inner self and the subtle dimensional realms. Spiritual practices, psychological therapies, metaphysical studies, artistic creativity, and altruistic activities all provide positive channels for the expression of progressed Balsamic phase energies that will help you to move through this final stage of cyclic process.

As you prepare your seed capsule you may feel the urge to resolve the past by distilling the wisdom you have gained into some kind of form that will become the basis for what is to emerge. Releasing the past, you begin to envision the future. You yearn for something new, fresh, vital. In your daydreams and night dreams you weave the images of what is waiting to be born, something which will satisfy your vague inner longings. It will be in answer to this need that the new will come forth. As this phase draws to its conclusion, you may sense the future and dedicate and commit yourself to following the course that opens up to you, even though you may have no idea where it will eventually lead.

1. What aspects of my life dissolved or ended? In what ways did I feel withdrawn and unconnected?

2. What did I sum up and distill?

3. What did I yearn and long for? How did I envision the future-to-be?

4. Can I now see how this emptying out was the prelude and preparation for the new cycle to begin fresh and unencumbered?

Finding My Way Through the Dark
Here are some questions that will help you to further apply the lunation cycle archetypes to your own life.

A. The dates of my previous progressed Balsamic phases are

_____

     1. What ended for me?

     2. How did I experience this dark phase of the moon?

B. My most recent progressed New Moon Phase began

_____

     1. What or who was trying to emerge?

C. In my current lunation cycle, I am in the _____ phase.

     This began _____ and will end _____.

     1. My current challenges are:

     2. How aware am I of how the seed impulse initiated at the progressed New Moon Phase is developing?

D. Can I now see the meaning of my life purpose unfolding as a series of spirals with the events of each phase integrated into a larger holistic pattern?

How To Determine Your Lunation Phase

There are three methods of determining your birth lunation phase.

1) If you do not know the sign and degree positions of your Sun and Moon, you can have a birth chart printed out by Astro-Communications Services, using the order form in Appendix C. If you have an ACS chart, on the left hand side about 1/3 down the page you will see

ANGLE = some number.

If this number is:

0.00 -45.00	your lunation phase is New Moon
45.01 -90.00	your lunation phase is Crescent Moon
90.01 -135.00	your lunation phase is First Quarter Moon
135.01 -180.00	your lunation phase is Gibbous Moon
180.01 -225.00	your lunation phase is Full Moon
225.01 -270.00	your lunation phase is Disseminating Moon
270.01 -315.00	your lunation phase is Last Quarter Moon
315.01 -360.00	your lunation phase is Balsamic Moon

2) If you know the sign and degree positions of your Sun and Moon, you can ask a competent astrologer to calculate your moon phase or 3) you can *find your lunation phase* by assembling a Moon Phase and Aspect Wheel. The directions for how to do this appear on the following pages.

Instructions for Assembling Your Moon Phase and Aspect Wheel

To begin, **cut out** or **photocopy** Figures 3 and 4. You will be needing to cut and paste these two diagrams to form your own measuring instrument.

Begin by cutting out the smaller cirlce, Figure 3. Place it tin the center of the larger circle, Figure 4. Align the centers and connect them with a paper fastener so that the inner wheel turns inside the outer wheel. Mounting and pasting on light weight cardboard will make your wheel more durable.

To determine your Moon Phase, rotate the black arrow on the inner wheel to the sign and degree of your Sun. For example, if your *Sun were in 13 degrees of Leo,* you would place the arrow as indicated in the sample Moon Phase Wheel in figure 2.

Next, holding the wheel in place, locate with your finger, the sign and degree of your moon. In our figure, the *Moon is in 10 degrees of Gemini.* Then point your finger toward the center of the wheel; it will be pointing towards your correct Moon Phase.

Suppoe the Sun were still at 13 degrees of Leo and the *Moon were at 20 degrees of Aries.* What would be the Moon Phase? The answer shown in Figure 2 is the Disseminating Moon Phase. Now proceed to determine your own Moon Phase!

Figure 2: Sample Moon Phase Wheel

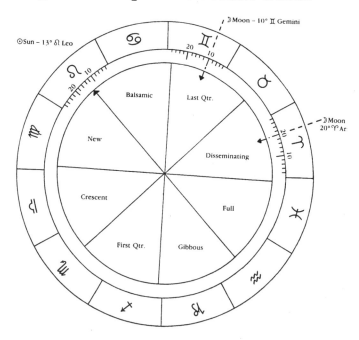

Figure 3: Inner Moon Phase Wheel

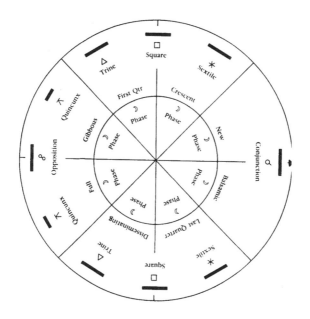

Figure 4: Outer Moon Phase Wheel

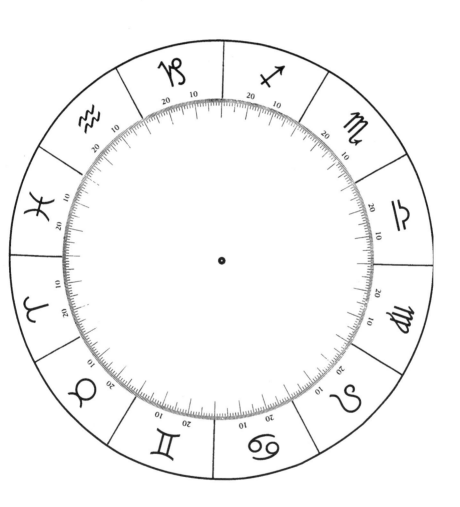

CHAPTER 3

THE TWELFTH HOUSE: THE GREAT UNKNOWN

There exists an area in the human psyche that is hidden from our conscious awareness and difficult to access with the rational mind. This sphere contains all that lies beneath the surface of consciousness, the reservoir of forgotten memories of the past and intimations of the future. Western psychology refers to this dimension of the psyche as the UnconsciousUnconscious, and Eastern philosophy describes it in terms of *Karma*. In astrology, the twelfth house is a symbol for the influence of both unconscious and karmic forces in our life. A discussion of the twelfth house raises the underlying question pondered in both Western and Eastern thought: *"How is it that unconscious hidden forces from the past can dominate our actions and shape our life circumstances?"*

The wheel of houses in astrology portrays a mandala of the meaning of the totality of human experiences. In astrology, the birth chart is a circular map that symbolically indicates the vibrational pattern of planetary energies existing at the precise moment of our first breath, that we, as individuals, share with the cosmos. It is a mandala of our personal meaning. One major astrological perspective in interpreting this pattern yields a twelvefold division of this circular mandala into a wheel of twelve houses. Each house describes one of the twelve basic compartments of life activities and environments such as health, finances, relationships, family, children, career, friends, education etc.

As the final sector of the wheel of houses, the twelfth house is directly related to the dark moon phase of the lunation cycle.

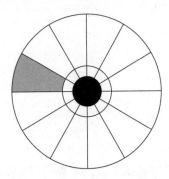

The Twelfth House as the Closure Phase of Cyclic process

Both the dark phase of the moon and the twelfth house symbolize the closure phase of cyclic process. Historically the dark slice of the cycle in all conceptual systems symbolizes the great, dark unknown that evokes human emotions of fear, denial, and repression. This pattern also exists in astrology where classical interpretations of the twelfth house assign it rulership of fate, self-undoing, hidden enemies, demons, bondage, obstacles, limitations, karmic retribution, sacrifice, victimization, suffering, confinement, alienation, and imprisonment. As a polarity to the negative and evil influences of the twelfth house, there also exist traces in the astrological lore that associate it with hidden treasures and spiritual transcendence.

The experiences of this phase occur during the absence of the moon's light where, under the cover of darkness, they are concealed from the gaze of the waking eye. The twelfth house contains all that is hidden from the conscious mind, as well as what transpires behind the scenes and what emerges when we retreat from the outer world into the veiled solitude of our inner spaces.

The purpose of the final sector of cyclic process is completion and renewal. Here is where a physical, emotional or mental form that has fulfilled its function disintegrates back into the formless state of energy. The wisdom essence of that form's purpose is distilled and concentrated into a seed capsule which is placed in the dark Underground, Underworld, or Unconscious, and awaits renewal with the initiation of the next cycle. This twelfth sector contains the accumulated contents of the past which composts into the soil that nourishes the seed of the future.

The twelfth house is the womb of the soul. It describes a critical juncture between the world of the living and that of the dead and unborn. We enter the twelfth house through death and leave it through rebirth. During this intermediate stage, in the womb of becoming, the essence of our wisdom from the past, our habits and what is unresolved from the previous cycle, all fuse with our intentions for the future. In the developing fetal stage of our physical or psychological gestation, this pattern is imprinted into the neural circuits that web the unconscious dimension of our psyche.

In the closure sector of cyclic process, all returns back to source and merges with the larger whole. The energies of the twelfth phase magnetically draw us down and under into the undifferentiated waters of the vast cosmic ocean of unity. This immersion in the awareness of our oneness with all life is later felt, when we are in physical incarnation, as the mystical yearning for that connectedness that might heal the pain of separation and isolation in our life. Both spiritual quests and chemical addictions are paths modern individuals follow in their longing for the peace and serenity of that dimly remembered other realm.

In this space between worlds and time between incarnations, the twelfth house provides an opening into the underworld of our unconscious where we can access the entire universe of past, present and future flowing into our psyche. It is the repository of hidden wisdom and secret teachings embodied in universal, mythic and archetypal images. Buddhist tradition teaches that in this intermediate state called the Bardo, we encounter the Peaceful and Wrathful Deities. Dane Rudhyar writes that this is where we meet both the Angels of Light and the Guardians of the Threshold (9).

In this deep recess of our psyche, our angels can guide us to our source of transcendent understanding, creative inspiration, and the highest aspirations of selfless love and service. Intertwined with the angels are our demons whose faces mirror all of our failures, frustrations, denials, fears, anger, greed, jealousy, hatred and ignorance. The roots of our angels and demons reach back into both the joys and the pain of the past, and their branches extend out toward the possibilities of our future.

It is through the twelfth house that each of us is linked to the past and future. The twelfth dimension, which lies hidden beneath the surface of conscious awareness, holds the storehouse of forgotten memories from the past and the potentialities of future possibilities. The sum total of our personal and collective past is recorded in the many layers of the unconscious - from the forgotten images of personal experiences from this lifetime, infancy, the cycle of our death, conception, gestation and birth, past lives, and then deeper into the transpersonal strata of the collective unconscious. While this psychic material is not normally accessible to the conscious mind, it nevertheless has a powerful effect on how we perceive and interact with the world and it shapes the actions and circumstances of our lives. It is the soil from which our conscious experiences and circumstances are formed and nourished. Whether this force is called karma or unconscious motivation, both Eastern and Western thought agrees to the existence of a pattern running through the unconscious that weaves the ancient threads of our future. It is only by going into the dark time of inner space and coming to peace with our memories that a way opens toward healing, renewal, inspired creativity and merging with the soul of the cosmos.

The twelfth house is a metaphor for the unseen real of all that happens before we can remember. In ancient times, rites of initiation were the means used to descend into the Underworld so that individuals could remember the experiences of their death and rebirth. There exists a spectrum of ancient Oriental spiritual practices developed over several millennia that are designed to enter and explore this inner dimension of consciousness.

Only within the last century have modern individuals in Western culture begun to explore the knowledge hidden in the depths of the mind. Sigmund Freud and Carl Jung helped to usher in the birth of a psychology that seeks to understand the workings of the Unconscious. Today many psychotherapeutic techniques are providing the passageway into the Unconscious in order to uncover the forgotten treasures in the underworld of our psyche. Current depth therapies such as rebirthing, rolfing, holotropic breathwork, shamanic counseling, and dreamwork are enabling people to access their infantile, birth and death experiences and travel into the subtle dimensions of other realms. Regression and hypnosis are assisting people to explore their past lives. A proliferation of information on death and dying is bringing much needed guidance and compassion to help prepare individuals for the closure phase of their lives. The spread of Buddhism to the West is revealing ancient teachings on the nature of the mind and the causes of suffering. Women, in academic and spiritual areas, are rediscovering their ancient history and old religion.

As we evolve, we begin to stretch and expand the boundaries of our awareness. By reaching into the unconscious, we can reclaim knowledge of our past, understand the circumstances of the present, and intuit visions of the future. In this process it is inevitable that our terror of the unknown that keeps us frozen and constricted in pain will dissolve, and our images of the dark will have to be revised. This is a courageous movement toward accepting the wholeness of our being that challenges our misogynic cultural conditioning of fearing the great dark unknown.

The final sector in the wheel of life experiences is a symbol for this mysterious realm of the unseen real where both Eastern karmic patterns and Western collective memories are hidden and stored in the unconscious dimension of the psyche. The following discussion of these matters will hopefully expand upon the traditional interpretations of this closure sector of cyclic process.

The Twelfth House and Karma

The twelfth house is often called the house of karma. In this context, it refers to the unconscious material we carry over from the past.

Karma and Reincarnation

The concepts of karma and reincarnation form the basis of a supposition that moral laws operate in the sphere of consciousness. Eastern philosophers have used this view to explain how unconscious forces from the past affect the present and the future.

Karma is the law of cause and effect; it is the result of any previous action whose seed will eventually bear a fruit. This law implies that it is inevitable that we will at some time encounter the results of all our previous actions. Positive activity will bear joyous and enriching life circumstances; negative activity will yield misery and misfortune. *Reincarnation* proposes that we have not one, but many lives, one right after the other, here on earth. These two principles working together imply that throughout countless lifetimes, we reap the results of our actions.

This view holds that our present circumstances are due to our own making by our actions in past lives. There exists both individual karma and group karma, the latter being the conditions created by the collective attitudes and actions of a family, generation, group, race or nation. However, the theory of karma does not remain static in simply keeping the account of a cosmic balance sheet of rewards and punishments from one life to the next. It further goes on to suggest that how we respond to the present conditions of our karma will determine our future. A Buddhist adage teaches,

"If you want to know who you were in your past life, look to your present circumstances. If you want to know who you will be in your future life, look to your present actions."

Karma and Fate

The discussion of karma always brings up the question of fate. To what extent is our life fated–that is, already predetermined by forces that are now beyond our control? Does free will exist? Do we have any possibility or power to influence our future? The resolution to this query is not an "either/or" answer, but "both/and" the realization that at each moment we are simultaneously subject to fate and offered free-will.

To the ancient Greeks, fate was personified by the three daughters of Nyx, Goddess of Night, who reflect the dark side of the goddess, and in our soul represent the primal elements in the dark unconscious parts of our being. The Greeks called her Moira, whose name means "part," or a person's allotted portion in life. As a Triple Moon Goddess, Moira is known in her three lunar aspects as *Klotho* who spins the thread of life from her distaff, *Lachesis* who measures it against her rod, and *Atropos*, the "inevitable" who cuts it with her shears.(4) The Moirai within us spin our fate and are an embodiment of our destinies. No one can go against their decree.

Fate is the inevitable ripening of our karma. It is unavoidable and unalterable. Up to the ever-present now, everything that occurs to us has been preordained by our own personal or groups' former actions and thoughts. This is our fate, and it has not been imposed upon us from the outside, but is a product of our own inner creation. Where the possibility of free will exists is in how we respond to our fate. The intentions and motivations that underlie the choices we make and actions we take in the present determines our destiny. Our free will exists as the choice and opportunity to create the future according to our level of wisdom and compassion in th present.

From the perspective of karma, reincarnation and fate, the twelfth house signifies that area of our life experiences where we reap the results of our prior actions from this or previous lifetimes; and, by our response, sow the seeds of future circumstances. The twelfth house experiences may not be the product of this lifetime, but are those sources of hidden wisdom, advantageous ingrained talents, as well as the painful issues, unfinished lessons and unresolved relationships that we carry over from before. In this sense, the twelfth house represents the ghosts from the past.

What is seen by the conscious eye in this temporal reality is but the tip of a situation whose antecedent causes extend deep into the past. When we consider our unconscious past in this light, we can gain clarity and compassion in understanding the causes of the suffering, loss, pain, and seemingly unfair burdens that are so often found in the twelfth house.

When we do not willingly face our unfinished business from the past, the universe forces us to do so. This is why the twelfth house is associated with involuntary confinement– imprisonment, hospitalization, and institutionalization in all its forms. The confinement continues until we have resolved the issues, or in the case of imprisonment, paid back our karmic debts.

The experiences of the twelfth house offer us the opportunity to fulfill our karmic moral obligations, voluntarily assume our outstanding debts, and thus bring unresolved issues from the past to a state of balance and completion. Twelfth house energies can sustain us by offering vast hidden resources of strength and wisdom to fulfill our purpose. However, when what we feel is the pervasive pain of our wounds, the teaching of the twelfth house is that our soul will not heal until we realize the necessity of transforming the attitudes and actions that have created these results. As we become aware of the workings of the law cause and effect, our karma seems to accelerate and the results ripen more quickly. We can rapidly burn through much old karma as we willingly seek to make the necessary amends and consciously change our behavior from harmful to beneficial activity. This is the karmic lesson of the twelfth house that offers a gift of healing during the dark night of the soul. Biblical scripture sums up the law of karma in the following three verses.

"As ye sow, so shall ye reap."
"An eye for an eye, and a tooth for a tooth."
"Do unto others as you would have others do unto you."

Karma and Transcendence

To the extent that our level of awareness operates in a dualistic world where we perceive reality as polarized into a separation between *object and subject* or *self and other*, we are bound by the karmic law of cause and effect. The twelfth house, as a symbol of the closure phase of cyclic process, is where all merges back to source. It contains the possibility of the direct experience of "oneness," which has been referred to as the Law of Grace, "Christ Consciousness," and "Buddha Mind." The law of grace transcends the law of karma when the distinction between self and other dissolves into a more inclusive awareness of the fundamental unity of all life.

In the East, the term *bodhisattva* describes the being who has achieved enlightenment through having fulfilled and completed his or her karma. However, rather than remaining in the clear light, this person chooses to continue incarnating in this dualistic dimension for the purpose of benefiting others. The bodhisattva's life is motivated by the desire to relieve suffering and guide others toward healing and liberation.

Our twelfth house energies can point to our commitments to emulate the bodhisattva ideal. On the level where the law of grace, or oneness, is operative, the twelfth house burdens of pain and suffering are not karmic retribution, but rather the additional responsibilities we have voluntarily taken on in order to help others. The pattern that often unfolds is that of the *wounded healer,* which in Western traditions is linked with the image of the shamanic healer who has always been first wounded. In the early part of life, we experience some great pain, loss or denial which is actually the training ground for deepening our capacity for empathy and sensitivity. In later life, from the power and wisdom of our own experience, we operate in a helping and healing capacity for others in similar situations. Hence, the twelfth house rules "redemptive suffering."

From this perspective, twelfth house energies may also indicate the difficulties we encounter when we function as the release valve for purifying the karma and toxic accumulation, not only for ourselves, but for the family or group that we are a part of. In dysfunctional families, the most open and vulnerable member will usually serve in this capacity; and in society, the scapegoat assumes the role of the martyr. Twelfth house factors may indicate the commitments we take on to resolve a collective or archetypal problem, and like the hundredth monkey theory, the healing of an individual will have a rippling, cumulative effect throughout the group. The twelfth house can also point to living a symbolic life where what come through us are not personal, but collective issues.

When karma and reincarnation are linked with the concepts of evolution and progression, they become the means by which consciousness comes into self-realization. (10) Karma is the principle by which we shape our personality and reality according to our choices and actions. Moving through eons of time, reincarnation offers us many lifetimes and varied experiences through which to understand, practice and perfect the act of creation. The Eastern path teaches that the goal of enlightenment is liberation from illusion of duality which precipitates rebirth and the endless suffering of human condition. Western occult traditions speak to developing total awareness of being a unit of consciousness within the larger mind and living in harmony with the earth and all living things. This is the inner meaning of the twelfth house as sacrifice (that is *to make sacred*), selfless service, spiritual practice, and enlightenment.

The Twelfth House and Our Hidden Life

Entering the twelfth domain of consciousness entails developing a relationship with all that is hidden. While the vast portion of the twelfth realm holds our forgotten past, this symbol also pertains to that part of our conscious waking life that we keep hidden from others. Twelfth house factors address our need for solitude, time alone, privacy and seclusion so that all those aspects of ourselves that operate only when we are by ourselves may emerge.

The twelfth house is where we pull inward from the myriad demands of other people and the outer world in order to secure a state of peace and clarity within ourselves. For some of us the dark moments of our solitude speak to a rich inner life of contemplation, introspection, spiritual practice and artistic self-expression. Here we can get in touch with our visions and dreams and connect with the hidden gifts of our unconscious. We are comfortable with being alone and are not lonely. It is a centering and creative experience whereby we can recharge our energy, tap our inner wisdom, and heal ourselves.

However, for some people the experience of being alone brings up feelings of alienation. Our overriding emotional reaction is one of being cut off from others, and we feel abandoned, alienated, unloved and unwanted. We panic, are anxious, frightened and desperate when we are by ourselves or have empty time in our lives without anyone or anything to fill it up.

The twelfth house also shows our need to leave the outer world and voluntarily withdraw into places of retreat such as temples, monasteries, ashrams, sanctuaries, or nature; or involuntarily in places of exile and isolation from society such as institutions, prisons, hospitals, asylums, and reformatories.

This hidden dimension contains what we keep to ourselves. It is our tendency to be a private person and remain anonymous, to operate behind the scenes, or live as a hermit. The twelfth house gives us a space in which to relate to our personal interests, "au natural" appearance, bodily functions, and daily routines that we do not care for others to see or know about.

In a more problematical manner, we may use the twelfth house energies of withdrawal to create a shell of protection around us which conceals our hidden activities or shameful secrets. When the dark energies are used in this way, we shun public exposure, remain aloof, and act evasive. We become obsessed with preventing others from discovering our deceptions, illegal activities, clandestine relationships and love affairs, physical dysfunctions, addictions and family problems.

In the process of reclaiming the dark closure phase of cyclic process, we must heal our relationship to the hidden parts of our waking lives when we are alone. When our experience of aloneness reinforces our sense of isolation and exclusion or when we pull into ourselves to conceal our wrongdoing and shame, we block our source of regeneration and deplete our vital force. Then we are not able to use the energies of the twelfth house in positive and self-affirming ways.

The Twelfth House and thePsychological Dimensions of the Unconscious

Like the other water houses (the fourth and eighth), the twelfth house in astrology is linked to the concept of the unconscious. In this context, it refers to those patterns, urges, motivations, compulsions, and drives in our life that operate from below the surface of conscious awareness. Today many people are familiar with the psychological definition of the unconscious as that area of our psyche which contains latent, forgotten and unretrievable thoughts, images and impressions. While we are not consciously aware of the workings of these hidden forces, they exert a powerful influence in affecting our choices, actions and attitudes in life. Continued exploration into the unconscious is revealing the existence of many layers of the past in this dimension of psyche.

The Personal Layer of the Unconscious

It was less than one hundred years ago that Sigmund Freud first pioneered the exploration of the unconscious background of consciousness. He postulated the existence of a vast portion of the mind which includes instinctual desires and personal experiences going as far back as infancy which were frightening, painful, or unacceptable and have been long since repressed and forgotten. In his practice, Freud found that the symptoms of hysterical patients could be directly traced to these apparently forgotten psychic traumas in early life, and that they represented undischarged emotional energy. These neurotic behavior patterns could be neutralized if the person could clearly recall the painful experiences which had caused a deep impression or emotional shock and thereby release the blocked energy .

The Collective Layer of the Unconscious

Carl Jung later elaborated upon his mentor's work, and one of his greatest contributions to psychology was his theory of the *collective unconscious*. He proposed that there are two dimensions to the unconscious: a personal layer that Freud discovered consisting of an individual's own biographical repressed material, and a second layer called the collective unconscious whose contents have never been conscious and are not acquired from a person's own memories and experiences. These inherited propensities in the human psyche extend back beyond the pre-infantile period into the residues of ancestral life. Jung gave the name "archetypes" to these primordial images in the collective unconscious which are "the most ancient and universal thought forms of humanity." This second system in the unconscious contains the preexistent thought forms in the psyche that are universal, impersonal mental and emotional patterns which are identical in all people throughout time reoccurring cross-culturally in humanity as themes in mythology, religion and fairy tales.

The collective unconscious not only contains the repository of ancestral memories from the past, but it is also the storehouse of latent potentialities and dreams of the yet-to-be future of the conscious mind. Completely new thoughts and creative ideas which have never been conscious before can present themselves from the unconscious. This forms an important part of our subliminal psyche where germinal ideas for the future can arise from the dark depths of the mind. The collective unconscious can be conceived of as a treasure house which is the source of all inspiration, creativity and wisdom.

The Prenatal Level of the Unconscious:
There exists a belief among some contemporary psychologists such as Stanislov Grof that there exists a third layer to the unconscious which consists of the womb and birth experience which is the interface between the collective and the personal dimensions.(11) Observations show that many forms of psychopathology and unconscious motivations have deep roots in the biological aspects of birth. The spiritual process of rebirth parallels the biological process of birth. When our birth transitions are encoded with difficult experiences, they emerge later in life as the forms of our dis-eases. The inner healer in each individual, who is always moving toward a state of wholeness, will attract or recreate situations in life that carry a similar emotional charge. This process gives us the opportunity to reconfront, release, and heal the painful unconscious issues arising from our birth/death experiences that shape our lives.

The Hidden Enemies of the Twelfth House: The Shadow and The Demons

The twelfth house, as a symbol of our unconscious past, encompasses this vast multidimensional realm hidden within our psyche where powerful, compulsive forces arise that cause confusion and pain in our life. These are the wounds in our soul. Because these forces are not easily seen or understood, astrological terminology calls the twelfth house the place of hidden enemies and self-undoing. In reality, these secret enemies who would subversively seek to deceive, hurt or destroy us are the hidden aspects of ourselves.

The twelfth house is an indicator of what is passed on to us from our forgotten past, and can show us the nature of our unconscious motivations and their resultant complexes. Twelfth house symbols can indicate what happened to us in the time before we can remember —in our shared archetypal and collective memories, previous incarnations, the cycle of our death, conception and birth, and our early childhood. They also point to how we absorbed into our unconscious programming our mother's physical, emotional and mental state and our parents' relationship, which, as young children, we did not distinguish as being separate from our own.

The causal factors of these compulsions that make us act in ways we don't understand and eventually result in harm to ourselves or others are rooted in our unconscious habit patterns, deeply ingrained beliefs, karmic accumulations, and forgotten traumas. Certain issues may become lifelong themes that maintain a continuous expression and emotional charge through the many layers of the past. These themes manifest as repeated cycles of physical and emotional trauma and subsequent suffering. Twelfth house symbols can evoke memories of just one experience which can then reveal the meaning of the entire strand.

Western psychology proposes that the unconscious motivations that propel us toward self-destructive behavior come from repressed energies of forgotten traumas and absorbed impressions which we have not been able to assimilate and integrate. Our defense system tends to repress the memories associated with powerful experiences involving fear, failure, pain, loss or danger. When we cannot acknowledge or release the residual feelings that accompany these traumatic experiences, they become locked into the unconscious webbing of our psyche. Here, contained under pressure and confinement, they fester and autointoxicate our system. These poisonous contents of our psyche distort our perception and color our view of what life is all about. The blocked, emotionally charged energies are the source of the seemingly irrational fears, phobias, compulsions, guilt and shame that plague us, and also are the basis of the psychosomatic symptoms of disease in our physical body. Healing requires that we recall, understand, and release the charged feeling associated with the trauma.

However, our conscious mind resists uncovering these lurking, dark images because we believe the realizations might be more than we could handle and would overwhelm and shatter us. Herein lies our conditioned fear of the dark. Much of our life energy in the twelfth house is used to hold back these threatening and potentially destructive forces. Twelfth house factors point to the nature of these hidden fears and the kinds of energy we use to keep them repressed. The more the conscious mind shuts off, the more our self-image develops apart from the wholeness of our being.

The *shadow,* in Jungian psychology, is the dark, rejected part of the psyche. We repress into the unconscious dimension of our being not only frightening and painful memories, but also those aspects of ourselves that we dislike and find unacceptable because they make us feel uncomfortable or inadequate. To the extent that we are unable or unwilling to accept these traits and deny their existence, they become our hidden enemies.

The shadow is the messenger of the unconscious. When we repress the shadow aspect of ourselves, rather than withering away, it seems to grow, flourish and acquire a strength that subversively dominates our personality. During our most vulnerable moments of weariness, crisis, stress, or unguardedness, this alien forces can suddenly erupt with great power and violence. We then act in negative and self-destructive ways that we scarcely recognize and can't understand. When the shadow, as the distorted aspects of our hidden self, is activated in emotionally charged situations, it threatens our sense of control and shatters our self-image as a reasonable, calm and civilized being.

The twelfth house symbolizes the ways in which we both repress and project the unconscious hidden parts of ourselves. When we repress these energies, their toxic accumulation becomes the source of our chronic physical and mental illnesses, as well as the cause of depression and the depletion of our vital force. Through our distorted perception, we notice in others and take offense at those qualities we cannot accept in ourselves. When we project our shadowy unconscious, we externalize these images and magnetically attract those people who embody what we most fear and those conditions that confine, limit or deny us.

Demons are another class of hidden enemies found in twelfth house interpretations. Buddhist teachings explain the phenomena of demons as those habitual, deeply ingrained concepts in our mind that are the accumulated residue of our mistaken beliefs and wrong actions. All of our suffering arises from the basic misperception of the illusion of separateness, and the subsequent attachment to the self and aversion to anything that threatens it. Our demons are the negative emotions of ignorance, greed, hatred, pride and jealousy that perpetuate our self-important attitudes and actions. These are the poisons of the mind which pollute our thoughts and actions, distort our perceptions of reality, and, when projected onto others in our environment, take on the demonic appearance of our external enemies who seek to harm and destroy us. These projections confuse our relationships with others by creating conflict and mistrust.

Healing in the twelfth house demands that we acknowledge our hidden enemies as our hidden self. From a psychological perspective, we must recover these lost parts of ourselves, and integrate them into the wholeness of our being. From a spiritual perspective, the energy bound up in these destructive emotions needs to be released and purified, so it can be transmuted into corresponding wisdom qualities inherent in the depths of the twelfth house.(12) These qualities can take the shape of those guardian angels and spirit guides who function as protectors and benevolent, unseen forces in our lives.

The Twelfth House and Healing The Soul

Healing the soul is one of the core issues of the twelfth house. The twelfth sphere is the place of our deep wounds in the psyche. Both Western psychology and Eastern philosophy are concerned with the processes in our unconscious past that yield the painful conditions of the present. The healing of a person's psychic wounds is the task of Jungian psychology, and the relief from suffering is the aim of Eastern enlightenment. Both traditions seek to heal the wound of the soul and effect a spiritual transformation toward self-realization and enlightened awareness.

Jung's process moves toward actualizing individual wholeness by establishing a network of communication between the conscious and unconscious, and integrating and harmonizing these components of our being. With self-realization comes the awareness of an ethical responsibility in that we can no longer conduct our life as though unaware of the hidden workings of our unconscious.(13) Buddhist practice reaches toward enlightened awareness of our true nature, for the sake of all beings. The causes of our suffering are known to be the illusion of separateness and subsequent results of our prior tendencies and actions to see ourselves as something separate and more important than others. This realization precipitates a shift in our behavior and conduct.

Wounding comes from separation from the unity of source. As we descend into the underworld of our consciousness, we encounter our angels and demons, the deep wounds in our psyche and the cures for healing the soul. It is the place where we are the most painfully alone until we realize our connectedness with a larger whole. Healing entails moving toward a state of wholeness within oneself and with the rest of life.

The Healing Power of the Lunar Darkness

Healing takes place in the dark, during the absence of the moon's light, when the final phase of cyclic process does its work of completion and renewal. The wounded wild animal instinctively withdraws into the silent stillness of the dark empty cave in order to heal itself; likewise the psyche requires that we go down into the depths of the unconscious in order to heal the soul. It is here that we can uncover the hidden causes of the wounds in our psyche, and align ourselves with the closure phase energies of release and transformation to effect a healing.

As we journey between worlds, from the dimension of conscious manifest reality to the unconscious phenomenal realm, we must alter our perception to enter the tunnel leading to the underworld of psyche. There exist many different methods to access the unconscious spanning the psychological, spiritual, metaphysical, artistic and pharmaceutical disciplines. When encountering the contents of the unconscious, it is important to have the proper safeguards and take appropriate precautions; otherwise this process can overwhelm the conscious mind and cause its collapse. Different people according to their precondition will choose or be chosen by a more or less structured and supervised path.

The spiritual path includes meditation, prayer, ritual, trance, vision quest, chanting, mantra, shamanic trance journey, yoga, breath, spirit guides and initiation. Metaphysical disciplines such as astrology, tarot, numerology, and palmistry can help one to decipher the subtle vibrational patterns that influence the hidden workings of our lives. The psychological modalities encompass psychotherapy, guided imagery, dreamwork, hypnosis, regression, holotropic breathwork, rebirthing, primal scream, rolfing, and bioenergetics. Many individuals are releasing the pain of the past and overcoming addictions and unconscious compulsions through the twelve-step recovery programs and other counseling techniques found in support groups of AA, NA, adult children of dysfunctional families, and survivors of rape, incest, and abuse. We can access our unconscious, and archetypal and mythological motifs through the artistic-creative processes of painting, sculpture, music, ecstatic dance, poetry and inspired writing. Mind-altering substances such as psychedelics, herbs and mushrooms can induce non-ordinary states of consciousness leading to visionary and cathartic experiences.

The essential process of twelfth-house closure-phase healing found in many of the above paths is recognition, release, purification, transformation and commitment. The first step is to recognize that there is a wound and to admit the existence of pain and confusion in our life. Our conscious mind resists acknowledging that which threatens to overwhelm us, and many behavior patterns of avoidance found in the twelfth house are manifestations of this denial. In fact, drug, alcohol and other chemical addictions are coping mechanisms to numb painful memories and their corresponding bad feelings, thereby creating the illusion of well being.

The feelings of these rejected memories are locked into the circuitry of our emotional and physical bodies. The second phase involves recalling these painful experiences and releasing the emotional charge of the blocked energy. The third phase is purifying the toxic accumulation from the festering repressed energies. Cleansing the psychic system will clarify our perceptions of reality and the causal effect of our actions.

As we come to know the faces of our hidden tendencies and accept these components of our being as within us, not external to us, the next phase of twelfth house healing is transmuting the negative energies into their positive nature. Buddhist teachings hold that there exist five basic groups of negative emotional energies such as anger, greed, and envy. When the energy of the emotion is purified and transmuted, it expresses as a particular "wisdom" or aspect of the awakened state of mind. For example, the energy within us that manifests negatively as anger, when transformed becomes mirror-like wisdom whose essence is clarity, luminosity, and seeing things as they are.(14)

As we heal, we approach a state of wholeness within ourselves, and that awareness precipitates a realization of our connectedness with all of life. The transcendent function of the twelfth house is activated when we begin to consider others as not separate from ourselves, and act accordingly. At this point we begin to utilize the very same energy that was previously blocked and distorted in a way that no longer harms others or ourselves, and may actively help.

Ultimately the way to deal with problematical twelfth house energies is from an altruistic point of view. These energies are not to be used solely for personal ends. In helping others, we heal ourselves. Twelfth house factors show the commitments we make to heal certain aspects of ourselves through selfless love and service to others. This is the foundation for traditional twelfth house interpretations such as sensitivity to people in need, empathy and compassion, carrying others' burdens, sacrifice, caring for the ill, volunteer work, community service, and charitable activities. This activity may manifest as the fixer and rescuer who takes on the causes of others. The twelfth house straddles the fine line here between selfless love and service on one hand and compulsive caregiving and co-dependency on the other hand, where we live in a shifting reality between *healer and healee* or *savior and victim*. Nevertheless, by integrating our twelfth house energies into an expanded perception of the wholeness of our life, we discover the source of our hidden strengths and talents.

The Twelfth House and Hidden Treasures

The twelfth house is the veil behind which we enter into the realm of the unseen real, and shows the path to penetrating the deep recesses of our mind to uncover secret wisdom. The twelfth house is the treasure house of all inspired creativity and wisdom. It is the gateway into the collective unconscious where we can access universal knowledge and become the mediators and transmitters of eternal themes. The archetypal symbols in this realm can speak to us directly in a language that has meaning for all people in all time.

We can apprehend the secret wisdom of the past and future inwardly, through the power of our imagination, visions, dreams, and fantasies; and outwardly, through the mythological motifs that appear in religious rites, artistic symbols and fairy tales. Joseph Campbell says the myths are the representations of the unconscious energies within us and give clues to the spiritual meaning of life. All the gods and goddesses reside within us as the wisdom beings, spirit guides, and inner teachers who lead us to this rich vein of psychic material in our unconscious.

The experiences we encounter in the twelfth realm of consciousness provide us with the opportunities to connect with sources of metaphysical knowledge and spiritual beliefs. In this place where all merges back into source, the faith and knowing that arise from direct experience transcend intellectual concepts and rational logic. This is the temple of the mysteries where through ritual, prayer, and meditation we can align ourselves with cosmic or divine energies and channel inspired creations. In this subtle realm we are receptive to higher states of consciousness and can activate our psychic and telepathic abilities. It is the source of our inner power that we draw upon in crises.

The twelfth house, above all, is the domain of the "Mysteries." This sector reveals the descent into the Underworld where we encounter the reality of the nonphysical dimension and experience the secrets of death and rebirth, renewal and regeneration. In this world of spirit reside the memories of the past and dreams of the future. When either of the two lights, the Sun and Moon, is found in the twelfth house, our purpose involves illuminating the mysteries. These gifts of spirit from the angelic worlds are our secret, or hidden, resources and talents.

Twelfth House Concepts
That Which is Hidden

Hidden Treasures
The Source of Our Talents, Strengths and Resources Which
Unite Us With The Riches and Wealth of the Underworld

Collective unconscious
  Memory Banks Of The Past and Akashic Records
  Museums and Libraries
  Creative Inspiration From the Unconscious -
    Genius and Dreaming the Future
  Universal Visions, Ideals of Truth and Beauty
  Access to Universal Symbols, Mythological Motifs,
    Archetypal Images
Transcendent and Ecstatic Experiences
  Unity With All Of Life - Transcendence and Grace
  Longing For Union With Source
  Experience of Oneness and Being Part of a Larger Unity
  Self-Realization Through Following a Spiritual,
    Mystical, Religious, Occult or Esoteric Path
  Initiation to the Mysteries
  Near-Death Experiences
Receptivity To The Subtle Realms
  Imagination, Dreams, and Fantasy
  Psychic Abilities-Clairvoyance, Telepathy, Empathy,
    Precognition, Premonition
  Spirit Guides, Wisdom Beings, Inner Teachers

Hidden Enemies

The Source of Our Weaknesses That Are Responsible
For Our Self-Undoing and Suffering

Traumas and Ghosts From The Forgotten Past
  Wounds of the Soul
  Separation From Wholeness
  Painful and Unresolved Issues From Our
    Collective Past, Prior Lives,

Death and Birth Memories, Infancy, Early Childhood
and Parental Relationship
Negative Karmic Patterns
Victimization and Exploitation - Experiences of
Violence, Violation, Loss, Denial, Rejection,
Abandonment, Grief
Repressed Energies and Rejected Aspects of Ourselves
Shadows and Demons Toxic Accumulations
Poisons of the Mindstream - Negative Emotions of
Ignorance, Hatred and Greed
Chronic Physical, Mental, Emotional or Spiritual Illness
Reality Colored by Misery, Misfortune, Suffering
Life Experiences of Frustration, Limitation, Bondage,
Madness, Disintegration
Psychological Problems and Complexes
Phobias, Self-Pity, Escapism, Addictions, Self-
Destructive Tendencies
Unconscious Motivations and Habit Patterns
Projecting those Qualities We Fear, Reject and
Deny in Ourselves

Our Hidden Life

Need For Privacy, Seclusion and Solitude
What Emerges When We Are Alone
Rich Inner Life and/or Loneliness, Alienation, Fear
Personal Habits and Natural Appearance
Secret Addictions
Secrets and Clandestine Affairs
Fantasies and Dreams
Desire For Anonymity and Operating Behind the Scenes
Places of Retreat
Temples, Monasteries, Ashrams, Sanctuaries, Nature
Places of Exile
Institutions, Prisons, Asylums, Hospitals,
Reformatories

Healing The Soul

Completion and Renewal
Transformation
Death and Rebirth
Endings and Beginnings

Recalling, Releasing, Purifying, Transforming
and Transcending
Psychological Therapy
Self-Redemption
Karmic Purification
Resolving Past Karma and Karmic Debts
Completing Unfinished Business
Coming to Terms With Moral Obligations
Renunciation and Repentance
Rendering Service To Others
Bodhisattva Intention to Benefit Others
Wounded Healer
Carrying Additional Burdens
Sensitivity, Empathy and Compassion Towards Others
Altruism and Sacrifice
Volunteer work, Community Service, Charitable Activities

Ways To Access The Twelfth House

Meditation, Prayer, Ritual, Faith, Devotion, Yoga and Breath
Trance, Vision Quest, Dreams, Channeling, Nature, Crystals,
Flower Essences
Astrology, Tarot, Numerology, Palmistry
Psychotherapy, Guided Imagery, Dreamwork, Hypnosis, Regression, Holotropic Breathwork, Primal Scream, Rebirthing, Bioenergetics, Rolfing
Soul Retrieval, Shamanic Trance Journey
Twelve Step Programs
Creative Inspiration - Artistic, Scientific, Philosophical
Ecstatic Experiences
Ecstatic Dance, Chant, Music, Drumming, Rattles
Pharmaceutical Substances - Psychedelics, Herbs,
Mushrooms
Alcohol

Twelfth House Questions To Consider

The following questions speak to issues that are associated with the twelfth house. Read them over and answer any that particularly speak to you.

1. Are there parts of my life that I can no longer remember? What feelings come up when I try to force myself to recall these time periods?

2. Am I vaguely aware of, but don't know the details of difficult experiences that occurred during my mother's pregnancy with me, my birth, or in my early family life? Do I have memories or a sense of past lives, mine or others?

3. Do I sometimes act in ways that are totally unlike my usual behavior? Do I unconsciously do things that are ultimately harmful to myself or others? Do I get upset when I lose control? Do I cry, scream, rebel, get violent, freeze, or run away? Do I feel mortified if others have seen this display?

4. The thought of what circumstances or kinds of people bring up the greatest fears in me? To what extent are my fears part of my reality, either as phobias or actual situations? Am I paranoid about others being out to get me, and therefore over protect myself?

5. What qualities do I most dislike in other people? How do I feel when I am interacting with a person who has these qualities? If I look closely, will I recognize any of these qualities in myself? How does even the possibility of this idea make me feel right now?

6. To what extent are negative emotions of prejudice, narrow mindedness, greed, neurotic desires, anger, hatred, aggression, pride, arrogance, envy, and jealousy, a part of my life? Have I harmed myself or others by using this emotional energy in a destructive manner? Can I envision a way to utilize the energy of these powerful feelings in a more harmonious, skillful, and helpful manner?

7. In what ways do things or relationships that I have not resolved or completed in the past continue to influence my present circumstances?

8. Do I have regular time in my life when I am private and alone? Is there too much or too little of this time and space? How do I feel when I don't get this time or have my privacy invaded? What kinds of things do I only do when I am alone? Is this a positive experience—relaxing, healing, centering, creative, productive? Or does being alone make me feel uncomfortable, lonely, fearful, or desperate?

9. What aspects of myself and my life do I actively conceal from others - natural appearance, sexuality, personal habits, finances, fantasies, religious beliefs, unusual interests? What things about myself don't I like or think others won't approve of? How much of my vital energy is utilized in shielding this part of my life?

10. To what extent do I experience a deep and pervasive suffering in some area of my life? What might be a wound in my soul? Does this painful condition continue to reoccur as a pattern in my life, like a bad dream? How have I reacted in the past? What might be a different way to respond in the future when this arises again?

11. Is following a spiritual, religious, or mystical path an important consideration in my life?

12. Do I have inspirations that seem to "come out of the blue" that are creative or give helpful solutions to problems?

13. Do I sense deep veins of hidden strengths or wisdom within me that I am reluctant to trust or bring forth? What might they be? Can I imagine allowing these hidden powers into my life? How would my life be different?

14. Is it easy or difficult for me to help others and be altruistic? Do I consider myself to be a loner? Do I yearn to be part of something larger than myself?

15. To what extent do I find it difficult to live in this world, hold things together, know who I am and where I'm going?

Workbook For Interpreting The Twelfth House

The twelfth house indicates the forces operating in our unconscious past and private life. It is the place of the deep wounds in our soul that are seeking to be healed. When these energies are repressed, we express them in distorted ways as the hidden weaknesses that motivate our unconscious self-destructive behavior. As these energies become healed in our movement toward wholeness, we express them as our hidden strengths and talents that serve and benefit ourselves and others.

A. The Sign on the Twelfth House

1. The sign on the cusp (or beginning) of my twelfth house is

_____.

The sign on the cusp of the twelfth house shows what psychological need is involved in our wounding and healing process, and is an indicator of our hidden weaknesses and hidden strengths. In order to heal ourselves and others, it is important that we acknowledge, release and transform the repressed energy associated with this need. When we are in soul pain, we will experience ourselves, others or the conditions of our life as the negative qualities of that sign. As we move toward healing, we will increasingly experience the positive qualities of that sign in ourselves and others. The part of the physical body that is associated with this sign will be the area that is most vulnerable to the toxic accumulation of our repressed contents.

In order to heal my soul and that of significant others in my life I must acknowledge and express _____.
(fill in sign keyphrase from Table 1, Appendix A).

When I am in touch with this need, I may experience my hidden strengths and talents in a _____
manner.
(Fill in skillful sign keywords from Table 2, Appendix A)

When I deny or repress this need, I may experience my hidden weaknesses and self undoing in a _____
manner.
(Fill in unskillful sign keywords from Table 2, Appendix A)

2. The Element of the twelfth house sign
If the element of our twelfth house sign is:

Fire (Aries, Leo or Sagittarius)—we need to heal our spiritual
body and capacity for purposeful direction
Air (Gemini, Libra or Aquarius— we need to heal our mental
body and capacity to communicate and interrelate;
Earth (Taurus, Virgo or Capricorn)—we need to heal our physical body and capacity to support our material needs
Water (Cancer, Scorpio or Pisces)—we need to heal our emotional body and capacity to feel.

My twelfth house sign's element is _____. Using the
table below, circle the response that is paired with this element.

ELEMENT	**WHAT I NEED TO HEAL IN MY SOUL**
Fire	My spirit
Air	My mind and relationships
Earth	My body
Water	My emotions

If you have an intercepted sign in the twelfth house, repeat
this exercise using the keywords of this additional sign. The energies of the intercepted sign will be even more unconscious and
difficult to discern. It is suggested that in the latter part of your
life (after 35), these energies may open up during transits of the
outer planets through this sector.

3. Optional Advanced Exercise
The position of the planet that rules the sign on the twelfth cusp
shows where (by house) we need experiences in order to fulfill our
karmic commitments, heal ourselves and benefit others. This
placement can also point to the area of life activities where we
encounter the most fear and inhibition that can transformed by
our actions. Additional information can be gained by studying the
aspects to this planet.

For example, if a person has the sign of Cancer on the cusp of
the twelfth house, this would indicate that the wound is in the
emotional body. Cancer is the need to give and receive emotional
warmth and security. This individual would repress and be out of
touch with his or her feelings, and be uncomfortable with and

detached from the emotional displays of others. Experiences of abandonment, rejection, and lack of nourishment may be part of the unconscious past. He or she might feel unloved, unwanted or unneeded and/or see others as being insensitive and uncaring. Hidden chronic illness may appear in the stomach or breasts. Healing will manifest as the increasing capacity to give others emotional support and sustenance. If the Moon (ruler of Cancer) is in the tenth house, it is through public or professional work that this individual can express his or her emotional energies to bring about healing, even though the thought of these activities may initially evoke feelings of panic and terror.

Now fill in the following sentences.

The sign on my 12th house cusp is _____.

The planetary ruler of that sign is _____.

SIGN	RULER
Aries	Mars
Taurus	Venus
Gemini	Mercury
Cancer	Moon
Leo	Sun
Virgo	Mercury
Libra	Venus
Scorpio	Pluto/Mars*
Sagittarius	Jupiter
Capricorn	Saturn
Aquarius	Uranus/Saturn*
Pisces	Neptune/Jupiter*

The planetary ruler is placed in this house _____.

House keywords _____.
(see Table 3, Appendix A)

This is an area where 12th house problems such as inhibitions or unconscious complexes from the past can manifest.

    *In the ancient classification of essential dignities, Mars was said to rule Aries and Scorpio, Saturn to rule Capricorn and Aquarius, and Jupiter to rule Sagittarius and Pisces. When the planets Uranus, Neptune, and Pluto were discovered, they were assigned to rule the signs of Aquarius, Pisces and Scorpio. You may want to use both the ancient and modern rulers to determine which work better for you; it may be the case that both are relevant.

B. Planets in the twelfth house

Planets in the twelfth house indicate the parts of our personality which tend to operate from unconscious motivations. They point to deep psychic traumas from our early childhood and unconscious past of infancy, birth, death, prior incarnations, and access to the suffering of the collective. These are the wounds in our soul whose energies we tend to repress, which may erupt as obsessive-compulsive behavior and negative emotions that dominate our personality. We may allow these parts of ourselves to function only behind the scenes or when we are alone.

Planets in the twelfth house also signify the empathy toward others that we develop through the conditions of our own suffering, and the commitments we then make to help and benefit others.

Furthermore, planets in the twelfth house point to our hidden strengths, talents, and aspects of ourselves that are involved in uncovering secret wisdom, inspired creativity and genius, spiritual and devotional practices, and illuminating the mysteries.

Aspects to twelfth house planets show what other parts of the personality are involved in this process. If these aspects are mostly trines and sextiles, then the twelfth house planets will be less problematical than usual and the energies will tend to flow more harmoniously. If the aspects are mostly squares, quincunxes or oppositions, then the twelfth house energies will tend to operate in more compulsive, disruptive, and problematical ways.

The qualities listed below may operate in a hidden, repressed, painful, or dysfunctional way in your life. If healed they can function as a positive resource.

1. PLANET _____ **SIGN** _____
PLANET KEYPHRASE _____
                                            (Table 4, Appendix A)
SIGN KEYPHRASE _____
                                            (Table 1, Appendix A)
2. PLANET _____ **SIGN** _____
PLANET KEYPHRASE _____
                                            (Table 4, Appendix A)
SIGN KEYPHRASE _____
                                            (Table 1, Appendix A)
3. PLANET _____ **SIGN** _____
PLANET KEYPHRASE _____
                                            (Table 4, Appendix A)
SIGN KEYPHRASE _____
                                            (Table 1, Appendix A)
4. PLANET _____ **SIGN** _____
PLANET KEYPHRASE _____
                                            (Table 4, Appendix A)
SIGN KEYPHRASE _____
                                            (Table 1, Appendix A)

In your own words, describe how these parts of your personality operate unconsciously, dysfunctionally or in ways that are painful and that you can't understand. How can you use these energies to help others and in the process heal yourself?

Optional advanced exercise
The house that each planet rules will indicate in what additional areas of life these energies will be hidden or inhibited until healing takes place (See pg. 113-114 for rulership information). For example, if the Sun is in your twelfth house, look to the house whose cusp is the sign of Leo. If the Moon is in your twelfth house, look to the house whose cusp is the sign of Cancer, etc. Fill in the sentences below.
My 12th House Planet _____
Sign this planet rules   _____
House of this sign in your chart _____
House keyphrase _____
                                            (Table 3, Appendix A)

C. Transits and Progressions Through the Twelfth House

Transits and progressions through the twelfth house indicate the timing when hidden issues from the unconscious will surface and require confrontation, release and healing. During such a period, we may experience disintegration, collapse, chaos, death and endings. We can transform much of the fear, suffering, loss and alienation commonly experienced during twelfth house transits by viewing these times as the opportunity to willingly let go of what is over, condense the essence of what was valuable from the past cycle, and carry it over into our intentions for the next cycle.

In order to determine the dates of these transits, you must know how to read an ephemeris. First find the sign and degree of your twelfth house cusp and the sign and degree of your Ascendant. Then go to the ephemeris and locate the dates of the passage of these planets through those zodiacal degrees. Be sure to double check for retrograde and direct periods. If you have planets in the twelfth house, then the dates of the transiting planet over your natal planet is especially important for activating the repressed energies of that part of your personality.

Because the Moon travels through the Zodiac every 29 days (and thus through the houses of the horoscope), each month the moon will spend 2-3 days transiting your twelfth house. In a similar fashion, the transiting Sun will pass through your twelfth house for approximately 1 month during each year.

The Transit of Mars
Mars will spend approximately two months of every two years moving through your twelfth house. Mars provides the opportunity to take altruistic actions or clear out the blocks to self-assertion. Mars can also bring to the surface repressed anger, frustration, violence and conflict when transiting through this house.

The dates of my Mars transits and any conjunctions to natal planets in the twelfth house _____.

The Transit of Jupiter
Jupiter will spend approximately one year of every twelve years moving through your twelfth house. Jupiter provides the oppor-

tunity to expand your spiritual horizons and experience higher states of consciousness. Jupiter transits can also bring up repressed excesses, over-indulgences and exaggerations when transiting through this house.

The dates of my Jupiter transits and any conjunctions to natal planets in the twelfth house_____.

The Transit of Saturn

Saturn will spend approximately two and one half years of every twenty-nine and one half years moving through your twelfth house. Saturn provides the opportunity to focus, define and manifest what you want and to tie up loose ends. Try to avoid brooding over past failures. Saturn transits can also bring to the surface repressed fears, limitations, and inhibitions when transiting through this house. It may also cause one to come out of denial and face the ghosts of the past.

The dates of my Saturn transits and any conjunctions to natal planets in the twelfth house_____.

The Transit of Uranus

Uranus will spend approximately seven years of every eighty-four years moving through your twelfth house. This can happen only once during a normal span lifetime. Uranus provides the opportunity to free yourself from past limitations. Uranus transits can also trigger repressed rebelliousness and erratic and unpredictable behavior to surface in yourself or others. Often the motivations for these behaviors will not be apparent. In the process, existing structures may be shattered.

The dates of my Uranus transits and any conjunctions to natal planets in the 12th house_____

The Transit of Neptune

Neptune will spend approximately fourteen years out of every one hundred and sixty four years moving through your twelfth house. Not everyone will have this transit during his or her life. Neptune provides the opportunity to experience a greater spiritual perspective and sensitivity. Neptune transits can also bring repressed addictions, phobias, deception and escapism to the surface when transiting through this house. In the process, existing structures may be dissolved.

The dates of my Neptune transits and any conjunctions to natal planets in the 12th house_____.

The Transit of Pluto

Pluto will spend approximately twenty-one years out of every two hundred and forty eight years moving through your twelfth house. Not everyone will have this transit during his or her life. Pluto provides the opportunity to transform and regenerate deep compulsions or fears. Pluto transits can also catalyze repressed self-destructive tendencies and emotionally charged experiences so that they may be healed. In the process, outmoded structures may be undermined so that new rebuilding can occur.

The dates of my Pluto transits and any conjunctions to natal planets in the 12th house_____.

CHAPTER 4

THE DARK MOON GODDESS IN ASTROLOGY

Early peoples noticed that the twenty-nine and one half days cycle of the moon's phases corresponded to the twenty-nine and one half days of a woman's menstrual cycle. They therefore surmised that the moon must be feminine, and personified it as the divine feminine Moon Goddess. The symbolism of the Triple Goddess grew out of the new, full and dark phases of the moon's cycle. The waxing new moon was conceptualized as the White Virgin Goddess who birthed new life, the full moon was likened to the Red Mother Goddess who nourished and sustained life, and the waning dark moon was envisioned as the Dark Crone Goddess who destroyed life and prepared it for renewal.

By observing the ever-renewing display of the moon's light, the ancients developed an intrinsic belief in cyclic rebirth. In the earliest societies that revered the moon as Goddess, they knew her in her third dark phase as a wise and compassionate being who ruled over the mysteries of death, transformation and renewal. It was the Dark Goddess who beckoned and received the souls of the dead; however her role was to purify, heal, and prepare them to be born anew. She destroyed in order to renew; and her underworld was not a place of torture but of salvation. The Dark Goddess was also the keeper of the secret traditions of magic, oracle, prophecy, and sacred sexuality as a vehicle for ecstasy, regenerative healing, and spiritual illumination.

Over the course of many millennia, solar cultures gradually replaced the moon worshippers, and knowledge of the cyclic nature of reality, as mirrored by the phases of the moon, was lost. The cosmologies of the solar gods denounced and outlawed belief in cyclic renewal. Death was no longer the precursor to rebirth, but rather the final ultimate conclusion of life that plunged one into endless suffering in the hellfires of damnation.

The meaning of the dark phase of cyclic process as a place of healing and transformation was forgotten, and the dark became associated with terror, evil, destruction, loss, and the finality of death. The Dark Goddess came to be understood only as a destroyer, and her sacred, ecstatic sexuality was cast out as dangerous and immoral.

Throughout many world mythologies the Dark Goddess was portrayed as the Temptress, the Terrible Mother and the Death-Bearing Crone. Her later biographers have recorded her as black, evil, venomous, demonic, horrifying, malevolent, fiery, and outraged. As patriarchal culture became more prevalent, she came to be a symbol of a devouring feminine sexuality that caused men to transgress their moral and religious convictions. She then consumed their vital essence and entwined them in an embrace of death.

In the mythic imagination of male-dominated cultures, the original nature of the Dark Goddess became distorted and she took on horrifying proportions. As Kali she appeared in cremation grounds adorned with a garland of skulls and holding the severed head of her mate Shiva dripping with blood. As Lilith, she flew through the night as a she-demon who seduced men, bred demons and killed infants. As Medusa, her beautiful abundant hair became a crown of hissing serpents and the gaze from her Evil Eye turned men to stone. And as Hekate, she stalked for men at the crossroads at night with her vicious hounds of hell.

We might well ask why the Dark Goddess presents such a terrifying image to mankind. In what ways does she, and her psychological counterpart of the dark feminine, threaten our security and create havoc in our lives? And how is her destructive power related to her healing qualities that bring renewal? In what ways has the Dark Goddess come to embody our fear of the dark, our fear of the occult, our fear of death and change, our fear of sex, and our fear of confronting our essential selves and our own interpretation of truth?

Psychologists are just beginning to discover that myth is the natural language of the collective unconscious. Joseph Campbell added that "all the gods and goddesses live within us" as the forces of our personality, and their stories represent the mythic themes that shape our lives. Our view of mythological deities has evolved over the millennia from personified gods and goddesses to properties of the psyche. From an astrological perspective their planetary namesakes symbolize the active forces of our personalities.

As the collective culture has banished and defamed the mythical Dark Goddess and her teachings, so have we as individuals been conditioned to deny and detest the parts of our personalities that correspond to the qualities of the Dark Goddess. The various goddesses of the dark moon were all queens of the underworld, and the underworld of the ancients is a metaphor for the unconscious mind of modern individuals. The ancient Dark Goddess who has been cast out and distorted is analogous to the Jungian shadow—the denied and rejected parts of the self which are exiled and repressed into the unconscious. The Dark Goddess has come to contain the rejected aspects of feminine wholeness, and, as such, now symbolizes the feminine shadow.

For the ancients, a safe and helpful relationship to the powers of the underworld was to be gained through a right approach to the Dark Goddess. Contemporary psychology reframes this ancient wisdom in suggesting that a safe and helpful relationship to the powers of the unconscious is to be gained through a right approach to the shadow. If we acknowledge and pay respect to the dark forces in our unconscious, our inner Dark Goddesses will be well disposed towards us and provide insight, healing, and renewal. It is when we demean and exile the dark that she (like the shadow self when rejected and denied) will, during our weakest moments, unexpectedly burst forth into our conscious reality. When the dark feminine shadow deities take over with a vengeful autonomy of their own, they then bring terror, destruction and madness into our lives.

As the Dark Goddess archetype evolved through patriarchal culture, she became an object of fear and persecution. Over the course of history, the healing and prophetic wisdom of the Dark Goddess has been distorted as sorcery, and her image has been demonized into the ugly death-bringing hag or the witch, consort of the devil. As we have lost our knowledge of her gifts of renewal and ecstatic sexuality, our fear of her ways has diminished our capacity to regenerate ourselves and has poisoned our relationships with loved ones. In order to heal ourselves and our relationships, we must enter into the darkness of our unconscious and develop an honorable, respectful and loving relationship with the Dark Goddesses in our midst.

In mythic-psychological astrology, the positions of the asteroids who share the same name with the goddesses of the dark moon represent the feminine shadow personalities as they operate within both men and women. Ephemerides and computer software are now available which can determine their astrological positions in a natal chart. Let us now explore how they operate in your birth chart.

The Dark Goddess and the Feminine Shadow

In *Finding Our Way Through The Dark*, we will be exploring the significance of the following dark goddess archetypes in our charts: Moira, Atropos, Nemesis, Lilith (asteroid, dark moon, and black moon), Hekate, Medusa, Persephone/Proserpina, and Pythia. In Appendix B we have included an ephemeris for each of these asteroids. For those of you who do not know how to read an ephemeris, ACS offer a printout listing their zodiacal position for your birthchart. See Appendix C. The workbook section contains a brief mythological description and astrological exercises for each one. The complete teachings on these goddesses can be found in Chapters Four, Five, and Six of *Mysteries of the Dark Moon*.

In addition to these, we have included short descriptions of a number of other dark goddesses. To obtain a list of their positions

in your chart, as well as the positions for the dark moon Lilith
and the black moon Lilith, send your birth data and $10 payable
to Astro Communications Service, Inc., Dark Goddesses, 5521
Ruffin Road, San Diego, CA 92123-1314 or use the order form in
Appendix C.

For more mythological information about each one, see *The
Women's Encyclopedia of Myths and Secrets* by Barbara Walker,
The Book of Goddesses and Heroines by Patricia Monaghan, and
Women of Classical Mythology by Robert E. Bell.

Once you have obtained the positions for the dark goddess
asteroids and moons from either the ephemeris in Appendix B or
the ACS printout, enter the sign and degree for each of them in
the space provided.   ·

You will then want to transfer this information to your natal
birth chart and place these asteroids in the correct house. The
importance of each dark goddess asteroid will vary from one person to another. Some asteroids will be more significant than others in any given chart. An asteroid is most significant when it is
conjunct or opposite the Sun, Moon, or on an angle (the 1st, 4th,
7th, or 10th house cusps). Its motifs also may be prominent in our
personality when it aspects any of the other personal planets, the
four major asteroids (Ceres, Pallas, Juno, Vesta) or Chiron. We
will also feel the energies of one of these dark goddess asteroids if
it completes a major aspect pattern or is receiving a transit from
an outer planet. Note any significant aspects (primarily the conjunction and opposition, to a lesser extent the square, and finally
the trine and sextile) that each one is making to planets, nodes or
angles. Use a 1-3 degree orb.

Table 1

Dark Goddess Asteroids and Moons

Asteroid	Zodiacal Position (Sign and Degree)
Moira, The Triple Goddess of Fate	_____
Atropos, the cutter of fate	_____
Nemesis, Goddess who protected the natural law and punished offenders	_____
Lilith, the Dark Maid	
*Dark Moon Lilith	_____

*Positions for the Dark Moon Lilith can be found in The Lilith Ephemeris *(AFA, 1983) by Delphine Jay.*

*Black Moon Lilith   _____

*Positions can be found in The Black Moon Book: *SUM Press, 1994) PO Box 2431, Fairfield Iowa 52556*

Hekate, Queen of the Night	_____
Medusa, the Serpent Haired Queen	_____
Persephone, Queen of the Underworld	_____
Proserpina, Latin name for Persephone	_____
Pythia, oracular serpent priestess of Delphi	_____

Other Dark Goddess Archetypes

Asteroid	Zodiacal Position (Sign and Degree)
Alekto, "unrelenting," one of the three Furies	_____
Tisiphone, "retaliation," one of the three Furies	_____
Megaira, "envious anger," one of the three Furies	_____
Klotho, the spinner of fate	_____
Lachesis, the measurer of fate	_____

(information about the above five asteroids can be found in *Mysteries of the Dark Moon*)

Arachne, spider or spinner, title of Athena   _____
as the Fate -weaver whose story was later told as
the mortal maid who challenged Athena to a weaving
contest who then transformed her into a spider for
her pride in her weaving skills.

Circe, a funerary priestess, enchantress and   _____
sorceress alledged to have transformed Odysseus's
men into swine. She sometimes was said to be the niece
of Hekate, and her geography connects her to Colchis on
the Black Sea (with Medea), and to the island of Aeaea
off the west coast of Italy.

Medea, "Wise One," medicine/healing goddess   _____
from Colchis on the Black Sea who could restore the
dead to life in her magic cauldron. Her story was retold
as a princess who enabled Jason to steal the Golden Fleece
and later murdered her children by him in retaliation
for his abandoning her to marry another.

Sirene, for the Sirens, bird-bodied, beautiful-   _____
headed prophetesses of the future and readers of the
past who were lated envisioned as enchanting female
sea spirits who sweetly and seductively sang sailors
to their deaths , servants of Persephone.

Melpomene, "Singing," muse of tragedy and   _____
mother of the Sirens

Eurydice, Mother of Fate, was the Orphic name for   _____
the underworld serpent goddess who received the
soul of Orpheus. Her story was later retold as the wife
of the poet Orpheus who died from a snake bite. Orpheus
descended into the underworld to reclaim her from the
dead, but he ignored Hades warning to not look back to
see if she was following him, and thus he lost her to
the world of the shades.

Niobe, an Analtolian mountain-goddess whose   _____
worshippers were destroyed by Hellenic Greeks.
Her story was later retold as being overcome with
grief at the slaughter of all her children due to her
pride in their beauty.

Semele, a subterranean composting and fructifying   _____
earth goddess from Asia Minor. Her story was retold
as the mortal mother of the wine-god Dionysus who was
consumed and destroyed by Zeus' brilliant light, and was
later restored to a divinity by her son who installed her on
Olympus as the foremost of his Maennads under the title
Thyone, "ecstatic madwoman."

Undina, a water spirit who could only obtain a   _____
soul by marrying a mortal and bearing a child.

Scylla, a beautiful maiden who frolicked with the   _____
sea nymphs. It was later said that Amphritite, out
of jealousy, or Circe, in an attempt to protect her from
being attacked, poisoned her bath with magic herbs that
caused her to be transformed into a twelve foot monster
with six barking dog heads lined with rows of sharp teeth
who devoured sailors.

Melusina, a water nymph as fish-tailed Aphrodite.   _____
Medieval legend made her the mystic bride of a French
count. She demanded privacy each Sunday when she
reclined in her bath as a mermaid, was later driven out
by Churchmen, and afterwards was said to haunt the
family as a banshee. It was said she could be seen bathing
only by men doomed to die.

Drakonia, a female dragon, guardian of oracular sites. _____

Gorgo, for the Gorgons, serpent crowned sisters of   _____
Medusa whose traditions included wrathful-looking
masked priestesses who guarded the secrets of women's
mysteries.

Sibylla , who came from Troad (Troy) in Asia Minor,   _____
one of the names of the first Siblys, the ten female
prophetesses of the ancient world.

Kassandra, princess of Troy, oracular priestess was   _____
 punished for refusing to have sex with Apollo. He
cursed her saying while her prophecies and vision
would be true, no one would believe her. When she
foretoldthe burning and sacking of Troy, she was
dismissed as a crazed madwoman.

Pele, Hawaiian volcano-fire goddess. _____

Nepthys, Egyptian goddess of the dead, sister to Isis, _____
wife of Set.

Sphinx, Egyptian underworld guardian goddess. _____

Skuld, Scandinavian sorceress, elf queen, goddess _____
of the future.

Urda, Scandinavian sorceress, elf queen, goddess _____
of the past.

Hel, Scandinavian goddess of the underworld _____

Nocturna, "nightly." _____

Isis, Great Goddess of Egypt associated with _____
mysteries of renewal.

The Daughters of Nyx

In Greek mythology, the Fates, the Furies, the Hesperides, Nemesis, and sometimes Hekate were all said to be the daughters of Nyx, Mother Night, envisioned as a great black winged spirit who laid a silver egg (the moon) in the gigantic lap of darkness. In her triple aspect, Nyx displayed herself as Night, Order and Justice. Her daughter's tasks were to ensure that the natural laws of the universe were carried out and maintained. These sisters also saw to the punishment of those who transgressed the boundaries of natural law.

Moira, Triple Goddess of Fate

Moira is the Goddess of Fate who spoke to the issue of fate, destiny, and the karmic patterning of the soul. Her position in the birth chart gives clues to how and where we experience our fate, for better or worse, as the inevitable ripening of our karma, or prior actions. The ancients believed that once the destiny of an individual was woven, it was irrevocable and could not be altered. In her triple aspect she is known as **Klotho** the Spinner who signifies how we spin our fate by our actions, **Lachesis** the Measurer who shows how we weave our fate into the daily fabric of our lives, and **Atropos** the Cutter who indicates the inevitable ending and has to do with our closures and terminations. These dark sisters represent the primal elements in the unconscious side of our beings who protest the violation of natural law.

The Fates operate from the unconscious level of our being. Because of our limited vision, we are often unable to see the full implications of how, or even when, our beginnings initiate a process that leads to an inescapable conclusion. By our prior actions, we spin the threads of our fate. By the nature of our response and actions in our present circumstances, we weave the pattern of our future destiny.

Journal Questions

1. Do I think that everything is fated or predetermined? Do I feel helpless to change anything? Do I feel that the course my life has taken is the result of the actions of others upon me, or simply good or bad luck? Do I think that I have free will to shape my future?

2. Do I assume any personal responsibility for my misfortune. Do I believe that victims are innocent, helpless bystanders who have been willfully abused by oppressors? Do I see any relationship between my own actions and the circumstances of my life?

Workbook

Moira is the Goddess of Fate. Her position in the birth chart indicates the nature of our fate as the ripening of karma, or prior actions, for better or worse.

Atropos is the third dark aspect of Moira known as the Cutter. Her position in the birth chart indicates shows how and where we bring our fate to its inevitable conclusion and how we cut our life thread when we experience endings, loss, closures and death.

While the three aspects of Moira are Klotho, Lachesis and Atropos, we have only included workbook exercises and ephemerides for Atropos because of our limited ephemeris space. You can find the locations of Lachesis and Atropos by sending away for the expanded asteroid list as described on page 123.

Using **Table 1 on pg. 124,** place Moira and Atropos in your birth chart. First take note of their sign and house placements. Then notice if the asteroid is conjunct or opposite the Sun, Moon, or on an angle (the 1st, 4th, 7th, or 10th house cusps). Secondly, note if any of the asteroids makes a close aspect (use a 1-3 degree orb) to any of the other personal planets, Chiron, the four major asteroids Ceres, Pallas, Juno, Vesta, or is completing a major aspect pattern.

Finally, note whether the asteroid is receiving a transit from an outer planet.

Asteroid	Planet Aspected	Planet Keyphrase
_____	_____	_____
_____	_____	_____
	_____	_____

If you find any major aspects or transits, ask yourself how the mythological themes of this dark goddess may be operating in your life or affecting other parts of your personality. You may also want to integrate the keywords of the asteroid with the keywords for its sign and house (See Appendix A -Keywords of the Astrological Alphabet).

Nemesis

Nemesis was the goddess of retribution who maintained the equilibrium of the human condition. She symbolizes our conscience, which urges us toward taking right action.

Journal Questions

1. Do I have a concept of right and wrong, and do I have a value system to determine the difference? Do I believe in a wrathful, punishing divine force that operates outside of my control? Or do I have a sense that it might be my own actions and attitudes that eventually lead to my punishment?

2. Do I try to "get away" with things? Am I dishonest when it is to my advantage? If I have fortunate luck, do I share my bounty with others? When I am caught, do I acknowledge my wrongdoing, or do I see it as bad luck? Do I see the law and authority figures as hostile powerful forces who are out to get me?

Workbook

Nemesis is the Goddess of swift retribution. Her position in the birth chart shows how our conscience and morality guide us towards right action and how, when we ignore those promptings, we suffer the consequences.

Using **Table 1 on pg. 124,** place Nemesis in your birth chart. First take note of its sign and house placement. Then notice if it is conjunct or opposite the Sun, Moon, or on an angle (the 1st, 4th, 7th, or 10th house cusps). Secondly, note if any of the asteroids makes a close aspect (use a 1-3 degree orb) to any of the other personal planets, Chiron, the four major asteroids Ceres, Pallas, Juno, Vesta, or is completing a major aspect pattern.

Finally, note whether the asteroid is receiving a transit from an outer planet.

Asteroid	Planet Aspected	Planet Keyphrase
Nemesis	_____	_____
	_____	_____

If you find any major aspects or transits, ask yourself how the mythological themes of this dark goddess may be operating in your life or affecting other parts of your personality. You may also want to integrate the keywords of the asteroid with the keywords for its sign and house (See Appendix A -Keywords of the Astrological Alphabet).

The Dark Goddess Lilith

The mythical biography of Lilith places her earliest origins in ancient Sumeria as the handmaiden of the Great Goddess Innana. It was Lilith who brought the people in from the fields to Innana's holy temple at Erech for the sacred sexual rites. She represented an aspect of feminine sexuality that is free, unfettered, instinctive, animating, ecstatic, healing and sacred. In order to suppress the worship of the Goddess, whose sexual rites lay at the core of her mysteries, the Babylonian solar hero Gilgamesh destroyed Lilith's home and cast her out into the desolate wilderness.

In Hebraic mythology Lilith is best known as the first wife of Adam who left her husband, choosing exile and loneliness rather than domination and sexual subjugation to Adam's will. She was subsequently distorted into a demoness by the nomadic patriarchal tribes for her instinctive sexuality and for defying male authority. Winged and wild-haired, she was said to fly through the night seducing men and killing babies. But by fifteenth-century Kabbalism, Lilith had risen to become the consort of God himself.

To the romantic poets of the nineteenth century, Lilith came to embody the image of woman as femme fatale—alluring, irresistible, and deadly. Now, at the close of the twentieth century, Lilith reasserts herself as the liberated feminine, exalting ecstatic sexuality, upholding integrity, and refusing submission.

Lilith, in the matriarchal world, was once an image of all that was the finest of a woman's sexual nature, especially in her fiery dark aspect which held the mysteries of using sexuality for spiritual illumination, magic, healing and regeneration. After the patriarchy repressed women's sexuality and the old goddess religion disappeared, Lilith came to represent men's fear of women's passion, psychic powers, and independence as something dark and evil. She was denounced, maligned, and banished, coming to embody many aspects of the feminine shadow.

In the mythic imagination of the patriarchy, Lilith came to be perceived as a demonic dark being, one personification of the ancient Dark Goddess. She was then feared, hated, and vilified as Torturous Serpent, Blood Sucker, Harlot, Impure Female, Alien Woman, Witch, Hag, and Enchantress, rather than revered for her powers of healing and renewal through sacred sexuality.

It is this negative image of Lilith that has come to dominate many of our modern astrological interpretations, but it is essential to recognize that she is not evil in her intrinsic nature, but has only become so through our denial and repression of this sacred aspect of feminine sexuality. In the words of Barbara Koltuv, "Images of humiliation, diminishment, flight and desolation, followed by fiery rage, and revenge as seductress and child killer, abound throughout Lilith's mythology."(15) Her story is one of repression, resentment, explosive rage, rejection, exile, suffering, alienation, revenge, redemption, and renewal.

The Three Faces of Lilith

In astrology there exist three distinct astronomical bodies that are all named Lilith:

The **asteroid Lilith** (# 1181) orbits around the Sun along with many other asteroids in the belt between Mars and Jupiter.

The **Dark Moon Lilith** is a possible second satellite of the Earth, orbiting three times farther way than our Moon, whose hypothesized existence has precipitated four hundred years of controversy.

The **Black Moon Lilith** is the energy vortex of the empty focal point in the Moon's orbit around the Earth. The Moon travels in an elliptical orbit around the Earth. The nature of an ellipse is that it has two focal points. The Earth is one of the focal points; what is called the Black Moon is the other. There is no actual body there. The Black Moon refers to a moving point in space which acts as an energy vortex that defines the Moon's orbit.

In addition to these three, the fixed star of **Agol** at twenty-five degrees of Taurus, representing the blinking eye in the head of the Gorgon Medusa, was also known as Lilith by the Hebrews.

My understanding of the three Liliths has evolved in stages. In 1980 I first began to use the position of the asteroid Lilith in the charts of my clients and observed her significance in their lives. I was marginally aware that some astrologers used another Lilith—the Dark Moon Lilith. My understanding at that time was that this body was a hypothetical satellite whose existence had not been confirmed by mainstream astronomers. I was already so obsessed with charting the significance of hundreds of asteroids which do exist that I could not justify incorporating bodies that might not. And so I dismissed considering the placements of the Dark Moon Lilith which, in the way of synchronicity, is consistent with her mythological dismissal over the millennia.

In 1987, while at the Fraternity of Canadian Astrologers conference, I attended a lecture by Montreal astrologer Marc Beriault entitled "Black Moon Lilith." I thought that this was the Dark moon, but was curious to hear his mythological and psychological interpretations. To my surprise I learned that the Black Moon Lilith was a third distinct astronomical point discovered by French astrologer Don Neroman at the turn of the century. It has been used by French and other astrologers for decades, but is virtually unknown in the United States.

This is the story that Marc related to clarify the confusion surrounding the Dark moon, invisible satellite of our Earth. This enigmatic tale begins in the seventeenth century with the eminent Jesuit astronomer Giovanni Riccioli, who helped to produce the map and nomenclature of the Moon's surface that is still used today. In the middle of his career, he ordered new parts for his telescope from the leading optical scientist of the time. He then proceeded to observe the Moon, and soon noticed a small body that reappeared night after night. He decided it was a previously unknown satellite and published his findings and an ephemeris. Several years later it was discovered that the new telescope lens had a defect which produced the optical illusion of the "new" moon. Riccioli advised his colleagues of the error and the matter was laid to rest.

Three centuries later in the 1920's, Robert Ambelain, a Kabbalist, self-proclaimed Grand-Master of a Templar Order and sometimes astrologer, found an old copy of Riccioli's ephemeris in an attic in Southern France. He associated the invisible moon with the Lilith of the Kabbalah, and produced an ephemeris for the 20th century.

The ephemeris was not used in France because the French were aware of this history, and they also had been successfully using Neroman's Black Moon point for some time in their research. However, this ephemeris made its way to the United States where it appealed to certain American astrologers who developed a body of work around the Dark Moon Lilith. (16)

This explanation strengthened my decision to not consider the Dark moon as a valid area of inquiry until nine months later when I once again returned to Canada to present teachings for the Ottawa Astrological Society. During the lecture break, someone approached me with the question, "What do I make of it that there are three Liliths in astrology?" I was about to respond that there were only two, not three Liliths when, like a Uranian thunderbolt, I realized that the Goddess always manifests in a triple form.

I went back to re-investigate the mystery of the Dark moon. Astronomically, she is difficult to locate, remains hidden from our sight most of the time, and has been repeatedly rejected as a valid astrological significator, all of which mirrors her mythical qualities. Delphine Jay's research documents more than one dozen separate sightings of this elusive body whose zodiacal positions are generally consistent with the proposed ephemeris. The controversy increases with the information that her suggested orbit is mathematically impossible (17). In recent times, reports on the continued observation of the dark satellite orbiting the earth have been published by Soviet scientists in the *Moscow News* (18).

Astronomical research suggests that the Dark moon is a dust cloud evoking Lilith's legendary nature as a wind spirit of the night. Occultists propose that the Dark moon exists on the astral level, which reflects her sojourn in exile. During the past years I have been experimenting with the placements of the Dark moon in my charts. I do not know if she is real, but where she shows up in the charts uncannily describes her mythical connections.

Lilith as the Triple Goddess

The three Liliths each contain the entire symbolic meaning of the archetype. However if we were to attempt to distinguish between them, I can propose a tentative theory with which astrologers can experiment: the three astronomical Liliths correspond to the three phases of the Triple Moon Goddess as maiden, mother and crone. The **asteroid Lilith** describes the first stage of Lilith's mythical journey where she is suppressed, humiliated, and flees in a fiery rage to the desolate wilderness. The **Dark Moon Lilith** depicts the pain of her exile where she plots and executes her revenge. The **Black Moon Lilith** shows how she transmutes her distorted image back into its natural healthy expression.

The Asteroid Lilith and Confrontation

The asteroid Lilith describes how we find ourselves in those repressive situations where we are not free to express ourselves and not valued and accepted for who we intrinsically are. We are prevented from acting, moving, choosing and determining our life circumstances. We may feel forced to obey others against our better judgment, and pressured to suppress the qualities that others find unacceptable and threatening, especially the sexual, independent, and rebellious parts of our personality. Experiences of humiliation and denial also contribute to the build-up of smoldering resentment.

The inner pressure that accumulates when any energy is confined and constricted eventually precipitates a violent explosion. In the forceful expression of our repressed anger, we have the capacity to see and speak our truth. However, this clarity can also destroy the false pretensions that give form to our relationships with our partners, parents, bosses, spiritual and academic teachers, or groups. We cannot go back to them and resume our relationship as if nothing happened. In the face of these irreconcilable differences, we can no longer accept our subjugation and feel forced to leave. We experience our flight in a fiery rage and feel wounded by the spears of rejection and betrayal.

In chart analysis, the asteroid Lilith shows where we want to be free to move, to act, to chooose, to determine, to speak our truth and to be acknowledged for our wisdom. When the energy of this dark maid is blocked or denied, the asteroid Liliths shows how and where we experience the themes of suppression, resentment, explosive anger, rejection and flight in our lives.

Dark Moon Lilith and Exile

Kabbalistically, Lilith's name corresponds to the screech owl—the night owl who remains in the shadows. Likewise the Dark Moon Lilith describes our period of exile where the rejected shadow becomes distorted by the anguish of our pain. As it festers, it poisons our psyche with images of revenge and retaliation.

When we internalize this energy, we turn it against ourselves and become bitter, hateful, blaming and vengeful. We may become a loner who feels rejected by and alienated from others. Suppressing Lilith's sexual energy can lead to misogyny in men and self-hatred in women, accompanied in both sexes by barrenness, frigidity, impotence, emotional coldness and detachment, or indiscriminate, destructive sexual expression, and experiences of triangulation and betrayal.

When we project and externalize our shadow Lilith, we become the victims and perpetuators of Lilith's dysfunctions which include seduction, sexual manipulation, abuse, and ostracism. Our inner distorted Lilith images create an outer reality where demonic enemies, who may be alluring, bewitching or beguiling, are out to destroy us through their sexual power.

Dark Moon Lilith also describes how we plot our revenge and execute our retaliation. The seeds of these thoughts and actions yield a crop of continued suppression and rejection in our future. This is why Ivy Goldstein-Jacobson, who pioneered Dark Moon Lilith research, observed her characteristics as, "Sinister and malevolent... denying, frustrating, and catastrophic, bringing chaos to the affairs ruled by that house....rules temptation, betrayal,... poisoning, abortions, and stillbirth," (19) Yet, through her grotesque manifestation in our life, the Dark moon offers us a mirror which reflects our pain in the dark shadows of the psyche.

In chart analysis, the Dark Moon Lilith shows how and where we withdraw and isolate ourselves when we experience the distorted aspects of Lilith in our lives—our anguish, bitterness, alienation, desire for revenge, fear and hatred of our sexuality. The placement of Dark Moon Lilith also points to a channel whereby we can release our rage and grief over the pain of having been betrayed and rejected.

The Black Moon Lilith and Release
The resolution phase of the Lilith's cyclic process is depicted by the transmuting and healing activities of the Black Moon Lilith.

The secret of Lilith's alchemical transformation lies in the darkness of the final phase of her threefold process where the dark goddess of the dark moon destroys in order to renew. Many old amulets for protection against Lilith are in the form of knives which represent Lilith's quality to instinctively cut to the essential nature of things. The Hebrew Lilith, the "Flame of the Revolving Sword" is an ally of the Hindu Kali and the Tibetan Black Dakini. The Eastern image of the Black Mother is often depicted as a wildly dancing figure in a charnel ground emanating fiery sparks, brandishing her curved knife in one hand and in the other holding up a severed head.

Her fiery sparks illuminate the truth that shatters delusions and allows us to see and name things as they are. The Dark Goddess's crescent-shaped knife cuts away all that is false, inessential and inauthentic in our lives. For many people it is a very frightening thing to see ourselves stripped of our illusions and false pretensions. She forces us to look at ourselves with utter, naked honesty and makes us demand the truth of things, from our families, partners, groups and government. She is ruthless in destroying any of our life structures or relationships that are built upon a foundation of deception and disrespect, or do not express our true individuality or appropriate life path. The Black Moon will lead us to our goal, not by revealing what it is, but rather by eliminating everything that it is not, and this stark aspect of Lilith slams shut all the wrong doors that open to us.

The enforced clarity of the Black Moon enables us to penetrate the delusion of our false needs which have forced us into roles that are not in accordance with our true selves. She makes us dissatisfied with the part of our lives that pressure us to deny our needs and beliefs. She makes us reject sexual partners who do not honor or allow us to express our full erotic passion and abandon. She is a warrior goddess of revolution who creates troubling disruption as she moves us to protest against those who have a vested interest in keeping us submissive and subservient.

The Dark Goddess is a goddess of the self, not in the sense of selfishness or separateness, but from a stance of upholding individual integrity. The Black Moon in us will accept nothing less than the expression of our true individuality. When we are secure in acknowledging and expressing our authentic self, we are less likely to falsify ourselves in order to be accepted by others. We are then not so vulnerable to becoming entrapped in situations which deny and disempower us, which is where Lilith's self-destructive cycle begins.

In chart analysis, the **Black Moon Lilith** describes how and where we cut away our pretensions, false roles, and delusions and actualize our true, essential selves. Healing arises when we can enter into our darkness, release our pain, and purify and eliminate our toxic accumulations. We can then reclaim the lost and rejected parts of ourselves and integrate them into the wholeness of our being.

Journal Questions

1. Where in my life do I feel repressed and unacknowledged by others? Do I find myself in situations where others are forcing me to do things that I don't want to do, and therefore I act in ways that are not aligned with my true self? Does my repressed anger sometimes break through my facade and explode in tears, accusations, fury, rage or flight as I reveal my dissatisfaction? To what extent am I then rejected, dismissed, hated or ostracized by others when I am trying to be myself, speak my truth, and act upon my beliefs?

2. How do I feel about my sexuality? What is my relationship with the wild woman within me whose sexuality is instinctual, uninhibited, unrestrained and animating? Do I think that erotic experiences are sacred or dirty? Do I allow the wild woman, or do my partner(s) allow her expression? If I deny, fear or disapprove of this aspect in myself, how do I react to others who openly express it?

3. If I am a man, am I secretly attracted to erotic women while overtly denouncing them? Do I think they are sexually manipulative and basically evil or dangerous so that I need to protect myself against their sexual power? If I am a woman, do I hate sex? Do I find it degrading and humiliating? Am I frigid, impotent, sexually cold or emotionally detached? Am I indiscriminately promiscuous?

4. Have I been a victim of rape or others forms of sexual or emotional abuse? Have I ever been blamed for it afterwards and told that I "was asking for it?" To what extent am I attracted to dark, intriguing, forbidden lovers whose sexual power over me I fear? Do I refer to my lovers as bewitching or beguiling? Like the spider who makes love with her mate and then kills it, have I ever had sex with someone and tried to hurt or destroy him or her? Have I ever been a victim of this activity? Might it have anything to do with my fear of their sexual power?

Workbook

In chart analysis, *the Asteroid Lilith* shows how and where wee experience the themes of suppression, resentment, explosive anger, rejection, and flight in our lives. She also indicates the ways in which we need to assert our own truths.

In chart analysis, *the Dark Moon Lilith* signifies how and where we experience the distorted aspects of Lilith in our lives—her anguish, bitterness, betrayal, alienation, fear and hatred of sexuality, and revenge.

In chart analysis, *the Black Moon Lilith* shows how and where we cut away our pretensions, false roles, and delusions and actualize who we essentially are.

Using the **Table 1** on pg. 124, place these Liliths in your birth chart. First take note of the sign and house placement for each. Then notice any conjunctions or oppositions to the Sun, Moon, or on an angle (the 1st, 4th, 7th, or 10th house cusps). Secondly, note if any of the Liliths makes a close aspect (use a 1-3 degree orb) to any of the other personal planets, Chiron, the four major asteroids Ceres, Pallas, Juno, Vesta, or is completing a major aspect pattern.

Finally, note whether the asteroid is receiving a transit from an outer planet.

Asteroid or Moon	Planet Aspected	Planet Keyphrase
_____	_____	_____
_____	_____	_____
_____	_____	_____
_____	_____	_____

If you find any major aspects or transits, ask yourself how the mythological themes of this Dark Goddess may be operating in your life or affecting other parts of your personality. You may also want to integrate the keywords of the asteroid with the keywords for its sign and house (See Appendix A—Keywords of the Astrological Alphabet)

Hekate, Queen of the Night

Hekate is one of the most ancient images from the preGrecian stratum of mythology and an original embodiment of the Triple Goddess. This lunar goddess could be seen walking the remote roads of ancient Greece accompanied by her howling dogs and blazing torches. She dwelt in caves, made love on the vast seas, and was the force that moved the moon. She is often linked with the dark of the moon, and presides over magic, ritual, prophetic dreams and visions, and madness. As Queen of the Dead, Hekate is a ruler of the Underworld where she is a wardress and conveyor of souls. She was honored at places where three roads converged; here, at dead of night, her worshippers would leave offerings of ritual food known as Hekate's Suppers. Because Hekate was a mysterious figure, the Hellenes later emphasized only her

destructive qualities and the Medieval Church distorted her figure into the ugly hag Queen of the Witches.

In the birth chart, Hekate is a guardian figure of our unconscious who enables us to converse with the hidden parts of our
psyche. She is the archetypal shaman as she moves between the
visible and invisible worlds in a fluid and facile way, delving for
insight into the magical realms for the ultimate purpose of effect-
ing healing and regeneration. When our relationship with Hekate is positive, we may experience her as inspiration, or prophetic
dreams and visions. When we deny and reject Hekate, her shadow nature may make itself known as madness, nightmares, stu-
por, depression, stagnation, blocked creative energy, or real/imag-
ined persecution.

Journal Questions

1. Do I ever have foretellings through dreams, visions, voices or
sudden insights? Can I honor my extrasensory wisdom or am I
frightened when these prophecies come true? If they are bad, do I
fear that I caused them to happen because I thought of them?

2. What comes up for me at those times when I feel as if I am
going crazy because of seeing things or imagining voices? Can I
follow these inner promptings or am I afraid without knowing
why?

3. Have there been times when I've felt as if I were plunged into
darkness, feeling lost, confused, depressed, despondent, inactive,
or unproductive? Have I ever felt as if I didn't know who I was or
where I was supposed to be going? Was I vulnerable at those times
to my addictions, which helped to numb and block my awareness
of reality? In retrospect can I see some of these dark times as
preceding creative bursts or new beginnings?

Workbook

In chart analysis, the **asteroid Hekate** shows how I can best access my unconscious and communicate with the spirit realms.

Using **Table 1 on pg. 124,** place the asteroid Hekate in your birth chart. First take note of its sign and house placement. Then notice if it is conjunct or opposite the Sun, Moon, or on an angle (the 1st, 4th, 7th, or 10th house cusps). Secondly, note if Hekate makes a close aspect (use a 1-3 degree orb) to any of the other personal planets, Chiron, the four major asteroids Ceres, Pallas, Juno, Vesta, or is completing a major aspect pattern.

Finally, note whether the asteroid is receiving a transit from an outer planet.

Asteroid	Planet Aspected	Planet Keyphrase
Hekate	_____	_____
	_____	_____

If you find any major aspects or transits, ask yourself how the mythological themes of this dark goddess may be operating in your life or affecting other parts of your personality. You may also want to integrate the keywords of the asteroid with the keywords for its sign and house (See Appendix A—Keywords of the Astrological Alphabet).

The Serpent-Haired Queen Medusa

Medusa was originally the Libyan serpent goddess of female wisdom, and, as the third or dark moon aspect of her trinity, ruled over oracle, prophecy, healing, magic and women's blood mysteries. The Greeks portrayed Medusa as the once-beautiful third Gorgon sister who wore a crown of hissing serpents and whose evil gaze petrified any approaching man. Thus was she punished by Athena for making love with Poseidon (Neptune) in one of Athena's sanctuaries. The Gorgon sisters were subsequently feared as gruesome sea monsters who wielded deadly power. Medusa was later decapitated by the solar hero Perseus, and Athena displayed the Gorgon's head in the center of her breastplate. From Medusa's severed neck sprang the winged horse Pegasus and the hero of the golden sword, Chrysaor. Vials of her blood were given to Asklepius, which he used to heal the living and regenerate the dead.

Medusa represents our serpent wisdom energy arising from our instinctive sexuality which we can transform into our powers to create, regenerate, and recognize truth. In the lineage of the distortion of the Dark Goddess, Sigmund Freud saw in Medusa a symbol of the terrible, castrating, devouring Mother. In the birth chart when Medusa is active in the masculine psyche, she may express as a man's experience of his mother as manipulating and controlling. He later projects this disturbing inner image onto his partners who appear to threaten his sexual potency. When Medusa is active in the feminine psyche, she may indicate our propensity to wear a hideous mask (giving a look that can kill) that repels others in order to protect our vulnerability and to frighten away those who would invade, threaten or disempower us.

Journal Questions

1. How do I feel about snakes? How do I respond to the sight of hair on a woman's vulva? Do I find it beautiful? Am I somewhat fascinated but repulsed at the same time? Can I remember my childhood reactions when I first saw pubic hairs on my mother or some other woman?

2. If I am a man, have I ever felt that a woman's sexuality and power was something potentially threatening to me? Have I had experiences where I felt sexually manipulated or psychologically castrated by a woman? If I have had sexually devastating relationships, have I considered that the kinds of difficult experiences that I seem to attract may reflect my unconscious inner images of the dark feminine?

3. If I am a woman, do I feel insecure and inadequate in my ability to express my sexuality, wisdom and power in my life? Have I ever put on a wrathful face or given a look that could kill in order to protect myself from being exposed? Have I ever felt shunned and rejected by others because of my appearance or personality? Can I acknowledge and honor my female serpent power as my inner source of creativity, actualization and strength in my life?

Workbook

In chart analysis, the **asteroid Medusa** shows how I can best access my sexual serpent power to create, regenerate, and recognize truth and how, when I experience the shadow side, I may feel impotent (as a man) or repulsive (as a woman).

Using **Table 1 on pg. 124,** place the asteroid Medusa in your birth chart. First take note of its sign and house placement. Then notice if it is conjunct or opposite the Sun, Moon, or on an angle (the 1st, 4th, 7th, or 10th house cusps). Secondly, note if Medusa makes a close aspect (use a 1-3 degree orb) to any of the other personal planets, Chiron, the four major asteroids Ceres, Pallas, Juno, Vesta, or is completing a major aspect pattern.

Finally, note whether the asteroid is receiving a transit from an outer planet.

Asteroid	Planet Aspected	Planet Keyphrase
Medusa	_____	_____
	_____	_____

If you find any major aspects or transits, ask yourself how the mythological themes of this dark goddess may be operating in your life or affecting other parts of your personality. You may also want to integrate the keywords of the asteroid with the keywords for its sign and house (See Appendix A—Keywords of the Astrological Alphabet).

Persephone, Queen of the Underworld

Persephone, the daughter of the Great Earth Mother Demeter (Ceres), was abducted, dragged off into the Underworld and ravished by Hades (Pluto). There she reigned as Queen, watching over the souls of the dead and initiating them into the rites of rebirth. Her annual return to her mother each Spring was a symbol, for the Greeks, of the promise of the renewal of life after death.

In the archaic form of Demeter as a triple goddess, her full moon mother aspect was known by the name of Ploutos. In the pre-Hellenic version of her myth, Persephone voluntarily went into the Underworld for part of each year to tend to the dead. The story of her rape and abduction was a later adjunct to the myth first recorded by Homer in the 8th century B.C. which spoke to the patriarchal takeover by the God Pluto of the Great Mother's rulership over death and rebirth.

In the birth chart Persephone, as a daughter of the patriarchy, symbolizes the process of a child's separation from its mother. Persephone can indicate how and where, either physically or psychologically, we may be abducted and plunged into an underworld experience (sometimes at an early age) where we encounter terror, loss, and confusion, and feelings of abandonment. This descent can enable us to develop a relationship with the hidden forces in our unconscious, activate our psychic abilities, release the past, discover a new sense of our adult self and strengths, and emerge transformed and renewed. Some individuals who experience Persephone as a tragedy from which they have never recovered may react by developing patterns of distrust, withdrawal, fear of sexuality and intimacy, fantasy life, depression, chemical addictions, separation anxieties, victimization, passivity and powerlessness, and being acted upon by the strong will of others.

Journal Questions

1. As I grew up, in what ways did I experience a power struggle with my mother as I tried to obtain more freedom and autonomy, especially in the area of relating to the opposite sex? Did I feel that she did not understand or trust me? As a mother, what fears and concerns did I have when my daughter came of age showing signs of sexual development and interest? In what ways did I try to protect her? How did I react to her resistance to my rules and values?

2. Did this power struggle between my mother and/or my daughter result in an estrangement? Have we been able to reconnect? In what ways was I different when I was finally able to reunite with my mother or daughter?

3. Did I experience a tragic event in my childhood that led to the loss of physical or emotional security in my life? Did I feel abandoned or unprotected by my mother? Did I react by retreating into myself and survive by creating a fantasy life? Can I see how this process gave me the opportunity to become more sensitive to the subtleties of the inner world? Have I been able to actualize my latent psychic or empathic abilities or have I tried to dissociate from the pain of my early life through patterns of addictive substance use or behaviors?

4. Have I ever had fantasies or actual experiences of myself as an innocent and pure maiden with unvoiced longings who is ravished by a dark lover and finds subsequent horror at my violation or the awakening of my sexuality?

Workbook

In chart analysis, the **asteroid Persephone** shows how I can best access my psychic and regenerative powers and how, when I experience her shadow side, I may feel powerless and victimized.

Using **Table 1 on pg. 124** place the asteroid Persephone in your birth chart. First take note of its sign and house placement. Then notice if it is conjunct or opposite the Sun, Moon, or on an angle (the 1st, 4th, 7th, or 10th house cusps). Secondly, note if Persephone makes a close aspect (use a 1-3 degree orb) to any of the other personal planets, Chiron, the four major asteroids Ceres, Pallas, Juno, Vesta, or is completing a major aspect pattern.

Finally, note whether the asteroid is receiving a transit from an outer planet.

Asteroid	Planet Aspected	Planet Keyphrase
Persephone	_____	_____
	_____	_____

If you find any major aspects or transits, ask yourself how the mythological themes of this dark goddess may be operating in your life or affecting other parts of your personality. You may also want to integrate the keywords of the asteroid with the keywords for its sign and house (See Appendix A—Keywords of the Astrological Alphabet).

Optional or on your own. Repeat this exercise using the position of Proserpina (the Roman name for Persephone).

Pythia, Priestess of the Delphic Oracle

The Pythia were the name given to the priestesses of the Delphic Oracle. Pythia is derived from Python, the great serpent who guarded the oracular chasm and cave of Gaia's original oracle on Mt. Parnassus above Delphi. This serpent-dragon was also known as Drakonia and Delphyne. Serpents were always raised and honored as sacred animals at oracular sites because the ingestion of a small amounts of certain venom can induce ecstatic states that are conducive to receiving oracular messages.

Apollo, son of the great Zeus, as part of his heroic initiation, slayed the female dragon at Delphi, claimed the oracle for himself, and retained the former priestesses in his own service.

In chart analysis, Pythia represents the oracular part of ourselves through which we can perceive and communicate prophetic words or images that are divinely inspired. Sometimes this flow of information is symbolic and needs to be deciphered before the meaning is apparent. The patriarchal society feared the visionary, oracular and prophetic aspect of the feminine. Thus many people today who carry the Pythia archetype are often dismissed and ridiculed as crazy and hysterical.

Workbook

In chart analysis, Pythia indicates how I channel prophetic inspiration. When I experience the shadow side, I may fear or distrust my visions.

Using **Table 1 on pg. 124,** place the asteroid Pythia in your birth chart. First take note of its sign and house placement. Then notice if it is conjunct or opposite the Sun, Moon, or on an angle (the 1st, 4th, 7th, or 10th house cusps). Secondly, note if Pythia makes a close aspect (use a 1-3 degree orb) to any of the other personal planets, Chiron, the four major asteroids Ceres, Pallas, Juno, Vesta, or is completing a major aspect pattern.

Finally, note whether the asteroid is receiving a transit from an outer planet.

Asteroid	**Planet Aspected**	**Planet Keyphrase**
Pythia	_____	_____
	_____	_____

If you find any major aspects or transits, ask yourself how the mythological themes of this dark goddess may be operating in your life or affecting other parts of your personality. You may also want to integrate the keywords of the asteroid with the keywords for its sign and house (See Appendix A—Keywords of the Astrological Alphabet).

CHAPTER 5

OTHER SIGNIFICATORS
OF THE DARK MOON ENERGIES

Thus far we have spoken of the balsamic moon phase, the twelfth house, and the dark moon goddesses as indicators of the shadowy lunar symbolism of the dark moon. In addition, we will briefly mention a number of other significators—the planet Pluto, and other derivatives of the moon's cycle—the South Node of the Moon, the void-of-course moon, and eclipses.

Pluto

Persephone enthroned, with Pluto at her side

In the Olympic pantheon Pluto, called Hades by the Greeks, was awarded dominion over the Underworld by his brother Zeus/Jupiter, supreme king of all the gods. This was a province that previously had been the dominion of various dark goddesses of matriarchal cultures. It was through the rape and abduction of

Persephone, daughter of Great Mother Demeter/Ceres who had ruled over both birth and death, that Pluto secured his kingdom. With Persephone at his side as the Queen of the Underworld, Pluto took over rulership of the realm of the dead. Many of the qualities of the dark feminine that some astrologers have correlated with Pluto are actually aspects of Persephone and other dark goddesses who preceded her.

While Persephone alternated moving between the world of the living and that of the dead, Pluto remained a prisoner in his own domain. There exist few mythological references to his ever leaving the Underworld, and when he did he always wore a cap of invisibility. This is the core of Pluto's manifestation as a center of repressed energy that gains its tremendous power from the buildup of internal pressure, a power that controls us from the unconscious level. When Plutonian energies eventually erupt in the upper world on the conscious level, they often explode with a rage and violence that can make a person lose control.

Astrologers have correlated Pluto's discovery in 1930 with a global depression that destroyed the economic security of millions, with the birth of modern depth psychology, with an era of gangsters and racketeering, with the spread of Fascism throughout Europe as dictators sought to control and manipulate the masses, and with the detonation of the first atomic bomb.

The mysteries of death and destruction include those of regeneration and rebirth. As such, Pluto in the birth chart represents our capacity for self-transformation and self-renewal. But we are required to journey into the underworld of our unconscious where we must first meet our inner demons and die to the old before we can be reborn.

This is the process that occurs when we experience a Pluto transit. The transit of Pluto over a sensitive point in our birth chart is another important indicator of the dark moon phase closure energies that move us through transformation. Pluto is the farthest planet from the Sun, and it takes 248 years to make one complete revolution. Therefore Pluto can spend several years activating a particular planet (part of personality) or point (angle, node) in our chart. Pluto's process of transformation is slow, deep, and irreversible.

The underworld is a metaphor for the unconscious. Whenever we have Pluto transits, Pluto goes to the deepest level of our unconscious where crystallized habits, fears, anger, distortions, resentments, traumas, and a sense of inadequacy and failure are stored. By the very definition of the unconscious, we don't even know that this material is there, but it has a very powerful effect upon our actions, often manifesting as compulsive behaviors.

The volcano is an apt symbol for Pluto. Through the volcano's incredible inner pressure, it turns our rock-hard, crystallized psychological and emotional material into a state of molten lava. As this material loosens up, it expands. Our body's natural channels of elimination then begin to purge this old and often toxic material, leading to a healing crisis. All of our suppressed anger and unhappiness comes spewing up from the depths of our being. This process can occur on the physical level as tumors, fevers, eruptions, and other kinds of illnesses. It can also occur on the emotional level as outbursts of rage and tears that we can no longer hold back. And psychologically it can manifest as those situations where we remember or learn something about our past that we had been previously unaware, and that knowledge has the power to destroy the assumptions upon which we had based our lives. The Plutonian process of elimination can also surface as mental disturbances when we feel as if we are going crazy or are out-of-control.

If we understand Pluto as essentially a process of transformation and regeneration, this is the first stage of purification which gives us the opportunity to eliminate the old patterning that keeps us locked into self-destructive and self-defeating behaviors. We can clear this material out, and instead of being bound to a past of which we are not even aware, we are freed to consciously imprint new patterns that are more in alignment with our future aspirations. However, the interim process of being called to destroy all the aspects of our previous life that have no function or value in our future and forced to give up that which we think we can't live without is often terrifying and very painful.

If we project this Plutonian energy, we may rage at others who we think are the cause of our misery and unhappiness and blame them for our predicament. We may also at this time magnetize people who will press all of our sensitive buttons and set off our crazy, irrational reactions and obsessive behaviors. It is helpful if we can occasionally step back and honor these people for being catalysts strong enough to activate the process of elimination and purification which is necessary to release self-destructive, repressed, and therefore toxic patterns.

During Pluto transits, we experience endings of an old way of life, similar to the experience that occurs during the balsamic moon phase. Death, chaos and disintegration are precursors to the re-birth and renewal that are to follow. As I stated in *Mysteries of the Dark Moon*, "The naked awareness of the Dark Goddess is to see the death and destruction of the old and joyfully embrace it as a sign of imminent renewal."

You can determine times of major Pluto transits in your life by looking in the ephemeris to see when transiting Pluto makes major aspects to your planets or angles*. Each aspected point rep-resents a different part of our personality whose psychological issues need to be transformed. While Pluto is an important sig-nificator of the dark moon energies of death and renewal, I am only mentioning it in passing because of the wealth of material that already exists on Pluto—i.e. *Pluto, the Evolutionary Journey of the Soul* by Jeffrey Green, Donna Cunningham's *Healing Pluto Problems*, Steven Forrest's *Book of Pluto*, Liz Greene's discussion of Pluto in *The Astrology of Fate,* and Ariel Guttman's chapter on Pluto in *Mythic Astrology*.

The South Node of the Moon
We have included the Moon's South Node in this text because, like the other dark moon points, it has been partly misunderstood and therefore unfairly maligned. The South Node of the Moon, like its counterpoint the North Node, arises from the intersection of the moon's orbit with the plane of the ecliptic (the path of the sun and the planets as they appear to revolve around the earth).

The nodes are not physical bodies as are the planets, but rather points in space. This may suggest that they carry a cosmic mean-ing rather than one related solely to the physical world. The north or *ascending node* shows where the Moon crosses the ecliptic from south to north. The south or *descending node* is conversely indi-cated by the Moon's path from a northerly to southerly celestial latitude. The Nodes have an 18-year cycle through the signs of the zodiac.

---

*Astro also offers Pluto Passages, which lists the aspects made and dates of all Pluto transits (including progressions and directions) to your birth chart.

The Hindu astrologers envisioned the Nodes as a vast cosmic dragon. The cosmic dragon, the mother of all the serpents who shed their skin and renew themselves, is an ancient image of the goddess's mysteries of death and rebirth. The image of the uroborous, the serpent wrapped around the world egg biting its tail, is a symbol of undifferentiated cosmic unity existing in eternal time. Medieval astrologers referred to the Nodes as the Dragon's Head (the North Node) and the Dragon's Tail (the South Node). The depiction of the serpent cut, severing the head from the tail, points to the beginning of temporal linear time.

Our lunar consciousness symbolized by the Moon contains, among other things, our lineage and the storehouse of all our memories from the past. The Nodes of the moon represent eternal karmic issues as they manifest within the temporal time frame of a particular incarnation.

Our Western culture generally equates the Eastern concept of karma as something bad, as in the phrase that someone has bad karma. Karma, as we spoke about in Section II, simply means the results of all of our previous actions, both positive and negative. Many people reap the results of good karma, although we don't generally hear this phrase bandied about as much as the other one. Because every new cycle is related to the previous one, in every new life of existence, some of the karma, or the results of previous actions, is carried over into the next cycle of activity. The Nodes can be seen as an axis of where we reap old karma from a previous cycle and sow the seeds of new karma in the present cycle.

According to the traditional astrological interpretation of the Nodes, (including what Douglas Bloch and I wrote in *Astrology For Yourself*) the North Node is a symbol of spiritual power and integration. It is said to depict the future and represents how new learning experiences can lead to personal growth. By contrast the South Node, lying directly opposite, is a symbol of the past, and represents the path of least resistance. It depicts deeply ingrained habit patterns that may limit the development of future potential.

There is a general acceptance that the South Node refers to bad karma, as in the astrological descriptor of this point as a karmic affliction. Many teachings about the South Node neglect to mention the good karma, or positive wisdom and skills carried over from the past, that is also contained in the meaning of the South Node.

This negative view of the South Node arises from the metaphysical bias of the solar consciousness of patriarchal cultures that value northward and upward motion, as depicted in the North Node, as the ascent of the spirit. They likewise devalue southward and downward motion as depicted by the South Node as the descent of the soul into matter. And it is the earth, the body, the soul, the emotions, the underworld, and the unconscious that are linked with the feminine lunar energies which have been feared and rejected. This is one reason why the interpretations of the South Node of the Moon have been so negative.

Our conditioning to fear the great dark unknown has colored our astrological interpretations, teaching astrology students that the activities of the South Node are to be avoided at all costs. Conjunctions of the South Node to personal planets or to planets in another's birth chart are looked upon as karmic afflictions, and viewed with fear and trepidation.

In *Finding Our Way Through the Dark*, we want to present a more holistic understanding of the South Node, one that reclaims its "dark moon phase denied qualities." The South Node describes where from where we have come out of eternity with the total accumulation of our memories from the past. Its meaning includes both the subconscious memory of our successes where we utilized our knowledge, skills, capacities, and wisdom in the fulfillment of our potential as well as the subconscious memory of our failures which act as a kind of inertia that blocks personal fulfillment.

As an empowering symbol of the past, the South Node represents a resource, innate talent or ability with which we have been born, and it often expresses itself at an early age. It points to our base of operation—the sum total of knowledge that we have carried over from the past. The South Node indicates where we can be a teacher or role model for others. It is our soul's memory through which we can access the power of our unconscious as a source of wisdom and enlightenment. We can use our South Node skills to enhance our lives and to make a contribution to others and to society, as seen in Table 1. Thus, the sign and house qualities of the South Node are not to be avoided, but to be utilized.

Our strength comes from what we carry over from the past. However, because South Node functioning feels so natural, easy, and comfortable, we are vulnerable to overemphasizing these qualities and thus getting stuck there. Eventually we may become bored, limited, stunted in our growth, and depleted of energy. When we devalue the wisdom of the dark, we may have difficulty in expressing our positive South Node qualities, and can instead experience anxiety, insecurity and a wide range phobias. Problems arise when we remain fixated in the South's Nodes realm and, because of our fear of failure, avoid the path of future development depicted by the North Node's sign and house position.

The nodes after all represent a **polarity**. For the polarity to remain balanced, both sides must be equally represented. When either side becomes emphasized to the detriment of the other, dis-ease occurs. Healing takes place when we are able to use the skills and talents of our South Node past in ways that enable us to stay focused and acting skillfully upon what lies ahead. New growth takes place when we stretch to incorporate the North Node's sign and house qualities into our ever-evolving self. Table 2 shows how this can occur.

We encourage the reader to recognize and reclaim the innate gifts of his or her South Node as a precious foundation that can support and sustain the building of new skills and capacities.

Void of course moon

The moon travels through the Zodiac every 28 days and spends about 2 and 1/3 days in each sign. In the course of her stay in each sign, the Moon makes aspects to other planets. As she leaves one sign and goes into another, she makes a final major aspect (conjunction, sextile, square, trine or opposition) to the planet that is in the latest degree of the zodiac on that day. The period of time between this final aspect and the time when the moon moves into the next sign is called the of "void-of-course moon." These times are indicated on many astrological calendars and are abbreviated as VOC. They can last from a few minutes, to several hours, and occasionally an entire day or more. The void-of-course moon is the final or closure phase of the moon's journey through each sign.

Many astrologers say a void-of-course moon indicates a bad time to conduct business, sign contracts, make important decisions or initiate events. However, it is said to be a good time for

Table 1

South Node	Innate Talent of Ability
♈ Aries/1st house	Ability to function as an indepoendent individual.
♉ Taurus/2nd house	Ability to connect to the material world and it's resources.
♊ Gemini/3rd house	Ability to gather information and to effectively communicate it to others.
♋ Cancer/4th house	Ability to nurture and express one's feeling nature.
♌ Leo/5th house	Ability to express creativity.
♍ Virgo/6th house	Ability to perfect and refine form.
♎ Libra/7th house	Ability to share and relate to others.
♏ Scoprio/8th house	Ability to perceive the secret workings behind manifest form.
♐ Sagittarius/9th house	Ability to see systems holistically and to understand how the parts fit into the whole.
♑ Capricorn/10th house	Ability to translate ideals into reality.
♒ Aquraius/11th house	Ability to serve a larger group or humanitarian purpose and to be original.
♓ Pisces/12th house	Ability to use one's empathy and compassion to perceive the unity in all things.

Table 2

SOUTH NODE	OVEREMPHASIS	NORTH NODE	BALANCE PROVIDED
Aries/ 1st house	Overemphasis on self and on own independence	Libra/ 7th house	Understands the importance of others, learns to cooperate, develops partnerships
Taurus/ 2nd house	Attachment to form, resistance to change, over importance of possessions, compromise values for financial security	Scorpio/ 8th house	Destroys old forms to make way for the new, shares physical and emotional resources, develops financial and sexual integrity
Gemini/ 3rd house	Overemphasis on facts, immersion in trivia and gossip, limited world-view	Sagittarius/ 9th house	Understands how the facts fit into a larger whole, develops a more wide ranging perspective, pursues philosophical Truth
Cancer/ 4th house	Drowning in emotions and insecurities, being at the mercy of feelings, overemphasis on family matters, reluctance to leave home	Capricorn/ 10th house	Uses self discipline to direct one's emotions so that one can focus in the objective realm, develops a professional life and assumes authority
Leo/ 5th house	Excessive pride, elitism, and self-importance, over-involvement with personal creativity, children, play, or love affairs	Aquarius/11th house	Develops an impersonal humanitarian outlook, focuses on group endeavors, friendships, and community concerns
Virgo/ 6th house	Overemphasis on functionality, details, efficiency, and day-to-day routines and responsibilities, excessive judgementalness, worry and fear	Pisces/12th house	Trusts the universe, learns compassion, develops a spiritual world view and a spiritual practice
Libra/ 7th house	Over dependency on others, doing what others want, giving away power, indecision	Aries/1st house	Builds self reliance, develops a stronger sense of self, learns to take action
Scorpio/ 8th house	Excessive emotional extremism, intensity or psychological processing, financial reliance on others	Taurus/2nd house	Maintains calmness and stability through being grounded in the physical world, develops own financial security through the use of one's skills and talents
Sagittarius/ 9th house	Involvement in abstract, overly impractical concerns, excessive education or travel	Gemini/ 3rd house	Brings abstract ideas into everyday reality, leans how to make personal observations, research and communicate the facts
Capricorn/ 10th house	Excessive ambition, workaholic, fear of vulnerability, over-attachment to one's reputation and outer forms	Cancer/4th house	Learns to nurture oneself and accept one's feelings, creates a home and values a family as the basis of personal foundations
Aquarius/ 11th house	Excessive detachment, impersonality, inconsistency, and rebelliousness, overemphasis on freedom or on group activity	Leo/ 5th house	Develops warmth, creativity, and leadership, learns to relate to others in a personal way
Pisces/ 12th house	Excessive escapism, lack of realism, and victimization, overemphasis on the "other world"	Virgo/ 6th house	Learns the skills to function in the daily world, develops discrimination, ease with mundane responsibilities, and useful service to others

inner work, spiritual practices and relaxation. It's like taking a siesta or putting an "out to lunch sign" on your door. After the moon has related to all of the planets in a particular sign, when she goes void-of-course, it is her opportunity to plop down on the couch, put her feet up and take a breather before she moves into the next sign.

In a world that places a premium on productivity and activity, void-of-course moon times have been seen as a hindrance and nuisance. As a result we miss the valuable renewal function that this time offers. The feminine is devalued in a culture that emphasizes *doing* rather than *being*. Therefore, we encourage the reader to make use of void-of-course moon periods to access deep sources of creativity, inspiration and illumination that are available during these subtle dark moon phases of the monthly cycle.

Eclipses

The ancients regarded eclipses with awe and terror, as the Sun or Moon would suddenly, and without warning, disappear from the heavens. It appeared as if these celestial bodies were being swallowed by a cosmic dragon or some other invisible entity. We know from monuments such as Stonehenge that early priest-astrologers devoted much study to the prediction of eclipses, especially since they gained power and reverence from their ability to foretell the movements of the gods.

In astrological interpretation, eclipses have been seen as indicators of calamity, disaster, and otherwise difficult times. Once again, the Moon's movement, as she participates in the creation of darkness during an eclipse, has been feared and subsequently demonized. As such, eclipses fall into the category of the Dark Moon Phase energies needing to be revisioned.

Eclipses occur when either of the two lights, the Sun or the Moon, are in exact alignment at the New Moon or the Full Moon, on the ecliptic and therefore near the Nodes.

An eclipse of the Sun takes place when the Moon is exactly between the Earth and the Sun at New Moon. During a solar eclipse, the Moon's shadow falls on the Earth, and blocks the light of the Sun. Astrologically, the Sun and Moon are in the same degree of the zodiac and conjunct one of the two Nodes at which point the orbits of the Earth and Moon intersect.

An eclipse of the Moon takes place when the Earth is exactly between the Moon and the Sun at the Full Moon. During a lunar eclipse, the Earth's shadow falls on the Moon, and her light is obscured from the sky. Astrologically, the Sun and Moon are in opposite degrees of the zodiac and conjunct one of the two nodes.

In general, eclipses are said to be negative, but this is a misunderstanding of the shadow function. In both solar and lunar eclipses, the light of either the Sun or Moon is obstructed from reaching the Earth. When the light of consciousness is temporarily blocked, something else is revealed—that which is normally hidden. Called windows into secret realms and open doorways into the subconscious, eclipses allow us to access that which has been concealed or repressed in our lives. Eclipses are said to be karmic in nature, because they relate to issues that lie outside of our consciousness.

If we are out of touch with this hidden material which Carl Jung calls "the shadow," then we may judge it as bad and destructive. We are shocked because this material seems to come out of nowhere, when in fact it was with us all along. To the extent that we have tried to repress the shadow material, we will call the results of the eclipse disastrous. But to the extent that we are open to the unconscious and the surfacing of hidden problems, we will experience the emergence of this material as neutral, revelatory or healing.

Dane Rudhyar said that at the New Moon solar eclipse, the present is blotted out by the past, while at the Full Moon lunar eclipse, the past is obscured by the present. This statement suggests that at a solar eclipse, the Sun—which represents our consciousness awareness—when obscured, allows the forces of the past which lie buried in the unconscious as psychic complexes, to be seen, confronted, and experienced with the possibility of integrating these previously unconscious energies into the present awareness. During a lunar eclipse, it is the past, symbolized by the Moon, which is obscured and can be released. In the absence of the conditioning of the past, the possibility emerges of meeting experiences in a new manner.

Eclipses are linked to nodal axes, and thus they stimulate the possibility of personal integration of the past and future. In addition to differentiating between solar and lunar eclipses, eclipses can be categorized as to whether the Sun (during either a solar or lunar eclipse) is conjunct the North Node or the South Node. When the sun is conjunct the South Node, which symbolizes what has been carried over from previous lifetimes, growth can come from focusing upon, resolving, revisioning and releasing old karmic issues. When the Sun is conjunct the North Node, which symbolizes future possibilities of growth on the basis of what has been accomplished in the past, the eclipse can awaken new illuminations about the future and activate new ways of doing things.

Solar and lunar eclipses occur in pairs across the zodiac, following each other within two weeks. There are at least two solar eclipses each year. Eclipses represent major tests that are presented to us in those areas of the chart where the eclipse falls. This is neither good nor bad—it does mean, however, that during a solar eclipse or one where the Sun is conjunct the South Node we are called upon to confront and resolve some aspect of our unconscious or of our past which we had not been previously aware. At lunar eclipses or when the Sun is conjunct the North Node, we are called upon to face the necessity of manifesting new ways to move into our future, Hence, eclipses often correspond to stress, crisis and change in our lives.

The repercussions of solar and lunar eclipses are said to be felt long after the actual eclipse has taken place. Some astrologers suggest that the significance of a solar eclipse can last for up to six months, and those of a lunar eclipse for several weeks. Tibetan Buddhists say that the ramifications of any activity performed during an eclipse are greatly amplified—including any negative actions which can be multiplied many times and extend far into the future. Thus, they suggest that people do meditation practices and other positive activities on the eclipses to benefit not only themselves, but also all other beings.

The planets that receive aspects from the eclipse show the parts of our personality that are affected by this new awareness. The house that the eclipse falls in shows where the revelations and/or difficulties take place. An eclipse will be far more significant when it makes a close aspect to a planet or angle in the chart.

Below we have listed the solar and lunar eclipse points from 1987 to 2000. You may want to place these points in your chart and note what changes, challenges or insights occurred in your life during these times. Remember, the resolution of the events precipitated by the eclipses can take many months and may also be felt a few months before the actual eclipse takes place. More extensive information on eclipses can be found in the work of Georgia Stathis (her tapes are available from STARCYCLES), and in Bernadette Brady's *The Eagle and the Lark.*

Solar Eclipse		Lunar Eclipse	
September 23, 1987	29 Virgo 34	October 7, 1987	13 Aries 22
March 18, 1988	27 Pisces 42	March 3, 1988	3 Virgo 18
September 11, 1988	18 Virgo 40	August 27, 1988	4 Pisces 23
March 7, 1989	17 Pisces 10	February 20, 1989	1 Virgo 59
August 31, 1989	7 Virgo 48	August 17, 1989	24 Aquarius 12
January 26, 1990	6 Aquarius 35	February 9, 1990	20 Leo 47
July 22, 1990	29 Cancer 04	August 6, 1990	13 Aquarius 52
January 15, 1991	25 Capricorn 20	January 30, 1991	19 Leo 51
July 11, 1991	18 Cancer 59	July 26, 1991	3 Aquarius 16
January 4, 1992	13 Capricorn 51	December 21, 1991	29 Gemini 03
June 30, 1992	8 Cancer 57	June 15, 1992	24 Sag 20
December 24, 1992	2 Capricorn 28	December 9, 1992	18 Gemini 10
May 21, 1993	0 Gemini 31	June 4, 1993	13 Sag 55
November 13, 1993	21 Scorpio 32	November 29, 1993	7 Gemini 03
May 10, 1994	19 Taurus 48	May 25, 1994	3 Sag 43
November 3, 1994	10 Scorpio 54	November 18, 1994	25 Taurus 42
April 29, 1995	8 Taurus 56	April 15, 1995	25 Libra 04
October 23, 1995	0 Scorpio 18	October 8, 1995	14 Aries 54
April 17, 1996	28 Aries 12	April 4, 1996	14 Libra 31
October 12, 1996	19 Libra 32	September 27, 1996	4 Aries 17
March 9, 1997	18 Pisces 31	March 24, 1997	3 Libra 35
September 1, 1997	9 Virgo 34	September 16, 1997	23 Pisces 56
February 26, 1998	7 Pisces 55	March 13, 1998	22 Virgo 24
August 22, 1998	28 Leo 48	August 8, 1998	15 Aquarius 21
		September 6, 1998	13 Pisces 40
February 16, 1999	27 Aquarius 08	January 31, 1999	11 Leo 20
August 11, 1999	18 Leo 21	July 28, 1999	4 Aquarius 58
February 5, 2000	16 Aquarius 02	January 21, 2000	0 Leo 26
July 1, 2000	10 Cancer 14	July 16, 2000	24 Capr 19
July 31, 2000	8 Leo 12		
December 25, 2000	4 Capricorn 14		

In closing, the following table lists the many times and the many ways in which we experience the dark moon phase energies.

Table 3 — Dark Moon Phase Periods

* Every night in the last hours before waking
* Every few days when the moon goes "void-of-course"
* Every month when women menstruate
* Every month, in the 3½ days of the balsamic moon phase, just before the New Moon.
* Every month when the Moon passes through the twelfth house of our birth chart for several days
* Every year in the month before our birthday
* Every year when the Sun passes through the twelfth house of our birth chart for a month
* Every year during the shortest daylight hours in the time before the Winter Solstice
* Every twenty-eight years when our progressed Moon passes through our twelfth house for 2½ years
* Every twenty-nine years when our progressed Balsamic phase occurs for 3½ years
* During all twelfth house transits, especially by the outer planets—Jupiter, Saturn, Chiron, Uranus, Neptune, and Pluto
* During eclipses
* In the final years of any planetary return cycle, *i.e.*, the years before our Saturn return or progressed lunar return
* During major Pluto transits to sensitive points
* During transits to the dark goddess asteroids, the Dark Moon, and the Black Moon.
* After menopause
* The final days, weeks, months or years before physical death.

We have been conditioned by our lack of night vision to feel lost, confused and frightened when we pass through the many dark moon times in our lives. The experience of loss, alienation, and grief that we normally feel can be intensified by our lack of knowledge concerning the nature, purpose and potential outcome contained in the mysteries which bridge the dark and light, the old and new. We encourage you to learn to recognize these times and to begin to use the special qualities available during the dark closure phase of any cycle to heal, transform and empower yourself and others.

Footnotes

1. Alexander Marshack, *The Roots of Civilization: The Cognitive Beginnings of Man's first Art, Symbols and Notation*, (New York: McGraw-Hill, 1972)

2. Dane Rudhyar, *The Lunation Cycle* (The Netherlands: Servire-Wassenaar, 1967), 37.

3. Diane Stein, *Casting the Circle: A Woman's Book of Ritual* (Freedom, CA: The Crossing Press, 1990), 93.

4. Joanne Wickenberg and Virginia Ewbank, *The Spiral of Life* (Seattle, WA: 1974), 33.

5. Dane Rudhyar, *Astrological Aspects: A Process Oriented Approach* (Santa Fe, NM: Aurora Press), 67.

6. Ibid., 74.

7. Marc Robertson, *Cosmopsychology 1: The Engine of Destiny* (Seattle:WA, Astrology Center of the Northwest, 1976).

8. Dane Rudhyar, from *The Lunation Process in Astrological Guidance* by Leyla Rael, p. 3.

9. Dane Rudhyar, *The Astrological Houses*, (New York: Doubleday & Co., 1972.), 132.

10. John Algeo, *Reincarnation Explored*, (The Theosophical Publishing House, 1987.), 7.

11. Stanislav Grof, *The Adventure of Self Discovery* (New York: State University of New York, 1988).

12. Chogyam Trungpa, *Cutting Through Spiritual Materialism.* (Berkeley: Shambhala, 1973).

13. Radmilla Moacanin, *Jung's Psychology and Tibetan Buddhism* (London: Wisdom Publications, 1986). 45.

14. Op. Cit., Trungpa.

15. Barbara Black Koltuv, *The Book of Lilith*, (Nicholas Hayes, Inc., 1986)

16. Marc Beriault, "The Dark Moon," from the magazine *Considerations.*

17. J. Lee Lehman, Ph.D., *The Ultimate Asteroid Book* (Pennsylvania: Whitford Press, 1988), 77.

18. Delphine Jay, *Interpretating Lilith* (Tempe, AZ, AFA, 1983), 6.

19. Ivy Goldstein-Jacobson, *The Dark Moon Lilith in Astrology,* (Alhambra, CA: Frank Severy Publishing, 1961), 6.

Bibliography

Marc Beriault, "The Dark Moon," from the magazine *Considerations.*

Demetra George, *Mysteries of the Dark Moon: The Healing Power of the Dark Goddess,* (San Francisco: Harper SanFrancisco, 1992).

Ivy Goldstein-Jacobson, *The Dark Moon Lilith in Astrology.* (Alhambra, CA: Frank Severy Publishing, 1961).

Delphine Jay, *Interpretating Lilith* (Tempe, AZ, AFA, 1983).

Tracy Marks, *Your Secret Self: Illuminating the Mysteries of the Twelfth House,* (Sebastopol, CA: CRCS Publications, 1989).

Michael Meyers, *A Handbook For The Humanistic Astrologer.* (New York: Anchor Press/Doubleday , 1974).

Rael, Leyla. *The Lunation Process in Astrological Guidance.,* a pamphlet.

Marc Robertson, *Cosmopsychology I: The Engine of Destiny.*(Tempe, AZ, American Federation of Astrologers, 1975).

_____ *Not a Sign in the Sky, But A Living Person.* (Tempe, AZ, American Federation of Astrologers, 1975).

_____ *Time Out of Mind.*, (Tempe, Arizona, American Federation of Astrologers, 1972).

Dane Rudhyar,*The Lunation Cycle.* (Sante Fe, N M: Aurora Press. 1986).

_____ *An Astrological Mandala.* (New York: Random House, 1973).

_____ *Astrological Aspects: A Process Oriented Approach* (Santa Fe, NM: Aurora Press).

_____ *The Astrological Houses*, (New York: Doubleday, 1972).

Maria Kay Simms,*Circle of the Cosmic Muse,* (St. Paul, MN: Llewllyn Publications, 1994)

Joanne Wickenburg and Virginia Ewbank, *The Spiral of Life.* (Seattle: 1974).

Appendix A

KEYWORDS OF THE ASTROLOGICAL ALPHABET

Table 1: SIGN KEY PHRASES

♈ Aries	My need to be independent and develop self awareness
♉ Taurus	My need to be resourceful, productive and stable
♊ Gemini	My need to communicate with and learn from others
♋ Cancer	My need to give and receive emotional warmth and security
♌ Leo	My need to express myself creatively and be appreciated by others
♍ Virgo	My need to bring order into my life and function efficiently
♎ Libra	My need to cooperate with others and create harmony and balance in my life
♏ Scorpio	My need for deep involvements and intense transformations
♐ Sagittarius	My need to explore and expand the horizons of my mind and world
♑ Capricorn	My need for structure, authority, and social accomplishment
♒ Aquarius	My need to be innovative, original and create social change
♓ Pisces	My need to commit myself to a dream or ideal and strive towards its realization

Table 2: SIGN KEYWORDS

♈ Aries	Courageous, independent, assertive, spontaneous, inconsiderate, self-centered, pushy
♉ Taurus	Grounded, consistent, dependable, practical, sensual, stubborn, hoarding, possessive
♊ Gemini	Intellectual, curious, communicative, versatile, superficial, unreliable, scattered
♋ Cancer	Nurturing, caring, protective, sympathetic, intuitive, clinging, dependent, needy
♌ Leo	Confident, creative, dramatic, generous, proud, arrogant, boastful, egocentric

♍ Virgo	Analytic, useful, discriminating, perfecting, efficient, nagging, critical, neurotic
♎ Libra	Sharing, cooperative, fair, charming, interactive, graceful, manipulative, indecisive
♏ Scorpio	Deep, intense, penetrating, passionate, transforming, vengeful, compulsive, suspicious
♐ Sagittarius	Open-minded, adventurous, philosophical, optimistic, wise, self-indulgent, opinionated
♑ Capricorn	Mature, successful, industrious, structured, authoritative, controlling, rigid
♒ Aquarius	Unique, innovative, reforming, eccentric, futuristic, visionary, erratic, unreliable
♓ Pisces	Sensitive, compassionate, spiritual, psychic, imaginative, confused, victimized

Table 3: HOUSE KEYWORDS

1st House	Physical appearance, identity, personality
2nd House	The use of my talents to generate resources necessary for my survival: income, money, possessions.
3rd House	Communicating, interacting in my immediate environment, siblings
4th House	Home, family, personal foundations
5th House	Creative self-expression, children, love affairs, recreation, risks
6th House	Efficient functioning in health, job, and everyday routines
7th House	Relationships: mate, business, client
8th House	Shared emotional, financial and sexual resources; death
9th House	Larger viewpoints, far-reaching environments, philosophical beliefs
10th House	Position in the outer world, professional identity, public reputation
11th House	Friends, causes, groups, politics, goals, and social visions for the future
12th House	Spiritual quest, selfless service to others, confinements; karma, facing ghosts of the past, transcendence

Table 4: PLANET & POINT KEYWORDS

☉ Sun	my life-purpose self; my basic identity and life purpose	
☽ Moon	my emotional self; my emotions, feelings, and daily habits	
☿ Mercury	my mental self; my capacity to think, speak, learn, and reason	
♀ Venus	my erotic self; my capacity to attract people and things I love and value	
♂ Mars	my action-taking self; my capacity to act and assert myself based on personal desire	
⚳ Ceres	my maternal self; my capacity to unconditionally love and nurture myself and others	
⚴ Pallas	my creative self; my capacity for creative wisdom and original perceptions	
⚵ Juno	my partnering self; my capacity for meaningful, committed relationships	
⚶ Vesta	my priest/priestess self; my capacity to integrate and focus my energies	
♃ Jupiter	my expansive self; my search for meaning, truth, and ethical values	
♄ Saturn	my structured self; my capacity to create order, form, and discipline in my life	
⚷ Chiron	my core wound and healing self; my capacity for holistic understanding	
♅ Uranus	my individualistic self; my capacity to liberate myself from past limitations, my unique individuality	
♆ Neptune	my idealistic self; my capacity to transcend the finite self through feeling unity with a greater whole	
♇/ Pluto	my transformative self; my capacity to transform and renew myself	
Ascendant	(1st house cusp) -my way of presenting my outer personality to the world	
Descendant	(7th house cusp)-my relating self and what I seek from others	
IC	(4th house cusp) - my private self and personal foundations	

MC   (10th house cusp)- my public, social, and profes-
               sional self

♌ North Node my future direction of growth and the skills and
               talents I need to develop

☋ South Node my skills and knowledge from the past that I
               can draw upon, but also where I may be vulner-
               able to repeating old habit patterns

APPENDIX B:
MIDNIGHT EPHEMERIDES
FOR THE DARK GODDESS ASTEROIDS

	ATROPOS	HEKATE	LILITH	MEDUSA	MOIRA	NEMESIS	PERSEPHONE	PROSERPINA	PYTHIA
Jan 1, 1920	19 ♈ 19	02 ♌ 55	09 ♐ 20	11 ♑ 46	08 ♍ 03	16 ♎ 31	13 ♈ 08	21 ♓ 37	25 ♊ 07
Jan 11, 1920	21 ♈ 24	01 ♋ 06	12 ♐ 41	16 ♑ 52	08 ♍ 07	18 ♎ 22	14 ♈ 45	24 ♓ 38	22 ♊ 50
Jan 21, 1920	23 ♈ 55	29 ♋ 06	15 ♐ 55	21 ♑ 59	07 ♍ 30	19 ♎ 43	16 ♈ 46	27 ♓ 53	21 ♊ 06
Jan 31, 1920	26 ♈ 48	27 ♋ 07	19 ♐ 02	27 ♑ 06	06 ♍ 12	20 ♎ 43	19 ♈ 06	01 ♈ 19	20 ♊ 02
Feb 10, 1920	00 ♉ 00	25 ♋ 19	21 ♐ 59	02 ♒ 13	04 ♍ 20	21 ♎ 06	21 ♈ 43	04 ♈ 53	19 ♊ 42
Feb 20, 1920	03 ♉ 26	23 ♋ 52	24 ♐ 44	07 ♒ 19	02 ♍ 04	20 ♎ 55	24 ♈ 34	08 ♉ 35	20 ♊ 02
Mar 1, 1920	07 ♉ 05	23 ♋ 51	27 ♐ 15	12 ♒ 23	29 ♌ 42	20 ♎ 01	27 ♈ 37	12 ♉ 23	21 ♊ 01
Mar 11, 1920	10 ♉ 53	22 ♋ 20	29 ♐ 30	17 ♒ 26	27 ♌ 32	18 ♎ 46	00 ♉ 50	16 ♉ 14	22 ♊ 33
Mar 21, 1920	14 ♉ 48	22 ♋ 19	01 ♑ 25	22 ♒ 25	25 ♌ 50	16 ♎ 58	04 ♉ 11	20 ♈ 09	24 ♊ 34
Mar 31, 1920	18 ♉ 50	22 ♋ 47	04 ♑ 58	27 ♒ 22	24 ♌ 46	14 ♎ 50	07 ♉ 38	24 ♈ 05	26 ♊ 60
Apr 10, 1920	22 ♉ 56	23 ♋ 41	04 ♑ 05	07 ♓ 13	24 ♌ 25	12 ♎ 38	11 ♉ 10	28 ♈ 03	29 ♊ 45
Apr 20, 1920	27 ♉ 05	24 ♋ 59	04 ♑ 43	07 ♓ 00	24 ♌ 48	10 ♎ 33	14 ♉ 47	02 ♉ 01	02 ♋ 48
Apr 30, 1920	01 ♊ 17	26 ♋ 37	04 ♑ 50	11 ♓ 41	25 ♌ 52	08 ♎ 48	18 ♉ 26	05 ♉ 59	06 ♋ 06
May 10, 1920	05 ♊ 30	28 ♋ 33	03 ♑ 22	16 ♓ 14	27 ♌ 33	07 ♎ 31	22 ♉ 07	09 ♉ 56	09 ♋ 36
May 20, 1920	09 ♊ 44	00 ♌ 44	03 ♑ 21	20 ♓ 39	29 ♌ 46	06 ♎ 47	25 ♉ 50	13 ♉ 50	13 ♋ 16
May 30, 1920	13 ♊ 59	03 ♌ 08	01 ♑ 49	24 ♓ 53	02 ♍ 26	06 ♎ 27	29 ♉ 32	17 ♉ 42	17 ♋ 06
Jun 9, 1920	18 ♊ 12	05 ♌ 42	29 ♐ 52	28 ♓ 54	05 ♍ 30	07 ♎ 00	03 ♊ 14	21 ♉ 30	21 ♋ 03
Jun 19, 1920	22 ♊ 24	08 ♌ 26	27 ♐ 41	02 ♈ 41	08 ♍ 54	07 ♎ 54	06 ♊ 55	25 ♉ 14	25 ♋ 07
Jun 29, 1920	26 ♊ 35	11 ♌ 18	25 ♐ 28	06 ♈ 08	12 ♍ 35	09 ♎ 15	10 ♊ 34	28 ♉ 53	29 ♋ 17
Jul 9, 1920	00 ♋ 42	14 ♌ 15	23 ♐ 27	09 ♈ 14	16 ♍ 31	11 ♎ 01	14 ♊ 09	02 ♊ 26	03 ♌ 31
Jul 19, 1920	04 ♋ 47	17 ♌ 18	21 ♐ 47	11 ♈ 53	20 ♍ 40	13 ♎ 07	17 ♊ 40	05 ♊ 51	07 ♌ 51
Jul 29, 1920	08 ♋ 48	20 ♌ 24	20 ♐ 37	13 ♈ 60	24 ♍ 59	15 ♎ 32	21 ♊ 06	09 ♊ 07	12 ♌ 14
Aug 8, 1920	12 ♋ 44	23 ♌ 33	20 ♐ 01	15 ♈ 28	29 ♍ 28	18 ♎ 11	24 ♊ 25	12 ♊ 12	16 ♌ 40
Aug 18, 1920	16 ♋ 35	26 ♌ 45	20 ♐ 35	16 ♈ 11	04 ♎ 05	21 ♎ 05	27 ♊ 37	15 ♊ 04	21 ♌ 09
Aug 28, 1920	20 ♋ 19	29 ♌ 57	21 ♐ 41	16 ♈ 05	08 ♎ 49	24 ♎ 09	00 ♋ 26	17 ♊ 42	25 ♌ 41
Sep 7, 1920	23 ♋ 54	03 ♍ 09	23 ♐ 15	15 ♈ 06	13 ♎ 39	27 ♎ 23	03 ♋ 26	20 ♊ 01	00 ♍ 14
Sep 17, 1920	27 ♋ 20	06 ♍ 20	25 ♐ 14	13 ♈ 19	18 ♎ 34	00 ♏ 46	06 ♋ 00	21 ♊ 59	04 ♍ 50
Sep 27, 1920	00 ♌ 34	09 ♍ 29	27 ♐ 36	10 ♈ 56	23 ♎ 33	04 ♏ 15	08 ♋ 17	23 ♊ 31	09 ♍ 26
Oct 7, 1920	03 ♌ 34	12 ♍ 35	00 ♑ 17	08 ♈ 18	28 ♎ 36	07 ♏ 50	10 ♋ 12	24 ♊ 35	14 ♍ 02
Oct 17, 1920	06 ♌ 16	15 ♍ 37	03 ♑ 15	05 ♈ 50	03 ♏ 42	11 ♏ 31	11 ♋ 43	25 ♊ 06	18 ♍ 38
Oct 27, 1920	08 ♌ 39	18 ♍ 32	06 ♑ 28	03 ♈ 54	08 ♏ 50	15 ♏ 14	12 ♋ 44	24 ♊ 60	23 ♍ 12
Nov 6, 1920	10 ♌ 37	21 ♍ 20	09 ♑ 53	02 ♈ 47	13 ♏ 59	19 ♏ 01	13 ♋ 13	24 ♊ 16	27 ♍ 45
Nov 16, 1920	12 ♌ 06	23 ♍ 58	13 ♑ 30	02 ♈ 34	19 ♏ 09	22 ♏ 50	13 ♋ 06	22 ♊ 54	02 ♎ 14
Nov 26, 1920	13 ♌ 01	26 ♍ 24	17 ♑ 16	03 ♈ 15	24 ♏ 19	26 ♏ 39	12 ♋ 21	21 ♊ 02	06 ♎ 38
Dec 6, 1920	13 ♌ 18	28 ♍ 37	17 ♑ 16	04 ♈ 45	29 ♏ 28	00 ♐ 29	11 ♋ 02	18 ♊ 48	10 ♎ 56

	ATROPOS	HEKATE	LILITH	MEDUSA	MOIRA	NEMESIS	PERSEPHONE	PROSERPINA	PYTHIA
Dec 16, 1920	12 ♌ 52	00 ♎ 32	21 ♑ 11	06 ♈ 58	04 ♐ 35	04 ♐ 18	09 ♋ 13	16 ♊ 27	15 ♎ 06
Dec 26, 1920	11 ♌ 42	02 ♎ 07	25 ♑ 12	09 ♈ 48	09 ♐ 39	08 ♐ 05	07 ♋ 05	14 ♊ 15	19 ♎ 06
Jan 5, 1921	09 ♌ 50	03 ♎ 05	29 ♑ 19	13 ♈ 08	14 ♐ 40	11 ♐ 48	04 ♋ 53	12 ♊ 26	22 ♎ 52
Jan 15, 1921	07 ♌ 25	04 ♎ 05	03 ♒ 32	16 ♈ 53	19 ♐ 36	15 ♐ 28	02 ♋ 51	11 ♊ 10	26 ♎ 22
Jan 25, 1921	04 ♌ 40	04 ♎ 21	07 ♒ 48	20 ♈ 58	24 ♐ 26	19 ♐ 01	01 ♋ 13	10 ♊ 32	29 ♎ 31
Feb 4, 1921	01 ♌ 55	04 ♎ 06	12 ♒ 08	25 ♈ 20	29 ♐ 09	22 ♐ 28	00 ♋ 08	10 ♊ 34	02 ♏ 15
Feb 14, 1921	29 ♋ 27	03 ♎ 19	16 ♒ 30	29 ♈ 56	03 ♑ 44	25 ♐ 45	29 ♊ 40	11 ♊ 13	04 ♏ 28
Feb 24, 1921	27 ♋ 32	02 ♎ 02	20 ♒ 54	04 ♉ 43	08 ♑ 09	28 ♐ 52	29 ♊ 50	12 ♊ 26	06 ♏ 03
Mar 6, 1921	26 ♋ 17	00 ♎ 21	25 ♒ 19	09 ♉ 38	12 ♑ 22	01 ♑ 46	00 ♋ 36	14 ♊ 08	06 ♏ 56
Mar 16, 1921	25 ♋ 47	28 ♍ 24	29 ♒ 44	14 ♉ 41	16 ♑ 21	04 ♑ 24	01 ♋ 54	16 ♊ 16	06 ♏ 59
Mar 26, 1921	25 ♋ 58	26 ♍ 22	04 ♓ 09	19 ♉ 50	20 ♑ 05	06 ♑ 44	03 ♋ 41	18 ♊ 46	06 ♏ 12
Apr 5, 1921	26 ♋ 49	24 ♍ 27	08 ♓ 32	25 ♉ 03	23 ♑ 34	08 ♑ 43	05 ♋ 52	21 ♊ 34	04 ♏ 36
Apr 15, 1921	28 ♋ 14	22 ♍ 49	12 ♓ 54	00 ♊ 19	26 ♑ 34	10 ♑ 17	08 ♋ 24	24 ♊ 37	02 ♏ 22
Apr 25, 1921	00 ♌ 08	21 ♍ 36	17 ♓ 13	05 ♊ 39	29 ♑ 12	11 ♑ 21	11 ♋ 13	27 ♊ 54	29 ♎ 51
May 5, 1921	02 ♌ 27	20 ♍ 54	21 ♓ 28	10 ♊ 60	01 ♒ 22	11 ♑ 54	14 ♋ 17	01 ♋ 21	27 ♎ 24
May 15, 1921	05 ♌ 07	20 ♍ 43	25 ♓ 38	16 ♊ 22	02 ♒ 58	11 ♑ 51	17 ♋ 33	04 ♋ 51	25 ♎ 25
May 25, 1921	08 ♌ 05	21 ♍ 05	29 ♓ 42	21 ♊ 45	03 ♒ 56	11 ♑ 11	21 ♋ 00	08 ♋ 41	24 ♎ 10
Jun 4, 1921	11 ♌ 19	21 ♍ 55	03 ♈ 38	27 ♊ 09	04 ♒ 14	09 ♑ 57	24 ♋ 35	12 ♋ 32	23 ♎ 47
Jun 14, 1921	14 ♌ 45	23 ♍ 12	07 ♈ 25	02 ♋ 32	03 ♒ 50	07 ♑ 12	28 ♋ 17	16 ♋ 27	24 ♎ 16
Jun 24, 1921	18 ♌ 23	24 ♍ 53	11 ♈ 00	07 ♋ 55	02 ♒ 44	06 ♑ 07	02 ♌ 05	20 ♋ 27	25 ♎ 34
Jul 4, 1921	22 ♌ 10	26 ♍ 55	14 ♈ 21	13 ♋ 17	01 ♒ 02	03 ♑ 55	05 ♌ 58	24 ♋ 31	27 ♎ 35
Jul 14, 1921	26 ♌ 06	29 ♍ 16	17 ♈ 25	18 ♋ 38	28 ♑ 57	01 ♑ 50	09 ♌ 55	28 ♋ 37	00 ♏ 13
Jul 24, 1921	00 ♍ 10	01 ♎ 52	20 ♈ 07	23 ♋ 57	26 ♑ 43	00 ♑ 07	13 ♌ 55	02 ♌ 46	03 ♏ 22
Aug 3, 1921	04 ♍ 20	04 ♎ 42	22 ♈ 23	29 ♋ 15	24 ♑ 38	28 ♐ 54	17 ♌ 57	06 ♌ 57	06 ♏ 56
Aug 13, 1921	08 ♍ 37	07 ♎ 43	24 ♈ 07	04 ♌ 31	22 ♑ 55	28 ♐ 18	22 ♌ 00	11 ♌ 08	10 ♏ 53
Aug 23, 1921	12 ♍ 59	10 ♎ 55	25 ♈ 15	09 ♌ 44	21 ♑ 46	28 ♐ 21	26 ♌ 04	15 ♌ 20	15 ♏ 08
Sep 2, 1921	17 ♍ 25	14 ♎ 16	25 ♈ 41	14 ♌ 53	21 ♑ 16	29 ♐ 01	00 ♍ 09	19 ♌ 31	19 ♏ 38
Sep 12, 1921	21 ♍ 57	17 ♎ 45	24 ♈ 17	19 ♌ 60	21 ♑ 25	00 ♑ 17	04 ♍ 12	23 ♌ 41	24 ♏ 21
Sep 22, 1921	26 ♍ 33	21 ♎ 20	22 ♈ 33	25 ♌ 02	22 ♑ 12	02 ♑ 04	08 ♍ 14	27 ♌ 50	29 ♏ 14
Oct 2, 1921	01 ♎ 12	25 ♎ 00	20 ♈ 23	29 ♌ 59	23 ♑ 33	04 ♑ 18	12 ♍ 14	01 ♍ 55	04 ♐ 16
Oct 12, 1921	05 ♎ 55	28 ♎ 45	18 ♈ 08	04 ♍ 50	25 ♑ 24	06 ♑ 58	16 ♍ 10	05 ♍ 57	09 ♐ 26
Oct 22, 1921	10 ♎ 41	02 ♏ 34	16 ♈ 09	09 ♍ 34	27 ♑ 41	09 ♑ 58	20 ♍ 02	09 ♍ 54	14 ♐ 43
Nov 1, 1921	15 ♎ 29	06 ♏ 25	14 ♈ 43	14 ♍ 09	00 ♒ 19	13 ♑ 16	23 ♍ 48	13 ♍ 44	20 ♐ 04
Nov 11, 1921	20 ♎ 20	10 ♏ 19	14 ♈ 09	18 ♍ 35	03 ♒ 15	16 ♑ 50	27 ♍ 27	17 ♍ 25	25 ♐ 30
Nov 21, 1921	25 ♎ 12	14 ♏ 13	14 ♈ 04	22 ♍ 49	06 ♒ 27	20 ♑ 37	00 ♎ 56	20 ♍ 56	00 ♑ 59

	ATROPOS	HEKATE	LILITH	MEDUSA	MOIRA	NEMESIS	PERSEPHONE	PROSERPINA	PYTHIA
Dec 1, 1921	00 ♏ 05	18 ♏ 07	14 ♈ 15	26 ♍ 49	09 ♒ 51	24 ♑ 37	04 ♎ 15	24 ♍ 15	06 ♑ 31
Dec 11, 1921	04 ♏ 58	21 ♏ 59	15 ♈ 15	00 ♎ 31	13 ♒ 25	28 ♑ 46	07 ♎ 20	27 ♍ 17	12 ♑ 04
Dec 21, 1921	09 ♏ 51	25 ♏ 50	17 ♈ 00	03 ♎ 53	17 ♒ 07	03 ♒ 03	10 ♎ 00	00 ♎ 00	17 ♑ 38
Dec 31, 1921	14 ♏ 42	29 ♏ 37	19 ♈ 24	06 ♎ 50	20 ♒ 56	07 ♒ 28	12 ♎ 39	02 ♎ 20	23 ♑ 13
Jan 10, 1922	19 ♏ 30	03 ♐ 19	22 ♈ 21	09 ♎ 18	24 ♒ 51	11 ♒ 59	14 ♎ 45	04 ♎ 12	28 ♑ 47
Jan 20, 1922	24 ♏ 14	06 ♐ 55	25 ♈ 46	11 ♎ 12	28 ♒ 49	16 ♒ 35	16 ♎ 25	05 ♎ 32	04 ♒ 20
Jan 30, 1922	28 ♏ 52	10 ♐ 23	29 ♈ 34	12 ♎ 24	02 ♓ 49	21 ♒ 14	17 ♎ 34	06 ♎ 14	09 ♒ 52
Feb 9, 1922	03 ♐ 23	13 ♐ 41	03 ♉ 40	12 ♎ 50	06 ♓ 51	25 ♒ 57	18 ♎ 08	06 ♎ 15	15 ♒ 21
Feb 19, 1922	07 ♐ 43	16 ♐ 47	08 ♉ 02	12 ♎ 26	10 ♓ 54	00 ♓ 42	18 ♎ 05	05 ♎ 33	20 ♒ 47
Mar 1, 1922	11 ♐ 50	19 ♐ 38	12 ♉ 35	12 ♎ 11	14 ♓ 56	05 ♓ 29	17 ♎ 24	04 ♎ 11	26 ♒ 10
Mar 11, 1922	15 ♐ 40	22 ♐ 12	17 ♉ 18	09 ♎ 11	18 ♓ 57	10 ♓ 16	16 ♎ 06	02 ♎ 15	01 ♓ 29
Mar 21, 1922	19 ♐ 08	24 ♐ 25	22 ♉ 09	06 ♎ 40	22 ♓ 55	15 ♓ 03	14 ♎ 20	29 ♍ 60	06 ♓ 42
Mar 31, 1922	22 ♐ 10	26 ♐ 13	27 ♉ 06	03 ♎ 57	26 ♓ 51	19 ♓ 49	12 ♎ 15	27 ♍ 42	11 ♓ 50
Apr 10, 1922	24 ♐ 38	27 ♐ 34	02 ♊ 06	01 ♎ 23	00 ♈ 43	24 ♓ 34	10 ♎ 07	25 ♍ 39	16 ♓ 52
Apr 20, 1922	26 ♐ 25	28 ♐ 24	07 ♊ 10	29 ♍ 20	04 ♈ 30	29 ♓ 17	08 ♎ 09	24 ♍ 07	21 ♓ 47
Apr 30, 1922	27 ♐ 25	28 ♐ 38	12 ♊ 16	27 ♍ 60	08 ♈ 12	03 ♈ 56	06 ♎ 35	23 ♍ 13	26 ♓ 33
May 10, 1922	27 ♐ 30	28 ♐ 16	17 ♊ 24	27 ♍ 27	11 ♈ 47	08 ♈ 32	05 ♎ 34	23 ♍ 03	01 ♈ 11
May 20, 1922	26 ♐ 39	27 ♐ 19	22 ♊ 31	27 ♍ 42	15 ♈ 15	13 ♈ 02	05 ♎ 08	23 ♍ 35	05 ♈ 39
May 30, 1922	24 ♐ 55	25 ♐ 51	27 ♊ 39	28 ♍ 41	18 ♈ 34	17 ♈ 27	05 ♎ 20	24 ♍ 46	09 ♈ 56
Jun 9, 1922	22 ♐ 35	24 ♐ 00	02 ♋ 45	00 ♎ 18	21 ♈ 42	21 ♈ 45	06 ♎ 06	26 ♍ 31	13 ♈ 59
Jun 19, 1922	20 ♐ 02	22 ♐ 00	07 ♋ 50	02 ♎ 27	24 ♈ 39	25 ♈ 54	07 ♎ 24	28 ♍ 47	17 ♈ 48
Jun 29, 1922	17 ♐ 44	20 ♐ 05	12 ♋ 54	05 ♎ 04	27 ♈ 22	29 ♈ 53	09 ♎ 09	01 ♎ 28	21 ♈ 20
Jul 9, 1922	16 ♐ 04	18 ♐ 28	17 ♋ 54	08 ♎ 04	29 ♈ 48	03 ♉ 40	11 ♎ 19	04 ♎ 31	24 ♈ 32
Jul 19, 1922	15 ♐ 17	17 ♐ 19	22 ♋ 52	11 ♎ 24	03 ♉ 56	08 ♉ 12	13 ♎ 50	07 ♎ 53	27 ♈ 20
Jul 29, 1922	15 ♐ 26	16 ♐ 46	27 ♋ 47	14 ♎ 59	03 ♉ 42	10 ♉ 26	16 ♎ 38	11 ♎ 30	29 ♈ 42
Aug 8, 1922	16 ♐ 29	16 ♐ 51	02 ♌ 38	18 ♎ 49	05 ♉ 04	13 ♉ 20	19 ♎ 41	15 ♎ 21	01 ♉ 32
Aug 18, 1922	18 ♐ 20	17 ♐ 33	07 ♌ 25	22 ♎ 50	05 ♉ 57	15 ♉ 49	22 ♎ 57	19 ♎ 23	02 ♉ 46
Aug 28, 1922	20 ♐ 52	18 ♐ 50	12 ♌ 07	27 ♎ 01	06 ♉ 19	17 ♉ 49	26 ♎ 23	23 ♎ 35	03 ♉ 18
Sep 7, 1922	23 ♐ 57	20 ♐ 37	16 ♌ 43	01 ♏ 21	06 ♉ 06	19 ♉ 14	29 ♎ 59	27 ♎ 56	03 ♉ 05
Sep 17, 1922	27 ♐ 28	22 ♐ 52	21 ♌ 13	05 ♏ 48	05 ♉ 19	20 ♉ 01	03 ♏ 42	02 ♏ 23	02 ♉ 06
Sep 27, 1922	01 ♑ 22	25 ♐ 31	25 ♌ 35	10 ♏ 21	03 ♉ 58	20 ♉ 04	07 ♏ 31	06 ♏ 57	00 ♉ 23
Oct 7, 1922	05 ♑ 33	28 ♐ 31	29 ♌ 49	14 ♏ 60	02 ♉ 09	19 ♉ 23	11 ♏ 26	11 ♏ 35	28 ♈ 05
Oct 17, 1922	09 ♑ 58	01 ♑ 48	03 ♍ 54	19 ♏ 43	00 ♉ 01	18 ♉ 00	15 ♏ 25	16 ♏ 18	25 ♈ 27
Oct 27, 1922	14 ♑ 34	05 ♑ 21	07 ♍ 46	24 ♏ 30	27 ♈ 46	16 ♉ 04	19 ♏ 26	21 ♏ 04	22 ♈ 49
Nov 6, 1922	19 ♑ 20	09 ♑ 06	11 ♍ 26	29 ♏ 21	25 ♈ 38	13 ♉ 49	23 ♏ 30	25 ♏ 53	20 ♈ 30

	ATROPOS	HEKATE	LILITH	MEDUSA	MOIRA	NEMESIS	PERSEPHONE	PROSERPINA	PYTHIA
Nov 16, 1922	24 ♑ 12	13 ♑ 02	14 ♍ 49	04 ♐ 14	23 ♈ 49	11 ♉ 34	27 ♏ 35	00 ♐ 43	18 ♈ 45
Nov 26, 1922	29 ♑ 09	17 ♑ 07	17 ♍ 55	09 ♐ 10	22 ♈ 28	09 ♉ 38	01 ♐ 41	05 ♐ 35	17 ♈ 42
Dec 6, 1922	04 ♒ 11	21 ♑ 19	20 ♍ 39	14 ♐ 07	21 ♈ 41	08 ♉ 15	05 ♐ 46	10 ♐ 27	17 ♈ 24
Dec 16, 1922	09 ♒ 16	25 ♑ 38	22 ♍ 58	19 ♐ 05	21 ♈ 29	07 ♉ 34	09 ♐ 49	15 ♐ 18	17 ♈ 50
Dec 26, 1922	14 ♒ 23	00 ♒ 02	24 ♍ 47	24 ♐ 04	21 ♈ 53	08 ♉ 38	13 ♐ 49	20 ♐ 09	18 ♈ 54
Jan 5, 1923	19 ♒ 31	04 ♒ 29	26 ♍ 03	29 ♐ 02	22 ♈ 47	08 ♉ 23	17 ♐ 46	24 ♐ 57	20 ♈ 32
Jan 15, 1923	24 ♒ 40	08 ♒ 60	26 ♍ 41	03 ♑ 59	24 ♈ 10	09 ♉ 48	21 ♐ 37	29 ♐ 42	22 ♈ 39
Jan 25, 1923	29 ♒ 49	13 ♒ 32	26 ♍ 39	08 ♑ 55	25 ♈ 58	11 ♉ 46	25 ♐ 23	04 ♑ 24	25 ♈ 11
Feb 4, 1923	04 ♓ 58	18 ♒ 04	25 ♍ 54	13 ♑ 49	28 ♈ 07	14 ♉ 12	29 ♐ 01	09 ♑ 00	28 ♈ 02
Feb 14, 1923	10 ♓ 05	22 ♒ 37	24 ♍ 30	18 ♑ 39	00 ♉ 33	17 ♉ 01	02 ♑ 29	13 ♑ 31	01 ♉ 09
Feb 24, 1923	15 ♓ 11	27 ♒ 08	22 ♍ 33	23 ♑ 26	03 ♉ 15	20 ♉ 10	05 ♑ 47	17 ♑ 55	04 ♉ 29
Mar 6, 1923	20 ♓ 14	01 ♓ 38	20 ♍ 15	28 ♑ 08	06 ♉ 08	23 ♉ 35	08 ♑ 52	22 ♑ 10	08 ♉ 00
Mar 16, 1923	25 ♓ 15	06 ♓ 05	17 ♍ 53	02 ♒ 44	09 ♉ 12	27 ♉ 12	11 ♑ 41	26 ♑ 15	11 ♉ 40
Mar 26, 1923	00 ♈ 14	10 ♓ 28	15 ♍ 41	07 ♒ 14	12 ♉ 24	01 ♊ 00	14 ♑ 13	00 ♒ 08	15 ♉ 27
Apr 5, 1923	05 ♈ 08	14 ♓ 47	13 ♍ 53	11 ♒ 35	15 ♉ 42	04 ♊ 56	16 ♑ 25	03 ♒ 48	19 ♉ 19
Apr 15, 1923	09 ♈ 59	19 ♓ 01	12 ♍ 39	15 ♒ 47	19 ♉ 06	08 ♊ 59	18 ♑ 13	07 ♒ 12	23 ♉ 15
Apr 25, 1923	14 ♈ 46	23 ♓ 08	12 ♍ 02	19 ♒ 47	22 ♉ 34	13 ♊ 06	19 ♑ 35	10 ♒ 17	27 ♉ 15
May 5, 1923	19 ♈ 28	27 ♓ 07	12 ♍ 03	23 ♒ 33	26 ♉ 05	17 ♊ 18	20 ♑ 26	12 ♒ 60	01 ♊ 16
May 15, 1923	24 ♈ 05	00 ♈ 58	12 ♍ 38	27 ♒ 03	29 ♉ 37	21 ♊ 32	20 ♑ 45	15 ♒ 18	05 ♊ 19
May 25, 1923	28 ♈ 35	04 ♈ 38	13 ♍ 44	00 ♓ 13	03 ♊ 11	25 ♊ 47	20 ♑ 30	17 ♒ 07	09 ♊ 23
Jun 4, 1923	02 ♉ 59	08 ♈ 07	15 ♍ 18	02 ♓ 59	06 ♊ 45	00 ♋ 04	19 ♑ 40	18 ♒ 22	13 ♊ 28
Jun 14, 1923	07 ♉ 16	11 ♈ 21	17 ♍ 15	05 ♓ 17	10 ♊ 18	04 ♋ 21	18 ♑ 19	19 ♒ 00	17 ♊ 31
Jun 24, 1923	11 ♉ 24	14 ♈ 19	19 ♍ 31	07 ♓ 01	13 ♊ 50	08 ♋ 38	16 ♑ 34	18 ♒ 58	21 ♊ 34
Jul 4, 1923	15 ♉ 21	16 ♈ 59	22 ♍ 04	08 ♓ 06	17 ♊ 19	12 ♋ 53	14 ♑ 33	18 ♒ 15	25 ♊ 35
Jul 14, 1923	19 ♉ 08	19 ♈ 17	24 ♍ 51	08 ♓ 26	20 ♊ 46	17 ♋ 08	12 ♑ 30	16 ♒ 53	29 ♊ 34
Jul 24, 1923	22 ♉ 41	21 ♈ 09	27 ♍ 49	07 ♓ 57	24 ♊ 08	21 ♋ 20	10 ♑ 36	15 ♒ 01	03 ♋ 30
Aug 3, 1923	25 ♉ 58	22 ♈ 33	00 ♎ 57	06 ♓ 39	27 ♊ 25	25 ♋ 29	09 ♑ 03	12 ♒ 50	07 ♋ 22
Aug 13, 1923	28 ♉ 57	23 ♈ 25	04 ♎ 13	04 ♓ 39	00 ♋ 36	29 ♋ 35	07 ♑ 58	10 ♒ 37	11 ♋ 10
Aug 23, 1923	01 ♊ 34	23 ♈ 41	07 ♎ 35	02 ♓ 10	03 ♋ 38	03 ♌ 36	07 ♑ 26	08 ♒ 36	14 ♋ 52
Sep 2, 1923	03 ♊ 44	23 ♈ 19	11 ♎ 02	29 ♒ 34	06 ♋ 31	07 ♌ 33	07 ♑ 26	07 ♒ 04	18 ♋ 27
Sep 12, 1923	05 ♊ 24	22 ♈ 22	14 ♎ 34	27 ♒ 12	09 ♋ 12	11 ♌ 23	07 ♑ 59	06 ♒ 06	21 ♋ 54
Sep 22, 1923	06 ♊ 27	20 ♈ 52	18 ♎ 08	25 ♒ 26	11 ♋ 38	15 ♌ 07	09 ♑ 01	05 ♒ 49	25 ♋ 11
Oct 2, 1923	06 ♊ 49	18 ♈ 58	21 ♎ 45	24 ♒ 28	13 ♋ 48	18 ♌ 41	10 ♑ 30	06 ♒ 11	28 ♋ 16
Oct 12, 1923	06 ♊ 26	16 ♈ 53	25 ♎ 24	24 ♒ 22	15 ♋ 36	22 ♌ 05	12 ♑ 22	07 ♒ 09	01 ♌ 06
Oct 22, 1923	05 ♊ 15	14 ♈ 51	29 ♎ 03	25 ♒ 08	17 ♋ 01	25 ♌ 17	14 ♑ 34	08 ♒ 41	03 ♌ 38

	ATROPOS	HEKATE	LILITH	MEDUSA	MOIRA	NEMESIS	PERSEPHONE	PROSERPINA	PYTHIA
Nov 1, 1923	03 ♊ 19	13 ♈ 06	02 ♏ 41	26 ♒ 40	17 ♋ 57	28 ♌ 15	17 ♑ 04	10 ♒ 42	05 ♌ 48
Nov 11, 1923	00 ♊ 49	11 ♈ 49	06 ♏ 18	28 ♒ 54	18 ♋ 21	00 ♍ 55	19 ♑ 48	13 ♒ 08	07 ♌ 33
Nov 21, 1923	27 ♉ 59	11 ♈ 05	09 ♏ 52	01 ♓ 43	18 ♋ 09	03 ♍ 15	22 ♑ 45	15 ♒ 54	08 ♌ 46
Dec 1, 1923	25 ♉ 12	10 ♈ 58	13 ♏ 23	05 ♓ 01	17 ♋ 21	05 ♍ 11	25 ♑ 52	18 ♒ 58	09 ♌ 23
Dec 11, 1923	22 ♉ 46	11 ♈ 27	16 ♏ 50	08 ♓ 44	15 ♋ 57	06 ♍ 39	29 ♑ 07	22 ♒ 17	09 ♌ 19
Dec 21, 1923	20 ♉ 58	12 ♈ 29	20 ♏ 10	12 ♓ 48	14 ♋ 03	07 ♍ 35	02 ♒ 29	25 ♒ 48	08 ♌ 32
Dec 31, 1923	19 ♉ 54	13 ♈ 60	23 ♏ 23	17 ♓ 09	11 ♋ 49	07 ♍ 55	05 ♒ 56	29 ♒ 29	07 ♌ 02
Jan 10, 1924	19 ♉ 37	15 ♈ 56	26 ♏ 26	21 ♓ 44	09 ♋ 28	07 ♍ 38	09 ♒ 28	03 ♓ 18	04 ♌ 54
Jan 20, 1924	20 ♉ 05	18 ♈ 14	29 ♏ 19	26 ♓ 32	07 ♋ 17	06 ♍ 42	13 ♒ 02	07 ♓ 14	02 ♌ 20
Jan 30, 1924	21 ♉ 12	20 ♈ 50	01 ♐ 58	01 ♈ 29	05 ♋ 29	05 ♍ 11	16 ♒ 38	11 ♓ 14	29 ♋ 39
Feb 9, 1924	22 ♉ 53	23 ♈ 40	04 ♐ 22	06 ♈ 34	04 ♋ 13	03 ♍ 12	20 ♒ 14	15 ♓ 18	27 ♋ 08
Feb 19, 1924	25 ♉ 02	26 ♈ 43	06 ♐ 27	11 ♈ 47	03 ♋ 35	00 ♍ 57	23 ♒ 49	19 ♓ 25	25 ♋ 05
Feb 29, 1924	27 ♉ 35	29 ♈ 56	08 ♐ 12	17 ♈ 04	03 ♋ 36	28 ♌ 41	27 ♒ 23	23 ♓ 33	23 ♋ 43
Mar 10, 1924	00 ♊ 28	03 ♉ 17	09 ♐ 31	22 ♈ 26	04 ♋ 13	26 ♌ 39	00 ♓ 54	27 ♓ 42	23 ♋ 05
Mar 20, 1924	03 ♊ 37	06 ♉ 43	10 ♐ 23	27 ♈ 51	05 ♋ 24	25 ♌ 01	04 ♓ 22	01 ♈ 51	23 ♋ 13
Mar 30, 1924	06 ♊ 58	10 ♉ 14	10 ♐ 44	03 ♉ 19	07 ♋ 05	23 ♌ 56	07 ♓ 45	05 ♈ 59	24 ♋ 03
Apr 9, 1924	10 ♊ 30	13 ♉ 48	10 ♐ 32	08 ♉ 49	09 ♋ 12	23 ♌ 27	11 ♓ 01	10 ♈ 05	25 ♋ 31
Apr 19, 1924	14 ♊ 10	17 ♉ 25	09 ♐ 46	14 ♉ 21	11 ♋ 41	23 ♌ 34	14 ♓ 11	14 ♈ 08	25 ♋ 31
Apr 29, 1924	17 ♊ 57	21 ♉ 02	08 ♐ 29	19 ♉ 53	14 ♋ 30	24 ♌ 14	17 ♓ 12	18 ♈ 08	29 ♋ 60
May 9, 1924	21 ♊ 49	24 ♉ 40	06 ♐ 43	25 ♉ 25	17 ♋ 34	25 ♌ 25	20 ♓ 03	22 ♈ 05	02 ♋ 53
May 19, 1924	25 ♊ 45	28 ♉ 17	04 ♐ 39	00 ♊ 57	20 ♋ 52	27 ♌ 01	22 ♓ 42	25 ♈ 56	06 ♌ 06
May 29, 1924	29 ♊ 45	01 ♊ 52	02 ♐ 27	06 ♊ 29	24 ♋ 22	29 ♌ 00	25 ♓ 07	29 ♈ 41	09 ♌ 36
Jun 8, 1924	03 ♋ 47	05 ♊ 24	00 ♐ 20	11 ♊ 59	28 ♋ 03	01 ♍ 18	27 ♓ 16	03 ♉ 20	13 ♌ 21
Jun 18, 1924	07 ♋ 50	08 ♊ 54	28 ♏ 29	17 ♊ 29	01 ♌ 52	03 ♍ 53	29 ♓ 07	06 ♉ 50	17 ♌ 19
Jun 28, 1924	11 ♋ 54	12 ♊ 19	27 ♏ 03	22 ♊ 57	05 ♌ 49	06 ♍ 40	00 ♈ 37	10 ♉ 11	21 ♌ 29
Jul 8, 1924	15 ♋ 58	15 ♊ 39	26 ♏ 07	28 ♊ 22	09 ♌ 53	09 ♍ 40	01 ♈ 42	13 ♉ 21	25 ♌ 48
Jul 18, 1924	20 ♋ 02	18 ♊ 53	25 ♏ 45	03 ♋ 46	14 ♌ 02	12 ♍ 49	02 ♈ 20	16 ♉ 18	00 ♍ 16
Jul 28, 1924	24 ♋ 05	21 ♊ 60	25 ♏ 56	09 ♋ 06	18 ♌ 17	16 ♍ 05	02 ♈ 28	19 ♉ 00	04 ♍ 52
Aug 7, 1924	28 ♋ 06	24 ♊ 58	26 ♏ 38	14 ♋ 23	22 ♌ 36	19 ♍ 29	02 ♈ 05	21 ♉ 24	09 ♍ 35
Aug 17, 1924	02 ♌ 05	27 ♊ 46	27 ♏ 49	19 ♋ 37	26 ♌ 58	22 ♍ 58	01 ♈ 10	23 ♉ 27	14 ♍ 25
Aug 27, 1924	06 ♌ 00	00 ♋ 21	29 ♏ 24	24 ♋ 45	01 ♍ 25	26 ♍ 31	29 ♓ 47	25 ♉ 06	19 ♍ 20
Sep 6, 1924	09 ♌ 52	02 ♋ 42	01 ♐ 22	29 ♋ 48	05 ♍ 53	00 ♎ 08	28 ♓ 01	26 ♉ 16	24 ♍ 20
Sep 16, 1924	13 ♌ 39	04 ♋ 47	03 ♐ 40	04 ♌ 45	10 ♍ 24	03 ♎ 47	26 ♓ 00	26 ♉ 54	29 ♍ 25
Sep 26, 1924	17 ♌ 20	06 ♋ 32	06 ♐ 14	09 ♌ 34	14 ♍ 56	07 ♎ 28	23 ♓ 57	26 ♉ 56	04 ♎ 34
Oct 6, 1924	20 ♌ 52	07 ♋ 55	09 ♐ 03	14 ♌ 14	19 ♍ 30	11 ♎ 09	22 ♓ 02	26 ♉ 21	09 ♎ 47

	ATROPOS	HEKATE	LILITH	MEDUSA	MOIRA	NEMESIS	PERSEPHONE	PROSERPINA	PYTHIA
Oct 16, 1924	24 ♌ 16	08 ♋ 53	12 ♐ 05	18 ♌ 44	24 ♍ 03	14 ♎ 51	20 ♓ 27	25 ♉ 09	15 ♎ 02
Oct 26, 1924	27 ♌ 28	09 ♋ 22	15 ♐ 17	23 ♌ 00	28 ♍ 35	18 ♎ 31	19 ♓ 19	23 ♉ 24	20 ♎ 21
Nov 5, 1924	00 ♍ 27	09 ♋ 20	18 ♐ 39	27 ♌ 02	03 ♎ 06	22 ♎ 10	18 ♓ 42	21 ♉ 15	25 ♎ 42
Nov 15, 1924	03 ♍ 09	08 ♋ 46	22 ♐ 08	00 ♍ 44	07 ♎ 34	25 ♎ 45	18 ♓ 38	18 ♉ 56	01 ♏ 04
Nov 25, 1924	05 ♍ 30	07 ♋ 41	25 ♐ 44	04 ♍ 04	11 ♎ 58	29 ♎ 16	19 ♓ 07	16 ♉ 42	06 ♏ 27
Dec 5, 1924	07 ♍ 27	06 ♋ 09	29 ♐ 26	06 ♍ 58	16 ♎ 17	02 ♏ 42	20 ♓ 05	14 ♉ 47	11 ♏ 50
Dec 15, 1924	08 ♍ 55	04 ♋ 17	03 ♑ 12	09 ♍ 18	20 ♎ 28	06 ♏ 01	21 ♓ 30	13 ♉ 22	17 ♏ 12
Dec 25, 1924	09 ♍ 49	02 ♋ 15	07 ♑ 01	11 ♍ 01	24 ♎ 30	09 ♏ 10	23 ♓ 19	12 ♉ 34	22 ♏ 32
Jan 4, 1925	10 ♍ 03	00 ♋ 14	10 ♑ 53	11 ♍ 58	28 ♎ 20	12 ♏ 09	25 ♓ 28	12 ♉ 24	27 ♏ 50
Jan 14, 1925	09 ♍ 34	28 ♊ 26	14 ♑ 46	12 ♍ 05	01 ♏ 56	14 ♏ 55	27 ♓ 55	12 ♉ 52	03 ♐ 04
Jan 24, 1925	08 ♍ 20	27 ♊ 01	18 ♑ 40	11 ♍ 18	05 ♏ 14	17 ♏ 26	00 ♈ 36	13 ♉ 54	08 ♐ 14
Feb 3, 1925	06 ♍ 24	26 ♊ 04	22 ♑ 33	09 ♍ 41	08 ♏ 10	19 ♏ 38	03 ♈ 30	15 ♉ 27	13 ♐ 16
Feb 13, 1925	03 ♍ 56	25 ♊ 37	26 ♑ 25	07 ♍ 22	10 ♏ 41	21 ♏ 29	06 ♈ 35	17 ♉ 26	18 ♐ 11
Feb 23, 1925	01 ♍ 09	25 ♊ 42	00 ♒ 14	04 ♍ 39	12 ♏ 40	22 ♏ 55	09 ♈ 47	19 ♉ 48	22 ♐ 55
Mar 5, 1925	28 ♌ 23	26 ♊ 16	04 ♒ 00	01 ♍ 56	14 ♏ 02	23 ♏ 52	13 ♈ 07	22 ♉ 28	27 ♐ 28
Mar 15, 1925	25 ♌ 57	27 ♊ 16	07 ♒ 42	29 ♌ 36	14 ♏ 44	24 ♏ 18	16 ♈ 32	25 ♉ 24	01 ♑ 45
Mar 25, 1925	24 ♌ 06	28 ♊ 40	11 ♒ 18	27 ♌ 56	14 ♏ 40	24 ♏ 09	20 ♈ 01	28 ♉ 34	05 ♑ 45
Apr 4, 1925	22 ♌ 58	00 ♋ 24	14 ♒ 46	27 ♌ 04	13 ♏ 52	23 ♏ 25	23 ♈ 33	01 ♊ 54	09 ♑ 22
Apr 14, 1925	22 ♌ 36	02 ♋ 26	18 ♒ 05	27 ♌ 04	12 ♏ 23	22 ♏ 08	27 ♈ 07	05 ♊ 24	12 ♑ 34
Apr 24, 1925	22 ♌ 58	04 ♋ 42	21 ♒ 14	27 ♌ 49	10 ♏ 25	20 ♏ 23	00 ♉ 42	09 ♊ 00	15 ♑ 15
May 4, 1925	24 ♌ 00	07 ♋ 10	24 ♒ 09	29 ♌ 17	08 ♏ 14	18 ♏ 18	04 ♉ 17	12 ♊ 43	17 ♑ 18
May 14, 1925	25 ♌ 39	09 ♋ 49	26 ♒ 49	01 ♍ 19	06 ♏ 11	16 ♏ 07	07 ♉ 51	16 ♊ 31	18 ♑ 39
May 24, 1925	27 ♌ 48	12 ♋ 36	29 ♒ 11	03 ♍ 52	04 ♏ 32	14 ♏ 02	11 ♉ 24	20 ♊ 23	19 ♑ 12
Jun 3, 1925	00 ♍ 24	15 ♋ 29	01 ♓ 10	06 ♍ 49	03 ♏ 30	12 ♏ 15	14 ♉ 54	24 ♊ 17	18 ♑ 52
Jun 13, 1925	03 ♍ 22	18 ♋ 28	02 ♓ 43	10 ♍ 06	03 ♏ 12	10 ♏ 56	18 ♉ 21	28 ♊ 14	17 ♑ 41
Jun 23, 1925	06 ♍ 41	21 ♋ 31	03 ♓ 46	13 ♍ 40	03 ♏ 38	10 ♏ 09	21 ♉ 42	02 ♋ 13	15 ♑ 48
Jul 3, 1925	10 ♍ 17	24 ♋ 37	04 ♓ 15	17 ♍ 28	04 ♏ 47	09 ♏ 58	24 ♉ 58	06 ♋ 12	13 ♑ 28
Jul 13, 1925	14 ♍ 07	27 ♋ 45	04 ♓ 05	21 ♍ 28	06 ♏ 33	10 ♏ 21	28 ♉ 07	10 ♋ 11	11 ♑ 04
Jul 23, 1925	18 ♍ 11	00 ♌ 54	03 ♓ 17	25 ♍ 37	08 ♏ 51	11 ♏ 15	01 ♊ 08	14 ♋ 10	08 ♑ 58
Aug 2, 1925	22 ♍ 27	04 ♌ 03	01 ♓ 50	29 ♍ 55	11 ♏ 37	12 ♏ 39	03 ♊ 57	18 ♋ 08	07 ♑ 30
Aug 12, 1925	26 ♍ 54	07 ♌ 12	29 ♒ 53	04 ♎ 20	14 ♏ 46	14 ♏ 28	06 ♊ 35	22 ♋ 03	06 ♑ 49
Aug 22, 1925	01 ♎ 31	10 ♌ 18	27 ♒ 37	08 ♎ 51	18 ♏ 14	16 ♏ 39	08 ♊ 57	25 ♋ 56	06 ♑ 58
Sep 1, 1925	06 ♎ 17	13 ♌ 22	25 ♒ 19	13 ♎ 27	21 ♏ 58	19 ♏ 10	11 ♊ 01	29 ♋ 45	07 ♑ 56
Sep 11, 1925	11 ♎ 11	16 ♌ 22	23 ♒ 16	18 ♎ 07	25 ♏ 56	21 ♏ 58	12 ♊ 44	03 ♌ 29	09 ♑ 38
Sep 21, 1925	16 ♎ 13	19 ♌ 16	21 ♒ 43	22 ♎ 51	00 ♐ 05	25 ♏ 01	14 ♊ 02	07 ♌ 07	11 ♑ 56

Date	ATROPOS	HEKATE	LILITH	MEDUSA	MOIRA	NEMESIS	PERSEPHONE	PROSERPINA	PYTHIA
Oct 1, 1925	21 ♎ 23	22 ♌ 04	20 ♒ 49	27 ♎ 38	04 ♐ 24	28 ♏ 16	14 ♊ 52	10 ♌ 38	14 ♈ 47
Oct 11, 1925	26 ♎ 39	24 ♌ 43	20 ♒ 40	02 ♏ 27	08 ♐ 49	01 ♐ 42	15 ♊ 42	13 ♌ 58	18 ♈ 03
Oct 21, 1925	02 ♏ 02	27 ♌ 12	21 ♒ 15	07 ♏ 19	13 ♐ 21	05 ♐ 18	14 ♊ 53	17 ♌ 07	21 ♈ 41
Oct 31, 1925	07 ♏ 30	29 ♌ 29	22 ♒ 32	12 ♏ 11	17 ♐ 58	09 ♐ 01	14 ♊ 01	20 ♌ 01	25 ♈ 36
Nov 10, 1925	13 ♏ 04	01 ♍ 31	24 ♒ 26	17 ♏ 05	22 ♐ 39	12 ♐ 52	12 ♊ 35	22 ♌ 38	29 ♈ 46
Nov 20, 1925	18 ♏ 43	03 ♍ 16	26 ♒ 54	21 ♏ 60	27 ♐ 23	16 ♐ 48	10 ♊ 43	24 ♌ 54	04 ♉ 08
Nov 30, 1925	24 ♏ 26	04 ♍ 39	29 ♒ 51	26 ♏ 54	02 ♑ 09	20 ♐ 49	08 ♊ 35	26 ♌ 44	08 ♉ 40
Dec 10, 1925	00 ♐ 12	05 ♍ 40	03 ♓ 12	01 ♐ 47	06 ♑ 55	24 ♐ 54	06 ♊ 25	28 ♌ 04	13 ♉ 19
Dec 20, 1925	06 ♐ 01	06 ♍ 14	06 ♓ 55	06 ♐ 39	11 ♑ 42	29 ♐ 02	04 ♊ 27	28 ♌ 49	18 ♉ 04
Dec 30, 1925	11 ♐ 51	06 ♍ 18	10 ♓ 56	11 ♐ 28	16 ♑ 29	03 ♑ 12	02 ♊ 53	28 ♌ 56	22 ♉ 54
Jan 9, 1926	17 ♐ 42	05 ♍ 52	15 ♓ 12	16 ♐ 15	21 ♑ 14	07 ♑ 23	01 ♊ 51	28 ♌ 21	27 ♉ 47
Jan 19, 1926	23 ♐ 33	04 ♍ 55	19 ♓ 42	20 ♐ 58	25 ♑ 57	11 ♑ 34	01 ♊ 26	27 ♌ 06	02 ♊ 42
Jan 29, 1926	29 ♐ 23	03 ♍ 31	24 ♓ 23	25 ♐ 36	00 ♒ 38	15 ♑ 44	01 ♊ 38	25 ♌ 16	07 ♊ 39
Feb 8, 1926	05 ♑ 10	01 ♍ 45	29 ♓ 13	00 ♑ 08	05 ♒ 14	19 ♑ 53	02 ♊ 25	23 ♌ 03	12 ♊ 36
Feb 18, 1926	10 ♑ 53	29 ♌ 47	04 ♈ 11	04 ♑ 34	09 ♒ 47	23 ♑ 60	03 ♊ 44	20 ♌ 40	17 ♊ 33
Feb 28, 1926	16 ♑ 30	27 ♌ 47	09 ♈ 16	08 ♑ 51	14 ♒ 14	28 ♑ 02	05 ♊ 30	18 ♌ 28	22 ♊ 28
Mar 10, 1926	22 ♑ 01	25 ♌ 56	14 ♈ 26	12 ♑ 58	18 ♒ 35	02 ♒ 00	07 ♊ 41	16 ♌ 39	27 ♊ 22
Mar 20, 1926	27 ♑ 23	24 ♌ 24	19 ♈ 41	16 ♑ 53	22 ♒ 49	05 ♒ 52	10 ♊ 12	15 ♌ 27	02 ♋ 14
Mar 30, 1926	02 ♒ 34	23 ♌ 17	24 ♈ 59	20 ♑ 33	26 ♒ 55	09 ♒ 37	13 ♊ 01	14 ♌ 56	07 ♋ 03
Apr 9, 1926	07 ♒ 32	22 ♌ 39	00 ♉ 20	23 ♑ 57	00 ♓ 51	13 ♒ 12	16 ♊ 04	15 ♌ 07	11 ♋ 48
Apr 19, 1926	12 ♒ 15	22 ♌ 33	05 ♉ 43	27 ♑ 01	04 ♓ 37	16 ♒ 37	19 ♊ 19	15 ♌ 57	16 ♋ 29
Apr 29, 1926	16 ♒ 40	22 ♌ 55	11 ♉ 07	29 ♑ 40	08 ♓ 11	19 ♒ 48	22 ♊ 44	17 ♌ 23	21 ♋ 06
May 9, 1926	20 ♒ 43	23 ♌ 45	16 ♉ 32	01 ♒ 52	11 ♓ 31	22 ♒ 44	26 ♊ 17	19 ♌ 20	25 ♋ 38
May 19, 1926	24 ♒ 21	25 ♌ 00	21 ♉ 57	03 ♒ 29	14 ♓ 35	25 ♒ 21	29 ♊ 57	21 ♌ 44	00 ♌ 04
May 29, 1926	27 ♒ 29	26 ♌ 37	27 ♉ 21	04 ♒ 28	17 ♓ 21	27 ♒ 36	03 ♋ 43	24 ♌ 30	04 ♌ 23
Jun 8, 1926	00 ♓ 01	28 ♌ 33	02 ♊ 44	04 ♒ 42	19 ♓ 46	29 ♒ 26	07 ♋ 33	27 ♌ 36	08 ♌ 36
Jun 18, 1926	01 ♓ 51	00 ♍ 45	08 ♊ 05	04 ♒ 09	21 ♓ 47	00 ♓ 44	11 ♋ 27	00 ♍ 59	12 ♌ 40
Jun 28, 1926	02 ♓ 54	02 ♍ 12	13 ♊ 24	04 ♒ 50	23 ♓ 20	01 ♓ 28	15 ♋ 23	04 ♍ 36	16 ♌ 35
Jul 8, 1926	03 ♓ 04	05 ♍ 50	18 ♊ 39	00 ♒ 49	24 ♓ 14	01 ♓ 34	19 ♋ 22	08 ♍ 24	20 ♌ 20
Jul 18, 1926	02 ♓ 18	08 ♍ 40	23 ♊ 51	28 ♑ 20	24 ♓ 48	00 ♓ 60	23 ♋ 21	12 ♍ 23	23 ♌ 53
Jul 28, 1926	00 ♓ 40	11 ♍ 38	28 ♊ 59	25 ♑ 44	24 ♓ 38	29 ♒ 47	27 ♋ 21	16 ♍ 31	27 ♌ 12
Aug 7, 1926	28 ♒ 20	14 ♍ 43	04 ♋ 00	23 ♑ 20	23 ♓ 50	28 ♒ 02	01 ♌ 20	20 ♍ 46	00 ♍ 15
Aug 17, 1926	25 ♒ 36	17 ♍ 55	08 ♋ 56	21 ♑ 29	22 ♓ 27	25 ♒ 56	05 ♌ 19	25 ♍ 07	02 ♍ 58
Aug 27, 1926	22 ♒ 54	21 ♍ 12	13 ♋ 44	20 ♑ 23	20 ♓ 34	23 ♒ 44	09 ♌ 15	29 ♍ 35	05 ♍ 20
Sep 6, 1926	20 ♒ 37	24 ♍ 33	18 ♋ 23	20 ♑ 06	18 ♓ 23	21 ♒ 44	13 ♌ 09	04 ♎ 07	07 ♍ 16

	ATROPOS	HEKATE	LILITH	MEDUSA	MOIRA	NEMESIS	PERSEPHONE	PROSERPINA	PYTHIA
Sep 16, 1926	19 ♒ 00	27 ♍ 57	22 ♋ 51	20 ♑ 38	16 ♓ 07	20 ♒ 12	16 ♌ 59	08 ♎ 43	08 ♊ 41
Sep 26, 1926	18 ♒ 14	01 ♎ 24	27 ♋ 07	21 ♑ 56	14 ♓ 02	19 ♒ 17	20 ♌ 44	13 ♎ 23	09 ♊ 32
Oct 6, 1926	18 ♒ 18	04 ♎ 52	01 ♌ 08	23 ♑ 54	12 ♓ 19	19 ♒ 04	24 ♌ 22	18 ♎ 05	09 ♊ 44
Oct 16, 1926	19 ♒ 09	08 ♎ 20	04 ♌ 51	26 ♑ 27	11 ♓ 07	19 ♒ 34	27 ♌ 53	22 ♎ 50	09 ♊ 12
Oct 26, 1926	20 ♒ 43	11 ♎ 48	08 ♌ 14	29 ♑ 30	10 ♓ 31	20 ♒ 45	01 ♍ 13	27 ♎ 35	07 ♊ 59
Nov 5, 1926	22 ♒ 51	15 ♎ 14	11 ♌ 11	02 ♒ 58	10 ♓ 32	22 ♒ 33	04 ♍ 22	02 ♏ 22	06 ♊ 05
Nov 15, 1926	25 ♒ 30	18 ♎ 37	13 ♌ 39	06 ♒ 47	11 ♓ 09	24 ♒ 52	07 ♍ 17	07 ♏ 08	03 ♊ 42
Nov 25, 1926	28 ♒ 34	21 ♎ 56	15 ♌ 33	10 ♒ 55	12 ♓ 17	27 ♒ 40	09 ♍ 54	11 ♏ 54	01 ♊ 04
Dec 5, 1926	01 ♓ 57	25 ♎ 09	16 ♌ 47	15 ♒ 18	13 ♓ 53	00 ♓ 51	12 ♍ 10	16 ♏ 38	28 ♉ 29
Dec 15, 1926	05 ♓ 38	28 ♎ 15	17 ♌ 15	19 ♒ 54	15 ♓ 54	04 ♓ 22	14 ♍ 01	21 ♏ 20	26 ♉ 14
Dec 25, 1926	09 ♓ 32	01 ♏ 12	16 ♌ 57	24 ♒ 41	18 ♓ 15	08 ♓ 09	15 ♍ 24	25 ♏ 58	24 ♉ 33
Jan 4, 1927	13 ♓ 36	03 ♏ 57	15 ♌ 51	29 ♒ 37	20 ♓ 54	12 ♓ 11	16 ♍ 14	00 ♐ 31	23 ♉ 32
Jan 14, 1927	17 ♓ 50	06 ♏ 28	14 ♌ 03	04 ♓ 41	23 ♓ 47	16 ♓ 24	16 ♍ 27	04 ♐ 58	23 ♉ 15
Jan 24, 1927	22 ♓ 11	08 ♏ 42	11 ♌ 47	09 ♓ 52	26 ♓ 51	20 ♓ 47	16 ♍ 01	09 ♐ 18	23 ♉ 38
Feb 3, 1927	26 ♓ 38	10 ♏ 37	09 ♌ 20	15 ♓ 08	00 ♈ 06	25 ♓ 17	14 ♍ 58	13 ♐ 28	24 ♉ 39
Feb 13, 1927	01 ♈ 08	12 ♏ 07	07 ♌ 04	20 ♓ 29	03 ♈ 28	29 ♓ 54	13 ♍ 21	17 ♐ 28	26 ♉ 13
Feb 23, 1927	05 ♈ 42	13 ♏ 11	05 ♌ 13	25 ♓ 53	06 ♈ 56	04 ♈ 36	11 ♍ 21	21 ♐ 14	28 ♉ 14
Mar 5, 1927	10 ♈ 18	13 ♏ 45	04 ♌ 01	01 ♈ 20	10 ♈ 29	09 ♈ 21	09 ♍ 10	24 ♐ 45	00 ♊ 38
Mar 15, 1927	14 ♈ 56	13 ♏ 46	03 ♌ 32	06 ♈ 50	14 ♈ 04	14 ♈ 09	07 ♍ 04	27 ♐ 57	03 ♊ 22
Mar 25, 1927	19 ♈ 34	13 ♏ 13	03 ♌ 46	12 ♈ 21	17 ♈ 42	18 ♈ 59	05 ♍ 17	00 ♑ 47	06 ♊ 23
Apr 4, 1927	24 ♈ 12	12 ♏ 07	04 ♌ 39	17 ♈ 54	21 ♈ 22	23 ♈ 50	04 ♍ 00	03 ♑ 12	09 ♊ 37
Apr 14, 1927	28 ♈ 49	10 ♏ 33	06 ♌ 06	23 ♈ 26	25 ♈ 01	28 ♈ 41	03 ♍ 19	05 ♑ 06	13 ♊ 02
Apr 24, 1927	03 ♉ 25	08 ♏ 38	08 ♌ 02	28 ♈ 59	28 ♈ 39	03 ♉ 31	03 ♍ 16	06 ♑ 25	16 ♊ 36
May 4, 1927	07 ♉ 59	06 ♏ 35	10 ♌ 23	04 ♉ 32	02 ♉ 16	08 ♉ 20	03 ♍ 48	07 ♑ 05	20 ♊ 18
May 14, 1927	12 ♉ 30	04 ♏ 37	13 ♌ 03	10 ♉ 04	05 ♉ 51	13 ♉ 08	04 ♍ 55	07 ♑ 04	24 ♊ 06
May 24, 1927	16 ♉ 59	02 ♏ 55	16 ♌ 00	15 ♉ 35	09 ♉ 22	17 ♉ 53	06 ♍ 31	06 ♑ 20	27 ♊ 60
Jun 3, 1927	21 ♉ 24	01 ♏ 40	19 ♌ 11	21 ♉ 04	12 ♉ 49	22 ♉ 35	08 ♍ 32	04 ♑ 57	01 ♋ 57
Jun 13, 1927	25 ♉ 44	00 ♏ 58	22 ♌ 32	26 ♉ 32	16 ♉ 11	27 ♉ 14	10 ♍ 56	03 ♑ 03	05 ♋ 59
Jun 23, 1927	29 ♉ 60	00 ♏ 50	26 ♌ 02	01 ♊ 57	19 ♉ 26	01 ♊ 48	13 ♍ 38	00 ♑ 53	10 ♋ 03
Jul 3, 1927	04 ♊ 10	01 ♏ 17	29 ♌ 39	07 ♊ 19	22 ♉ 34	06 ♊ 17	16 ♍ 37	28 ♐ 43	14 ♋ 09
Jul 13, 1927	08 ♊ 13	02 ♏ 16	03 ♍ 22	12 ♊ 37	25 ♉ 33	10 ♊ 40	19 ♍ 49	26 ♐ 50	18 ♋ 18
Jul 23, 1927	12 ♊ 09	03 ♏ 45	07 ♍ 10	17 ♊ 51	28 ♉ 21	14 ♊ 56	23 ♍ 12	25 ♐ 27	22 ♋ 27
Aug 2, 1927	15 ♊ 55	05 ♏ 41	11 ♍ 01	23 ♊ 01	00 ♊ 57	19 ♊ 05	26 ♍ 45	24 ♐ 43	26 ♋ 36
Aug 12, 1927	19 ♊ 31	08 ♏ 00	14 ♍ 54	28 ♊ 05	03 ♊ 17	23 ♊ 03	00 ♎ 26	24 ♐ 40	00 ♌ 46
Aug 22, 1927	22 ♊ 54	10 ♏ 39	18 ♍ 49	03 ♋ 01	05 ♊ 21	26 ♊ 51	04 ♎ 14	25 ♐ 17	04 ♌ 55

	ATROPOS	HEKATE	LILITH	MEDUSA	MOIRA	NEMESIS	PERSEPHONE	PROSERPINA	PYTHIA
Sep 1, 1927	26 ♊ 02	13 ♏ 36	22 ♍ 45	07 ♋ 50	07 ♊ 04	00 ♋ 26	08 ♎ 07	26 ♐ 32	09 ♌ 03
Sep 11, 1927	28 ♊ 51	16 ♏ 48	26 ♍ 42	12 ♋ 28	08 ♊ 23	03 ♋ 45	12 ♎ 06	28 ♐ 19	13 ♌ 09
Sep 21, 1927	01 ♋ 20	20 ♏ 14	00 ♎ 37	16 ♋ 55	09 ♊ 15	06 ♋ 46	16 ♎ 08	00 ♑ 35	17 ♌ 12
Oct 1, 1927	03 ♋ 23	23 ♏ 50	04 ♎ 32	21 ♋ 07	09 ♊ 36	09 ♋ 25	20 ♎ 13	03 ♑ 15	21 ♌ 12
Oct 11, 1927	04 ♋ 56	27 ♏ 37	08 ♎ 25	25 ♋ 02	09 ♊ 24	11 ♋ 39	24 ♎ 19	06 ♑ 16	25 ♌ 06
Oct 21, 1927	05 ♋ 53	01 ♐ 33	12 ♎ 15	28 ♋ 36	08 ♊ 37	13 ♋ 23	28 ♎ 28	09 ♑ 34	28 ♌ 53
Oct 31, 1927	06 ♋ 11	05 ♐ 36	16 ♎ 01	01 ♌ 44	07 ♊ 16	14 ♋ 33	02 ♏ 36	13 ♑ 07	02 ♍ 32
Nov 10, 1927	05 ♋ 44	09 ♐ 45	19 ♎ 42	04 ♌ 22	05 ♊ 27	15 ♋ 04	06 ♏ 44	16 ♑ 52	06 ♍ 01
Nov 20, 1927	04 ♋ 31	13 ♐ 59	23 ♎ 18	06 ♌ 22	03 ♊ 19	14 ♋ 53	10 ♏ 51	20 ♑ 46	09 ♍ 16
Nov 30, 1927	02 ♋ 35	18 ♐ 17	26 ♎ 46	07 ♌ 39	01 ♊ 03	13 ♋ 59	14 ♏ 55	24 ♑ 50	12 ♍ 15
Dec 10, 1927	00 ♋ 06	22 ♐ 39	00 ♏ 06	08 ♌ 05	28 ♉ 53	12 ♋ 27	18 ♏ 56	28 ♑ 60	14 ♍ 54
Dec 20, 1927	27 ♊ 19	27 ♐ 03	03 ♏ 15	07 ♌ 36	27 ♉ 02	10 ♋ 23	22 ♏ 42	03 ♒ 15	17 ♍ 08
Dec 30, 1927	24 ♊ 33	01 ♑ 29	06 ♏ 12	06 ♌ 13	25 ♉ 39	08 ♋ 04	26 ♏ 42	07 ♒ 35	18 ♍ 51
Jan 9, 1928	22 ♊ 07	05 ♑ 55	08 ♏ 54	04 ♌ 03	24 ♉ 51	05 ♋ 46	00 ♐ 21	11 ♒ 57	19 ♍ 59
Jan 29, 1928	20 ♊ 16	10 ♑ 21	11 ♏ 19	01 ♌ 23	24 ♉ 39	03 ♋ 45	03 ♐ 58	16 ♒ 21	20 ♍ 25
Feb 8, 1928	19 ♊ 08	14 ♑ 45	13 ♏ 24	28 ♋ 37	25 ♉ 01	02 ♋ 15	07 ♐ 21	20 ♒ 47	20 ♍ 05
Feb 18, 1928	18 ♊ 45	19 ♑ 07	15 ♏ 05	26 ♋ 11	25 ♉ 56	01 ♋ 24	10 ♐ 30	25 ♒ 13	18 ♍ 57
Feb 28, 1928	19 ♊ 04	23 ♑ 26	16 ♏ 19	24 ♋ 25	27 ♉ 19	01 ♋ 13	13 ♐ 25	29 ♒ 38	17 ♍ 05
Mar 9, 1928	20 ♊ 02	27 ♑ 40	17 ♏ 04	23 ♋ 29	29 ♉ 07	01 ♋ 42	16 ♐ 00	04 ♓ 01	14 ♍ 38
Mar 19, 1928	21 ♊ 34	01 ♒ 49	17 ♏ 15	23 ♋ 26	01 ♊ 17	02 ♋ 46	18 ♐ 15	08 ♓ 22	11 ♍ 56
Mar 29, 1928	23 ♊ 33	05 ♒ 51	16 ♏ 51	24 ♋ 13	03 ♊ 45	04 ♋ 21	20 ♐ 05	12 ♓ 41	09 ♍ 20
Apr 8, 1928	25 ♊ 57	09 ♒ 44	15 ♏ 52	25 ♋ 44	06 ♊ 29	06 ♋ 23	21 ♐ 26	16 ♓ 55	07 ♍ 12
Apr 18, 1928	28 ♊ 40	13 ♒ 27	14 ♏ 22	27 ♋ 52	09 ♊ 26	08 ♋ 47	22 ♐ 16	21 ♓ 05	05 ♍ 45
Apr 28, 1928	01 ♋ 39	16 ♒ 58	12 ♏ 27	00 ♌ 30	12 ♊ 33	11 ♋ 30	22 ♐ 32	25 ♓ 10	05 ♍ 08
May 8, 1928	04 ♋ 51	20 ♒ 15	10 ♏ 16	03 ♌ 35	15 ♊ 49	14 ♋ 28	22 ♐ 11	29 ♓ 08	05 ♍ 21
May 18, 1928	08 ♋ 14	23 ♒ 14	08 ♏ 03	07 ♌ 00	19 ♊ 13	17 ♋ 38	21 ♐ 15	02 ♈ 58	06 ♍ 22
May 28, 1928	11 ♋ 47	25 ♒ 55	05 ♏ 60	10 ♌ 42	22 ♊ 43	20 ♋ 58	19 ♐ 48	06 ♈ 40	08 ♍ 04
Jun 7, 1928	15 ♋ 27	28 ♒ 12	04 ♏ 17	14 ♌ 38	26 ♊ 19	24 ♋ 27	17 ♐ 57	10 ♈ 12	10 ♍ 24
Jun 17, 1928	19 ♋ 13	00 ♓ 02	03 ♏ 04	18 ♌ 45	29 ♊ 58	28 ♋ 02	15 ♐ 53	13 ♈ 32	13 ♍ 15
Jun 27, 1928	23 ♋ 04	01 ♓ 21	02 ♏ 22	23 ♌ 02	03 ♋ 40	01 ♌ 43	13 ♐ 51	16 ♈ 39	16 ♍ 32
Jul 7, 1928	26 ♋ 59	02 ♓ 06	02 ♏ 14	27 ♌ 26	07 ♋ 25	05 ♌ 28	12 ♐ 02	19 ♈ 30	20 ♍ 11
Jul 17, 1928	00 ♌ 57	02 ♓ 14	02 ♏ 37	01 ♍ 57	11 ♋ 12	09 ♌ 16	10 ♐ 37	22 ♈ 03	24 ♍ 10
Jul 27, 1928	04 ♌ 59	01 ♓ 44	03 ♏ 30	06 ♍ 33	15 ♋ 00	13 ♌ 07	09 ♐ 44	24 ♈ 15	28 ♍ 25
Aug 6, 1928	09 ♌ 02	00 ♓ 37	04 ♏ 50	11 ♍ 14	18 ♋ 48	16 ♌ 59	09 ♐ 24	26 ♈ 03	02 ♎ 54
	13 ♌ 06	29 ♒ 01	06 ♏ 32	15 ♍ 58	22 ♋ 36	20 ♌ 51	09 ♐ 39	27 ♈ 21	07 ♎ 35

	ATROPOS	HEKATE	LILITH	MEDUSA	MOIRA	NEMESIS	PERSEPHONE	PROSERPINA	PYTHIA
Aug 16, 1928	17 ♌ 12	27 ♒ 05	08 ♏ 35	20 ♍ 45	26 ♋ 23	24 ♌ 44	10 ♐ 26	28 ♈ 08	12 ♎ 26
Aug 26, 1928	21 ♌ 17	25 ♒ 05	10 ♏ 55	25 ♍ 35	00 ♌ 07	28 ♌ 36	11 ♐ 43	28 ♈ 19	17 ♎ 26
Sep 5, 1928	25 ♌ 23	23 ♒ 16	13 ♏ 30	00 ♎ 26	03 ♌ 49	02 ♍ 27	13 ♐ 25	27 ♈ 53	22 ♎ 35
Sep 15, 1928	29 ♌ 27	21 ♒ 50	16 ♏ 17	05 ♎ 20	07 ♌ 26	06 ♍ 15	15 ♐ 30	26 ♈ 48	27 ♎ 50
Sep 25, 1928	03 ♍ 30	20 ♒ 57	19 ♏ 16	10 ♎ 14	10 ♌ 58	10 ♍ 01	17 ♐ 54	25 ♈ 10	03 ♏ 12
Oct 5, 1928	07 ♍ 31	20 ♒ 42	22 ♏ 24	15 ♎ 09	14 ♌ 42	13 ♍ 42	20 ♐ 35	23 ♈ 06	08 ♏ 38
Oct 15, 1928	11 ♍ 28	21 ♒ 05	25 ♏ 40	20 ♎ 04	17 ♌ 40	17 ♍ 18	23 ♐ 30	20 ♈ 49	14 ♏ 09
Oct 25, 1928	15 ♍ 20	22 ♒ 04	29 ♏ 02	24 ♎ 59	20 ♌ 45	20 ♍ 48	26 ♐ 36	18 ♈ 34	19 ♏ 44
Nov 4, 1928	19 ♍ 07	23 ♒ 36	02 ♐ 29	29 ♎ 54	23 ♌ 37	24 ♍ 10	29 ♐ 53	16 ♈ 36	25 ♏ 22
Nov 14, 1928	22 ♍ 46	25 ♒ 37	06 ♐ 01	04 ♏ 46	26 ♌ 12	27 ♍ 22	03 ♑ 17	15 ♈ 06	01 ♐ 03
Nov 24, 1928	26 ♍ 16	28 ♒ 04	09 ♐ 36	09 ♏ 37	28 ♌ 27	00 ♎ 23	06 ♑ 48	14 ♈ 12	06 ♐ 46
Dec 4, 1928	29 ♍ 34	00 ♓ 51	13 ♐ 13	14 ♏ 25	00 ♍ 17	03 ♎ 10	10 ♑ 25	13 ♈ 56	12 ♐ 29
Dec 14, 1928	02 ♎ 38	03 ♓ 56	16 ♐ 51	19 ♏ 09	01 ♍ 37	05 ♎ 40	14 ♑ 05	14 ♈ 19	18 ♐ 14
Dec 24, 1928	05 ♎ 24	07 ♓ 15	20 ♐ 30	23 ♏ 49	02 ♍ 24	07 ♎ 51	17 ♑ 48	15 ♈ 16	23 ♐ 58
Jan 3, 1929	07 ♎ 48	10 ♓ 47	24 ♐ 07	28 ♏ 24	02 ♍ 33	09 ♎ 39	21 ♑ 33	16 ♈ 44	29 ♐ 41
Jan 13, 1929	09 ♎ 46	14 ♓ 29	27 ♐ 42	02 ♐ 52	01 ♍ 60	11 ♎ 00	25 ♑ 18	18 ♈ 40	05 ♑ 24
Jan 23, 1929	11 ♎ 12	18 ♓ 19	01 ♑ 14	07 ♐ 11	00 ♍ 47	11 ♎ 51	29 ♑ 02	20 ♈ 58	11 ♑ 03
Feb 2, 1929	12 ♎ 01	22 ♓ 15	04 ♑ 42	11 ♐ 21	28 ♌ 58	12 ♎ 09	02 ♒ 45	23 ♈ 37	16 ♑ 40
Feb 12, 1929	12 ♎ 07	26 ♓ 15	08 ♑ 04	15 ♐ 20	26 ♌ 44	11 ♎ 50	06 ♒ 26	26 ♈ 31	22 ♑ 14
Feb 22, 1929	11 ♎ 25	00 ♈ 19	11 ♑ 18	19 ♐ 05	24 ♌ 21	10 ♎ 56	10 ♒ 02	29 ♈ 39	27 ♑ 43
Mar 4, 1929	09 ♎ 56	04 ♈ 25	14 ♑ 24	22 ♐ 33	22 ♌ 08	09 ♎ 29	13 ♒ 34	02 ♉ 58	03 ♒ 06
Mar 14, 1929	07 ♎ 44	08 ♈ 32	17 ♑ 19	25 ♐ 42	20 ♌ 19	07 ♎ 35	16 ♒ 60	06 ♉ 26	08 ♒ 23
Mar 24, 1929	05 ♎ 02	12 ♈ 40	20 ♑ 01	28 ♐ 28	19 ♌ 07	05 ♎ 25	20 ♒ 18	10 ♉ 01	13 ♒ 33
Apr 3, 1929	02 ♎ 10	16 ♈ 46	22 ♑ 28	00 ♑ 46	18 ♌ 38	03 ♎ 12	23 ♒ 28	13 ♉ 43	18 ♒ 35
Apr 13, 1929	29 ♍ 29	20 ♈ 51	24 ♑ 37	02 ♑ 32	18 ♌ 52	01 ♎ 10	26 ♒ 28	17 ♉ 29	23 ♒ 26
Apr 23, 1929	27 ♍ 21	24 ♈ 54	26 ♑ 24	03 ♑ 40	19 ♌ 47	29 ♍ 30	29 ♒ 16	21 ♉ 18	28 ♒ 07
May 3, 1929	25 ♍ 58	28 ♈ 54	27 ♑ 47	03 ♑ 06	21 ♌ 20	28 ♍ 19	01 ♓ 50	25 ♉ 10	02 ♓ 34
May 13, 1929	25 ♍ 27	02 ♉ 49	28 ♑ 42	03 ♑ 45	23 ♌ 25	27 ♍ 43	04 ♓ 09	29 ♉ 03	06 ♓ 45
May 23, 1929	25 ♍ 47	06 ♉ 40	29 ♑ 05	02 ♑ 38	25 ♌ 59	27 ♍ 40	06 ♓ 08	02 ♊ 58	10 ♓ 39
Jun 2, 1929	26 ♍ 55	10 ♉ 26	28 ♑ 54	00 ♑ 47	28 ♌ 56	28 ♍ 11	07 ♓ 47	06 ♊ 52	14 ♓ 12
Jun 12, 1929	28 ♍ 46	14 ♉ 04	28 ♑ 07	28 ♐ 25	02 ♍ 15	29 ♍ 11	09 ♓ 01	10 ♊ 46	17 ♓ 20
Jun 22, 1929	01 ♎ 14	17 ♉ 35	26 ♑ 47	25 ♐ 48	05 ♍ 51	00 ♎ 39	09 ♓ 49	14 ♊ 39	19 ♓ 59
Jul 2, 1929	04 ♎ 14	20 ♉ 58	24 ♑ 57	23 ♐ 17	09 ♍ 42	02 ♎ 29	10 ♓ 07	18 ♊ 29	22 ♓ 04
Jul 12, 1929	07 ♎ 42	24 ♉ 10	22 ♑ 47	21 ♐ 11	13 ♍ 47	04 ♎ 39	09 ♓ 54	22 ♊ 17	23 ♓ 29
Jul 22, 1929	11 ♎ 34	27 ♉ 09	20 ♑ 31	19 ♐ 45	18 ♍ 02	07 ♎ 07	09 ♓ 09	26 ♊ 01	24 ♓ 10

	ATROPOS	HEKATE	LILITH	MEDUSA	MOIRA	NEMESIS	PERSEPHONE	PROSERPINA	PYTHIA
Aug 1, 1929	15 ♎ 46	29 ♉ 55	18 ♑ 22	19 ♐ 05	22 ♍ 27	09 ♎ 50	07 ♓ 54	29 ♊ 41	24 ♓ 01
Aug 11, 1929	20 ♎ 16	02 ♊ 25	16 ♑ 33	19 ♐ 14	27 ♍ 01	12 ♎ 45	06 ♓ 14	03 ♋ 15	23 ♓ 02
Aug 21, 1929	25 ♎ 01	04 ♊ 36	15 ♑ 16	20 ♐ 08	01 ♎ 42	15 ♎ 50	04 ♓ 17	06 ♋ 42	21 ♓ 17
Aug 31, 1929	00 ♏ 00	06 ♊ 25	14 ♑ 35	21 ♐ 42	06 ♎ 30	19 ♎ 05	02 ♓ 15	10 ♋ 00	18 ♓ 58
Sep 10, 1929	05 ♏ 11	07 ♊ 50	14 ♑ 32	23 ♐ 53	11 ♎ 23	22 ♎ 28	00 ♓ 17	13 ♋ 08	16 ♓ 21
Sep 20, 1929	10 ♏ 33	08 ♊ 46	15 ♑ 08	26 ♐ 34	16 ♎ 21	25 ♎ 57	28 ♒ 36	16 ♋ 03	13 ♓ 50
Sep 30, 1929	16 ♏ 03	09 ♊ 11	16 ♑ 18	29 ♐ 41	21 ♎ 22	29 ♎ 31	27 ♒ 20	18 ♋ 44	11 ♓ 45
Oct 10, 1929	21 ♏ 42	09 ♊ 02	18 ♑ 01	03 ♑ 10	26 ♎ 27	03 ♏ 10	26 ♒ 34	21 ♋ 06	10 ♓ 18
Oct 20, 1929	27 ♏ 27	08 ♊ 19	20 ♑ 11	06 ♑ 58	01 ♏ 35	06 ♏ 52	26 ♒ 20	23 ♋ 06	09 ♓ 39
Oct 30, 1929	03 ♐ 17	07 ♊ 04	22 ♑ 47	11 ♑ 02	06 ♏ 44	10 ♏ 37	26 ♒ 38	24 ♋ 41	09 ♓ 47
Nov 9, 1929	09 ♐ 12	05 ♊ 21	25 ♑ 44	15 ♑ 21	11 ♏ 55	14 ♏ 23	27 ♒ 26	25 ♋ 45	10 ♓ 40
Nov 19, 1929	15 ♐ 10	03 ♊ 22	28 ♑ 60	19 ♑ 51	17 ♏ 05	18 ♏ 10	28 ♒ 41	26 ♋ 15	12 ♓ 11
Nov 29, 1929	21 ♐ 11	01 ♊ 16	02 ♒ 32	24 ♑ 31	22 ♏ 16	21 ♏ 57	00 ♓ 21	26 ♋ 07	14 ♓ 16
Dec 9, 1929	27 ♐ 13	29 ♉ 17	06 ♒ 18	29 ♑ 20	27 ♏ 25	25 ♏ 42	02 ♓ 22	25 ♋ 20	16 ♓ 49
Dec 19, 1929	03 ♑ 15	27 ♉ 38	10 ♒ 17	04 ♒ 17	02 ♐ 31	29 ♏ 25	04 ♓ 42	23 ♋ 54	19 ♓ 44
Dec 29, 1929	09 ♑ 16	26 ♉ 25	14 ♒ 27	09 ♒ 20	07 ♐ 35	03 ♐ 04	07 ♓ 16	21 ♋ 58	22 ♓ 59
Jan 8, 1930	15 ♑ 16	25 ♉ 44	18 ♒ 45	14 ♒ 28	12 ♐ 34	06 ♐ 38	10 ♓ 04	19 ♋ 41	26 ♓ 29
Jan 18, 1930	21 ♑ 13	25 ♉ 37	23 ♒ 12	19 ♒ 41	17 ♐ 29	10 ♐ 06	13 ♓ 03	17 ♋ 19	00 ♈ 12
Jan 28, 1930	27 ♑ 07	26 ♉ 02	27 ♒ 46	24 ♒ 58	22 ♐ 16	13 ♐ 26	16 ♓ 10	15 ♋ 09	04 ♈ 05
Feb 7, 1930	02 ♒ 57	26 ♉ 56	02 ♓ 25	00 ♓ 18	26 ♐ 56	16 ♐ 37	19 ♓ 25	13 ♋ 25	08 ♈ 05
Feb 17, 1930	08 ♒ 42	28 ♉ 17	07 ♓ 10	05 ♓ 40	01 ♑ 26	19 ♐ 35	22 ♓ 46	12 ♋ 16	12 ♈ 12
Feb 27, 1930	14 ♒ 22	00 ♊ 00	11 ♓ 59	11 ♓ 05	05 ♑ 46	22 ♐ 20	26 ♓ 11	11 ♋ 47	16 ♈ 23
Mar 9, 1930	19 ♒ 55	02 ♊ 03	16 ♓ 52	16 ♓ 30	09 ♑ 52	24 ♐ 48	29 ♓ 38	11 ♋ 59	20 ♈ 37
Mar 19, 1930	25 ♒ 21	04 ♊ 23	21 ♓ 47	21 ♓ 56	13 ♑ 42	26 ♐ 56	03 ♈ 08	12 ♋ 48	24 ♈ 54
Mar 29, 1930	00 ♓ 40	06 ♊ 55	26 ♓ 45	27 ♓ 23	17 ♑ 15	28 ♐ 41	06 ♈ 39	14 ♋ 11	29 ♈ 12
Apr 8, 1930	05 ♓ 51	09 ♊ 39	01 ♈ 44	02 ♈ 49	20 ♑ 27	29 ♐ 59	10 ♈ 10	16 ♋ 04	03 ♉ 31
Apr 18, 1930	10 ♓ 52	12 ♊ 31	06 ♈ 44	08 ♈ 15	23 ♑ 14	00 ♑ 47	13 ♈ 39	18 ♋ 22	07 ♉ 50
Apr 28, 1930	15 ♓ 43	15 ♊ 31	11 ♈ 45	13 ♈ 40	25 ♑ 33	01 ♑ 02	17 ♈ 07	21 ♋ 01	12 ♉ 08
May 8, 1930	20 ♓ 22	18 ♊ 37	16 ♈ 46	19 ♈ 03	27 ♑ 19	01 ♑ 40	20 ♈ 32	23 ♋ 59	16 ♉ 24
May 18, 1930	24 ♓ 49	21 ♊ 46	21 ♈ 45	24 ♈ 24	28 ♑ 29	29 ♐ 44	23 ♈ 53	27 ♋ 13	20 ♉ 38
May 28, 1930	29 ♓ 02	24 ♊ 59	26 ♈ 44	29 ♈ 42	28 ♑ 57	28 ♐ 14	27 ♈ 09	00 ♌ 39	24 ♉ 50
Jun 7, 1930	02 ♈ 58	28 ♊ 14	01 ♉ 40	04 ♉ 58	28 ♑ 42	26 ♐ 19	00 ♉ 19	04 ♌ 17	28 ♉ 59
Jun 17, 1930	06 ♈ 36	01 ♋ 29	06 ♉ 34	10 ♉ 09	27 ♑ 45	24 ♐ 09	03 ♉ 21	08 ♌ 04	03 ♊ 04
Jun 27, 1930	09 ♈ 53	04 ♋ 45	11 ♉ 23	15 ♉ 16	26 ♑ 10	21 ♐ 59	06 ♉ 14	11 ♌ 59	07 ♊ 05
Jul 7, 1930	12 ♈ 45	08 ♋ 00	16 ♉ 07	20 ♉ 18	24 ♑ 09	20 ♐ 02	08 ♉ 56	16 ♌ 01	10 ♊ 60

	ATROPOS	HEKATE	LILITH	MEDUSA	MOIRA	NEMESIS	PERSEPHONE	PROSERPINA	PYTHIA
Jul 17, 1930	15 ♈ 07	11 ♋ 14	20 ♉ 45	25 ♉ 13	21 ♑ 56	18 ♐ 30	11 ♉ 26	20 ♌ 09	14 ♊ 49
Jul 27, 1930	16 ♈ 56	14 ♋ 24	25 ♉ 15	29 ♉ 60	19 ♑ 48	17 ♐ 31	13 ♉ 41	24 ♌ 22	18 ♊ 32
Aug 6, 1930	18 ♈ 05	17 ♋ 31	29 ♉ 34	04 ♊ 37	18 ♑ 01	17 ♐ 09	15 ♉ 37	28 ♌ 40	22 ♊ 06
Aug 16, 1930	18 ♈ 29	20 ♋ 33	03 ♊ 40	09 ♊ 03	16 ♑ 47	17 ♐ 24	17 ♉ 13	03 ♍ 00	25 ♊ 30
Aug 26, 1930	18 ♈ 04	23 ♋ 30	07 ♊ 32	13 ♊ 15	16 ♑ 11	18 ♐ 16	18 ♉ 25	07 ♍ 24	28 ♊ 43
Sep 5, 1930	16 ♈ 49	26 ♋ 19	11 ♊ 04	17 ♊ 10	16 ♑ 16	19 ♐ 40	19 ♉ 08	11 ♍ 51	01 ♋ 42
Sep 15, 1930	14 ♈ 49	28 ♋ 59	14 ♊ 12	20 ♊ 44	16 ♑ 59	21 ♐ 33	19 ♉ 21	16 ♍ 19	04 ♋ 25
Sep 25, 1930	12 ♈ 14	01 ♌ 28	16 ♊ 53	23 ♊ 53	18 ♑ 17	23 ♐ 52	19 ♉ 02	20 ♍ 48	06 ♋ 49
Oct 5, 1930	09 ♈ 23	03 ♌ 45	18 ♊ 59	26 ♊ 32	20 ♑ 05	26 ♐ 33	18 ♉ 08	25 ♍ 17	08 ♋ 50
Oct 15, 1930	06 ♈ 40	05 ♌ 46	20 ♊ 24	28 ♊ 33	22 ♑ 20	29 ♐ 34	16 ♉ 43	29 ♍ 46	10 ♋ 23
Oct 25, 1930	04 ♈ 23	07 ♌ 30	21 ♊ 04	29 ♊ 50	24 ♑ 57	02 ♑ 52	14 ♉ 54	04 ♎ 14	11 ♋ 25
Nov 4, 1930	02 ♈ 48	08 ♌ 53	20 ♊ 54	00 ♋ 16	27 ♑ 53	06 ♑ 24	12 ♉ 48	08 ♎ 41	11 ♋ 50
Nov 14, 1930	02 ♈ 01	09 ♌ 52	19 ♊ 54	29 ♊ 47	01 ♒ 05	10 ♑ 09	10 ♉ 40	13 ♎ 04	11 ♋ 34
Nov 24, 1930	02 ♈ 02	10 ♌ 24	18 ♊ 10	28 ♊ 23	04 ♒ 29	14 ♑ 05	08 ♉ 43	17 ♎ 23	10 ♋ 37
Dec 4, 1930	02 ♈ 49	10 ♌ 28	15 ♊ 59	26 ♊ 12	08 ♒ 05	18 ♑ 10	07 ♉ 07	21 ♎ 37	08 ♋ 58
Dec 14, 1930	04 ♈ 16	10 ♌ 01	13 ♊ 41	23 ♊ 33	11 ♒ 48	22 ♑ 23	06 ♉ 02	25 ♎ 44	06 ♋ 45
Dec 24, 1930	06 ♈ 17	09 ♌ 03	11 ♊ 38	20 ♊ 50	15 ♒ 39	26 ♑ 43	05 ♉ 32	29 ♎ 42	04 ♋ 11
Jan 3, 1931	08 ♈ 47	07 ♌ 38	10 ♊ 10	18 ♊ 31	19 ♒ 35	01 ♒ 09	05 ♉ 38	03 ♏ 29	01 ♋ 32
Jan 13, 1931	11 ♈ 40	05 ♌ 52	09 ♊ 27	16 ♊ 54	23 ♒ 35	05 ♒ 39	06 ♉ 18	07 ♏ 03	29 ♊ 07
Jan 23, 1931	14 ♈ 52	03 ♌ 54	09 ♊ 33	16 ♊ 11	27 ♒ 38	10 ♒ 13	07 ♉ 29	10 ♏ 21	27 ♊ 11
Feb 2, 1931	18 ♈ 20	01 ♌ 54	10 ♊ 27	16 ♊ 22	01 ♓ 42	14 ♒ 50	09 ♉ 08	13 ♏ 50	25 ♊ 53
Feb 12, 1931	22 ♈ 01	00 ♌ 03	12 ♊ 03	17 ♊ 25	05 ♓ 47	19 ♒ 28	11 ♉ 11	15 ♏ 55	25 ♊ 18
Feb 22, 1931	25 ♈ 53	28 ♋ 31	14 ♊ 15	19 ♊ 12	09 ♓ 52	24 ♒ 08	13 ♉ 35	18 ♏ 03	25 ♊ 26
Mar 4, 1931	29 ♈ 52	27 ♋ 25	16 ♊ 57	21 ♊ 37	13 ♓ 56	28 ♒ 48	16 ♉ 16	19 ♏ 38	26 ♊ 14
Mar 14, 1931	03 ♉ 58	26 ♋ 47	20 ♊ 03	24 ♊ 33	17 ♓ 58	03 ♓ 28	19 ♉ 12	20 ♏ 36	27 ♊ 36
Mar 24, 1931	08 ♉ 09	26 ♋ 39	23 ♊ 29	27 ♊ 54	21 ♓ 57	08 ♓ 07	22 ♉ 21	20 ♏ 53	29 ♊ 30
Apr 3, 1931	12 ♉ 23	27 ♋ 01	27 ♊ 11	01 ♋ 36	25 ♓ 53	12 ♓ 44	25 ♉ 40	20 ♏ 26	01 ♋ 49
Apr 13, 1931	16 ♉ 40	27 ♋ 49	01 ♋ 05	05 ♋ 34	29 ♓ 44	17 ♓ 19	29 ♉ 07	19 ♏ 18	04 ♋ 30
Apr 23, 1931	20 ♉ 59	29 ♋ 02	05 ♋ 10	09 ♋ 46	03 ♈ 30	21 ♓ 50	02 ♊ 41	17 ♏ 34	07 ♋ 29
May 3, 1931	25 ♉ 19	00 ♌ 35	09 ♋ 22	14 ♋ 08	07 ♈ 10	26 ♓ 16	06 ♊ 21	15 ♏ 27	10 ♋ 45
May 13, 1931	29 ♉ 39	02 ♌ 27	13 ♋ 40	18 ♋ 39	10 ♈ 42	00 ♈ 37	10 ♊ 06	11 ♏ 13	14 ♋ 13
May 23, 1931	03 ♊ 58	04 ♌ 34	18 ♋ 03	23 ♋ 17	14 ♈ 06	04 ♈ 51	13 ♊ 53	11 ♏ 10	17 ♋ 53
Jun 2, 1931	08 ♊ 17	06 ♌ 55	22 ♋ 29	28 ♋ 00	17 ♈ 20	08 ♈ 57	17 ♊ 44	09 ♏ 35	21 ♋ 43
Jun 12, 1931	12 ♊ 33	09 ♌ 27	26 ♋ 57	02 ♌ 48	20 ♈ 23	12 ♈ 53	21 ♊ 36	08 ♏ 36	25 ♋ 41
Jun 22, 1931	16 ♊ 48	12 ♌ 09	01 ♌ 26	07 ♌ 40	23 ♈ 12	16 ♈ 38	25 ♊ 29	08 ♏ 20	29 ♋ 47

	ATROPOS	HEKATE	LILITH	MEDUSA	MOIRA	NEMESIS	PERSEPHONE	PROSERPINA	PYTHIA
Jul 2, 1931	20 ♊ 59	14 ♌ 58	05 ♌ 57	12 ♌ 35	25 ♈ 46	20 ♈ 08	29 ♊ 22	08 ♏ 46	03 ♌ 58
Jul 12, 1931	25 ♊ 07	17 ♌ 54	10 ♌ 27	17 ♌ 32	28 ♈ 03	23 ♈ 21	03 ♋ 14	09 ♏ 51	08 ♌ 15
Jul 22, 1931	29 ♊ 10	20 ♌ 56	14 ♌ 57	22 ♌ 31	29 ♈ 59	26 ♈ 15	07 ♋ 05	11 ♏ 32	12 ♌ 38
Aug 1, 1931	03 ♋ 08	24 ♌ 01	19 ♌ 26	27 ♌ 31	01 ♉ 31	28 ♈ 44	10 ♋ 54	13 ♏ 44	17 ♌ 04
Aug 11, 1931	07 ♋ 00	27 ♌ 09	23 ♌ 53	02 ♍ 32	02 ♉ 36	00 ♉ 44	14 ♋ 40	16 ♏ 23	21 ♌ 35
Aug 21, 1931	10 ♋ 44	00 ♍ 20	28 ♌ 19	07 ♍ 33	03 ♉ 11	02 ♉ 11	18 ♋ 21	19 ♏ 24	26 ♌ 08
Aug 31, 1931	14 ♋ 20	03 ♍ 32	02 ♍ 42	12 ♍ 35	03 ♉ 13	03 ♉ 00	21 ♋ 58	22 ♏ 45	00 ♍ 45
Sep 10, 1931	17 ♋ 45	06 ♍ 44	07 ♍ 01	17 ♍ 36	02 ♉ 40	03 ♉ 07	25 ♋ 27	26 ♏ 20	05 ♍ 24
Sep 20, 1931	20 ♋ 57	09 ♍ 56	11 ♍ 17	22 ♍ 37	01 ♉ 32	02 ♉ 30	28 ♋ 48	00 ♐ 09	10 ♍ 05
Sep 30, 1931	23 ♋ 54	13 ♍ 05	15 ♍ 28	27 ♍ 36	29 ♈ 53	01 ♉ 11	01 ♌ 58	04 ♐ 10	14 ♍ 48
Oct 10, 1931	26 ♋ 33	16 ♍ 12	19 ♍ 34	02 ♎ 34	27 ♈ 52	29 ♈ 19	04 ♌ 56	08 ♐ 21	19 ♍ 31
Oct 20, 1931	28 ♋ 50	19 ♍ 14	23 ♍ 34	07 ♎ 30	25 ♈ 38	27 ♈ 06	07 ♌ 38	12 ♐ 40	24 ♍ 15
Oct 30, 1931	00 ♌ 42	22 ♍ 11	27 ♍ 26	12 ♎ 24	23 ♈ 25	24 ♈ 53	10 ♌ 03	17 ♐ 05	28 ♍ 58
Nov 9, 1931	02 ♌ 03	25 ♍ 01	01 ♎ 10	17 ♎ 14	21 ♈ 27	22 ♈ 57	12 ♌ 05	21 ♐ 36	03 ♎ 40
Nov 19, 1931	02 ♌ 48	27 ♍ 41	04 ♎ 43	22 ♎ 00	19 ♈ 54	21 ♈ 34	13 ♌ 41	26 ♐ 12	08 ♎ 19
Nov 29, 1931	02 ♌ 53	00 ♎ 10	08 ♎ 04	26 ♎ 41	18 ♈ 53	20 ♈ 52	14 ♌ 46	00 ♑ 50	12 ♎ 55
Dec 9, 1931	02 ♌ 14	02 ♎ 25	11 ♎ 11	01 ♏ 16	18 ♈ 27	20 ♈ 54	15 ♌ 18	05 ♑ 32	17 ♎ 26
Dec 19, 1931	00 ♌ 52	04 ♎ 24	14 ♎ 01	05 ♏ 44	18 ♈ 36	21 ♈ 40	15 ♌ 12	10 ♑ 15	21 ♎ 50
Dec 29, 1931	28 ♋ 49	06 ♎ 04	16 ♎ 31	10 ♏ 02	19 ♈ 18	23 ♈ 06	14 ♌ 28	14 ♑ 59	26 ♎ 05
Jan 8, 1932	26 ♋ 16	07 ♎ 21	18 ♎ 39	14 ♏ 10	20 ♈ 30	25 ♈ 05	13 ♌ 07	19 ♑ 42	00 ♏ 10
Jan 18, 1932	23 ♋ 29	08 ♎ 11	20 ♎ 20	18 ♏ 06	22 ♈ 09	27 ♈ 34	11 ♌ 17	24 ♑ 25	04 ♏ 01
Jan 28, 1932	20 ♋ 47	08 ♎ 34	21 ♎ 30	21 ♏ 46	24 ♈ 09	00 ♉ 27	09 ♌ 08	29 ♑ 06	07 ♏ 34
Feb 7, 1932	18 ♋ 28	08 ♎ 25	22 ♎ 07	25 ♏ 08	26 ♈ 29	03 ♉ 41	06 ♌ 56	03 ♒ 45	10 ♏ 47
Feb 17, 1932	16 ♋ 44	07 ♎ 44	22 ♎ 06	28 ♏ 09	29 ♈ 04	07 ♉ 11	04 ♌ 57	08 ♒ 21	13 ♏ 32
Feb 27, 1932	15 ♋ 43	06 ♎ 33	21 ♎ 28	00 ♐ 44	01 ♉ 53	10 ♉ 54	03 ♌ 22	12 ♒ 53	15 ♏ 47
Mar 8, 1932	15 ♋ 25	04 ♎ 56	20 ♎ 13	02 ♐ 49	04 ♉ 53	14 ♉ 48	02 ♌ 21	17 ♒ 19	17 ♏ 23
Mar 18, 1932	15 ♋ 49	03 ♎ 01	18 ♎ 26	04 ♐ 18	08 ♉ 01	18 ♉ 51	01 ♌ 57	21 ♒ 40	18 ♏ 14
Mar 28, 1932	16 ♋ 50	00 ♎ 58	16 ♎ 18	05 ♐ 07	11 ♉ 17	23 ♉ 00	02 ♌ 12	25 ♒ 54	18 ♏ 17
Apr 7, 1932	18 ♋ 23	29 ♍ 01	13 ♎ 60	05 ♐ 10	14 ♉ 39	27 ♉ 15	03 ♌ 02	29 ♒ 59	18 ♏ 28
Apr 17, 1932	20 ♋ 25	27 ♍ 18	11 ♎ 47	04 ♐ 26	18 ♉ 05	01 ♊ 34	04 ♌ 24	03 ♓ 56	15 ♏ 50
Apr 27, 1932	22 ♋ 49	26 ♍ 00	09 ♎ 52	02 ♐ 55	21 ♉ 34	05 ♊ 55	06 ♌ 14	07 ♓ 41	13 ♏ 37
May 7, 1932	25 ♋ 33	25 ♍ 11	08 ♎ 24	00 ♐ 46	25 ♉ 05	10 ♊ 19	08 ♌ 28	11 ♓ 15	11 ♏ 07
May 17, 1932	28 ♋ 34	24 ♍ 54	07 ♎ 30	28 ♏ 13	28 ♉ 38	14 ♊ 44	11 ♌ 03	14 ♓ 33	08 ♏ 45
May 27, 1932	01 ♌ 48	25 ♍ 09	07 ♎ 10	25 ♏ 34	02 ♊ 11	19 ♊ 09	13 ♌ 54	17 ♓ 35	06 ♏ 52
Jun 6, 1932	05 ♌ 14	25 ♍ 54	07 ♎ 25	23 ♏ 12	05 ♊ 44	23 ♊ 33	17 ♌ 00	20 ♓ 18	05 ♏ 44

	ATROPOS	HEKATE	LILITH	MEDUSA	MOIRA	NEMESIS	PERSEPHONE	PROSERPINA	PYTHIA
Jun 16, 1932	08 ♌ 50	27 ♍ 07	08 ♎ 10	21 ♏ 22	09 ♊ 16	27 ♊ 57	20 ♌ 19	22 ♓ 38	05 ♏ 27
Jun 26, 1932	12 ♌ 35	28 ♍ 44	09 ♎ 24	20 ♏ 15	12 ♊ 45	02 ♋ 19	23 ♌ 47	24 ♓ 32	06 ♏ 03
Jul 6, 1932	16 ♌ 27	00 ♎ 43	11 ♎ 01	19 ♏ 55	16 ♊ 12	06 ♋ 39	27 ♌ 24	25 ♓ 56	07 ♏ 27
Jul 16, 1932	20 ♌ 26	03 ♎ 01	13 ♎ 00	20 ♏ 22	19 ♊ 35	10 ♋ 57	01 ♍ 08	26 ♓ 47	09 ♏ 32
Jul 26, 1932	24 ♌ 30	05 ♎ 35	15 ♎ 17	21 ♏ 30	22 ♊ 53	15 ♋ 11	04 ♍ 59	27 ♓ 00	12 ♏ 14
Aug 5, 1932	28 ♌ 39	08 ♎ 23	17 ♎ 49	23 ♏ 16	26 ♋ 05	19 ♋ 22	08 ♍ 54	26 ♓ 34	15 ♏ 26
Aug 15, 1932	02 ♍ 53	11 ♎ 24	20 ♎ 34	25 ♏ 23	29 ♋ 09	23 ♋ 27	12 ♍ 53	25 ♓ 29	19 ♏ 04
Aug 25, 1932	07 ♍ 10	14 ♎ 35	23 ♎ 29	28 ♏ 20	02 ♋ 04	27 ♋ 21	16 ♍ 55	23 ♓ 50	23 ♏ 02
Sep 4, 1932	11 ♍ 31	17 ♎ 56	26 ♎ 34	01 ♐ 29	04 ♋ 48	01 ♌ 21	21 ♍ 00	21 ♓ 46	27 ♏ 18
Sep 14, 1932	15 ♍ 55	21 ♎ 25	29 ♎ 47	04 ♐ 58	07 ♋ 18	05 ♌ 06	25 ♍ 07	19 ♓ 29	01 ♐ 49
Sep 24, 1932	20 ♍ 21	25 ♎ 00	03 ♏ 06	08 ♐ 43	09 ♋ 32	08 ♌ 42	29 ♍ 14	17 ♓ 17	06 ♐ 31
Oct 4, 1932	24 ♍ 49	28 ♎ 42	06 ♏ 30	12 ♐ 44	11 ♋ 22	12 ♌ 07	03 ♎ 22	15 ♓ 23	11 ♐ 25
Oct 14, 1932	29 ♍ 19	02 ♏ 28	09 ♏ 58	16 ♐ 57	12 ♋ 59	15 ♌ 19	07 ♎ 28	13 ♓ 59	16 ♐ 26
Oct 24, 1932	03 ♎ 50	06 ♏ 18	13 ♏ 29	21 ♐ 20	14 ♋ 04	18 ♌ 16	11 ♎ 34	13 ♓ 12	21 ♐ 35
Nov 3, 1932	08 ♎ 21	10 ♏ 12	17 ♏ 02	25 ♐ 53	14 ♋ 39	20 ♌ 54	15 ♎ 37	13 ♓ 05	26 ♐ 50
Nov 13, 1932	12 ♎ 52	14 ♏ 07	20 ♏ 36	00 ♑ 35	14 ♋ 39	23 ♌ 10	19 ♎ 36	13 ♓ 35	02 ♑ 09
Nov 23, 1932	17 ♎ 22	18 ♏ 03	24 ♏ 11	05 ♑ 23	14 ♋ 03	25 ♌ 01	23 ♎ 31	14 ♓ 40	07 ♑ 33
Dec 3, 1932	21 ♎ 49	22 ♏ 00	27 ♏ 44	10 ♑ 17	12 ♋ 50	26 ♌ 23	27 ♎ 19	16 ♓ 16	12 ♑ 59
Dec 13, 1932	26 ♎ 14	25 ♏ 56	01 ♐ 15	15 ♑ 16	11 ♋ 06	27 ♌ 10	01 ♏ 00	18 ♓ 20	18 ♑ 27
Dec 23, 1932	00 ♏ 35	29 ♏ 50	04 ♐ 43	20 ♑ 19	08 ♋ 58	27 ♌ 21	04 ♏ 32	20 ♓ 46	23 ♑ 56
Jan 2, 1933	04 ♏ 49	03 ♐ 42	08 ♐ 07	25 ♑ 27	06 ♋ 38	26 ♌ 52	07 ♏ 53	23 ♓ 31	29 ♑ 26
Jan 12, 1933	08 ♏ 56	07 ♐ 29	11 ♐ 25	00 ♒ 37	04 ♋ 22	25 ♌ 45	10 ♏ 60	26 ♓ 33	04 ♒ 56
Jan 22, 1933	12 ♏ 53	11 ♐ 10	14 ♐ 36	05 ♒ 49	02 ♋ 25	24 ♌ 03	13 ♏ 50	29 ♓ 47	10 ♒ 25
Feb 1, 1933	16 ♏ 36	14 ♐ 43	17 ♐ 37	11 ♒ 04	00 ♋ 56	21 ♌ 57	16 ♏ 22	03 ♈ 13	15 ♒ 52
Feb 11, 1933	20 ♏ 04	18 ♐ 08	20 ♐ 28	16 ♒ 30	00 ♋ 28	19 ♌ 39	18 ♏ 30	06 ♈ 47	21 ♒ 17
Feb 21, 1933	23 ♏ 11	21 ♐ 21	23 ♐ 06	21 ♒ 35	29 ♊ 50	17 ♌ 25	20 ♏ 13	10 ♈ 29	26 ♒ 40
Mar 3, 1933	25 ♏ 53	24 ♐ 21	25 ♐ 29	26 ♒ 51	00 ♋ 14	15 ♌ 30	21 ♏ 25	14 ♈ 16	01 ♓ 59
Mar 13, 1933	28 ♏ 03	27 ♐ 05	27 ♐ 34	02 ♓ 07	01 ♋ 12	14 ♌ 03	22 ♏ 04	18 ♈ 08	07 ♓ 13
Mar 23, 1933	00 ♐ 23	29 ♐ 29	29 ♐ 18	07 ♓ 21	02 ♋ 42	13 ♌ 12	22 ♏ 06	22 ♈ 02	12 ♓ 24
Apr 2, 1933	00 ♐ 19	01 ♑ 30	01 ♑ 29	12 ♓ 35	04 ♋ 38	12 ♌ 58	21 ♏ 31	25 ♈ 59	17 ♓ 29
Apr 12, 1933	29 ♏ 36	03 ♑ 05	01 ♑ 51	17 ♓ 46	06 ♋ 58	13 ♌ 19	20 ♏ 20	29 ♈ 56	22 ♓ 27
Apr 22, 1933	29 ♏ 21	04 ♑ 10	01 ♑ 39	22 ♓ 54	09 ♋ 39	14 ♌ 13	18 ♏ 40	03 ♉ 55	27 ♓ 20
May 2, 1933	27 ♏ 33	04 ♑ 40	00 ♑ 54	27 ♓ 60	12 ♋ 36	15 ♌ 37	16 ♏ 39	07 ♉ 52	02 ♈ 05
May 12, 1933	25 ♏ 08	04 ♑ 35	29 ♐ 36	03 ♈ 01	15 ♋ 47	17 ♌ 25	14 ♏ 33	11 ♉ 49	06 ♈ 41
May 22, 1933	22 ♏ 27	03 ♑ 53	29 ♐ 36	07 ♈ 57	19 ♋ 12	19 ♌ 35	12 ♏ 34	15 ♉ 43	11 ♈ 08

	ATROPOS	HEKATE	LILITH	MEDUSA	NEMESIS	MOIRA	PERSEPHONE	PROSERPINA	PYTHIA
Jun 1, 1933	19 ♏ 58	02 ♑ 37	27 ♐ 51	12 ♈ 48	22 ♌ 02	22 ♋ 47	10 ♏ 56	19 ♊ 35	15 ♈ 24
Jun 11, 1933	18 ♏ 06	00 ♑ 55	25 ♐ 46	17 ♈ 32	24 ♌ 45	26 ♋ 31	09 ♏ 47	23 ♊ 23	19 ♈ 28
Jun 21, 1933	17 ♏ 06	28 ♐ 57	23 ♐ 33	22 ♈ 07	27 ♌ 40	00 ♌ 23	09 ♏ 12	27 ♊ 07	23 ♈ 19
Jul 1, 1933	17 ♏ 05	26 ♐ 58	21 ♐ 24	26 ♈ 33	00 ♍ 46	04 ♌ 22	09 ♏ 13	00 ♋ 46	26 ♈ 54
Jul 11, 1933	18 ♏ 01	25 ♐ 12	19 ♐ 33	00 ♉ 46	04 ♍ 00	08 ♌ 27	09 ♏ 48	04 ♋ 19	00 ♉ 10
Jul 21, 1933	19 ♏ 48	23 ♐ 52	18 ♐ 07	04 ♉ 45	07 ♍ 22	12 ♌ 37	10 ♏ 55	07 ♋ 44	03 ♉ 05
Jul 31, 1933	22 ♏ 20	23 ♐ 06	17 ♐ 14	08 ♉ 26	10 ♍ 50	16 ♌ 52	12 ♏ 31	10 ♋ 60	05 ♉ 34
Aug 10, 1933	25 ♏ 28	22 ♐ 57	16 ♐ 56	11 ♉ 46	14 ♍ 22	21 ♌ 11	14 ♏ 30	14 ♋ 05	07 ♉ 35
Aug 20, 1933	29 ♏ 07	23 ♐ 27	17 ♐ 12	14 ♉ 39	17 ♍ 59	25 ♌ 33	16 ♏ 51	16 ♋ 58	09 ♉ 02
Aug 30, 1933	03 ♐ 10	24 ♐ 33	18 ♐ 01	16 ♉ 60	21 ♍ 38	29 ♌ 58	19 ♏ 30	19 ♋ 35	09 ♉ 50
Sep 9, 1933	07 ♐ 33	26 ♐ 11	19 ♐ 19	18 ♉ 43	25 ♍ 19	04 ♍ 26	22 ♏ 24	21 ♋ 54	09 ♉ 55
Sep 19, 1933	12 ♐ 13	28 ♐ 19	21 ♐ 04	19 ♉ 40	29 ♍ 02	08 ♍ 24	25 ♏ 32	23 ♋ 52	09 ♉ 14
Sep 29, 1933	17 ♐ 05	00 ♑ 52	23 ♐ 13	19 ♉ 46	02 ♎ 44	13 ♍ 24	28 ♏ 50	25 ♋ 25	07 ♉ 48
Oct 9, 1933	22 ♐ 07	03 ♑ 47	25 ♐ 42	18 ♉ 58	06 ♎ 27	17 ♍ 54	02 ♐ 18	26 ♋ 29	05 ♉ 44
Oct 19, 1933	27 ♐ 17	07 ♑ 01	28 ♐ 29	17 ♉ 18	10 ♎ 08	22 ♍ 24	05 ♐ 53	26 ♋ 60	03 ♉ 13
Oct 29, 1933	02 ♑ 34	10 ♑ 31	01 ♑ 32	14 ♉ 57	13 ♎ 46	26 ♍ 52	09 ♐ 34	26 ♋ 54	00 ♉ 32
Nov 8, 1933	07 ♑ 55	14 ♑ 15	04 ♑ 48	12 ♉ 18	17 ♎ 21	01 ♎ 18	13 ♐ 21	26 ♋ 10	28 ♈ 03
Nov 18, 1933	13 ♑ 19	18 ♑ 10	08 ♑ 16	09 ♉ 44	20 ♎ 52	05 ♎ 40	17 ♐ 11	24 ♋ 49	26 ♈ 00
Nov 28, 1933	18 ♑ 46	22 ♑ 15	11 ♑ 54	07 ♉ 42	24 ♎ 16	09 ♎ 57	21 ♐ 04	22 ♋ 56	24 ♈ 37
Dec 8, 1933	24 ♑ 14	26 ♑ 28	15 ♑ 41	06 ♉ 28	27 ♎ 33	14 ♎ 08	24 ♐ 58	20 ♋ 43	23 ♈ 58
Dec 18, 1933	29 ♑ 43	00 ♒ 48	19 ♑ 35	06 ♉ 08	00 ♏ 40	18 ♎ 40	28 ♐ 53	18 ♋ 22	24 ♈ 03
Dec 28, 1933	05 ♒ 12	05 ♒ 12	23 ♑ 35	06 ♉ 44	03 ♏ 36	21 ♎ 59	02 ♑ 48	16 ♋ 10	24 ♈ 49
Jan 7, 1934	10 ♒ 39	09 ♒ 41	27 ♑ 41	08 ♉ 10	06 ♏ 19	25 ♎ 35	06 ♑ 41	14 ♋ 21	26 ♈ 10
Jan 17, 1934	16 ♒ 06	14 ♒ 13	01 ♒ 51	10 ♉ 19	08 ♏ 45	28 ♎ 55	10 ♑ 32	13 ♋ 05	28 ♈ 03
Jan 27, 1934	21 ♒ 30	18 ♒ 47	06 ♒ 04	13 ♉ 05	10 ♏ 52	01 ♏ 52	14 ♑ 20	12 ♋ 27	00 ♉ 21
Feb 6, 1934	26 ♒ 53	23 ♒ 21	10 ♒ 20	16 ♉ 21	12 ♏ 37	04 ♏ 26	18 ♑ 02	12 ♋ 28	03 ♉ 02
Feb 16, 1934	02 ♓ 12	27 ♒ 56	14 ♒ 38	20 ♉ 01	13 ♏ 56	06 ♏ 29	21 ♑ 39	13 ♋ 07	05 ♉ 60
Feb 26, 1934	07 ♓ 28	02 ♓ 30	18 ♒ 57	24 ♉ 01	14 ♏ 45	07 ♏ 56	25 ♑ 09	14 ♋ 19	09 ♉ 12
Mar 8, 1934	12 ♓ 41	07 ♓ 02	23 ♒ 16	28 ♉ 16	15 ♏ 01	08 ♏ 43	28 ♑ 30	16 ♋ 01	12 ♉ 37
Mar 18, 1934	17 ♓ 50	11 ♓ 32	27 ♒ 35	02 ♊ 45	14 ♏ 43	08 ♏ 45	01 ♒ 41	18 ♋ 09	16 ♉ 11
Mar 28, 1934	22 ♓ 54	15 ♓ 58	01 ♓ 53	07 ♊ 24	13 ♏ 50	08 ♏ 02	04 ♒ 40	20 ♋ 39	19 ♉ 52
Apr 7, 1934	27 ♓ 54	20 ♓ 20	06 ♓ 08	12 ♊ 12	12 ♏ 25	06 ♏ 38	07 ♒ 25	23 ♋ 26	23 ♉ 40
Apr 17, 1934	02 ♈ 48	24 ♓ 38	10 ♓ 21	17 ♊ 06	10 ♏ 33	04 ♏ 42	09 ♒ 54	26 ♋ 30	27 ♉ 33
Apr 27, 1934	07 ♈ 37	28 ♓ 49	14 ♓ 29	22 ♊ 05	08 ♏ 26	02 ♏ 31	12 ♒ 04	29 ♋ 46	01 ♊ 30
May 7, 1934	12 ♈ 19	02 ♈ 53	18 ♓ 33	27 ♊ 08	06 ♏ 15	00 ♏ 25	13 ♒ 15	03 ♋ 13	05 ♊ 29

	ATROPOS	HEKATE	LILITH	MEDUSA	MOIRA	NEMESIS	PERSEPHONE	PROSERPINA	PYTHIA
May 17, 1934	16 ♈ 54	06 ♈ 49	22 ♓ 30	02 ♋ 15	28 ♎ 42	04 ♏ 14	15 ♒ 18	06 ♋ 49	09 ♊ 31
May 27, 1934	21 ♈ 22	10 ♈ 35	26 ♓ 20	07 ♋ 24	27 ♎ 35	02 ♏ 33	16 ♒ 15	10 ♋ 32	13 ♊ 34
Jun 6, 1934	25 ♈ 41	14 ♈ 10	29 ♓ 60	12 ♋ 35	27 ♎ 12	01 ♏ 22	16 ♒ 43	14 ♋ 22	17 ♊ 37
Jun 16, 1934	29 ♈ 50	17 ♈ 32	03 ♈ 28	17 ♋ 47	27 ♎ 34	00 ♏ 44	16 ♒ 38	18 ♋ 18	21 ♊ 41
Jun 26, 1934	03 ♉ 48	20 ♈ 39	06 ♈ 42	22 ♋ 59	28 ♎ 39	00 ♏ 41	16 ♒ 01	22 ♋ 18	25 ♊ 44
Jul 6, 1934	07 ♉ 33	23 ♈ 29	09 ♈ 38	28 ♋ 12	00 ♏ 22	01 ♏ 10	14 ♒ 52	26 ♋ 21	29 ♊ 45
Jul 16, 1934	11 ♉ 03	25 ♈ 59	12 ♈ 13	03 ♌ 25	02 ♏ 11	02 ♏ 11	13 ♒ 16	00 ♌ 27	03 ♋ 45
Jul 26, 1934	14 ♉ 16	28 ♈ 05	14 ♈ 22	08 ♌ 38	05 ♏ 23	03 ♏ 39	11 ♒ 22	04 ♌ 36	07 ♋ 43
Aug 5, 1934	17 ♉ 08	29 ♈ 45	15 ♈ 60	13 ♌ 49	08 ♏ 32	05 ♏ 31	09 ♒ 19	08 ♌ 46	11 ♋ 38
Aug 15, 1934	19 ♉ 35	00 ♉ 54	17 ♈ 02	19 ♌ 00	11 ♏ 60	07 ♏ 45	07 ♒ 20	12 ♌ 57	15 ♋ 29
Aug 25, 1934	21 ♉ 33	01 ♉ 29	17 ♈ 22	24 ♌ 10	15 ♏ 45	10 ♏ 17	05 ♒ 36	17 ♌ 09	19 ♋ 14
Sep 4, 1934	22 ♉ 58	01 ♉ 27	16 ♈ 58	29 ♌ 17	19 ♏ 44	13 ♏ 05	04 ♒ 16	21 ♌ 20	22 ♋ 54
Sep 14, 1934	23 ♉ 43	00 ♉ 48	15 ♈ 50	04 ♍ 23	23 ♏ 54	16 ♏ 06	03 ♒ 25	25 ♌ 30	26 ♋ 26
Sep 24, 1934	23 ♉ 43	29 ♈ 34	14 ♈ 04	09 ♍ 26	28 ♏ 14	19 ♏ 20	03 ♒ 06	29 ♌ 38	29 ♋ 50
Oct 4, 1934	22 ♉ 56	27 ♈ 51	11 ♈ 54	14 ♍ 26	02 ♐ 42	22 ♏ 43	03 ♒ 20	03 ♍ 43	03 ♌ 02
Oct 14, 1934	21 ♉ 22	25 ♈ 49	09 ♈ 37	19 ♍ 21	07 ♐ 16	26 ♏ 16	04 ♒ 04	07 ♍ 45	06 ♌ 00
Oct 24, 1934	19 ♉ 07	23 ♈ 43	07 ♈ 37	24 ♍ 12	11 ♐ 55	29 ♏ 56	05 ♒ 16	11 ♍ 41	08 ♌ 42
Nov 3, 1934	16 ♉ 24	21 ♈ 46	06 ♈ 10	28 ♍ 58	16 ♐ 39	03 ♐ 42	06 ♒ 53	15 ♍ 31	11 ♌ 04
Nov 13, 1934	13 ♉ 32	20 ♈ 12	05 ♈ 28	03 ♎ 37	21 ♐ 25	07 ♐ 33	08 ♒ 51	19 ♍ 12	13 ♌ 02
Nov 23, 1934	10 ♉ 54	19 ♈ 09	05 ♈ 36	08 ♎ 30	26 ♐ 14	11 ♐ 29	11 ♒ 08	22 ♍ 43	14 ♌ 31
Dec 3, 1934	08 ♉ 47	18 ♈ 41	06 ♈ 33	12 ♎ 30	01 ♑ 03	15 ♐ 41	13 ♒ 41	26 ♍ 01	15 ♌ 25
Dec 13, 1934	07 ♉ 23	18 ♈ 50	08 ♈ 15	16 ♎ 40	05 ♑ 54	19 ♐ 29	16 ♒ 27	29 ♍ 03	15 ♌ 41
Dec 23, 1934	06 ♉ 47	19 ♈ 33	10 ♈ 36	20 ♎ 37	10 ♑ 44	23 ♐ 31	19 ♒ 25	01 ♎ 46	15 ♌ 13
Jan 2, 1935	06 ♉ 57	20 ♈ 47	13 ♈ 31	24 ♎ 17	15 ♑ 33	27 ♐ 35	22 ♒ 32	04 ♎ 05	14 ♌ 01
Jan 12, 1935	07 ♉ 49	22 ♈ 29	16 ♈ 54	27 ♎ 38	20 ♑ 20	01 ♑ 39	25 ♒ 46	05 ♎ 56	12 ♌ 07
Jan 22, 1935	09 ♉ 19	24 ♈ 34	20 ♈ 41	00 ♏ 36	25 ♑ 04	05 ♑ 39	29 ♒ 06	07 ♎ 15	09 ♌ 42
Feb 1, 1935	11 ♉ 20	26 ♈ 58	24 ♈ 47	03 ♏ 06	29 ♑ 45	09 ♑ 38	02 ♓ 31	07 ♎ 57	07 ♌ 01
Feb 11, 1935	13 ♉ 47	29 ♈ 39	29 ♈ 09	05 ♏ 03	04 ♒ 22	13 ♑ 34	05 ♓ 59	07 ♎ 57	04 ♌ 23
Feb 21, 1935	16 ♉ 36	02 ♉ 34	03 ♉ 43	06 ♏ 12	08 ♒ 54	17 ♑ 25	09 ♓ 20	07 ♎ 15	02 ♌ 08
Mar 3, 1935	19 ♉ 42	05 ♉ 39	08 ♉ 28	06 ♏ 57	13 ♒ 20	21 ♑ 10	12 ♓ 60	05 ♎ 52	00 ♌ 29
Mar 13, 1935	23 ♉ 03	08 ♉ 53	13 ♉ 21	06 ♏ 45	17 ♒ 40	24 ♑ 48	16 ♓ 31	03 ♎ 55	29 ♋ 34
Mar 23, 1935	26 ♉ 35	12 ♉ 14	18 ♉ 20	05 ♏ 43	21 ♒ 51	28 ♑ 17	20 ♓ 01	01 ♎ 40	29 ♋ 26
Apr 2, 1935	00 ♊ 17	15 ♉ 40	23 ♉ 25	03 ♏ 56	25 ♒ 54	01 ♒ 36	23 ♓ 28	29 ♍ 22	00 ♌ 02
Apr 12, 1935	04 ♊ 06	19 ♉ 09	28 ♉ 33	01 ♏ 33	29 ♒ 47	04 ♒ 41	26 ♓ 53	27 ♍ 20	01 ♌ 18
Apr 22, 1935	08 ♊ 00	22 ♉ 42	03 ♊ 43	28 ♎ 53	03 ♓ 28	07 ♒ 30	00 ♈ 13	25 ♍ 48	03 ♌ 09

	ATROPOS	HEKATE	LILITH	MEDUSA	MOIRA	NEMESIS	PERSEPHONE	PROSERPINA	PYTHIA
May 2, 1935	11 ♊ 59	26 ♉ 16	08 ♊ 55	26 ♎ 17	06 ♓ 56	10 ♒ 02	03 ♈ 28	24 ♍ 55	05 ♌ 31
May 12, 1935	16 ♊ 02	29 ♉ 51	14 ♊ 08	24 ♎ 04	10 ♓ 04	12 ♒ 31	06 ♈ 37	24 ♍ 45	08 ♌ 19
May 22, 1935	20 ♊ 07	03 ♊ 25	19 ♊ 21	22 ♎ 29	13 ♓ 04	13 ♒ 55	09 ♈ 37	25 ♍ 17	11 ♌ 28
Jun 1, 1935	24 ♊ 13	06 ♊ 58	24 ♊ 33	21 ♎ 40	15 ♓ 39	15 ♒ 09	12 ♈ 29	26 ♍ 28	14 ♌ 56
Jun 11, 1935	28 ♊ 21	10 ♊ 29	29 ♊ 44	21 ♎ 38	17 ♓ 51	15 ♒ 50	15 ♈ 10	26 ♍ 14	18 ♌ 41
Jun 21, 1935	02 ♋ 28	13 ♊ 57	04 ♋ 54	22 ♎ 21	19 ♓ 37	15 ♒ 54	17 ♈ 38	00 ♎ 30	22 ♌ 39
Jul 1, 1935	06 ♋ 36	17 ♊ 21	10 ♋ 01	23 ♎ 44	20 ♓ 52	15 ♒ 19	19 ♈ 50	03 ♎ 11	26 ♌ 50
Jul 11, 1935	10 ♋ 42	20 ♊ 41	15 ♋ 06	25 ♎ 41	21 ♓ 34	14 ♒ 07	21 ♈ 45	06 ♎ 14	01 ♍ 10
Jul 21, 1935	14 ♋ 46	23 ♊ 55	20 ♋ 08	28 ♎ 08	21 ♓ 40	12 ♒ 23	23 ♈ 20	09 ♎ 36	05 ♍ 41
Jul 31, 1935	18 ♋ 48	27 ♊ 03	25 ♋ 06	01 ♏ 00	21 ♓ 07	10 ♒ 17	24 ♈ 31	13 ♎ 14	10 ♍ 19
Aug 10, 1935	22 ♋ 48	00 ♋ 02	29 ♋ 60	04 ♏ 13	19 ♓ 57	08 ♒ 03	25 ♈ 16	17 ♎ 05	15 ♍ 05
Aug 20, 1935	26 ♋ 43	02 ♋ 51	04 ♌ 49	07 ♏ 44	18 ♓ 15	06 ♒ 03	25 ♈ 31	21 ♎ 07	19 ♍ 58
Aug 30, 1935	00 ♌ 34	05 ♋ 29	09 ♌ 32	11 ♏ 30	16 ♓ 10	04 ♒ 25	25 ♈ 14	25 ♎ 20	24 ♍ 57
Sep 9, 1935	04 ♌ 19	07 ♋ 54	14 ♌ 10	15 ♏ 29	13 ♓ 54	03 ♒ 22	24 ♈ 25	29 ♎ 40	00 ♎ 01
Sep 19, 1935	07 ♌ 56	10 ♋ 03	18 ♌ 41	19 ♏ 40	11 ♓ 43	02 ♒ 60	23 ♈ 06	04 ♏ 08	05 ♎ 10
Sep 29, 1935	11 ♌ 26	11 ♋ 59	23 ♌ 03	23 ♏ 59	09 ♓ 50	03 ♒ 20	21 ♈ 22	08 ♏ 42	10 ♎ 24
Oct 9, 1935	14 ♌ 45	13 ♋ 24	27 ♌ 17	28 ♏ 27	08 ♓ 25	04 ♒ 20	19 ♈ 21	13 ♏ 21	15 ♎ 41
Oct 19, 1935	17 ♌ 51	14 ♋ 29	01 ♍ 19	03 ♐ 03	07 ♓ 35	05 ♒ 56	17 ♈ 15	18 ♏ 04	21 ♎ 02
Oct 29, 1935	20 ♌ 42	15 ♋ 07	05 ♍ 09	07 ♐ 44	07 ♓ 22	08 ♒ 05	15 ♈ 16	22 ♏ 50	26 ♎ 26
Nov 8, 1935	23 ♌ 15	15 ♋ 15	08 ♍ 43	12 ♐ 31	07 ♓ 46	10 ♒ 42	13 ♈ 37	27 ♏ 39	01 ♏ 51
Nov 18, 1935	25 ♌ 26	14 ♋ 52	12 ♍ 01	17 ♐ 22	08 ♓ 43	13 ♒ 44	12 ♈ 25	02 ♐ 30	07 ♏ 19
Nov 28, 1935	27 ♌ 11	13 ♋ 57	14 ♍ 58	22 ♐ 17	10 ♓ 09	17 ♒ 06	11 ♈ 45	07 ♐ 22	12 ♏ 47
Dec 8, 1935	28 ♌ 24	12 ♋ 33	17 ♍ 31	27 ♐ 16	12 ♓ 01	20 ♒ 46	11 ♈ 39	12 ♐ 15	18 ♏ 16
Dec 18, 1935	29 ♌ 01	10 ♋ 47	19 ♍ 37	02 ♑ 17	14 ♓ 16	24 ♒ 40	12 ♈ 07	17 ♐ 07	23 ♏ 44
Dec 28, 1935	28 ♌ 58	08 ♋ 47	21 ♍ 10	07 ♑ 20	16 ♓ 49	28 ♒ 47	13 ♈ 06	21 ♐ 58	29 ♏ 10
Jan 7, 1936	28 ♌ 10	06 ♋ 44	22 ♍ 06	12 ♑ 24	19 ♓ 37	03 ♓ 05	14 ♈ 33	26 ♐ 46	04 ♐ 35
Jan 17, 1936	26 ♌ 39	04 ♋ 51	22 ♍ 22	17 ♑ 29	22 ♓ 38	07 ♓ 32	16 ♈ 25	01 ♑ 32	09 ♐ 56
Jan 27, 1936	24 ♌ 29	03 ♋ 17	21 ♍ 55	22 ♑ 34	25 ♓ 50	12 ♓ 06	18 ♈ 38	06 ♑ 14	15 ♐ 12
Feb 6, 1936	21 ♌ 52	02 ♋ 09	20 ♍ 46	27 ♑ 39	29 ♓ 10	16 ♓ 45	21 ♈ 09	10 ♑ 51	20 ♐ 23
Feb 16, 1936	19 ♌ 04	01 ♋ 31	19 ♍ 01	02 ♒ 42	02 ♈ 37	21 ♓ 30	23 ♈ 55	15 ♑ 22	25 ♐ 27
Feb 26, 1936	16 ♌ 25	01 ♋ 24	16 ♍ 48	07 ♒ 45	06 ♈ 09	26 ♓ 18	26 ♈ 54	19 ♑ 46	00 ♑ 22
Mar 7, 1936	14 ♌ 11	01 ♋ 47	14 ♍ 25	12 ♒ 44	09 ♈ 44	01 ♈ 08	00 ♉ 04	24 ♑ 02	05 ♑ 06
Mar 17, 1936	12 ♌ 36	02 ♋ 37	12 ♍ 06	17 ♒ 41	13 ♈ 22	06 ♈ 06	03 ♉ 23	28 ♑ 07	09 ♑ 37
Mar 27, 1936	11 ♌ 44	03 ♋ 52	10 ♍ 08	22 ♒ 34	17 ♈ 02	10 ♈ 54	06 ♉ 49	02 ♒ 01	13 ♑ 53
Apr 6, 1936	11 ♌ 36	05 ♋ 27	08 ♍ 42	27 ♒ 23	20 ♈ 42	15 ♈ 47	10 ♉ 20	05 ♒ 41	17 ♑ 50

	ATROPOS	HEKATE	LILITH	MEDUSA	MOIRA	NEMESIS	PERSEPHONE	PROSERPINA	PYTHIA
Apr 16, 1936	12 ♌ 11	07 ♋ 22	07 ♍ 52	02 ♓ 06	24 ♈ 22	20 ♈ 40	13 ♉ 56	09 ♒ 05	21 ♑ 25
Apr 26, 1936	13 ♌ 22	09 ♋ 31	07 ♍ 41	06 ♓ 42	28 ♈ 00	25 ♈ 31	17 ♉ 36	12 ♒ 11	24 ♑ 34
May 6, 1936	15 ♌ 07	11 ♋ 54	08 ♍ 06	11 ♓ 11	01 ♉ 37	00 ♉ 37	21 ♉ 18	14 ♒ 55	27 ♑ 10
May 16, 1936	17 ♌ 20	14 ♋ 27	09 ♍ 05	15 ♓ 31	05 ♉ 10	05 ♉ 09	25 ♉ 02	17 ♒ 14	29 ♑ 09
May 26, 1936	19 ♌ 57	17 ♋ 10	10 ♍ 32	19 ♓ 39	08 ♉ 39	09 ♉ 53	28 ♉ 46	19 ♒ 03	00 ♒ 25
Jun 5, 1936	22 ♌ 54	19 ♋ 59	12 ♍ 24	23 ♓ 34	12 ♉ 04	14 ♉ 33	02 ♊ 31	20 ♒ 19	00 ♒ 52
Jun 15, 1936	26 ♌ 10	22 ♋ 55	14 ♍ 37	27 ♓ 12	15 ♉ 22	19 ♉ 09	06 ♊ 14	20 ♒ 58	00 ♒ 27
Jun 25, 1936	29 ♌ 40	25 ♋ 55	17 ♍ 07	00 ♈ 32	18 ♉ 34	23 ♉ 39	09 ♊ 56	20 ♒ 57	29 ♑ 11
Jul 5, 1936	03 ♍ 24	28 ♋ 59	19 ♍ 52	03 ♈ 28	21 ♉ 37	28 ♉ 03	13 ♊ 35	20 ♒ 15	27 ♑ 14
Jul 15, 1936	07 ♍ 19	02 ♌ 05	22 ♍ 49	05 ♈ 55	24 ♉ 31	02 ♊ 20	17 ♊ 10	18 ♒ 54	24 ♑ 52
Jul 25, 1936	11 ♍ 26	05 ♌ 12	25 ♍ 56	07 ♈ 49	27 ♉ 12	06 ♊ 27	20 ♊ 41	17 ♒ 02	22 ♑ 26
Aug 4, 1936	15 ♍ 41	08 ♌ 20	29 ♍ 11	09 ♈ 02	29 ♉ 40	10 ♊ 24	24 ♊ 06	14 ♒ 51	20 ♑ 21
Aug 14, 1936	20 ♍ 05	11 ♌ 28	02 ♎ 34	09 ♈ 30	01 ♊ 51	14 ♊ 09	27 ♊ 23	12 ♒ 38	18 ♑ 53
Aug 24, 1936	24 ♍ 37	14 ♌ 34	06 ♎ 01	09 ♈ 06	03 ♊ 44	17 ♊ 39	00 ♋ 32	10 ♒ 37	18 ♑ 13
Sep 3, 1936	29 ♍ 16	17 ♌ 37	09 ♎ 34	07 ♈ 52	05 ♊ 14	20 ♊ 52	03 ♋ 29	09 ♒ 03	18 ♑ 23
Sep 13, 1936	04 ♎ 09	20 ♌ 37	13 ♎ 09	05 ♈ 53	06 ♊ 18	23 ♊ 44	06 ♋ 14	08 ♒ 06	19 ♑ 21
Sep 23, 1936	08 ♎ 55	23 ♌ 33	16 ♎ 48	03 ♈ 23	06 ♊ 53	26 ♊ 12	08 ♋ 42	07 ♒ 47	21 ♑ 01
Oct 3, 1936	13 ♎ 53	26 ♌ 22	20 ♎ 27	00 ♈ 46	06 ♊ 56	28 ♊ 12	10 ♋ 51	08 ♒ 09	23 ♑ 18
Oct 13, 1936	18 ♎ 57	29 ♌ 03	24 ♎ 08	28 ♓ 25	06 ♊ 25	29 ♊ 39	12 ♋ 38	09 ♒ 07	26 ♑ 06
Oct 23, 1936	24 ♎ 07	01 ♍ 35	27 ♎ 48	26 ♓ 42	05 ♊ 19	00 ♋ 27	13 ♋ 57	10 ♒ 39	29 ♑ 19
Nov 2, 1936	29 ♎ 21	03 ♍ 54	01 ♏ 28	25 ♓ 49	03 ♊ 42	00 ♋ 34	14 ♋ 46	12 ♒ 40	02 ♒ 54
Nov 12, 1936	04 ♏ 39	06 ♍ 00	05 ♏ 05	25 ♓ 51	01 ♊ 41	29 ♊ 57	15 ♋ 01	15 ♒ 05	06 ♒ 46
Nov 22, 1936	10 ♏ 01	07 ♍ 49	08 ♏ 39	26 ♓ 45	29 ♉ 27	28 ♊ 38	14 ♋ 38	17 ♒ 51	10 ♒ 52
Dec 2, 1936	15 ♏ 27	09 ♍ 18	12 ♏ 10	28 ♓ 27	27 ♉ 13	26 ♊ 44	13 ♋ 38	20 ♒ 56	15 ♒ 09
Dec 12, 1936	20 ♏ 56	10 ♍ 25	15 ♏ 34	00 ♈ 50	25 ♉ 12	24 ♊ 29	12 ♋ 05	24 ♒ 14	19 ♒ 36
Dec 22, 1936	26 ♏ 26	11 ♍ 06	18 ♏ 52	03 ♈ 48	23 ♉ 36	22 ♊ 08	10 ♋ 06	27 ♒ 45	24 ♒ 10
Jan 1, 1937	01 ♐ 58	11 ♍ 18	22 ♏ 02	07 ♈ 15	22 ♉ 32	20 ♊ 01	07 ♋ 54	01 ♓ 26	28 ♒ 50
Jan 11, 1937	07 ♐ 30	11 ♍ 59	25 ♏ 02	11 ♈ 06	22 ♉ 03	18 ♊ 23	05 ♋ 45	05 ♓ 15	03 ♓ 33
Jan 21, 1937	13 ♐ 02	10 ♍ 10	27 ♏ 49	15 ♈ 16	22 ♉ 10	17 ♊ 22	03 ♋ 52	09 ♓ 10	08 ♓ 20
Jan 31, 1937	18 ♐ 31	08 ♍ 53	00 ♐ 28	19 ♈ 42	22 ♉ 50	17 ♊ 04	02 ♋ 28	13 ♓ 11	13 ♓ 09
Feb 10, 1937	23 ♐ 58	07 ♍ 12	02 ♐ 38	24 ♈ 22	24 ♉ 00	17 ♊ 26	01 ♋ 39	17 ♓ 15	17 ♓ 59
Feb 20, 1937	29 ♐ 20	05 ♍ 16	04 ♐ 34	29 ♈ 12	25 ♉ 38	18 ♊ 26	01 ♋ 29	21 ♓ 21	22 ♓ 49
Mar 2, 1937	04 ♑ 35	03 ♍ 16	06 ♐ 07	04 ♉ 16	27 ♉ 38	19 ♊ 60	01 ♋ 56	25 ♓ 30	27 ♓ 39
Mar 12, 1937	09 ♑ 41	01 ♍ 21	07 ♐ 15	09 ♉ 16	29 ♉ 58	22 ♊ 02	02 ♋ 57	29 ♓ 38	02 ♈ 27
Mar 22, 1937	14 ♑ 36	29 ♌ 43	07 ♐ 52	14 ♉ 28	02 ♊ 34	24 ♊ 27	04 ♋ 30	03 ♈ 47	07 ♈ 13

	ATROPOS	HEKATE	LILITH	MEDUSA	MOIRA	NEMESIS	PERSEPHONE	PROSERPINA	PYTHIA
Apr 1, 1937	19 ♑ 17	28 ♌ 28	07 ♐ 58	19 ♉ 43	05 ♊ 24	27 ♊ 12	06 ♋ 28	07 ♈ 55	11 ♈ 57
Apr 11, 1937	23 ♑ 40	27 ♌ 43	07 ♐ 29	25 ♉ 02	08 ♊ 26	00 ♋ 14	08 ♋ 50	12 ♈ 01	16 ♈ 38
Apr 21, 1937	27 ♑ 42	27 ♌ 27	06 ♐ 28	00 ♊ 24	11 ♊ 38	03 ♋ 29	11 ♋ 31	16 ♈ 04	21 ♈ 16
May 1, 1937	01 ♒ 17	27 ♌ 42	04 ♐ 56	05 ♊ 47	14 ♊ 58	06 ♋ 54	14 ♋ 28	20 ♈ 04	25 ♈ 49
May 11, 1937	04 ♒ 21	28 ♌ 25	02 ♐ 60	11 ♊ 12	18 ♊ 24	10 ♋ 28	17 ♋ 38	24 ♈ 00	00 ♉ 17
May 21, 1937	06 ♒ 45	29 ♌ 33	00 ♐ 50	16 ♊ 38	21 ♊ 56	14 ♋ 09	21 ♋ 00	27 ♈ 51	04 ♉ 41
May 31, 1937	08 ♒ 25	01 ♍ 04	28 ♏ 39	22 ♊ 03	25 ♊ 33	17 ♋ 56	24 ♋ 31	01 ♉ 37	08 ♉ 58
Jun 10, 1937	09 ♒ 12	02 ♍ 55	26 ♏ 38	27 ♊ 29	29 ♊ 13	21 ♋ 46	28 ♋ 10	05 ♉ 15	13 ♉ 09
Jun 20, 1937	09 ♒ 02	05 ♍ 03	24 ♏ 58	02 ♋ 54	02 ♋ 56	25 ♋ 41	01 ♌ 56	08 ♉ 45	17 ♉ 13
Jun 30, 1937	07 ♒ 56	07 ♍ 26	23 ♏ 46	08 ♋ 18	06 ♋ 40	29 ♋ 37	05 ♌ 47	12 ♉ 07	21 ♉ 07
Jul 10, 1937	05 ♒ 59	10 ♍ 02	23 ♏ 06	13 ♋ 41	10 ♋ 26	03 ♌ 35	09 ♌ 42	15 ♉ 17	24 ♉ 52
Jul 20, 1937	03 ♒ 29	12 ♍ 49	23 ♏ 00	19 ♋ 02	14 ♋ 12	07 ♌ 34	13 ♌ 40	18 ♉ 14	28 ♉ 26
Jul 30, 1937	00 ♒ 50	15 ♍ 46	23 ♏ 26	24 ♋ 22	17 ♋ 58	11 ♌ 33	17 ♌ 42	20 ♉ 56	01 ♊ 47
Aug 9, 1937	28 ♑ 27	18 ♍ 50	24 ♏ 22	29 ♋ 39	21 ♋ 44	15 ♌ 31	21 ♌ 45	23 ♉ 20	04 ♊ 53
Aug 19, 1937	26 ♑ 41	22 ♍ 01	25 ♏ 44	04 ♌ 53	25 ♋ 27	19 ♌ 28	25 ♌ 49	25 ♉ 23	07 ♊ 41
Aug 29, 1937	25 ♑ 46	25 ♍ 18	27 ♏ 30	10 ♌ 05	29 ♋ 07	23 ♌ 23	29 ♌ 53	27 ♉ 01	10 ♊ 08
Sep 8, 1937	25 ♑ 42	28 ♍ 39	29 ♏ 37	15 ♌ 13	02 ♌ 44	27 ♌ 16	03 ♍ 58	28 ♉ 12	12 ♊ 11
Sep 18, 1937	26 ♑ 29	02 ♎ 04	02 ♐ 02	20 ♌ 16	06 ♌ 16	01 ♍ 05	08 ♍ 01	28 ♉ 50	13 ♊ 46
Sep 28, 1937	27 ♑ 60	05 ♎ 31	04 ♐ 43	25 ♌ 14	09 ♌ 41	04 ♍ 49	12 ♍ 02	28 ♉ 52	14 ♊ 47
Oct 8, 1937	00 ♒ 09	09 ♎ 01	07 ♐ 37	00 ♍ 06	12 ♌ 58	08 ♍ 28	16 ♍ 01	28 ♉ 17	15 ♊ 11
Oct 18, 1937	02 ♒ 50	12 ♎ 31	10 ♐ 42	04 ♍ 51	16 ♌ 05	11 ♍ 59	19 ♍ 55	27 ♉ 05	14 ♊ 53
Oct 28, 1937	05 ♒ 56	16 ♎ 01	13 ♐ 58	09 ♍ 28	18 ♌ 59	15 ♍ 23	23 ♍ 45	25 ♉ 21	13 ♊ 53
Nov 7, 1937	09 ♒ 24	19 ♎ 30	17 ♐ 22	13 ♍ 54	21 ♌ 37	18 ♍ 36	27 ♍ 28	23 ♉ 12	12 ♊ 11
Nov 17, 1937	13 ♒ 10	22 ♎ 56	20 ♐ 53	18 ♍ 08	23 ♌ 56	21 ♍ 37	01 ♎ 03	20 ♉ 53	09 ♊ 56
Nov 27, 1937	17 ♒ 10	26 ♎ 19	24 ♐ 30	22 ♍ 08	25 ♌ 52	24 ♍ 23	04 ♎ 28	18 ♉ 38	07 ♊ 21
Dec 7, 1937	21 ♒ 21	29 ♎ 36	28 ♐ 12	25 ♍ 50	27 ♌ 20	26 ♍ 53	07 ♎ 41	16 ♉ 43	04 ♊ 43
Dec 17, 1937	25 ♒ 42	02 ♏ 47	01 ♑ 58	29 ♍ 12	28 ♌ 16	29 ♍ 01	10 ♎ 39	15 ♉ 18	02 ♊ 20
Dec 27, 1937	00 ♓ 10	05 ♏ 49	05 ♑ 46	02 ♎ 08	28 ♌ 35	00 ♎ 46	13 ♎ 20	14 ♉ 29	00 ♊ 27
Jan 6, 1938	04 ♓ 45	08 ♏ 41	09 ♑ 37	04 ♎ 34	28 ♌ 14	02 ♎ 03	15 ♎ 40	14 ♉ 19	29 ♉ 13
Jan 16, 1938	09 ♓ 24	11 ♏ 20	13 ♑ 28	06 ♎ 24	27 ♌ 12	02 ♎ 49	17 ♎ 36	14 ♉ 47	28 ♉ 41
Jan 26, 1938	14 ♓ 06	13 ♏ 42	17 ♑ 19	07 ♎ 33	25 ♌ 33	03 ♎ 00	19 ♎ 03	15 ♉ 49	28 ♉ 51
Feb 5, 1938	18 ♓ 51	15 ♏ 47	21 ♑ 09	07 ♎ 55	23 ♌ 25	02 ♎ 35	19 ♎ 57	17 ♉ 21	29 ♉ 40
Feb 15, 1938	23 ♓ 38	17 ♏ 29	24 ♑ 57	07 ♎ 26	21 ♌ 04	01 ♎ 33	20 ♎ 15	19 ♉ 20	01 ♊ 03
Feb 25, 1938	28 ♓ 25	18 ♏ 45	28 ♑ 42	06 ♎ 06	18 ♌ 45	29 ♍ 59	19 ♎ 56	21 ♉ 41	02 ♊ 56
Mar 7, 1938	03 ♈ 13	19 ♏ 32	02 ♒ 22	04 ♎ 02	16 ♌ 46	27 ♍ 59	18 ♎ 59	24 ♉ 21	05 ♊ 13

	ATROPOS	HEKATE	LILITH	MEDUSA	MOIRA	NEMESIS	PERSEPHONE	PROSERPINA	PYTHIA
Mar 17, 1938	08 ♈ 01	19 ♏ 47	05 ♒ 57	01 ♎ 27	15 ♌ 21	25 ♍ 47	17 ♎ 28	27 ♉ 17	07 ♊ 51
Mar 27, 1938	12 ♈ 47	19 ♏ 29	09 ♒ 26	28 ♍ 44	14 ♌ 37	23 ♍ 34	15 ♎ 33	00 ♊ 26	10 ♊ 46
Apr 6, 1938	17 ♈ 32	18 ♏ 35	12 ♒ 45	26 ♍ 13	14 ♌ 36	21 ♍ 36	13 ♎ 25	03 ♊ 47	13 ♊ 56
Apr 16, 1938	22 ♈ 15	17 ♏ 12	15 ♒ 55	24 ♍ 14	15 ♌ 17	20 ♍ 01	11 ♎ 19	07 ♊ 16	17 ♊ 18
Apr 26, 1938	26 ♈ 55	15 ♏ 24	18 ♒ 52	22 ♍ 59	16 ♌ 36	18 ♍ 59	09 ♎ 30	10 ♊ 52	20 ♊ 50
May 6, 1938	01 ♉ 33	13 ♏ 20	21 ♒ 34	22 ♍ 33	18 ♌ 29	18 ♍ 31	08 ♎ 09	14 ♊ 35	24 ♊ 31
May 16, 1938	06 ♉ 06	11 ♏ 20	23 ♒ 59	22 ♍ 54	20 ♌ 52	18 ♍ 52	07 ♎ 21	18 ♊ 22	28 ♊ 18
May 26, 1938	10 ♉ 36	09 ♏ 31	26 ♒ 03	23 ♍ 58	23 ♌ 40	19 ♍ 16	07 ♎ 10	22 ♊ 14	02 ♋ 11
Jun 5, 1938	15 ♉ 00	08 ♏ 05	27 ♒ 42	25 ♍ 40	26 ♌ 50	20 ♍ 23	07 ♎ 36	26 ♊ 08	06 ♋ 09
Jun 15, 1938	19 ♉ 20	06 ♏ 10	28 ♒ 52	27 ♍ 54	00 ♍ 18	21 ♍ 57	08 ♎ 34	00 ♋ 05	10 ♋ 11
Jun 25, 1938	23 ♉ 32	06 ♏ 50	29 ♒ 29	00 ♎ 35	04 ♍ 02	23 ♍ 53	10 ♎ 03	04 ♋ 03	14 ♋ 16
Jul 5, 1938	27 ♉ 38	07 ♏ 55	29 ♒ 29	03 ♎ 38	07 ♍ 60	26 ♍ 08	11 ♎ 58	08 ♋ 02	18 ♋ 25
Jul 15, 1938	01 ♊ 35	07 ♏ 16	28 ♒ 51	07 ♎ 01	12 ♍ 09	28 ♍ 40	14 ♎ 15	12 ♋ 01	22 ♋ 35
Jul 25, 1938	05 ♊ 22	09 ♏ 16	27 ♒ 35	10 ♎ 39	16 ♍ 29	01 ♎ 25	16 ♎ 52	15 ♋ 60	26 ♋ 46
Aug 4, 1938	08 ♊ 57	11 ♏ 05	25 ♒ 46	14 ♎ 30	20 ♍ 57	04 ♎ 22	19 ♎ 45	19 ♋ 58	00 ♌ 59
Aug 14, 1938	12 ♊ 18	13 ♏ 18	23 ♒ 35	18 ♎ 32	25 ♍ 34	07 ♎ 30	22 ♎ 52	23 ♋ 53	05 ♌ 13
Aug 24, 1938	15 ♊ 24	15 ♏ 53	21 ♒ 16	22 ♎ 45	00 ♎ 17	10 ♎ 45	26 ♎ 11	27 ♋ 46	09 ♌ 26
Sep 3, 1938	18 ♊ 10	18 ♏ 48	19 ♒ 06	27 ♎ 05	05 ♎ 06	14 ♎ 08	29 ♎ 40	01 ♌ 35	13 ♌ 39
Sep 13, 1938	20 ♊ 32	21 ♏ 58	17 ♒ 21	01 ♏ 32	09 ♎ 60	17 ♎ 37	03 ♏ 17	05 ♌ 19	17 ♌ 50
Sep 23, 1938	22 ♊ 28	25 ♏ 23	16 ♒ 13	06 ♏ 06	14 ♎ 58	21 ♎ 11	07 ♏ 02	08 ♌ 57	21 ♌ 59
Oct 3, 1938	23 ♊ 51	29 ♏ 00	15 ♒ 47	10 ♏ 45	20 ♎ 00	24 ♎ 49	10 ♏ 52	12 ♌ 27	26 ♌ 05
Oct 13, 1938	24 ♊ 37	02 ♐ 48	16 ♒ 05	15 ♏ 28	25 ♎ 05	28 ♎ 29	14 ♏ 47	15 ♌ 48	00 ♍ 07
Oct 23, 1938	24 ♊ 40	06 ♐ 45	17 ♒ 05	20 ♏ 15	00 ♏ 13	02 ♏ 12	18 ♏ 45	18 ♌ 56	04 ♍ 03
Nov 2, 1938	23 ♊ 57	10 ♐ 50	18 ♒ 44	25 ♏ 05	05 ♏ 21	05 ♏ 55	22 ♏ 46	21 ♌ 50	07 ♍ 53
Nov 12, 1938	22 ♊ 28	15 ♐ 01	20 ♒ 57	29 ♏ 58	10 ♏ 34	09 ♏ 39	26 ♏ 49	24 ♌ 27	11 ♍ 33
Nov 22, 1938	20 ♊ 19	19 ♐ 18	23 ♒ 40	04 ♐ 53	15 ♏ 40	13 ♏ 22	00 ♐ 52	26 ♌ 42	15 ♍ 01
Dec 2, 1938	17 ♊ 40	23 ♐ 40	26 ♒ 49	09 ♐ 49	20 ♏ 49	17 ♏ 03	04 ♐ 56	28 ♌ 32	18 ♍ 15
Dec 12, 1938	14 ♊ 50	28 ♐ 06	00 ♓ 21	14 ♐ 46	25 ♏ 56	20 ♏ 41	08 ♐ 58	29 ♌ 52	21 ♍ 11
Dec 22, 1938	12 ♊ 09	02 ♑ 34	04 ♓ 12	19 ♐ 44	01 ♐ 00	24 ♏ 16	12 ♐ 58	00 ♍ 37	23 ♍ 45
Jan 1, 1939	09 ♊ 55	07 ♑ 05	08 ♓ 19	24 ♐ 41	06 ♐ 01	27 ♏ 44	16 ♐ 55	00 ♍ 44	25 ♍ 55
Jan 11, 1939	08 ♊ 20	11 ♑ 36	12 ♓ 40	29 ♐ 37	10 ♐ 57	01 ♐ 06	20 ♐ 47	00 ♍ 09	27 ♍ 26
Jan 21, 1939	07 ♊ 30	16 ♑ 07	17 ♓ 13	04 ♑ 31	15 ♐ 47	04 ♐ 19	24 ♐ 34	28 ♌ 54	28 ♍ 22
Jan 31, 1939	07 ♊ 26	21 ♑ 37	21 ♓ 56	09 ♑ 23	20 ♐ 30	07 ♐ 21	28 ♐ 14	27 ♌ 03	28 ♍ 34
Feb 10, 1939	08 ♊ 04	25 ♑ 06	26 ♓ 48	14 ♑ 12	25 ♐ 04	10 ♐ 11	01 ♑ 46	24 ♌ 50	27 ♍ 57
Feb 20, 1939	09 ♊ 18	29 ♑ 32	01 ♈ 48	18 ♑ 56	29 ♐ 27	12 ♐ 45	05 ♑ 07	22 ♌ 27	26 ♍ 33

	ATROPOS	HEKATE	LILITH	MEDUSA	MOIRA	NEMESIS	PERSEPHONE	PROSERPINA	PYTHIA
Mar 2, 1939	11 ♊ 04	03 ♒ 54	06 ♈ 53	23 ♑ 36	03 ♑ 38	15 ♐ 01	08 ♑ 17	20 ♌ 15	24 ♍ 27
Mar 12, 1939	13 ♊ 17	08 ♒ 11	12 ♈ 04	28 ♑ 10	07 ♑ 35	16 ♐ 56	11 ♑ 12	18 ♌ 27	21 ♍ 53
Mar 22, 1939	15 ♊ 52	12 ♒ 21	17 ♈ 18	02 ♒ 37	11 ♑ 31	18 ♐ 26	13 ♑ 52	17 ♌ 15	19 ♍ 11
Apr 1, 1939	18 ♊ 45	16 ♒ 25	22 ♈ 36	06 ♒ 55	14 ♑ 32	19 ♐ 28	16 ♑ 12	16 ♌ 44	16 ♍ 46
Apr 11, 1939	21 ♊ 52	20 ♒ 19	27 ♈ 56	11 ♒ 03	17 ♑ 27	19 ♐ 58	18 ♑ 10	16 ♌ 55	14 ♍ 55
Apr 21, 1939	25 ♊ 12	24 ♒ 03	03 ♉ 19	14 ♒ 59	19 ♑ 55	19 ♐ 54	19 ♑ 43	17 ♌ 45	13 ♍ 50
May 1, 1939	28 ♊ 42	27 ♒ 34	08 ♉ 42	18 ♒ 40	21 ♑ 50	19 ♐ 15	20 ♑ 48	19 ♌ 11	13 ♍ 37
May 11, 1939	02 ♋ 19	00 ♓ 51	14 ♉ 06	22 ♒ 04	23 ♑ 10	18 ♐ 01	21 ♑ 21	21 ♌ 08	14 ♍ 14
May 21, 1939	06 ♋ 04	03 ♓ 50	19 ♉ 29	25 ♒ 08	23 ♑ 49	16 ♐ 18	21 ♑ 21	23 ♌ 32	15 ♍ 37
May 31, 1939	09 ♋ 53	06 ♓ 28	24 ♉ 52	27 ♒ 46	23 ♑ 44	14 ♐ 14	20 ♑ 46	26 ♌ 19	17 ♍ 40
Jun 10, 1939	13 ♋ 47	08 ♓ 42	00 ♊ 13	29 ♒ 55	22 ♑ 57	12 ♐ 03	19 ♑ 39	29 ♌ 25	20 ♍ 17
Jun 20, 1939	17 ♋ 44	10 ♓ 28	05 ♊ 33	01 ♓ 29	21 ♑ 31	09 ♐ 57	18 ♑ 04	02 ♍ 48	23 ♍ 23
Jun 30, 1939	21 ♋ 44	11 ♓ 42	10 ♊ 50	02 ♓ 23	19 ♑ 34	08 ♐ 10	16 ♑ 09	06 ♍ 25	26 ♍ 55
Jul 10, 1939	25 ♋ 45	12 ♓ 21	16 ♊ 03	02 ♓ 31	17 ♑ 23	06 ♐ 50	14 ♑ 06	10 ♍ 13	00 ♎ 47
Jul 20, 1939	29 ♋ 48	12 ♓ 21	21 ♊ 13	01 ♓ 50	15 ♑ 13	06 ♐ 05	12 ♑ 06	14 ♍ 12	04 ♎ 56
Jul 30, 1939	03 ♌ 51	11 ♓ 43	26 ♊ 17	00 ♓ 21	13 ♑ 21	05 ♐ 57	10 ♑ 22	18 ♍ 20	09 ♎ 21
Aug 9, 1939	07 ♌ 55	10 ♓ 30	01 ♋ 16	28 ♒ 12	12 ♑ 01	06 ♐ 24	09 ♑ 04	22 ♍ 35	13 ♎ 59
Aug 19, 1939	11 ♌ 57	08 ♓ 47	06 ♋ 08	25 ♒ 40	11 ♑ 19	07 ♐ 25	08 ♑ 16	26 ♍ 57	18 ♎ 48
Aug 29, 1939	15 ♌ 59	06 ♓ 49	10 ♋ 51	23 ♒ 05	11 ♑ 17	08 ♐ 57	08 ♑ 01	01 ♎ 25	23 ♎ 47
Sep 8, 1939	19 ♌ 59	04 ♓ 49	15 ♋ 24	20 ♒ 50	11 ♑ 54	10 ♐ 55	08 ♑ 18	05 ♎ 34	28 ♎ 53
Sep 18, 1939	23 ♌ 56	03 ♓ 03	19 ♋ 46	19 ♒ 13	13 ♑ 08	13 ♐ 17	09 ♑ 07	10 ♎ 34	04 ♏ 08
Sep 28, 1939	27 ♌ 49	01 ♓ 43	23 ♋ 53	18 ♒ 25	14 ♑ 53	16 ♐ 00	10 ♑ 23	15 ♎ 14	09 ♏ 28
Oct 8, 1939	01 ♍ 38	00 ♓ 58	27 ♋ 44	18 ♒ 29	17 ♑ 05	19 ♐ 01	12 ♑ 05	19 ♎ 56	14 ♏ 54
Oct 18, 1939	05 ♍ 21	00 ♓ 51	01 ♌ 16	19 ♒ 24	19 ♑ 40	22 ♐ 17	14 ♑ 08	24 ♎ 41	20 ♏ 24
Oct 28, 1939	08 ♍ 56	01 ♓ 23	04 ♌ 23	21 ♒ 04	22 ♑ 35	25 ♐ 47	16 ♑ 29	29 ♎ 27	25 ♏ 59
Nov 7, 1939	12 ♍ 23	02 ♓ 30	07 ♌ 02	23 ♒ 23	25 ♑ 45	29 ♐ 28	19 ♑ 06	04 ♏ 14	01 ♐ 36
Nov 17, 1939	15 ♍ 38	04 ♓ 09	09 ♌ 08	26 ♒ 17	29 ♑ 10	03 ♑ 19	21 ♑ 57	09 ♏ 01	07 ♐ 16
Nov 27, 1939	18 ♍ 39	06 ♓ 16	10 ♌ 36	29 ♒ 39	02 ♒ 45	07 ♑ 19	24 ♑ 59	13 ♏ 47	12 ♐ 58
Dec 7, 1939	21 ♍ 23	08 ♓ 47	11 ♌ 19	03 ♓ 25	06 ♒ 30	11 ♑ 27	28 ♑ 10	18 ♏ 32	18 ♐ 41
Dec 17, 1939	23 ♍ 46	11 ♓ 38	11 ♌ 15	07 ♓ 31	10 ♒ 21	15 ♑ 40	01 ♒ 29	23 ♏ 14	24 ♐ 25
Dec 27, 1939	25 ♍ 44	14 ♓ 46	10 ♌ 22	11 ♓ 53	14 ♒ 19	19 ♑ 59	04 ♒ 54	27 ♏ 52	00 ♑ 08
Jan 6, 1940	27 ♍ 12	18 ♓ 08	08 ♌ 45	16 ♓ 30	18 ♒ 21	24 ♑ 22	08 ♒ 23	02 ♐ 25	05 ♑ 51
Jan 16, 1940	28 ♍ 04	21 ♓ 41	06 ♌ 35	21 ♓ 18	22 ♒ 26	28 ♑ 49	11 ♒ 56	06 ♐ 53	11 ♑ 32
Jan 26, 1940	28 ♍ 23	25 ♓ 23	04 ♌ 10	26 ♓ 16	26 ♒ 32	03 ♒ 18	15 ♒ 31	11 ♐ 13	17 ♑ 11
Feb 5, 1940	27 ♍ 42	29 ♓ 12	01 ♌ 49	01 ♈ 22	00 ♓ 40	07 ♒ 48	19 ♒ 07	15 ♐ 24	22 ♑ 48

	ATROPOS	HEKATE	LILITH	MEDUSA	MOIRA	NEMESIS	PERSEPHONE	PROSERPINA	PYTHIA
Feb 15, 1940	26 ♍ 22	03 ♈ 07	29 ♋ 52	06 ♈ 35	04 ♓ 48	12 ♒ 20	22 ♒ 43	19 ♐ 24	28 ♑ 21
Feb 25, 1940	24 ♍ 20	07 ♈ 06	28 ♋ 31	11 ♈ 53	08 ♓ 55	16 ♒ 51	26 ♒ 17	23 ♐ 11	03 ♒ 49
Mar 6, 1940	21 ♍ 45	11 ♈ 08	27 ♋ 54	17 ♈ 16	13 ♓ 01	21 ♒ 22	29 ♒ 50	26 ♐ 42	09 ♒ 13
Mar 16, 1940	18 ♍ 54	15 ♈ 11	27 ♋ 60	22 ♈ 42	17 ♓ 04	25 ♒ 51	03 ♓ 19	29 ♐ 55	14 ♒ 30
Mar 26, 1940	16 ♍ 09	19 ♈ 15	28 ♋ 47	28 ♈ 10	21 ♓ 03	00 ♓ 18	06 ♓ 44	02 ♑ 45	19 ♒ 41
Apr 5, 1940	13 ♍ 49	23 ♈ 19	00 ♌ 09	03 ♉ 41	24 ♓ 59	04 ♓ 41	10 ♓ 04	05 ♑ 10	24 ♒ 43
Apr 15, 1940	12 ♍ 08	27 ♈ 21	02 ♌ 03	09 ♉ 13	28 ♓ 49	09 ♓ 01	13 ♓ 17	07 ♑ 05	29 ♒ 36
Apr 25, 1940	11 ♍ 15	01 ♉ 22	04 ♌ 22	14 ♉ 45	02 ♈ 34	13 ♓ 14	16 ♓ 22	08 ♑ 25	04 ♓ 19
May 5, 1940	11 ♍ 10	05 ♉ 20	07 ♌ 02	20 ♉ 18	06 ♈ 11	17 ♓ 22	19 ♓ 18	09 ♑ 07	08 ♓ 50
May 15, 1940	11 ♍ 52	09 ♉ 14	09 ♌ 60	25 ♉ 51	09 ♈ 41	21 ♓ 21	22 ♓ 03	09 ♑ 06	13 ♓ 06
May 25, 1940	13 ♍ 17	13 ♉ 05	13 ♌ 11	01 ♊ 23	13 ♈ 01	25 ♓ 10	24 ♓ 35	08 ♑ 24	17 ♓ 06
Jun 4, 1940	15 ♍ 18	16 ♉ 50	16 ♌ 34	06 ♊ 54	16 ♈ 10	28 ♓ 48	26 ♓ 52	07 ♑ 01	20 ♓ 47
Jun 14, 1940	17 ♍ 51	20 ♉ 29	20 ♌ 06	12 ♊ 25	19 ♈ 07	02 ♈ 12	28 ♓ 51	05 ♑ 08	24 ♓ 05
Jun 24, 1940	20 ♍ 52	24 ♉ 01	23 ♌ 45	17 ♊ 53	21 ♈ 49	05 ♈ 19	00 ♈ 31	02 ♑ 58	26 ♓ 57
Jul 4, 1940	24 ♍ 16	27 ♉ 25	27 ♌ 30	23 ♊ 19	24 ♈ 15	08 ♈ 06	01 ♈ 48	00 ♑ 48	29 ♓ 18
Jul 14, 1940	28 ♍ 02	00 ♊ 39	01 ♍ 20	28 ♊ 43	26 ♈ 21	10 ♈ 29	02 ♈ 39	28 ♐ 55	01 ♈ 03
Jul 24, 1940	02 ♎ 05	03 ♊ 43	05 ♍ 14	04 ♋ 04	28 ♈ 05	12 ♈ 24	03 ♈ 01	27 ♐ 31	02 ♈ 06
Aug 3, 1940	06 ♎ 25	06 ♊ 34	09 ♍ 10	09 ♋ 22	29 ♈ 24	13 ♈ 45	02 ♈ 52	26 ♐ 46	02 ♈ 23
Aug 13, 1940	10 ♎ 59	09 ♊ 10	13 ♍ 08	14 ♋ 35	00 ♉ 13	14 ♈ 29	02 ♈ 12	26 ♐ 42	01 ♈ 50
Aug 23, 1940	15 ♎ 45	11 ♊ 28	17 ♍ 06	19 ♋ 44	00 ♉ 30	14 ♈ 30	01 ♈ 01	27 ♐ 19	00 ♈ 29
Sep 2, 1940	20 ♎ 43	13 ♊ 27	21 ♍ 06	24 ♋ 47	00 ♉ 12	13 ♈ 49	29 ♓ 24	28 ♐ 32	28 ♓ 26
Sep 12, 1940	25 ♎ 51	15 ♊ 02	25 ♍ 05	29 ♋ 44	29 ♈ 19	12 ♈ 27	27 ♓ 29	00 ♑ 19	25 ♓ 56
Sep 22, 1940	01 ♏ 09	16 ♊ 12	29 ♍ 03	04 ♌ 33	27 ♈ 54	10 ♈ 34	25 ♓ 25	02 ♑ 34	23 ♓ 18
Oct 2, 1940	06 ♏ 35	16 ♊ 51	02 ♎ 59	09 ♌ 13	26 ♈ 01	08 ♈ 23	23 ♓ 25	05 ♑ 14	20 ♓ 54
Oct 12, 1940	12 ♏ 06	16 ♊ 59	06 ♎ 53	13 ♌ 42	23 ♈ 51	06 ♈ 12	21 ♓ 40	08 ♑ 14	19 ♓ 02
Oct 22, 1940	17 ♏ 50	16 ♊ 33	10 ♎ 43	17 ♌ 58	21 ♈ 36	04 ♈ 21	20 ♓ 19	11 ♑ 32	17 ♓ 53
Nov 1, 1940	23 ♏ 36	15 ♊ 33	14 ♎ 29	21 ♌ 57	19 ♈ 30	03 ♈ 02	19 ♓ 28	15 ♑ 05	17 ♓ 30
Nov 11, 1940	29 ♏ 28	14 ♊ 04	18 ♎ 10	25 ♌ 38	17 ♈ 45	02 ♈ 26	19 ♓ 10	18 ♑ 49	17 ♓ 54
Nov 21, 1940	05 ♐ 23	12 ♊ 12	21 ♎ 44	28 ♌ 56	16 ♈ 30	02 ♈ 35	19 ♓ 25	22 ♑ 44	18 ♓ 60
Dec 1, 1940	11 ♐ 22	10 ♊ 07	25 ♎ 10	01 ♍ 49	15 ♈ 49	03 ♈ 27	20 ♓ 10	26 ♑ 47	20 ♓ 42
Dec 11, 1940	17 ♐ 23	08 ♊ 03	28 ♎ 26	04 ♍ 03	15 ♈ 44	04 ♈ 59	21 ♓ 25	00 ♒ 57	22 ♓ 55
Dec 21, 1940	23 ♐ 25	06 ♊ 12	01 ♏ 31	05 ♍ 40	16 ♈ 13	07 ♈ 05	23 ♓ 04	05 ♒ 12	25 ♓ 34
Dec 31, 1940	29 ♐ 27	04 ♊ 43	04 ♏ 23	06 ♍ 31	17 ♈ 13	09 ♈ 41	25 ♓ 05	09 ♒ 31	28 ♓ 35
Jan 10, 1941	05 ♑ 29	03 ♊ 44	06 ♏ 58	06 ♍ 30	18 ♈ 41	12 ♈ 41	27 ♓ 26	13 ♒ 54	01 ♈ 52
Jan 20, 1941	11 ♑ 29	03 ♊ 17	09 ♏ 15	05 ♍ 36	20 ♈ 32	16 ♈ 02	00 ♈ 02	18 ♒ 18	05 ♈ 24

	ATROPOS	HEKATE	LILITH	MEDUSA	MOIRA	NEMESIS	PERSEPHONE	PROSERPINA	PYTHIA
Jan 30, 1941	17 ♑ 26	03 ♊ 23	11 ♏ 09	03 ♍ 51	22 ♈ 45	19 ♈ 40	02 ♈ 51	22 ♒ 43	09 ♈ 07
Feb 9, 1941	23 ♑ 19	03 ♊ 59	12 ♏ 38	01 ♍ 27	25 ♈ 14	23 ♈ 32	05 ♈ 53	27 ♒ 08	12 ♈ 59
Feb 19, 1941	29 ♑ 07	05 ♊ 04	13 ♏ 39	28 ♌ 42	27 ♈ 58	27 ♈ 34	09 ♈ 03	01 ♓ 33	16 ♈ 58
Mar 1, 1941	04 ♒ 49	06 ♊ 33	14 ♏ 07	26 ♌ 01	00 ♉ 53	01 ♉ 46	12 ♈ 21	05 ♓ 56	21 ♈ 03
Mar 11, 1941	10 ♒ 25	08 ♊ 22	14 ♏ 02	23 ♌ 47	03 ♉ 59	06 ♉ 05	15 ♈ 45	10 ♓ 17	25 ♈ 12
Mar 21, 1941	15 ♒ 52	10 ♊ 30	13 ♏ 20	23 ♌ 15	07 ♉ 12	10 ♉ 29	19 ♈ 13	14 ♓ 35	29 ♈ 23
Mar 31, 1941	21 ♒ 11	12 ♊ 52	12 ♏ 05	21 ♌ 33	10 ♉ 32	14 ♉ 57	22 ♈ 46	18 ♓ 50	03 ♉ 37
Apr 10, 1941	26 ♒ 19	15 ♊ 27	10 ♏ 21	21 ♌ 41	13 ♉ 56	19 ♉ 29	26 ♈ 20	22 ♓ 59	07 ♉ 52
Apr 20, 1941	01 ♓ 16	18 ♊ 11	08 ♏ 16	22 ♌ 36	17 ♉ 24	24 ♉ 02	29 ♈ 56	27 ♓ 03	12 ♉ 07
Apr 30, 1941	05 ♓ 60	21 ♊ 04	06 ♏ 02	24 ♌ 11	20 ♉ 55	28 ♉ 37	03 ♉ 33	01 ♈ 01	16 ♉ 22
May 10, 1941	10 ♓ 29	24 ♊ 03	03 ♏ 52	26 ♌ 21	24 ♉ 27	03 ♊ 12	07 ♉ 09	04 ♈ 51	20 ♉ 36
May 20, 1941	14 ♓ 41	27 ♊ 07	01 ♏ 58	28 ♌ 60	27 ♉ 60	07 ♊ 47	10 ♉ 44	08 ♈ 33	24 ♉ 48
May 30, 1941	18 ♓ 34	00 ♋ 15	00 ♏ 30	02 ♍ 02	01 ♊ 33	12 ♊ 21	14 ♉ 17	12 ♈ 05	28 ♉ 58
Jun 9, 1941	22 ♓ 04	03 ♋ 26	29 ♎ 33	05 ♍ 24	05 ♊ 05	16 ♊ 53	17 ♉ 47	15 ♈ 25	03 ♊ 06
Jun 19, 1941	25 ♓ 09	06 ♋ 38	29 ♎ 08	09 ♍ 02	08 ♊ 35	21 ♊ 23	21 ♉ 13	18 ♈ 31	07 ♊ 10
Jun 29, 1941	27 ♓ 44	09 ♋ 51	29 ♎ 17	12 ♍ 53	12 ♊ 02	25 ♊ 51	24 ♉ 34	21 ♈ 23	11 ♊ 10
Jul 9, 1941	29 ♓ 43	13 ♋ 03	29 ♎ 57	16 ♍ 56	15 ♊ 26	00 ♋ 16	27 ♉ 49	23 ♈ 55	15 ♊ 06
Jul 19, 1941	01 ♈ 02	16 ♋ 15	01 ♏ 04	21 ♍ 08	18 ♊ 45	04 ♋ 36	00 ♊ 55	26 ♈ 07	18 ♊ 56
Jul 29, 1941	01 ♈ 35	19 ♋ 24	02 ♏ 36	25 ♍ 28	21 ♊ 59	08 ♋ 53	03 ♊ 53	27 ♈ 54	22 ♊ 40
Aug 8, 1941	01 ♈ 17	22 ♋ 30	04 ♏ 30	29 ♍ 55	25 ♊ 05	13 ♋ 03	06 ♊ 38	29 ♈ 13	26 ♊ 16
Aug 18, 1941	00 ♈ 08	25 ♋ 32	06 ♏ 42	04 ♎ 28	28 ♊ 03	17 ♋ 08	09 ♊ 11	29 ♈ 60	29 ♊ 43
Aug 28, 1941	28 ♓ 11	28 ♋ 29	09 ♏ 10	09 ♎ 05	00 ♋ 51	21 ♋ 06	11 ♊ 27	00 ♉ 11	02 ♋ 59
Sep 7, 1941	25 ♓ 38	01 ♌ 18	11 ♏ 51	13 ♎ 46	03 ♋ 26	24 ♋ 54	13 ♊ 23	29 ♈ 44	06 ♋ 03
Sep 17, 1941	22 ♓ 49	04 ♌ 00	14 ♏ 45	18 ♎ 31	05 ♋ 45	28 ♋ 33	14 ♊ 57	28 ♈ 40	08 ♋ 51
Sep 27, 1941	20 ♓ 06	06 ♌ 32	17 ♏ 48	23 ♎ 19	07 ♋ 47	01 ♌ 60	16 ♊ 03	27 ♈ 02	11 ♋ 21
Oct 7, 1941	17 ♓ 51	08 ♌ 52	21 ♏ 00	28 ♎ 09	09 ♋ 27	05 ♌ 12	16 ♊ 40	24 ♈ 58	13 ♋ 29
Oct 17, 1941	16 ♓ 17	10 ♌ 58	24 ♏ 19	03 ♏ 00	10 ♋ 42	08 ♌ 09	16 ♊ 43	22 ♈ 41	15 ♋ 12
Oct 27, 1941	15 ♓ 31	12 ♌ 47	27 ♏ 44	07 ♏ 53	11 ♋ 28	10 ♌ 45	16 ♊ 11	20 ♈ 25	16 ♋ 24
Nov 6, 1941	15 ♓ 36	14 ♌ 16	01 ♐ 13	12 ♏ 47	11 ♋ 42	12 ♌ 58	15 ♊ 03	18 ♈ 27	17 ♋ 01
Nov 16, 1941	16 ♓ 26	15 ♌ 23	04 ♐ 46	17 ♏ 41	11 ♋ 20	14 ♌ 44	13 ♊ 25	16 ♈ 57	16 ♋ 59
Nov 26, 1941	17 ♓ 56	16 ♌ 04	08 ♐ 22	22 ♏ 35	10 ♋ 22	15 ♌ 58	11 ♊ 25	16 ♈ 02	16 ♋ 14
Dec 6, 1941	20 ♓ 01	16 ♌ 18	11 ♐ 59	27 ♏ 28	08 ♋ 49	16 ♌ 37	09 ♊ 14	15 ♈ 47	14 ♋ 48
Dec 16, 1941	22 ♓ 34	16 ♌ 01	15 ♐ 36	02 ♐ 20	06 ♋ 50	16 ♌ 37	07 ♊ 08	16 ♈ 09	12 ♋ 44
Dec 26, 1941	25 ♓ 32	15 ♌ 13	19 ♐ 13	07 ♐ 09	04 ♋ 56	15 ♌ 56	05 ♊ 19	17 ♈ 06	10 ♋ 15
Jan 5, 1942	28 ♓ 49	13 ♌ 57	22 ♐ 49	11 ♐ 55	02 ♋ 16	14 ♌ 37	03 ♊ 59	18 ♈ 34	07 ♋ 35

	ATROPOS	HEKATE	LILITH	MEDUSA	MOIRA	NEMESIS	PERSEPHONE	PROSERPINA	PYTHIA
Jan 15, 1942	02 ♈ 22	12 ♌ 18	26 ♐ 22	16 ♐ 37	00 ♋ 10	12 ♌ 45	03 ♊ 14	20 ♈ 29	05 ♋ 04
Jan 25, 1942	06 ♈ 09	10 ♌ 22	29 ♐ 51	21 ♐ 14	28 ♊ 29	10 ♌ 32	03 ♊ 07	22 ♈ 48	02 ♋ 57
Feb 4, 1942	10 ♈ 05	08 ♌ 22	03 ♑ 31	25 ♐ 45	27 ♊ 21	08 ♌ 13	03 ♊ 36	25 ♈ 26	01 ♋ 27
Feb 14, 1942	14 ♈ 10	06 ♌ 26	06 ♑ 40	00 ♑ 09	26 ♊ 50	06 ♌ 03	04 ♊ 39	28 ♈ 20	00 ♋ 39
Feb 24, 1942	18 ♈ 22	04 ♌ 47	09 ♑ 40	04 ♑ 24	26 ♊ 57	04 ♌ 16	06 ♊ 12	01 ♉ 28	00 ♋ 35
Mar 6, 1942	22 ♈ 39	03 ♌ 30	12 ♑ 39	08 ♑ 28	27 ♊ 40	03 ♌ 02	08 ♊ 11	04 ♉ 47	01 ♋ 12
Mar 16, 1942	27 ♈ 00	02 ♌ 42	15 ♑ 26	12 ♑ 21	28 ♊ 56	02 ♌ 26	10 ♊ 32	08 ♉ 15	02 ♋ 26
Mar 26, 1942	01 ♉ 24	02 ♌ 23	17 ♑ 58	15 ♑ 58	00 ♋ 39	02 ♌ 27	13 ♊ 12	11 ♉ 50	04 ♋ 11
Apr 5, 1942	05 ♉ 50	02 ♌ 34	20 ♑ 14	19 ♑ 18	02 ♋ 47	03 ♌ 04	16 ♊ 08	15 ♉ 32	06 ♋ 24
Apr 15, 1942	10 ♉ 16	03 ♌ 12	22 ♑ 10	22 ♑ 18	05 ♋ 17	04 ♌ 13	19 ♊ 18	19 ♉ 18	09 ♋ 01
Apr 25, 1942	14 ♉ 43	04 ♌ 16	23 ♑ 43	24 ♑ 52	08 ♋ 04	05 ♌ 50	22 ♊ 38	23 ♉ 07	11 ♋ 57
May 5, 1942	19 ♉ 10	05 ♌ 42	24 ♑ 49	26 ♑ 57	11 ♋ 07	07 ♌ 50	26 ♊ 07	26 ♉ 59	15 ♋ 10
May 15, 1942	23 ♉ 35	07 ♌ 27	25 ♑ 25	28 ♑ 27	14 ♋ 23	10 ♌ 11	29 ♊ 44	00 ♊ 53	18 ♋ 37
May 25, 1942	27 ♉ 59	09 ♌ 29	25 ♑ 28	29 ♑ 17	17 ♋ 50	12 ♌ 48	03 ♋ 28	04 ♊ 47	22 ♋ 16
Jun 4, 1942	02 ♊ 21	11 ♌ 45	24 ♑ 56	29 ♑ 23	21 ♋ 27	15 ♌ 39	07 ♋ 16	08 ♊ 42	26 ♋ 06
Jun 14, 1942	06 ♊ 39	14 ♌ 13	23 ♑ 48	28 ♑ 42	25 ♋ 11	18 ♌ 42	11 ♋ 08	12 ♊ 36	00 ♌ 04
Jun 24, 1942	10 ♊ 55	16 ♌ 52	22 ♑ 10	27 ♑ 13	29 ♋ 03	21 ♌ 54	15 ♋ 03	16 ♊ 29	04 ♌ 10
Jul 4, 1942	15 ♊ 06	19 ♌ 39	20 ♑ 08	25 ♑ 07	03 ♌ 01	25 ♌ 14	19 ♋ 01	20 ♊ 20	08 ♌ 24
Jul 14, 1942	19 ♊ 12	22 ♌ 33	18 ♑ 53	22 ♑ 35	07 ♌ 05	28 ♌ 41	22 ♋ 60	24 ♊ 08	12 ♌ 43
Jul 24, 1942	23 ♊ 13	25 ♌ 33	15 ♑ 40	19 ♑ 59	11 ♌ 13	02 ♍ 13	26 ♋ 60	27 ♊ 53	17 ♌ 08
Aug 3, 1942	27 ♊ 07	28 ♌ 38	13 ♑ 42	17 ♑ 40	15 ♌ 25	05 ♍ 49	00 ♌ 59	01 ♋ 33	21 ♌ 37
Aug 13, 1942	00 ♋ 52	01 ♍ 47	12 ♑ 10	15 ♑ 55	19 ♌ 40	09 ♍ 29	04 ♌ 58	05 ♋ 08	26 ♌ 11
Aug 23, 1942	04 ♋ 28	04 ♍ 58	11 ♑ 12	14 ♑ 56	23 ♌ 58	13 ♍ 11	08 ♌ 56	08 ♋ 35	00 ♍ 48
Sep 2, 1942	07 ♋ 52	08 ♍ 11	10 ♑ 51	14 ♑ 46	28 ♌ 18	16 ♍ 54	12 ♌ 51	11 ♋ 54	05 ♍ 29
Sep 12, 1942	11 ♋ 03	11 ♍ 25	11 ♑ 09	15 ♑ 24	02 ♍ 40	20 ♍ 38	16 ♌ 42	15 ♋ 03	10 ♍ 13
Sep 22, 1942	13 ♋ 58	14 ♍ 39	12 ♑ 02	16 ♑ 48	07 ♍ 02	24 ♍ 22	20 ♌ 30	17 ♋ 59	14 ♍ 59
Oct 2, 1942	16 ♋ 33	17 ♍ 52	13 ♑ 29	18 ♑ 50	11 ♍ 25	28 ♍ 06	24 ♌ 11	20 ♋ 41	19 ♍ 47
Oct 12, 1942	18 ♋ 45	21 ♍ 02	15 ♑ 25	21 ♑ 26	15 ♍ 47	01 ♎ 47	27 ♌ 46	23 ♋ 04	24 ♍ 36
Oct 22, 1942	20 ♋ 30	24 ♍ 08	17 ♑ 47	24 ♑ 31	20 ♍ 08	05 ♎ 26	01 ♍ 11	25 ♋ 05	29 ♍ 26
Nov 1, 1942	21 ♋ 42	27 ♍ 10	20 ♑ 31	28 ♑ 00	24 ♍ 26	09 ♎ 00	04 ♍ 26	26 ♋ 41	04 ♎ 16
Nov 11, 1942	22 ♋ 17	00 ♎ 05	23 ♑ 35	01 ♒ 50	28 ♍ 40	12 ♎ 30	07 ♍ 28	27 ♋ 47	09 ♎ 06
Nov 21, 1942	22 ♋ 10	02 ♎ 52	26 ♑ 57	05 ♒ 58	02 ♎ 49	15 ♎ 53	10 ♍ 14	28 ♋ 18	13 ♎ 53
Dec 1, 1942	21 ♋ 19	05 ♎ 29	00 ♒ 34	10 ♒ 21	06 ♎ 51	19 ♎ 08	12 ♍ 51	28 ♋ 11	18 ♎ 38
Dec 11, 1942	19 ♋ 43	07 ♎ 53	04 ♒ 23	14 ♒ 57	10 ♎ 45	22 ♎ 14	14 ♍ 41	27 ♋ 25	23 ♎ 20
Dec 21, 1942	17 ♋ 29	10 ♎ 02	08 ♒ 24	19 ♒ 43	14 ♎ 27	25 ♎ 07	16 ♍ 23	26 ♋ 01	27 ♎ 55

	ATROPOS	HEKATE	LILITH	MEDUSA	MOIRA	NEMESIS	PERSEPHONE	PROSERPINA	PYTHIA
Dec 31, 1942	14 ♋ 50	11 ♎ 53	12 ♒ 34	24 ♒ 38	17 ♎ 56	27 ♎ 47	17 ♍ 30	24 ♋ 05	02 ♏ 24
Jan 10, 1943	12 ♋ 02	13 ♎ 23	16 ♒ 53	29 ♒ 42	21 ♎ 07	00 ♏ 12	18 ♍ 03	21 ♋ 48	06 ♏ 43
Jan 20, 1943	09 ♋ 25	14 ♎ 28	21 ♒ 20	04 ♓ 51	23 ♎ 57	02 ♏ 12	17 ♍ 14	19 ♋ 27	10 ♏ 50
Jan 30, 1943	07 ♋ 15	15 ♎ 05	25 ♒ 52	10 ♓ 07	26 ♎ 21	03 ♏ 51	17 ♍ 14	17 ♋ 16	14 ♏ 43
Feb 9, 1943	05 ♋ 45	15 ♎ 12	00 ♓ 30	15 ♓ 26	28 ♎ 15	05 ♏ 03	15 ♍ 55	15 ♋ 32	18 ♏ 17
Feb 19, 1943	04 ♋ 58	14 ♎ 47	09 ♓ 13	20 ♓ 50	29 ♎ 33	05 ♏ 45	14 ♍ 06	14 ♋ 22	21 ♏ 29
Mar 1, 1943	04 ♋ 55	13 ♎ 50	09 ♓ 59	26 ♓ 16	00 ♏ 11	05 ♏ 53	11 ♍ 59	13 ♋ 53	24 ♏ 14
Mar 11, 1943	05 ♋ 32	12 ♎ 24	14 ♓ 48	01 ♈ 45	00 ♏ 04	05 ♏ 26	09 ♍ 49	14 ♋ 04	26 ♏ 25
Mar 21, 1943	06 ♋ 45	10 ♎ 35	19 ♓ 40	07 ♈ 15	29 ♎ 12	04 ♏ 25	07 ♍ 50	14 ♋ 53	27 ♏ 57
Mar 31, 1943	08 ♋ 28	08 ♎ 34	24 ♓ 33	12 ♈ 47	27 ♎ 41	02 ♏ 52	06 ♍ 16	16 ♋ 16	28 ♏ 43
Apr 10, 1943	10 ♋ 38	06 ♎ 32	29 ♓ 28	18 ♈ 19	25 ♎ 40	00 ♏ 55	05 ♍ 14	18 ♋ 08	28 ♏ 39
Apr 20, 1943	13 ♋ 09	04 ♎ 41	04 ♈ 23	23 ♈ 51	23 ♎ 27	28 ♎ 45	04 ♍ 49	20 ♋ 27	27 ♏ 43
Apr 30, 1943	15 ♋ 58	03 ♎ 11	09 ♈ 18	29 ♈ 23	21 ♎ 21	26 ♎ 35	05 ♍ 01	23 ♋ 06	26 ♏ 01
May 10, 1943	19 ♋ 03	02 ♎ 09	14 ♈ 12	04 ♉ 55	19 ♎ 40	24 ♎ 37	05 ♍ 49	26 ♋ 04	23 ♏ 45
May 20, 1943	22 ♋ 20	01 ♎ 38	19 ♈ 06	10 ♉ 25	18 ♎ 37	23 ♎ 03	07 ♍ 07	29 ♋ 18	21 ♏ 17
May 30, 1943	25 ♋ 47	01 ♎ 41	23 ♈ 57	15 ♉ 54	18 ♎ 19	21 ♎ 59	08 ♍ 54	02 ♌ 45	19 ♏ 00
Jun 9, 1943	29 ♋ 24	02 ♎ 15	28 ♈ 45	21 ♉ 20	18 ♎ 45	21 ♎ 29	11 ♍ 04	06 ♌ 23	17 ♏ 16
Jun 19, 1943	03 ♌ 08	03 ♎ 18	03 ♉ 30	26 ♉ 45	19 ♎ 55	21 ♎ 32	13 ♍ 35	10 ♌ 11	16 ♏ 19
Jun 29, 1943	06 ♌ 58	04 ♎ 48	08 ♉ 09	02 ♊ 06	21 ♎ 42	22 ♎ 09	16 ♍ 23	14 ♌ 06	16 ♏ 13
Jul 9, 1943	10 ♌ 54	06 ♎ 41	12 ♉ 42	07 ♊ 24	24 ♎ 02	23 ♎ 15	19 ♍ 26	18 ♌ 09	16 ♏ 58
Jul 19, 1943	14 ♌ 54	08 ♎ 55	17 ♉ 07	12 ♊ 37	26 ♎ 51	24 ♎ 47	22 ♍ 42	22 ♌ 18	18 ♏ 31
Jul 29, 1943	18 ♌ 59	11 ♎ 26	21 ♉ 23	17 ♊ 46	00 ♏ 03	26 ♎ 43	26 ♍ 07	26 ♌ 31	20 ♏ 44
Aug 8, 1943	23 ♌ 06	14 ♎ 14	25 ♉ 26	22 ♊ 49	03 ♏ 34	28 ♎ 58	29 ♍ 42	00 ♍ 49	23 ♏ 32
Aug 18, 1943	27 ♌ 17	17 ♎ 14	29 ♉ 14	27 ♊ 44	07 ♏ 23	01 ♏ 32	03 ♎ 24	05 ♍ 11	26 ♏ 49
Aug 28, 1943	01 ♍ 29	20 ♎ 27	02 ♊ 43	02 ♋ 31	11 ♏ 25	04 ♏ 20	07 ♎ 13	09 ♍ 35	00 ♐ 30
Sep 7, 1943	05 ♍ 44	23 ♎ 50	05 ♊ 50	07 ♋ 08	15 ♏ 39	07 ♏ 21	11 ♎ 07	14 ♍ 02	04 ♐ 32
Sep 17, 1943	09 ♍ 59	27 ♎ 21	08 ♊ 28	11 ♋ 33	20 ♏ 02	10 ♏ 34	15 ♎ 05	18 ♍ 31	08 ♐ 50
Sep 27, 1943	14 ♍ 15	01 ♏ 00	10 ♊ 34	15 ♋ 43	24 ♏ 34	13 ♏ 56	19 ♎ 06	23 ♍ 01	13 ♐ 23
Oct 7, 1943	18 ♍ 32	04 ♏ 46	11 ♊ 59	19 ♋ 35	29 ♏ 12	17 ♏ 26	23 ♎ 10	27 ♍ 31	18 ♐ 07
Oct 17, 1943	22 ♍ 47	08 ♏ 38	12 ♊ 39	23 ♋ 05	03 ♐ 55	21 ♏ 03	27 ♎ 15	02 ♎ 01	23 ♐ 01
Oct 27, 1943	27 ♍ 02	12 ♏ 34	12 ♊ 30	26 ♋ 09	08 ♐ 43	24 ♏ 46	01 ♏ 21	06 ♎ 29	28 ♐ 02
Nov 6, 1943	01 ♎ 14	16 ♏ 33	11 ♊ 32	00 ♌ 34	13 ♐ 34	28 ♏ 34	05 ♏ 27	10 ♎ 56	03 ♑ 11
Nov 16, 1943	05 ♎ 23	20 ♏ 36	09 ♊ 51	01 ♌ 42	18 ♐ 27	02 ♐ 25	09 ♏ 32	15 ♎ 20	08 ♑ 24
Nov 26, 1943	09 ♎ 28	24 ♏ 41	07 ♊ 41	01 ♌ 42	23 ♐ 22	06 ♐ 19	13 ♏ 35	19 ♎ 40	13 ♑ 42
Dec 6, 1943	13 ♎ 27	28 ♏ 46	05 ♊ 23	01 ♌ 58	28 ♐ 17	10 ♐ 16	17 ♏ 35	23 ♎ 55	19 ♑ 03

	ATROPOS	HEKATE	LILITH	MEDUSA	MOIRA	NEMESIS	PERSEPHONE	PROSERPINA	PYTHIA
Dec 16, 1943	17 ♎ 19	02 ♐ 52	03 ♊ 21	01 ♌ 19	03 ♑ 12	14 ♐ 13	21 ♏ 31	28 ♎ 02	24 ♑ 27
Dec 26, 1943	21 ♎ 00	06 ♐ 57	01 ♊ 53	29 ♋ 46	08 ♑ 00	18 ♐ 10	25 ♏ 22	02 ♏ 01	29 ♑ 52
Jan 5, 1944	24 ♎ 30	10 ♐ 60	01 ♊ 11	27 ♋ 28	13 ♑ 00	22 ♐ 07	29 ♏ 05	05 ♏ 49	05 ♒ 18
Jan 15, 1944	27 ♎ 45	14 ♐ 60	01 ♊ 18	24 ♋ 46	17 ♑ 51	26 ♐ 01	02 ♐ 41	09 ♏ 24	10 ♒ 43
Jan 25, 1944	00 ♏ 40	18 ♐ 55	03 ♊ 13	22 ♋ 02	22 ♑ 38	29 ♐ 53	06 ♐ 06	12 ♏ 43	16 ♒ 08
Feb 4, 1944	03 ♏ 12	22 ♐ 45	03 ♊ 51	19 ♋ 44	27 ♑ 22	03 ♑ 40	09 ♐ 19	15 ♏ 43	21 ♒ 32
Feb 14, 1944	05 ♏ 16	26 ♐ 27	06 ♊ 05	18 ♋ 08	02 ♒ 00	07 ♑ 22	12 ♐ 17	18 ♏ 20	26 ♒ 53
Feb 24, 1944	06 ♏ 45	00 ♑ 00	08 ♊ 50	17 ♋ 24	06 ♒ 34	10 ♑ 58	14 ♐ 59	20 ♏ 29	02 ♓ 12
Mar 5, 1944	07 ♏ 32	03 ♑ 22	12 ♊ 00	17 ♋ 34	11 ♒ 00	14 ♑ 24	17 ♐ 20	22 ♏ 07	07 ♓ 28
Mar 15, 1944	07 ♏ 33	06 ♑ 31	15 ♊ 30	18 ♋ 32	15 ♒ 19	17 ♑ 41	19 ♐ 18	23 ♏ 27	12 ♓ 40
Mar 25, 1944	06 ♏ 43	09 ♑ 23	19 ♊ 16	20 ♋ 14	19 ♒ 30	20 ♑ 45	20 ♐ 49	23 ♏ 04	17 ♓ 47
Apr 4, 1944	05 ♏ 03	11 ♑ 56	23 ♊ 16	22 ♋ 31	23 ♒ 34	23 ♑ 34	21 ♐ 50	21 ♏ 58	22 ♓ 49
Apr 14, 1944	02 ♏ 41	14 ♑ 07	27 ♊ 25	25 ♋ 18	27 ♒ 20	26 ♑ 05	22 ♐ 18	20 ♏ 17	27 ♓ 45
Apr 24, 1944	29 ♎ 55	15 ♑ 51	01 ♋ 42	28 ♋ 30	00 ♓ 57	28 ♑ 16	22 ♐ 10	18 ♏ 11	02 ♈ 36
May 4, 1944	27 ♎ 09	17 ♑ 05	06 ♋ 05	02 ♌ 01	04 ♓ 18	00 ♒ 03	21 ♐ 27	15 ♏ 57	07 ♈ 19
May 14, 1944	24 ♎ 48	17 ♑ 45	10 ♋ 33	05 ♌ 49	07 ♓ 21	01 ♒ 21	20 ♐ 10	13 ♏ 53	11 ♈ 54
May 24, 1944	23 ♎ 10	17 ♑ 49	15 ♋ 04	09 ♌ 49	10 ♓ 08	02 ♒ 08	18 ♐ 27	12 ♏ 15	16 ♈ 20
Jun 3, 1944	22 ♎ 28	17 ♑ 14	19 ♋ 38	14 ♌ 01	12 ♓ 30	02 ♒ 18	16 ♐ 26	11 ♏ 13	20 ♈ 36
Jun 13, 1944	22 ♎ 42	16 ♑ 05	24 ♋ 13	18 ♌ 21	14 ♓ 27	01 ♒ 51	14 ♐ 22	10 ♏ 53	24 ♈ 40
Jun 23, 1944	23 ♎ 50	14 ♑ 27	28 ♋ 27	22 ♌ 49	15 ♓ 54	00 ♒ 47	12 ♐ 27	11 ♏ 15	28 ♈ 32
Jul 3, 1944	25 ♎ 47	12 ♑ 31	03 ♌ 24	27 ♌ 23	16 ♓ 48	29 ♑ 10	10 ♐ 52	12 ♏ 18	02 ♉ 09
Jul 13, 1944	28 ♎ 25	10 ♑ 32	07 ♌ 60	02 ♍ 02	17 ♓ 05	27 ♑ 09	09 ♐ 46	13 ♏ 55	05 ♉ 29
Jul 23, 1944	01 ♏ 38	08 ♑ 45	12 ♌ 34	06 ♍ 44	16 ♓ 44	24 ♑ 57	09 ♐ 14	16 ♏ 04	08 ♉ 29
Aug 2, 1944	05 ♏ 22	07 ♑ 23	17 ♌ 07	11 ♍ 31	15 ♓ 45	22 ♑ 50	09 ♐ 16	18 ♏ 40	11 ♉ 05
Aug 12, 1944	09 ♏ 30	06 ♑ 36	21 ♌ 37	16 ♍ 20	14 ♓ 11	21 ♑ 02	09 ♐ 51	21 ♏ 38	13 ♉ 15
Aug 22, 1944	13 ♏ 58	06 ♑ 26	26 ♌ 06	21 ♍ 11	12 ♓ 10	19 ♑ 46	10 ♐ 56	24 ♏ 56	14 ♉ 53
Sep 1, 1944	18 ♏ 44	08 ♑ 55	00 ♍ 31	26 ♍ 04	09 ♓ 56	19 ♑ 08	12 ♐ 28	28 ♏ 30	15 ♉ 54
Sep 11, 1944	23 ♏ 44	08 ♑ 01	04 ♍ 52	00 ♎ 59	07 ♓ 42	19 ♑ 10	14 ♐ 25	02 ♐ 18	16 ♉ 15
Sep 21, 1944	28 ♏ 56	09 ♑ 41	09 ♍ 09	05 ♎ 54	05 ♓ 43	19 ♑ 53	16 ♐ 41	06 ♐ 17	15 ♉ 51
Oct 1, 1944	04 ♐ 18	11 ♑ 50	13 ♍ 21	10 ♎ 50	04 ♓ 12	21 ♑ 12	19 ♐ 16	10 ♐ 26	14 ♉ 41
Oct 11, 1944	09 ♐ 47	14 ♑ 26	17 ♍ 27	15 ♎ 45	03 ♓ 14	23 ♑ 05	22 ♐ 05	14 ♐ 43	12 ♉ 51
Oct 21, 1944	15 ♐ 22	17 ♑ 23	21 ♍ 26	20 ♎ 41	02 ♓ 54	25 ♑ 27	25 ♐ 07	19 ♐ 07	10 ♉ 28
Oct 31, 1944	21 ♐ 02	20 ♑ 39	25 ♍ 17	25 ♎ 35	03 ♓ 11	28 ♑ 15	28 ♐ 20	23 ♐ 37	07 ♉ 49
Nov 10, 1944	26 ♐ 46	24 ♑ 11	28 ♍ 58	00 ♏ 28	04 ♓ 02	01 ♒ 24	01 ♑ 41	28 ♐ 11	05 ♉ 13
Nov 20, 1944	02 ♑ 31	27 ♑ 57	02 ♎ 28	05 ♏ 19	05 ♓ 24	04 ♒ 52	05 ♑ 10		02 ♉ 57

	ATROPOS	HEKATE	LILITH	MEDUSA	MOIRA	NEMESIS	PERSEPHONE	PROSERPINA	PYTHIA
Nov 30, 1944	08 ♑ 18	01 ♒ 54	05 ♎ 44	10 ♏ 07	07 ♓ 13	08 ♒ 37	08 ♑ 44	02 ♑ 48	01 ♉ 17
Dec 10, 1944	14 ♑ 05	06 ♒ 00	08 ♎ 45	14 ♏ 51	09 ♓ 25	12 ♒ 35	12 ♑ 23	07 ♑ 28	00 ♉ 19
Dec 20, 1944	19 ♑ 52	10 ♒ 14	11 ♎ 26	19 ♏ 30	11 ♓ 44	16 ♒ 04	16 ♑ 49	12 ♑ 10	00 ♉ 04
Dec 30, 1944	25 ♑ 38	14 ♒ 34	13 ♎ 47	24 ♏ 04	14 ♓ 44	21 ♒ 04	19 ♑ 34	16 ♑ 52	00 ♉ 32
Jan 9, 1945	01 ♒ 21	18 ♒ 59	15 ♎ 42	28 ♏ 31	17 ♓ 45	25 ♒ 31	23 ♑ 19	21 ♑ 35	01 ♉ 38
Jan 19, 1945	07 ♒ 03	23 ♒ 27	17 ♎ 08	02 ♐ 50	20 ♓ 57	00 ♓ 06	27 ♑ 19	26 ♑ 16	03 ♉ 17
Jan 29, 1945	12 ♒ 41	27 ♒ 58	18 ♎ 01	06 ♐ 59	24 ♓ 18	04 ♓ 46	01 ♒ 03	00 ♒ 56	05 ♉ 23
Feb 8, 1945	18 ♒ 15	02 ♓ 30	18 ♎ 18	10 ♐ 56	27 ♓ 46	09 ♓ 31	04 ♒ 44	05 ♒ 34	07 ♉ 53
Feb 18, 1945	23 ♒ 46	07 ♓ 03	17 ♎ 57	14 ♐ 38	01 ♈ 19	14 ♓ 19	08 ♒ 23	10 ♒ 08	10 ♉ 42
Feb 28, 1945	29 ♒ 12	11 ♓ 35	16 ♎ 58	18 ♐ 04	04 ♈ 57	19 ♓ 10	11 ♒ 57	14 ♒ 39	13 ♉ 47
Mar 10, 1945	04 ♓ 33	16 ♓ 06	16 ♎ 23	21 ♐ 10	08 ♈ 37	24 ♓ 02	15 ♒ 25	19 ♒ 04	17 ♉ 05
Mar 20, 1945	09 ♓ 49	20 ♓ 35	15 ♎ 22	23 ♐ 52	12 ♈ 19	28 ♓ 56	18 ♒ 47	23 ♒ 23	20 ♉ 33
Mar 30, 1945	14 ♓ 59	25 ♓ 01	13 ♎ 22	26 ♐ 06	16 ♈ 02	03 ♈ 49	22 ♒ 01	27 ♒ 36	24 ♉ 10
Apr 9, 1945	20 ♓ 02	29 ♓ 23	11 ♎ 06	27 ♐ 47	19 ♈ 44	08 ♈ 42	25 ♒ 05	01 ♓ 40	27 ♉ 54
Apr 19, 1945	24 ♓ 59	03 ♈ 41	08 ♎ 48	28 ♐ 49	23 ♈ 25	13 ♈ 34	27 ♒ 58	05 ♓ 36	01 ♊ 44
Apr 29, 1945	29 ♓ 48	07 ♈ 54	06 ♎ 44	29 ♐ 09	27 ♈ 05	18 ♈ 24	00 ♓ 38	09 ♓ 20	05 ♊ 38
May 9, 1945	04 ♈ 29	11 ♈ 60	05 ♎ 04	28 ♐ 41	00 ♉ 41	23 ♈ 11	03 ♓ 03	12 ♓ 52	09 ♊ 35
May 19, 1945	09 ♈ 01	15 ♈ 59	03 ♎ 56	27 ♐ 27	04 ♉ 14	27 ♈ 56	05 ♓ 10	16 ♓ 09	13 ♊ 35
May 29, 1945	13 ♈ 23	19 ♈ 49	03 ♎ 23	25 ♐ 31	07 ♉ 43	02 ♉ 36	06 ♓ 58	19 ♓ 10	17 ♊ 36
Jun 8, 1945	17 ♈ 34	23 ♈ 29	03 ♎ 25	23 ♐ 05	11 ♉ 05	07 ♉ 11	08 ♓ 22	21 ♓ 51	21 ♊ 39
Jun 18, 1945	21 ♈ 32	26 ♈ 59	03 ♎ 59	20 ♐ 27	14 ♉ 21	11 ♉ 40	09 ♓ 20	24 ♓ 10	25 ♊ 42
Jun 28, 1945	25 ♈ 14	00 ♉ 15	05 ♎ 03	17 ♐ 58	17 ♉ 29	16 ♉ 03	09 ♓ 50	26 ♓ 03	29 ♊ 45
Jul 8, 1945	28 ♈ 40	03 ♉ 16	06 ♎ 33	15 ♐ 57	20 ♉ 28	20 ♉ 17	09 ♓ 49	27 ♓ 25	03 ♋ 47
Jul 18, 1945	01 ♉ 46	05 ♉ 60	08 ♎ 25	14 ♐ 36	23 ♉ 16	24 ♉ 21	09 ♓ 16	28 ♓ 14	07 ♋ 49
Jul 28, 1945	04 ♉ 28	08 ♉ 23	10 ♎ 36	14 ♐ 03	25 ♉ 50	28 ♉ 14	08 ♓ 12	28 ♓ 26	11 ♋ 48
Aug 7, 1945	06 ♉ 42	10 ♉ 23	13 ♎ 03	14 ♐ 17	28 ♉ 10	01 ♊ 54	06 ♓ 41	27 ♓ 58	15 ♋ 44
Aug 17, 1945	08 ♉ 24	11 ♉ 56	15 ♎ 44	15 ♐ 15	00 ♊ 11	05 ♊ 17	04 ♓ 50	26 ♓ 52	19 ♋ 38
Aug 27, 1945	09 ♉ 27	12 ♉ 58	18 ♎ 37	16 ♐ 54	01 ♊ 51	08 ♊ 21	02 ♓ 48	25 ♓ 12	23 ♋ 27
Sep 6, 1945	09 ♉ 47	13 ♉ 27	21 ♎ 39	19 ♐ 07	03 ♊ 07	11 ♊ 02	00 ♓ 47	23 ♓ 07	27 ♋ 10
Sep 16, 1945	09 ♉ 20	13 ♉ 20	24 ♎ 50	21 ♐ 50	03 ♊ 55	13 ♊ 17	28 ♒ 59	20 ♓ 50	00 ♌ 47
Sep 26, 1945	08 ♉ 04	12 ♉ 36	28 ♎ 07	24 ♐ 58	04 ♊ 12	14 ♊ 60	27 ♒ 33	18 ♓ 38	04 ♌ 16
Oct 6, 1945	06 ♉ 03	11 ♉ 18	01 ♏ 30	28 ♐ 28	03 ♊ 56	16 ♊ 06	26 ♒ 35	16 ♓ 45	07 ♌ 35
Oct 16, 1945	03 ♉ 28	09 ♉ 32	04 ♏ 57	02 ♑ 08	03 ♊ 04	16 ♊ 31	26 ♒ 10	15 ♓ 23	10 ♌ 41
Oct 26, 1945	00 ♉ 38	07 ♉ 28	08 ♏ 28	06 ♑ 20	01 ♊ 40	16 ♊ 13	26 ♒ 17	14 ♓ 37	13 ♌ 32
Nov 5, 1945	27 ♈ 52	05 ♉ 21	12 ♏ 01	10 ♑ 38	29 ♉ 49	15 ♊ 11	26 ♒ 55	14 ♓ 31	16 ♌ 04

Date	ATROPOS	HEKATE	LILITH	MEDUSA	MOIRA	NEMESIS	PERSEPHONE	PROSERPINA	PYTHIA
Nov 15, 1945	25 ♈ 33	03 ♉ 25	19 ♏ 10	15 ♑ 08	27 ♉ 39	13 ♊ 30	28 ♒ 01	15 ♓ 02	18 ♌ 14
Nov 25, 1945	23 ♈ 54	01 ♉ 50	22 ♏ 44	19 ♑ 47	25 ♉ 23	11 ♊ 21	29 ♒ 33	16 ♓ 08	19 ♌ 57
Dec 5, 1945	23 ♈ 02	00 ♉ 47	26 ♏ 16	24 ♑ 35	23 ♉ 16	09 ♊ 01	01 ♓ 28	17 ♓ 46	21 ♌ 07
Dec 15, 1945	22 ♈ 59	00 ♉ 18	29 ♏ 46	29 ♑ 30	21 ♉ 28	06 ♊ 48	03 ♓ 42	19 ♓ 50	21 ♌ 40
Dec 25, 1945	23 ♈ 40	00 ♉ 25	03 ♐ 12	04 ♒ 32	20 ♉ 09	05 ♊ 00	06 ♓ 12	22 ♓ 17	21 ♌ 31
Jan 4, 1946	25 ♈ 01	01 ♉ 05	06 ♐ 33	09 ♒ 39	19 ♉ 25	03 ♊ 48	08 ♓ 56	25 ♓ 02	20 ♌ 37
Jan 14, 1946	26 ♈ 56	02 ♉ 16	09 ♐ 47	14 ♒ 51	19 ♉ 16	03 ♊ 18	11 ♓ 52	28 ♓ 04	18 ♌ 59
Jan 24, 1946	29 ♈ 19	03 ♉ 54	12 ♐ 53	20 ♒ 06	19 ♉ 42	03 ♊ 31	14 ♓ 58	01 ♈ 20	16 ♌ 45
Feb 3, 1946	02 ♉ 05	05 ♉ 54	15 ♐ 49	25 ♒ 25	20 ♉ 39	04 ♊ 24	18 ♓ 12	04 ♈ 46	14 ♌ 08
Feb 13, 1946	05 ♉ 11	08 ♉ 13	18 ♐ 33	00 ♓ 46	22 ♉ 05	05 ♊ 52	21 ♓ 31	08 ♈ 21	11 ♌ 26
Feb 23, 1946	08 ♉ 32	10 ♉ 49	21 ♐ 03	06 ♓ 09	23 ♉ 55	07 ♊ 50	24 ♓ 56	12 ♈ 02	08 ♌ 59
Mar 5, 1946	12 ♉ 06	13 ♉ 37	23 ♐ 16	11 ♓ 33	26 ♉ 06	10 ♊ 15	28 ♓ 24	15 ♈ 50	07 ♌ 05
Mar 15, 1946	15 ♉ 50	16 ♉ 36	25 ♐ 09	16 ♓ 58	28 ♉ 34	13 ♊ 00	01 ♈ 55	19 ♈ 42	05 ♌ 54
Mar 25, 1946	19 ♉ 41	19 ♉ 44	26 ♐ 39	22 ♓ 23	01 ♊ 18	16 ♊ 03	05 ♈ 27	23 ♈ 36	05 ♌ 30
Apr 4, 1946	23 ♉ 40	22 ♉ 58	27 ♐ 44	27 ♓ 48	04 ♊ 14	19 ♊ 21	08 ♈ 59	27 ♈ 33	05 ♌ 52
Apr 14, 1946	27 ♉ 43	26 ♉ 17	28 ♐ 19	03 ♈ 12	07 ♊ 20	22 ♊ 49	12 ♈ 31	01 ♉ 31	06 ♌ 56
Apr 24, 1946	01 ♊ 50	29 ♉ 40	28 ♐ 22	08 ♈ 35	10 ♊ 35	26 ♊ 27	16 ♈ 01	05 ♉ 29	08 ♌ 38
May 4, 1946	05 ♊ 59	03 ♊ 06	27 ♐ 51	13 ♈ 57	13 ♊ 57	00 ♋ 13	19 ♈ 28	09 ♉ 27	10 ♌ 52
May 14, 1946	10 ♊ 11	06 ♊ 33	26 ♐ 47	19 ♈ 16	17 ♊ 25	04 ♋ 04	22 ♈ 52	13 ♉ 24	13 ♌ 34
May 24, 1946	14 ♊ 23	10 ♊ 01	25 ♐ 13	24 ♈ 33	20 ♊ 58	08 ♋ 00	26 ♈ 12	17 ♉ 19	16 ♌ 40
Jun 3, 1946	18 ♊ 35	13 ♊ 28	23 ♐ 16	29 ♈ 46	24 ♊ 34	11 ♋ 60	29 ♈ 26	21 ♉ 11	20 ♌ 05
Jun 13, 1946	22 ♊ 47	16 ♊ 54	21 ♐ 05	04 ♉ 56	28 ♊ 13	16 ♋ 01	02 ♉ 33	24 ♉ 59	23 ♌ 48
Jun 23, 1946	26 ♊ 58	20 ♊ 18	18 ♐ 54	10 ♉ 00	01 ♋ 54	20 ♋ 05	05 ♉ 32	28 ♉ 44	27 ♌ 46
Jul 3, 1946	01 ♋ 08	23 ♊ 39	16 ♐ 53	14 ♉ 59	05 ♋ 37	24 ♋ 09	08 ♉ 21	02 ♊ 23	01 ♍ 57
Jul 13, 1946	05 ♋ 15	26 ♊ 56	15 ♐ 15	19 ♉ 52	09 ♋ 20	28 ♋ 14	10 ♉ 58	05 ♊ 56	06 ♍ 19
Jul 23, 1946	09 ♋ 19	00 ♋ 08	14 ♐ 07	24 ♉ 36	13 ♋ 03	02 ♌ 18	13 ♉ 21	09 ♊ 21	10 ♍ 51
Aug 2, 1946	13 ♋ 20	03 ♋ 14	13 ♐ 33	29 ♉ 10	16 ♋ 45	06 ♌ 21	15 ♉ 28	12 ♊ 38	15 ♍ 31
Aug 12, 1946	17 ♋ 16	06 ♋ 13	13 ♐ 33	03 ♊ 32	20 ♋ 25	10 ♌ 23	17 ♉ 15	15 ♊ 43	20 ♍ 20
Aug 22, 1946	21 ♋ 07	09 ♋ 04	14 ♐ 06	07 ♊ 39	24 ♋ 02	14 ♌ 21	18 ♉ 39	18 ♊ 36	25 ♍ 15
Sep 1, 1946	24 ♋ 51	11 ♋ 44	15 ♐ 10	11 ♊ 29	27 ♋ 36	18 ♌ 17	19 ♉ 37	21 ♊ 14	00 ♎ 17
Sep 11, 1946	28 ♋ 28	14 ♋ 12	16 ♐ 42	14 ♊ 57	01 ♌ 04	22 ♌ 09	20 ♉ 06	23 ♊ 33	05 ♎ 25
Sep 21, 1946	01 ♌ 55	16 ♋ 26	18 ♐ 39	17 ♊ 59	04 ♌ 27	25 ♌ 56	20 ♉ 02	25 ♊ 32	10 ♎ 38
Oct 1, 1946	05 ♌ 11	18 ♋ 23	20 ♐ 57	20 ♊ 28	07 ♌ 41	29 ♌ 36	19 ♉ 25	27 ♊ 05	15 ♎ 55
Oct 11, 1946	08 ♌ 13	20 ♋ 01	23 ♐ 34	22 ♊ 19	10 ♌ 46	03 ♍ 10	18 ♉ 14	28 ♊ 09	21 ♎ 16
Oct 21, 1946	10 ♌ 58	21 ♋ 16	26 ♐ 27	23 ♊ 24	13 ♌ 38	06 ♍ 34	16 ♉ 36	28 ♊ 39	26 ♎ 41

Date	ATROPOS	HEKATE	LILITH	MEDUSA	MOIRA	NEMESIS	PERSEPHONE	PROSERPINA	PYTHIA
Oct 31, 1946	13 ♌ 24	22 ♋ 06	29 ♐ 34	23 ♊ 37	16 ♌ 15	09 ♍ 48	14 ♉ 36	28 ♊ 33	02 ♏ 09
Nov 10, 1946	15 ♌ 26	22 ♋ 27	02 ♑ 54	22 ♊ 54	18 ♌ 33	12 ♍ 49	12 ♉ 28	27 ♊ 49	07 ♏ 39
Nov 20, 1946	17 ♌ 00	22 ♋ 17	06 ♑ 25	21 ♊ 18	20 ♌ 59	15 ♍ 34	10 ♉ 24	26 ♊ 27	13 ♏ 11
Nov 30, 1946	18 ♌ 01	21 ♋ 37	10 ♑ 04	18 ♊ 59	22 ♌ 57	18 ♍ 02	08 ♉ 37	24 ♊ 34	18 ♏ 43
Dec 10, 1946	18 ♌ 24	20 ♋ 26	13 ♑ 52	16 ♊ 17	23 ♌ 20	20 ♍ 09	07 ♉ 17	22 ♊ 20	24 ♏ 16
Dec 20, 1946	18 ♌ 05	18 ♋ 51	17 ♑ 46	13 ♊ 38	23 ♌ 03	21 ♍ 50	06 ♉ 31	19 ♊ 60	29 ♏ 49
Dec 30, 1946	17 ♌ 02	16 ♋ 56	21 ♑ 45	11 ♊ 29	22 ♌ 07	23 ♍ 03	06 ♉ 21	17 ♊ 48	05 ♐ 21
Jan 9, 1947	15 ♌ 16	14 ♋ 54	25 ♑ 50	10 ♊ 06	20 ♌ 33	23 ♍ 43	06 ♉ 46	15 ♊ 59	10 ♐ 50
Jan 19, 1947	12 ♌ 56	12 ♋ 56	29 ♑ 57	09 ♊ 37	18 ♌ 29	23 ♍ 48	07 ♉ 43	14 ♊ 44	16 ♐ 17
Jan 29, 1947	10 ♌ 13	11 ♋ 11	04 ♒ 08	10 ♊ 04	16 ♌ 09	23 ♍ 16	09 ♉ 11	14 ♊ 07	21 ♐ 39
Feb 8, 1947	07 ♌ 27	09 ♋ 50	08 ♒ 20	11 ♊ 20	13 ♌ 48	22 ♍ 07	11 ♉ 04	14 ♊ 10	26 ♐ 56
Feb 18, 1947	04 ♌ 55	08 ♋ 56	12 ♒ 34	13 ♊ 19	11 ♌ 44	20 ♍ 26	13 ♉ 19	14 ♊ 49	02 ♑ 07
Feb 28, 1947	02 ♌ 54	08 ♋ 33	16 ♒ 48	15 ♊ 55	10 ♌ 11	18 ♍ 22	15 ♉ 54	16 ♊ 03	07 ♑ 10
Mar 10, 1947	01 ♌ 32	08 ♋ 39	21 ♒ 02	18 ♊ 60	09 ♌ 16	16 ♍ 07	18 ♉ 44	17 ♊ 46	12 ♑ 04
Mar 20, 1947	00 ♌ 55	09 ♋ 14	25 ♒ 14	22 ♊ 29	09 ♌ 04	13 ♍ 56	21 ♉ 48	19 ♊ 55	16 ♑ 46
Mar 30, 1947	01 ♌ 01	10 ♋ 15	29 ♒ 24	26 ♊ 17	09 ♌ 34	12 ♍ 01	25 ♉ 03	22 ♊ 25	21 ♑ 14
Apr 9, 1947	01 ♌ 46	11 ♋ 39	03 ♓ 31	00 ♋ 22	10 ♌ 42	10 ♍ 33	28 ♉ 27	25 ♊ 14	25 ♑ 26
Apr 19, 1947	03 ♌ 07	13 ♋ 22	07 ♓ 34	04 ♋ 38	12 ♌ 24	09 ♍ 38	01 ♊ 58	28 ♊ 18	29 ♑ 19
Apr 29, 1947	04 ♌ 57	15 ♋ 22	11 ♓ 32	09 ♋ 06	14 ♌ 37	09 ♍ 18	05 ♊ 36	01 ♋ 35	02 ♒ 49
May 9, 1947	07 ♌ 14	17 ♋ 36	15 ♓ 24	13 ♋ 41	17 ♌ 15	09 ♍ 33	09 ♊ 19	05 ♋ 02	05 ♒ 51
May 19, 1947	09 ♌ 53	20 ♋ 03	19 ♓ 08	18 ♋ 23	20 ♌ 16	10 ♍ 20	13 ♊ 05	08 ♋ 39	08 ♒ 20
May 29, 1947	12 ♌ 51	22 ♋ 39	22 ♓ 42	23 ♋ 10	23 ♌ 35	11 ♍ 35	16 ♊ 55	12 ♋ 24	10 ♒ 11
Jun 8, 1947	16 ♌ 04	25 ♋ 24	26 ♓ 04	28 ♋ 01	27 ♌ 11	13 ♍ 16	20 ♊ 46	16 ♋ 10	11 ♒ 17
Jun 18, 1947	19 ♌ 31	28 ♋ 15	29 ♓ 57	02 ♌ 56	01 ♍ 01	15 ♍ 17	24 ♊ 39	20 ♋ 10	11 ♒ 34
Jun 28, 1947	23 ♌ 10	01 ♌ 11	02 ♈ 18	07 ♌ 53	05 ♍ 53	17 ♍ 37	28 ♊ 32	24 ♋ 11	10 ♒ 58
Jul 8, 1947	26 ♌ 59	04 ♌ 12	04 ♈ 30	12 ♌ 53	09 ♍ 15	20 ♍ 13	02 ♋ 25	28 ♋ 15	09 ♒ 34
Jul 18, 1947	00 ♍ 58	07 ♌ 16	06 ♈ 33	17 ♌ 54	13 ♍ 36	23 ♍ 02	06 ♋ 17	02 ♌ 22	07 ♒ 30
Jul 28, 1947	05 ♍ 04	10 ♌ 22	08 ♈ 05	22 ♌ 56	18 ♍ 06	26 ♍ 02	10 ♋ 06	06 ♌ 31	05 ♒ 04
Aug 7, 1947	09 ♍ 18	13 ♌ 29	09 ♈ 01	27 ♌ 59	22 ♍ 42	29 ♍ 11	13 ♋ 53	10 ♌ 42	02 ♒ 38
Aug 17, 1947	13 ♍ 38	16 ♌ 37	09 ♈ 17	03 ♍ 02	27 ♍ 25	02 ♎ 29	17 ♋ 37	14 ♌ 54	00 ♒ 36
Aug 27, 1947	18 ♍ 05	19 ♌ 43	08 ♈ 50	08 ♍ 05	02 ♎ 13	05 ♎ 53	21 ♋ 15	19 ♌ 06	29 ♑ 13
Sep 6, 1947	22 ♍ 36	22 ♌ 48	07 ♈ 39	13 ♍ 08	07 ♎ 06	09 ♎ 23	24 ♋ 47	23 ♌ 18	28 ♑ 39
Sep 16, 1947	27 ♍ 14	25 ♌ 50	05 ♈ 52	18 ♍ 10	12 ♎ 03	12 ♎ 57	28 ♋ 11	27 ♌ 29	28 ♑ 53
Sep 26, 1947	01 ♎ 55	28 ♌ 48	03 ♈ 40	23 ♍ 10	17 ♎ 03	16 ♎ 34	01 ♌ 26	01 ♍ 38	29 ♑ 55
Oct 6, 1947	06 ♎ 41	01 ♍ 40	01 ♈ 24	28 ♍ 10	22 ♎ 01	20 ♎ 14	04 ♌ 29	05 ♍ 44	01 ♒ 39

	ATROPOS	HEKATE	LILITH	MEDUSA	MOIRA	NEMESIS	PERSEPHONE	PROSERPINA	PYTHIA
Oct 16, 1947	11 ♎ 31	04 ♍ 26	29 ♓ 22	03 ♎ 06	22 ♎ 06	23 ♎ 56	07 ♌ 19	09 ♍ 46	03 ♒ 57
Oct 26, 1947	16 ♎ 25	07 ♍ 03	27 ♓ 52	08 ♎ 01	27 ♎ 11	27 ♎ 38	09 ♌ 51	13 ♍ 43	06 ♒ 46
Nov 5, 1947	21 ♎ 22	09 ♍ 29	27 ♓ 07	12 ♎ 51	02 ♏ 17	01 ♏ 20	12 ♌ 03	17 ♍ 34	09 ♒ 59
Nov 15, 1947	26 ♎ 22	11 ♍ 42	27 ♓ 11	17 ♎ 38	07 ♏ 24	05 ♏ 01	13 ♌ 50	21 ♍ 16	13 ♒ 33
Nov 25, 1947	01 ♏ 24	13 ♍ 40	28 ♓ 04	22 ♎ 19	12 ♏ 30	08 ♏ 40	15 ♌ 10	24 ♍ 48	17 ♒ 23
Dec 5, 1947	06 ♏ 27	15 ♍ 19	29 ♓ 41	26 ♎ 54	17 ♏ 36	12 ♏ 16	15 ♌ 57	28 ♍ 06	21 ♒ 26
Dec 15, 1947	11 ♏ 32	16 ♍ 37	01 ♈ 58	01 ♏ 22	22 ♏ 39	15 ♏ 47	16 ♌ 08	01 ♎ 09	25 ♒ 41
Dec 25, 1947	16 ♏ 36	17 ♍ 30	04 ♈ 49	05 ♏ 41	27 ♏ 39	19 ♏ 12	15 ♌ 40	03 ♎ 53	00 ♓ 04
Jan 4, 1948	21 ♏ 41	17 ♍ 56	08 ♈ 08	09 ♏ 49	02 ♐ 35	22 ♏ 30	14 ♌ 36	06 ♎ 13	04 ♓ 34
Jan 14, 1948	26 ♏ 43	17 ♍ 53	11 ♈ 52	13 ♏ 43	07 ♐ 25	25 ♏ 38	12 ♌ 58	08 ♎ 06	09 ♓ 09
Jan 24, 1948	01 ♐ 42	17 ♍ 18	15 ♈ 56	17 ♏ 23	12 ♐ 09	28 ♏ 35	10 ♌ 56	09 ♎ 26	13 ♓ 48
Feb 3, 1948	06 ♐ 37	16 ♍ 13	20 ♈ 16	20 ♏ 44	16 ♐ 44	01 ♐ 19	08 ♌ 44	10 ♎ 09	18 ♓ 29
Feb 13, 1948	11 ♐ 25	14 ♍ 42	24 ♈ 50	23 ♏ 43	21 ♐ 09	03 ♐ 46	06 ♌ 37	10 ♎ 11	23 ♓ 12
Feb 23, 1948	16 ♐ 05	12 ♍ 51	29 ♈ 35	26 ♏ 16	25 ♐ 22	05 ♐ 54	04 ♌ 49	09 ♎ 30	27 ♓ 56
Mar 4, 1948	20 ♐ 34	10 ♍ 51	04 ♉ 28	28 ♏ 18	29 ♐ 21	07 ♐ 40	03 ♌ 32	08 ♎ 09	02 ♈ 40
Mar 14, 1948	24 ♐ 48	08 ♍ 51	09 ♉ 29	29 ♏ 44	03 ♑ 03	08 ♐ 60	02 ♌ 50	06 ♎ 14	07 ♈ 23
Mar 24, 1948	28 ♐ 44	07 ♍ 04	14 ♉ 35	00 ♐ 29	06 ♑ 24	09 ♐ 50	02 ♌ 47	03 ♎ 59	12 ♈ 05
Apr 3, 1948	02 ♑ 17	05 ♍ 38	19 ♉ 45	00 ♐ 27	09 ♑ 22	10 ♐ 08	03 ♌ 20	01 ♎ 42	16 ♈ 44
Apr 13, 1948	05 ♑ 21	04 ♍ 39	24 ♉ 59	29 ♏ 38	11 ♑ 52	09 ♐ 51	04 ♌ 26	29 ♍ 38	21 ♈ 21
Apr 23, 1948	07 ♑ 49	04 ♍ 10	00 ♊ 14	28 ♏ 03	13 ♑ 49	08 ♐ 59	06 ♌ 02	28 ♍ 05	25 ♈ 55
May 3, 1948	09 ♑ 36	04 ♍ 12	05 ♊ 31	25 ♏ 50	15 ♑ 10	07 ♐ 35	08 ♌ 04	27 ♍ 11	00 ♉ 25
May 13, 1948	10 ♑ 31	04 ♍ 43	10 ♊ 48	23 ♏ 15	15 ♑ 50	05 ♐ 44	10 ♌ 28	26 ♍ 59	04 ♉ 51
May 23, 1948	10 ♑ 31	05 ♍ 42	16 ♊ 05	20 ♏ 17	15 ♑ 46	03 ♐ 37	13 ♌ 10	27 ♍ 29	09 ♉ 12
Jun 2, 1948	09 ♑ 34	07 ♍ 05	21 ♊ 21	18 ♏ 17	14 ♑ 58	01 ♐ 26	16 ♌ 08	28 ♍ 39	13 ♉ 27
Jun 12, 1948	07 ♑ 45	08 ♍ 49	26 ♊ 35	16 ♏ 31	13 ♑ 31	29 ♏ 24	19 ♌ 19	00 ♎ 23	17 ♉ 37
Jun 22, 1948	05 ♑ 22	10 ♍ 52	01 ♋ 48	15 ♏ 29	11 ♑ 34	27 ♏ 45	22 ♌ 41	02 ♎ 37	21 ♉ 39
Jul 2, 1948	02 ♑ 49	13 ♍ 11	06 ♋ 58	15 ♏ 14	09 ♑ 24	26 ♏ 36	26 ♌ 12	05 ♎ 17	25 ♉ 34
Jul 12, 1948	00 ♑ 33	15 ♍ 45	12 ♋ 06	15 ♏ 45	07 ♑ 16	26 ♏ 01	29 ♌ 51	08 ♎ 19	29 ♉ 19
Jul 22, 1948	28 ♐ 57	18 ♍ 30	17 ♋ 10	16 ♏ 57	05 ♑ 28	26 ♏ 02	03 ♍ 37	11 ♎ 40	02 ♊ 54
Aug 1, 1948	28 ♐ 13	21 ♍ 26	22 ♋ 10	18 ♏ 46	04 ♑ 13	26 ♏ 38	07 ♍ 28	15 ♎ 16	06 ♊ 17
Aug 11, 1948	28 ♐ 24	24 ♍ 31	27 ♋ 06	21 ♏ 06	03 ♑ 37	27 ♏ 45	11 ♍ 23	19 ♎ 06	09 ♊ 25
Aug 21, 1948	29 ♐ 28	27 ♍ 44	01 ♌ 56	23 ♏ 54	03 ♑ 42	29 ♏ 22	15 ♍ 22	23 ♎ 08	12 ♊ 17
Aug 31, 1948	01 ♑ 17	01 ♎ 03	06 ♌ 41	27 ♏ 04	04 ♑ 26	01 ♐ 24	19 ♍ 24	27 ♎ 19	14 ♊ 50
Sep 10, 1948	03 ♑ 44	04 ♎ 27	11 ♌ 19	00 ♐ 33	05 ♑ 47	03 ♐ 48	23 ♍ 28	01 ♏ 38	16 ♊ 59
Sep 20, 1948	06 ♑ 44	07 ♎ 56	15 ♌ 49	04 ♐ 20	07 ♑ 39	06 ♐ 31	27 ♍ 32	06 ♏ 05	18 ♊ 42

Date	ATROPOS	HEKATE	LILITH	MEDUSA	MOIRA	NEMESIS	PERSEPHONE	PROSERPINA	PYTHIA
Sep 30, 1948	10 ♑ 10	11 ♎ 28	20 ♌ 10	08 ♐ 20	09 ♑ 57	09 ♐ 32	01 ♎ 38	10 ♏ 38	19 ♊ 53
Oct 10, 1948	13 ♑ 56	15 ♎ 03	24 ♌ 21	12 ♐ 33	12 ♑ 39	12 ♐ 47	05 ♎ 43	15 ♏ 16	20 ♊ 28
Oct 20, 1948	17 ♑ 60	18 ♎ 39	28 ♌ 19	16 ♐ 56	15 ♑ 40	16 ♐ 14	09 ♎ 46	19 ♏ 58	20 ♊ 23
Oct 30, 1948	22 ♑ 17	22 ♎ 16	02 ♍ 04	21 ♐ 28	18 ♑ 57	19 ♐ 52	13 ♎ 48	24 ♏ 44	19 ♊ 36
Nov 9, 1948	26 ♑ 45	25 ♎ 53	05 ♍ 32	26 ♐ 08	22 ♑ 27	23 ♐ 40	17 ♎ 47	29 ♏ 32	18 ♊ 06
Nov 19, 1948	01 ♒ 22	29 ♎ 28	08 ♍ 40	00 ♑ 55	26 ♑ 08	27 ♐ 36	21 ♎ 41	04 ♐ 22	16 ♊ 01
Nov 29, 1948	06 ♒ 06	03 ♏ 01	11 ♍ 26	05 ♑ 48	29 ♑ 58	01 ♑ 39	25 ♎ 30	09 ♐ 13	13 ♊ 31
Dec 9, 1948	10 ♒ 56	06 ♏ 30	13 ♍ 45	10 ♑ 45	03 ♒ 56	05 ♑ 47	29 ♎ 11	14 ♐ 04	10 ♊ 52
Dec 19, 1948	15 ♒ 49	09 ♏ 54	15 ♍ 33	15 ♑ 47	07 ♒ 58	10 ♑ 01	02 ♏ 44	18 ♐ 55	08 ♊ 22
Dec 29, 1948	20 ♒ 46	13 ♏ 11	16 ♍ 45	20 ♑ 53	12 ♒ 06	14 ♑ 18	06 ♏ 07	23 ♐ 45	06 ♊ 18
Jan 8, 1949	25 ♒ 46	16 ♏ 19	17 ♍ 16	26 ♑ 02	16 ♒ 16	18 ♑ 38	09 ♏ 16	28 ♐ 32	04 ♊ 51
Jan 18, 1949	00 ♓ 47	19 ♏ 15	17 ♍ 05	01 ♒ 12	20 ♒ 28	23 ♑ 00	12 ♏ 11	03 ♑ 17	04 ♊ 05
Jan 28, 1949	05 ♓ 48	21 ♏ 59	16 ♍ 10	06 ♒ 25	24 ♒ 42	27 ♑ 23	14 ♏ 47	07 ♑ 58	04 ♊ 02
Feb 7, 1949	10 ♓ 50	24 ♏ 27	14 ♍ 36	11 ♒ 38	28 ♒ 55	01 ♒ 47	17 ♏ 01	12 ♑ 33	04 ♊ 39
Feb 17, 1949	15 ♓ 51	26 ♏ 35	12 ♍ 30	16 ♒ 52	03 ♓ 08	06 ♒ 11	18 ♏ 51	17 ♑ 03	05 ♊ 52
Feb 27, 1949	20 ♓ 51	28 ♏ 21	10 ♍ 08	22 ♒ 06	07 ♓ 19	10 ♒ 33	20 ♏ 11	21 ♑ 26	07 ♊ 35
Mar 9, 1949	25 ♓ 50	29 ♏ 41	07 ♍ 45	27 ♒ 19	11 ♓ 27	14 ♒ 53	20 ♏ 59	25 ♑ 40	09 ♊ 45
Mar 19, 1949	00 ♈ 46	00 ♐ 30	05 ♍ 39	02 ♓ 31	15 ♓ 32	19 ♒ 09	21 ♏ 12	29 ♑ 44	12 ♊ 16
Mar 29, 1949	05 ♈ 40	00 ♐ 47	04 ♍ 03	07 ♓ 42	19 ♓ 34	23 ♒ 22	20 ♏ 47	03 ♒ 37	15 ♊ 07
Apr 8, 1949	10 ♈ 31	00 ♐ 29	03 ♍ 03	12 ♓ 50	23 ♓ 30	27 ♒ 30	19 ♏ 46	07 ♒ 15	18 ♊ 13
Apr 18, 1949	15 ♈ 17	00 ♐ 42	02 ♍ 42	17 ♓ 56	27 ♓ 20	01 ♓ 31	18 ♏ 14	10 ♒ 38	21 ♊ 31
Apr 28, 1949	20 ♈ 03	28 ♏ 11	02 ♍ 59	22 ♓ 58	01 ♈ 04	05 ♓ 18	16 ♏ 18	13 ♒ 42	25 ♊ 01
May 8, 1949	24 ♈ 42	26 ♏ 22	03 ♍ 51	-27 ♓ 56	04 ♈ 40	09 ♓ 08	14 ♏ 12	16 ♒ 24	28 ♊ 39
May 18, 1949	29 ♈ 17	24 ♏ 21	05 ♍ 13	02 ♈ 48	08 ♈ 07	12 ♓ 40	12 ♏ 10	18 ♒ 41	02 ♋ 26
May 28, 1949	03 ♉ 46	22 ♏ 19	07 ♍ 01	07 ♈ 35	11 ♈ 24	15 ♓ 58	10 ♏ 24	20 ♒ 29	06 ♋ 18
Jun 7, 1949	08 ♉ 09	20 ♏ 32	09 ♍ 11	12 ♈ 14	14 ♈ 28	19 ♓ 00	09 ♏ 06	21 ♒ 43	10 ♋ 16
Jun 17, 1949	12 ♉ 24	19 ♏ 10	11 ♍ 39	16 ♈ 45	17 ♈ 19	21 ♓ 43	08 ♏ 21	22 ♒ 20	14 ♋ 18
Jun 27, 1949	16 ♉ 32	18 ♏ 21	14 ♍ 23	21 ♈ 05	19 ♈ 53	24 ♓ 01	08 ♏ 11	22 ♒ 16	18 ♋ 25
Jul 7, 1949	20 ♉ 29	18 ♏ 08	17 ♍ 20	25 ♈ 11	22 ♈ 09	25 ♓ 52	08 ♏ 36	22 ♒ 32	22 ♋ 34
Jul 17, 1949	24 ♉ 16	18 ♏ 32	20 ♍ 27	29 ♈ 03	24 ♈ 04	27 ♓ 11	09 ♏ 33	20 ♒ 10	26 ♋ 46
Jul 27, 1949	27 ♉ 51	19 ♏ 31	23 ♍ 42	02 ♉ 36	25 ♈ 33	27 ♓ 53	10 ♏ 60	18 ♒ 16	00 ♌ 60
Aug 6, 1949	01 ♊ 10	21 ♏ 02	27 ♍ 05	05 ♉ 45	26 ♈ 35	27 ♓ 54	12 ♏ 52	16 ♒ 05	05 ♌ 15
Aug 16, 1949	04 ♊ 11	23 ♏ 01	00 ♎ 34	08 ♉ 27	27 ♈ 05	27 ♓ 14	15 ♏ 07	13 ♒ 52	09 ♌ 32
Aug 26, 1949	06 ♊ 51	25 ♏ 24	04 ♎ 07	10 ♉ 36	27 ♈ 02	25 ♓ 54	17 ♏ 40	11 ♒ 52	13 ♌ 49
Sep 5, 1949	09 ♊ 06	28 ♏ 10	07 ♎ 44	12 ♉ 03	26 ♈ 22	24 ♓ 02	20 ♏ 30	10 ♒ 20	18 ♌ 06

	ATROPOS	HEKATE	LILITH	MEDUSA	MOIRA	NEMESIS	PERSEPHONE	PROSERPINA	PYTHIA
Sep 15, 1949	10 ♊ 51	01 ♐ 15	11 ♎ 24	12 ♉ 44	25 ♈ 09	21 ♓ 53	23 ♏ 33	09 ♒ 24	22 ♌ 22
Sep 25, 1949	12 ♊ 01	04 ♐ 36	15 ♎ 05	12 ♉ 33	23 ♈ 25	19 ♓ 42	26 ♏ 48	09 ♒ 07	26 ♌ 37
Oct 5, 1949	12 ♊ 31	08 ♐ 11	18 ♎ 47	11 ♉ 28	21 ♈ 19	17 ♓ 49	00 ♐ 13	09 ♒ 30	00 ♍ 49
Oct 15, 1949	12 ♊ 16	11 ♐ 58	22 ♎ 30	09 ♉ 35	19 ♈ 04	16 ♓ 28	03 ♐ 46	10 ♒ 30	04 ♍ 58
Oct 25, 1949	11 ♊ 14	15 ♐ 56	26 ♎ 11	07 ♉ 06	16 ♈ 53	15 ♓ 48	07 ♐ 26	12 ♒ 03	09 ♍ 02
Nov 4, 1949	09 ♊ 27	20 ♐ 03	29 ♎ 51	04 ♉ 26	14 ♈ 59	15 ♓ 53	11 ♐ 11	14 ♒ 04	13 ♍ 00
Nov 14, 1949	07 ♊ 02	24 ♐ 18	03 ♏ 28	02 ♉ 01	13 ♈ 33	16 ♓ 40	14 ♐ 60	16 ♒ 31	16 ♍ 50
Nov 24, 1949	04 ♊ 15	28 ♐ 39	07 ♏ 02	00 ♉ 12	12 ♈ 39	18 ♓ 08	18 ♐ 52	19 ♒ 18	20 ♍ 31
Dec 4, 1949	01 ♊ 26	03 ♑ 05	10 ♏ 31	29 ♈ 14	12 ♈ 21	20 ♓ 11	22 ♐ 47	22 ♒ 22	23 ♍ 58
Dec 14, 1949	28 ♉ 55	07 ♑ 36	13 ♏ 53	29 ♈ 11	12 ♈ 38	22 ♓ 44	26 ♐ 42	25 ♒ 41	27 ♍ 10
Dec 24, 1949	26 ♉ 44	12 ♑ 10	17 ♏ 08	00 ♉ 03	13 ♈ 28	25 ♓ 42	00 ♑ 37	29 ♒ 13	00 ♎ 02
Jan 3, 1950	25 ♉ 44	16 ♑ 47	20 ♏ 13	01 ♉ 43	14 ♈ 47	29 ♓ 03	04 ♑ 32	02 ♓ 54	02 ♎ 30
Jan 13, 1950	25 ♉ 17	21 ♑ 24	23 ♏ 07	04 ♉ 04	16 ♈ 31	02 ♈ 41	08 ♑ 24	06 ♓ 43	04 ♎ 29
Jan 23, 1950	25 ♉ 35	26 ♑ 03	25 ♏ 48	06 ♉ 60	18 ♈ 36	06 ♈ 34	12 ♑ 13	10 ♓ 38	05 ♎ 52
Feb 2, 1950	26 ♉ 34	00 ♒ 41	28 ♏ 13	10 ♉ 24	21 ♈ 01	10 ♈ 38	15 ♑ 58	14 ♓ 39	06 ♎ 34
Feb 12, 1950	28 ♉ 07	05 ♒ 18	00 ♐ 19	14 ♉ 12	23 ♈ 40	14 ♈ 53	19 ♑ 38	18 ♓ 43	06 ♎ 29
Feb 22, 1950	00 ♊ 10	09 ♒ 53	02 ♐ 04	18 ♉ 18	26 ♈ 32	19 ♈ 15	23 ♑ 10	22 ♓ 49	05 ♎ 35
Mar 4, 1950	02 ♊ 37	14 ♒ 25	03 ♐ 24	22 ♉ 40	29 ♈ 35	23 ♈ 44	26 ♑ 35	26 ♓ 57	03 ♎ 54
Mar 14, 1950	05 ♊ 25	18 ♒ 53	03 ♐ 15	27 ♉ 14	02 ♉ 46	28 ♈ 17	29 ♑ 50	01 ♈ 06	01 ♎ 36
Mar 24, 1950	08 ♊ 29	23 ♒ 16	04 ♐ 36	01 ♊ 57	06 ♉ 04	02 ♉ 54	02 ♒ 54	05 ♈ 14	28 ♍ 57
Apr 3, 1950	11 ♊ 46	27 ♒ 33	04 ♐ 23	06 ♊ 49	09 ♉ 27	07 ♉ 33	05 ♒ 45	09 ♈ 22	26 ♍ 21
Apr 13, 1950	15 ♊ 14	01 ♓ 43	03 ♐ 37	11 ♊ 47	12 ♉ 55	12 ♉ 14	08 ♒ 20	13 ♈ 28	24 ♍ 09
Apr 23, 1950	18 ♊ 52	05 ♓ 43	02 ♐ 18	16 ♊ 50	16 ♉ 25	16 ♉ 55	10 ♒ 37	17 ♈ 31	22 ♍ 39
May 3, 1950	22 ♊ 36	09 ♓ 34	00 ♐ 31	21 ♊ 57	19 ♉ 57	21 ♉ 37	12 ♒ 34	21 ♈ 30	21 ♍ 58
May 13, 1950	26 ♊ 26	13 ♓ 12	28 ♏ 27	27 ♊ 07	23 ♉ 30	26 ♉ 18	14 ♒ 08	25 ♈ 26	22 ♍ 10
May 23, 1950	00 ♋ 21	16 ♓ 36	26 ♏ 14	02 ♋ 19	27 ♉ 03	00 ♊ 57	15 ♒ 15	29 ♈ 17	23 ♍ 10
Jun 2, 1950	04 ♋ 18	19 ♓ 43	24 ♏ 07	07 ♋ 33	00 ♊ 35	05 ♊ 35	15 ♒ 53	03 ♉ 02	24 ♍ 54
Jun 12, 1950	08 ♋ 19	22 ♓ 30	22 ♏ 16	12 ♋ 47	04 ♊ 06	10 ♊ 11	15 ♒ 59	06 ♉ 40	27 ♍ 16
Jun 22, 1950	12 ♋ 21	24 ♓ 55	20 ♏ 51	18 ♋ 03	07 ♊ 34	14 ♊ 43	15 ♒ 33	10 ♉ 10	00 ♎ 10
Jul 2, 1950	16 ♋ 24	26 ♓ 53	19 ♏ 57	23 ♋ 18	10 ♊ 59	19 ♊ 12	14 ♒ 34	13 ♉ 31	03 ♎ 32
Jul 12, 1950	20 ♋ 28	28 ♓ 21	19 ♏ 35	28 ♌ 33	14 ♊ 20	23 ♊ 37	13 ♒ 07	16 ♉ 40	07 ♎ 16
Jul 22, 1950	24 ♋ 32	29 ♓ 15	19 ♏ 46	03 ♌ 48	17 ♊ 35	27 ♊ 57	11 ♒ 17	19 ♉ 37	11 ♎ 19
Aug 1, 1950	28 ♋ 35	29 ♓ 31	20 ♏ 28	09 ♌ 02	20 ♊ 44	02 ♋ 11	09 ♒ 16	22 ♉ 18	15 ♎ 39
Aug 11, 1950	02 ♌ 36	29 ♓ 08	21 ♏ 38	14 ♌ 15	23 ♊ 44	06 ♋ 15	07 ♒ 15	24 ♉ 41	20 ♎ 53
Aug 21, 1950	06 ♌ 36	28 ♓ 07	23 ♏ 13	19 ♌ 27	26 ♊ 35	10 ♋ 17	05 ♒ 25	26 ♉ 43	24 ♎ 59

Date	ATROPOS	HEKATE	LILITH	MEDUSA	MOIRA	NEMESIS	PERSEPHONE	PROSERPINA	PYTHIA
Aug 31, 1950	10 ♌ 33	26 ♓ 35	25 ♏ 10	24 ♌ 36	29 ♊ 13	14 ♋ 07	03 ♒ 57	28 ♉ 20	29 ♎ 56
Sep 10, 1950	14 ♌ 26	24 ♓ 39	27 ♏ 26	29 ♌ 43	01 ♋ 38	17 ♋ 46	02 ♒ 57	29 ♉ 29	05 ♏ 01
Sep 20, 1950	18 ♌ 14	22 ♓ 36	29 ♏ 59	04 ♍ 48	03 ♋ 46	21 ♋ 12	02 ♒ 28	00 ♊ 06	10 ♏ 13
Sep 30, 1950	21 ♌ 57	20 ♓ 39	02 ♐ 45	09 ♍ 49	05 ♋ 33	24 ♋ 52	02 ♒ 33	00 ♊ 29	15 ♏ 33
Oct 10, 1950	25 ♌ 33	19 ♓ 04	05 ♐ 44	14 ♍ 46	06 ♋ 57	27 ♋ 15	03 ♒ 08	28 ♉ 15	20 ♏ 58
Oct 20, 1950	28 ♌ 60	17 ♓ 59	08 ♐ 54	19 ♍ 38	07 ♋ 53	29 ♋ 47	04 ♒ 12	26 ♉ 29	26 ♏ 27
Oct 30, 1950	02 ♍ 16	17 ♓ 32	12 ♐ 12	24 ♍ 25	08 ♋ 18	01 ♌ 53	05 ♒ 43	24 ♉ 19	02 ♐ 01
Nov 9, 1950	05 ♍ 19	17 ♓ 43	15 ♐ 39	29 ♍ 05	08 ♋ 09	03 ♌ 30	07 ♒ 35	21 ♉ 60	07 ♐ 38
Nov 19, 1950	08 ♍ 06	18 ♓ 30	19 ♐ 11	03 ♎ 36	07 ♋ 24	04 ♌ 33	09 ♒ 48	19 ♉ 46	13 ♐ 17
Nov 29, 1950	10 ♍ 34	19 ♓ 51	22 ♐ 49	07 ♎ 58	06 ♋ 04	04 ♌ 59	12 ♒ 17	17 ♉ 52	18 ♐ 59
Dec 9, 1950	12 ♍ 39	21 ♓ 41	26 ♐ 30	12 ♎ 09	04 ♋ 13	04 ♌ 44	15 ♒ 00	16 ♉ 29	24 ♐ 41
Dec 19, 1950	14 ♍ 15	23 ♓ 56	00 ♑ 15	16 ♎ 06	02 ♋ 02	03 ♌ 48	17 ♒ 56	15 ♉ 43	00 ♑ 25
Dec 29, 1950	15 ♍ 18	26 ♓ 33	04 ♑ 02	19 ♎ 46	29 ♊ 43	02 ♌ 14	21 ♒ 01	15 ♉ 35	06 ♑ 08
Jan 8, 1951	15 ♍ 43	29 ♓ 27	07 ♑ 50	23 ♎ 06	27 ♊ 31	00 ♌ 11	24 ♒ 14	16 ♉ 05	11 ♑ 50
Jan 18, 1951	15 ♍ 26	02 ♈ 36	11 ♑ 39	26 ♎ 03	25 ♊ 40	27 ♋ 52	27 ♒ 34	17 ♉ 09	17 ♑ 31
Jan 28, 1951	14 ♍ 23	05 ♈ 56	15 ♒ 26	28 ♎ 31	24 ♊ 18	25 ♋ 35	00 ♓ 58	17 ♉ 09	23 ♑ 10
Feb 7, 1951	12 ♍ 36	09 ♈ 26	19 ♒ 12	00 ♏ 26	23 ♊ 33	23 ♋ 33	04 ♓ 27	18 ♉ 43	28 ♑ 46
Feb 17, 1951	10 ♍ 14	13 ♈ 04	22 ♒ 54	01 ♏ 42	23 ♊ 25	22 ♋ 01	07 ♓ 57	20 ♉ 44	04 ♒ 19
Feb 27, 1951	07 ♍ 29	16 ♈ 47	26 ♒ 33	02 ♏ 14	23 ♊ 54	21 ♋ 05	11 ♓ 29	23 ♉ 07	09 ♒ 48
Mar 9, 1951	04 ♍ 40	20 ♈ 35	00 ♒ 06	01 ♏ 57	24 ♊ 56	20 ♋ 49	15 ♓ 02	25 ♉ 48	15 ♒ 11
Mar 19, 1951	02 ♍ 08	24 ♈ 26	03 ♒ 33	00 ♏ 50	26 ♊ 29	21 ♋ 10	18 ♓ 33	28 ♉ 45	20 ♒ 29
Mar 29, 1951	00 ♍ 08	28 ♈ 18	06 ♒ 51	28 ♎ 59	28 ♊ 26	22 ♋ 06	22 ♓ 03	01 ♊ 55	25 ♒ 41
Apr 8, 1951	28 ♌ 51	02 ♉ 12	10 ♒ 00	26 ♎ 33	00 ♋ 47	23 ♋ 32	25 ♓ 30	05 ♊ 16	00 ♓ 44
Apr 18, 1951	28 ♌ 20	06 ♉ 05	12 ♒ 57	23 ♎ 52	03 ♋ 26	25 ♋ 25	28 ♓ 53	08 ♊ 46	05 ♓ 39
Apr 28, 1951	28 ♌ 35	09 ♉ 57	15 ♒ 39	21 ♎ 17	06 ♋ 21	27 ♋ 40	02 ♈ 11	12 ♊ 24	10 ♓ 24
May 8, 1951	29 ♌ 32	13 ♉ 48	18 ♒ 04	19 ♎ 07	09 ♋ 31	00 ♌ 13	05 ♈ 23	16 ♊ 07	14 ♓ 58
May 18, 1951	01 ♍ 06	17 ♉ 36	20 ♒ 09	17 ♎ 37	12 ♋ 51	03 ♌ 02	08 ♈ 28	19 ♊ 55	19 ♓ 19
May 28, 1951	03 ♍ 13	21 ♉ 20	21 ♒ 50	16 ♎ 53	16 ♋ 22	06 ♌ 03	11 ♈ 25	23 ♊ 47	23 ♓ 24
Jun 7, 1951	05 ♍ 48	25 ♉ 01	23 ♒ 03	16 ♎ 56	20 ♋ 02	09 ♌ 15	14 ♈ 11	27 ♊ 42	27 ♓ 12
Jun 17, 1951	08 ♍ 47	28 ♉ 36	23 ♒ 44	17 ♎ 44	23 ♋ 49	12 ♌ 36	16 ♈ 45	01 ♋ 39	00 ♈ 39
Jun 27, 1951	12 ♍ 07	02 ♊ 05	23 ♒ 49	19 ♎ 11	27 ♋ 42	16 ♌ 03	19 ♈ 04	05 ♋ 38	03 ♈ 43
Jul 7, 1951	15 ♍ 45	05 ♊ 28	23 ♒ 17	21 ♎ 12	01 ♌ 41	19 ♌ 37	21 ♈ 08	09 ♋ 38	06 ♈ 18
Jul 17, 1951	19 ♍ 39	08 ♊ 42	22 ♒ 07	23 ♎ 42	05 ♌ 44	23 ♌ 15	22 ♈ 51	13 ♋ 38	08 ♈ 20
Jul 27, 1951	23 ♍ 47	11 ♊ 47	20 ♒ 23	26 ♎ 37	09 ♌ 52	26 ♌ 56	24 ♈ 13	17 ♋ 37	09 ♈ 44
Aug 6, 1951	28 ♍ 08	14 ♊ 40	18 ♒ 15	29 ♎ 52	14 ♌ 02	00 ♍ 40	25 ♈ 08	21 ♋ 35	10 ♈ 24

	ATROPOS	HEKATE	LILITH	MEDUSA	MOIRA	NEMESIS	PERSEPHONE	PROSERPINA	PYTHIA
Aug 16, 1951	02 ♎ 40	17 ♊ 21	15 ♒ 56	03 ♏ 24	18 ♌ 16	04 ♍ 26	25 ♈ 36	25 ♋ 31	10 ♈ 17
Aug 26, 1951	07 ♎ 23	19 ♊ 46	13 ♒ 43	07 ♏ 11	22 ♌ 32	08 ♍ 13	25 ♈ 32	29 ♋ 24	09 ♈ 21
Sep 5, 1951	12 ♎ 15	21 ♊ 54	11 ♒ 51	11 ♏ 11	26 ♌ 49	12 ♍ 00	24 ♈ 56	03 ♌ 14	07 ♈ 39
Sep 15, 1951	17 ♎ 16	23 ♊ 41	10 ♒ 33	15 ♏ 21	01 ♍ 07	15 ♍ 47	23 ♈ 49	06 ♌ 59	05 ♈ 21
Sep 25, 1951	22 ♎ 25	25 ♊ 05	09 ♒ 59	19 ♏ 41	05 ♍ 26	19 ♍ 32	22 ♈ 14	10 ♌ 37	02 ♈ 44
Oct 5, 1951	27 ♎ 42	26 ♊ 02	09 ♒ 46	24 ♏ 09	09 ♍ 44	23 ♍ 16	20 ♈ 19	14 ♌ 08	00 ♈ 08
Oct 15, 1951	03 ♏ 06	26 ♊ 29	10 ♒ 46	28 ♏ 44	14 ♍ 00	26 ♍ 56	18 ♈ 14	17 ♌ 29	27 ♓ 55
Oct 25, 1951	08 ♏ 36	26 ♊ 24	12 ♒ 12	03 ♐ 24	18 ♍ 14	00 ♎ 31	16 ♈ 11	20 ♌ 38	26 ♓ 18
Nov 4, 1951	14 ♏ 12	25 ♊ 47	14 ♒ 13	08 ♐ 10	22 ♍ 25	04 ♎ 02	14 ♈ 23	23 ♌ 32	26 ♓ 26
Nov 14, 1951	19 ♏ 53	24 ♊ 37	16 ♒ 45	13 ♐ 01	26 ♍ 30	07 ♎ 25	12 ♈ 60	26 ♌ 09	25 ♓ 22
Nov 24, 1951	25 ♏ 38	23 ♊ 00	19 ♒ 43	17 ♐ 55	00 ♎ 29	10 ♎ 41	12 ♈ 07	28 ♌ 25	26 ♓ 01
Dec 4, 1951	01 ♐ 28	21 ♊ 04	23 ♒ 04	22 ♐ 52	04 ♎ 20	13 ♎ 45	11 ♈ 48	00 ♍ 15	27 ♈ 19
Dec 14, 1951	07 ♐ 20	18 ♊ 59	26 ♒ 46	27 ♐ 52	07 ♎ 60	16 ♎ 38	12 ♈ 03	01 ♍ 34	29 ♈ 12
Dec 24, 1951	13 ♐ 14	16 ♊ 58	00 ♓ 44	02 ♑ 53	11 ♎ 16	19 ♎ 16	12 ♈ 50	02 ♍ 20	01 ♈ 33
Jan 3, 1952	19 ♐ 10	15 ♊ 13	04 ♓ 57	07 ♑ 56	14 ♎ 35	21 ♎ 36	14 ♈ 06	02 ♍ 26	04 ♈ 18
Jan 13, 1952	25 ♐ 05	13 ♊ 51	09 ♓ 23	12 ♑ 59	17 ♎ 24	23 ♎ 35	15 ♈ 49	01 ♍ 50	07 ♈ 22
Jan 23, 1952	00 ♑ 59	12 ♊ 59	13 ♓ 60	18 ♑ 03	19 ♎ 47	25 ♎ 10	17 ♈ 53	00 ♍ 35	10 ♈ 42
Feb 2, 1952	06 ♑ 51	12 ♊ 39	18 ♓ 45	23 ♑ 06	21 ♎ 41	26 ♎ 17	20 ♈ 17	28 ♌ 44	14 ♈ 15
Feb 12, 1952	12 ♑ 40	12 ♊ 51	23 ♓ 39	28 ♑ 08	22 ♎ 59	26 ♎ 53	22 ♈ 57	26 ♌ 30	17 ♈ 59
Feb 22, 1952	18 ♑ 24	13 ♊ 32	28 ♓ 40	03 ♒ 08	23 ♎ 38	26 ♎ 55	25 ♈ 51	24 ♌ 08	21 ♈ 50
Mar 3, 1952	24 ♑ 03	14 ♊ 40	03 ♈ 46	08 ♒ 05	23 ♎ 32	26 ♎ 21	28 ♈ 57	21 ♌ 56	25 ♈ 48
Mar 13, 1952	29 ♑ 33	16 ♊ 11	08 ♈ 57	12 ♒ 59	22 ♎ 41	25 ♎ 12	02 ♉ 11	20 ♌ 09	29 ♈ 51
Mar 23, 1952	04 ♒ 55	18 ♊ 01	14 ♈ 12	17 ♒ 50	21 ♎ 10	23 ♎ 34	05 ♉ 34	18 ♌ 58	03 ♉ 57
Apr 2, 1952	10 ♒ 06	20 ♊ 09	19 ♈ 29	22 ♒ 35	19 ♎ 10	21 ♎ 33	09 ♉ 02	18 ♌ 27	08 ♉ 06
Apr 12, 1952	15 ♒ 05	22 ♊ 30	24 ♈ 49	27 ♒ 15	16 ♎ 56	19 ♎ 21	12 ♉ 36	18 ♌ 39	12 ♉ 16
Apr 22, 1952	19 ♒ 49	25 ♊ 03	00 ♉ 11	01 ♓ 48	14 ♎ 48	17 ♎ 12	16 ♉ 13	19 ♌ 30	16 ♉ 28
May 2, 1952	24 ♒ 15	27 ♊ 46	05 ♉ 34	06 ♓ 13	13 ♎ 04	15 ♎ 18	19 ♉ 53	20 ♌ 57	20 ♉ 39
May 12, 1952	28 ♒ 22	00 ♋ 37	10 ♉ 57	10 ♓ 27	11 ♎ 57	13 ♎ 50	23 ♉ 35	22 ♌ 55	24 ♉ 50
May 22, 1952	02 ♓ 05	03 ♋ 33	16 ♉ 20	14 ♓ 30	11 ♎ 35	12 ♎ 53	27 ♉ 18	25 ♌ 20	29 ♉ 00
Jun 1, 1952	05 ♓ 20	06 ♋ 35	21 ♉ 42	18 ♓ 19	11 ♎ 58	12 ♎ 30	01 ♊ 01	28 ♌ 07	03 ♊ 09
Jun 11, 1952	08 ♓ 03	09 ♋ 40	27 ♉ 02	21 ♓ 51	13 ♎ 05	12 ♎ 41	04 ♊ 43	01 ♍ 14	07 ♊ 15
Jun 21, 1952	10 ♓ 09	12 ♋ 48	02 ♊ 21	25 ♓ 02	14 ♎ 50	13 ♎ 24	08 ♊ 24	04 ♍ 37	11 ♊ 18
Jul 1, 1952	11 ♓ 30	15 ♋ 57	07 ♊ 37	27 ♓ 49	17 ♎ 08	14 ♎ 36	12 ♊ 02	08 ♍ 14	15 ♊ 18
Jul 11, 1952	12 ♓ 02	19 ♋ 06	12 ♊ 49	00 ♈ 05	19 ♎ 55	16 ♎ 13	15 ♊ 37	12 ♍ 03	19 ♊ 13
Jul 21, 1952	11 ♓ 41	22 ♋ 16	17 ♊ 57	01 ♈ 47	23 ♎ 06	18 ♎ 12	19 ♊ 07	16 ♍ 02	23 ♊ 04

Date	ATROPOS	HEKATE	LILITH	MEDUSA	MOIRA	NEMESIS	PERSEPHONE	PROSERPINA	PYTHIA
Jul 31, 1952	10 ♓ 26	25 ♋ 23	22 ♊ 59	02 ♈ 46	26 ♎ 37	20 ♎ 31	22 ♊ 32	20 ♍ 11	26 ♊ 49
Aug 10, 1952	08 ♓ 24	28 ♋ 29	27 ♊ 55	02 ♈ 59	00 ♏ 25	23 ♎ 06	25 ♊ 50	24 ♍ 26	00 ♋ 26
Aug 20, 1952	05 ♓ 49	01 ♌ 31	02 ♋ 43	02 ♈ 20	04 ♏ 28	25 ♎ 55	28 ♊ 60	28 ♍ 49	03 ♋ 55
Aug 30, 1952	03 ♓ 01	04 ♌ 29	07 ♋ 22	00 ♈ 52	08 ♏ 07	28 ♎ 57	01 ♋ 58	03 ♎ 17	07 ♋ 15
Sep 9, 1952	00 ♓ 26	07 ♌ 21	11 ♋ 50	28 ♓ 43	13 ♏ 07	02 ♏ 09	04 ♋ 45	07 ♎ 49	10 ♋ 22
Sep 19, 1952	28 ♒ 23	10 ♌ 06	16 ♋ 04	26 ♓ 09	17 ♏ 39	05 ♏ 31	07 ♋ 16	12 ♎ 26	13 ♋ 15
Sep 29, 1952	27 ♒ 06	12 ♌ 42	20 ♋ 03	23 ♓ 34	22 ♏ 19	08 ♏ 59	09 ♋ 29	17 ♎ 06	15 ♋ 51
Oct 9, 1952	26 ♒ 39	15 ♌ 08	23 ♋ 42	21 ♓ 22	27 ♏ 04	12 ♏ 35	11 ♋ 20	21 ♎ 49	18 ♋ 07
Oct 19, 1952	27 ♒ 01	17 ♌ 21	26 ♋ 59	19 ♓ 51	01 ♐ 53	16 ♏ 15	12 ♋ 46	26 ♎ 34	19 ♋ 59
Oct 29, 1952	28 ♒ 09	19 ♌ 18	29 ♋ 49	19 ♓ 12	06 ♐ 46	19 ♏ 60	13 ♋ 42	01 ♏ 21	21 ♋ 21
Nov 8, 1952	29 ♒ 55	20 ♌ 58	02 ♌ 06	19 ♓ 27	11 ♐ 42	23 ♏ 48	14 ♋ 06	06 ♏ 08	22 ♋ 10
Nov 18, 1952	02 ♓ 14	22 ♌ 16	03 ♌ 46	20 ♓ 33	16 ♐ 39	27 ♏ 39	13 ♋ 53	10 ♏ 55	22 ♋ 21
Nov 28, 1952	05 ♓ 01	23 ♌ 11	04 ♌ 42	22 ♓ 25	21 ♐ 38	01 ♐ 31	13 ♋ 03	15 ♏ 41	21 ♋ 50
Dec 8, 1952	08 ♓ 10	23 ♌ 38	04 ♌ 51	24 ♓ 57	26 ♐ 36	05 ♐ 24	11 ♋ 38	20 ♏ 25	20 ♋ 36
Dec 18, 1952	11 ♓ 39	23 ♌ 46	04 ♌ 10	28 ♓ 02	01 ♑ 34	09 ♐ 16	09 ♋ 46	25 ♏ 07	18 ♋ 43
Dec 28, 1952	15 ♓ 22	23 ♌ 06	02 ♌ 42	01 ♈ 34	06 ♑ 31	13 ♐ 07	07 ♋ 37	29 ♏ 45	16 ♋ 20
Jan 7, 1953	19 ♓ 18	22 ♌ 04	00 ♌ 39	05 ♈ 30	11 ♑ 26	16 ♐ 55	05 ♋ 26	04 ♐ 18	13 ♋ 41
Jan 17, 1953	23 ♓ 24	20 ♌ 36	28 ♋ 15	09 ♈ 44	16 ♑ 19	20 ♐ 40	03 ♋ 27	08 ♐ 45	11 ♋ 04
Jan 27, 1953	27 ♓ 38	18 ♌ 48	25 ♋ 52	14 ♈ 14	21 ♑ 05	24 ♐ 20	01 ♋ 53	13 ♐ 05	08 ♋ 48
Feb 6, 1953	01 ♈ 59	16 ♌ 49	23 ♋ 50	18 ♈ 56	25 ♑ 49	27 ♐ 53	00 ♋ 53	17 ♐ 15	07 ♋ 06
Feb 16, 1953	06 ♈ 25	14 ♌ 49	22 ♋ 24	23 ♈ 49	00 ♒ 27	01 ♑ 19	00 ♋ 30	21 ♐ 15	06 ♋ 05
Feb 26, 1953	10 ♈ 54	13 ♌ 00	21 ♋ 41	28 ♈ 50	04 ♒ 59	04 ♑ 35	00 ♋ 45	25 ♐ 01	05 ♋ 49
Mar 8, 1953	15 ♈ 26	11 ♌ 31	21 ♋ 42	03 ♉ 58	09 ♒ 40	07 ♑ 39	01 ♋ 35	28 ♐ 32	06 ♋ 14
Mar 18, 1953	19 ♈ 60	10 ♌ 27	22 ♋ 26	09 ♉ 12	13 ♒ 40	10 ♑ 30	02 ♋ 56	01 ♑ 44	07 ♋ 18
Mar 28, 1953	24 ♈ 35	09 ♌ 53	23 ♋ 47	14 ♉ 29	17 ♒ 47	13 ♑ 04	04 ♋ 45	04 ♑ 34	08 ♋ 56
Apr 7, 1953	29 ♈ 10	09 ♌ 48	25 ♋ 40	19 ♉ 51	21 ♒ 43	15 ♑ 19	06 ♋ 58	06 ♑ 58	11 ♋ 03
Apr 17, 1953	03 ♉ 44	10 ♌ 13	27 ♋ 60	25 ♉ 14	25 ♒ 26	17 ♑ 10	09 ♋ 31	08 ♑ 52	13 ♋ 34
Apr 27, 1953	08 ♉ 18	11 ♌ 04	00 ♌ 42	00 ♊ 40	28 ♒ 55	18 ♑ 35	12 ♋ 21	10 ♑ 11	16 ♋ 27
May 7, 1953	12 ♉ 50	12 ♌ 19	03 ♌ 41	06 ♊ 06	02 ♓ 08	19 ♑ 30	15 ♋ 25	10 ♑ 52	19 ♋ 38
May 17, 1953	17 ♉ 19	13 ♌ 55	06 ♌ 55	11 ♊ 33	05 ♓ 02	19 ♑ 51	18 ♋ 41	10 ♑ 51	23 ♋ 03
May 27, 1953	21 ♉ 46	15 ♌ 49	10 ♌ 21	17 ♊ 01	07 ♓ 34	19 ♑ 36	22 ♋ 06	10 ♑ 08	26 ♋ 42
Jun 6, 1953	26 ♊ 10	17 ♌ 59	13 ♌ 56	22 ♊ 28	09 ♓ 40	18 ♑ 43	25 ♋ 41	08 ♑ 45	00 ♌ 32
Jun 16, 1953	00 ♊ 30	20 ♌ 23	17 ♌ 38	27 ♊ 55	11 ♓ 18	17 ♑ 17	29 ♋ 22	06 ♑ 52	04 ♌ 31
Jun 26, 1953	04 ♊ 45	22 ♌ 58	21 ♌ 27	03 ♋ 20	12 ♓ 24	15 ♑ 24	03 ♌ 08	04 ♑ 42	08 ♌ 39
Jul 6, 1953	08 ♊ 54	25 ♌ 42	25 ♌ 20	08 ♋ 45	12 ♓ 54	13 ♑ 14	06 ♌ 59	02 ♑ 32	12 ♌ 54

	ATROPOS	HEKATE	LILITH	MEDUSA	MOIRA	NEMESIS	PERSEPHONE	PROSERPINA	PYTHIA
Jul 16, 1953	12 ♊ 57	28 ♍ 35	29 ♌ 17	14 ♋ 08	12 ♓ 45	11 ♑ 03	10 ♌ 54	00 ♑ 38	17 ♌ 16
Jul 26, 1953	16 ♊ 52	01 ♍ 35	03 ♍ 17	19 ♋ 29	11 ♓ 57	09 ♑ 06	14 ♌ 52	29 ♐ 15	21 ♌ 44
Aug 5, 1953	20 ♊ 39	04 ♍ 40	07 ♍ 18	24 ♋ 47	10 ♓ 33	07 ♑ 34	18 ♌ 51	28 ♐ 30	26 ♌ 17
Aug 15, 1953	24 ♊ 15	07 ♍ 50	11 ♍ 20	00 ♌ 03	08 ♓ 40	06 ♑ 37	22 ♌ 52	28 ♐ 26	00 ♍ 55
Aug 25, 1953	27 ♊ 39	11 ♍ 03	15 ♍ 23	05 ♌ 15	06 ♓ 28	06 ♑ 19	26 ♌ 54	29 ♐ 02	05 ♍ 37
Sep 4, 1953	00 ♋ 49	14 ♍ 19	19 ♍ 26	10 ♌ 24	04 ♓ 12	06 ♑ 40	00 ♍ 55	00 ♑ 55	10 ♍ 22
Sep 14, 1953	03 ♋ 40	17 ♍ 37	23 ♍ 27	15 ♌ 28	02 ♓ 08	07 ♑ 38	04 ♍ 55	02 ♑ 02	15 ♍ 11
Sep 24, 1953	06 ♋ 11	20 ♍ 55	27 ♍ 27	20 ♌ 27	00 ♓ 28	09 ♑ 10	08 ♍ 54	04 ♑ 17	20 ♍ 03
Oct 4, 1953	08 ♋ 18	24 ♍ 13	01 ♎ 25	25 ♌ 20	29 ♒ 21	11 ♑ 12	12 ♍ 50	06 ♑ 56	24 ♍ 57
Oct 14, 1953	09 ♋ 54	27 ♍ 29	05 ♎ 19	00 ♍ 06	28 ♒ 51	13 ♑ 42	16 ♍ 42	09 ♑ 56	29 ♍ 54
Oct 24, 1953	10 ♋ 57	00 ♎ 43	09 ♎ 10	04 ♍ 42	28 ♒ 58	16 ♑ 34	20 ♍ 29	13 ♑ 13	04 ♎ 51
Nov 3, 1953	10 ♋ 20	03 ♎ 54	12 ♎ 55	09 ♍ 09	29 ♒ 41	19 ♑ 46	24 ♍ 11	16 ♑ 45	09 ♎ 49
Nov 13, 1953	10 ♋ 59	06 ♎ 59	16 ♎ 35	13 ♍ 23	00 ♓ 56	23 ♑ 15	27 ♍ 44	20 ♑ 30	14 ♎ 47
Nov 23, 1953	09 ♋ 53	09 ♎ 57	20 ♎ 07	17 ♍ 22	02 ♓ 39	26 ♑ 59	01 ♎ 07	24 ♑ 24	19 ♎ 44
Dec 3, 1953	08 ♋ 03	12 ♎ 46	23 ♎ 30	21 ♍ 04	04 ♓ 46	00 ♒ 56	04 ♎ 19	28 ♑ 26	24 ♎ 39
Dec 13, 1953	05 ♋ 38	15 ♎ 25	26 ♎ 43	24 ♍ 24	07 ♓ 13	05 ♒ 03	07 ♎ 17	02 ♒ 35	29 ♎ 31
Dec 23, 1953	02 ♋ 53	17 ♎ 51	29 ♎ 42	27 ♍ 18	09 ♓ 58	09 ♒ 20	09 ♎ 57	06 ♒ 50	04 ♏ 19
Jan 2, 1954	00 ♋ 06	20 ♎ 01	02 ♏ 27	29 ♍ 42	12 ♓ 56	13 ♒ 44	12 ♎ 17	11 ♒ 09	09 ♏ 01
Jan 12, 1954	27 ♊ 36	21 ♎ 52	04 ♏ 55	01 ♎ 29	16 ♓ 07	18 ♒ 15	14 ♎ 13	15 ♒ 30	13 ♏ 35
Jan 22, 1954	25 ♊ 39	23 ♎ 20	07 ♏ 01	02 ♎ 33	19 ♓ 27	22 ♒ 51	15 ♎ 41	19 ♒ 54	17 ♏ 60
Feb 1, 1954	24 ♊ 24	24 ♎ 24	08 ♏ 44	02 ♎ 50	22 ♓ 54	27 ♒ 32	16 ♎ 36	24 ♒ 18	22 ♏ 12
Feb 11, 1954	23 ♊ 54	24 ♎ 58	10 ♏ 00	02 ♎ 15	26 ♓ 28	02 ♓ 16	16 ♎ 56	28 ♒ 43	26 ♏ 09
Feb 21, 1954	24 ♊ 07	25 ♎ 01	10 ♏ 45	00 ♎ 50	00 ♈ 06	07 ♓ 04	16 ♎ 39	03 ♓ 07	29 ♏ 47
Mar 3, 1954	24 ♊ 59	24 ♎ 30	10 ♏ 57	28 ♍ 41	03 ♈ 47	11 ♓ 50	15 ♎ 44	07 ♓ 29	03 ♐ 02
Mar 13, 1954	26 ♊ 25	23 ♎ 28	10 ♏ 32	26 ♍ 03	07 ♈ 30	16 ♓ 39	14 ♎ 15	11 ♓ 49	05 ♐ 49
Mar 23, 1954	28 ♊ 21	21 ♎ 57	09 ♏ 33	23 ♍ 19	11 ♈ 14	21 ♓ 28	12 ♎ 21	16 ♓ 07	08 ♐ 01
Apr 2, 1954	00 ♋ 40	20 ♎ 05	08 ♏ 01	20 ♍ 51	14 ♈ 59	26 ♓ 16	10 ♎ 13	20 ♓ 20	08 ♐ 34
Apr 12, 1954	03 ♋ 19	18 ♎ 02	06 ♏ 05	18 ♍ 58	18 ♈ 42	01 ♈ 04	08 ♎ 07	24 ♓ 29	10 ♐ 20
Apr 22, 1954	06 ♋ 15	16 ♎ 01	03 ♏ 53	17 ♍ 50	22 ♈ 23	05 ♈ 49	06 ♎ 16	28 ♓ 32	10 ♐ 16
May 2, 1954	09 ♋ 25	14 ♎ 13	01 ♏ 39	17 ♍ 30	26 ♈ 02	10 ♈ 31	04 ♎ 53	02 ♈ 28	09 ♐ 19
May 12, 1954	12 ♋ 47	12 ♎ 49	29 ♎ 36	17 ♍ 58	29 ♈ 38	15 ♈ 10	04 ♎ 03	06 ♈ 18	07 ♐ 37
May 22, 1954	16 ♋ 17	11 ♎ 55	27 ♎ 54	19 ♍ 09	03 ♉ 09	19 ♈ 45	03 ♎ 50	09 ♈ 58	05 ♐ 22
Jun 1, 1954	19 ♋ 56	11 ♎ 35	26 ♎ 42	20 ♍ 56	06 ♉ 35	24 ♈ 14	04 ♎ 12	13 ♈ 29	02 ♐ 55
Jun 11, 1954	23 ♋ 41	11 ♎ 48	26 ♎ 02	23 ♍ 15	09 ♉ 55	28 ♈ 37	05 ♎ 09	16 ♈ 48	00 ♐ 42
Jun 21, 1954	27 ♋ 31	12 ♎ 33	25 ♎ 56	25 ♍ 60	13 ♉ 07	02 ♉ 52	06 ♎ 36	19 ♈ 53	29 ♏ 02

Date	ATROPOS	HEKATE	LILITH	MEDUSA	MOIRA	NEMESIS	PERSEPHONE	PROSERPINA	PYTHIA
Jul 1, 1954	01 ♌ 26	13 ♎ 48	26 ♎ 21	29 ♍ 07	16 ♉ 10	06 ♉ 58	08 ♎ 29	22 ♈ 43	28 ♏ 09
Jul 11, 1954	05 ♌ 25	15 ♎ 29	27 ♎ 16	02 ♎ 32	19 ♉ 03	10 ♉ 52	10 ♎ 45	25 ♈ 14	28 ♏ 07
Jul 21, 1954	09 ♌ 27	17 ♎ 33	28 ♎ 37	06 ♎ 12	21 ♉ 43	14 ♉ 34	13 ♎ 21	27 ♈ 24	28 ♏ 57
Jul 31, 1954	13 ♌ 30	19 ♎ 58	00 ♏ 21	10 ♎ 06	24 ♉ 09	18 ♉ 01	16 ♎ 13	29 ♈ 09	00 ♐ 32
Aug 10, 1954	17 ♌ 36	22 ♎ 41	02 ♏ 24	14 ♎ 10	26 ♉ 18	21 ♉ 08	19 ♎ 20	00 ♉ 25	02 ♐ 48
Aug 20, 1954	21 ♌ 43	25 ♎ 39	04 ♏ 45	18 ♎ 23	28 ♉ 08	23 ♉ 54	22 ♎ 39	01 ♉ 10	05 ♐ 38
Aug 30, 1954	25 ♌ 50	28 ♎ 51	07 ♏ 21	22 ♎ 45	29 ♉ 34	26 ♉ 14	26 ♎ 07	01 ♉ 18	08 ♐ 56
Sep 9, 1954	29 ♌ 58	02 ♏ 14	10 ♏ 08	27 ♎ 13	00 ♊ 34	28 ♉ 03	29 ♎ 45	00 ♉ 48	12 ♐ 39
Sep 19, 1954	04 ♍ 05	05 ♏ 48	13 ♏ 07	01 ♏ 47	01 ♊ 03	29 ♉ 16	03 ♏ 30	29 ♈ 42	16 ♐ 40
Sep 29, 1954	08 ♍ 11	09 ♏ 31	16 ♏ 14	06 ♏ 26	01 ♊ 01	29 ♉ 49	07 ♏ 20	28 ♈ 01	20 ♐ 59
Oct 9, 1954	12 ♍ 15	13 ♏ 21	19 ♏ 30	11 ♏ 09	00 ♊ 23	29 ♉ 37	11 ♏ 16	25 ♈ 56	25 ♐ 31
Oct 19, 1954	16 ♍ 16	17 ♏ 18	22 ♏ 51	15 ♏ 56	29 ♉ 12	28 ♉ 42	15 ♏ 15	23 ♈ 38	00 ♑ 14
Oct 29, 1954	20 ♍ 13	21 ♏ 21	26 ♏ 17	20 ♏ 46	27 ♉ 30	27 ♉ 07	19 ♏ 21	21 ♈ 23	05 ♑ 06
Nov 8, 1954	24 ♍ 05	25 ♏ 28	29 ♏ 48	25 ♏ 39	25 ♉ 27	25 ♉ 03	23 ♏ 21	19 ♈ 27	10 ♑ 06
Nov 18, 1954	27 ♍ 50	29 ♏ 39	03 ♐ 21	00 ♐ 33	23 ♉ 12	22 ♉ 45	27 ♏ 27	17 ♈ 59	15 ♑ 12
Nov 28, 1954	01 ♎ 27	03 ♐ 53	06 ♐ 57	05 ♐ 29	20 ♉ 59	20 ♉ 33	01 ♐ 32	17 ♈ 07	20 ♑ 22
Dec 8, 1954	04 ♎ 53	08 ♐ 09	10 ♐ 33	10 ♐ 25	19 ♉ 03	18 ♉ 43	05 ♐ 36	16 ♈ 54	25 ♑ 37
Dec 18, 1954	08 ♎ 06	12 ♐ 26	14 ♐ 09	15 ♐ 22	17 ♉ 32	17 ♉ 30	09 ♐ 38	17 ♈ 19	00 ♒ 54
Dec 28, 1954	11 ♎ 03	16 ♐ 43	17 ♐ 44	20 ♐ 18	16 ♉ 33	16 ♉ 59	13 ♐ 38	18 ♈ 18	06 ♒ 14
Jan 7, 1955	13 ♎ 39	20 ♐ 60	21 ♐ 17	25 ♐ 13	16 ♉ 10	17 ♉ 12	17 ♐ 33	19 ♈ 48	11 ♒ 34
Jan 17, 1955	15 ♎ 51	25 ♐ 15	24 ♐ 46	00 ♑ 06	16 ♉ 22	18 ♉ 06	21 ♐ 23	21 ♈ 45	16 ♒ 54
Jan 27, 1955	17 ♎ 33	29 ♐ 26	28 ♐ 11	04 ♑ 57	17 ♉ 07	19 ♉ 37	25 ♐ 07	24 ♈ 05	22 ♒ 14
Feb 6, 1955	18 ♎ 40	03 ♑ 34	01 ♑ 29	09 ♑ 44	18 ♉ 22	21 ♉ 40	28 ♐ 42	26 ♈ 45	27 ♒ 32
Feb 16, 1955	19 ♎ 05	07 ♑ 37	04 ♑ 40	14 ♑ 27	20 ♉ 02	24 ♉ 09	02 ♑ 08	29 ♈ 40	02 ♓ 49
Feb 26, 1955	18 ♎ 44	11 ♑ 33	07 ♑ 42	19 ♑ 05	22 ♉ 05	26 ♉ 60	05 ♑ 22	02 ♉ 49	08 ♓ 03
Mar 8, 1955	17 ♎ 34	15 ♑ 20	10 ♑ 32	23 ♑ 36	24 ♉ 26	00 ♊ 09	08 ♑ 23	06 ♉ 08	13 ♓ 14
Mar 18, 1955	15 ♎ 38	18 ♑ 57	13 ♑ 09	28 ♑ 00	27 ♉ 04	03 ♊ 33	11 ♑ 07	09 ♉ 37	18 ♓ 22
Mar 28, 1955	13 ♎ 05	22 ♑ 22	15 ♑ 30	02 ♒ 16	29 ♉ 55	07 ♊ 09	13 ♑ 34	13 ♉ 13	23 ♓ 25
Apr 7, 1955	10 ♎ 14	25 ♑ 32	17 ♑ 32	06 ♒ 20	02 ♊ 57	10 ♊ 55	15 ♑ 38	16 ♉ 54	28 ♓ 23
Apr 17, 1955	07 ♎ 27	28 ♑ 24	19 ♑ 13	10 ♒ 12	06 ♊ 08	14 ♊ 48	17 ♑ 18	20 ♉ 41	03 ♈ 16
Apr 27, 1955	05 ♎ 06	00 ♒ 56	20 ♑ 28	13 ♒ 49	09 ♊ 27	18 ♊ 48	18 ♑ 30	24 ♉ 30	08 ♈ 03
May 7, 1955	03 ♎ 29	03 ♒ 03	21 ♑ 14	17 ♒ 07	12 ♊ 52	22 ♊ 51	19 ♑ 11	28 ♉ 22	12 ♈ 43
May 17, 1955	02 ♎ 43	04 ♒ 43	21 ♑ 29	20 ♒ 04	16 ♊ 22	26 ♊ 59	19 ♑ 19	02 ♊ 16	17 ♈ 16
May 27, 1955	02 ♎ 50	05 ♒ 49	21 ♑ 09	22 ♒ 35	19 ♊ 57	01 ♋ 09	18 ♑ 52	06 ♊ 11	21 ♈ 40
Jun 6, 1955	03 ♎ 47	06 ♒ 21	20 ♑ 14	24 ♒ 36	23 ♊ 34	05 ♋ 20	17 ♑ 51	10 ♊ 06	25 ♈ 55

	ATROPOS	HEKATE	LILITH	MEDUSA	MOIRA	NEMESIS	PERSEPHONE	PROSERPINA	PYTHIA
Jun 16, 1955	05 ♎ 30	06 ♒ 14	18 ♑ 47	26 ♒ 00	27 ♊ 13	09 ♋ 33	16 ♑ 20	14 ♋ 00	29 ♈ 59
Jun 26, 1955	07 ♎ 53	05 ♒ 29	16 ♑ 53	26 ♒ 42	00 ♋ 54	13 ♋ 45	14 ♑ 28	17 ♋ 53	03 ♉ 52
Jul 6, 1955	10 ♎ 50	04 ♒ 10	14 ♑ 42	26 ♒ 38	04 ♋ 36	17 ♋ 57	12 ♑ 25	21 ♋ 44	07 ♉ 30
Jul 16, 1955	14 ♎ 17	02 ♒ 25	12 ♑ 26	25 ♒ 46	08 ♋ 18	22 ♋ 09	10 ♑ 24	25 ♋ 33	10 ♉ 52
Jul 26, 1955	18 ♎ 08	00 ♒ 27	10 ♑ 21	24 ♒ 07	11 ♋ 58	26 ♋ 18	08 ♑ 37	29 ♋ 17	13 ♉ 56
Aug 5, 1955	22 ♎ 21	28 ♑ 31	08 ♑ 38	21 ♒ 52	15 ♋ 38	00 ♌ 25	07 ♑ 14	02 ♌ 58	16 ♉ 38
Aug 15, 1955	26 ♎ 52	26 ♑ 53	07 ♑ 26	19 ♒ 17	19 ♋ 14	04 ♌ 29	06 ♑ 21	06 ♌ 32	18 ♉ 55
Aug 25, 1955	01 ♏ 40	25 ♑ 43	06 ♑ 49	16 ♒ 44	22 ♋ 48	08 ♌ 30	06 ♑ 02	09 ♌ 60	20 ♉ 43
Sep 4, 1955	06 ♏ 41	25 ♑ 10	06 ♑ 51	14 ♒ 36	26 ♋ 16	12 ♌ 26	06 ♑ 15	13 ♌ 19	21 ♉ 57
Sep 14, 1955	11 ♏ 54	25 ♑ 16	07 ♑ 28	13 ♒ 08	29 ♋ 39	16 ♌ 16	07 ♑ 00	16 ♌ 27	22 ♉ 32
Sep 24, 1955	17 ♏ 17	26 ♑ 01	08 ♑ 40	12 ♒ 30	02 ♌ 54	19 ♌ 60	08 ♑ 14	19 ♌ 23	22 ♉ 24
Oct 4, 1955	22 ♏ 49	27 ♑ 22	10 ♑ 22	12 ♒ 44	05 ♌ 60	23 ♌ 35	09 ♑ 53	22 ♌ 04	21 ♉ 31
Oct 14, 1955	28 ♏ 29	29 ♑ 14	12 ♑ 30	13 ♒ 46	08 ♌ 54	27 ♌ 02	11 ♑ 54	24 ♌ 26	19 ♉ 56
Oct 24, 1955	04 ♐ 14	01 ♒ 34	15 ♑ 03	15 ♒ 33	11 ♌ 34	00 ♍ 16	14 ♑ 15	26 ♌ 27	17 ♉ 44
Nov 3, 1955	10 ♐ 04	04 ♒ 19	17 ♑ 56	17 ♒ 58	13 ♌ 56	03 ♍ 18	16 ♑ 52	28 ♌ 02	15 ♉ 10
Nov 13, 1955	15 ♐ 58	07 ♒ 23	21 ♑ 08	20 ♒ 55	15 ♌ 58	06 ♍ 03	19 ♑ 42	29 ♌ 06	12 ♉ 30
Nov 23, 1955	21 ♐ 55	10 ♒ 45	24 ♑ 35	24 ♒ 20	17 ♌ 34	08 ♍ 29	22 ♑ 45	29 ♌ 36	10 ♉ 04
Dec 3, 1955	27 ♐ 53	14 ♒ 21	28 ♑ 15	28 ♒ 08	18 ♌ 40	10 ♍ 32	25 ♑ 56	29 ♌ 27	08 ♉ 08
Dec 13, 1955	03 ♑ 52	18 ♒ 09	02 ♒ 07	02 ♓ 16	19 ♌ 13	12 ♍ 10	29 ♑ 16	28 ♌ 39	06 ♉ 51
Dec 23, 1955	09 ♑ 51	22 ♒ 07	06 ♒ 10	06 ♓ 40	19 ♌ 08	13 ♍ 17	02 ♒ 42	27 ♌ 13	06 ♉ 17
Jan 2, 1956	15 ♑ 48	26 ♒ 13	10 ♒ 22	11 ♓ 17	18 ♌ 22	13 ♍ 50	06 ♒ 13	25 ♌ 15	06 ♉ 27
Jan 12, 1956	21 ♑ 43	00 ♓ 24	14 ♒ 41	16 ♓ 06	16 ♌ 59	13 ♍ 46	09 ♒ 48	22 ♌ 58	07 ♉ 16
Jan 22, 1956	27 ♑ 36	04 ♓ 41	19 ♒ 07	21 ♓ 05	15 ♌ 03	13 ♍ 04	13 ♒ 25	20 ♌ 36	08 ♉ 39
Feb 1, 1956	03 ♒ 24	09 ♓ 01	23 ♒ 38	26 ♓ 11	12 ♌ 46	11 ♍ 46	17 ♒ 03	18 ♌ 27	10 ♉ 33
Feb 11, 1956	09 ♒ 09	13 ♓ 24	28 ♒ 14	01 ♈ 24	10 ♌ 23	09 ♍ 57	20 ♒ 41	16 ♌ 44	12 ♉ 51
Feb 21, 1956	14 ♒ 49	17 ♓ 47	02 ♓ 54	06 ♈ 42	08 ♌ 13	07 ♍ 47	24 ♒ 18	15 ♌ 37	15 ♉ 31
Mar 2, 1956	20 ♒ 24	22 ♓ 11	07 ♓ 38	12 ♈ 05	06 ♌ 29	05 ♍ 31	27 ♒ 53	15 ♌ 10	18 ♉ 27
Mar 12, 1956	25 ♒ 52	26 ♓ 35	12 ♓ 24	17 ♈ 31	05 ♌ 21	03 ♍ 22	01 ♓ 26	15 ♌ 15	21 ♉ 38
Mar 22, 1956	01 ♓ 14	00 ♈ 57	17 ♓ 12	22 ♈ 60	04 ♌ 55	01 ♍ 34	04 ♓ 54	16 ♌ 15	25 ♉ 01
Apr 1, 1956	06 ♓ 28	05 ♈ 17	22 ♓ 01	28 ♈ 31	05 ♌ 11	00 ♍ 16	08 ♓ 17	17 ♌ 40	28 ♉ 33
Apr 11, 1956	11 ♓ 34	09 ♈ 34	26 ♓ 51	04 ♉ 03	06 ♌ 05	29 ♌ 33	11 ♓ 35	19 ♌ 35	02 ♊ 13
Apr 21, 1956	16 ♓ 32	13 ♈ 47	01 ♈ 41	09 ♉ 36	07 ♌ 36	29 ♌ 25	14 ♓ 44	21 ♌ 55	05 ♊ 59
May 1, 1956	21 ♓ 20	17 ♈ 56	06 ♈ 31	15 ♉ 09	09 ♌ 37	29 ♌ 52	17 ♓ 44	24 ♌ 37	09 ♊ 50
May 11, 1956	25 ♓ 57	21 ♈ 59	11 ♈ 19	20 ♉ 42	12 ♌ 06	00 ♍ 50	20 ♓ 35	27 ♌ 37	13 ♊ 45
May 21, 1956	00 ♈ 22	25 ♈ 56	16 ♈ 06	26 ♉ 15	14 ♌ 58	02 ♍ 16	23 ♓ 12	00 ♌ 52	17 ♊ 43

	ATROPOS	HEKATE	LILITH	MEDUSA	MOIRA	NEMESIS	PERSEPHONE	PROSERPINA	PYTHIA
May 31, 1956	04 ♈ 34	29 ♈ 46	20 ♈ 50	01 ♊ 47	18 ♌ 09	04 ♍ 06	25 ♓ 36	04 ♌ 21	21 ♊ 43
Jun 10, 1956	08 ♈ 31	03 ♉ 27	25 ♈ 30	07 ♊ 17	21 ♌ 37	06 ♍ 16	27 ♓ 42	08 ♌ 00	25 ♊ 45
Jun 20, 1956	12 ♈ 11	06 ♉ 59	00 ♉ 05	12 ♊ 46	25 ♌ 20	08 ♍ 43	29 ♓ 30	11 ♌ 09	29 ♊ 48
Jun 30, 1956	15 ♈ 30	10 ♉ 19	04 ♉ 35	18 ♊ 13	29 ♌ 16	11 ♍ 25	00 ♈ 55	15 ♌ 47	03 ♋ 51
Jul 10, 1956	18 ♈ 26	13 ♉ 27	08 ♉ 56	23 ♊ 37	03 ♍ 22	14 ♍ 20	01 ♈ 56	19 ♌ 51	07 ♋ 54
Jul 20, 1956	20 ♈ 54	16 ♉ 19	13 ♉ 08	28 ♊ 59	07 ♍ 38	17 ♍ 24	02 ♈ 28	24 ♌ 01	11 ♋ 56
Jul 30, 1956	22 ♈ 50	18 ♉ 55	17 ♉ 09	04 ♋ 17	12 ♍ 02	20 ♍ 38	02 ♈ 31	28 ♌ 16	15 ♋ 57
Aug 9, 1956	24 ♈ 08	21 ♉ 10	20 ♉ 54	09 ♋ 31	16 ♍ 33	23 ♍ 58	02 ♈ 01	02 ♍ 35	19 ♋ 56
Aug 19, 1956	24 ♈ 44	23 ♉ 03	24 ♉ 21	14 ♋ 40	21 ♍ 11	27 ♍ 25	01 ♈ 00	06 ♍ 58	23 ♋ 53
Aug 29, 1956	24 ♈ 32	24 ♉ 29	27 ♉ 26	19 ♋ 43	25 ♍ 55	00 ♎ 56	29 ♓ 32	11 ♍ 24	27 ♋ 45
Sep 8, 1956	23 ♈ 29	25 ♉ 25	00 ♊ 04	24 ♋ 40	00 ♎ 43	04 ♎ 31	27 ♓ 41	15 ♍ 52	01 ♌ 33
Sep 18, 1956	21 ♈ 40	25 ♉ 48	02 ♊ 09	29 ♋ 29	05 ♎ 36	08 ♎ 39	25 ♓ 39	20 ♍ 22	05 ♌ 15
Sep 28, 1956	19 ♈ 13	25 ♉ 36	03 ♊ 35	04 ♌ 09	10 ♎ 32	11 ♎ 50	23 ♓ 37	24 ♍ 53	08 ♌ 50
Oct 8, 1956	16 ♈ 24	24 ♉ 48	04 ♊ 16	08 ♌ 37	15 ♎ 31	15 ♎ 32	21 ♓ 46	29 ♍ 25	12 ♌ 16
Oct 18, 1956	13 ♈ 36	23 ♉ 28	04 ♊ 08	12 ♌ 52	20 ♎ 33	19 ♎ 13	20 ♓ 16	03 ♎ 57	15 ♌ 30
Oct 28, 1956	11 ♈ 10	21 ♉ 41	03 ♊ 12	16 ♌ 51	25 ♎ 36	22 ♎ 55	19 ♓ 15	08 ♎ 27	18 ♌ 30
Nov 7, 1956	09 ♈ 22	19 ♉ 38	01 ♊ 32	20 ♌ 30	00 ♏ 40	26 ♎ 34	18 ♓ 46	12 ♎ 55	21 ♌ 14
Nov 17, 1956	08 ♈ 21	17 ♉ 31	29 ♉ 24	23 ♌ 45	05 ♏ 44	00 ♏ 11	18 ♓ 50	17 ♎ 21	23 ♌ 37
Nov 27, 1956	08 ♈ 08	15 ♉ 34	27 ♉ 08	26 ♌ 32	10 ♏ 47	03 ♏ 45	19 ♓ 26	21 ♎ 42	25 ♌ 35
Dec 7, 1956	08 ♈ 43	13 ♉ 59	25 ♉ 06	28 ♌ 45	15 ♏ 48	07 ♏ 13	20 ♓ 31	25 ♎ 58	27 ♌ 03
Dec 17, 1956	09 ♈ 59	12 ♉ 53	23 ♉ 39	00 ♍ 17	20 ♏ 47	10 ♏ 35	22 ♓ 03	00 ♏ 07	27 ♌ 55
Dec 27, 1956	11 ♈ 50	12 ♉ 22	22 ♉ 57	01 ♍ 01	25 ♏ 42	13 ♏ 48	23 ♓ 57	04 ♏ 08	28 ♌ 07
Jan 6, 1957	14 ♈ 11	12 ♉ 25	23 ♉ 06	00 ♍ 54	00 ♐ 32	16 ♏ 52	26 ♓ 11	07 ♏ 57	27 ♌ 34
Jan 16, 1957	16 ♈ 58	13 ♉ 00	24 ♉ 02	29 ♌ 52	05 ♐ 16	19 ♏ 43	28 ♓ 42	11 ♏ 34	26 ♌ 16
Jan 26, 1957	20 ♈ 04	14 ♉ 05	25 ♉ 43	28 ♌ 00	09 ♐ 52	22 ♏ 21	01 ♈ 27	14 ♏ 55	24 ♌ 16
Feb 5, 1957	23 ♈ 27	15 ♉ 37	27 ♉ 60	25 ♌ 31	14 ♐ 18	24 ♏ 41	04 ♈ 25	17 ♏ 57	21 ♌ 46
Feb 15, 1957	27 ♈ 04	17 ♉ 31	00 ♊ 49	22 ♌ 45	18 ♐ 33	26 ♏ 40	07 ♈ 32	20 ♏ 35	19 ♌ 03
Feb 25, 1957	00 ♉ 51	19 ♉ 43	04 ♊ 02	20 ♌ 07	22 ♐ 34	28 ♏ 16	10 ♈ 47	22 ♏ 47	16 ♌ 28
Mar 7, 1957	04 ♉ 47	22 ♉ 11	07 ♊ 37	17 ♌ 59	26 ♐ 18	29 ♏ 25	14 ♈ 08	24 ♏ 27	14 ♌ 18
Mar 17, 1957	08 ♉ 50	24 ♉ 53	11 ♊ 28	16 ♌ 35	29 ♐ 42	00 ♐ 04	17 ♈ 35	25 ♏ 30	12 ♌ 49
Mar 27, 1957	12 ♉ 58	27 ♉ 44	15 ♊ 33	16 ♌ 03	02 ♑ 43	00 ♐ 09	21 ♈ 05	25 ♏ 52	12 ♌ 07
Apr 6, 1957	17 ♉ 10	00 ♊ 45	19 ♊ 47	16 ♌ 21	05 ♑ 17	29 ♏ 39	24 ♈ 38	25 ♏ 32	12 ♌ 12
Apr 16, 1957	21 ♉ 25	03 ♊ 52	24 ♊ 10	17 ♌ 24	07 ♑ 19	28 ♏ 35	28 ♈ 13	24 ♏ 29	13 ♌ 03
Apr 26, 1957	25 ♉ 42	07 ♊ 04	28 ♊ 39	19 ♌ 08	08 ♑ 45	26 ♏ 60	01 ♉ 49	22 ♏ 49	14 ♌ 33
May 6, 1957	29 ♉ 60	10 ♊ 20	03 ♋ 13	21 ♌ 25	09 ♑ 29	25 ♏ 02	05 ♉ 24	20 ♏ 45	16 ♌ 39

	ATROPOS	HEKATE	LILITH	MEDUSA	MOIRA	NEMESIS	PERSEPHONE	PROSERPINA	PYTHIA
May 16, 1957	04 ♊ 18	13 ♊ 38	07 ♋ 50	24 ♌ 09	09 ♑ 31	22 ♏ 52	08 ♉ 58	18 ♏ 31	19 ♌ 14
May 26, 1957	08 ♊ 36	16 ♊ 59	12 ♋ 29	27 ♌ 17	08 ♑ 48	20 ♏ 43	12 ♉ 30	16 ♏ 26	22 ♌ 15
Jun 5, 1957	12 ♊ 53	20 ♊ 19	17 ♋ 10	00 ♍ 44	07 ♑ 24	18 ♏ 47	15 ♉ 60	14 ♏ 46	25 ♌ 38
Jun 15, 1957	17 ♊ 08	23 ♊ 40	21 ♋ 52	04 ♍ 26	05 ♑ 30	17 ♏ 17	19 ♉ 25	13 ♏ 43	29 ♌ 19
Jun 25, 1957	21 ♊ 21	26 ♊ 59	26 ♋ 33	08 ♍ 21	03 ♑ 20	16 ♏ 18	22 ♉ 46	13 ♏ 20	03 ♍ 17
Jul 5, 1957	25 ♊ 32	00 ♋ 16	01 ♌ 14	12 ♍ 27	01 ♑ 12	15 ♏ 53	26 ♉ 01	13 ♏ 40	07 ♍ 28
Jul 15, 1957	29 ♊ 39	03 ♋ 31	05 ♌ 54	16 ♍ 42	29 ♐ 23	16 ♏ 47	29 ♉ 08	14 ♏ 40	11 ♍ 51
Jul 25, 1957	03 ♋ 42	06 ♋ 41	10 ♌ 32	21 ♍ 04	28 ♐ 06	16 ♏ 01	02 ♊ 06	16 ♏ 16	16 ♍ 25
Aug 4, 1957	07 ♋ 40	09 ♋ 46	15 ♌ 08	25 ♍ 33	28 ♐ 28	18 ♏ 01	04 ♊ 53	18 ♏ 23	21 ♍ 08
Aug 14, 1957	11 ♋ 31	12 ♋ 45	19 ♌ 42	00 ♎ 07	27 ♐ 31	19 ♏ 42	07 ♊ 27	20 ♏ 57	25 ♍ 60
Aug 24, 1957	15 ♋ 51	15 ♋ 37	24 ♌ 13	04 ♎ 46	28 ♐ 14	21 ♏ 47	09 ♊ 45	23 ♏ 54	00 ♎ 59
Sep 3, 1957	18 ♋ 51	18 ♋ 20	28 ♌ 40	09 ♎ 28	29 ♐ 34	24 ♏ 12	11 ♊ 45	27 ♏ 10	06 ♎ 04
Sep 13, 1957	22 ♋ 17	20 ♋ 51	03 ♍ 03	14 ♎ 14	01 ♑ 25	26 ♏ 56	13 ♊ 22	00 ♐ 43	11 ♎ 16
Sep 23, 1957	25 ♋ 30	23 ♋ 15	07 ♍ 21	19 ♎ 02	03 ♑ 44	29 ♏ 55	14 ♊ 35	04 ♐ 30	16 ♎ 32
Oct 3, 1957	28 ♋ 28	25 ♋ 15	11 ♍ 33	23 ♎ 53	06 ♑ 27	03 ♐ 28	15 ♊ 17	08 ♐ 28	21 ♎ 54
Oct 13, 1957	01 ♌ 09	27 ♋ 01	15 ♍ 39	28 ♎ 45	09 ♑ 28	06 ♐ 33	15 ♊ 28	12 ♐ 36	27 ♎ 20
Oct 23, 1957	03 ♌ 29	28 ♋ 27	19 ♍ 37	03 ♏ 38	12 ♑ 46	10 ♐ 07	15 ♊ 03	16 ♐ 52	02 ♏ 49
Nov 2, 1957	05 ♌ 23	28 ♋ 29	23 ♍ 26	08 ♏ 32	16 ♑ 18	13 ♐ 50	14 ♊ 04	21 ♐ 15	08 ♏ 21
Nov 12, 1957	06 ♌ 47	00 ♌ 05	27 ♍ 04	13 ♏ 26	20 ♑ 00	17 ♐ 41	12 ♊ 32	25 ♐ 43	13 ♏ 55
Nov 22, 1957	07 ♌ 37	00 ♌ 11	00 ♎ 29	18 ♏ 19	23 ♑ 52	21 ♐ 38	10 ♊ 36	00 ♑ 16	19 ♏ 31
Dec 2, 1957	07 ♌ 47	29 ♋ 47	03 ♎ 40	23 ♏ 12	27 ♑ 51	25 ♐ 40	08 ♊ 27	04 ♑ 53	25 ♏ 09
Dec 12, 1957	07 ♌ 13	28 ♋ 53	06 ♎ 34	28 ♏ 03	01 ♒ 56	29 ♐ 47	06 ♊ 19	09 ♑ 31	00 ♐ 46
Dec 22, 1957	05 ♌ 56	27 ♋ 30	09 ♎ 07	02 ♐ 51	06 ♒ 06	03 ♑ 57	04 ♊ 25	14 ♑ 12	06 ♐ 24
Jan 1, 1958	03 ♌ 57	25 ♋ 45	11 ♎ 16	07 ♐ 36	10 ♒ 18	08 ♑ 09	02 ♊ 57	18 ♑ 53	12 ♐ 00
Jan 11, 1958	01 ♌ 27	23 ♋ 47	12 ♎ 58	12 ♐ 17	14 ♒ 33	12 ♑ 23	02 ♊ 02	23 ♑ 34	17 ♐ 35
Jan 21, 1958	28 ♋ 41	21 ♋ 46	14 ♎ 09	16 ♐ 53	18 ♒ 50	16 ♑ 37	01 ♊ 44	28 ♑ 15	23 ♐ 07
Jan 31, 1958	25 ♋ 58	19 ♋ 53	14 ♎ 44	21 ♐ 22	23 ♒ 06	20 ♑ 52	02 ♊ 02	02 ♒ 53	28 ♐ 35
Feb 10, 1958	23 ♋ 35	18 ♋ 18	14 ♎ 42	25 ♐ 44	27 ♒ 22	25 ♑ 05	02 ♊ 55	07 ♒ 29	03 ♑ 58
Feb 20, 1958	21 ♋ 46	17 ♋ 08	13 ♎ 60	29 ♐ 58	01 ♓ 37	29 ♑ 16	04 ♊ 18	12 ♒ 02	09 ♑ 16
Mar 2, 1958	20 ♋ 39	16 ♋ 27	12 ♎ 41	03 ♑ 60	05 ♓ 49	03 ♒ 25	06 ♊ 09	16 ♒ 31	14 ♑ 26
Mar 12, 1958	20 ♋ 16	16 ♋ 16	10 ♎ 50	07 ♑ 49	09 ♓ 58	07 ♒ 29	08 ♊ 22	20 ♒ 55	19 ♑ 28
Mar 22, 1958	20 ♋ 35	16 ♋ 35	08 ♎ 38	11 ♑ 23	14 ♓ 03	11 ♒ 28	10 ♊ 55	25 ♒ 13	24 ♑ 20
Apr 1, 1958	21 ♋ 31	17 ♋ 20	06 ♎ 19	14 ♑ 04	18 ♓ 04	15 ♒ 21	13 ♊ 45	29 ♒ 24	29 ♑ 00
Apr 11, 1958	23 ♋ 01	18 ♋ 30	04 ♎ 07	17 ♑ 34	21 ♓ 59	19 ♒ 05	16 ♊ 49	03 ♓ 27	03 ♒ 26
Apr 21, 1958	24 ♋ 59	20 ♋ 02	02 ♎ 14	20 ♑ 02	25 ♓ 47	22 ♒ 40	20 ♊ 04	07 ♓ 20	07 ♒ 35

	ATROPOS	HEKATE	LILITH	MEDUSA	MOIRA	NEMESIS	PERSEPHONE	PROSERPINA	PYTHIA
May 1, 1958	27♋21	21♋52	00♎52	22♑01	29♓28	26♒04	23♊28	11♓03	11♒24
May 11, 1958	00♌03	23♋57	00♎03	23♑24	03♈00	29♒13	27♊01	14♓33	14♒49
May 21, 1958	03♌02	26♋16	29♍51	24♑06	06♈22	02♓06	00♋40	17♓49	17♒46
May 31, 1958	06♌15	28♋46	00♎12	24♑02	09♈33	04♓40	04♋24	20♓47	20♒09
Jun 10, 1958	09♌41	01♌26	01♎04	23♑11	12♈30	06♓49	08♋13	23♓27	21♒53
Jun 20, 1958	13♌17	04♌13	02♎24	21♑35	15♈12	08♓32	12♋05	25♓44	22♒52
Jun 30, 1958	17♌03	07♌07	04♎08	19♑22	17♈36	09♓42	15♋59	27♓34	23♒01
Jul 10, 1958	20♌56	10♌06	06♎12	16♑49	19♈39	10♓10	19♋54	28♓55	22♒19
Jul 20, 1958	24♌56	13♌08	08♎34	14♑14	21♈19	10♓16	23♋51	29♓41	20♒48
Jul 30, 1958	29♌02	16♌14	11♎10	11♑59	22♈32	09♓24	27♋48	29♓51	18♒38
Aug 9, 1958	03♍13	19♌22	13♎59	10♑21	23♈14	08♓00	01♌44	29♓21	16♒09
Aug 19, 1958	07♍30	22♌30	16♎58	09♑29	23♈22	06♓07	05♌39	28♓13	13♒43
Aug 29, 1958	11♍50	25♌39	20♎06	09♑26	22♈56	03♓56	09♌31	26♓31	11♒41
Sep 8, 1958	16♍15	28♌46	23♎21	10♑11	21♈54	01♓47	13♌20	24♓26	10♒20
Sep 18, 1958	20♍42	01♍52	26♎42	11♑39	20♈19	29♒55	17♌05	22♓09	09♒46
Sep 28, 1958	25♍13	04♍54	00♏08	13♑45	18♈20	28♒35	20♌44	19♓57	10♒02
Oct 8, 1958	29♍47	07♍52	03♏38	16♑24	16♈07	27♒55	24♌17	18♓05	11♒04
Oct 18, 1958	04♎22	10♍44	07♏10	19♑31	13♈53	27♒59	27♌41	16♓44	12♒46
Oct 28, 1958	08♎59	13♍29	10♏44	23♑02	11♈52	28♒46	00♍54	15♓59	15♒04
Nov 7, 1958	13♎37	16♍04	14♏19	26♑52	10♈16	00♓12	03♍54	15♓54	17♒50
Nov 17, 1958	18♎16	18♍28	17♏54	01♒00	09♈11	02♓14	06♍39	16♓26	21♒00
Nov 27, 1958	22♎55	20♍38	20♏28	05♒23	08♈42	04♓46	09♍05	17♓34	24♒30
Dec 7, 1958	27♎32	22♍31	24♏59	09♒58	08♈48	07♓44	11♍09	19♓11	28♒16
Dec 17, 1958	02♏07	24♍05	28♏27	14♒44	09♈27	11♓04	12♍47	21♓16	02♓15
Dec 27, 1958	06♏39	25♍17	01♐50	19♒38	10♈37	14♓43	13♍54	23♓43	06♓25
Jan 6, 1959	11♏07	26♍02	05♐08	24♒41	12♈14	18♓37	14♍27	26♓29	10♓42
Jan 16, 1959	15♏28	26♍19	08♐18	29♒50	14♈14	22♓43	14♍23	29♓31	15♓06
Jan 26, 1959	19♏41	26♍04	11♐19	05♓04	16♈33	27♓01	13♍40	02♈46	19♓36
Feb 5, 1959	23♏43	25♍19	14♐08	10♓23	19♈08	01♈27	12♍22	06♈12	24♓08
Feb 15, 1959	27♏32	24♍04	17♐45	15♓45	21♈57	05♈59	10♍33	09♈46	28♓43
Feb 25, 1959	01♐03	22♍24	19♐06	21♓11	24♈58	10♈38	08♍27	13♈28	03♈20
Mar 7, 1959	04♐12	20♍28	21♐08	26♓39	28♈07	15♈20	06♍16	17♈15	07♈57
Mar 17, 1959	06♐54	18♍26	22♐50	02♈08	01♉24	20♈05	04♍17	21♈06	12♈33
Mar 27, 1959	09♐02	16♍29	24♐06	07♈39	04♉46	24♈53	02♍41	25♈01	17♈09
Apr 6, 1959	10♐29	14♍49	24♐55	13♈10	08♉13	29♈41	01♍38	28♈57	21♈43

	ATROPOS	HEKATE	LILITH	MEDUSA	MOIRA	NEMESIS	PERSEPHONE	PROSERPINA	PYTHIA
Apr 16, 1959	11 ♐ 09	13 ♍ 32	25 ♐ 13	18 ♈ 42	11 ♉ 43	04 ♉ 31	01 ♍ 11	02 ♉ 55	26 ♈ 16
Apr 26, 1959	10 ♐ 55	12 ♍ 45	24 ♐ 58	24 ♈ 13	15 ♉ 15	09 ♉ 19	01 ♍ 22	06 ♉ 52	00 ♉ 45
May 6, 1959	09 ♐ 46	12 ♍ 30	24 ♐ 09	29 ♈ 44	18 ♉ 48	14 ♉ 08	02 ♍ 08	10 ♉ 50	05 ♉ 11
May 16, 1959	07 ♐ 49	12 ♍ 45	22 ♐ 48	05 ♉ 14	22 ♉ 22	18 ♉ 54	03 ♍ 26	14 ♉ 46	09 ♉ 34
May 26, 1959	05 ♐ 20	13 ♍ 30	21 ♐ 01	10 ♉ 42	25 ♉ 55	23 ♉ 38	05 ♍ 11	18 ♉ 40	13 ♉ 52
Jun 5, 1959	02 ♐ 43	14 ♍ 41	18 ♐ 55	16 ♉ 08	29 ♉ 27	28 ♉ 20	07 ♍ 21	22 ♉ 32	18 ♉ 05
Jun 15, 1959	00 ♐ 27	16 ♍ 16	16 ♐ 43	21 ♉ 32	02 ♊ 56	02 ♊ 58	09 ♍ 51	26 ♉ 30	22 ♉ 13
Jun 25, 1959	28 ♏ 54	18 ♍ 12	14 ♐ 36	26 ♉ 52	06 ♊ 22	07 ♊ 33	12 ♍ 39	00 ♊ 04	26 ♉ 14
Jul 5, 1959	28 ♏ 16	20 ♍ 26	12 ♐ 47	02 ♊ 10	09 ♊ 45	12 ♊ 03	15 ♍ 42	03 ♊ 43	00 ♊ 07
Jul 15, 1959	28 ♏ 36	22 ♍ 56	11 ♐ 24	07 ♊ 22	13 ♊ 02	16 ♊ 27	18 ♍ 57	07 ♊ 15	03 ♊ 53
Jul 25, 1959	29 ♏ 52	25 ♍ 39	10 ♐ 33	12 ♊ 30	16 ♊ 13	20 ♊ 45	22 ♍ 23	10 ♊ 40	07 ♊ 28
Aug 4, 1959	01 ♐ 55	28 ♍ 35	10 ♐ 16	17 ♊ 32	19 ♊ 16	24 ♊ 55	25 ♍ 58	13 ♊ 56	10 ♊ 53
Aug 14, 1959	04 ♐ 39	01 ♎ 40	10 ♐ 33	22 ♊ 26	22 ♊ 10	28 ♊ 57	29 ♍ 40	17 ♊ 01	14 ♊ 04
Aug 24, 1959	07 ♐ 56	04 ♎ 55	11 ♐ 22	27 ♊ 12	24 ♊ 53	02 ♋ 48	03 ♎ 29	19 ♊ 53	16 ♊ 60
Sep 3, 1959	11 ♐ 40	08 ♎ 17	12 ♐ 39	01 ♋ 47	27 ♊ 22	06 ♋ 28	07 ♎ 24	22 ♊ 30	19 ♊ 37
Sep 13, 1959	15 ♐ 47	11 ♎ 45	14 ♐ 23	06 ♋ 09	29 ♊ 36	09 ♋ 53	11 ♎ 22	24 ♊ 48	21 ♊ 53
Sep 23, 1959	20 ♐ 11	15 ♎ 19	16 ♐ 29	10 ♋ 17	01 ♋ 30	13 ♋ 02	15 ♎ 24	26 ♊ 45	23 ♊ 43
Oct 3, 1959	24 ♐ 50	18 ♎ 57	18 ♐ 55	14 ♋ 06	03 ♋ 02	15 ♋ 51	19 ♎ 29	28 ♊ 16	25 ♊ 04
Oct 13, 1959	29 ♐ 39	22 ♎ 39	21 ♐ 38	17 ♋ 32	04 ♋ 08	18 ♋ 17	23 ♎ 36	29 ♊ 18	25 ♊ 51
Oct 23, 1959	04 ♑ 38	26 ♎ 24	24 ♐ 36	20 ♋ 30	04 ♋ 45	20 ♋ 15	27 ♎ 43	29 ♊ 46	25 ♊ 59
Nov 2, 1959	09 ♑ 43	00 ♏ 10	27 ♐ 48	22 ♋ 56	04 ♋ 48	21 ♋ 42	01 ♏ 11	29 ♊ 38	25 ♊ 25
Nov 12, 1959	14 ♑ 54	03 ♏ 57	01 ♑ 10	24 ♋ 41	04 ♋ 15	22 ♋ 32	05 ♏ 57	28 ♊ 51	24 ♊ 09
Nov 22, 1959	20 ♑ 08	07 ♏ 44	04 ♑ 42	25 ♋ 40	03 ♋ 07	22 ♋ 42	10 ♏ 02	27 ♊ 27	22 ♊ 14
Dec 2, 1959	25 ♑ 26	11 ♏ 30	08 ♑ 23	25 ♋ 47	01 ♋ 27	22 ♋ 09	14 ♏ 05	25 ♊ 32	19 ♊ 51
Dec 12, 1959	00 ♒ 45	15 ♏ 13	12 ♑ 10	24 ♋ 57	29 ♊ 05	20 ♋ 56	18 ♏ 03	23 ♊ 17	17 ♊ 12
Dec 22, 1959	06 ♒ 05	18 ♏ 53	16 ♑ 04	23 ♋ 14	27 ♊ 05	19 ♋ 07	21 ♏ 56	20 ♊ 56	14 ♊ 38
Jan 1, 1960	11 ♒ 26	22 ♏ 28	20 ♑ 02	20 ♋ 50	24 ♊ 49	16 ♋ 54	25 ♏ 43	18 ♊ 46	12 ♊ 24
Jan 11, 1960	16 ♒ 46	25 ♏ 56	24 ♑ 04	18 ♋ 05	22 ♊ 49	14 ♋ 32	29 ♏ 22	16 ♊ 59	10 ♊ 43
Jan 21, 1960	22 ♒ 06	29 ♏ 16	28 ♑ 09	15 ♋ 25	21 ♊ 16	12 ♋ 21	02 ♐ 51	15 ♊ 47	09 ♊ 43
Jan 31, 1960	27 ♒ 24	02 ♐ 25	02 ♒ 16	13 ♋ 15	20 ♊ 17	10 ♋ 33	06 ♐ 08	15 ♊ 13	09 ♊ 26
Feb 10, 1960	02 ♓ 41	05 ♐ 22	06 ♒ 25	11 ♋ 51	19 ♊ 55	09 ♋ 20	09 ♐ 11	15 ♊ 18	09 ♊ 50
Feb 20, 1960	07 ♓ 55	08 ♐ 03	10 ♒ 34	11 ♋ 20	20 ♊ 11	08 ♋ 47	11 ♐ 58	16 ♊ 01	10 ♊ 51
Mar 1, 1960	13 ♓ 06	10 ♐ 26	14 ♒ 42	11 ♋ 42	21 ♊ 00	08 ♋ 53	14 ♐ 25	17 ♊ 17	12 ♊ 25
Mar 11, 1960	18 ♓ 14	12 ♐ 27	18 ♒ 49	12 ♋ 52	22 ♊ 21	09 ♋ 37	16 ♐ 29	19 ♊ 03	14 ♊ 26
Mar 21, 1960	23 ♓ 19	14 ♐ 03	22 ♒ 54	14 ♋ 44	24 ♊ 08	10 ♋ 54	18 ♐ 06	21 ♊ 14	16 ♊ 51

	ATROPOS	HEKATE	LILITH	MEDUSA	MOIRA	NEMESIS	PERSEPHONE	PROSERPINA	PYTHIA
Mar 31, 1960	28 ♓ 19	15 ♐ 09	26 ♒ 56	17 ♋ 11	26 ♊ 19	12 ♋ 40	19 ♐ 14	23 ♊ 46	19 ♊ 36
Apr 10, 1960	03 ♈ 16	15 ♐ 43	00 ♓ 54	20 ♋ 06	28 ♊ 51	14 ♋ 50	19 ♐ 49	26 ♊ 37	22 ♊ 38
Apr 20, 1960	08 ♈ 07	15 ♐ 42	04 ♓ 47	23 ♋ 25	01 ♋ 39	17 ♋ 20	19 ♐ 48	29 ♊ 42	25 ♊ 53
Apr 30, 1960	12 ♈ 53	15 ♐ 04	08 ♓ 33	27 ♋ 02	04 ♋ 41	20 ♋ 08	19 ♐ 11	03 ♋ 01	29 ♊ 20
May 10, 1960	17 ♈ 34	13 ♐ 52	12 ♓ 11	00 ♌ 55	07 ♋ 56	23 ♋ 09	17 ♐ 59	06 ♋ 30	02 ♋ 57
May 20, 1960	22 ♈ 07	12 ♐ 12	15 ♓ 40	05 ♌ 01	11 ♋ 21	26 ♋ 22	16 ♐ 20	10 ♋ 08	06 ♋ 42
May 30, 1960	26 ♈ 34	10 ♐ 14	18 ♓ 56	09 ♌ 17	14 ♋ 56	29 ♋ 44	14 ♐ 21	13 ♋ 54	10 ♋ 34
Jun 9, 1960	00 ♉ 52	08 ♐ 13	21 ♓ 58	13 ♌ 41	18 ♋ 38	03 ♌ 13	12 ♐ 16	17 ♋ 46	14 ♋ 32
Jun 19, 1960	05 ♉ 01	06 ♐ 21	24 ♓ 42	18 ♌ 12	22 ♋ 26	06 ♌ 49	10 ♐ 19	21 ♋ 43	18 ♋ 36
Jun 29, 1960	08 ♉ 60	04 ♐ 53	27 ♓ 05	22 ♌ 49	26 ♋ 20	10 ♌ 29	08 ♐ 41	25 ♋ 45	22 ♋ 43
Jul 9, 1960	12 ♉ 46	03 ♐ 57	29 ♓ 03	27 ♌ 30	00 ♌ 19	14 ♌ 13	07 ♐ 32	29 ♋ 50	26 ♋ 54
Jul 19, 1960	16 ♉ 18	03 ♐ 37	00 ♈ 30	02 ♍ 15	04 ♌ 22	18 ♌ 00	06 ♐ 55	03 ♌ 58	01 ♌ 08
Jul 29, 1960	19 ♉ 33	03 ♐ 55	00 ♈ 22	07 ♍ 04	08 ♌ 28	21 ♌ 50	06 ♐ 54	08 ♌ 09	05 ♌ 25
Aug 8, 1960	22 ♉ 28	04 ♐ 50	01 ♈ 35	11 ♍ 55	12 ♌ 37	25 ♌ 40	07 ♐ 26	12 ♌ 21	09 ♌ 44
Aug 18, 1960	24 ♉ 60	06 ♐ 19	01 ♈ 05	16 ♍ 48	16 ♌ 48	29 ♌ 31	08 ♐ 30	16 ♌ 34	14 ♌ 05
Aug 28, 1960	27 ♉ 04	08 ♐ 17	29 ♓ 53	21 ♍ 42	21 ♌ 01	03 ♍ 21	10 ♐ 01	20 ♌ 48	18 ♌ 26
Sep 7, 1960	28 ♉ 35	10 ♐ 42	28 ♓ 05	26 ♍ 05	25 ♌ 14	07 ♍ 11	11 ♐ 56	25 ♌ 01	22 ♌ 48
Sep 17, 1960	29 ♉ 38	13 ♐ 29	25 ♓ 53	01 ♎ 34	29 ♌ 28	10 ♍ 59	14 ♐ 13	29 ♌ 13	27 ♌ 10
Sep 27, 1960	29 ♉ 38	16 ♐ 37	23 ♓ 35	06 ♎ 31	03 ♍ 41	14 ♍ 44	16 ♐ 47	03 ♍ 23	01 ♍ 31
Oct 7, 1960	29 ♉ 00	20 ♐ 01	21 ♓ 31	11 ♎ 27	07 ♍ 53	18 ♍ 25	19 ♐ 37	07 ♍ 31	05 ♍ 50
Oct 17, 1960	27 ♉ 36	23 ♐ 40	19 ♓ 58	16 ♎ 23	12 ♍ 02	22 ♍ 02	22 ♐ 40	11 ♍ 35	10 ♍ 07
Oct 27, 1960	25 ♉ 28	27 ♐ 31	19 ♓ 08	21 ♎ 18	16 ♍ 09	25 ♍ 34	25 ♐ 54	15 ♍ 33	14 ♍ 21
Nov 6, 1960	22 ♉ 49	01 ♑ 33	19 ♓ 06	26 ♎ 11	20 ♍ 09	28 ♍ 57	29 ♐ 17	19 ♍ 25	18 ♍ 29
Nov 16, 1960	19 ♉ 58	05 ♑ 44	19 ♓ 52	01 ♏ 02	24 ♍ 03	02 ♎ 12	02 ♑ 47	23 ♍ 09	22 ♍ 31
Nov 26, 1960	17 ♉ 15	09 ♑ 03	21 ♓ 23	05 ♏ 50	27 ♍ 50	05 ♎ 16	06 ♑ 23	26 ♍ 42	26 ♍ 25
Dec 6, 1960	15 ♉ 00	14 ♑ 28	23 ♓ 34	10 ♏ 34	01 ♎ 25	08 ♎ 07	10 ♑ 04	00 ♎ 02	00 ♎ 07
Dec 16, 1960	13 ♉ 26	18 ♑ 58	26 ♓ 19	15 ♏ 14	04 ♎ 47	10 ♎ 43	13 ♑ 48	03 ♎ 06	03 ♎ 37
Dec 26, 1960	12 ♉ 39	23 ♑ 31	29 ♓ 33	19 ♏ 47	07 ♎ 52	13 ♎ 00	17 ♑ 35	05 ♎ 52	06 ♎ 49
Jan 5, 1961	12 ♉ 38	28 ♑ 08	03 ♈ 12	24 ♏ 14	10 ♎ 37	14 ♎ 56	21 ♑ 22	08 ♎ 14	09 ♎ 40
Jan 15, 1961	13 ♉ 21	02 ♒ 47	07 ♈ 12	28 ♏ 32	12 ♎ 58	16 ♎ 27	25 ♑ 10	10 ♎ 08	12 ♎ 06
Jan 25, 1961	14 ♉ 42	07 ♒ 27	11 ♈ 29	02 ♐ 40	14 ♎ 48	17 ♎ 29	28 ♑ 57	11 ♎ 30	14 ♎ 00
Feb 4, 1961	16 ♉ 35	12 ♒ 07	16 ♈ 01	06 ♐ 35	16 ♎ 04	17 ♎ 58	02 ♒ 42	12 ♎ 15	15 ♎ 17
Feb 14, 1961	18 ♉ 56	16 ♒ 46	20 ♈ 44	10 ♐ 17	16 ♎ 40	17 ♎ 53	06 ♒ 23	12 ♎ 18	15 ♎ 51
Feb 24, 1961	21 ♉ 39	21 ♒ 24	25 ♈ 37	13 ♐ 41	16 ♎ 33	17 ♎ 12	10 ♒ 01	11 ♎ 39	15 ♎ 36
Mar 6, 1961	24 ♉ 40	25 ♒ 59	00 ♉ 37	16 ♐ 44	15 ♎ 41	15 ♎ 56	13 ♒ 33	10 ♎ 19	14 ♎ 31

	ATROPOS	HEKATE	LILITH	MEDUSA	MOIRA	NEMESIS	PERSEPHONE	PROSERPINA	PYTHIA
Mar 16, 1961	27 ♉ 56	00 ♓ 31	05 ♉ 44	19 ♐ 24	14 ♎ 09	14 ♎ 11	16 ♒ 59	08 ♎ 25	12 ♎ 40
Mar 26, 1961	01 ♊ 24	04 ♓ 58	10 ♉ 56	21 ♐ 34	12 ♎ 07	12 ♎ 06	20 ♒ 18	06 ♎ 11	10 ♎ 16
Apr 5, 1961	05 ♊ 02	09 ♓ 20	16 ♉ 11	23 ♐ 10	09 ♎ 52	09 ♎ 53	23 ♒ 27	03 ♎ 50	07 ♎ 37
Apr 15, 1961	08 ♊ 48	13 ♓ 36	21 ♉ 29	24 ♐ 08	07 ♎ 42	07 ♎ 46	26 ♒ 25	01 ♎ 50	05 ♎ 08
Apr 25, 1961	12 ♊ 39	17 ♓ 45	26 ♉ 49	24 ♐ 21	05 ♎ 56	05 ♎ 57	29 ♒ 11	00 ♎ 16	03 ♎ 09
May 5, 1961	16 ♊ 36	21 ♓ 45	02 ♊ 09	23 ♐ 48	04 ♎ 47	04 ♎ 34	01 ♓ 42	29 ♍ 21	01 ♎ 56
May 15, 1961	20 ♊ 36	25 ♓ 35	07 ♊ 30	22 ♐ 28	04 ♎ 22	03 ♎ 44	03 ♓ 57	29 ♍ 09	01 ♎ 35
May 25, 1961	24 ♊ 39	29 ♓ 13	12 ♊ 51	20 ♐ 27	04 ♎ 42	03 ♎ 29	05 ♓ 52	29 ♍ 39	02 ♎ 05
Jun 4, 1961	28 ♊ 44	02 ♈ 37	18 ♊ 10	17 ♐ 58	05 ♎ 46	03 ♎ 47	07 ♓ 25	00 ♎ 47	03 ♎ 24
Jun 14, 1961	02 ♋ 49	05 ♈ 46	23 ♊ 28	15 ♐ 20	07 ♎ 28	04 ♎ 36	08 ♓ 33	02 ♎ 31	05 ♎ 24
Jun 24, 1961	06 ♋ 56	08 ♈ 36	28 ♊ 44	12 ♐ 54	09 ♎ 44	05 ♎ 53	09 ♓ 13	04 ♎ 45	08 ♎ 01
Jul 4, 1961	11 ♋ 02	11 ♈ 04	03 ♋ 57	10 ♐ 57	12 ♎ 29	07 ♎ 35	09 ♓ 23	07 ♎ 25	11 ♎ 08
Jul 14, 1961	15 ♋ 07	13 ♈ 08	09 ♋ 08	09 ♐ 41	15 ♎ 39	09 ♎ 37	09 ♓ 00	10 ♎ 27	14 ♎ 42
Jul 24, 1961	19 ♋ 11	14 ♈ 42	14 ♋ 14	09 ♐ 13	19 ♎ 09	11 ♎ 59	08 ♓ 06	13 ♎ 47	18 ♎ 36
Aug 3, 1961	23 ♋ 12	15 ♈ 44	19 ♋ 17	09 ♐ 31	22 ♎ 56	14 ♎ 36	06 ♓ 44	17 ♎ 24	22 ♎ 49
Aug 13, 1961	27 ♋ 11	16 ♈ 11	24 ♋ 14	10 ♐ 34	26 ♎ 58	17 ♎ 26	04 ♓ 58	21 ♎ 14	27 ♎ 18
Aug 23, 1961	01 ♌ 07	15 ♈ 59	29 ♋ 06	12 ♐ 15	01 ♏ 12	20 ♎ 28	02 ♓ 58	25 ♎ 15	01 ♏ 60
Sep 2, 1961	04 ♌ 57	15 ♈ 10	03 ♌ 52	14 ♐ 31	05 ♏ 36	23 ♎ 40	00 ♓ 55	29 ♎ 26	06 ♏ 52
Sep 12, 1961	08 ♌ 43	13 ♈ 46	08 ♌ 30	17 ♐ 15	10 ♏ 09	27 ♎ 00	29 ♒ 02	03 ♏ 46	11 ♏ 54
Sep 22, 1961	12 ♌ 22	11 ♈ 56	12 ♌ 59	20 ♐ 25	14 ♏ 49	00 ♏ 28	27 ♒ 28	08 ♏ 13	17 ♏ 05
Oct 2, 1961	15 ♌ 52	09 ♈ 51	17 ♌ 19	23 ♐ 55	19 ♏ 34	04 ♏ 01	26 ♒ 21	12 ♏ 45	22 ♏ 22
Oct 12, 1961	19 ♌ 13	07 ♈ 48	21 ♌ 27	27 ♐ 43	24 ♏ 25	07 ♏ 39	25 ♒ 45	17 ♏ 23	27 ♏ 45
Oct 22, 1961	22 ♌ 21	05 ♈ 60	25 ♌ 22	01 ♑ 47	29 ♏ 20	11 ♏ 21	25 ♒ 41	22 ♏ 05	03 ♐ 14
Nov 1, 1961	25 ♌ 15	04 ♈ 38	29 ♌ 01	06 ♑ 05	04 ♐ 17	15 ♏ 06	26 ♒ 09	26 ♏ 50	08 ♐ 46
Nov 11, 1961	27 ♌ 51	03 ♈ 51	02 ♍ 20	10 ♑ 33	09 ♐ 16	18 ♏ 53	27 ♒ 07	01 ♐ 38	14 ♐ 22
Nov 21, 1961	00 ♍ 06	03 ♈ 41	05 ♍ 20	15 ♑ 11	14 ♐ 17	22 ♏ 41	28 ♒ 31	06 ♐ 27	20 ♐ 00
Dec 1, 1961	01 ♍ 55	04 ♈ 08	07 ♍ 53	19 ♑ 58	19 ♐ 18	26 ♏ 28	00 ♓ 18	11 ♐ 18	25 ♐ 41
Dec 11, 1961	03 ♍ 14	05 ♈ 08	09 ♍ 57	24 ♑ 52	24 ♐ 19	00 ♐ 16	02 ♓ 26	16 ♐ 09	01 ♑ 22
Dec 21, 1961	03 ♍ 58	06 ♈ 39	11 ♍ 25	29 ♑ 53	29 ♐ 19	04 ♐ 01	04 ♓ 51	20 ♐ 59	07 ♑ 05
Dec 31, 1961	04 ♍ 01	08 ♈ 37	12 ♍ 14	04 ♒ 58	04 ♑ 17	07 ♐ 43	07 ♓ 31	25 ♐ 48	12 ♑ 47
Jan 10, 1962	03 ♍ 21	10 ♈ 56	12 ♍ 20	10 ♒ 08	09 ♑ 13	11 ♐ 21	10 ♓ 23	00 ♑ 35	18 ♑ 28
Jan 20, 1962	01 ♍ 56	13 ♈ 34	11 ♍ 42	15 ♒ 22	14 ♑ 05	14 ♐ 53	13 ♓ 25	05 ♑ 19	24 ♑ 08
Jan 30, 1962	29 ♌ 51	16 ♈ 28	10 ♍ 21	20 ♒ 39	18 ♑ 53	18 ♐ 18	16 ♓ 36	09 ♑ 58	29 ♑ 46
Feb 9, 1962	27 ♌ 17	19 ♈ 34	08 ♍ 24	25 ♒ 59	23 ♑ 36	21 ♐ 35	19 ♓ 53	14 ♑ 33	05 ♒ 21
Feb 19, 1962	24 ♌ 30	22 ♈ 51	06 ♍ 05	01 ♓ 20	28 ♑ 13	24 ♐ 40	23 ♓ 15	19 ♑ 02	10 ♒ 53

	ATROPOS	HEKATE	LILITH	MEDUSA	MOIRA	NEMESIS	PERSEPHONE	PROSERPINA	PYTHIA
Mar 1, 1962	21 ♌ 48	26 ♈ 15	03 ♍ 40	06 ♓ 42	02 ♒ 43	27 ♐ 33	26 ♓ 42	23 ♑ 24	16 ♒ 21
Mar 11, 1962	19 ♌ 29	29 ♈ 46	01 ♍ 26	12 ♓ 05	07 ♒ 05	00 ♑ 10	00 ♈ 11	27 ♑ 37	21 ♒ 44
Mar 21, 1962	17 ♌ 47	03 ♉ 22	29 ♌ 40	17 ♓ 28	11 ♒ 17	02 ♑ 27	03 ♈ 41	01 ♒ 40	27 ♒ 01
Mar 31, 1962	16 ♌ 49	07 ♉ 00	28 ♌ 28	22 ♓ 51	15 ♒ 19	04 ♑ 27	07 ♈ 13	05 ♒ 31	02 ♓ 12
Apr 10, 1962	16 ♌ 36	10 ♉ 41	27 ♌ 57	28 ♓ 13	19 ♒ 09	05 ♑ 60	10 ♈ 43	09 ♒ 09	07 ♓ 16
Apr 20, 1962	17 ♌ 05	14 ♉ 24	28 ♌ 05	03 ♈ 34	22 ♒ 45	07 ♑ 04	14 ♈ 13	12 ♒ 30	12 ♓ 12
Apr 30, 1962	18 ♌ 13	18 ♉ 06	28 ♌ 49	08 ♈ 53	26 ♒ 04	07 ♑ 36	17 ♈ 40	15 ♒ 33	16 ♓ 58
May 10, 1962	19 ♌ 55	21 ♉ 48	00 ♍ 05	14 ♈ 11	29 ♒ 06	07 ♑ 33	21 ♈ 04	18 ♒ 14	21 ♓ 34
May 20, 1962	22 ♌ 06	25 ♉ 28	01 ♍ 49	19 ♈ 25	01 ♓ 45	06 ♑ 53	24 ♈ 23	20 ♒ 29	25 ♓ 57
May 30, 1962	24 ♌ 42	29 ♉ 05	03 ♍ 56	24 ♈ 36	04 ♓ 01	05 ♑ 39	27 ♈ 37	22 ♒ 16	00 ♈ 06
Jun 9, 1962	27 ♌ 40	02 ♊ 40	06 ♍ 23	29 ♈ 42	05 ♓ 48	03 ♑ 55	00 ♉ 45	23 ♒ 29	03 ♈ 60
Jun 19, 1962	00 ♍ 56	06 ♊ 10	09 ♍ 05	04 ♉ 44	07 ♓ 02	01 ♑ 51	03 ♉ 44	24 ♒ 04	07 ♈ 35
Jun 29, 1962	04 ♍ 28	09 ♊ 36	12 ♍ 01	09 ♉ 40	07 ♓ 42	29 ♐ 39	06 ♉ 34	24 ♒ 00	10 ♈ 48
Jul 9, 1962	08 ♍ 14	12 ♊ 56	15 ♍ 08	14 ♉ 28	07 ♓ 43	27 ♐ 33	09 ♉ 13	23 ♒ 15	13 ♈ 35
Jul 19, 1962	12 ♍ 12	16 ♊ 08	18 ♍ 25	19 ♉ 08	07 ♓ 04	25 ♐ 48	11 ♉ 38	21 ♒ 52	15 ♈ 53
Jul 29, 1962	16 ♍ 22	19 ♊ 13	21 ♍ 48	23 ♉ 38	05 ♓ 48	24 ♐ 34	13 ♉ 47	19 ♒ 59	17 ♈ 36
Aug 8, 1962	20 ♍ 41	22 ♊ 08	25 ♍ 18	27 ♉ 55	03 ♓ 59	23 ♐ 55	15 ♉ 37	17 ♒ 47	18 ♈ 39
Aug 18, 1962	25 ♍ 09	24 ♊ 51	28 ♍ 53	01 ♊ 56	01 ♓ 51	23 ♐ 55	17 ♉ 06	15 ♒ 34	18 ♈ 57
Aug 28, 1962	29 ♍ 46	27 ♊ 21	02 ♎ 31	05 ♊ 39	29 ♒ 35	24 ♐ 32	18 ♉ 09	13 ♒ 34	18 ♈ 28
Sep 7, 1962	04 ♎ 31	29 ♊ 35	06 ♎ 12	08 ♊ 59	27 ♒ 28	25 ♐ 43	18 ♉ 44	12 ♒ 02	17 ♈ 11
Sep 17, 1962	09 ♎ 23	01 ♋ 31	09 ♎ 55	11 ♊ 52	25 ♒ 43	27 ♐ 26	18 ♉ 47	11 ♒ 06	15 ♈ 12
Sep 27, 1962	14 ♎ 21	03 ♋ 07	13 ♎ 40	14 ♊ 11	24 ♒ 30	29 ♐ 37	18 ♉ 17	10 ♒ 49	12 ♈ 43
Oct 7, 1962	19 ♎ 27	04 ♋ 18	17 ♎ 24	15 ♊ 49	23 ♒ 54	02 ♑ 11	17 ♉ 14	11 ♒ 11	10 ♈ 03
Oct 17, 1962	24 ♎ 37	05 ♋ 01	21 ♎ 09	16 ♊ 40	23 ♒ 56	05 ♑ 07	15 ♉ 41	12 ♒ 11	07 ♈ 33
Oct 27, 1962	29 ♎ 54	05 ♋ 15	24 ♎ 51	16 ♊ 38	24 ♒ 33	08 ♑ 21	13 ♉ 46	13 ♒ 43	05 ♈ 30
Nov 6, 1962	05 ♏ 15	04 ♋ 57	28 ♎ 32	15 ♊ 40	25 ♒ 44	11 ♑ 51	11 ♉ 39	15 ♒ 44	04 ♈ 08
Nov 16, 1962	10 ♏ 41	04 ♋ 07	02 ♏ 09	13 ♊ 50	27 ♒ 24	15 ♑ 34	09 ♉ 33	18 ♒ 10	03 ♈ 31
Nov 26, 1962	16 ♏ 12	02 ♋ 47	05 ♏ 42	11 ♊ 23	29 ♒ 28	19 ♑ 29	07 ♉ 41	20 ♒ 57	03 ♈ 40
Dec 6, 1962	21 ♏ 45	01 ♋ 03	09 ♏ 09	08 ♊ 40	01 ♓ 54	23 ♑ 35	06 ♉ 14	24 ♒ 01	04 ♈ 31
Dec 16, 1962	27 ♏ 21	29 ♊ 04	12 ♏ 29	06 ♊ 08	04 ♓ 38	27 ♑ 48	05 ♉ 18	27 ♒ 19	05 ♈ 60
Dec 26, 1962	02 ♐ 60	26 ♊ 60	15 ♏ 40	04 ♊ 10	07 ♓ 36	02 ♒ 09	04 ♉ 57	00 ♓ 50	07 ♈ 59
Jan 5, 1963	08 ♐ 40	25 ♊ 04	18 ♏ 42	03 ♊ 03	10 ♓ 47	06 ♒ 37	05 ♉ 12	04 ♓ 30	10 ♈ 26
Jan 15, 1963	14 ♐ 19	23 ♊ 26	21 ♏ 30	02 ♊ 51	14 ♓ 07	11 ♒ 09	06 ♉ 00	08 ♓ 19	13 ♈ 14
Jan 25, 1963	19 ♐ 58	22 ♊ 14	24 ♏ 04	03 ♊ 33	17 ♓ 35	15 ♒ 45	07 ♉ 18	12 ♓ 13	16 ♈ 20
Feb 4, 1963	25 ♐ 35	21 ♊ 32	26 ♏ 21	05 ♊ 04	21 ♓ 10	20 ♒ 25	09 ♉ 03	16 ♓ 13	19 ♈ 41

	ATROPOS	HEKATE	LILITH	MEDUSA	MOIRA	NEMESIS	PERSEPHONE	PROSERPINA	PYTHIA
Feb 14, 1963	01 ♑ 09	21 ♊ 21	28 ♏ 18	07 ♊ 15	24 ♓ 49	25 ♒ 07	11 ♉ 11	20 ♓ 16	23 ♈ 14
Feb 24, 1963	06 ♑ 37	21 ♊ 41	29 ♏ 51	10 ♊ 01	28 ♓ 32	29 ♒ 50	13 ♉ 39	24 ♓ 22	26 ♈ 56
Mar 6, 1963	11 ♑ 59	22 ♊ 29	00 ♐ 58	13 ♊ 16	02 ♈ 17	04 ♓ 35	16 ♉ 23	28 ♓ 30	00 ♉ 46
Mar 16, 1963	17 ♑ 12	23 ♊ 42	01 ♐ 35	16 ♊ 53	06 ♈ 03	09 ♓ 19	19 ♉ 21	02 ♈ 38	04 ♉ 41
Mar 26, 1963	22 ♑ 14	25 ♊ 17	01 ♐ 40	20 ♊ 48	09 ♈ 50	14 ♓ 03	22 ♉ 30	06 ♈ 45	08 ♉ 42
Apr 5, 1963	27 ♑ 02	27 ♊ 10	01 ♐ 10	24 ♊ 59	13 ♈ 36	18 ♓ 45	25 ♉ 50	10 ♈ 52	12 ♉ 45
Apr 15, 1963	01 ♒ 34	29 ♊ 20	00 ♐ 07	29 ♊ 21	17 ♈ 20	23 ♓ 25	29 ♉ 17	14 ♈ 57	16 ♉ 51
Apr 25, 1963	05 ♒ 46	01 ♋ 42	28 ♏ 33	03 ♋ 53	21 ♈ 02	28 ♓ 02	02 ♊ 51	18 ♈ 59	20 ♉ 58
May 5, 1963	09 ♒ 33	04 ♋ 16	26 ♏ 37	08 ♋ 33	24 ♈ 40	02 ♈ 35	06 ♊ 30	22 ♈ 58	25 ♉ 06
May 15, 1963	12 ♒ 50	06 ♋ 58	24 ♏ 26	13 ♋ 19	28 ♈ 14	07 ♈ 03	10 ♊ 13	26 ♈ 53	29 ♉ 14
May 25, 1963	15 ♒ 33	09 ♋ 48	22 ♏ 15	18 ♋ 50	01 ♉ 43	11 ♈ 26	13 ♊ 59	00 ♉ 43	03 ♊ 22
Jun 4, 1963	17 ♒ 34	12 ♋ 44	20 ♏ 14	23 ♋ 05	05 ♉ 07	15 ♈ 41	17 ♊ 47	04 ♉ 27	07 ♊ 28
Jun 14, 1963	18 ♒ 47	15 ♋ 45	18 ♏ 36	28 ♋ 03	08 ♉ 22	19 ♈ 47	21 ♊ 37	08 ♉ 05	11 ♊ 33
Jun 24, 1963	19 ♒ 06	18 ♋ 48	17 ♏ 25	03 ♌ 04	11 ♉ 30	23 ♈ 44	25 ♊ 27	11 ♉ 34	15 ♊ 35
Jul 4, 1963	18 ♒ 27	21 ♋ 55	16 ♏ 47	08 ♌ 06	14 ♉ 27	27 ♈ 27	29 ♊ 17	14 ♉ 53	19 ♊ 35
Jul 14, 1963	16 ♒ 55	25 ♋ 02	16 ♏ 42	13 ♌ 10	17 ♉ 12	00 ♉ 56	03 ♋ 06	18 ♉ 01	23 ♊ 30
Jul 24, 1963	14 ♒ 39	28 ♋ 10	17 ♏ 08	18 ♌ 14	19 ♉ 44	04 ♉ 08	06 ♋ 53	20 ♉ 57	27 ♊ 22
Aug 3, 1963	11 ♒ 60	01 ♌ 17	18 ♏ 04	23 ♌ 19	21 ♉ 60	06 ♉ 57	10 ♋ 38	23 ♉ 36	01 ♋ 08
Aug 13, 1963	09 ♒ 21	04 ♌ 23	19 ♏ 27	28 ♌ 25	23 ♉ 56	09 ♉ 22	14 ♋ 18	25 ♉ 58	04 ♋ 48
Aug 23, 1963	07 ♒ 08	07 ♌ 08	21 ♏ 12	03 ♍ 30	25 ♉ 31	11 ♉ 17	17 ♋ 54	27 ♉ 58	08 ♋ 20
Sep 2, 1963	05 ♒ 37	10 ♌ 26	23 ♏ 18	08 ♍ 34	26 ♉ 40	12 ♉ 36	21 ♋ 24	29 ♉ 33	11 ♋ 43
Sep 12, 1963	04 ♒ 57	13 ♌ 21	25 ♏ 41	13 ♍ 37	27 ♉ 21	13 ♉ 17	24 ♋ 47	00 ♊ 40	14 ♋ 55
Sep 22, 1963	05 ♒ 08	16 ♌ 10	28 ♏ 20	18 ♍ 40	27 ♉ 30	13 ♉ 13	28 ♋ 00	01 ♊ 13	17 ♋ 55
Oct 2, 1963	06 ♒ 07	18 ♌ 51	01 ♐ 11	23 ♍ 40	27 ♉ 04	12 ♉ 26	01 ♌ 02	01 ♊ 11	20 ♋ 38
Oct 12, 1963	07 ♒ 48	21 ♌ 23	04 ♐ 14	28 ♍ 38	26 ♉ 05	10 ♉ 58	03 ♌ 50	00 ♊ 32	23 ♋ 02
Oct 22, 1963	10 ♒ 05	23 ♌ 43	07 ♐ 27	03 ♎ 33	24 ♉ 33	08 ♉ 58	06 ♌ 21	29 ♉ 15	25 ♋ 04
Nov 1, 1963	12 ♒ 51	25 ♌ 50	10 ♐ 47	08 ♎ 25	22 ♉ 36	06 ♉ 43	08 ♌ 32	27 ♉ 26	26 ♋ 39
Nov 11, 1963	16 ♒ 01	27 ♌ 40	14 ♐ 15	13 ♎ 12	20 ♉ 24	04 ♉ 31	10 ♌ 20	25 ♉ 16	27 ♋ 42
Nov 21, 1963	19 ♒ 32	29 ♌ 11	17 ♐ 48	17 ♎ 55	18 ♉ 10	02 ♉ 41	11 ♌ 39	22 ♉ 56	27 ♋ 08
Dec 1, 1963	23 ♒ 19	00 ♍ 20	21 ♐ 25	22 ♎ 30	16 ♉ 06	01 ♉ 25	12 ♌ 27	20 ♉ 43	27 ♋ 53
Dec 11, 1963	27 ♒ 19	01 ♍ 03	25 ♐ 06	26 ♎ 58	14 ♉ 25	00 ♉ 53	12 ♌ 39	18 ♉ 51	26 ♋ 55
Dec 21, 1963	01 ♓ 30	01 ♍ 18	28 ♐ 50	01 ♏ 17	13 ♉ 15	01 ♉ 05	12 ♌ 13	17 ♉ 31	25 ♋ 16
Dec 31, 1963	05 ♓ 17	01 ♍ 04	02 ♑ 35	05 ♏ 25	12 ♉ 39	01 ♉ 59	11 ♌ 09	16 ♉ 47	23 ♋ 02
Jan 10, 1964	10 ♓ 17	00 ♍ 19	06 ♑ 20	09 ♏ 20	12 ♉ 39	03 ♉ 31	09 ♌ 33	16 ♉ 42	20 ♋ 26
Jan 20, 1964	14 ♓ 50	29 ♌ 05	10 ♑ 05	12 ♏ 58	13 ♉ 12	05 ♉ 36	07 ♌ 32	17 ♉ 14	17 ♋ 46

	ATROPOS	HEKATE	LILITH	MEDUSA	MOIRA	NEMESIS	PERSEPHONE	PROSERPINA	PYTHIA
Jan 30, 1964	19 ♓ 27	27 ♌ 27	13 ♑ 48	16 ♏ 19	14 ♉ 16	08 ♉ 09	05 ♋ 20	18 ♊ 21	15 ♋ 21
Feb 9, 1964	24 ♓ 07	25 ♌ 32	17 ♑ 29	19 ♏ 16	15 ♉ 47	11 ♉ 04	03 ♋ 12	19 ♊ 57	13 ♋ 25
Feb 19, 1964	28 ♓ 50	23 ♌ 31	21 ♑ 06	21 ♏ 47	17 ♉ 42	14 ♉ 19	01 ♋ 23	21 ♊ 59	12 ♋ 09
Feb 29, 1964	03 ♈ 33	21 ♌ 35	24 ♑ 38	23 ♏ 47	19 ♉ 56	17 ♉ 49	00 ♋ 03	24 ♊ 23	11 ♋ 37
Mar 10, 1964	08 ♈ 18	19 ♌ 54	28 ♑ 03	25 ♏ 10	22 ♉ 28	21 ♉ 32	29 ♊ 19	27 ♊ 06	11 ♋ 49
Mar 20, 1964	13 ♈ 02	18 ♌ 36	01 ♒ 21	25 ♏ 50	25 ♉ 13	25 ♉ 25	29 ♊ 13	00 ♋ 04	12 ♋ 42
Mar 30, 1964	17 ♈ 46	18 ♌ 46	04 ♒ 29	25 ♏ 44	28 ♉ 11	29 ♉ 26	29 ♊ 44	03 ♋ 15	14 ♋ 10
Apr 9, 1964	22 ♈ 29	17 ♌ 25	07 ♒ 26	24 ♏ 50	01 ♊ 18	03 ♊ 33	00 ♋ 49	06 ♋ 36	16 ♋ 10
Apr 19, 1964	27 ♈ 10	17 ♌ 35	10 ♒ 08	23 ♏ 11	04 ♊ 33	07 ♊ 44	02 ♋ 24	10 ♋ 07	18 ♋ 36
Apr 29, 1964	01 ♉ 48	18 ♌ 12	12 ♒ 35	20 ♏ 54	07 ♊ 55	11 ♊ 60	04 ♋ 24	13 ♋ 44	21 ♋ 25
May 9, 1964	06 ♉ 24	19 ♌ 16	14 ♒ 42	18 ♏ 18	11 ♊ 22	16 ♊ 18	06 ♋ 47	17 ♋ 28	24 ♋ 33
May 19, 1964	10 ♉ 56	20 ♌ 42	16 ♒ 25	15 ♏ 40	14 ♊ 53	20 ♊ 37	09 ♋ 29	21 ♋ 17	27 ♋ 57
May 29, 1964	15 ♉ 25	22 ♌ 28	17 ♒ 42	13 ♏ 23	18 ♊ 28	24 ♊ 58	12 ♋ 26	25 ♋ 09	01 ♌ 35
Jun 8, 1964	19 ♉ 48	24 ♌ 32	18 ♒ 29	11 ♏ 41	22 ♊ 05	29 ♊ 18	15 ♋ 37	29 ♋ 04	05 ♌ 25
Jun 18, 1964	24 ♉ 07	26 ♌ 51	18 ♒ 41	10 ♏ 44	25 ♊ 43	03 ♋ 39	18 ♋ 59	03 ♌ 01	09 ♌ 26
Jun 28, 1964	28 ♉ 19	29 ♌ 22	18 ♒ 16	10 ♏ 33	29 ♊ 22	07 ♋ 58	22 ♋ 31	07 ♌ 00	13 ♌ 36
Jul 8, 1964	02 ♊ 25	02 ♍ 04	17 ♒ 14	11 ♏ 08	03 ♋ 02	12 ♋ 15	26 ♋ 10	11 ♌ 00	17 ♌ 54
Jul 18, 1964	06 ♊ 22	04 ♍ 56	15 ♒ 38	12 ♏ 24	06 ♋ 40	16 ♋ 30	29 ♋ 56	14 ♌ 50	22 ♌ 19
Jul 28, 1964	10 ♊ 09	07 ♍ 55	13 ♒ 35	14 ♏ 17	10 ♋ 17	20 ♋ 43	03 ♌ 48	18 ♌ 59	26 ♌ 51
Aug 7, 1964	13 ♊ 45	11 ♍ 01	11 ♒ 18	16 ♏ 39	13 ♋ 51	24 ♋ 52	07 ♌ 44	22 ♌ 58	01 ♍ 28
Aug 17, 1964	17 ♊ 08	14 ♍ 13	09 ♒ 02	19 ♏ 29	17 ♋ 22	28 ♋ 56	11 ♌ 44	26 ♌ 54	06 ♍ 11
Aug 27, 1964	20 ♊ 14	17 ♍ 29	07 ♒ 03	22 ♏ 40	20 ♋ 49	02 ♌ 56	15 ♌ 46	00 ♍ 47	10 ♍ 58
Sep 6, 1964	23 ♊ 03	20 ♍ 48	05 ♒ 33	26 ♏ 10	24 ♋ 09	06 ♌ 50	19 ♌ 51	04 ♍ 37	15 ♍ 49
Sep 16, 1964	25 ♊ 28	24 ♍ 10	04 ♒ 41	29 ♏ 57	27 ♋ 23	10 ♌ 36	23 ♌ 57	08 ♍ 21	20 ♍ 45
Sep 26, 1964	27 ♊ 27	27 ♍ 34	04 ♒ 31	03 ♐ 57	00 ♌ 27	14 ♌ 14	28 ♌ 04	11 ♍ 60	25 ♍ 43
Oct 6, 1964	28 ♊ 54	00 ♎ 58	05 ♒ 02	08 ♐ 47	03 ♌ 20	17 ♌ 41	02 ♍ 10	15 ♍ 30	00 ♎ 45
Oct 16, 1964	29 ♊ 45	04 ♎ 22	06 ♒ 13	12 ♐ 32	05 ♌ 59	20 ♌ 57	06 ♍ 16	18 ♍ 51	05 ♎ 48
Oct 26, 1964	29 ♊ 54	07 ♎ 44	07 ♒ 59	17 ♐ 04	08 ♌ 21	23 ♌ 58	10 ♍ 19	21 ♍ 59	10 ♎ 54
Nov 5, 1964	29 ♊ 18	11 ♎ 04	10 ♒ 17	21 ♐ 43	10 ♌ 23	26 ♌ 42	14 ♍ 20	24 ♍ 53	16 ♎ 01
Nov 15, 1964	27 ♊ 55	14 ♎ 19	13 ♒ 02	26 ♐ 29	12 ♌ 01	29 ♌ 06	18 ♍ 17	27 ♍ 29	21 ♎ 08
Nov 25, 1964	25 ♊ 51	17 ♎ 30	16 ♒ 11	01 ♑ 20	13 ♌ 10	01 ♍ 07	22 ♍ 08	29 ♍ 44	26 ♎ 15
Dec 5, 1964	23 ♊ 16	20 ♎ 33	19 ♒ 41	06 ♑ 16	13 ♌ 46	02 ♍ 40	25 ♍ 53	01 ♎ 32	01 ♏ 21
Dec 15, 1964	20 ♊ 26	23 ♎ 28	23 ♒ 28	11 ♑ 17	13 ♌ 44	03 ♍ 41	29 ♍ 30	02 ♎ 50	06 ♏ 24
Dec 25, 1964	17 ♊ 43	26 ♎ 11	27 ♒ 31	16 ♑ 21	13 ♌ 04	04 ♍ 07	02 ♎ 56	03 ♎ 33	11 ♏ 24
Jan 4, 1965	15 ♊ 24	28 ♎ 41	01 ♓ 47	21 ♑ 28	11 ♌ 46	03 ♍ 55	06 ♎ 10	03 ♎ 37	16 ♏ 20

Date	ATROPOS	HEKATE	LILITH	MEDUSA	MOIRA	NEMESIS	PERSEPHONE	PROSERPINA	PYTHIA
Jan 14, 1965	13 Ⅱ 43	00 ♏ 55	06 ♓ 15	26 ♑ 37	09 ♌ 54	03 ♍ 03	09 ♏ 10	02 ♍ 60	21 ♏ 09
Jan 24, 1965	12 Ⅱ 46	02 ♏ 49	10 ♓ 52	01 ♒ 47	07 ♌ 39	01 ♍ 36	11 ♏ 12	01 ♍ 42	25 ♏ 51
Feb 3, 1965	12 Ⅱ 34	04 ♏ 21	15 ♓ 38	06 ♒ 59	05 ♌ 17	29 ♌ 40	14 ♏ 12	29 ♌ 50	00 ♐ 23
Feb 13, 1965	13 Ⅱ 05	05 ♏ 26	20 ♓ 32	12 ♒ 11	03 ♌ 03	27 ♌ 26	16 ♏ 08	27 ♌ 35	04 ♐ 41
Feb 23, 1965	14 Ⅱ 13	06 ♏ 02	25 ♓ 31	17 ♒ 22	01 ♌ 12	25 ♌ 09	17 ♏ 35	25 ♌ 13	08 ♐ 45
Mar 5, 1965	15 Ⅱ 53	06 ♏ 06	00 ♈ 36	22 ♒ 34	29 ♋ 34	23 ♌ 04	18 ♏ 31	23 ♌ 01	12 ♐ 30
Mar 15, 1965	18 Ⅱ 01	05 ♏ 35	05 ♈ 45	27 ♒ 43	29 ♋ 22	21 ♌ 23	18 ♏ 50	21 ♌ 16	15 ♐ 51
Mar 25, 1965	20 Ⅱ 31	04 ♏ 32	10 ♈ 57	02 ♓ 52	29 ♋ 28	20 ♌ 14	18 ♏ 33	20 ♌ 07	18 ♐ 44
Apr 4, 1965	23 Ⅱ 20	03 ♏ 00	16 ♈ 13	07 ♓ 57	00 ♌ 13	19 ♌ 42	17 ♏ 38	19 ♌ 40	21 ♐ 04
Apr 14, 1965	26 Ⅱ 24	01 ♏ 07	21 ♈ 30	13 ♓ 00	01 ♌ 35	19 ♌ 46	16 ♏ 11	19 ♌ 55	22 ♐ 43
Apr 24, 1965	29 Ⅱ 40	29 ♎ 04	26 ♈ 50	17 ♓ 59	03 ♌ 28	20 ♌ 24	14 ♏ 18	20 ♌ 48	23 ♐ 37
May 4, 1965	03 ♋ 07	27 ♎ 03	02 ♉ 10	22 ♓ 54	05 ♌ 48	21 ♌ 32	12 ♏ 12	22 ♌ 18	23 ♐ 40
May 14, 1965	06 ♋ 43	25 ♎ 17	07 ♉ 30	27 ♓ 43	08 ♌ 32	23 ♌ 08	10 ♏ 08	24 ♌ 18	22 ♐ 51
May 24, 1965	10 ♋ 25	23 ♎ 57	12 ♉ 51	02 ♈ 25	11 ♌ 37	25 ♌ 06	08 ♏ 19	26 ♌ 44	21 ♐ 15
Jun 3, 1965	14 ♋ 12	23 ♎ 08	18 ♉ 10	06 ♈ 60	14 ♌ 58	27 ♌ 23	06 ♏ 57	29 ♌ 33	19 ♐ 04
Jun 13, 1965	18 ♋ 05	22 ♎ 54	23 ♉ 28	11 ♈ 25	18 ♌ 35	29 ♌ 57	06 ♏ 07	02 ♍ 42	16 ♐ 39
Jun 23, 1965	22 ♋ 01	23 ♎ 15	28 ♉ 44	15 ♈ 40	22 ♌ 24	02 ♍ 45	05 ♏ 53	06 ♍ 06	14 ♐ 24
Jul 3, 1965	25 ♋ 59	24 ♎ 08	03 Ⅱ 57	19 ♈ 40	26 ♌ 25	05 ♍ 44	06 ♏ 15	09 ♍ 45	12 ♐ 40
Jul 13, 1965	00 ♌ 00	25 ♎ 31	09 Ⅱ 05	23 ♈ 24	00 ♍ 35	08 ♍ 53	07 ♏ 10	13 ♍ 35	11 ♐ 42
Jul 23, 1965	04 ♌ 02	27 ♎ 21	14 Ⅱ 10	26 ♈ 49	04 ♍ 54	12 ♍ 10	08 ♏ 35	17 ♍ 36	11 ♐ 34
Aug 2, 1965	08 ♌ 06	29 ♎ 35	19 Ⅱ 08	29 ♈ 49	09 ♍ 20	15 ♍ 34	10 ♏ 26	21 ♍ 45	12 ♐ 17
Aug 12, 1965	12 ♌ 09	02 ♏ 09	23 Ⅱ 60	02 ♉ 20	13 ♍ 53	19 ♍ 03	12 ♏ 40	26 ♍ 02	13 ♐ 47
Aug 22, 1965	16 ♌ 12	05 ♏ 01	28 Ⅱ 42	04 ♉ 15	18 ♍ 32	22 ♍ 36	15 ♏ 14	00 ♎ 26	15 ♐ 57
Sep 1, 1965	20 ♌ 15	08 ♏ 09	03 ♋ 15	05 ♉ 29	23 ♍ 16	26 ♍ 13	18 ♏ 04	04 ♎ 55	18 ♐ 42
Sep 11, 1965	24 ♌ 15	11 ♏ 31	07 ♋ 34	05 ♉ 54	28 ♍ 05	29 ♍ 52	21 ♏ 08	09 ♎ 29	21 ♐ 55
Sep 21, 1965	28 ♌ 14	15 ♏ 04	11 ♋ 39	05 ♉ 26	02 ♎ 57	03 ♎ 33	24 ♏ 24	14 ♎ 07	25 ♐ 32
Oct 1, 1965	02 ♍ 09	18 ♏ 48	15 ♋ 25	04 ♉ 06	07 ♎ 53	07 ♎ 15	27 ♏ 51	18 ♎ 48	29 ♐ 30
Oct 11, 1965	05 ♍ 60	22 ♏ 40	18 ♋ 49	02 ♉ 01	12 ♎ 51	10 ♎ 25	01 ♐ 25	23 ♎ 32	03 ♑ 43
Oct 21, 1965	09 ♍ 45	26 ♏ 40	21 ♋ 48	29 ♈ 27	17 ♎ 51	14 ♎ 38	05 ♐ 07	28 ♎ 18	08 ♑ 10
Oct 31, 1965	13 ♍ 24	00 ♐ 47	24 ♋ 14	26 ♈ 49	22 ♎ 53	18 ♎ 17	08 ♐ 54	03 ♏ 05	12 ♑ 49
Nov 10, 1965	16 ♍ 54	04 ♐ 60	26 ♋ 03	24 ♈ 32	27 ♎ 54	21 ♎ 53	12 ♐ 46	07 ♏ 53	17 ♑ 36
Nov 20, 1965	20 ♍ 13	09 ♐ 17	27 ♋ 10	22 ♈ 57	02 ♏ 56	25 ♎ 25	16 ♐ 40	12 ♏ 41	22 ♑ 30
Nov 30, 1965	23 ♍ 19	13 ♐ 37	27 ♋ 29	22 ♈ 15	07 ♏ 57	28 ♎ 51	20 ♐ 37	17 ♏ 28	27 ♑ 31
Dec 10, 1965	26 ♍ 09	18 ♐ 01	26 ♋ 57	22 ♈ 29	12 ♏ 55	02 ♏ 11	24 ♐ 36	22 ♏ 13	02 ♒ 36
Dec 20, 1965	28 ♍ 39	22 ♐ 26	25 ♋ 38	23 ♈ 35	17 ♏ 50	05 ♏ 22	28 ♐ 34	26 ♏ 56	07 ♒ 44

	ATROPOS	HEKATE	LILITH	MEDUSA	MOIRA	NEMESIS	PERSEPHONE	PROSERPINA	PYTHIA
Dec 30, 1965	00 ♎ 45	26 ♐ 53	23 ♋ 39	25 ♈ 27	22 ♏ 41	08 ♏ 22	02 ♑ 32	01 ♐ 35	12 ♒ 55
Jan 9, 1966	02 ♎ 22	01 ♑ 19	21 ♋ 18	27 ♈ 59	27 ♏ 26	11 ♏ 10	06 ♑ 27	06 ♐ 09	18 ♒ 07
Jan 19, 1966	03 ♎ 25	05 ♑ 45	18 ♋ 55	01 ♉ 04	02 ♐ 03	13 ♏ 43	10 ♑ 20	10 ♐ 37	23 ♒ 20
Jan 29, 1966	03 ♎ 47	10 ♑ 09	16 ♋ 51	04 ♉ 36	06 ♐ 32	15 ♏ 58	14 ♑ 09	14 ♐ 57	28 ♒ 32
Feb 8, 1966	03 ♎ 25	14 ♑ 30	15 ♋ 22	08 ♉ 31	10 ♐ 49	17 ♏ 51	17 ♑ 53	19 ♐ 08	03 ♓ 44
Feb 18, 1966	02 ♎ 16	18 ♑ 47	14 ♋ 38	12 ♉ 43	14 ♐ 53	19 ♏ 20	21 ♑ 31	23 ♐ 09	08 ♓ 54
Feb 28, 1966	00 ♎ 22	22 ♑ 59	14 ♋ 39	17 ♉ 10	18 ♐ 40	20 ♏ 22	25 ♑ 01	26 ♐ 56	14 ♓ 02
Mar 10, 1966	27 ♍ 53	27 ♑ 05	15 ♋ 23	21 ♉ 48	22 ♐ 09	20 ♏ 51	28 ♑ 22	00 ♑ 27	19 ♓ 08
Mar 20, 1966	25 ♍ 04	01 ♒ 03	16 ♋ 47	26 ♉ 36	25 ♐ 14	20 ♏ 47	01 ♒ 32	03 ♑ 40	24 ♓ 09
Mar 30, 1966	22 ♍ 15	04 ♒ 51	18 ♋ 43	01 ♊ 32	27 ♐ 52	20 ♏ 07	04 ♒ 29	06 ♑ 30	29 ♓ 07
Apr 9, 1966	17 ♍ 48	08 ♒ 27	21 ♋ 06	06 ♊ 34	29 ♐ 58	18 ♏ 54	07 ♒ 12	08 ♑ 55	04 ♈ 01
Apr 19, 1966	17 ♍ 58	11 ♒ 50	23 ♋ 52	11 ♊ 40	01 ♑ 38	17 ♏ 38	09 ♒ 38	10 ♑ 50	08 ♈ 49
Apr 29, 1966	16 ♍ 56	14 ♒ 57	26 ♋ 56	16 ♊ 50	02 ♑ 17	15 ♏ 10	11 ♒ 44	12 ♑ 10	13 ♈ 32
May 9, 1966	16 ♍ 44	17 ♒ 44	00 ♌ 15	22 ♊ 03	02 ♑ 21	12 ♏ 59	13 ♒ 28	12 ♑ 52	18 ♈ 09
May 19, 1966	17 ♍ 20	20 ♒ 09	03 ♌ 46	27 ♊ 18	01 ♑ 41	10 ♏ 52	14 ♒ 46	12 ♑ 52	22 ♈ 38
May 29, 1966	18 ♍ 41	22 ♒ 08	07 ♌ 27	02 ♋ 34	00 ♑ 20	09 ♏ 02	15 ♒ 36	12 ♑ 09	27 ♈ 00
Jun 8, 1966	20 ♍ 39	23 ♒ 37	11 ♌ 14	07 ♋ 52	28 ♐ 27	07 ♏ 39	15 ♒ 55	10 ♑ 48	01 ♉ 13
Jun 18, 1966	23 ♍ 12	24 ♒ 31	15 ♌ 08	13 ♋ 09	26 ♐ 18	06 ♏ 48	15 ♒ 40	08 ♑ 55	05 ♉ 16
Jun 28, 1966	26 ♍ 13	24 ♒ 48	19 ♌ 07	18 ♋ 27	24 ♐ 11	06 ♏ 31	14 ♒ 53	06 ♑ 45	09 ♉ 08
Jul 8, 1966	29 ♍ 40	24 ♒ 27	23 ♌ 09	23 ♋ 45	22 ♐ 23	06 ♏ 49	13 ♒ 36	04 ♑ 35	12 ♉ 47
Jul 18, 1966	03 ♎ 28	23 ♒ 28	27 ♌ 13	29 ♋ 02	21 ♐ 07	07 ♏ 39	11 ♒ 53	02 ♑ 41	16 ♉ 11
Jul 28, 1966	07 ♎ 35	21 ♒ 57	01 ♍ 20	04 ♌ 17	20 ♐ 32	08 ♏ 58	09 ♒ 55	01 ♑ 16	19 ♉ 18
Aug 7, 1966	11 ♎ 58	20 ♒ 05	05 ♍ 27	09 ♌ 32	20 ♐ 39	10 ♏ 42	07 ♒ 52	00 ♑ 31	22 ♉ 06
Aug 17, 1966	16 ♎ 37	18 ♒ 05	09 ♍ 35	14 ♌ 45	21 ♐ 26	12 ♏ 49	05 ♒ 56	00 ♑ 26	24 ♉ 30
Aug 27, 1966	21 ♎ 28	16 ♒ 13	13 ♍ 42	19 ♌ 56	22 ♐ 50	15 ♏ 17	04 ♒ 19	01 ♑ 01	26 ♉ 26
Sep 6, 1966	26 ♎ 31	14 ♒ 44	17 ♍ 49	25 ♌ 05	24 ♐ 46	18 ♏ 01	03 ♒ 08	02 ♑ 14	27 ♉ 51
Sep 16, 1966	01 ♏ 45	13 ♒ 47	21 ♍ 54	00 ♍ 10	27 ♐ 09	20 ♏ 59	02 ♒ 28	03 ♑ 59	28 ♉ 40
Sep 26, 1966	07 ♏ 08	13 ♒ 27	25 ♍ 57	05 ♍ 13	29 ♐ 56	24 ♏ 11	02 ♒ 20	06 ♑ 14	28 ♉ 48
Oct 6, 1966	12 ♏ 39	13 ♒ 27	29 ♍ 56	10 ♍ 11	03 ♑ 02	27 ♏ 34	02 ♒ 45	08 ♑ 53	28 ♉ 12
Oct 16, 1966	18 ♏ 18	12 ♒ 44	03 ♎ 53	15 ♍ 04	06 ♑ 24	01 ♐ 06	03 ♒ 39	11 ♑ 52	26 ♉ 53
Oct 26, 1966	24 ♏ 03	14 ♒ 44	07 ♎ 44	19 ♍ 51	10 ♑ 00	04 ♐ 46	05 ♒ 01	15 ♑ 09	24 ♉ 55
Nov 5, 1966	29 ♏ 53	16 ♒ 15	11 ♎ 30	24 ♍ 32	13 ♑ 48	08 ♐ 33	06 ♒ 46	18 ♑ 41	22 ♉ 28
Nov 15, 1966	05 ♐ 48	18 ♒ 15	15 ♎ 09	29 ♍ 04	17 ♑ 44	12 ♐ 26	08 ♒ 51	22 ♑ 24	19 ♉ 48
Nov 25, 1966	11 ♐ 47	20 ♒ 42	18 ♎ 39	03 ♎ 26	21 ♑ 47	16 ♐ 24	11 ♒ 15	26 ♑ 18	17 ♉ 15
Dec 5, 1966	17 ♐ 48	23 ♒ 31	21 ♎ 60	07 ♎ 37	25 ♑ 57	20 ♐ 25	13 ♒ 53	00 ♒ 20	15 ♉ 05

Date	ATROPOS	HEKATE	LILITH	MEDUSA	MOIRA	NEMESIS	PERSEPHONE	PROSERPINA	PYTHIA
Dec 15, 1966	23 ♐ 50	29 ♒ 60	25 ♎ 09	11 ♎ 34	00 ♒ 11	24 ♐ 30	16 ♒ 44	04 ♒ 29	13 ♉ 30
Dec 25, 1966	29 ♐ 53	03 ♓ 35	28 ♎ 04	15 ♎ 13	04 ♒ 28	28 ♐ 36	19 ♒ 46	08 ♒ 43	12 ♉ 38
Jan 4, 1967	05 ♑ 56	07 ♓ 20	00 ♏ 43	18 ♎ 33	08 ♒ 48	02 ♑ 44	22 ♒ 56	13 ♒ 01	12 ♉ 28
Jan 14, 1967	11 ♑ 57	11 ♓ 14	03 ♏ 03	21 ♎ 28	13 ♒ 09	06 ♑ 52	26 ♒ 13	17 ♒ 22	12 ♉ 60
Jan 24, 1967	17 ♑ 55	15 ♓ 14	05 ♏ 01	23 ♎ 54	17 ♒ 30	10 ♑ 59	29 ♒ 36	21 ♒ 45	14 ♉ 08
Feb 3, 1967	23 ♑ 51	19 ♓ 19	06 ♏ 33	25 ♎ 47	21 ♒ 50	15 ♑ 04	03 ♓ 03	26 ♒ 09	15 ♉ 48
Feb 13, 1967	29 ♑ 42	23 ♓ 28	07 ♏ 35	26 ♎ 59	26 ♒ 10	19 ♑ 07	06 ♓ 32	00 ♓ 33	17 ♉ 55
Feb 23, 1967	05 ♒ 28	27 ♓ 40	08 ♏ 05	27 ♎ 27	00 ♓ 27	23 ♑ 06	10 ♓ 04	04 ♓ 57	20 ♉ 25
Mar 5, 1967	11 ♒ 07	01 ♈ 52	08 ♏ 01	27 ♎ 05	04 ♓ 41	27 ♑ 00	13 ♓ 35	09 ♓ 18	23 ♉ 13
Mar 15, 1967	16 ♒ 40	06 ♈ 06	07 ♏ 20	25 ♎ 53	08 ♓ 52	00 ♒ 48	17 ♓ 07	13 ♓ 38	26 ♉ 17
Mar 25, 1967	22 ♒ 05	10 ♈ 18	06 ♏ 04	23 ♎ 57	12 ♓ 58	04 ♒ 28	20 ♓ 36	17 ♓ 54	29 ♉ 34
Apr 4, 1967	27 ♒ 21	14 ♈ 29	04 ♏ 19	21 ♎ 29	16 ♓ 58	07 ♒ 59	24 ♓ 04	22 ♓ 07	03 ♊ 01
Apr 14, 1967	02 ♓ 27	18 ♈ 38	02 ♏ 12	18 ♎ 47	20 ♓ 52	11 ♒ 19	27 ♓ 28	26 ♓ 15	06 ♊ 37
Apr 24, 1967	07 ♓ 22	22 ♈ 45	29 ♎ 57	16 ♎ 13	24 ♓ 39	14 ♒ 25	00 ♈ 47	00 ♈ 17	10 ♊ 20
May 4, 1967	12 ♓ 05	26 ♈ 47	27 ♎ 47	14 ♎ 07	28 ♓ 18	17 ♒ 16	04 ♈ 07	04 ♈ 13	14 ♊ 08
May 14, 1967	16 ♓ 33	00 ♉ 45	25 ♎ 53	12 ♎ 41	01 ♈ 46	19 ♒ 47	07 ♈ 07	08 ♈ 02	18 ♊ 01
May 24, 1967	20 ♓ 46	04 ♉ 38	24 ♎ 24	12 ♎ 03	05 ♈ 04	21 ♒ 55	10 ♈ 06	11 ♈ 41	21 ♊ 58
Jun 3, 1967	24 ♓ 41	08 ♉ 24	23 ♎ 28	12 ♎ 12	08 ♈ 09	23 ♒ 37	12 ♈ 55	15 ♈ 11	25 ♊ 58
Jun 13, 1967	28 ♓ 15	12 ♉ 03	23 ♎ 05	13 ♎ 04	10 ♈ 59	24 ♒ 48	15 ♈ 32	18 ♈ 29	29 ♊ 59
Jun 23, 1967	01 ♈ 25	15 ♉ 34	23 ♎ 14	14 ♎ 36	13 ♈ 32	25 ♒ 24	17 ♈ 56	21 ♈ 33	04 ♋ 03
Jul 3, 1967	04 ♈ 07	18 ♉ 55	23 ♎ 55	16 ♎ 41	15 ♈ 46	25 ♒ 22	20 ♈ 04	24 ♈ 22	08 ♋ 07
Jul 13, 1967	06 ♈ 16	22 ♉ 05	25 ♎ 04	19 ♎ 14	17 ♈ 37	24 ♒ 40	21 ♈ 53	26 ♈ 52	12 ♋ 12
Jul 23, 1967	07 ♈ 47	25 ♉ 02	26 ♎ 37	22 ♎ 11	19 ♈ 02	23 ♒ 22	23 ♈ 21	29 ♈ 01	16 ♋ 16
Aug 2, 1967	08 ♈ 34	27 ♉ 44	28 ♎ 31	25 ♎ 27	19 ♈ 57	21 ♒ 32	24 ♈ 25	00 ♉ 45	20 ♋ 20
Aug 12, 1967	08 ♈ 33	00 ♊ 08	00 ♏ 43	29 ♎ 01	20 ♈ 20	19 ♒ 24	25 ♈ 01	02 ♉ 00	24 ♋ 22
Aug 22, 1967	07 ♈ 40	02 ♊ 13	03 ♏ 12	02 ♏ 50	20 ♈ 08	17 ♒ 13	25 ♈ 08	02 ♉ 43	28 ♋ 22
Sep 1, 1967	05 ♈ 59	03 ♊ 54	05 ♏ 53	06 ♏ 50	19 ♈ 20	15 ♒ 16	24 ♈ 42	02 ♉ 50	02 ♌ 19
Sep 11, 1967	03 ♈ 36	05 ♊ 09	08 ♏ 47	11 ♏ 01	17 ♈ 58	13 ♒ 47	23 ♈ 44	02 ♉ 19	06 ♌ 13
Sep 21, 1967	00 ♈ 57	05 ♊ 53	11 ♏ 49	15 ♏ 01	16 ♈ 08	12 ♒ 56	22 ♈ 18	01 ♉ 11	10 ♌ 01
Oct 1, 1967	28 ♓ 02	06 ♊ 06	15 ♏ 00	19 ♏ 49	13 ♈ 58	12 ♒ 47	20 ♈ 28	29 ♈ 30	13 ♌ 43
Oct 11, 1967	25 ♓ 33	05 ♊ 43	18 ♏ 18	24 ♏ 23	11 ♈ 43	13 ♒ 20	18 ♈ 25	27 ♈ 23	17 ♌ 17
Oct 21, 1967	23 ♓ 42	04 ♊ 47	21 ♏ 42	29 ♏ 04	09 ♈ 35	14 ♒ 34	16 ♈ 20	25 ♈ 06	20 ♌ 42
Oct 31, 1967	22 ♓ 38	03 ♊ 20	25 ♏ 09	03 ♐ 47	07 ♈ 48	16 ♒ 23	14 ♈ 26	22 ♈ 51	23 ♌ 54
Nov 10, 1967	22 ♓ 24	01 ♊ 28	28 ♏ 41	08 ♐ 39	06 ♈ 30	18 ♒ 44	12 ♈ 53	20 ♈ 55	26 ♌ 50
Nov 20, 1967	22 ♓ 57	29 ♉ 24	02 ♐ 14	13 ♐ 32	05 ♈ 46	21 ♒ 33	11 ♈ 49	19 ♈ 28	29 ♌ 29

Date	ATROPOS	HEKATE	LILITH	MEDUSA	NEMESIS	MOIRA	PERSEPHONE	PROSERPINA	PYTHIA
Nov 30, 1967	24 ♓ 12	27 ♉ 19	05 ♐ 49	18 ♐ 28	24 ♒ 44	05 ♈ 38	11 ♈ 18	18 ♈ 37	01 ♍ 44
Dec 10, 1967	26 ♓ 04	25 ♉ 26	09 ♐ 25	23 ♐ 27	28 ♒ 15	06 ♈ 05	11 ♈ 21	18 ♈ 25	03 ♍ 32
Dec 20, 1967	28 ♓ 27	23 ♉ 56	12 ♐ 59	28 ♐ 27	02 ♓ 03	07 ♈ 04	11 ♈ 57	18 ♈ 51	04 ♍ 48
Dec 30, 1967	01 ♈ 15	22 ♉ 55	16 ♐ 32	03 ♑ 29	06 ♓ 05	08 ♈ 30	13 ♈ 03	19 ♈ 50	05 ♍ 25
Jan 9, 1968	04 ♈ 24	22 ♉ 28	20 ♐ 02	08 ♑ 31	10 ♓ 18	10 ♈ 22	14 ♈ 35	21 ♈ 21	05 ♍ 18
Jan 19, 1968	07 ♈ 51	22 ♉ 34	24 ♐ 27	13 ♑ 33	14 ♓ 41	12 ♈ 34	16 ♈ 32	23 ♈ 19	04 ♍ 25
Jan 29, 1968	11 ♈ 31	23 ♉ 12	26 ♐ 47	18 ♑ 34	19 ♓ 12	15 ♈ 03	18 ♈ 48	25 ♈ 39	02 ♍ 48
Feb 8, 1968	15 ♈ 23	24 ♉ 18	00 ♑ 01	23 ♑ 34	23 ♓ 49	17 ♈ 47	21 ♈ 22	28 ♈ 18	00 ♍ 32
Feb 18, 1968	19 ♈ 24	25 ♉ 49	03 ♑ 05	28 ♑ 32	28 ♓ 31	20 ♈ 44	24 ♈ 10	01 ♉ 14	27 ♌ 54
Feb 28, 1968	23 ♈ 32	27 ♉ 41	05 ♑ 59	03 ♒ 28	03 ♈ 17	23 ♈ 50	27 ♈ 11	04 ♉ 22	25 ♌ 12
Mar 9, 1968	27 ♈ 45	29 ♉ 52	08 ♑ 41	08 ♒ 20	08 ♈ 21	27 ♈ 04	00 ♉ 21	07 ♉ 42	22 ♌ 47
Mar 19, 1968	02 ♉ 03	02 ♊ 17	11 ♑ 08	13 ♒ 08	12 ♈ 58	00 ♉ 24	03 ♉ 40	11 ♉ 10	20 ♌ 57
Mar 29, 1968	06 ♉ 24	04 ♊ 55	13 ♑ 17	17 ♒ 51	17 ♈ 50	03 ♉ 49	07 ♉ 06	14 ♉ 45	19 ♌ 52
Apr 8, 1968	10 ♉ 47	07 ♊ 43	15 ♑ 06	22 ♒ 27	22 ♈ 42	07 ♉ 18	10 ♉ 37	18 ♉ 27	19 ♌ 36
Apr 18, 1968	15 ♉ 11	10 ♊ 40	16 ♑ 31	26 ♒ 57	27 ♈ 35	10 ♉ 49	14 ♉ 11	22 ♉ 12	20 ♌ 08
Apr 28, 1968	19 ♉ 35	13 ♊ 42	17 ♑ 29	01 ♓ 17	02 ♉ 26	14 ♉ 22	17 ♉ 50	26 ♉ 02	21 ♌ 23
May 8, 1968	23 ♉ 60	16 ♊ 50	17 ♑ 56	05 ♓ 28	07 ♉ 15	17 ♉ 55	21 ♉ 30	29 ♉ 54	23 ♌ 16
May 18, 1968	28 ♉ 23	20 ♊ 01	17 ♑ 50	09 ♓ 25	12 ♉ 02	21 ♉ 28	25 ♉ 11	03 ♊ 47	25 ♌ 42
May 28, 1968	02 ♊ 45	23 ♊ 15	17 ♑ 10	13 ♓ 08	16 ♉ 47	24 ♉ 59	28 ♉ 53	07 ♊ 41	28 ♌ 36
Jun 7, 1968	07 ♊ 05	26 ♊ 31	15 ♑ 55	16 ♓ 33	21 ♉ 28	28 ♉ 29	02 ♊ 34	11 ♊ 36	01 ♍ 54
Jun 17, 1968	11 ♊ 23	29 ♊ 47	14 ♑ 12	19 ♓ 37	26 ♉ 04	01 ♊ 56	06 ♊ 14	15 ♊ 29	05 ♍ 32
Jun 27, 1968	15 ♊ 37	03 ♋ 03	12 ♑ 07	22 ♓ 14	00 ♊ 36	05 ♊ 19	09 ♊ 51	19 ♊ 22	09 ♍ 28
Jul 7, 1968	19 ♊ 47	06 ♋ 17	09 ♑ 52	24 ♓ 20	05 ♊ 01	08 ♊ 37	13 ♊ 26	23 ♊ 13	13 ♍ 38
Jul 17, 1968	23 ♊ 52	09 ♋ 29	07 ♑ 41	25 ♓ 50	09 ♊ 20	11 ♊ 49	16 ♊ 57	27 ♊ 00	18 ♍ 02
Jul 27, 1968	27 ♊ 51	12 ♋ 38	05 ♑ 47	26 ♓ 36	13 ♊ 30	14 ♊ 55	20 ♊ 22	00 ♋ 45	22 ♍ 37
Aug 6, 1968	01 ♋ 44	15 ♋ 43	04 ♑ 20	26 ♓ 34	17 ♊ 32	17 ♊ 51	23 ♊ 41	04 ♋ 24	27 ♍ 22
Aug 16, 1968	05 ♋ 29	18 ♋ 43	03 ♑ 27	25 ♓ 42	21 ♊ 22	20 ♊ 37	26 ♊ 52	07 ♋ 58	02 ♎ 15
Aug 26, 1968	09 ♋ 05	21 ♋ 36	03 ♑ 10	24 ♓ 01	24 ♊ 59	23 ♊ 10	29 ♊ 52	11 ♋ 25	07 ♎ 17
Sep 5, 1968	12 ♋ 29	24 ♋ 22	03 ♑ 30	21 ♓ 44	28 ♊ 20	25 ♊ 28	02 ♋ 41	14 ♋ 43	12 ♎ 25
Sep 15, 1968	15 ♋ 41	26 ♋ 57	04 ♑ 24	19 ♓ 08	01 ♋ 23	27 ♊ 28	05 ♋ 16	17 ♋ 51	17 ♎ 40
Sep 25, 1968	18 ♋ 36	29 ♋ 21	05 ♑ 50	16 ♓ 36	04 ♋ 05	29 ♊ 08	07 ♋ 33	20 ♋ 46	22 ♎ 59
Oct 5, 1968	21 ♋ 12	01 ♌ 32	07 ♑ 44	14 ♓ 33	06 ♋ 21	00 ♋ 22	09 ♋ 29	23 ♋ 26	28 ♎ 24
Oct 15, 1968	23 ♋ 26	03 ♌ 26	10 ♑ 03	13 ♓ 14	08 ♋ 07	01 ♋ 09	11 ♋ 01	25 ♋ 47	03 ♏ 53
Oct 25, 1968	25 ♋ 13	05 ♌ 01	12 ♑ 43	12 ♓ 47	09 ♋ 19	01 ♋ 23	12 ♋ 05	27 ♋ 46	09 ♏ 26
Nov 4, 1968	26 ♋ 29	06 ♌ 15	15 ♑ 43	13 ♓ 15	09 ♋ 51	01 ♋ 03	12 ♋ 36	29 ♋ 19	15 ♏ 01

	ATROPOS	HEKATE	LILITH	MEDUSA	MOIRA	NEMESIS	PERSEPHONE	PROSERPINA	PYTHIA
Nov 14, 1968	27 ♋ 07	07 ♌ 03	18 ♑ 59	14 ♓ 32	00 ♋ 07	09 ♋ 42	12 ♋ 33	00 ♌ 21	20 ♏ 39
Nov 24, 1968	27 ♋ 05	07 ♌ 24	22 ♑ 29	16 ♓ 33	28 ♊ 37	08 ♋ 49	11 ♋ 52	00 ♌ 49	26 ♏ 18
Dec 4, 1968	26 ♋ 18	07 ♌ 15	26 ♑ 12	19 ♓ 12	26 ♊ 41	07 ♋ 16	10 ♋ 35	00 ♌ 38	01 ♐ 59
Dec 14, 1968	24 ♋ 47	06 ♌ 36	00 ♒ 06	22 ♓ 22	24 ♊ 27	05 ♋ 13	08 ♋ 49	29 ♋ 47	07 ♐ 40
Dec 24, 1968	22 ♋ 37	06 ♌ 27	04 ♒ 09	25 ♓ 60	22 ♊ 09	02 ♋ 54	06 ♋ 43	28 ♋ 18	13 ♐ 20
Jan 3, 1969	19 ♋ 60	03 ♌ 53	08 ♒ 20	29 ♓ 59	20 ♊ 02	00 ♋ 35	04 ♋ 30	26 ♋ 19	19 ♐ 00
Jan 13, 1969	17 ♋ 12	02 ♌ 00	12 ♒ 38	04 ♈ 17	18 ♊ 18	28 ♊ 36	02 ♋ 27	24 ♋ 01	24 ♐ 38
Jan 23, 1969	14 ♋ 33	29 ♋ 60	17 ♒ 02	08 ♈ 49	17 ♊ 05	27 ♊ 07	00 ♋ 46	21 ♋ 39	00 ♑ 13
Feb 2, 1969	12 ♋ 19	28 ♋ 02	21 ♒ 31	13 ♈ 34	16 ♊ 29	26 ♊ 18	29 ♊ 36	19 ♋ 31	05 ♑ 45
Feb 12, 1969	10 ♋ 44	26 ♋ 17	26 ♒ 04	18 ♈ 29	16 ♊ 29	26 ♊ 09	29 ♊ 04	17 ♋ 50	11 ♑ 13
Feb 22, 1969	09 ♋ 51	24 ♋ 54	00 ♓ 40	23 ♈ 32	17 ♊ 05	26 ♊ 41	29 ♊ 09	16 ♋ 46	16 ♑ 35
Mar 4, 1969	09 ♋ 42	23 ♋ 58	05 ♓ 20	28 ♈ 42	18 ♊ 13	27 ♊ 48	29 ♊ 50	16 ♋ 21	21 ♑ 51
Mar 14, 1969	10 ♋ 13	23 ♋ 32	10 ♓ 01	03 ♉ 57	19 ♊ 50	29 ♊ 27	01 ♋ 04	16 ♋ 37	26 ♑ 59
Mar 24, 1969	11 ♋ 21	23 ♋ 35	14 ♓ 44	09 ♉ 16	21 ♊ 51	01 ♋ 32	02 ♋ 47	17 ♋ 31	01 ♒ 58
Apr 3, 1969	13 ♋ 01	24 ♋ 07	19 ♓ 28	14 ♉ 39	24 ♊ 13	03 ♋ 59	04 ♋ 55	18 ♋ 58	06 ♒ 46
Apr 13, 1969	15 ♋ 06	25 ♋ 05	24 ♓ 12	20 ♉ 04	26 ♊ 53	06 ♋ 45	07 ♋ 23	20 ♋ 55	11 ♒ 22
Apr 23, 1969	17 ♋ 34	26 ♋ 26	28 ♓ 55	25 ♉ 31	29 ♊ 48	09 ♋ 46	10 ♋ 10	23 ♋ 17	15 ♒ 43
May 3, 1969	20 ♋ 21	28 ♋ 07	03 ♈ 38	00 ♊ 59	02 ♋ 57	12 ♋ 60	13 ♋ 11	25 ♋ 60	19 ♒ 46
May 13, 1969	23 ♋ 23	00 ♌ 05	08 ♈ 18	06 ♊ 28	06 ♋ 16	16 ♋ 23	16 ♋ 25	29 ♋ 01	23 ♒ 29
May 23, 1969	26 ♋ 39	02 ♌ 17	12 ♈ 56	11 ♊ 57	09 ♋ 45	19 ♋ 55	19 ♋ 49	02 ♌ 17	26 ♒ 48
Jun 2, 1969	00 ♌ 05	04 ♌ 42	17 ♈ 31	17 ♊ 25	13 ♋ 21	23 ♋ 34	23 ♋ 23	05 ♌ 47	29 ♒ 37
Jun 12, 1969	03 ♌ 41	07 ♌ 18	22 ♈ 01	22 ♊ 53	17 ♋ 04	27 ♋ 17	27 ♋ 03	09 ♌ 27	01 ♓ 52
Jun 22, 1969	07 ♌ 25	10 ♌ 02	26 ♈ 24	28 ♊ 20	20 ♋ 54	01 ♌ 05	00 ♌ 49	13 ♌ 18	03 ♓ 27
Jul 2, 1969	11 ♌ 15	12 ♌ 54	00 ♉ 41	03 ♋ 46	24 ♋ 48	04 ♌ 56	04 ♌ 40	17 ♌ 16	04 ♓ 17
Jul 12, 1969	15 ♌ 11	15 ♌ 51	04 ♉ 48	09 ♋ 10	28 ♋ 46	08 ♌ 48	08 ♌ 35	21 ♌ 21	04 ♓ 17
Jul 22, 1969	19 ♌ 13	18 ♌ 54	08 ♉ 43	14 ♋ 32	02 ♌ 48	12 ♌ 43	12 ♌ 33	25 ♌ 32	03 ♓ 25
Aug 1, 1969	23 ♌ 18	21 ♌ 60	12 ♉ 23	19 ♋ 52	06 ♌ 52	16 ♌ 38	16 ♌ 34	29 ♌ 48	01 ♓ 47
Aug 11, 1969	27 ♌ 27	25 ♌ 09	15 ♉ 46	25 ♋ 09	10 ♌ 59	20 ♌ 33	20 ♌ 36	04 ♍ 08	29 ♒ 32
Aug 21, 1969	01 ♍ 40	28 ♌ 19	18 ♉ 47	00 ♌ 32	15 ♌ 07	24 ♌ 27	24 ♌ 39	08 ♍ 32	26 ♒ 59
Aug 31, 1969	05 ♍ 55	01 ♍ 30	21 ♉ 22	05 ♌ 32	19 ♌ 16	28 ♌ 20	28 ♌ 41	12 ♍ 59	24 ♒ 32
Sep 10, 1969	10 ♍ 12	04 ♍ 42	23 ♉ 23	10 ♌ 37	23 ♌ 26	02 ♍ 11	02 ♍ 44	17 ♍ 28	22 ♒ 31
Sep 20, 1969	14 ♍ 31	07 ♍ 51	24 ♉ 46	15 ♌ 37	27 ♌ 35	05 ♍ 58	06 ♍ 45	21 ♍ 59	21 ♒ 11
Sep 30, 1969	18 ♍ 51	10 ♍ 59	25 ♉ 26	20 ♌ 31	01 ♍ 43	09 ♍ 42	10 ♍ 43	26 ♍ 32	20 ♒ 40
Oct 10, 1969	23 ♍ 12	14 ♍ 03	25 ♉ 17	25 ♌ 17	05 ♍ 48	13 ♍ 20	14 ♍ 38	01 ♎ 05	20 ♒ 56
Oct 20, 1969	27 ♍ 33	17 ♍ 02	24 ♉ 19	29 ♌ 54	09 ♍ 50	16 ♍ 53	18 ♍ 29	05 ♎ 37	21 ♒ 58

	ATROPOS	HEKATE	LILITH	MEDUSA	MOIRA	NEMESIS	PERSEPHONE	PROSERPINA	PYTHIA
Oct 30, 1969	01 ♎ 53	19 ♍ 55	22 ♉ 40	04 ♍ 21	13 ♍ 48	20 ♍ 17	22 ♍ 14	10 ♎ 09	23 ♒ 40
Nov 9, 1969	06 ♎ 12	22 ♍ 40	20 ♉ 32	08 ♍ 35	17 ♍ 39	23 ♍ 32	25 ♍ 52	14 ♎ 38	25 ♒ 55
Nov 19, 1969	10 ♎ 28	25 ♍ 15	18 ♉ 16	12 ♍ 34	21 ♍ 22	26 ♍ 36	29 ♍ 21	19 ♎ 05	28 ♒ 38
Nov 29, 1969	14 ♎ 41	27 ♍ 38	16 ♉ 16	16 ♍ 14	24 ♍ 54	29 ♍ 27	02 ♎ 39	23 ♎ 28	01 ♓ 45
Dec 9, 1969	18 ♎ 50	29 ♍ 46	14 ♉ 51	19 ♍ 33	28 ♍ 14	02 ♎ 01	05 ♎ 44	27 ♎ 45	05 ♓ 11
Dec 19, 1969	22 ♎ 51	01 ♎ 36	14 ♉ 12	22 ♍ 26	01 ♎ 17	04 ♎ 16	08 ♎ 32	01 ♏ 56	08 ♓ 53
Dec 29, 1969	26 ♎ 45	03 ♎ 06	14 ♉ 23	24 ♍ 47	04 ♎ 01	06 ♎ 20	11 ♎ 02	05 ♏ 58	12 ♓ 47
Jan 8, 1970	00 ♏ 28	04 ♎ 11	15 ♉ 33	26 ♍ 31	06 ♎ 20	07 ♎ 36	13 ♎ 08	09 ♏ 49	16 ♓ 51
Jan 18, 1970	03 ♏ 58	04 ♎ 50	17 ♉ 07	27 ♍ 31	08 ♎ 11	08 ♎ 33	14 ♎ 48	13 ♏ 28	21 ♓ 03
Jan 28, 1970	07 ♏ 11	04 ♎ 58	19 ♉ 29	27 ♍ 43	09 ♎ 27	08 ♎ 56	15 ♎ 57	16 ♏ 50	25 ♓ 22
Feb 7, 1970	10 ♏ 04	04 ♎ 35	22 ♉ 22	27 ♍ 02	10 ♎ 03	08 ♎ 45	16 ♎ 31	19 ♏ 54	29 ♓ 45
Feb 17, 1970	12 ♏ 31	03 ♎ 40	25 ♉ 41	25 ♍ 31	09 ♎ 57	07 ♎ 56	16 ♎ 28	22 ♏ 34	04 ♈ 11
Feb 27, 1970	14 ♏ 26	02 ♎ 16	29 ♉ 21	23 ♍ 17	09 ♎ 07	06 ♎ 34	15 ♎ 46	24 ♏ 48	08 ♈ 39
Mar 9, 1970	15 ♏ 44	00 ♎ 30	03 ♊ 19	20 ♍ 37	07 ♎ 36	04 ♎ 43	14 ♎ 29	26 ♏ 30	13 ♈ 09
Mar 19, 1970	16 ♏ 17	28 ♍ 30	07 ♊ 29	17 ♍ 54	05 ♎ 34	02 ♎ 35	12 ♎ 43	27 ♏ 35	17 ♈ 40
Mar 29, 1970	15 ♏ 60	26 ♍ 28	11 ♊ 50	15 ♍ 29	03 ♎ 17	00 ♎ 21	10 ♎ 38	28 ♏ 00	22 ♈ 09
Apr 8, 1970	14 ♏ 50	24 ♍ 35	16 ♊ 20	13 ♍ 41	01 ♎ 05	28 ♍ 16	08 ♎ 29	27 ♏ 42	26 ♈ 38
Apr 18, 1970	12 ♏ 52	23 ♍ 02	20 ♊ 56	12 ♍ 40	29 ♍ 15	26 ♍ 32	06 ♎ 32	26 ♏ 41	01 ♉ 06
Apr 28, 1970	10 ♏ 20	21 ♍ 57	25 ♊ 36	12 ♍ 28	28 ♍ 03	25 ♍ 16	04 ♎ 58	25 ♏ 03	05 ♉ 31
May 8, 1970	07 ♏ 33	21 ♍ 22	00 ♋ 21	13 ♍ 03	27 ♍ 34	24 ♍ 34	03 ♎ 56	22 ♏ 59	09 ♉ 53
May 18, 1970	04 ♏ 59	21 ♍ 19	05 ♋ 07	14 ♍ 20	27 ♎ 51	24 ♍ 51	03 ♎ 31	20 ♏ 46	14 ♉ 13
May 28, 1970	03 ♏ 01	21 ♍ 48	09 ♋ 55	16 ♍ 13	28 ♍ 52	24 ♍ 53	03 ♎ 42	18 ♏ 41	18 ♉ 28
Jun 7, 1970	01 ♏ 55	22 ♍ 45	14 ♋ 43	18 ♍ 37	00 ♎ 32	25 ♍ 49	04 ♎ 28	16 ♏ 60	22 ♉ 39
Jun 17, 1970	01 ♏ 46	24 ♍ 09	19 ♋ 32	21 ♍ 26	02 ♎ 46	27 ♍ 12	05 ♎ 47	15 ♏ 55	26 ♉ 45
Jun 27, 1970	02 ♏ 35	25 ♍ 56	24 ♋ 20	24 ♍ 37	05 ♎ 30	28 ♍ 59	07 ♎ 33	15 ♏ 32	00 ♊ 45
Jul 7, 1970	04 ♏ 15	28 ♍ 03	29 ♋ 06	28 ♍ 05	08 ♎ 39	01 ♎ 07	09 ♎ 43	15 ♏ 51	04 ♊ 38
Jul 17, 1970	06 ♏ 41	00 ♎ 28	03 ♌ 52	01 ♎ 48	12 ♎ 09	03 ♎ 32	12 ♎ 14	16 ♏ 51	08 ♊ 24
Jul 27, 1970	09 ♏ 44	03 ♎ 09	08 ♌ 35	05 ♎ 44	15 ♎ 57	06 ♎ 12	15 ♎ 02	18 ♏ 26	12 ♊ 01
Aug 6, 1970	13 ♏ 19	06 ♎ 02	13 ♌ 15	09 ♎ 50	19 ♎ 59	09 ♎ 05	18 ♎ 06	20 ♏ 33	15 ♊ 27
Aug 16, 1970	17 ♏ 21	09 ♎ 08	17 ♌ 53	14 ♎ 05	24 ♎ 15	12 ♎ 09	21 ♎ 23	23 ♏ 07	18 ♊ 41
Aug 26, 1970	21 ♏ 44	12 ♎ 24	22 ♌ 27	18 ♎ 27	28 ♎ 41	15 ♎ 22	24 ♎ 50	26 ♏ 04	21 ♊ 40
Sep 5, 1970	26 ♏ 25	15 ♎ 48	26 ♌ 57	22 ♎ 56	03 ♏ 15	18 ♎ 43	28 ♎ 26	29 ♏ 21	24 ♊ 23
Sep 15, 1970	06 ♐ 21	19 ♎ 20	01 ♍ 22	27 ♎ 31	07 ♏ 58	22 ♎ 10	02 ♏ 10	02 ♐ 54	26 ♊ 46
Sep 25, 1970	06 ♐ 28	22 ♎ 58	05 ♍ 42	02 ♏ 11	12 ♏ 46	25 ♎ 43	06 ♏ 00	06 ♐ 40	28 ♊ 44
Oct 5, 1970	11 ♐ 45	26 ♎ 41	09 ♍ 56	06 ♏ 54	17 ♏ 40	29 ♎ 20	09 ♏ 56	10 ♐ 39	00 ♋ 15

	ATROPOS	HEKATE	LILITH	MEDUSA	MOIRA	NEMESIS	PERSEPHONE	PROSERPINA	PYTHIA
Oct 15, 1970	17 ♐ 10	00 ♏ 29	14 ♍ 02	11 ♏ 41	22 ♏ 37	03 ♏ 01	13 ♏ 56	14 ♐ 47	01 ♋ 13
Oct 25, 1970	22 ♐ 40	04 ♏ 21	17 ♍ 59	16 ♏ 31	27 ♏ 38	06 ♏ 44	17 ♏ 59	19 ♐ 03	01 ♋ 34
Nov 4, 1970	28 ♐ 15	08 ♏ 15	21 ♍ 47	21 ♏ 23	02 ♐ 47	10 ♏ 14	22 ♏ 10	23 ♐ 27	01 ♋ 15
Nov 14, 1970	03 ♑ 53	12 ♏ 11	25 ♍ 23	26 ♏ 17	07 ♐ 46	14 ♏ 14	26 ♏ 10	27 ♐ 55	00 ♋ 13
Nov 24, 1970	09 ♑ 32	16 ♏ 08	28 ♍ 45	01 ♐ 12	12 ♐ 52	17 ♏ 60	00 ♐ 17	02 ♑ 28	28 ♊ 31
Dec 4, 1970	15 ♑ 13	20 ♏ 05	01 ♎ 50	06 ♐ 08	17 ♐ 57	21 ♐ 44	04 ♐ 23	07 ♑ 05	26 ♊ 15
Dec 14, 1970	20 ♑ 54	24 ♏ 00	04 ♎ 37	11 ♐ 04	23 ♐ 02	25 ♐ 25	08 ♐ 28	11 ♑ 44	23 ♊ 40
Dec 24, 1970	26 ♑ 35	27 ♏ 53	07 ♎ 02	15 ♐ 59	28 ♐ 05	29 ♏ 03	12 ♐ 30	16 ♑ 24	21 ♊ 02
Jan 3, 1971	02 ♒ 14	01 ♐ 43	09 ♎ 01	20 ♐ 53	03 ♑ 06	02 ♐ 36	16 ♐ 29	21 ♑ 06	18 ♊ 40
Jan 13, 1971	07 ♒ 52	05 ♐ 28	10 ♎ 31	25 ♐ 44	08 ♑ 04	06 ♐ 03	20 ♐ 22	25 ♑ 47	16 ♊ 46
Jan 23, 1971	13 ♒ 27	09 ♐ 07	11 ♎ 26	00 ♑ 33	12 ♑ 58	09 ♐ 22	24 ♐ 10	00 ♒ 27	15 ♊ 32
Feb 2, 1971	18 ♒ 59	12 ♐ 38	11 ♎ 45	05 ♑ 19	17 ♑ 48	12 ♐ 32	27 ♐ 50	05 ♒ 06	15 ♊ 01
Feb 12, 1971	24 ♒ 28	15 ♐ 58	11 ♎ 24	10 ♑ 00	22 ♑ 31	15 ♐ 29	01 ♑ 21	09 ♒ 42	15 ♊ 11
Feb 22, 1971	29 ♒ 53	19 ♐ 07	10 ♎ 23	14 ♑ 36	27 ♑ 08	18 ♐ 13	04 ♑ 42	14 ♒ 14	16 ♊ 00
Mar 4, 1971	05 ♓ 14	22 ♐ 00	08 ♎ 47	19 ♑ 05	01 ♒ 37	20 ♐ 40	07 ♑ 49	18 ♒ 43	17 ♊ 24
Mar 14, 1971	10 ♓ 31	24 ♐ 37	06 ♎ 44	23 ♑ 26	05 ♒ 58	22 ♐ 48	10 ♑ 42	23 ♒ 06	19 ♊ 17
Mar 24, 1971	15 ♓ 42	26 ♐ 52	04 ♎ 26	27 ♑ 38	10 ♒ 08	24 ♐ 33	13 ♑ 18	27 ♒ 24	21 ♊ 35
Apr 3, 1971	20 ♓ 48	28 ♐ 43	02 ♎ 07	01 ♒ 39	14 ♒ 06	25 ♐ 51	15 ♑ 33	01 ♓ 35	24 ♊ 15
Apr 13, 1971	25 ♓ 48	00 ♑ 05	00 ♎ 03	05 ♒ 26	17 ♒ 51	26 ♐ 39	17 ♑ 25	05 ♓ 37	27 ♊ 12
Apr 23, 1971	00 ♈ 42	00 ♑ 56	28 ♍ 24	08 ♒ 58	21 ♒ 21	26 ♐ 54	18 ♑ 50	09 ♓ 30	00 ♋ 25
May 3, 1971	05 ♈ 29	01 ♑ 11	27 ♍ 19	12 ♒ 11	24 ♒ 33	26 ♐ 33	19 ♑ 46	13 ♓ 13	03 ♋ 50
May 13, 1971	10 ♈ 08	00 ♑ 50	26 ♍ 50	15 ♒ 01	27 ♒ 24	25 ♐ 38	20 ♑ 09	16 ♓ 43	07 ♋ 25
May 23, 1971	14 ♈ 38	29 ♐ 53	26 ♍ 55	17 ♒ 24	29 ♒ 53	24 ♐ 09	19 ♑ 58	19 ♓ 58	11 ♋ 10
Jun 2, 1971	18 ♈ 60	28 ♐ 24	27 ♍ 34	19 ♒ 16	01 ♓ 53	22 ♐ 15	19 ♑ 12	22 ♓ 57	15 ♋ 02
Jun 12, 1971	23 ♈ 10	26 ♐ 33	28 ♍ 43	20 ♒ 30	03 ♓ 24	20 ♐ 06	17 ♑ 55	25 ♓ 36	19 ♋ 01
Jun 22, 1971	27 ♈ 08	24 ♐ 33	00 ♎ 17	21 ♒ 01	04 ♓ 19	17 ♐ 55	16 ♑ 11	27 ♓ 53	23 ♋ 06
Jul 2, 1971	00 ♉ 53	22 ♐ 38	02 ♎ 13	20 ♒ 45	04 ♓ 37	15 ♐ 57	14 ♑ 12	29 ♓ 44	27 ♋ 15
Jul 12, 1971	04 ♉ 21	21 ♐ 02	04 ♎ 28	19 ♒ 41	04 ♓ 14	14 ♐ 23	12 ♑ 08	01 ♈ 05	01 ♌ 29
Jul 22, 1971	07 ♉ 30	19 ♐ 57	06 ♎ 58	17 ♒ 53	03 ♓ 12	13 ♐ 22	10 ♑ 13	01 ♈ 53	05 ♌ 46
Aug 1, 1971	10 ♉ 17	19 ♐ 27	09 ♎ 43	15 ♒ 31	01 ♓ 35	12 ♐ 57	08 ♑ 38	02 ♈ 07	10 ♌ 07
Aug 11, 1971	12 ♉ 37	19 ♐ 36	12 ♎ 38	12 ♒ 55	29 ♒ 33	13 ♐ 08	07 ♑ 30	01 ♈ 34	14 ♌ 30
Aug 21, 1971	14 ♉ 27	20 ♐ 23	15 ♎ 43	10 ♒ 26	27 ♒ 18	13 ♐ 55	06 ♑ 54	00 ♈ 27	18 ♌ 55
Aug 31, 1971	15 ♉ 40	21 ♐ 44	18 ♎ 56	08 ♒ 24	25 ♒ 05	15 ♐ 15	06 ♑ 52	28 ♓ 46	23 ♌ 22
Sep 10, 1971	16 ♉ 11	23 ♐ 37	22 ♎ 15	07 ♒ 06	23 ♒ 10	17 ♐ 04	07 ♑ 23	26 ♓ 41	27 ♌ 49
Sep 20, 1971	15 ♉ 56	25 ♐ 57	25 ♎ 39	06 ♒ 37	21 ♒ 45	19 ♐ 18	08 ♑ 23	24 ♓ 24	02 ♍ 18

	ATROPOS	HEKATE	LILITH	MEDUSA	MOIRA	NEMESIS	PERSEPHONE	PROSERPINA	PYTHIA
Sep 30, 1971	14 ♉ 52	28 ♐ 41	29 ♎ 08	06 ♒ 60	20 ♒ 55	21 ♐ 55	09 ♑ 50	22 ♓ 12	06 ♍ 46
Oct 10, 1971	13 ♉ 02	01 ♑ 45	02 ♏ 40	08 ♒ 10	20 ♒ 43	24 ♐ 51	11 ♑ 41	20 ♓ 19	11 ♍ 14
Oct 20, 1971	10 ♉ 35	05 ♑ 07	06 ♏ 14	10 ♒ 03	21 ♒ 08	28 ♐ 04	13 ♑ 53	18 ♓ 55	15 ♍ 40
Oct 30, 1971	07 ♉ 46	08 ♑ 44	09 ♏ 49	12 ♒ 32	22 ♒ 08	01 ♑ 31	16 ♑ 22	18 ♓ 09	20 ♍ 03
Nov 9, 1971	04 ♉ 57	12 ♑ 34	13 ♏ 25	15 ♒ 33	23 ♒ 38	05 ♑ 11	19 ♑ 06	18 ♓ 02	24 ♍ 23
Nov 19, 1971	02 ♉ 29	16 ♑ 34	16 ♏ 33	19 ♒ 01	25 ♒ 35	09 ♑ 02	22 ♑ 02	18 ♓ 33	28 ♍ 38
Nov 29, 1971	00 ♉ 38	20 ♑ 43	20 ♏ 33	22 ♒ 51	27 ♒ 55	13 ♑ 03	25 ♑ 09	19 ♓ 38	02 ♎ 45
Dec 9, 1971	29 ♈ 32	24 ♑ 60	24 ♏ 03	26 ♒ 60	00 ♓ 33	17 ♑ 11	28 ♑ 24	21 ♓ 14	06 ♎ 44
Dec 19, 1971	29 ♈ 14	29 ♑ 23	27 ♏ 29	01 ♓ 24	03 ♓ 27	21 ♑ 26	01 ♒ 47	23 ♓ 17	10 ♎ 32
Dec 29, 1971	29 ♈ 43	03 ♒ 50	00 ♐ 51	06 ♓ 02	06 ♓ 35	25 ♑ 47	05 ♒ 15	25 ♓ 43	14 ♎ 06
Jan 8, 1972	00 ♉ 52	08 ♒ 21	04 ♐ 05	10 ♓ 52	09 ♓ 53	00 ♒ 13	08 ♒ 46	28 ♓ 28	17 ♎ 22
Jan 18, 1972	02 ♉ 37	12 ♒ 54	07 ♐ 11	15 ♓ 50	13 ♓ 20	04 ♒ 42	12 ♒ 21	01 ♈ 28	20 ♎ 16
Jan 28, 1972	04 ♉ 51	17 ♒ 29	10 ♐ 07	20 ♓ 57	16 ♓ 54	09 ♒ 14	15 ♒ 58	04 ♈ 42	22 ♎ 43
Feb 7, 1972	07 ♉ 29	22 ♒ 05	12 ♐ 51	26 ♓ 09	20 ♓ 33	13 ♒ 49	19 ♒ 35	08 ♈ 07	24 ♎ 38
Feb 17, 1972	10 ♉ 28	26 ♒ 40	15 ♐ 21	01 ♈ 28	24 ♓ 16	18 ♒ 24	23 ♒ 12	11 ♈ 40	25 ♎ 53
Feb 27, 1972	13 ♉ 43	01 ♓ 15	17 ♐ 34	06 ♈ 50	28 ♓ 01	23 ♒ 00	26 ♒ 47	15 ♈ 21	26 ♎ 24
Mar 8, 1972	17 ♉ 12	05 ♓ 47	19 ♐ 27	12 ♈ 16	01 ♈ 48	27 ♒ 36	00 ♓ 19	19 ♈ 07	26 ♎ 05
Mar 18, 1972	20 ♉ 51	10 ♓ 16	20 ♐ 57	17 ♈ 45	05 ♈ 36	02 ♓ 10	03 ♓ 48	22 ♈ 57	24 ♎ 56
Mar 28, 1972	24 ♉ 39	14 ♓ 42	22 ♐ 02	23 ♈ 16	09 ♈ 23	06 ♓ 43	07 ♓ 13	26 ♈ 50	23 ♎ 02
Apr 7, 1972	28 ♉ 33	19 ♓ 03	22 ♐ 36	28 ♈ 48	13 ♈ 10	11 ♓ 13	10 ♓ 31	00 ♉ 46	20 ♎ 37
Apr 17, 1972	02 ♊ 32	23 ♓ 18	22 ♐ 39	04 ♉ 22	16 ♈ 54	15 ♓ 39	13 ♓ 43	04 ♉ 42	18 ♎ 01
Apr 27, 1972	06 ♊ 36	27 ♈ 27	22 ♐ 09	09 ♉ 55	20 ♈ 35	20 ♓ 01	16 ♓ 46	08 ♉ 39	15 ♎ 38
May 7, 1972	10 ♊ 42	01 ♈ 29	22 ♐ 05	15 ♉ 29	24 ♈ 12	24 ♓ 16	19 ♓ 39	12 ♉ 36	13 ♎ 49
May 17, 1972	14 ♊ 51	05 ♈ 22	19 ♐ 31	21 ♉ 02	27 ♈ 44	28 ♓ 25	22 ♓ 21	16 ♉ 31	12 ♎ 48
May 27, 1972	19 ♊ 00	09 ♈ 04	17 ♐ 34	26 ♉ 34	01 ♉ 11	02 ♈ 26	24 ♓ 49	20 ♉ 25	12 ♎ 40
Jun 6, 1972	23 ♊ 11	12 ♈ 35	15 ♐ 24	02 ♊ 05	04 ♉ 31	06 ♈ 16	27 ♓ 01	24 ♉ 15	13 ♎ 22
Jun 16, 1972	27 ♊ 21	15 ♈ 52	13 ♐ 12	07 ♊ 35	07 ♉ 43	09 ♈ 55	28 ♓ 55	28 ♉ 03	14 ♎ 52
Jun 26, 1972	01 ♋ 30	18 ♈ 53	11 ♐ 13	13 ♊ 02	10 ♉ 46	13 ♈ 18	00 ♈ 29	01 ♊ 46	17 ♎ 04
Jul 6, 1972	05 ♋ 37	21 ♈ 36	09 ♐ 35	18 ♊ 27	13 ♉ 38	16 ♈ 24	01 ♈ 38	05 ♊ 24	19 ♎ 50
Jul 16, 1972	09 ♋ 43	23 ♈ 57	08 ♐ 26	23 ♊ 49	16 ♉ 17	19 ♈ 09	02 ♈ 21	08 ♊ 55	23 ♎ 06
Jul 26, 1972	13 ♋ 46	25 ♈ 54	07 ♐ 50	29 ♊ 07	18 ♉ 40	21 ♈ 29	02 ♈ 35	12 ♊ 19	26 ♎ 46
Aug 5, 1972	17 ♋ 46	27 ♈ 22	07 ♐ 48	04 ♋ 22	20 ♉ 47	23 ♈ 19	02 ♈ 17	15 ♊ 34	00 ♏ 48
Aug 15, 1972	21 ♋ 41	28 ♈ 19	08 ♐ 19	09 ♋ 31	22 ♉ 32	24 ♈ 35	01 ♈ 28	18 ♊ 39	05 ♏ 06
Aug 25, 1972	25 ♋ 31	28 ♈ 40	09 ♐ 21	14 ♋ 35	23 ♉ 54	25 ♈ 12	00 ♈ 09	21 ♊ 30	09 ♏ 40
Sep 4, 1972	29 ♋ 15	28 ♈ 25	10 ♐ 49	19 ♋ 32	24 ♉ 49	25 ♈ 07	28 ♓ 26	24 ♊ 06	14 ♏ 26

	ATROPOS	HEKATE	LILITH	MEDUSA	MOIRA	NEMESIS	PERSEPHONE	PROSERPINA	PYTHIA
Sep 14, 1972	02 ♌ 52	27 ♈ 32	12 ♐ 42	24 ♋ 21	25 ♉ 14	24 ♈ 18	26 ♓ 27	26 ♊ 23	19 ♏ 22
Sep 24, 1972	06 ♌ 19	26 ♈ 06	14 ♐ 56	29 ♋ 00	25 ♉ 05	22 ♈ 49	24 ♓ 24	28 ♊ 19	24 ♏ 27
Oct 4, 1972	09 ♌ 35	24 ♈ 15	17 ♐ 29	03 ♌ 28	24 ♉ 22	20 ♈ 51	22 ♓ 27	29 ♊ 49	29 ♏ 40
Oct 14, 1972	12 ♌ 38	22 ♈ 10	20 ♐ 17	07 ♌ 42	23 ♉ 05	18 ♈ 37	20 ♓ 48	00 ♋ 50	04 ♐ 59
Oct 24, 1972	15 ♌ 25	20 ♈ 05	23 ♐ 20	11 ♌ 40	21 ♉ 19	16 ♈ 28	19 ♓ 34	01 ♋ 17	10 ♐ 24
Nov 3, 1972	17 ♌ 53	18 ♈ 16	26 ♐ 35	15 ♌ 17	19 ♉ 13	14 ♈ 40	18 ♓ 52	01 ♋ 07	15 ♐ 53
Nov 13, 1972	19 ♌ 58	16 ♈ 52	29 ♐ 60	18 ♌ 30	16 ♉ 58	13 ♈ 43	18 ♓ 43	00 ♋ 18	21 ♐ 25
Nov 23, 1972	21 ♌ 35	16 ♈ 02	03 ♑ 34	21 ♌ 13	14 ♉ 47	12 ♈ 59	19 ♓ 06	28 ♊ 53	27 ♐ 01
Dec 3, 1972	22 ♌ 40	15 ♈ 47	07 ♑ 15	23 ♌ 21	12 ♉ 54	13 ♈ 15	19 ♓ 59	26 ♊ 57	02 ♑ 38
Dec 13, 1972	23 ♌ 07	16 ♈ 09	11 ♑ 03	24 ♌ 47	11 ♉ 28	14 ♈ 13	21 ♓ 20	24 ♊ 41	08 ♑ 17
Dec 23, 1972	22 ♌ 53	17 ♈ 04	14 ♑ 56	25 ♌ 25	10 ♉ 35	15 ♈ 50	23 ♓ 05	22 ♊ 21	13 ♑ 56
Jan 2, 1973	21 ♌ 55	18 ♈ 28	18 ♑ 54	25 ♌ 10	10 ♉ 18	17 ♈ 60	25 ♓ 11	20 ♊ 11	19 ♑ 35
Jan 12, 1973	20 ♌ 14	20 ♈ 19	22 ♑ 54	23 ♌ 60	10 ♉ 35	20 ♈ 38	27 ♓ 35	18 ♊ 25	25 ♑ 13
Jan 22, 1973	17 ♌ 57	22 ♈ 32	26 ♑ 57	22 ♌ 01	11 ♉ 25	23 ♈ 39	00 ♈ 14	17 ♊ 14	00 ♒ 50
Feb 1, 1973	15 ♌ 16	25 ♈ 02	01 ♒ 02	19 ♌ 27	12 ♉ 43	27 ♈ 00	03 ♈ 05	16 ♊ 41	06 ♒ 25
Feb 11, 1973	12 ♌ 29	27 ♈ 49	05 ♒ 07	16 ♌ 41	14 ♉ 26	00 ♉ 37	06 ♈ 37	16 ♊ 48	11 ♒ 58
Feb 21, 1973	09 ♌ 55	00 ♉ 47	09 ♒ 12	14 ♌ 07	16 ♉ 31	04 ♉ 27	09 ♈ 19	17 ♊ 32	17 ♒ 27
Mar 3, 1973	07 ♌ 49	03 ♉ 56	13 ♒ 17	12 ♌ 06	18 ♉ 55	08 ♉ 28	12 ♈ 37	18 ♊ 49	22 ♒ 52
Mar 13, 1973	06 ♌ 23	07 ♉ 13	17 ♒ 19	10 ♌ 52	21 ♉ 33	12 ♉ 37	16 ♈ 01	20 ♊ 35	28 ♒ 12
Mar 23, 1973	05 ♌ 41	10 ♉ 36	21 ♒ 18	10 ♌ 29	24 ♉ 25	16 ♉ 52	19 ♈ 29	22 ♊ 47	03 ♓ 27
Apr 2, 1973	05 ♌ 41	14 ♉ 03	25 ♒ 13	10 ♌ 57	27 ♉ 27	21 ♉ 12	23 ♈ 00	25 ♊ 20	08 ♓ 36
Apr 12, 1973	06 ♌ 23	17 ♉ 34	29 ♒ 03	12 ♌ 10	00 ♊ 38	25 ♉ 36	26 ♈ 34	28 ♊ 11	13 ♓ 38
Apr 22, 1973	07 ♌ 40	21 ♉ 07	02 ♓ 47	14 ♌ 02	03 ♊ 57	00 ♊ 03	00 ♉ 08	01 ♋ 17	18 ♓ 32
May 2, 1973	09 ♌ 29	24 ♉ 42	06 ♓ 24	16 ♌ 26	07 ♊ 21	04 ♊ 31	03 ♉ 42	04 ♋ 36	23 ♓ 17
May 12, 1973	11 ♌ 44	28 ♉ 16	09 ♓ 50	19 ♌ 17	10 ♊ 50	09 ♊ 01	07 ♉ 16	08 ♋ 06	27 ♓ 53
May 22, 1973	14 ♌ 22	01 ♊ 50	13 ♓ 05	22 ♌ 31	14 ♊ 22	13 ♊ 30	10 ♉ 48	11 ♋ 44	02 ♈ 17
Jun 1, 1973	17 ♌ 19	05 ♊ 23	16 ♓ 06	26 ♌ 02	17 ♊ 57	17 ♊ 60	14 ♉ 18	15 ♋ 31	06 ♈ 28
Jun 11, 1973	20 ♌ 33	08 ♊ 53	18 ♓ 50	29 ♌ 49	21 ♊ 34	22 ♊ 28	17 ♉ 44	19 ♋ 23	10 ♈ 24
Jun 21, 1973	24 ♌ 01	12 ♊ 19	21 ♓ 14	03 ♍ 47	25 ♊ 12	26 ♊ 55	21 ♉ 06	23 ♋ 21	14 ♈ 03
Jul 1, 1973	27 ♌ 41	15 ♊ 42	23 ♓ 13	07 ♍ 57	28 ♊ 50	01 ♋ 19	24 ♉ 22	27 ♋ 23	17 ♈ 23
Jul 11, 1973	01 ♍ 32	18 ♊ 60	24 ♓ 43	12 ♍ 14	02 ♋ 27	05 ♋ 41	27 ♉ 31	01 ♌ 29	20 ♈ 19
Jul 21, 1973	05 ♍ 33	22 ♊ 11	25 ♓ 40	16 ♍ 39	06 ♋ 04	09 ♋ 59	00 ♊ 31	05 ♌ 38	22 ♈ 48
Jul 31, 1973	09 ♍ 43	25 ♊ 15	25 ♓ 58	21 ♍ 10	09 ♋ 38	14 ♋ 14	03 ♊ 22	09 ♌ 49	24 ♈ 46
Aug 10, 1973	14 ♍ 00	28 ♊ 11	25 ♓ 35	25 ♍ 46	13 ♋ 09	18 ♋ 24	05 ♊ 59	14 ♌ 02	26 ♈ 06
Aug 20, 1973	18 ♍ 24	00 ♋ 56	24 ♓ 30	00 ♎ 26	16 ♋ 36	22 ♋ 27	08 ♊ 23	18 ♌ 16	26 ♈ 46

	ATROPOS	HEKATE	LILITH	MEDUSA	MOIRA	NEMESIS	PERSEPHONE	PROSERPINA	PYTHIA
Aug 30, 1973	22 ♍ 55	03 ♋ 29	22 ♓ 48	05 ♎ 10	19 ♋ 58	26 ♋ 25	10 ♊ 28	22 ♌ 30	26 ♈ 40
Sep 9, 1973	27 ♍ 32	05 ♋ 48	20 ♓ 40	09 ♎ 56	23 ♋ 13	00 ♌ 14	12 ♊ 13	26 ♌ 44	25 ♈ 46
Sep 19, 1973	02 ♎ 15	07 ♋ 50	18 ♓ 21	14 ♎ 45	26 ♋ 19	03 ♌ 54	13 ♊ 34	00 ♍ 57	24 ♈ 08
Sep 29, 1973	07 ♎ 03	09 ♋ 33	16 ♓ 12	19 ♎ 36	29 ♋ 15	07 ♌ 24	14 ♊ 26	05 ♍ 09	21 ♈ 52
Oct 9, 1973	11 ♎ 55	10 ♋ 54	14 ♓ 29	24 ♎ 29	01 ♌ 58	10 ♌ 40	14 ♊ 47	09 ♍ 17	19 ♈ 16
Oct 19, 1973	16 ♎ 52	11 ♋ 49	13 ♓ 26	29 ♎ 23	04 ♌ 26	13 ♌ 40	14 ♊ 34	13 ♍ 22	16 ♈ 37
Oct 29, 1973	21 ♎ 54	12 ♋ 16	13 ♓ 09	04 ♏ 17	06 ♌ 35	16 ♌ 23	13 ♊ 45	17 ♍ 22	14 ♈ 16
Nov 8, 1973	26 ♎ 59	12 ♋ 12	13 ♓ 40	09 ♏ 11	08 ♌ 21	18 ♌ 44	12 ♊ 24	21 ♍ 15	12 ♈ 29
Nov 18, 1973	02 ♏ 07	11 ♋ 37	14 ♓ 56	14 ♏ 04	09 ♌ 41	20 ♌ 40	10 ♊ 35	24 ♍ 60	11 ♈ 25
Nov 28, 1973	07 ♏ 18	10 ♋ 30	16 ♓ 52	18 ♏ 56	10 ♌ 29	22 ♌ 06	08 ♊ 28	28 ♍ 34	11 ♈ 06
Dec 8, 1973	12 ♏ 31	08 ♋ 57	19 ♓ 25	23 ♏ 47	10 ♌ 42	22 ♌ 59	06 ♊ 18	01 ♎ 56	11 ♈ 31
Dec 18, 1973	17 ♏ 46	07 ♋ 05	22 ♓ 28	28 ♏ 34	10 ♌ 16	23 ♌ 14	04 ♊ 17	05 ♎ 02	12 ♈ 36
Dec 28, 1973	23 ♏ 01	05 ♋ 03	25 ♓ 57	03 ♐ 19	09 ♌ 12	22 ♌ 50	02 ♊ 39	07 ♎ 48	14 ♈ 15
Jan 7, 1974	28 ♏ 17	03 ♋ 02	29 ♓ 48	07 ♐ 59	07 ♌ 33	21 ♌ 46	01 ♊ 33	10 ♎ 12	16 ♈ 23
Jan 17, 1974	03 ♐ 31	01 ♋ 15	03 ♈ 57	12 ♐ 34	05 ♌ 26	20 ♌ 07	01 ♊ 03	12 ♎ 08	18 ♈ 56
Jan 27, 1974	08 ♐ 43	29 ♊ 50	08 ♈ 22	17 ♐ 03	03 ♌ 04	18 ♌ 02	01 ♊ 10	13 ♎ 32	21 ♈ 49
Feb 6, 1974	13 ♐ 51	28 ♊ 53	12 ♈ 60	21 ♐ 23	00 ♌ 45	15 ♌ 44	01 ♊ 52	14 ♎ 19	24 ♈ 58
Feb 16, 1974	18 ♐ 54	28 ♊ 27	17 ♈ 48	25 ♐ 35	28 ♋ 44	13 ♌ 29	03 ♊ 06	14 ♎ 24	28 ♈ 21
Feb 26, 1974	23 ♐ 49	28 ♊ 31	22 ♈ 45	29 ♐ 35	27 ♋ 13	11 ♌ 31	04 ♊ 48	13 ♎ 47	01 ♉ 54
Mar 8, 1974	28 ♐ 34	29 ♊ 04	27 ♈ 48	03 ♑ 22	26 ♋ 20	10 ♌ 02	06 ♊ 55	12 ♎ 28	05 ♉ 37
Mar 18, 1974	03 ♑ 07	00 ♋ 04	02 ♉ 58	06 ♑ 53	26 ♋ 09	09 ♌ 09	09 ♊ 23	10 ♎ 36	09 ♉ 26
Mar 28, 1974	07 ♑ 23	01 ♋ 27	08 ♉ 12	10 ♑ 06	26 ♋ 38	08 ♌ 53	12 ♊ 08	08 ♎ 22	13 ♉ 20
Apr 7, 1974	11 ♑ 19	03 ♋ 10	13 ♉ 29	12 ♑ 56	27 ♋ 44	09 ♌ 13	15 ♊ 08	06 ♎ 04	17 ♉ 19
Apr 17, 1974	14 ♑ 49	05 ♋ 10	18 ♉ 48	15 ♑ 20	29 ♋ 23	10 ♌ 07	18 ♊ 20	04 ♎ 01	21 ♉ 20
Apr 27, 1974	17 ♑ 48	07 ♋ 25	24 ♉ 09	17 ♑ 13	01 ♌ 31	11 ♌ 30	21 ♊ 43	02 ♎ 26	25 ♉ 24
May 7, 1974	20 ♑ 08	09 ♋ 52	29 ♉ 31	18 ♑ 29	04 ♌ 04	13 ♌ 19	25 ♊ 14	01 ♎ 31	28 ♉ 29
May 17, 1974	21 ♑ 43	12 ♋ 29	04 ♊ 53	19 ♑ 04	06 ♌ 58	15 ♌ 29	28 ♊ 52	01 ♎ 18	03 ♊ 35
May 27, 1974	22 ♑ 24	15 ♋ 15	10 ♊ 15	18 ♑ 52	10 ♌ 11	17 ♌ 57	02 ♋ 36	01 ♎ 47	07 ♊ 41
Jun 6, 1974	22 ♑ 09	18 ♋ 07	15 ♊ 35	17 ♑ 54	13 ♌ 39	20 ♌ 41	06 ♋ 24	02 ♎ 56	11 ♊ 46
Jun 16, 1974	20 ♑ 56	21 ♋ 04	20 ♊ 54	16 ♑ 11	17 ♌ 21	23 ♌ 37	10 ♋ 16	04 ♎ 39	15 ♊ 49
Jun 26, 1974	18 ♑ 55	24 ♋ 06	26 ♊ 11	13 ♑ 54	21 ♌ 15	26 ♌ 44	14 ♋ 11	06 ♎ 54	19 ♊ 52
Jul 6, 1974	16 ♑ 26	27 ♋ 10	01 ♋ 24	11 ♑ 18	25 ♌ 19	29 ♌ 60	18 ♋ 08	09 ♎ 34	23 ♊ 51
Jul 16, 1974	13 ♑ 52	00 ♌ 17	06 ♋ 35	08 ♑ 45	29 ♌ 32	03 ♍ 23	22 ♋ 06	12 ♎ 36	27 ♊ 48
Jul 26, 1974	11 ♑ 42	03 ♌ 25	11 ♋ 42	06 ♑ 35	03 ♍ 53	06 ♍ 51	26 ♋ 04	15 ♎ 57	01 ♋ 41
Aug 5, 1974	10 ♑ 14	06 ♌ 32	16 ♋ 44	05 ♑ 02	08 ♍ 21	10 ♍ 25	00 ♌ 02	19 ♎ 35	05 ♋ 29

	ATROPOS	HEKATE	LILITH	MEDUSA	MOIRA	NEMESIS	PERSEPHONE	PROSERPINA	PYTHIA
Aug 15, 1974	09 ♑ 39	09 ♌ 39	21 ♋ 41	04 ♑ 17	12 ♍ 54	14 ♍ 02	03 ♌ 59	23 ♎ 25	09 ♋ 12
Aug 25, 1974	09 ♑ 57	12 ♌ 44	26 ♋ 33	04 ♑ 20	17 ♍ 34	17 ♍ 42	07 ♌ 54	27 ♎ 27	12 ♋ 48
Sep 4, 1974	11 ♑ 06	15 ♌ 47	01 ♌ 17	05 ♑ 10	22 ♍ 18	21 ♍ 25	11 ♌ 47	01 ♏ 40	16 ♋ 15
Sep 14, 1974	12 ♑ 58	18 ♌ 45	05 ♌ 53	06 ♑ 42	27 ♍ 06	25 ♍ 08	15 ♌ 35	05 ♏ 60	19 ♋ 33
Sep 24, 1974	15 ♑ 26	21 ♌ 38	10 ♌ 20	08 ♑ 52	01 ♎ 58	28 ♍ 52	19 ♌ 19	10 ♏ 27	22 ♋ 39
Oct 4, 1974	18 ♑ 25	24 ♌ 24	14 ♌ 36	11 ♑ 33	06 ♎ 52	02 ♎ 35	22 ♌ 56	15 ♏ 01	25 ♋ 30
Oct 14, 1974	21 ♑ 48	27 ♌ 01	18 ♌ 40	14 ♑ 42	11 ♎ 49	06 ♎ 17	26 ♌ 26	19 ♏ 40	28 ♋ 04
Oct 24, 1974	25 ♑ 32	29 ♌ 28	22 ♌ 28	18 ♑ 13	16 ♎ 47	09 ♎ 56	29 ♌ 46	24 ♏ 22	00 ♌ 16
Nov 3, 1974	29 ♑ 32	01 ♍ 43	25 ♌ 59	22 ♑ 05	21 ♎ 46	13 ♎ 32	02 ♍ 54	29 ♏ 08	02 ♌ 04
Nov 13, 1974	03 ♒ 45	03 ♍ 42	29 ♌ 10	26 ♑ 12	26 ♎ 46	17 ♎ 04	05 ♍ 48	03 ♐ 57	03 ♌ 21
Nov 23, 1974	08 ♒ 08	05 ♍ 24	01 ♍ 56	00 ♒ 35	01 ♏ 44	20 ♎ 30	08 ♍ 24	08 ♐ 47	04 ♌ 04
Dec 3, 1974	12 ♒ 41	06 ♍ 45	04 ♍ 14	05 ♒ 09	06 ♏ 41	23 ♎ 48	10 ♍ 40	13 ♐ 38	04 ♌ 07
Dec 13, 1974	17 ♒ 20	07 ♍ 42	05 ♍ 58	09 ♒ 54	11 ♏ 36	26 ♎ 58	12 ♍ 31	18 ♐ 30	03 ♌ 27
Dec 23, 1974	22 ♒ 05	08 ♍ 12	07 ♍ 04	14 ♒ 48	16 ♏ 26	29 ♎ 56	13 ♍ 54	23 ♐ 21	02 ♌ 04
Jan 2, 1975	26 ♒ 53	08 ♍ 13	07 ♍ 28	19 ♒ 49	21 ♏ 11	02 ♏ 41	14 ♍ 43	28 ♐ 10	00 ♌ 02
Jan 12, 1975	01 ♓ 45	07 ♍ 43	07 ♍ 07	24 ♒ 57	25 ♏ 57	05 ♏ 11	14 ♍ 57	02 ♑ 58	27 ♋ 33
Jan 22, 1975	06 ♓ 40	06 ♍ 43	06 ♍ 00	00 ♓ 10	00 ♐ 19	07 ♏ 21	14 ♍ 32	07 ♑ 42	24 ♋ 51
Feb 1, 1975	11 ♓ 35	05 ♍ 15	04 ♍ 15	05 ♓ 28	04 ♐ 39	09 ♏ 09	13 ♍ 29	12 ♑ 22	22 ♋ 18
Feb 11, 1975	16 ♓ 32	03 ♍ 28	02 ♍ 02	10 ♓ 49	08 ♐ 46	10 ♏ 33	11 ♍ 53	16 ♑ 58	20 ♋ 09
Feb 21, 1975	21 ♓ 28	01 ♍ 28	29 ♌ 36	16 ♓ 14	12 ♐ 37	11 ♏ 26	09 ♍ 53	21 ♑ 27	18 ♋ 37
Mar 3, 1975	26 ♓ 24	29 ♌ 28	27 ♌ 17	21 ♓ 41	16 ♐ 10	11 ♏ 48	07 ♍ 42	25 ♑ 49	17 ♋ 50
Mar 13, 1975	01 ♈ 18	27 ♌ 39	25 ♌ 20	27 ♓ 09	19 ♐ 21	11 ♏ 35	05 ♍ 35	00 ♒ 02	17 ♋ 47
Mar 23, 1975	06 ♈ 12	26 ♌ 09	23 ♌ 58	02 ♈ 39	22 ♐ 06	10 ♏ 47	03 ♍ 48	04 ♒ 06	18 ♌ 26
Apr 2, 1975	11 ♈ 02	25 ♌ 05	23 ♌ 15	08 ♈ 09	24 ♐ 21	09 ♏ 26	02 ♍ 30	07 ♒ 58	19 ♌ 44
Apr 12, 1975	15 ♈ 51	24 ♌ 31	23 ♌ 13	13 ♈ 40	25 ♐ 59	07 ♏ 38	01 ♍ 44	11 ♒ 36	21 ♌ 35
Apr 22, 1975	20 ♈ 36	24 ♌ 27	23 ♌ 48	19 ♈ 10	26 ♐ 58	05 ♏ 32	01 ♍ 44	14 ♒ 59	23 ♌ 55
May 2, 1975	25 ♈ 18	24 ♌ 53	24 ♌ 58	24 ♈ 39	27 ♐ 12	03 ♏ 21	02 ♍ 16	18 ♒ 03	26 ♌ 40
May 12, 1975	29 ♈ 56	25 ♌ 46	26 ♌ 37	00 ♉ 08	26 ♐ 42	01 ♏ 17	03 ♍ 22	20 ♒ 45	29 ♌ 44
May 22, 1975	04 ♉ 29	27 ♌ 04	28 ♌ 40	05 ♉ 35	25 ♐ 29	29 ♎ 33	04 ♍ 57	23 ♒ 02	03 ♍ 07
Jun 1, 1975	08 ♉ 56	28 ♌ 43	01 ♍ 04	10 ♉ 60	23 ♐ 42	28 ♎ 17	06 ♍ 59	24 ♒ 51	06 ♍ 45
Jun 11, 1975	13 ♉ 18	00 ♍ 41	03 ♍ 45	16 ♉ 22	21 ♐ 35	27 ♎ 33	09 ♍ 22	26 ♒ 06	10 ♌ 35
Jun 21, 1975	17 ♉ 33	02 ♍ 55	06 ♍ 41	21 ♉ 42	19 ♐ 26	27 ♎ 24	12 ♍ 05	26 ♒ 45	14 ♌ 38
Jul 1, 1975	21 ♉ 40	05 ♍ 24	09 ♍ 48	26 ♉ 57	17 ♐ 34	27 ♎ 49	15 ♍ 03	26 ♒ 43	18 ♌ 49
Jul 11, 1975	25 ♉ 38	08 ♍ 04	13 ♍ 05	02 ♊ 09	16 ♐ 12	28 ♎ 44	18 ♍ 15	26 ♒ 01	23 ♌ 10
Jul 21, 1975	29 ♉ 26	10 ♍ 55	16 ♍ 29	07 ♊ 15	15 ♐ 30	00 ♏ 08	21 ♍ 38	24 ♒ 41	27 ♌ 38

	ATROPOS	HEKATE	LILITH	MEDUSA	MOIRA	NEMESIS	PERSEPHONE	PROSERPINA	PYTHIA
Jul 31, 1975	03 ♊ 01	13 ♍ 54	20 ♍ 00	12 ♊ 14	15 ♐ 30	01 ♏ 56	25 ♍ 11	22 ♒ 49	02 ♍ 14
Aug 10, 1975	06 ♊ 21	17 ♍ 01	23 ♍ 36	17 ♊ 07	16 ♐ 11	04 ♏ 05	28 ♍ 53	20 ♒ 38	06 ♍ 55
Aug 20, 1975	09 ♊ 24	20 ♍ 15	27 ♍ 16	21 ♊ 50	17 ♐ 30	06 ♏ 33	02 ♎ 41	18 ♒ 24	11 ♍ 42
Aug 30, 1975	12 ♊ 07	23 ♍ 33	00 ♎ 59	26 ♊ 22	19 ♐ 22	09 ♏ 18	06 ♎ 35	16 ♒ 22	16 ♍ 35
Sep 9, 1975	14 ♊ 26	26 ♍ 56	04 ♎ 45	00 ♋ 42	21 ♐ 43	12 ♏ 16	10 ♎ 33	14 ♒ 47	21 ♍ 32
Sep 19, 1975	16 ♊ 15	00 ♎ 22	08 ♎ 31	04 ♋ 45	24 ♐ 28	15 ♏ 26	14 ♎ 36	13 ♒ 47	26 ♍ 33
Sep 29, 1975	17 ♊ 31	03 ♎ 50	12 ♎ 18	08 ♋ 29	27 ♐ 33	18 ♏ 46	18 ♎ 41	13 ♒ 26	01 ♎ 37
Oct 9, 1975	18 ♊ 08	07 ♎ 20	16 ♎ 05	11 ♋ 50	00 ♑ 54	22 ♏ 16	22 ♎ 49	13 ♒ 45	06 ♎ 45
Oct 19, 1975	18 ♊ 01	10 ♎ 50	19 ♎ 51	14 ♋ 42	04 ♑ 30	25 ♏ 52	26 ♎ 57	14 ♒ 41	11 ♎ 56
Oct 29, 1975	17 ♊ 07	14 ♎ 19	23 ♎ 35	16 ♋ 59	08 ♑ 17	29 ♏ 35	01 ♏ 07	16 ♒ 10	17 ♎ 08
Nov 8, 1975	15 ♊ 27	17 ♎ 47	27 ♎ 16	18 ♋ 36	12 ♑ 24	03 ♐ 24	05 ♏ 16	18 ♒ 08	22 ♎ 23
Nov 18, 1975	13 ♊ 08	21 ♎ 12	00 ♏ 53	19 ♋ 24	16 ♑ 19	07 ♐ 16	09 ♏ 23	20 ♒ 32	27 ♎ 38
Nov 28, 1975	10 ♊ 25	24 ♎ 33	04 ♏ 25	19 ♋ 18	20 ♑ 30	11 ♐ 12	13 ♏ 29	23 ♒ 16	02 ♏ 53
Dec 8, 1975	07 ♊ 34	27 ♎ 49	07 ♏ 51	18 ♋ 16	24 ♑ 46	15 ♐ 11	17 ♏ 31	26 ♒ 18	08 ♏ 08
Dec 18, 1975	04 ♊ 58	00 ♏ 56	11 ♏ 09	16 ♋ 23	29 ♑ 05	19 ♐ 11	21 ♏ 28	29 ♒ 34	13 ♏ 20
Dec 28, 1975	02 ♊ 54	03 ♏ 55	14 ♏ 18	13 ♋ 52	03 ♒ 27	23 ♐ 11	25 ♏ 20	03 ♓ 03	18 ♏ 31
Jan 7, 1976	01 ♊ 31	06 ♏ 42	17 ♏ 15	11 ♋ 06	07 ♒ 50	27 ♐ 11	29 ♏ 04	06 ♓ 42	23 ♏ 38
Jan 17, 1976	00 ♊ 54	09 ♏ 15	19 ♏ 58	08 ♋ 32	12 ♒ 14	01 ♑ 10	02 ♐ 40	10 ♓ 29	28 ♏ 39
Jan 27, 1976	01 ♊ 03	11 ♏ 31	22 ♏ 26	06 ♋ 32	16 ♒ 38	05 ♑ 06	06 ♐ 04	14 ♓ 22	03 ♐ 34
Feb 6, 1976	01 ♊ 52	13 ♏ 28	24 ♏ 35	05 ♋ 20	21 ♒ 01	08 ♑ 59	09 ♐ 16	18 ♓ 21	08 ♐ 21
Feb 16, 1976	03 ♊ 18	15 ♏ 00	26 ♏ 22	05 ♋ 04	25 ♒ 21	12 ♑ 47	12 ♐ 13	22 ♓ 23	12 ♐ 57
Feb 26, 1976	05 ♊ 13	16 ♏ 06	27 ♏ 45	05 ♋ 39	29 ♒ 40	16 ♑ 29	14 ♐ 51	26 ♓ 28	17 ♐ 20
Mar 7, 1976	07 ♊ 34	16 ♏ 42	28 ♏ 39	07 ♋ 02	03 ♓ 54	20 ♑ 04	17 ♐ 09	00 ♈ 34	21 ♐ 27
Mar 17, 1976	10 ♊ 16	16 ♏ 44	29 ♏ 01	09 ♋ 04	08 ♓ 05	23 ♑ 29	19 ♐ 01	04 ♈ 41	25 ♐ 15
Mar 27, 1976	13 ♊ 15	16 ♏ 12	28 ♏ 50	11 ♋ 40	12 ♓ 10	26 ♑ 44	20 ♐ 27	08 ♈ 48	28 ♐ 40
Apr 6, 1976	16 ♊ 28	15 ♏ 06	28 ♏ 05	14 ♋ 44	16 ♓ 09	29 ♑ 45	21 ♐ 20	12 ♈ 54	01 ♑ 37
Apr 16, 1976	19 ♊ 52	13 ♏ 32	26 ♏ 47	18 ♋ 10	20 ♓ 01	02 ♒ 31	21 ♐ 39	16 ♈ 58	03 ♑ 60
Apr 26, 1976	23 ♊ 26	11 ♏ 37	25 ♏ 02	21 ♋ 54	23 ♓ 46	04 ♒ 58	21 ♐ 22	20 ♈ 59	05 ♑ 43
May 6, 1976	27 ♊ 07	09 ♏ 34	22 ♏ 57	25 ♋ 52	27 ♓ 21	07 ♒ 03	20 ♐ 29	24 ♈ 58	06 ♑ 40
May 16, 1976	00 ♋ 54	07 ♏ 35	20 ♏ 44	00 ♌ 03	00 ♈ 45	08 ♒ 42	19 ♐ 03	28 ♈ 52	06 ♑ 48
May 26, 1976	04 ♋ 46	05 ♏ 54	18 ♏ 37	04 ♌ 23	03 ♈ 58	09 ♒ 51	17 ♐ 14	02 ♉ 42	06 ♑ 03
Jun 5, 1976	08 ♋ 41	04 ♏ 39	16 ♏ 45	08 ♌ 51	06 ♈ 56	10 ♒ 27	15 ♐ 10	06 ♉ 25	04 ♑ 30
Jun 15, 1976	12 ♋ 40	03 ♏ 57	15 ♏ 19	13 ♌ 26	09 ♈ 39	10 ♒ 25	13 ♐ 07	10 ♉ 02	02 ♑ 21
Jun 25, 1976	16 ♋ 40	03 ♏ 51	14 ♏ 24	18 ♌ 06	12 ♈ 03	09 ♒ 46	11 ♐ 17	13 ♉ 31	29 ♐ 57
Jul 5, 1976	20 ♋ 42	04 ♏ 21	14 ♏ 01	22 ♌ 50	14 ♈ 05	08 ♒ 30	09 ♐ 51	16 ♉ 50	27 ♐ 40

	ATROPOS	HEKATE	LILITH	MEDUSA	MOIRA	NEMESIS	PERSEPHONE	PROSERPINA	PYTHIA
Jul 15, 1976	24 ♋ 45	05 ♏ 23	14 ♏ 12	27 ♌ 38	15 ♈ 43	06 ♒ 43	08 ♐ 55	19 ♉ 58	25 ♐ 52
Jul 25, 1976	28 ♋ 47	06 ♏ 55	14 ♏ 53	02 ♍ 29	16 ♈ 53	04 ♒ 36	08 ♐ 34	22 ♉ 53	24 ♐ 49
Aug 4, 1976	02 ♌ 50	08 ♏ 54	16 ♏ 02	07 ♍ 22	17 ♈ 31	02 ♒ 24	08 ♐ 47	25 ♉ 33	24 ♐ 35
Aug 14, 1976	06 ♌ 51	11 ♏ 17	17 ♏ 35	12 ♍ 17	17 ♈ 36	00 ♒ 23	09 ♐ 33	27 ♉ 55	25 ♐ 13
Aug 24, 1976	10 ♌ 50	13 ♏ 60	19 ♏ 30	17 ♍ 13	17 ♈ 04	28 ♑ 47	10 ♐ 49	29 ♉ 55	26 ♐ 36
Sep 3, 1976	14 ♌ 47	17 ♏ 01	21 ♏ 45	22 ♍ 10	15 ♈ 57	27 ♑ 45	12 ♐ 30	01 ♊ 30	28 ♐ 40
Sep 13, 1976	18 ♌ 41	20 ♏ 17	24 ♏ 15	27 ♍ 08	14 ♈ 18	27 ♑ 25	14 ♐ 35	02 ♊ 37	01 ♑ 19
Sep 23, 1976	22 ♌ 31	23 ♏ 47	26 ♏ 60	02 ♎ 06	12 ♈ 15	27 ♑ 45	16 ♐ 59	03 ♊ 12	04 ♑ 27
Oct 3, 1976	26 ♌ 15	27 ♏ 28	29 ♏ 56	07 ♎ 03	10 ♈ 01	28 ♑ 44	19 ♐ 40	03 ♊ 10	07 ♑ 59
Oct 13, 1976	29 ♌ 52	01 ♐ 20	03 ♐ 03	12 ♎ 00	07 ♈ 48	00 ♒ 20	22 ♐ 35	02 ♊ 31	11 ♑ 51
Oct 23, 1976	03 ♍ 21	05 ♐ 20	06 ♐ 19	16 ♎ 56	05 ♈ 50	02 ♒ 28	25 ♐ 42	01 ♊ 15	15 ♑ 59
Nov 2, 1976	06 ♍ 40	09 ♐ 27	09 ♐ 42	21 ♎ 49	04 ♈ 19	05 ♒ 03	28 ♐ 59	29 ♉ 27	20 ♑ 20
Nov 12, 1976	09 ♍ 47	13 ♐ 41	13 ♐ 11	26 ♎ 41	03 ♈ 20	08 ♒ 03	02 ♑ 24	27 ♉ 16	24 ♑ 53
Nov 22, 1976	12 ♍ 38	18 ♐ 00	16 ♐ 45	01 ♏ 29	02 ♈ 57	11 ♒ 23	05 ♑ 56	24 ♉ 57	29 ♑ 34
Dec 2, 1976	15 ♍ 10	22 ♐ 24	20 ♐ 23	06 ♏ 14	03 ♈ 09	15 ♒ 01	09 ♑ 33	22 ♉ 44	04 ♒ 23
Dec 12, 1976	17 ♍ 20	26 ♐ 50	24 ♐ 04	10 ♏ 53	03 ♈ 55	18 ♒ 53	13 ♑ 14	20 ♉ 52	09 ♒ 17
Dec 22, 1976	19 ♍ 03	01 ♑ 20	27 ♐ 47	15 ♏ 27	05 ♈ 10	22 ♒ 58	16 ♑ 58	19 ♉ 30	14 ♒ 15
Jan 1, 1977	20 ♍ 13	05 ♑ 50	01 ♑ 31	19 ♏ 53	06 ♈ 52	27 ♒ 14	20 ♑ 44	18 ♉ 46	19 ♒ 17
Jan 11, 1977	20 ♍ 46	10 ♑ 22	04 ♑ 14	24 ♏ 10	08 ♈ 56	01 ♓ 39	24 ♑ 30	18 ♉ 41	24 ♒ 20
Jan 21, 1977	20 ♍ 37	14 ♑ 53	08 ♑ 56	28 ♏ 18	11 ♈ 19	06 ♓ 11	28 ♑ 16	19 ♉ 13	29 ♒ 25
Jan 31, 1977	19 ♍ 43	19 ♑ 23	12 ♑ 37	02 ♐ 13	13 ♈ 58	10 ♓ 50	02 ♒ 01	20 ♉ 19	04 ♓ 30
Feb 10, 1977	18 ♍ 04	23 ♑ 50	16 ♑ 13	05 ♐ 53	16 ♈ 50	15 ♓ 33	05 ♒ 42	21 ♉ 55	09 ♓ 35
Feb 20, 1977	15 ♍ 46	28 ♑ 15	19 ♑ 46	09 ♐ 15	19 ♈ 53	20 ♓ 20	09 ♒ 21	23 ♉ 56	14 ♓ 38
Mar 2, 1977	13 ♍ 03	02 ♒ 35	23 ♑ 12	12 ♐ 16	23 ♈ 04	25 ♓ 09	12 ♒ 54	26 ♉ 20	19 ♓ 40
Mar 12, 1977	10 ♍ 13	06 ♒ 50	26 ♑ 31	14 ♐ 53	26 ♈ 23	00 ♈ 01	16 ♒ 22	29 ♉ 02	24 ♓ 39
Mar 22, 1977	07 ♍ 36	10 ♒ 58	29 ♑ 41	16 ♐ 60	29 ♈ 47	04 ♈ 54	19 ♒ 43	02 ♊ 00	29 ♓ 36
Apr 1, 1977	05 ♍ 30	14 ♒ 58	02 ♒ 40	18 ♐ 32	03 ♉ 15	09 ♈ 47	22 ♒ 55	05 ♊ 11	04 ♈ 28
Apr 11, 1977	04 ♍ 06	18 ♒ 49	05 ♒ 26	19 ♐ 25	06 ♉ 46	14 ♈ 40	25 ♒ 58	08 ♊ 33	09 ♈ 17
Apr 21, 1977	04 ♍ 29	22 ♒ 28	07 ♒ 57	19 ♐ 33	10 ♉ 18	19 ♈ 32	28 ♒ 48	12 ♊ 03	14 ♈ 01
May 1, 1977	03 ♍ 38	25 ♒ 53	10 ♒ 10	18 ♐ 53	13 ♉ 52	24 ♈ 22	01 ♓ 25	15 ♊ 41	18 ♈ 40
May 11, 1977	04 ♍ 31	29 ♒ 03	12 ♒ 01	17 ♐ 28	17 ♉ 26	29 ♈ 10	03 ♓ 47	19 ♊ 24	23 ♈ 13
May 21, 1977	06 ♍ 03	01 ♓ 53	13 ♒ 26	15 ♐ 22	20 ♉ 59	03 ♉ 55	05 ♓ 50	23 ♊ 13	27 ♈ 40
May 31, 1977	08 ♍ 09	04 ♓ 22	14 ♒ 23	12 ♐ 51	24 ♉ 30	08 ♉ 36	07 ♓ 33	27 ♊ 05	01 ♉ 59
Jun 10, 1977	10 ♍ 44	06 ♓ 25	14 ♒ 47	10 ♐ 13	27 ♉ 59	13 ♉ 12	08 ♓ 52	01 ♋ 00	06 ♉ 10
Jun 20, 1977	13 ♍ 45	07 ♓ 59	14 ♒ 35	07 ♐ 49	01 ♊ 24	17 ♉ 44	09 ♓ 44	04 ♋ 58	10 ♉ 13

	ATROPOS	HEKATE	LILITH	MEDUSA	MOIRA	NEMESIS	PERSEPHONE	PROSERPINA	PYTHIA
Jun 30, 1977	17 ♍ 08	08 ♓ 59	13 ♒ 46	05 ♐ 56	04 ♊ 45	22 ♉ 08	10 ♓ 08	08 ♋ 57	14 ♉ 04
Jul 10, 1977	20 ♍ 49	09 ♓ 23	12 ♒ 22	04 ♐ 46	08 ♊ 00	26 ♉ 26	09 ♓ 60	12 ♋ 57	17 ♉ 44
Jul 20, 1977	24 ♍ 47	09 ♓ 08	10 ♒ 28	04 ♐ 23	11 ♊ 09	00 ♊ 34	09 ♓ 20	16 ♋ 57	21 ♉ 10
Jul 30, 1977	29 ♍ 00	08 ♓ 15	08 ♒ 15	04 ♐ 46	14 ♊ 10	04 ♊ 32	08 ♓ 09	20 ♋ 56	24 ♉ 20
Aug 9, 1977	03 ♎ 27	06 ♓ 49	05 ♒ 57	05 ♐ 53	17 ♊ 00	08 ♊ 17	06 ♓ 33	24 ♋ 55	27 ♉ 11
Aug 19, 1977	08 ♎ 05	04 ♓ 58	03 ♒ 50	07 ♐ 37	19 ♊ 40	11 ♊ 48	04 ♓ 38	28 ♋ 51	29 ♉ 41
Aug 29, 1977	12 ♎ 54	02 ♓ 57	02 ♒ 07	09 ♐ 55	22 ♊ 05	15 ♊ 02	02 ♓ 36	02 ♌ 45	01 ♊ 46
Sep 8, 1977	17 ♎ 53	01 ♓ 01	00 ♒ 59	12 ♐ 42	24 ♊ 14	17 ♊ 55	00 ♓ 37	06 ♌ 35	03 ♊ 21
Sep 18, 1977	23 ♎ 01	29 ♒ 24	00 ♒ 30	15 ♐ 52	26 ♊ 04	20 ♊ 23	28 ♒ 52	10 ♌ 20	04 ♊ 21
Sep 28, 1977	28 ♎ 18	28 ♒ 17	00 ♒ 42	19 ♐ 23	27 ♊ 30	22 ♊ 23	27 ♒ 32	13 ♌ 58	04 ♊ 43
Oct 8, 1977	03 ♏ 43	27 ♒ 47	01 ♒ 34	23 ♐ 47	28 ♊ 30	23 ♊ 49	26 ♒ 41	17 ♌ 29	04 ♊ 23
Oct 18, 1977	09 ♏ 14	27 ♒ 55	03 ♒ 02	27 ♐ 16	28 ♊ 60	24 ♊ 36	26 ♒ 22	20 ♌ 50	03 ♊ 18
Oct 28, 1977	14 ♏ 52	28 ♒ 41	05 ♒ 03	01 ♑ 32	28 ♊ 56	24 ♊ 42	26 ♒ 35	23 ♌ 59	01 ♊ 33
Nov 7, 1977	20 ♏ 36	00 ♓ 00	07 ♒ 33	05 ♑ 60	28 ♊ 17	24 ♊ 03	27 ♒ 18	26 ♌ 54	29 ♉ 16
Nov 17, 1977	26 ♏ 24	01 ♓ 50	10 ♒ 28	10 ♑ 37	28 ♊ 03	22 ♊ 42	28 ♒ 30	29 ♌ 30	26 ♉ 39
Nov 27, 1977	02 ♐ 17	04 ♓ 07	13 ♒ 44	15 ♑ 23	25 ♊ 19	20 ♊ 47	00 ♓ 06	01 ♍ 45	24 ♉ 02
Dec 7, 1977	08 ♐ 13	06 ♓ 45	17 ♒ 19	20 ♑ 16	23 ♊ 12	18 ♊ 31	02 ♓ 04	03 ♍ 35	21 ♉ 41
Dec 17, 1977	14 ♐ 11	09 ♓ 43	21 ♒ 10	25 ♑ 15	20 ♊ 55	16 ♊ 12	04 ♓ 21	04 ♍ 54	19 ♉ 52
Dec 27, 1977	20 ♐ 10	12 ♓ 56	25 ♒ 16	00 ♒ 19	18 ♊ 42	14 ♊ 07	06 ♓ 53	05 ♍ 37	18 ♉ 43
Jan 6, 1978	26 ♐ 11	16 ♓ 22	29 ♒ 33	05 ♒ 27	16 ♊ 45	12 ♊ 32	09 ♓ 39	05 ♍ 42	18 ♉ 17
Jan 16, 1978	02 ♑ 10	19 ♓ 58	04 ♓ 01	10 ♒ 39	15 ♊ 17	11 ♊ 36	12 ♓ 36	05 ♍ 06	18 ♉ 33
Jan 26, 1978	08 ♑ 08	23 ♓ 43	08 ♓ 38	15 ♒ 54	14 ♊ 23	11 ♊ 22	15 ♓ 42	03 ♍ 49	19 ♉ 27
Feb 5, 1978	14 ♑ 03	27 ♓ 34	13 ♓ 23	21 ♒ 12	14 ♊ 06	11 ♊ 50	18 ♓ 56	01 ♍ 57	20 ♉ 55
Feb 15, 1978	19 ♑ 54	01 ♈ 30	18 ♓ 14	26 ♒ 31	14 ♊ 25	12 ♊ 55	22 ♓ 15	29 ♌ 43	22 ♉ 51
Feb 25, 1978	25 ♑ 39	05 ♈ 30	23 ♓ 11	01 ♓ 52	15 ♊ 17	14 ♊ 34	25 ♓ 39	27 ♌ 21	25 ♉ 12
Mar 7, 1978	01 ♒ 19	09 ♈ 32	28 ♓ 13	07 ♓ 13	16 ♊ 40	16 ♊ 41	29 ♓ 07	25 ♌ 09	27 ♉ 53
Mar 17, 1978	06 ♒ 50	13 ♈ 36	03 ♈ 19	12 ♓ 34	18 ♊ 29	19 ♊ 11	02 ♈ 36	23 ♌ 23	00 ♊ 51
Mar 27, 1978	12 ♒ 13	17 ♈ 40	08 ♈ 27	17 ♓ 55	20 ♊ 40	22 ♊ 01	06 ♈ 06	22 ♌ 14	04 ♊ 02
Apr 6, 1978	17 ♒ 25	21 ♈ 43	13 ♈ 39	23 ♓ 15	23 ♊ 11	25 ♊ 07	09 ♈ 37	21 ♌ 46	07 ♊ 25
Apr 16, 1978	22 ♒ 25	25 ♈ 45	18 ♈ 52	28 ♓ 34	25 ♊ 58	28 ♊ 26	13 ♈ 06	21 ♌ 59	10 ♊ 58
Apr 26, 1978	27 ♒ 10	29 ♈ 45	24 ♈ 07	03 ♈ 51	28 ♊ 59	01 ♋ 56	16 ♈ 34	22 ♌ 52	14 ♊ 38
May 6, 1978	01 ♓ 40	03 ♉ 41	29 ♈ 23	09 ♈ 05	02 ♋ 12	05 ♋ 34	19 ♈ 59	24 ♌ 20	18 ♊ 25
May 16, 1978	05 ♓ 51	07 ♉ 34	04 ♉ 38	14 ♈ 17	05 ♋ 34	09 ♋ 19	23 ♈ 20	26 ♌ 20	22 ♊ 17
May 26, 1978	09 ♓ 40	11 ♉ 23	09 ♉ 54	19 ♈ 25	09 ♋ 06	13 ♋ 09	26 ♈ 36	28 ♌ 46	26 ♊ 13
Jun 5, 1978	13 ♓ 05	15 ♉ 06	15 ♉ 08	24 ♈ 29	12 ♋ 44	17 ♋ 03	29 ♈ 46	01 ♍ 34	00 ♋ 12

	ATROPOS	HEKATE	LILITH	MEDUSA	MOIRA	NEMESIS	PERSEPHONE	PROSERPINA	PYTHIA
Jun 15, 1978	15 ♓ 59	18 ♊ 42	20 ♉ 20	29 ♈ 27	16 ♋ 28	21 ♋ 01	02 ♉ 49	04 ♍ 42	04 ♋ 15
Jun 25, 1978	18 ♓ 20	22 ♊ 11	25 ♉ 30	04 ♉ 20	20 ♋ 18	25 ♋ 00	05 ♉ 43	08 ♍ 06	08 ♋ 19
Jul 5, 1978	20 ♓ 00	25 ♊ 32	00 ♊ 37	09 ♉ 05	24 ♋ 12	29 ♋ 01	08 ♉ 26	11 ♍ 44	12 ♋ 24
Jul 15, 1978	20 ♓ 55	28 ♊ 42	05 ♊ 39	13 ♉ 40	28 ♋ 09	03 ♌ 03	10 ♉ 57	15 ♍ 34	16 ♋ 31
Jul 25, 1978	20 ♓ 60	01 ♊ 40	10 ♊ 36	18 ♉ 05	02 ♌ 09	07 ♌ 05	13 ♉ 13	19 ♍ 35	20 ♋ 38
Aug 4, 1978	20 ♓ 11	04 ♊ 26	15 ♊ 27	22 ♉ 17	06 ♌ 12	11 ♌ 06	15 ♉ 12	23 ♍ 44	24 ♋ 44
Aug 14, 1978	18 ♓ 31	06 ♊ 55	20 ♊ 09	26 ♉ 12	10 ♌ 16	15 ♌ 06	16 ♉ 50	28 ♍ 00	28 ♋ 50
Aug 24, 1978	16 ♓ 10	09 ♊ 06	24 ♊ 42	29 ♉ 48	14 ♌ 21	19 ♌ 04	18 ♉ 04	02 ♎ 24	02 ♌ 54
Sep 3, 1978	13 ♓ 24	10 ♊ 56	29 ♊ 02	03 ♊ 00	18 ♌ 27	22 ♌ 59	18 ♉ 51	06 ♎ 52	06 ♌ 56
Sep 13, 1978	10 ♓ 38	12 ♊ 22	03 ♋ 08	05 ♊ 43	22 ♌ 32	26 ♌ 50	19 ♉ 08	11 ♎ 26	10 ♌ 55
Sep 23, 1978	08 ♓ 13	13 ♊ 47	06 ♋ 57	07 ♊ 51	26 ♌ 35	00 ♍ 37	18 ♉ 52	16 ♎ 04	14 ♌ 50
Oct 3, 1978	06 ♓ 28	13 ♊ 42	10 ♋ 24	09 ♊ 16	00 ♍ 37	04 ♍ 18	18 ♉ 03	20 ♎ 45	18 ♌ 39
Oct 13, 1978	05 ♓ 30	13 ♊ 02	13 ♋ 26	09 ♊ 52	04 ♍ 35	07 ♍ 53	16 ♉ 42	25 ♎ 29	22 ♌ 22
Oct 23, 1978	05 ♓ 23	11 ♊ 51	15 ♋ 57	09 ♊ 35	08 ♍ 29	11 ♍ 19	14 ♉ 55	00 ♏ 15	25 ♌ 56
Nov 2, 1978	06 ♓ 03	10 ♊ 11	17 ♋ 52	08 ♊ 22	12 ♍ 17	14 ♍ 35	12 ♉ 52	05 ♏ 02	29 ♌ 19
Nov 12, 1978	07 ♓ 26	08 ♊ 13	19 ♋ 04	06 ♊ 21	15 ♍ 57	17 ♍ 40	10 ♉ 44	09 ♏ 50	02 ♍ 28
Nov 22, 1978	09 ♓ 25	06 ♊ 08	19 ♋ 29	03 ♊ 47	19 ♍ 26	20 ♍ 30	08 ♉ 44	14 ♏ 37	05 ♍ 21
Dec 2, 1978	11 ♓ 54	04 ♊ 07	19 ♋ 03	01 ♊ 05	22 ♍ 44	23 ♍ 03	07 ♉ 05	19 ♏ 24	07 ♍ 54
Dec 12, 1978	14 ♓ 49	02 ♊ 24	17 ♋ 49	28 ♉ 42	25 ♍ 46	25 ♍ 16	05 ♉ 55	24 ♏ 09	10 ♍ 02
Dec 22, 1978	18 ♓ 05	01 ♊ 06	15 ♋ 54	26 ♉ 58	28 ♍ 28	27 ♍ 06	05 ♉ 20	28 ♏ 52	11 ♍ 40
Jan 1, 1979	21 ♓ 38	00 ♊ 19	13 ♋ 35	26 ♉ 06	00 ♎ 48	28 ♍ 29	05 ♉ 20	03 ♐ 30	12 ♍ 42
Jan 11, 1979	25 ♓ 24	00 ♊ 06	11 ♋ 13	26 ♉ 11	02 ♎ 39	29 ♍ 20	05 ♉ 54	08 ♐ 04	13 ♍ 02
Jan 21, 1979	29 ♓ 22	00 ♊ 24	09 ♋ 09	27 ♉ 08	03 ♎ 57	29 ♍ 37	07 ♉ 01	12 ♐ 32	12 ♍ 37
Jan 31, 1979	03 ♈ 29	01 ♊ 12	07 ♋ 40	28 ♉ 52	04 ♎ 37	29 ♍ 18	08 ♉ 35	16 ♐ 52	11 ♍ 26
Feb 10, 1979	07 ♈ 44	02 ♊ 27	06 ♋ 56	01 ♊ 16	04 ♎ 35	28 ♍ 21	10 ♉ 34	21 ♐ 03	09 ♍ 30
Feb 20, 1979	12 ♈ 04	04 ♊ 05	06 ♋ 58	04 ♊ 12	03 ♎ 50	26 ♍ 52	12 ♉ 54	25 ♐ 03	07 ♍ 03
Mar 2, 1979	16 ♈ 28	06 ♊ 03	07 ♋ 45	07 ♊ 35	02 ♎ 23	24 ♍ 55	15 ♉ 32	28 ♐ 50	04 ♍ 20
Mar 12, 1979	20 ♈ 56	08 ♊ 17	09 ♋ 11	11 ♊ 20	00 ♎ 24	22 ♍ 43	18 ♉ 25	02 ♑ 21	01 ♍ 44
Mar 22, 1979	25 ♈ 25	10 ♊ 45	11 ♋ 11	15 ♊ 23	28 ♍ 08	20 ♍ 27	21 ♉ 31	05 ♑ 34	29 ♌ 35
Apr 1, 1979	29 ♈ 56	13 ♊ 25	13 ♋ 38	19 ♊ 39	25 ♍ 52	18 ♍ 27	24 ♉ 47	08 ♑ 25	28 ♌ 06
Apr 11, 1979	04 ♉ 28	16 ♊ 14	16 ♋ 29	24 ♊ 07	23 ♍ 56	16 ♍ 49	28 ♉ 12	10 ♑ 50	27 ♌ 27
Apr 21, 1979	08 ♉ 59	19 ♊ 10	19 ♋ 39	28 ♊ 44	22 ♍ 34	15 ♍ 41	01 ♊ 44	12 ♑ 45	27 ♌ 36
May 1, 1979	13 ♉ 30	22 ♊ 12	23 ♋ 03	03 ♋ 29	21 ♍ 55	15 ♍ 09	05 ♊ 21	14 ♑ 06	28 ♌ 32
May 11, 1979	17 ♉ 59	25 ♊ 19	26 ♋ 39	08 ♋ 29	22 ♍ 02	15 ♍ 10	09 ♊ 04	14 ♑ 48	00 ♍ 10
May 21, 1979	22 ♉ 26		00 ♌ 25	13 ♋ 13	22 ♍ 52	15 ♍ 45	12 ♊ 50	14 ♑ 48	02 ♍ 24

	ATROPOS	HEKATE	LILITH	MEDUSA	MOIRA	NEMESIS	PERSEPHONE	PROSERPINA	PYTHIA
May 31, 1979	26 ♉ 51	28 ♊ 29	04 ♌ 19	18 ♋ 12	24 ♍ 22	16 ♍ 50	16 ♊ 38	14 ♑ 06	05 ♍ 08
Jun 10, 1979	01 ♊ 12	01 ♋ 41	08 ♌ 18	23 ♋ 13	26 ♍ 50	18 ♍ 20	20 ♊ 28	12 ♑ 45	08 ♍ 19
Jun 20, 1979	05 ♊ 30	04 ♋ 54	12 ♌ 22	28 ♋ 22	29 ♍ 03	20 ♍ 27	24 ♊ 19	10 ♑ 52	11 ♍ 52
Jun 30, 1979	09 ♊ 43	08 ♋ 08	16 ♌ 30	03 ♌ 28	02 ♎ 04	22 ♍ 27	28 ♊ 11	08 ♑ 42	15 ♍ 44
Jul 10, 1979	13 ♊ 51	11 ♋ 21	20 ♌ 40	08 ♌ 35	05 ♎ 27	24 ♍ 57	02 ♋ 02	06 ♑ 32	19 ♍ 52
Jul 20, 1979	17 ♊ 52	14 ♋ 32	24 ♌ 51	13 ♌ 42	09 ♎ 09	27 ♍ 40	05 ♋ 51	04 ♑ 38	24 ♍ 14
Jul 30, 1979	21 ♊ 47	17 ♋ 41	29 ♌ 04	18 ♌ 49	13 ♎ 06	00 ♎ 36	09 ♋ 38	03 ♑ 13	28 ♍ 49
Aug 9, 1979	25 ♊ 33	20 ♋ 47	03 ♍ 17	23 ♌ 56	17 ♎ 16	03 ♎ 42	13 ♋ 22	02 ♑ 26	03 ♎ 33
Aug 19, 1979	29 ♊ 08	23 ♋ 47	07 ♍ 30	28 ♌ 56	21 ♎ 38	06 ♎ 57	17 ♋ 02	02 ♑ 21	08 ♎ 27
Aug 29, 1979	02 ♋ 24	26 ♋ 42	11 ♍ 41	04 ♍ 02	26 ♎ 09	10 ♎ 18	20 ♋ 37	02 ♑ 56	13 ♎ 30
Sep 8, 1979	05 ♋ 42	29 ♋ 30	15 ♍ 52	09 ♍ 07	00 ♏ 48	13 ♎ 46	24 ♋ 04	04 ♑ 08	18 ♎ 39
Sep 18, 1979	08 ♋ 35	02 ♌ 09	19 ♍ 60	14 ♍ 11	05 ♏ 33	17 ♎ 19	27 ♋ 24	05 ♑ 53	23 ♎ 55
Sep 28, 1979	11 ♋ 07	04 ♌ 38	24 ♍ 05	19 ♍ 12	10 ♏ 25	20 ♎ 55	00 ♌ 33	08 ♑ 07	29 ♎ 16
Oct 8, 1979	13 ♋ 15	06 ♌ 53	28 ♍ 07	24 ♍ 11	15 ♏ 21	24 ♎ 35	03 ♌ 30	10 ♑ 46	04 ♏ 42
Oct 18, 1979	14 ♋ 55	08 ♌ 54	02 ♎ 04	29 ♍ 07	20 ♏ 20	28 ♎ 16	06 ♌ 11	13 ♑ 45	10 ♏ 13
Oct 28, 1979	16 ♋ 02	10 ♌ 37	05 ♎ 56	03 ♎ 60	25 ♏ 22	01 ♏ 59	08 ♌ 34	17 ♑ 02	15 ♏ 47
Nov 7, 1979	16 ♋ 29	11 ♌ 60	09 ♎ 42	08 ♎ 48	00 ♐ 27	05 ♏ 42	10 ♌ 35	20 ♑ 33	21 ♏ 23
Nov 17, 1979	16 ♋ 15	12 ♌ 59	13 ♎ 20	13 ♎ 30	05 ♐ 32	09 ♏ 24	12 ♌ 11	24 ♑ 17	27 ♏ 03
Nov 27, 1979	15 ♋ 14	13 ♌ 31	16 ♎ 49	18 ♎ 07	10 ♐ 38	13 ♏ 05	13 ♌ 16	28 ♑ 11	02 ♐ 44
Dec 7, 1979	13 ♋ 30	13 ♌ 34	20 ♎ 06	22 ♎ 35	15 ♐ 44	16 ♏ 42	13 ♌ 47	02 ♒ 13	08 ♐ 26
Dec 17, 1979	11 ♋ 10	13 ♌ 07	23 ♎ 11	26 ♎ 54	20 ♐ 49	20 ♏ 16	13 ♌ 42	06 ♒ 21	14 ♐ 08
Dec 27, 1979	08 ♋ 27	12 ♌ 10	26 ♎ 01	01 ♏ 01	25 ♐ 52	23 ♏ 44	12 ♌ 57	10 ♒ 35	19 ♐ 50
Jan 6, 1980	05 ♋ 39	10 ♌ 45	28 ♎ 33	04 ♏ 55	00 ♑ 52	27 ♏ 06	11 ♌ 37	14 ♒ 53	25 ♐ 31
Jan 16, 1980	03 ♋ 06	08 ♌ 59	00 ♏ 44	08 ♏ 33	05 ♑ 49	00 ♐ 19	09 ♌ 47	19 ♒ 14	01 ♑ 11
Jan 26, 1980	01 ♋ 03	07 ♌ 01	02 ♏ 31	11 ♏ 52	10 ♑ 42	03 ♐ 21	07 ♌ 39	23 ♒ 37	06 ♑ 48
Feb 5, 1980	29 ♊ 41	05 ♌ 01	03 ♏ 50	14 ♏ 48	15 ♑ 29	06 ♐ 11	05 ♌ 27	28 ♒ 01	12 ♑ 22
Feb 15, 1980	29 ♊ 04	03 ♌ 10	04 ♏ 38	17 ♏ 17	20 ♑ 10	08 ♐ 45	03 ♌ 27	02 ♓ 25	17 ♑ 52
Feb 25, 1980	29 ♊ 09	01 ♌ 38	04 ♏ 51	19 ♏ 14	24 ♑ 44	11 ♐ 02	01 ♌ 51	06 ♓ 49	23 ♑ 16
Mar 6, 1980	29 ♊ 54	00 ♌ 31	04 ♏ 28	20 ♏ 33	29 ♑ 09	12 ♐ 58	00 ♌ 49	11 ♓ 10	28 ♑ 35
Mar 16, 1980	01 ♋ 14	29 ♋ 53	03 ♏ 29	21 ♏ 09	03 ♒ 25	14 ♐ 30	00 ♌ 24	15 ♓ 30	03 ♒ 46
Mar 26, 1980	03 ♋ 04	29 ♋ 45	01 ♏ 56	20 ♏ 58	07 ♒ 29	15 ♐ 33	00 ♌ 38	19 ♓ 46	08 ♒ 50
Apr 5, 1980	05 ♋ 18	00 ♌ 06	29 ♎ 58	19 ♏ 59	11 ♒ 20	16 ♐ 05	01 ♌ 27	23 ♓ 59	13 ♒ 43
Apr 15, 1980	07 ♋ 54	00 ♌ 54	27 ♎ 45	18 ♏ 15	14 ♒ 56	16 ♐ 03	02 ♌ 48	28 ♓ 07	18 ♒ 25
Apr 25, 1980	10 ♋ 46	02 ♌ 07	25 ♎ 30	15 ♏ 55	18 ♒ 15	15 ♐ 26	04 ♌ 37	02 ♈ 09	22 ♒ 53
May 5, 1980	13 ♋ 53	03 ♌ 40	23 ♎ 27	13 ♏ 17	21 ♒ 13	14 ♐ 14	06 ♌ 51	06 ♈ 05	27 ♒ 06

	ATROPOS	HEKATE	LILITH	MEDUSA	MOIRA	NEMESIS	PERSEPHONE	PROSERPINA	PYTHIA
May 15, 1980	17 ♋ 12	05 ♌ 32	21 ♎ 45	10 ♏ 40	23 ♒ 49	12 ♐ 33	09 ♌ 24	09 ♈ 54	01 ♈ 01
May 25, 1980	20 ♋ 41	07 ♌ 40	20 ♎ 34	08 ♏ 26	25 ♒ 58	10 ♐ 31	12 ♌ 15	13 ♈ 33	04 ♈ 34
Jun 4, 1980	24 ♋ 18	10 ♌ 01	19 ♎ 55	06 ♏ 48	27 ♒ 37	08 ♐ 20	15 ♌ 21	17 ♈ 03	07 ♈ 41
Jun 14, 1980	28 ♋ 02	12 ♌ 34	19 ♎ 51	05 ♏ 56	28 ♒ 42	06 ♐ 13	18 ♌ 39	20 ♈ 21	10 ♓ 18
Jun 24, 1980	01 ♌ 52	15 ♌ 16	20 ♎ 18	05 ♏ 50	29 ♒ 08	04 ♐ 23	22 ♌ 07	23 ♈ 26	12 ♓ 19
Jul 4, 1980	05 ♌ 47	18 ♌ 07	21 ♎ 15	06 ♏ 30	28 ♒ 55	03 ♐ 01	25 ♌ 44	26 ♈ 15	13 ♓ 40
Jul 14, 1980	09 ♌ 46	21 ♌ 04	22 ♎ 38	07 ♏ 50	28 ♒ 01	02 ♐ 13	29 ♌ 28	28 ♈ 45	14 ♓ 13
Jul 24, 1980	13 ♌ 48	24 ♌ 06	24 ♎ 24	09 ♏ 45	26 ♒ 31	01 ♐ 60	03 ♍ 31	00 ♉ 55	13 ♓ 57
Aug 3, 1980	17 ♌ 53	27 ♌ 13	26 ♎ 29	12 ♏ 10	24 ♒ 33	02 ♐ 23	07 ♍ 13	02 ♉ 39	12 ♓ 50
Aug 13, 1980	22 ♌ 00	00 ♍ 23	28 ♎ 51	15 ♏ 01	22 ♒ 19	03 ♐ 20	11 ♍ 12	03 ♉ 55	10 ♓ 58
Aug 23, 1980	26 ♌ 09	03 ♍ 36	01 ♏ 28	18 ♏ 14	20 ♒ 06	04 ♐ 47	15 ♍ 15	04 ♉ 38	08 ♓ 34
Sep 2, 1980	00 ♍ 19	06 ♍ 49	04 ♏ 16	21 ♏ 45	18 ♒ 08	06 ♐ 41	19 ♍ 20	04 ♉ 45	05 ♓ 60
Sep 12, 1980	04 ♍ 29	10 ♍ 04	07 ♏ 15	25 ♏ 32	16 ♒ 38	08 ♐ 58	23 ♍ 27	04 ♉ 15	03 ♓ 35
Sep 22, 1980	08 ♍ 40	13 ♍ 17	10 ♏ 23	29 ♏ 33	15 ♒ 43	11 ♐ 37	27 ♍ 34	03 ♉ 07	01 ♓ 41
Oct 2, 1980	12 ♍ 49	16 ♍ 30	13 ♏ 38	03 ♐ 45	15 ♒ 27	14 ♐ 34	01 ♎ 42	01 ♉ 26	00 ♓ 30
Oct 12, 1980	16 ♍ 58	19 ♍ 39	16 ♏ 59	08 ♐ 07	15 ♒ 48	17 ♐ 46	05 ♎ 49	29 ♈ 20	00 ♓ 07
Oct 22, 1980	21 ♍ 04	22 ♍ 44	20 ♏ 25	12 ♐ 38	16 ♒ 45	21 ♐ 11	09 ♎ 55	27 ♈ 02	00 ♓ 32
Nov 1, 1980	25 ♍ 07	25 ♍ 44	23 ♏ 55	17 ♐ 16	18 ♒ 13	24 ♐ 49	13 ♎ 59	24 ♈ 48	01 ♓ 40
Nov 11, 1980	29 ♍ 06	28 ♍ 37	27 ♏ 27	22 ♐ 01	20 ♒ 08	28 ♐ 36	17 ♎ 59	22 ♈ 51	03 ♓ 26
Nov 21, 1980	02 ♎ 59	01 ♎ 21	01 ♐ 02	26 ♐ 51	22 ♒ 27	02 ♑ 32	21 ♎ 55	21 ♈ 24	05 ♓ 45
Dec 1, 1980	06 ♎ 44	03 ♎ 54	04 ♐ 37	01 ♑ 46	25 ♒ 00	06 ♑ 36	25 ♎ 44	20 ♈ 33	08 ♓ 30
Dec 11, 1980	10 ♎ 21	06 ♎ 14	08 ♐ 11	06 ♑ 46	27 ♒ 60	10 ♑ 46	29 ♎ 27	20 ♈ 20	11 ♓ 37
Dec 21, 1980	13 ♎ 45	08 ♎ 18	11 ♐ 45	11 ♑ 48	01 ♓ 08	15 ♑ 01	02 ♏ 60	20 ♈ 45	15 ♓ 02
Dec 31, 1980	16 ♎ 55	10 ♎ 02	15 ♐ 15	16 ♑ 53	04 ♓ 27	19 ♑ 20	06 ♏ 22	21 ♈ 45	18 ♓ 42
Jan 10, 1981	19 ♎ 47	11 ♎ 25	18 ♐ 43	22 ♑ 01	07 ♓ 56	23 ♑ 43	09 ♏ 30	23 ♈ 16	22 ♓ 34
Jan 20, 1981	22 ♎ 17	12 ♎ 21	22 ♐ 05	27 ♑ 10	11 ♓ 08	28 ♑ 08	12 ♏ 23	25 ♈ 13	26 ♓ 35
Jan 30, 1981	24 ♎ 19	12 ♎ 49	25 ♐ 21	02 ♒ 19	15 ♓ 13	02 ♒ 35	14 ♏ 56	27 ♈ 33	00 ♈ 44
Feb 9, 1981	25 ♎ 48	12 ♎ 46	28 ♐ 29	07 ♒ 30	18 ♓ 59	07 ♒ 03	17 ♏ 07	00 ♉ 13	04 ♈ 58
Feb 19, 1981	26 ♎ 38	12 ♎ 11	01 ♑ 27	12 ♒ 39	22 ♓ 47	11 ♒ 31	18 ♏ 52	03 ♉ 08	09 ♈ 17
Mar 1, 1981	26 ♎ 44	11 ♎ 04	04 ♑ 14	17 ♒ 49	26 ♓ 37	15 ♒ 58	20 ♏ 07	06 ♉ 16	13 ♈ 38
Mar 11, 1981	25 ♎ 60	09 ♎ 30	06 ♑ 47	22 ♒ 56	00 ♈ 28	20 ♒ 24	20 ♏ 48	09 ♉ 36	18 ♈ 02
Mar 21, 1981	24 ♎ 26	07 ♎ 37	09 ♑ 04	28 ♒ 02	04 ♈ 19	24 ♒ 47	20 ♏ 52	13 ♉ 04	22 ♈ 26
Mar 31, 1981	22 ♎ 10	05 ♎ 35	11 ♑ 01	03 ♓ 05	08 ♈ 09	29 ♒ 07	19 ♏ 19	16 ♉ 39	26 ♈ 51
Apr 10, 1981	19 ♎ 26	03 ♎ 36	12 ♑ 37	08 ♓ 05	11 ♈ 57	03 ♓ 22	19 ♏ 10	20 ♉ 21	01 ♉ 16
Apr 20, 1981	16 ♎ 35	01 ♎ 51	13 ♑ 46	13 ♓ 01	15 ♈ 42	07 ♓ 32	17 ♏ 31	24 ♉ 06	05 ♉ 39

	ATROPOS	HEKATE	LILITH	MEDUSA	MOIRA	NEMESIS	PERSEPHONE	PROSERPINA	PYTHIA
Apr 30, 1981	14 ♎ 01	00 ♎ 29	14 ♑ 26	17 ♓ 53	19 ♈ 23	11 ♓ 35	15 ♏ 32	27 ♉ 56	10 ♉ 01
May 10, 1981	12 ♎ 06	29 ♍ 37	14 ♑ 35	22 ♓ 38	23 ♈ 00	15 ♓ 30	13 ♏ 25	01 ♊ 47	14 ♉ 20
May 20, 1981	11 ♎ 01	29 ♍ 18	14 ♑ 09	27 ♓ 17	26 ♈ 32	19 ♓ 14	11 ♏ 25	05 ♊ 41	18 ♉ 37
May 30, 1981	10 ♎ 51	29 ♍ 31	13 ♑ 09	01 ♈ 47	29 ♈ 57	22 ♓ 47	09 ♏ 46	09 ♊ 35	22 ♉ 50
Jun 9, 1981	11 ♎ 35	00 ♎ 14	11 ♑ 38	06 ♈ 08	03 ♉ 14	26 ♓ 06	08 ♏ 36	13 ♊ 30	26 ♉ 60
Jun 19, 1981	13 ♎ 07	01 ♎ 26	09 ♑ 42	10 ♈ 17	06 ♉ 23	29 ♓ 07	08 ♏ 00	17 ♊ 23	01 ♊ 05
Jun 29, 1981	15 ♎ 23	03 ♎ 03	07 ♑ 30	14 ♈ 11	09 ♉ 21	01 ♈ 47	08 ♏ 01	21 ♊ 16	05 ♊ 04
Jul 9, 1981	18 ♎ 16	05 ♎ 03	05 ♑ 16	17 ♈ 48	12 ♉ 07	04 ♈ 03	08 ♏ 36	25 ♊ 07	08 ♊ 58
Jul 19, 1981	21 ♎ 40	07 ♎ 22	03 ♑ 14	21 ♈ 04	14 ♉ 39	05 ♈ 49	09 ♏ 43	28 ♊ 55	12 ♊ 44
Jul 29, 1981	25 ♎ 31	09 ♎ 57	01 ♑ 33	23 ♈ 55	16 ♉ 54	07 ♈ 02	11 ♏ 18	02 ♋ 39	16 ♊ 22
Aug 8, 1981	29 ♎ 45	12 ♎ 48	00 ♑ 24	26 ♈ 14	18 ♉ 49	07 ♈ 36	13 ♏ 18	06 ♋ 19	19 ♊ 50
Aug 18, 1981	04 ♏ 18	15 ♎ 51	29 ♐ 50	27 ♈ 57	20 ♉ 23	07 ♈ 29	15 ♏ 40	09 ♋ 53	23 ♊ 07
Aug 28, 1981	09 ♏ 08	19 ♎ 06	29 ♐ 52	28 ♈ 56	21 ♉ 30	06 ♈ 39	18 ♏ 20	13 ♋ 20	26 ♊ 11
Sep 7, 1981	14 ♏ 11	22 ♎ 30	00 ♑ 29	29 ♈ 05	22 ♉ 08	05 ♈ 10	21 ♏ 15	16 ♋ 39	28 ♊ 58
Sep 17, 1981	19 ♏ 26	26 ♎ 02	01 ♑ 38	28 ♈ 22	22 ♉ 14	03 ♈ 13	24 ♏ 23	19 ♋ 46	01 ♋ 27
Sep 27, 1981	24 ♏ 51	29 ♎ 41	03 ♑ 17	26 ♈ 47	21 ♉ 45	01 ♈ 01	27 ♏ 43	22 ♋ 42	03 ♋ 34
Oct 7, 1981	00 ♐ 25	03 ♏ 27	05 ♑ 22	24 ♈ 32	20 ♉ 42	28 ♓ 53	01 ♐ 11	25 ♋ 22	05 ♋ 14
Oct 17, 1981	06 ♐ 05	07 ♏ 18	07 ♑ 50	21 ♈ 55	19 ♉ 08	27 ♓ 07	04 ♐ 48	27 ♋ 43	06 ♋ 23
Oct 27, 1981	11 ♐ 50	11 ♏ 12	10 ♑ 38	19 ♈ 21	17 ♉ 09	25 ♓ 56	08 ♐ 30	29 ♋ 43	06 ♋ 57
Nov 6, 1981	17 ♐ 40	15 ♏ 11	13 ♑ 43	17 ♈ 15	14 ♉ 56	25 ♓ 28	12 ♐ 18	01 ♌ 16	06 ♋ 51
Nov 16, 1981	23 ♐ 32	19 ♏ 11	17 ♑ 03	15 ♈ 54	12 ♉ 42	25 ♓ 46	16 ♐ 10	02 ♌ 18	06 ♋ 03
Nov 26, 1981	29 ♐ 26	23 ♏ 13	20 ♑ 36	15 ♈ 27	10 ♉ 41	26 ♓ 45	20 ♐ 04	02 ♌ 46	04 ♋ 34
Dec 6, 1981	05 ♑ 22	27 ♏ 15	24 ♑ 20	15 ♈ 56	09 ♉ 03	28 ♓ 24	23 ♐ 60	02 ♌ 35	02 ♋ 28
Dec 16, 1981	11 ♑ 17	01 ♐ 17	28 ♑ 15	17 ♈ 15	07 ♉ 56	00 ♈ 36	27 ♐ 57	01 ♌ 45	29 ♊ 58
Dec 26, 1981	17 ♑ 11	05 ♐ 17	02 ♒ 17	19 ♈ 19	07 ♉ 24	03 ♈ 18	01 ♑ 53	00 ♌ 17	27 ♊ 18
Jan 5, 1982	23 ♑ 03	09 ♐ 16	06 ♒ 27	22 ♈ 01	07 ♉ 28	06 ♈ 23	05 ♑ 48	28 ♋ 18	24 ♊ 49
Jan 15, 1982	28 ♑ 53	13 ♐ 10	10 ♒ 44	25 ♈ 15	08 ♉ 04	09 ♈ 49	09 ♑ 41	25 ♋ 60	22 ♊ 45
Jan 25, 1982	04 ♒ 40	16 ♐ 59	15 ♒ 05	28 ♈ 54	09 ♉ 11	13 ♈ 31	13 ♑ 30	23 ♋ 38	21 ♊ 17
Feb 4, 1982	10 ♒ 23	20 ♐ 41	19 ♒ 31	02 ♉ 54	10 ♉ 45	17 ♈ 27	17 ♑ 15	21 ♋ 30	20 ♊ 32
Feb 14, 1982	16 ♒ 02	24 ♐ 14	24 ♒ 01	07 ♉ 12	12 ♉ 42	21 ♈ 33	20 ♑ 54	19 ♋ 49	20 ♊ 29
Feb 24, 1982	21 ♒ 37	27 ♐ 38	28 ♒ 33	11 ♉ 43	14 ♉ 58	25 ♈ 49	24 ♑ 26	18 ♋ 44	21 ♊ 07
Mar 6, 1982	27 ♒ 06	00 ♑ 49	03 ♓ 08	16 ♉ 26	17 ♉ 31	00 ♉ 11	27 ♑ 50	18 ♋ 19	22 ♊ 21
Mar 16, 1982	02 ♓ 29	03 ♑ 45	07 ♓ 44	21 ♉ 18	20 ♉ 18	04 ♉ 39	01 ♒ 04	18 ♋ 35	24 ♊ 05
Mar 26, 1982	07 ♓ 45	06 ♑ 23	12 ♓ 21	26 ♉ 17	23 ♉ 16	09 ♉ 11	04 ♒ 06	19 ♋ 28	26 ♊ 17
Apr 5, 1982	12 ♓ 55	08 ♑ 40	16 ♓ 58	01 ♊ 22	26 ♉ 24	13 ♉ 47	06 ♒ 54	20 ♋ 54	28 ♊ 52

	ATROPOS	HEKATE	LILITH	MEDUSA	MOIRA	NEMESIS	PERSEPHONE	PROSERPINA	PYTHIA
Apr 15, 1982	17 ♓ 57	10 ♑ 32	21 ♓ 35	06 ♊ 31	29 ♉ 39	18 ♉ 24	09 ♒ 27	22 ♋ 50	01 ♋ 45
Apr 25, 1982	22 ♓ 51	11 ♑ 56	26 ♓ 10	11 ♊ 44	03 ♊ 01	23 ♉ 02	11 ♒ 41	25 ♋ 12	04 ♋ 54
May 5, 1982	27 ♓ 36	12 ♑ 47	00 ♈ 44	16 ♊ 60	06 ♊ 28	27 ♉ 40	13 ♒ 35	27 ♋ 54	08 ♋ 17
May 15, 1982	02 ♈ 11	13 ♑ 04	05 ♈ 14	22 ♊ 17	09 ♊ 58	02 ♊ 19	15 ♒ 04	00 ♌ 55	11 ♋ 52
May 25, 1982	06 ♈ 35	12 ♑ 43	09 ♈ 41	27 ♊ 36	13 ♊ 31	06 ♊ 56	16 ♒ 07	04 ♌ 11	15 ♋ 36
Jun 4, 1982	10 ♈ 47	11 ♑ 46	14 ♈ 04	02 ♋ 55	17 ♊ 07	11 ♊ 32	16 ♒ 40	07 ♌ 40	19 ♋ 29
Jun 14, 1982	14 ♈ 44	10 ♑ 17	18 ♈ 20	08 ♋ 15	20 ♊ 43	16 ♊ 06	16 ♒ 06	11 ♌ 20	23 ♋ 28
Jun 24, 1982	18 ♈ 26	08 ♑ 27	22 ♈ 29	13 ♋ 35	24 ♊ 20	20 ♊ 37	16 ♒ 08	15 ♌ 10	27 ♋ 35
Jul 4, 1982	21 ♈ 49	06 ♑ 27	26 ♈ 28	18 ♋ 55	27 ♊ 57	25 ♊ 05	15 ♒ 04	19 ♌ 08	01 ♌ 46
Jul 14, 1982	24 ♈ 49	04 ♑ 34	00 ♉ 15	24 ♋ 13	01 ♋ 33	29 ♊ 29	13 ♒ 33	23 ♌ 12	06 ♌ 02
Jul 24, 1982	27 ♈ 25	02 ♑ 59	03 ♉ 48	29 ♋ 31	05 ♋ 06	03 ♋ 49	11 ♒ 41	27 ♌ 23	10 ♌ 22
Aug 3, 1982	29 ♈ 30	01 ♑ 55	07 ♉ 03	04 ♌ 47	08 ♋ 37	08 ♋ 50	09 ♒ 38	01 ♍ 39	14 ♌ 46
Aug 13, 1982	00 ♉ 60	01 ♑ 27	09 ♉ 56	10 ♌ 02	12 ♋ 03	12 ♋ 11	07 ♒ 38	05 ♍ 59	19 ♌ 13
Aug 23, 1982	01 ♉ 49	01 ♑ 38	12 ♉ 22	15 ♌ 14	15 ♋ 25	16 ♋ 12	05 ♒ 51	10 ♍ 22	23 ♌ 43
Sep 2, 1982	01 ♉ 52	02 ♑ 26	14 ♉ 16	20 ♌ 24	18 ♋ 40	20 ♋ 04	04 ♒ 26	14 ♍ 49	28 ♌ 15
Sep 12, 1982	01 ♉ 07	03 ♑ 48	15 ♉ 31	25 ♌ 31	21 ♋ 48	23 ♋ 46	03 ♒ 31	19 ♍ 18	02 ♍ 48
Sep 22, 1982	29 ♈ 33	05 ♑ 42	16 ♉ 03	00 ♍ 34	24 ♋ 45	27 ♋ 17	03 ♒ 07	23 ♍ 49	07 ♍ 22
Oct 2, 1982	27 ♈ 17	08 ♑ 03	15 ♉ 48	05 ♍ 34	27 ♋ 30	00 ♌ 33	03 ♒ 16	28 ♍ 21	11 ♍ 57
Oct 12, 1982	24 ♈ 34	10 ♑ 47	14 ♉ 45	10 ♍ 28	00 ♌ 01	03 ♌ 33	03 ♒ 56	02 ♎ 54	16 ♍ 32
Oct 22, 1982	21 ♈ 43	13 ♑ 51	13 ♉ 02	15 ♍ 16	02 ♌ 14	06 ♌ 13	05 ♒ 04	07 ♎ 26	21 ♍ 07
Nov 1, 1982	19 ♈ 06	17 ♑ 13	10 ♉ 53	19 ♍ 57	04 ♌ 06	08 ♌ 31	06 ♒ 31	11 ♎ 57	25 ♍ 39
Nov 11, 1982	17 ♈ 02	20 ♑ 49	08 ♉ 38	24 ♍ 30	05 ♌ 32	10 ♌ 21	08 ♒ 33	16 ♎ 27	00 ♎ 09
Nov 21, 1982	15 ♈ 43	24 ♑ 37	06 ♉ 40	28 ♍ 53	06 ♌ 28	11 ♌ 40	10 ♒ 47	20 ♎ 53	04 ♎ 34
Dec 1, 1982	15 ♈ 12	28 ♑ 36	05 ♉ 18	03 ♎ 03	06 ♌ 51	12 ♌ 24	13 ♒ 18	25 ♎ 15	08 ♎ 54
Dec 11, 1982	15 ♈ 28	02 ♒ 43	04 ♉ 43	06 ♎ 60	06 ♌ 37	12 ♌ 29	16 ♒ 02	29 ♎ 12	13 ♎ 07
Dec 21, 1982	16 ♈ 28	06 ♒ 57	04 ♉ 58	10 ♎ 39	05 ♌ 44	11 ♌ 52	18 ♒ 58	03 ♏ 43	17 ♎ 11
Dec 31, 1982	18 ♈ 05	11 ♒ 17	06 ♉ 02	13 ♎ 58	04 ♌ 15	10 ♌ 37	22 ♒ 04	07 ♏ 44	21 ♎ 03
Jan 10, 1983	20 ♈ 14	15 ♒ 41	07 ♉ 50	16 ♎ 52	02 ♌ 16	08 ♌ 47	25 ♒ 17	11 ♏ 35	24 ♎ 39
Jan 20, 1983	22 ♈ 50	20 ♒ 08	10 ♉ 16	19 ♎ 16	29 ♋ 58	06 ♌ 35	28 ♒ 37	15 ♏ 13	27 ♎ 58
Jan 30, 1983	25 ♈ 47	24 ♒ 37	13 ♉ 13	21 ♎ 06	27 ♋ 37	04 ♌ 15	02 ♓ 01	18 ♏ 35	00 ♏ 53
Feb 9, 1983	29 ♈ 02	29 ♒ 07	16 ♉ 37	22 ♎ 15	25 ♋ 29	02 ♌ 03	05 ♓ 29	21 ♏ 38	03 ♏ 21
Feb 19, 1983	02 ♉ 31	03 ♓ 37	20 ♉ 22	22 ♎ 39	23 ♋ 47	00 ♌ 14	08 ♓ 58	24 ♏ 18	05 ♏ 14
Mar 1, 1983	06 ♉ 12	08 ♓ 07	24 ♉ 24	22 ♎ 12	22 ♋ 40	28 ♋ 59	12 ♓ 29	26 ♏ 31	06 ♏ 27
Mar 11, 1983	10 ♉ 02	12 ♓ 34	28 ♉ 40	20 ♎ 56	22 ♋ 14	28 ♋ 20	16 ♓ 00	28 ♏ 13	06 ♏ 54
Mar 21, 1983	14 ♉ 00	16 ♓ 60	03 ♊ 07	18 ♎ 55	22 ♋ 27	28 ♋ 20	19 ♓ 30	29 ♏ 18	06 ♏ 30

Date	ATROPOS	HEKATE	LILITH	MEDUSA	MOIRA	NEMESIS	PERSEPHONE	PROSERPINA	PYTHIA
Mar 31, 1983	18 ♉ 03	21 ♓ 22	07 ♊ 42	16 ♎ 24	23 ♋ 19	28 ♋ 56	22 ♓ 58	29 ♏ 42	05 ♏ 16
Apr 10, 1983	22 ♉ 11	25 ♓ 40	12 ♊ 24	13 ♎ 42	24 ♋ 45	00 ♌ 04	26 ♓ 23	29 ♏ 23	03 ♏ 18
Apr 20, 1983	26 ♉ 22	29 ♓ 54	17 ♊ 11	11 ♎ 09	26 ♋ 40	01 ♌ 41	29 ♓ 44	28 ♏ 22	00 ♏ 52
Apr 30, 1983	00 ♊ 36	04 ♈ 01	22 ♊ 01	09 ♎ 07	29 ♋ 02	03 ♌ 42	02 ♈ 60	26 ♏ 44	28 ♎ 19
May 10, 1983	04 ♊ 50	08 ♈ 01	26 ♊ 54	07 ♎ 47	01 ♌ 45	06 ♌ 03	06 ♈ 09	24 ♏ 40	26 ♎ 04
May 20, 1983	09 ♊ 06	11 ♈ 54	01 ♋ 49	07 ♎ 14	04 ♌ 48	08 ♌ 41	09 ♈ 11	22 ♏ 27	24 ♎ 25
May 30, 1983	13 ♊ 21	15 ♈ 37	06 ♋ 44	07 ♎ 28	08 ♌ 08	11 ♌ 33	12 ♈ 04	20 ♏ 22	23 ♎ 36
Jun 9, 1983	17 ♊ 35	19 ♈ 09	11 ♋ 39	08 ♎ 26	11 ♌ 41	14 ♌ 37	14 ♈ 46	18 ♏ 42	23 ♎ 39
Jun 19, 1983	21 ♊ 48	22 ♈ 29	16 ♋ 34	10 ♎ 02	15 ♌ 26	17 ♌ 51	17 ♈ 16	17 ♏ 37	24 ♎ 33
Jun 29, 1983	25 ♊ 59	25 ♈ 34	21 ♋ 27	12 ♎ 11	19 ♌ 22	21 ♌ 12	19 ♈ 31	17 ♏ 14	26 ♎ 13
Jul 9, 1983	00 ♋ 08	28 ♈ 23	26 ♋ 19	14 ♎ 47	23 ♌ 27	24 ♌ 40	21 ♈ 28	17 ♏ 34	28 ♎ 33
Jul 19, 1983	04 ♋ 14	00 ♉ 52	01 ♌ 09	17 ♎ 47	27 ♌ 40	28 ♌ 14	23 ♈ 06	18 ♏ 34	01 ♏ 27
Jul 29, 1983	08 ♋ 15	02 ♉ 58	05 ♌ 56	21 ♎ 06	02 ♍ 00	01 ♍ 51	24 ♈ 20	20 ♏ 09	04 ♏ 49
Aug 8, 1983	12 ♋ 12	04 ♉ 39	10 ♌ 41	24 ♎ 41	06 ♍ 27	05 ♍ 32	25 ♈ 09	22 ♏ 16	08 ♏ 35
Aug 18, 1983	16 ♋ 02	05 ♉ 50	15 ♌ 22	28 ♎ 31	10 ♍ 59	09 ♍ 15	25 ♈ 28	24 ♏ 51	12 ♏ 41
Aug 28, 1983	19 ♋ 46	06 ♉ 29	19 ♌ 59	02 ♏ 32	15 ♍ 35	12 ♍ 59	25 ♈ 16	27 ♏ 48	17 ♏ 03
Sep 7, 1983	23 ♋ 22	06 ♉ 31	24 ♌ 31	06 ♏ 44	20 ♍ 16	16 ♍ 45	24 ♈ 32	01 ♐ 05	21 ♏ 40
Sep 17, 1983	26 ♋ 47	05 ♉ 57	28 ♌ 58	11 ♏ 04	25 ♍ 01	20 ♍ 30	23 ♈ 17	04 ♐ 38	26 ♏ 28
Sep 27, 1983	00 ♌ 01	04 ♉ 48	03 ♍ 19	15 ♏ 32	29 ♍ 48	24 ♍ 14	21 ♈ 37	08 ♐ 25	01 ♐ 26
Oct 7, 1983	03 ♌ 00	03 ♉ 09	07 ♍ 33	20 ♏ 07	04 ♎ 39	27 ♍ 57	19 ♈ 38	12 ♐ 24	06 ♐ 32
Oct 17, 1983	05 ♌ 42	01 ♉ 10	11 ♍ 39	24 ♏ 47	09 ♎ 30	01 ♎ 37	17 ♈ 32	16 ♐ 33	11 ♐ 46
Oct 27, 1983	08 ♌ 04	29 ♈ 04	15 ♍ 35	29 ♏ 32	14 ♎ 23	05 ♎ 13	15 ♈ 32	20 ♐ 49	17 ♐ 05
Nov 6, 1983	10 ♌ 01	27 ♈ 04	19 ♍ 20	04 ♐ 21	19 ♎ 16	08 ♎ 44	13 ♈ 49	25 ♐ 13	22 ♐ 29
Nov 16, 1983	11 ♌ 29	25 ♈ 24	22 ♍ 52	09 ♐ 13	24 ♎ 09	12 ♎ 09	12 ♈ 32	29 ♐ 42	27 ♐ 57
Nov 26, 1983	12 ♌ 23	24 ♈ 14	26 ♍ 09	14 ♐ 09	29 ♎ 00	15 ♎ 27	11 ♈ 47	04 ♑ 15	03 ♑ 27
Dec 6, 1983	12 ♌ 37	23 ♈ 37	29 ♍ 08	19 ♐ 06	03 ♏ 49	18 ♎ 35	11 ♈ 35	08 ♑ 52	09 ♑ 00
Dec 16, 1983	12 ♌ 09	23 ♈ 36	01 ♎ 46	24 ♐ 06	08 ♏ 35	21 ♎ 31	11 ♈ 57	13 ♑ 32	14 ♑ 35
Dec 26, 1983	10 ♌ 57	24 ♈ 10	03 ♎ 59	29 ♐ 06	13 ♏ 15	24 ♎ 13	12 ♈ 51	18 ♑ 12	20 ♑ 10
Jan 5, 1984	09 ♌ 04	25 ♈ 16	05 ♎ 44	04 ♑ 06	17 ♏ 49	26 ♎ 39	14 ♈ 13	22 ♑ 54	25 ♑ 45
Jan 15, 1984	06 ♌ 37	26 ♈ 49	06 ♎ 57	09 ♑ 07	22 ♏ 15	28 ♎ 46	16 ♈ 01	27 ♑ 35	01 ♒ 20
Jan 25, 1984	03 ♌ 53	28 ♈ 46	07 ♎ 33	14 ♑ 07	26 ♏ 30	00 ♏ 29	18 ♈ 10	02 ♒ 16	06 ♒ 53
Feb 4, 1984	01 ♌ 08	01 ♉ 03	07 ♎ 30	19 ♑ 05	00 ♐ 34	01 ♏ 47	20 ♈ 37	06 ♒ 54	12 ♒ 25
Feb 14, 1984	28 ♋ 42	03 ♉ 37	06 ♎ 46	23 ♑ 01	04 ♐ 21	02 ♏ 34	23 ♈ 20	11 ♒ 31	17 ♒ 54
Feb 24, 1984	26 ♋ 48	06 ♉ 25	05 ♎ 24	28 ♑ 54	07 ♐ 51	02 ♏ 48	26 ♈ 16	16 ♒ 03	23 ♒ 19
Mar 5, 1984	25 ♋ 35	09 ♉ 25	03 ♎ 30	03 ♒ 44	10 ♐ 58	02 ♏ 28	29 ♈ 24	20 ♒ 32	28 ♒ 41

	ATROPOS	HEKATE	LILITH	MEDUSA	MOIRA	NEMESIS	PERSEPHONE	PROSERPINA	PYTHIA
Mar 15, 1984	25♋06	12♉33	01♎15	08♒29	13♐39	01♏32	02♉40	24♒56	03♓58
Mar 25, 1984	25♋20	15♉49	28♍54	13♒09	15♐49	00♏04	06♉04	29♒13	09♓10
Apr 4, 1984	26♋11	19♉10	26♍41	17♒42	17♐23	28♎10	09♉33	03♓24	14♓17
Apr 14, 1984	27♋37	22♉35	24♍52	22♒08	18♐17	26♎01	13♉08	07♓27	19♓16
Apr 24, 1984	29♋32	26♉04	23♍33	26♒24	18♐26	23♎50	16♉46	11♓20	24♓09
May 4, 1984	01♌52	29♉34	22♍51	00♓30	17♐50	21♎49	20♉26	15♓03	28♓52
May 14, 1984	04♌32	03♊05	22♍45	04♓22	16♐32	20♎10	24♉08	18♓33	03♈27
May 24, 1984	07♌31	06♊35	23♍13	07♓58	14♐42	19♎01	27♉51	21♓49	07♈51
Jun 3, 1984	10♌44	10♊05	24♍13	11♓16	12♐34	18♎25	01♊34	24♓48	12♈02
Jun 13, 1984	14♌10	13♊33	25♍39	14♓33	10♐27	18♎23	05♊16	27♓28	16♈00
Jun 23, 1984	17♌47	16♊58	27♍30	16♓38	08♐40	18♎53	08♊57	29♓45	19♈45
Jul 3, 1984	21♌34	20♊20	29♍40	18♓33	07♐25	19♎54	12♊34	01♈36	23♈06
Jul 13, 1984	25♌29	23♊37	02♎07	19♓49	06♐51	21♎22	16♊09	02♈57	26♈09
Jul 23, 1984	29♌31	26♊48	04♎48	20♓22	06♐60	23♎14	19♊38	03♈45	28♈46
Aug 2, 1984	03♍40	29♊53	07♎42	20♓05	07♐49	25♎26	23♊02	03♈56	00♉54
Aug 12, 1984	07♍55	02♋50	10♎45	18♓59	09♐17	27♎40	26♊19	03♈27	02♉29
Aug 22, 1984	12♍15	05♋37	13♎56	17♓07	11♐17	00♏40	29♊27	02♈21	03♉25
Sep 1, 1984	16♍40	08♋13	17♎15	14♓42	13♐45	03♏38	02♋23	00♈40	03♉37
Sep 11, 1984	21♍10	10♋35	20♎39	12♓05	16♐37	06♏48	05♋07	28♓34	03♉03
Sep 21, 1984	25♍43	12♋42	24♎07	09♓39	19♐48	10♏07	07♋35	26♓18	01♉43
Oct 1, 1984	00♎20	14♋31	27♎40	07♓46	23♐16	13♏34	09♋44	24♓05	29♈42
Oct 11, 1984	05♎00	15♋58	01♏14	06♓39	26♐58	17♏09	11♋31	22♓12	27♈13
Oct 21, 1984	09♎43	17♋01	04♏50	06♓24	00♑51	20♏49	12♋51	20♓48	24♈32
Oct 31, 1984	14♎29	17♋37	08♏27	07♓03	04♑53	24♏34	13♋41	20♓02	22♈01
Nov 10, 1984	19♎16	17♋43	12♏03	08♓30	09♑03	28♏23	13♋57	19♓54	19♈56
Nov 20, 1984	24♎04	17♋17	15♏38	10♓39	13♑19	02♐15	13♋36	20♓25	18♈30
Nov 30, 1984	28♎53	16♋21	19♏11	13♓24	17♑41	06♐09	12♋38	21♓30	17♈49
Dec 10, 1984	03♏42	14♋56	22♏40	16♓41	21♑05	10♐04	11♋06	23♓06	17♈52
Dec 20, 1984	08♏30	13♋09	26♏05	20♓22	26♑32	13♐59	09♋09	25♓09	18♈37
Dec 30, 1984	13♏16	11♋09	29♏23	24♓25	01♒01	17♐53	06♋58	27♓35	19♈58
Jan 9, 1985	17♏59	09♋08	02♐34	28♓45	05♒30	21♐45	04♋48	00♈19	21♈51
Jan 19, 1985	22♏37	07♋16	05♐36	03♈20	09♒60	25♐34	02♋54	03♈20	24♈10
Jan 29, 1985	27♏09	05♋43	08♐27	08♈06	14♒28	29♐20	01♋20	06♈34	26♈51
Feb 8, 1985	01♐32	04♋36	11♐04	13♈03	18♒54	02♑59	00♋36	09♈58	29♈51
Feb 18, 1985	05♐44	03♋60	13♐26	18♈08	23♒18	06♑32	00♋22	13♈32	03♉05

	ATROPOS	HEKATE	LILITH	MEDUSA	MOIRA	NEMESIS	PERSEPHONE	PROSERPINA	PYTHIA
Feb 28, 1985	09 ♐ 42	03 ♋ 54	15 ♐ 29	23 ♈ 19	27 ♒ 38	09 ♑ 56	00 ♋ 46	17 ♈ 12	06 ♉ 31
Mar 10, 1985	13 ♐ 22	04 ♋ 18	17 ♐ 11	28 ♈ 35	01 ♓ 54	13 ♑ 10	01 ♋ 45	20 ♈ 58	10 ♉ 07
Mar 20, 1985	16 ♐ 38	05 ♋ 09	18 ♐ 28	03 ♉ 56	06 ♓ 05	16 ♑ 12	03 ♋ 15	24 ♈ 48	13 ♉ 51
Mar 30, 1985	19 ♐ 26	06 ♋ 25	19 ♐ 17	09 ♉ 20	10 ♓ 11	18 ♑ 58	05 ♋ 11	28 ♈ 41	17 ♉ 41
Apr 9, 1985	21 ♐ 39	08 ♋ 01	19 ♐ 36	14 ♉ 47	14 ♓ 09	21 ♑ 27	07 ♋ 31	02 ♉ 37	21 ♉ 35
Apr 19, 1985	23 ♐ 09	09 ♋ 56	19 ♐ 21	20 ♉ 15	17 ♓ 60	23 ♑ 35	10 ♋ 10	06 ♉ 33	25 ♉ 34
Apr 29, 1985	23 ♐ 49	12 ♋ 06	18 ♐ 33	25 ♉ 44	21 ♈ 41	25 ♑ 19	13 ♋ 05	10 ♉ 30	29 ♉ 35
May 9, 1985	23 ♐ 34	14 ♋ 29	17 ♐ 13	01 ♊ 14	25 ♈ 13	26 ♑ 34	16 ♋ 14	14 ♉ 26	03 ♊ 37
May 19, 1985	22 ♐ 23	17 ♋ 03	15 ♐ 26	06 ♊ 45	28 ♈ 32	27 ♑ 18	19 ♋ 34	18 ♉ 22	07 ♊ 41
May 29, 1985	20 ♐ 24	19 ♋ 46	13 ♐ 20	12 ♊ 15	01 ♈ 38	27 ♑ 26	23 ♋ 04	22 ♉ 15	11 ♊ 46
Jun 8, 1985	17 ♐ 56	22 ♋ 36	11 ♐ 08	17 ♊ 44	04 ♈ 29	26 ♑ 57	26 ♋ 42	26 ♉ 06	15 ♊ 50
Jun 18, 1985	15 ♐ 24	25 ♋ 32	09 ♐ 01	23 ♊ 13	07 ♈ 01	25 ♑ 51	00 ♌ 27	29 ♉ 53	19 ♊ 54
Jun 28, 1985	13 ♐ 16	28 ♋ 33	07 ♐ 12	28 ♊ 40	09 ♈ 13	24 ♑ 13	04 ♌ 17	03 ♊ 36	23 ♊ 56
Jul 8, 1985	11 ♐ 52	01 ♌ 37	05 ♐ 48	04 ♋ 05	11 ♈ 00	22 ♑ 11	08 ♌ 11	07 ♊ 14	27 ♊ 57
Jul 18, 1985	11 ♐ 23	04 ♌ 44	04 ♐ 56	09 ♋ 29	12 ♈ 21	19 ♑ 59	12 ♌ 09	10 ♊ 46	01 ♋ 54
Jul 28, 1985	11 ♐ 52	07 ♌ 52	04 ♐ 37	14 ♋ 50	13 ♈ 11	17 ♑ 52	16 ♌ 10	14 ♊ 10	05 ♋ 49
Aug 7, 1985	13 ♐ 13	11 ♌ 01	04 ♐ 52	20 ♋ 08	13 ♈ 27	16 ♑ 05	20 ♌ 12	17 ♊ 25	09 ♋ 40
Aug 17, 1985	15 ♐ 20	14 ♌ 09	05 ♐ 38	25 ♋ 23	13 ♈ 06	14 ♑ 48	24 ♌ 16	20 ♊ 29	13 ♋ 25
Aug 27, 1985	18 ♐ 05	17 ♌ 16	06 ♐ 53	00 ♌ 34	12 ♈ 10	14 ♑ 09	28 ♌ 20	23 ♊ 20	17 ♋ 05
Sep 6, 1985	21 ♐ 22	20 ♌ 21	08 ♐ 33	05 ♌ 40	10 ♈ 40	14 ♑ 10	02 ♍ 27	25 ♊ 56	20 ♋ 36
Sep 16, 1985	25 ♐ 04	23 ♌ 22	10 ♐ 36	10 ♌ 41	08 ♈ 43	14 ♑ 51	06 ♍ 27	28 ♊ 14	23 ♋ 59
Sep 26, 1985	29 ♐ 07	26 ♌ 18	12 ♐ 58	15 ♌ 35	06 ♈ 31	16 ♑ 08	10 ♍ 28	00 ♋ 10	27 ♋ 11
Oct 6, 1985	03 ♑ 26	29 ♌ 08	15 ♐ 38	20 ♌ 22	04 ♈ 16	17 ♑ 58	14 ♍ 26	01 ♋ 40	00 ♌ 10
Oct 16, 1985	07 ♑ 58	01 ♍ 51	18 ♐ 32	24 ♌ 60	02 ♈ 12	20 ♑ 17	18 ♍ 21	02 ♋ 41	02 ♌ 52
Oct 26, 1985	12 ♑ 41	04 ♍ 24	21 ♐ 39	29 ♌ 27	00 ♈ 33	23 ♑ 01	22 ♍ 10	03 ♋ 07	05 ♌ 15
Nov 5, 1985	17 ♑ 32	06 ♍ 45	24 ♐ 57	03 ♍ 41	29 ♓ 24	26 ♑ 07	25 ♍ 53	02 ♋ 58	07 ♌ 15
Nov 15, 1985	22 ♑ 29	08 ♍ 52	28 ♐ 24	07 ♍ 39	28 ♓ 52	29 ♑ 32	29 ♍ 29	02 ♋ 09	08 ♌ 46
Nov 25, 1985	27 ♑ 32	10 ♍ 42	02 ♑ 00	11 ♍ 19	28 ♓ 55	03 ♒ 13	02 ♎ 54	00 ♋ 44	09 ♌ 44
Dec 5, 1985	02 ♒ 38	12 ♍ 12	05 ♑ 42	14 ♍ 37	29 ♓ 33	07 ♒ 08	06 ♎ 07	28 ♊ 48	10 ♌ 03
Dec 15, 1985	07 ♒ 47	13 ♍ 20	09 ♑ 30	17 ♍ 28	00 ♈ 08	11 ♒ 14	09 ♎ 07	26 ♊ 32	09 ♌ 41
Dec 25, 1985	12 ♒ 58	14 ♍ 01	13 ♑ 23	19 ♍ 46	02 ♈ 17	15 ♒ 31	11 ♎ 48	24 ♊ 11	08 ♌ 34
Jan 4, 1986	18 ♒ 10	14 ♍ 14	17 ♑ 19	21 ♍ 27	04 ♈ 16	19 ♒ 56	14 ♎ 09	22 ♊ 01	06 ♌ 47
Jan 14, 1986	23 ♒ 22	13 ♍ 56	21 ♑ 18	21 ♍ 22	06 ♈ 36	24 ♒ 28	16 ♎ 06	20 ♊ 16	04 ♌ 26
Jan 24, 1986	28 ♒ 34	13 ♍ 08	25 ♑ 19	22 ♍ 28	09 ♈ 12	29 ♒ 05	17 ♎ 34	19 ♊ 05	01 ♌ 46
Feb 3, 1986	03 ♓ 45	11 ♍ 51	29 ♑ 21	21 ♍ 42	12 ♈ 02	03 ♓ 47	18 ♎ 30	18 ♊ 32	29 ♋ 07

	ATROPOS	HEKATE	LILITH	MEDUSA	MOIRA	NEMESIS	PERSEPHONE	PROSERPINA	PYTHIA
Feb 13, 1986	08 ♓ 55	10 ♍ 10	03 ♒ 23	20 ♍ 04	15 ♈ 03	08 ♓ 33	18 ♎ 50	18 ♊ 39	26 ♋ 47
Feb 23, 1986	14 ♓ 03	08 ♍ 14	07 ♒ 23	17 ♍ 46	18 ♈ 13	13 ♓ 22	18 ♎ 31	19 ♊ 22	25 ♋ 01
Mar 5, 1986	19 ♓ 09	06 ♍ 13	11 ♒ 22	15 ♍ 04	21 ♈ 31	18 ♓ 13	17 ♎ 35	20 ♊ 39	23 ♋ 58
Mar 15, 1986	24 ♓ 12	04 ♍ 18	15 ♒ 19	12 ♍ 21	24 ♈ 55	23 ♓ 04	16 ♎ 06	22 ♊ 26	23 ♋ 40
Mar 25, 1986	29 ♓ 40	02 ♍ 40	19 ♒ 11	10 ♍ 01	28 ♈ 24	27 ♓ 57	14 ♎ 11	24 ♊ 37	23 ♋ 07
Apr 4, 1986	04 ♈ 09	01 ♍ 26	22 ♒ 59	08 ♍ 19	01 ♉ 55	02 ♈ 48	12 ♎ 03	27 ♊ 10	25 ♋ 14
Apr 14, 1986	09 ♈ 02	00 ♍ 41	26 ♒ 41	07 ♍ 25	05 ♉ 29	07 ♈ 39	09 ♎ 57	00 ♋ 01	25 ♋ 56
Apr 24, 1986	13 ♈ 50	00 ♍ 27	00 ♓ 14	07 ♍ 21	09 ♉ 03	12 ♈ 28	08 ♎ 07	03 ♋ 07	26 ♋ 56
May 4, 1986	18 ♈ 33	00 ♍ 27	03 ♓ 39	08 ♍ 04	12 ♉ 38	17 ♈ 14	06 ♎ 45	06 ♋ 26	29 ♋ 09
May 14, 1986	23 ♈ 11	01 ♍ 27	06 ♓ 52	09 ♍ 27	16 ♉ 12	21 ♈ 58	05 ♎ 46	09 ♋ 56	01 ♌ 48
May 24, 1986	27 ♈ 43	02 ♍ 37	09 ♓ 52	11 ♍ 27	19 ♉ 45	26 ♈ 37	05 ♎ 46	13 ♋ 34	04 ♌ 50
Jun 3, 1986	02 ♉ 08	04 ♍ 10	12 ♓ 35	13 ♍ 56	23 ♉ 15	01 ♉ 11	06 ♎ 11	17 ♋ 20	08 ♌ 10
Jun 13, 1986	06 ♉ 26	06 ♍ 03	14 ♓ 59	16 ♍ 50	26 ♉ 42	05 ♉ 40	07 ♎ 09	21 ♋ 12	11 ♌ 47
Jun 23, 1986	10 ♉ 34	08 ♍ 14	16 ♓ 58	20 ♍ 04	00 ♊ 05	10 ♉ 02	08 ♎ 38	25 ♋ 10	15 ♌ 37
Jul 3, 1986	14 ♉ 32	10 ♍ 39	18 ♓ 30	23 ♍ 36	03 ♊ 23	14 ♉ 15	10 ♎ 33	29 ♋ 12	19 ♌ 40
Jul 13, 1986	18 ♉ 19	13 ♍ 18	19 ♓ 29	27 ♍ 22	06 ♊ 34	18 ♉ 19	12 ♎ 51	03 ♌ 18	23 ♌ 53
Jul 23, 1986	21 ♉ 52	16 ♍ 07	19 ♓ 52	01 ♎ 20	09 ♊ 38	22 ♉ 11	15 ♎ 29	07 ♌ 27	28 ♌ 15
Aug 2, 1986	25 ♉ 09	19 ♍ 06	19 ♓ 34	05 ♎ 28	12 ♊ 32	25 ♉ 49	18 ♎ 22	11 ♌ 38	02 ♍ 46
Aug 12, 1986	28 ♉ 08	22 ♍ 14	18 ♓ 34	09 ♎ 45	15 ♊ 15	29 ♉ 11	21 ♎ 30	15 ♌ 51	07 ♍ 24
Aug 22, 1986	00 ♊ 44	25 ♍ 28	16 ♓ 58	14 ♎ 09	17 ♊ 45	02 ♊ 13	24 ♎ 50	20 ♌ 05	12 ♍ 09
Sep 1, 1986	02 ♊ 53	28 ♍ 48	14 ♓ 53	18 ♎ 39	20 ♊ 00	04 ♊ 53	28 ♎ 20	24 ♌ 20	16 ♍ 59
Sep 11, 1986	04 ♊ 31	02 ♎ 12	12 ♓ 34	23 ♎ 14	21 ♊ 56	07 ♊ 05	01 ♏ 59	28 ♌ 34	21 ♍ 56
Sep 21, 1986	05 ♊ 33	05 ♎ 41	10 ♓ 21	27 ♎ 54	23 ♊ 31	08 ♊ 45	05 ♏ 44	02 ♍ 47	26 ♍ 57
Oct 1, 1986	05 ♊ 52	09 ♎ 12	08 ♓ 31	02 ♏ 38	24 ♊ 40	09 ♊ 48	09 ♏ 35	06 ♍ 58	02 ♎ 02
Oct 11, 1986	05 ♊ 26	12 ♎ 45	07 ♓ 17	07 ♏ 25	25 ♊ 20	10 ♊ 09	13 ♏ 31	11 ♍ 07	07 ♎ 11
Oct 21, 1986	04 ♊ 12	16 ♎ 19	06 ♓ 49	12 ♏ 15	25 ♊ 28	09 ♊ 47	17 ♏ 31	15 ♍ 12	12 ♎ 24
Oct 31, 1986	02 ♊ 13	19 ♎ 53	07 ♓ 07	17 ♏ 07	25 ♊ 01	08 ♊ 41	19 ♏ 33	19 ♍ 11	17 ♎ 40
Nov 10, 1986	29 ♉ 41	23 ♎ 27	08 ♓ 11	22 ♏ 01	23 ♊ 59	06 ♊ 56	25 ♏ 38	23 ♍ 05	22 ♎ 58
Nov 20, 1986	26 ♉ 51	26 ♎ 58	09 ♓ 56	26 ♏ 55	22 ♊ 25	04 ♊ 46	29 ♏ 43	26 ♍ 49	28 ♎ 17
Nov 30, 1986	24 ♉ 04	00 ♏ 25	12 ♓ 17	01 ♐ 50	20 ♊ 25	02 ♊ 27	03 ♐ 47	00 ♎ 24	03 ♏ 38
Dec 10, 1986	21 ♉ 40	03 ♏ 48	15 ♓ 11	06 ♐ 45	18 ♊ 10	00 ♊ 17	07 ♐ 51	03 ♎ 46	08 ♏ 59
Dec 20, 1986	19 ♉ 55	07 ♏ 04	18 ♓ 31	11 ♐ 39	15 ♊ 54	28 ♉ 34	11 ♐ 53	06 ♎ 52	14 ♏ 20
Dec 30, 1986	18 ♉ 55	10 ♏ 13	22 ♓ 14	16 ♐ 32	13 ♊ 50	27 ♉ 28	15 ♐ 52	09 ♎ 38	19 ♏ 40
Jan 9, 1987	18 ♉ 41	13 ♏ 11	26 ♓ 17	21 ♐ 23	12 ♊ 11	27 ♉ 05	19 ♐ 47	12 ♎ 02	24 ♏ 57
Jan 19, 1987	19 ♉ 12	15 ♏ 56	00 ♈ 36	26 ♐ 11	11 ♊ 04	27 ♉ 24	23 ♐ 36	13 ♎ 58	00 ♐ 11

	ATROPOS	HEKATE	LILITH	MEDUSA	MOIRA	NEMESIS	PERSEPHONE	PROSERPINA	PYTHIA
Jan 29, 1987	20 ♉ 22	18 ♏ 27	05 ♈ 08	00 ♑ 55	10 ♊ 33	28 ♉ 24	27 ♐ 18	15 ♎ 22	10 ♐ 25
Feb 8, 1987	22 ♉ 06	20 ♏ 39	09 ♈ 52	05 ♑ 35	10 ♊ 39	29 ♉ 59	00 ♑ 52	16 ♎ 09	15 ♐ 22
Feb 18, 1987	24 ♉ 18	22 ♏ 30	14 ♈ 46	10 ♑ 08	11 ♊ 19	02 ♊ 04	04 ♑ 16	16 ♎ 14	20 ♐ 09
Feb 28, 1987	26 ♉ 54	23 ♏ 57	19 ♈ 47	14 ♑ 35	12 ♊ 30	04 ♊ 34	07 ♑ 29	15 ♎ 37	24 ♐ 46
Mar 10, 1987	29 ♉ 48	24 ♏ 54	24 ♈ 54	18 ♑ 54	14 ♊ 09	07 ♊ 25	10 ♑ 28	14 ♎ 19	29 ♐ 08
Mar 20, 1987	02 ♊ 58	25 ♏ 21	00 ♉ 07	23 ♑ 03	16 ♊ 11	10 ♊ 33	13 ♑ 10	12 ♎ 26	03 ♑ 15
Mar 30, 1987	06 ♊ 21	25 ♏ 13	05 ♉ 23	27 ♑ 01	18 ♊ 34	13 ♊ 55	15 ♑ 35	10 ♎ 13	07 ♑ 01
Apr 9, 1987	09 ♊ 55	24 ♏ 30	10 ♉ 43	00 ≈ 44	21 ♊ 14	17 ♊ 29	17 ♑ 37	07 ♎ 55	10 ♑ 23
Apr 19, 1987	13 ♊ 36	23 ♏ 15	16 ♉ 04	04 ≈ 11	24 ♊ 09	21 ♊ 11	19 ♑ 14	05 ♎ 52	13 ♑ 16
Apr 29, 1987	17 ♊ 24	21 ♏ 33	21 ♉ 27	07 ≈ 19	27 ♊ 16	25 ♊ 01	20 ♑ 24	04 ♎ 17	15 ♑ 35
May 9, 1987	21 ♊ 17	19 ♏ 34	26 ♉ 51	10 ≈ 03	00 ♋ 34	28 ♊ 56	21 ♑ 03	03 ♎ 22	17 ♑ 14
May 19, 1987	25 ♊ 14	17 ♏ 32	02 ♊ 14	12 ≈ 19	04 ♋ 00	02 ♋ 56	21 ♑ 08	03 ♎ 09	18 ♑ 06
May 29, 1987	29 ♊ 14	15 ♏ 39	07 ♊ 37	14 ≈ 02	07 ♋ 34	06 ♋ 59	20 ♑ 38	03 ♎ 38	18 ♑ 07
Jun 8, 1987	03 ♋ 16	14 ♏ 07	12 ♊ 59	15 ≈ 07	11 ♋ 14	11 ♋ 05	19 ♑ 35	04 ♎ 46	17 ♑ 17
Jun 18, 1987	07 ♋ 20	13 ♏ 05	18 ♊ 18	15 ≈ 28	14 ♋ 59	15 ♋ 12	18 ♑ 03	06 ♎ 30	15 ♑ 39
Jun 28, 1987	11 ♋ 25	12 ♏ 37	23 ♊ 36	15 ≈ 01	18 ♋ 49	19 ♋ 19	16 ♑ 10	08 ♎ 44	13 ♑ 28
Jul 8, 1987	15 ♋ 29	12 ♏ 45	28 ♊ 50	13 ≈ 47	22 ♋ 43	23 ♋ 27	14 ♑ 07	11 ♎ 24	11 ♑ 02
Jul 18, 1987	19 ♋ 33	13 ♏ 29	04 ♋ 01	11 ≈ 51	26 ♋ 39	27 ♋ 34	12 ♑ 06	14 ♎ 26	08 ♑ 47
Jul 28, 1987	23 ♋ 36	14 ♏ 44	09 ♋ 08	09 ≈ 25	00 ♌ 38	01 ♌ 40	10 ♑ 20	17 ♎ 48	07 ♑ 01
Aug 7, 1987	27 ♋ 37	16 ♏ 29	14 ♋ 10	06 ≈ 48	04 ♌ 38	05 ♌ 45	08 ♑ 58	21 ♎ 25	06 ♑ 01
Aug 17, 1987	01 ♌ 36	18 ♏ 40	19 ♋ 07	04 ≈ 22	08 ♌ 39	09 ♌ 46	08 ♑ 06	25 ♎ 15	05 ♑ 50
Aug 27, 1987	05 ♌ 31	21 ♏ 13	23 ♋ 57	02 ≈ 28	12 ♌ 41	13 ♌ 45	07 ♑ 47	29 ♎ 18	06 ♑ 29
Sep 6, 1987	09 ♌ 22	24 ♏ 05	28 ♋ 39	01 ≈ 18	16 ♌ 42	17 ♌ 40	08 ♑ 01	03 ♏ 30	07 ♑ 54
Sep 16, 1987	13 ♌ 08	27 ♏ 15	03 ♌ 13	00 ≈ 58	20 ♌ 42	21 ♌ 29	08 ♑ 46	07 ♏ 50	09 ♑ 58
Sep 26, 1987	16 ♌ 48	00 ♐ 39	07 ♌ 37	01 ≈ 28	24 ♌ 40	25 ♌ 13	09 ♑ 59	12 ♏ 18	12 ♑ 37
Oct 6, 1987	20 ♌ 21	04 ♐ 16	11 ♌ 48	02 ≈ 45	28 ♌ 34	28 ♌ 49	11 ♑ 38	16 ♏ 52	15 ♑ 44
Oct 16, 1987	23 ♌ 43	08 ♐ 03	15 ♌ 45	04 ≈ 43	02 ♍ 24	02 ♍ 16	13 ♑ 39	21 ♏ 30	19 ♑ 14
Oct 26, 1987	26 ♌ 54	12 ♐ 00	19 ♌ 26	07 ≈ 17	06 ♍ 09	05 ♍ 33	15 ♑ 58	26 ♏ 13	23 ♑ 03
Nov 5, 1987	29 ♌ 52	16 ♐ 06	22 ♌ 47	10 ≈ 21	09 ♍ 45	08 ♍ 38	18 ♑ 34	00 ♐ 59	27 ♑ 09
Nov 15, 1987	02 ♍ 32	20 ♐ 18	25 ♌ 46	13 ≈ 51	13 ♍ 12	11 ♍ 27	21 ♑ 24	05 ♐ 48	01 ≈ 27
Nov 25, 1987	04 ♍ 51	24 ♐ 36	28 ♍ 16	17 ≈ 42	16 ♍ 27	13 ♍ 59	24 ♑ 25	10 ♐ 38	05 ≈ 56
Dec 5, 1987	06 ♍ 46	28 ♐ 58	00 ♍ 15	21 ≈ 52	19 ♍ 26	16 ♍ 10	27 ♑ 35	15 ♐ 30	10 ≈ 34
Dec 15, 1987	08 ♍ 12	03 ♑ 24	01 ♍ 38	26 ≈ 17	22 ♍ 07	17 ♍ 57	00 ≈ 54	20 ♐ 21	15 ≈ 18
Dec 25, 1987	07 ♍ 03	07 ♑ 53	02 ♍ 18	00 ♓ 56	24 ♍ 25	19 ♍ 15	04 ≈ 18	25 ♐ 12	20 ≈ 07
Jan 4, 1988	09 ♍ 14	12 ♑ 24	02 ♍ 13	05 ♓ 45	26 ♍ 16	20 ♍ 00	07 ≈ 48	00 ♑ 02	25 ≈ 00

	ATROPOS	HEKATE	LILITH	MEDUSA	MOIRA	NEMESIS	PERSEPHONE	PROSERPINA	PYTHIA
Jan 14, 1988	08 ♍ 42	16 ♑ 55	01 ♍ 23	10 ♓ 43	27 ♍ 34	20 ♍ 11	11 ♒ 20	04 ♑ 49	29 ♒ 56
Jan 24, 1988	07 ♍ 26	21 ♑ 27	29 ♌ 49	15 ♓ 50	28 ♍ 14	19 ♍ 44	14 ♒ 55	09 ♑ 33	04 ♓ 54
Feb 3, 1988	05 ♍ 28	25 ♑ 57	27 ♌ 43	21 ♓ 03	28 ♍ 13	18 ♍ 39	18 ♒ 32	14 ♑ 14	09 ♓ 52
Feb 13, 1988	02 ♍ 57	00 ♒ 26	25 ♌ 19	26 ♓ 21	27 ♍ 29	17 ♍ 02	22 ♒ 08	18 ♑ 49	14 ♓ 51
Feb 23, 1988	00 ♍ 10	04 ♒ 52	22 ♌ 56	01 ♈ 43	26 ♍ 04	14 ♍ 60	25 ♒ 43	23 ♑ 18	19 ♓ 49
Mar 4, 1988	27 ♌ 25	09 ♒ 14	20 ♌ 51	07 ♈ 09	24 ♍ 06	12 ♍ 45	29 ♒ 16	27 ♑ 40	24 ♓ 45
Mar 14, 1988	25 ♌ 01	13 ♒ 32	19 ♌ 17	12 ♈ 38	21 ♍ 49	10 ♍ 32	02 ♓ 46	01 ♒ 53	29 ♓ 40
Mar 24, 1988	23 ♌ 12	17 ♒ 43	18 ♌ 23	18 ♈ 09	19 ♍ 31	08 ♍ 34	06 ♓ 12	05 ♒ 57	04 ♈ 31
Apr 3, 1988	22 ♌ 06	21 ♒ 47	18 ♌ 11	23 ♈ 41	17 ♍ 32	07 ♍ 12	09 ♓ 33	09 ♒ 49	09 ♈ 20
Apr 13, 1988	21 ♌ 46	25 ♒ 42	18 ♌ 38	29 ♈ 14	16 ♍ 05	06 ♍ 03	12 ♓ 47	13 ♒ 27	14 ♈ 05
Apr 23, 1988	22 ♌ 10	29 ♒ 27	19 ♌ 40	04 ♉ 48	15 ♍ 21	05 ♍ 41	15 ♓ 54	16 ♒ 49	18 ♈ 46
May 3, 1988	23 ♌ 15	02 ♓ 60	21 ♌ 14	10 ♉ 21	15 ♍ 22	05 ♍ 53	18 ♓ 51	19 ♒ 53	23 ♈ 21
May 13, 1988	24 ♌ 54	06 ♓ 18	23 ♌ 13	15 ♉ 54	16 ♍ 07	06 ♍ 37	21 ♓ 38	22 ♒ 35	27 ♈ 52
May 23, 1988	27 ♌ 04	09 ♓ 19	25 ♌ 35	21 ♉ 27	17 ♍ 32	07 ♍ 50	24 ♓ 12	24 ♒ 53	02 ♉ 16
Jun 2, 1988	29 ♌ 40	12 ♓ 00	28 ♌ 14	26 ♉ 58	19 ♍ 33	09 ♍ 29	26 ♓ 32	26 ♒ 41	06 ♉ 34
Jun 12, 1988	02 ♍ 39	14 ♓ 19	01 ♍ 09	02 ♊ 27	22 ♍ 05	11 ♍ 29	28 ♓ 34	27 ♒ 57	10 ♉ 44
Jun 22, 1988	05 ♍ 57	16 ♓ 10	04 ♍ 16	07 ♊ 55	25 ♍ 03	13 ♍ 48	00 ♈ 17	28 ♒ 35	14 ♉ 45
Jul 2, 1988	09 ♍ 32	17 ♓ 31	07 ♍ 33	13 ♊ 20	28 ♍ 23	16 ♍ 23	01 ♈ 37	28 ♒ 34	18 ♉ 37
Jul 12, 1988	13 ♍ 22	18 ♓ 17	10 ♍ 58	18 ♊ 42	02 ♎ 02	19 ♍ 11	02 ♈ 32	27 ♒ 52	22 ♉ 17
Jul 22, 1988	17 ♍ 25	18 ♓ 26	14 ♍ 29	24 ♊ 00	05 ♎ 57	22 ♍ 11	02 ♈ 59	26 ♒ 32	25 ♉ 45
Aug 1, 1988	21 ♍ 39	17 ♓ 57	18 ♍ 07	29 ♊ 15	10 ♎ 06	25 ♍ 20	02 ♈ 55	24 ♒ 40	28 ♉ 58
Aug 11, 1988	26 ♍ 05	16 ♓ 51	21 ♍ 48	04 ♋ 24	14 ♎ 26	28 ♍ 37	02 ♈ 20	22 ♒ 29	01 ♊ 53
Aug 21, 1988	00 ♎ 40	15 ♓ 15	25 ♍ 33	09 ♋ 27	18 ♎ 56	02 ♎ 01	01 ♈ 13	20 ♒ 15	04 ♊ 28
Aug 31, 1988	05 ♎ 24	13 ♓ 19	29 ♍ 20	14 ♋ 24	23 ♎ 34	05 ♎ 30	29 ♓ 40	18 ♒ 13	06 ♊ 39
Sep 10, 1988	10 ♎ 16	11 ♓ 17	03 ♎ 08	19 ♋ 12	28 ♎ 20	09 ♎ 03	27 ♓ 47	16 ♒ 37	08 ♊ 22
Sep 20, 1988	15 ♎ 16	09 ♓ 24	06 ♎ 57	23 ♋ 51	03 ♏ 11	12 ♎ 41	25 ♓ 44	15 ♒ 37	09 ♊ 33
Sep 30, 1988	20 ♎ 23	07 ♓ 55	10 ♎ 47	28 ♋ 17	08 ♏ 07	16 ♎ 20	23 ♓ 43	15 ♒ 16	10 ♊ 06
Oct 10, 1988	25 ♎ 37	06 ♓ 58	14 ♎ 35	02 ♌ 30	13 ♏ 11	20 ♎ 02	21 ♓ 55	15 ♒ 35	09 ♊ 59
Oct 20, 1988	00 ♏ 58	06 ♓ 38	18 ♎ 22	06 ♌ 25	18 ♏ 11	23 ♎ 44	20 ♓ 30	16 ♒ 31	09 ♊ 08
Oct 30, 1988	06 ♏ 24	06 ♓ 56	22 ♎ 06	09 ♌ 60	23 ♏ 17	27 ♎ 26	19 ♓ 34	17 ♒ 60	07 ♊ 35
Nov 9, 1988	11 ♏ 55	07 ♓ 50	25 ♎ 47	13 ♌ 09	28 ♏ 24	01 ♏ 07	19 ♓ 10	19 ♒ 58	05 ♊ 27
Nov 19, 1988	17 ♏ 32	09 ♓ 17	29 ♎ 23	15 ♌ 48	03 ♐ 33	04 ♏ 46	19 ♓ 19	22 ♒ 21	02 ♊ 55
Nov 29, 1988	23 ♏ 12	11 ♓ 13	02 ♏ 53	17 ♌ 51	08 ♐ 41	08 ♏ 22	19 ♓ 60	25 ♒ 05	00 ♊ 16
Dec 9, 1988	28 ♏ 56	13 ♓ 33	06 ♏ 16	19 ♌ 10	13 ♐ 49	11 ♏ 53	21 ♓ 09	28 ♒ 06	27 ♉ 48
Dec 19, 1988	04 ♐ 42	16 ♓ 15	09 ♏ 31	19 ♌ 40	18 ♐ 55	15 ♏ 18	22 ♓ 44	01 ♓ 23	25 ♉ 48

	ATROPOS	HEKATE	LILITH	MEDUSA	MOIRA	NEMESIS	PERSEPHONE	PROSERPINA	PYTHIA
Dec 29, 1988	10 ♐ 30	19 ♈ 14	12 ♏ 35	19 ♌ 16	23 ♐ 59	18 ♏ 36	24 ♓ 42	04 ♓ 52	24 ♉ 25
Jan 8, 1989	16 ♐ 20	22 ♈ 27	15 ♏ 27	17 ♌ 57	28 ♐ 60	21 ♏ 45	26 ♓ 59	08 ♓ 30	23 ♉ 45
Jan 18, 1989	22 ♐ 09	25 ♓ 53	18 ♏ 04	15 ♌ 51	03 ♑ 57	24 ♏ 43	29 ♓ 32	12 ♓ 17	23 ♉ 47
Jan 28, 1989	27 ♐ 56	29 ♓ 28	20 ♏ 23	13 ♌ 13	08 ♑ 49	27 ♏ 28	02 ♈ 19	16 ♓ 10	24 ♉ 29
Feb 7, 1989	03 ♑ 42	03 ♈ 10	22 ♏ 22	10 ♌ 27	13 ♑ 35	29 ♏ 57	05 ♈ 18	20 ♓ 08	25 ♉ 45
Feb 17, 1989	09 ♑ 23	06 ♈ 59	23 ♏ 58	07 ♌ 57	18 ♑ 14	02 ♐ 06	08 ♈ 26	24 ♓ 10	27 ♉ 32
Feb 27, 1989	14 ♑ 59	10 ♈ 51	25 ♏ 07	06 ♌ 04	22 ♑ 45	03 ♐ 54	11 ♈ 42	28 ♓ 15	29 ♉ 45
Mar 9, 1989	20 ♑ 28	14 ♈ 47	25 ♏ 46	05 ♌ 00	27 ♑ 06	05 ♐ 17	15 ♈ 04	02 ♈ 21	02 ♊ 19
Mar 19, 1989	25 ♑ 49	18 ♈ 45	25 ♏ 52	04 ♌ 49	01 ♒ 17	06 ♐ 19	18 ♈ 32	06 ♈ 28	05 ♊ 11
Mar 29, 1989	00 ♒ 58	22 ♈ 44	25 ♏ 23	05 ♌ 27	05 ♒ 15	06 ♐ 31	22 ♈ 03	10 ♈ 34	08 ♊ 18
Apr 8, 1989	05 ♒ 55	26 ♈ 42	24 ♏ 21	06 ♌ 49	08 ♒ 58	06 ♐ 17	25 ♈ 36	14 ♈ 40	11 ♊ 38
Apr 18, 1989	10 ♒ 36	00 ♉ 40	22 ♏ 48	08 ♌ 49	12 ♒ 24	05 ♐ 29	29 ♈ 11	18 ♈ 43	15 ♊ 07
Apr 28, 1989	14 ♒ 58	04 ♉ 36	20 ♏ 51	11 ♌ 21	15 ♒ 31	04 ♐ 07	02 ♉ 47	22 ♈ 45	18 ♊ 45
May 8, 1989	18 ♒ 59	08 ♉ 30	18 ♏ 40	14 ♌ 19	18 ♒ 16	02 ♐ 18	06 ♉ 22	26 ♈ 43	22 ♊ 30
May 18, 1989	22 ♒ 32	12 ♉ 20	16 ♏ 28	17 ♌ 38	20 ♒ 35	00 ♐ 12	09 ♉ 56	00 ♉ 37	26 ♊ 21
May 28, 1989	25 ♒ 35	16 ♉ 06	14 ♏ 28	21 ♌ 14	22 ♒ 24	28 ♏ 01	13 ♉ 29	04 ♉ 26	00 ♋ 16
Jun 7, 1989	28 ♒ 01	19 ♉ 47	12 ♏ 48	25 ♌ 05	23 ♒ 39	25 ♏ 58	16 ♉ 58	08 ♉ 10	04 ♋ 15
Jun 17, 1989	29 ♒ 44	23 ♉ 22	11 ♏ 38	29 ♌ 08	24 ♒ 16	24 ♏ 16	20 ♉ 23	11 ♉ 46	08 ♋ 18
Jun 27, 1989	00 ♓ 38	26 ♉ 51	10 ♏ 59	03 ♍ 20	24 ♒ 14	23 ♏ 03	23 ♉ 44	15 ♉ 15	12 ♋ 22
Jul 7, 1989	00 ♓ 38	00 ♊ 11	10 ♏ 54	07 ♍ 40	23 ♒ 30	22 ♏ 24	26 ♉ 58	18 ♉ 34	16 ♋ 29
Jul 17, 1989	29 ♒ 42	03 ♊ 22	11 ♏ 21	12 ♍ 08	22 ♒ 08	22 ♏ 20	00 ♊ 04	21 ♉ 42	20 ♋ 37
Jul 27, 1989	27 ♒ 54	06 ♊ 21	12 ♏ 17	16 ♍ 41	20 ♒ 16	22 ♏ 51	03 ♊ 01	24 ♉ 37	24 ♋ 46
Aug 6, 1989	25 ♒ 28	09 ♊ 09	13 ♏ 39	21 ♍ 18	18 ♒ 04	23 ♏ 54	05 ♊ 47	27 ♉ 16	28 ♋ 55
Aug 16, 1989	22 ♒ 44	11 ♊ 41	15 ♏ 24	26 ♍ 00	15 ♒ 50	25 ♏ 25	08 ♊ 20	29 ♉ 38	03 ♌ 04
Aug 26, 1989	20 ♒ 06	13 ♊ 56	17 ♏ 29	00 ♎ 45	13 ♒ 47	27 ♏ 23	10 ♊ 36	01 ♊ 38	07 ♌ 11
Sep 5, 1989	17 ♒ 56	15 ♊ 51	19 ♏ 51	05 ♎ 33	12 ♒ 11	29 ♏ 42	12 ♊ 33	03 ♊ 13	11 ♌ 18
Sep 15, 1989	16 ♒ 31	17 ♊ 23	22 ♏ 29	10 ♎ 23	11 ♒ 09	02 ♐ 22	14 ♊ 08	04 ♊ 20	15 ♌ 21
Sep 25, 1989	15 ♒ 57	18 ♊ 28	25 ♏ 19	15 ♎ 15	10 ♒ 45	05 ♐ 18	15 ♊ 17	04 ♊ 54	19 ♌ 21
Oct 5, 1989	16 ♒ 13	19 ♊ 04	28 ♏ 21	20 ♎ 08	11 ♒ 00	08 ♐ 28	15 ♊ 56	04 ♊ 51	23 ♌ 16
Oct 15, 1989	17 ♒ 15	19 ♊ 08	01 ♐ 31	25 ♎ 02	11 ♒ 51	11 ♐ 52	16 ♊ 01	04 ♊ 12	27 ♌ 06
Oct 25, 1989	18 ♒ 58	18 ♊ 39	04 ♐ 50	29 ♎ 57	13 ♒ 14	15 ♐ 26	15 ♊ 32	02 ♊ 55	00 ♍ 48
Nov 4, 1989	21 ♒ 15	17 ♊ 36	08 ♐ 16	04 ♏ 51	15 ♒ 06	19 ♐ 10	14 ♊ 27	01 ♊ 06	04 ♍ 20
Nov 14, 1989	24 ♒ 01	16 ♊ 05	11 ♐ 46	09 ♏ 44	17 ♒ 21	23 ♐ 02	12 ♊ 51	28 ♉ 56	07 ♍ 40
Nov 24, 1989	27 ♒ 10	14 ♊ 12	15 ♐ 21	14 ♏ 37	19 ♒ 57	27 ♐ 01	10 ♊ 52	26 ♉ 36	10 ♍ 46
Dec 4, 1989	00 ♓ 39	12 ♊ 08	18 ♐ 60	19 ♏ 27	22 ♒ 50	01 ♑ 05	08 ♊ 42	24 ♉ 23	13 ♍ 33

	ATROPOS	HEKATE	LILITH	MEDUSA	MOIRA	NEMESIS	PERSEPHONE	PROSERPINA	PYTHIA
Dec 14, 1989	04 ♓ 24	10 ♊ 05	22 ♐ 40	24 ♏ 14	25 ♒ 58	05 ♑ 15	06 ♊ 35	22 ♉ 31	15 ♍ 57
Dec 24, 1989	08 ♓ 22	08 ♊ 16	26 ♐ 22	28 ♏ 58	29 ♒ 17	09 ♑ 28	04 ♊ 44	21 ♉ 10	17 ♍ 54
Jan 3, 1990	12 ♓ 30	06 ♊ 50	00 ♑ 05	03 ♐ 38	02 ♓ 45	13 ♑ 44	03 ♊ 21	20 ♉ 27	19 ♍ 18
Jan 13, 1990	16 ♓ 47	05 ♊ 53	03 ♑ 46	08 ♐ 12	06 ♓ 21	18 ♑ 03	02 ♊ 32	20 ♉ 22	20 ♍ 03
Jan 23, 1990	21 ♓ 10	05 ♊ 29	07 ♑ 25	12 ♐ 40	10 ♓ 04	22 ♑ 22	02 ♊ 21	20 ♉ 55	20 ♍ 03
Feb 2, 1990	25 ♓ 39	05 ♊ 37	11 ♑ 02	16 ♐ 59	13 ♓ 50	26 ♑ 42	02 ♊ 46	22 ♉ 01	19 ♍ 17
Feb 12, 1990	00 ♈ 12	06 ♊ 15	14 ♑ 34	21 ♐ 09	17 ♓ 40	01 ♒ 02	03 ♊ 45	23 ♉ 38	17 ♍ 43
Feb 22, 1990	04 ♈ 48	07 ♊ 21	18 ♑ 02	25 ♐ 08	21 ♓ 32	05 ♒ 20	05 ♊ 15	25 ♉ 40	15 ♍ 31
Mar 4, 1990	09 ♈ 26	08 ♊ 51	21 ♑ 22	28 ♐ 53	25 ♓ 25	09 ♒ 36	07 ♊ 11	28 ♉ 04	12 ♍ 53
Mar 14, 1990	14 ♈ 05	10 ♊ 42	24 ♑ 34	02 ♑ 22	29 ♓ 18	13 ♒ 48	09 ♊ 29	00 ♊ 47	10 ♍ 12
Mar 24, 1990	18 ♈ 44	12 ♊ 50	27 ♑ 35	05 ♑ 31	03 ♈ 10	17 ♒ 57	12 ♊ 07	03 ♊ 45	07 ♍ 48
Apr 3, 1990	23 ♈ 24	15 ♊ 13	00 ♒ 24	08 ♑ 17	07 ♈ 01	21 ♒ 60	15 ♊ 01	06 ♊ 57	05 ♍ 59
Apr 13, 1990	28 ♈ 02	17 ♊ 48	02 ♒ 59	10 ♑ 37	10 ♈ 48	25 ♒ 56	18 ♊ 09	10 ♊ 19	04 ♍ 57
Apr 23, 1990	02 ♉ 39	20 ♊ 32	05 ♒ 17	12 ♑ 24	14 ♈ 33	29 ♒ 44	21 ♊ 28	13 ♊ 50	04 ♍ 46
May 3, 1990	07 ♉ 14	23 ♊ 25	07 ♒ 13	13 ♑ 34	18 ♈ 13	03 ♓ 23	24 ♊ 56	17 ♊ 28	05 ♍ 23
May 13, 1990	11 ♉ 47	26 ♊ 25	08 ♒ 46	14 ♑ 01	21 ♈ 48	06 ♓ 32	28 ♊ 32	21 ♊ 12	06 ♍ 45
May 23, 1990	16 ♉ 16	29 ♊ 29	09 ♒ 52	13 ♑ 43	25 ♈ 17	10 ♓ 01	02 ♋ 14	25 ♊ 01	08 ♍ 46
Jun 2, 1990	20 ♉ 42	02 ♋ 37	10 ♒ 26	12 ♑ 37	28 ♈ 38	12 ♓ 57	06 ♋ 02	28 ♊ 54	11 ♍ 20
Jun 12, 1990	25 ♉ 04	05 ♋ 48	10 ♒ 25	10 ♑ 48	01 ♉ 51	15 ♓ 31	09 ♋ 53	02 ♋ 50	14 ♍ 23
Jun 22, 1990	29 ♉ 20	09 ♋ 00	09 ♒ 49	08 ♑ 26	04 ♉ 55	17 ♓ 42	13 ♋ 48	06 ♋ 48	17 ♍ 50
Jul 2, 1990	03 ♊ 31	12 ♋ 13	08 ♒ 36	05 ♑ 50	07 ♉ 46	19 ♓ 24	17 ♋ 45	10 ♋ 48	21 ♍ 38
Jul 12, 1990	07 ♊ 35	15 ♋ 26	06 ♒ 51	03 ♑ 19	10 ♉ 24	20 ♓ 34	21 ♋ 44	14 ♋ 48	25 ♍ 43
Jul 22, 1990	11 ♊ 31	18 ♋ 37	04 ♒ 44	01 ♑ 13	12 ♉ 46	21 ♓ 06	25 ♋ 43	18 ♋ 49	00 ♎ 03
Aug 1, 1990	15 ♊ 18	21 ♋ 47	02 ♒ 27	29 ♐ 46	14 ♉ 50	20 ♓ 57	29 ♋ 43	22 ♋ 50	04 ♎ 36
Aug 11, 1990	18 ♊ 53	24 ♋ 53	00 ♒ 15	29 ♐ 07	16 ♉ 32	20 ♓ 08	03 ♌ 42	26 ♋ 49	09 ♎ 21
Aug 21, 1990	22 ♊ 17	27 ♋ 55	28 ♑ 21	29 ♐ 17	17 ♉ 50	18 ♓ 40	07 ♌ 39	00 ♌ 47	14 ♎ 15
Aug 31, 1990	25 ♊ 24	00 ♌ 51	26 ♑ 59	00 ♑ 18	18 ♉ 40	16 ♓ 44	11 ♌ 34	04 ♌ 41	19 ♎ 17
Sep 10, 1990	28 ♊ 14	03 ♌ 41	26 ♑ 15	01 ♑ 48	18 ♉ 58	14 ♓ 33	15 ♌ 26	08 ♌ 32	24 ♎ 27
Sep 20, 1990	00 ♋ 42	06 ♌ 23	26 ♑ 10	04 ♑ 01	18 ♉ 43	12 ♓ 25	19 ♌ 14	12 ♌ 19	29 ♎ 44
Sep 30, 1990	02 ♋ 44	08 ♌ 54	26 ♑ 45	06 ♑ 45	17 ♉ 52	10 ♓ 37	22 ♌ 56	15 ♌ 59	05 ♏ 06
Oct 10, 1990	04 ♋ 16	11 ♌ 14	27 ♑ 58	09 ♑ 55	16 ♉ 29	09 ♓ 23	26 ♌ 31	19 ♌ 31	10 ♏ 34
Oct 20, 1990	05 ♋ 13	13 ♌ 19	29 ♑ 43	13 ♑ 27	14 ♉ 39	08 ♓ 51	29 ♌ 58	22 ♌ 53	16 ♏ 05
Oct 30, 1990	05 ♋ 28	15 ♌ 07	01 ♒ 59	17 ♑ 19	12 ♉ 30	09 ♓ 02	03 ♍ 14	26 ♌ 04	21 ♏ 41
Nov 9, 1990	04 ♋ 60	16 ♌ 36	04 ♒ 41	21 ♑ 27	10 ♉ 15	09 ♓ 57	06 ♍ 17	29 ♌ 00	27 ♏ 19
Nov 19, 1990	03 ♋ 45	17 ♌ 42	07 ♒ 45	25 ♑ 48	08 ♉ 07	11 ♓ 30	09 ♍ 05	01 ♍ 38	02 ♐ 59

	ATROPOS	HEKATE	LILITH	MEDUSA	MOIRA	NEMESIS	PERSEPHONE	PROSERPINA	PYTHIA
Nov 29, 1990	01 ♋ 48	18 ♌ 21	11 ♒ 10	00 ♒ 22	06 ♉ 19	13 ♓ 38	11 ♍ 33	03 ♍ 55	08 ♐ 42
Dec 9, 1990	29 ♊ 18	18 ♌ 33	14 ♒ 51	05 ♒ 06	04 ♉ 60	16 ♓ 16	13 ♍ 40	05 ♍ 47	14 ♐ 25
Dec 19, 1990	26 ♊ 30	18 ♌ 14	18 ♒ 46	09 ♒ 59	04 ♉ 14	19 ♓ 19	15 ♍ 21	07 ♍ 08	20 ♐ 09
Dec 29, 1990	23 ♊ 44	17 ♌ 25	22 ♒ 55	14 ♒ 59	04 ♉ 04	22 ♓ 42	16 ♍ 30	07 ♍ 54	25 ♐ 52
Jan 8, 1991	21 ♊ 20	16 ♌ 07	27 ♒ 15	20 ♒ 06	04 ♉ 29	26 ♓ 24	17 ♍ 06	08 ♍ 01	01 ♑ 35
Jan 18, 1991	19 ♊ 30	14 ♌ 26	01 ♓ 44	25 ♒ 18	05 ♉ 25	00 ♈ 19	17 ♍ 04	07 ♍ 27	07 ♑ 16
Jan 28, 1991	18 ♊ 24	12 ♌ 31	06 ♓ 21	00 ♓ 34	06 ♉ 49	04 ♈ 27	16 ♍ 24	06 ♍ 12	12 ♑ 55
Feb 7, 1991	18 ♊ 03	10 ♌ 30	11 ♓ 06	05 ♓ 54	08 ♉ 37	08 ♈ 44	15 ♍ 07	04 ♍ 22	18 ♑ 30
Feb 17, 1991	18 ♊ 25	08 ♌ 36	15 ♓ 56	11 ♓ 17	10 ♉ 46	13 ♈ 10	13 ♍ 20	02 ♍ 08	24 ♑ 02
Feb 27, 1991	19 ♊ 25	06 ♌ 59	20 ♓ 52	16 ♓ 43	13 ♉ 13	17 ♈ 41	11 ♍ 14	29 ♌ 47	29 ♑ 29
Mar 9, 1991	20 ♋ 59	05 ♌ 45	25 ♓ 52	22 ♓ 10	15 ♉ 55	22 ♈ 17	09 ♍ 04	27 ♌ 35	04 ♒ 50
Mar 19, 1991	23 ♋ 00	04 ♌ 59	00 ♈ 56	27 ♓ 38	18 ♉ 48	26 ♈ 57	07 ♍ 03	25 ♌ 48	10 ♒ 04
Mar 29, 1991	25 ♋ 25	04 ♌ 44	06 ♈ 02	03 ♈ 07	21 ♉ 52	01 ♉ 39	05 ♍ 27	24 ♌ 37	15 ♒ 11
Apr 8, 1991	28 ♋ 09	04 ♌ 57	11 ♈ 11	08 ♈ 36	25 ♉ 05	06 ♉ 23	04 ♍ 23	24 ♌ 07	20 ♒ 08
Apr 18, 1991	01 ♋ 09	05 ♌ 39	16 ♈ 21	14 ♈ 05	28 ♉ 24	11 ♉ 07	03 ♍ 55	24 ♌ 19	24 ♒ 55
Apr 28, 1991	04 ♋ 22	06 ♌ 45	21 ♈ 33	19 ♈ 33	01 ♊ 48	15 ♉ 52	04 ♍ 06	25 ♌ 11	29 ♒ 30
May 8, 1991	07 ♋ 46	08 ♌ 13	26 ♈ 44	25 ♈ 00	05 ♊ 17	20 ♉ 36	04 ♍ 51	26 ♌ 38	03 ♓ 50
May 18, 1991	11 ♋ 19	10 ♌ 01	01 ♉ 56	00 ♉ 26	08 ♊ 49	25 ♉ 19	06 ♍ 08	28 ♌ 37	07 ♓ 54
May 28, 1991	14 ♋ 60	12 ♌ 05	07 ♉ 07	05 ♉ 49	12 ♊ 23	00 ♊ 00	07 ♍ 54	01 ♍ 02	11 ♓ 38
Jun 7, 1991	18 ♋ 46	14 ♌ 23	12 ♉ 17	11 ♉ 10	15 ♊ 58	04 ♊ 39	10 ♍ 03	03 ♍ 50	14 ♓ 59
Jun 17, 1991	22 ♋ 37	16 ♌ 53	17 ♉ 24	16 ♉ 28	19 ♊ 34	09 ♊ 14	12 ♍ 34	06 ♍ 57	17 ♓ 53
Jun 27, 1991	26 ♋ 33	19 ♌ 33	22 ♉ 29	21 ♉ 42	23 ♊ 10	13 ♊ 46	15 ♍ 22	10 ♍ 21	20 ♓ 14
Jul 7, 1991	00 ♌ 31	22 ♌ 22	27 ♉ 29	26 ♉ 51	26 ♊ 45	18 ♊ 14	18 ♍ 25	13 ♍ 59	21 ♓ 59
Jul 17, 1991	04 ♌ 32	25 ♌ 18	02 ♊ 25	01 ♊ 55	00 ♋ 18	22 ♊ 37	21 ♍ 41	17 ♍ 49	23 ♓ 00
Jul 27, 1991	08 ♌ 35	28 ♌ 20	07 ♊ 15	06 ♊ 53	03 ♋ 48	26 ♊ 54	25 ♍ 07	21 ♍ 49	23 ♓ 14
Aug 6, 1991	12 ♌ 39	01 ♍ 26	11 ♊ 57	11 ♊ 43	07 ♋ 15	01 ♋ 04	28 ♍ 42	25 ♍ 58	22 ♓ 37
Aug 16, 1991	16 ♌ 44	04 ♍ 36	16 ♊ 30	16 ♊ 23	10 ♋ 37	05 ♋ 07	02 ♎ 25	00 ♎ 15	21 ♓ 12
Aug 26, 1991	20 ♌ 49	07 ♍ 49	20 ♊ 51	20 ♊ 53	13 ♋ 53	08 ♋ 60	06 ♎ 14	04 ♎ 38	19 ♓ 05
Sep 5, 1991	24 ♌ 54	11 ♍ 03	24 ♊ 59	25 ♊ 08	17 ♋ 01	12 ♋ 42	10 ♎ 09	09 ♎ 07	16 ♓ 34
Sep 15, 1991	28 ♌ 58	14 ♍ 19	28 ♊ 50	29 ♊ 08	20 ♋ 00	16 ♋ 11	14 ♎ 08	13 ♎ 41	13 ♓ 58
Sep 25, 1991	02 ♍ 59	17 ♍ 34	02 ♋ 20	02 ♋ 47	22 ♋ 48	19 ♋ 25	18 ♎ 10	18 ♎ 18	11 ♓ 41
Oct 5, 1991	06 ♍ 59	20 ♍ 47	05 ♋ 26	06 ♋ 02	25 ♋ 22	22 ♋ 21	22 ♎ 15	22 ♎ 59	09 ♓ 58
Oct 15, 1991	10 ♍ 54	23 ♍ 59	08 ♋ 02	08 ♋ 47	27 ♋ 39	24 ♋ 56	26 ♎ 21	27 ♎ 43	09 ♓ 00
Oct 25, 1991	14 ♍ 45	27 ♍ 06	10 ♋ 02	10 ♋ 55	29 ♋ 36	27 ♋ 06	00 ♏ 29	02 ♏ 29	08 ♓ 51
Nov 4, 1991	18 ♍ 30	00 ♎ 09	11 ♋ 20	12 ♋ 22	01 ♌ 09	28 ♋ 46	04 ♏ 36	07 ♏ 16	09 ♓ 27

Date	ATROPOS	HEKATE	LILITH	MEDUSA	MOIRA	NEMESIS	PERSEPHONE	PROSERPINA	PYTHIA
Nov 14, 1991	22 ♍ 07	03 ♎ 05	11 ♋ 52	12 ♋ 58	02 ♉ 14	29 ♋ 53	08 ♏ 43	12 ♏ 03	10 ♓ 45
Nov 24, 1991	25 ♍ 34	05 ♎ 53	11 ♋ 33	12 ♋ 40	02 ♉ 46	00 ♌ 22	12 ♏ 48	16 ♏ 51	12 ♓ 39
Dec 4, 1991	28 ♍ 50	08 ♎ 31	10 ♋ 25	11 ♋ 26	02 ♉ 43	00 ♌ 10	16 ♏ 49	21 ♏ 37	15 ♓ 03
Dec 14, 1991	01 ♎ 50	10 ♎ 56	08 ♋ 35	09 ♋ 22	02 ♉ 01	29 ♋ 16	20 ♏ 47	26 ♏ 22	17 ♓ 52
Dec 24, 1991	04 ♎ 33	13 ♎ 05	06 ♋ 19	06 ♋ 46	00 ♉ 42	27 ♋ 44	24 ♏ 40	01 ♐ 04	21 ♓ 01
Jan 3, 1992	06 ♎ 53	14 ♎ 57	03 ♋ 58	04 ♋ 01	28 ♋ 51	25 ♋ 42	28 ♏ 26	05 ♐ 42	24 ♓ 27
Jan 13, 1992	08 ♎ 46	16 ♎ 27	01 ♋ 52	01 ♋ 34	26 ♋ 38	23 ♋ 24	02 ♐ 04	10 ♐ 15	28 ♓ 07
Jan 23, 1992	10 ♎ 06	17 ♎ 32	00 ♋ 22	29 ♊ 45	24 ♋ 16	21 ♋ 05	05 ♐ 33	14 ♐ 43	01 ♈ 58
Feb 2, 1992	10 ♎ 49	18 ♎ 10	29 ♊ 35	28 ♊ 48	22 ♋ 02	19 ♋ 03	08 ♐ 49	19 ♐ 02	05 ♈ 57
Feb 12, 1992	10 ♎ 48	18 ♎ 17	29 ♊ 36	28 ♊ 46	20 ♋ 10	17 ♋ 30	11 ♐ 51	23 ♐ 13	10 ♈ 03
Feb 22, 1992	10 ♎ 00	17 ♎ 52	00 ♋ 23	29 ♊ 35	18 ♋ 52	16 ♋ 34	14 ♐ 37	27 ♐ 12	14 ♈ 14
Mar 3, 1992	08 ♎ 25	16 ♎ 55	01 ♋ 49	01 ♋ 10	18 ♋ 12	16 ♋ 17	17 ♐ 03	00 ♑ 58	18 ♈ 29
Mar 13, 1992	06 ♎ 08	15 ♎ 30	03 ♋ 51	03 ♋ 24	18 ♋ 12	16 ♋ 39	19 ♐ 06	04 ♑ 29	22 ♈ 47
Mar 23, 1992	03 ♎ 24	13 ♎ 42	06 ♋ 21	06 ♋ 10	18 ♋ 51	17 ♋ 35	20 ♐ 43	07 ♑ 41	27 ♈ 06
Apr 2, 1992	00 ♎ 32	11 ♎ 42	09 ♋ 15	09 ♋ 21	20 ♋ 05	19 ♋ 03	21 ♐ 51	10 ♑ 31	05 ♉ 46
Apr 12, 1992	27 ♍ 55	09 ♎ 40	12 ♋ 28	12 ♋ 55	21 ♋ 50	20 ♋ 57	22 ♐ 25	12 ♑ 56	10 ♉ 06
Apr 22, 1992	25 ♍ 51	07 ♎ 50	15 ♋ 56	16 ♋ 45	24 ♋ 02	23 ♋ 14	22 ♐ 24	14 ♑ 51	14 ♉ 24
May 2, 1992	24 ♍ 33	06 ♎ 20	19 ♋ 36	20 ♋ 50	26 ♋ 38	25 ♋ 49	21 ♐ 47	16 ♑ 12	18 ♉ 41
May 12, 1992	24 ♍ 06	05 ♎ 19	23 ♋ 27	25 ♋ 05	29 ♋ 33	28 ♋ 40	20 ♐ 36	16 ♑ 54	22 ♉ 55
May 22, 1992	24 ♍ 30	04 ♎ 49	27 ♋ 25	29 ♋ 30	02 ♌ 45	01 ♌ 43	18 ♐ 56	16 ♑ 55	27 ♉ 07
Jun 1, 1992	25 ♍ 41	04 ♎ 52	01 ♌ 28	04 ♌ 02	06 ♌ 12	04 ♌ 57	16 ♐ 58	16 ♑ 13	01 ♊ 15
Jun 11, 1992	27 ♍ 33	05 ♎ 26	05 ♌ 37	08 ♌ 41	09 ♌ 52	08 ♌ 19	14 ♐ 53	14 ♑ 52	05 ♊ 18
Jun 21, 1992	00 ♎ 02	06 ♎ 30	09 ♌ 49	13 ♌ 24	13 ♌ 42	11 ♌ 49	12 ♐ 55	13 ♑ 01	09 ♊ 17
Jul 1, 1992	03 ♎ 03	07 ♎ 60	14 ♌ 04	18 ♌ 12	17 ♌ 42	15 ♌ 24	11 ♐ 16	10 ♑ 51	13 ♊ 11
Jul 11, 1992	06 ♎ 30	09 ♎ 53	18 ♌ 20	23 ♌ 02	21 ♌ 50	19 ♌ 04	10 ♐ 05	08 ♑ 40	16 ♊ 57
Jul 21, 1992	10 ♎ 20	12 ♎ 06	22 ♌ 37	27 ♌ 55	26 ♌ 05	22 ♌ 47	09 ♐ 27	06 ♑ 45	20 ♊ 37
Jul 31, 1992	14 ♎ 31	14 ♎ 38	26 ♌ 54	02 ♍ 51	00 ♍ 27	26 ♌ 33	09 ♐ 23	05 ♑ 19	24 ♊ 07
Aug 10, 1992	18 ♎ 25	17 ♎ 25	01 ♍ 11	07 ♍ 48	04 ♍ 55	00 ♍ 20	09 ♐ 53	04 ♑ 31	27 ♊ 26
Aug 20, 1992	23 ♎ 42	20 ♎ 25	05 ♍ 28	12 ♍ 44	09 ♍ 27	04 ♍ 09	10 ♐ 54	04 ♑ 24	00 ♋ 33
Aug 30, 1992	28 ♎ 39	23 ♎ 37	09 ♍ 42	17 ♍ 44	14 ♍ 04	07 ♍ 57	12 ♐ 22	04 ♑ 56	03 ♋ 25
Sep 9, 1992	03 ♏ 47	26 ♎ 59	13 ♍ 55	22 ♍ 43	18 ♍ 45	11 ♍ 46	14 ♐ 15	06 ♑ 07	06 ♋ 00
Sep 19, 1992	09 ♏ 06	00 ♏ 30	18 ♍ 05	27 ♍ 42	23 ♍ 28	15 ♍ 32	16 ♐ 29	07 ♑ 50	08 ♋ 13
Sep 29, 1992	14 ♏ 35	04 ♏ 09	22 ♍ 15	02 ♎ 41	28 ♍ 15	19 ♍ 17	19 ♐ 01	10 ♑ 02	10 ♋ 02
Oct 9, 1992	20 ♏ 11	07 ♏ 54	26 ♍ 14	07 ♎ 39	03 ♎ 03	22 ♍ 59	21 ♐ 49	12 ♑ 39	11 ♋ 21
Oct 19, 1992	25 ♏ 54	11 ♏ 44	00 ♎ 12	12 ♎ 35	07 ♎ 53	26 ♍ 36	24 ♐ 49	15 ♑ 37	11 ♋ 55

	ATROPOS	HEKATE	LILITH	MEDUSA	MOIRA	NEMESIS	PERSEPHONE	PROSERPINA	PYTHIA
Oct 29, 1992	01 ♐ 42	15 ♏ 39	04 ♎ 03	17 ♎ 30	12 ♎ 43	00 ♎ 09	28 ♐ 00	18 ♑ 52	12 ♋ 06
Nov 8, 1992	07 ♐ 36	19 ♏ 38	07 ♎ 48	22 ♎ 22	17 ♎ 33	03 ♎ 34	01 ♑ 20	22 ♑ 23	12 ♋ 13
Nov 18, 1992	13 ♐ 32	23 ♏ 39	11 ♎ 23	27 ♎ 10	22 ♎ 22	06 ♎ 51	04 ♑ 48	26 ♑ 05	11 ♋ 38
Nov 28, 1992	19 ♐ 32	27 ♏ 42	14 ♎ 49	01 ♏ 55	27 ♎ 09	09 ♎ 59	08 ♑ 22	29 ♑ 58	10 ♋ 20
Dec 8, 1992	25 ♐ 33	01 ♐ 45	18 ♎ 02	06 ♏ 34	01 ♏ 53	12 ♎ 54	12 ♑ 00	03 ≈ 58	08 ♋ 25
Dec 18, 1992	01 ♑ 34	05 ♐ 49	21 ♎ 02	11 ♏ 08	06 ♏ 32	15 ♎ 35	15 ♑ 42	08 ≈ 06	06 ♋ 00
Dec 28, 1992	07 ♑ 36	09 ♐ 52	23 ♎ 44	15 ♏ 34	11 ♏ 05	17 ♎ 58	19 ♑ 26	12 ≈ 19	03 ♋ 21
Jan 7, 1993	13 ♑ 36	13 ♐ 52	26 ♎ 07	19 ♏ 51	15 ♏ 31	20 ♎ 01	23 ♑ 11	16 ≈ 36	00 ♋ 47
Jan 17, 1993	19 ♑ 33	17 ♐ 49	28 ♎ 07	23 ♏ 57	19 ♏ 46	21 ♎ 41	26 ♑ 57	20 ≈ 56	28 ♊ 33
Jan 27, 1993	25 ♑ 28	21 ♐ 41	29 ♎ 41	27 ♏ 51	23 ♏ 50	22 ♎ 53	00 ≈ 41	25 ≈ 18	26 ♊ 54
Feb 6, 1993	01 ≈ 18	25 ♐ 27	00 ♏ 45	01 ♐ 30	27 ♏ 39	23 ♎ 34	04 ≈ 23	29 ≈ 41	25 ♊ 55
Feb 16, 1993	07 ≈ 04	29 ♐ 05	01 ♏ 15	04 ♐ 51	01 ♐ 11	23 ♎ 42	08 ≈ 02	04 ♓ 04	25 ♊ 40
Feb 26, 1993	12 ≈ 45	02 ♑ 34	01 ♏ 09	07 ♐ 50	04 ♐ 20	23 ♎ 14	11 ≈ 37	08 ♓ 26	26 ♊ 07
Mar 8, 1993	18 ≈ 19	05 ♑ 51	00 ♏ 26	10 ♐ 23	07 ♐ 04	22 ♎ 10	15 ≈ 07	12 ♓ 47	27 ♊ 11
Mar 18, 1993	23 ≈ 46	08 ♑ 54	29 ♎ 08	12 ♐ 26	09 ♐ 18	20 ♎ 36	18 ≈ 30	17 ♓ 06	28 ♊ 47
Mar 28, 1993	29 ≈ 06	11 ♑ 41	27 ♎ 20	13 ♐ 54	10 ♐ 56	18 ♎ 37	21 ≈ 46	21 ♓ 21	00 ♋ 53
Apr 7, 1993	04 ♓ 17	14 ♑ 08	25 ♎ 12	14 ♐ 42	11 ♐ 54	16 ♎ 26	24 ≈ 52	25 ♓ 33	03 ♋ 22
Apr 17, 1993	09 ♓ 19	16 ♑ 12	22 ♎ 56	14 ♐ 44	12 ♐ 08	14 ♎ 16	27 ≈ 47	29 ♓ 40	06 ♋ 11
Apr 27, 1993	14 ♓ 10	17 ♑ 48	20 ♎ 45	13 ♐ 59	11 ♐ 36	12 ♎ 19	00 ♓ 30	03 ♈ 42	09 ♋ 17
May 7, 1993	18 ♓ 50	18 ♑ 55	18 ♎ 53	12 ♐ 28	10 ♐ 22	10 ♎ 46	02 ♓ 57	07 ♈ 37	12 ♋ 38
May 17, 1993	23 ♓ 17	19 ♑ 27	17 ♎ 27	10 ♐ 18	08 ♐ 34	09 ♎ 44	05 ♓ 08	11 ♈ 24	16 ♋ 11
May 27, 1993	27 ♓ 29	19 ♑ 22	16 ♎ 35	07 ♐ 45	06 ♐ 27	09 ♎ 16	06 ♓ 59	15 ♈ 03	19 ♋ 55
Jun 6, 1993	01 ♈ 25	18 ♑ 40	16 ♎ 16	05 ♐ 07	04 ♐ 20	09 ♎ 22	08 ♓ 28	18 ♈ 32	23 ♋ 48
Jun 16, 1993	05 ♈ 01	17 ♑ 25	16 ♎ 31	02 ♐ 46	02 ♐ 30	09 ♎ 60	09 ♓ 32	21 ♈ 50	27 ♋ 48
Jun 26, 1993	08 ♈ 16	15 ♑ 43	17 ♎ 16	00 ♐ 57	01 ♐ 13	11 ♎ 07	10 ♓ 07	24 ♈ 53	01 ♌ 56
Jul 6, 1993	11 ♈ 04	13 ♑ 46	18 ♎ 29	29 ♏ 52	00 ♐ 37	12 ♎ 40	10 ♓ 12	27 ♈ 41	06 ♌ 09
Jul 16, 1993	13 ♈ 23	11 ♑ 48	20 ♎ 06	29 ♏ 33	00 ♐ 43	14 ♎ 36	09 ♓ 45	00 ♉ 11	10 ♌ 27
Jul 26, 1993	15 ♈ 06	10 ♑ 04	22 ♎ 04	00 ♐ 01	01 ♐ 32	16 ♎ 51	08 ♓ 46	02 ♉ 18	14 ♌ 50
Aug 5, 1993	16 ♈ 25	08 ♑ 46	24 ♎ 19	01 ♐ 12	02 ♐ 58	19 ♎ 24	07 ♓ 20	04 ♉ 01	19 ♌ 17
Aug 15, 1993	16 ♈ 09	08 ♑ 02	26 ♎ 50	02 ♐ 60	04 ♐ 57	22 ♎ 10	05 ♓ 31	05 ♉ 16	23 ♌ 47
Aug 25, 1993	15 ♈ 52	07 ♑ 57	29 ♎ 34	05 ♐ 20	07 ♐ 25	25 ♎ 09	03 ♓ 31	05 ♉ 57	28 ♌ 21
Sep 4, 1993	14 ♈ 29	08 ♑ 29	02 ♏ 29	08 ♐ 08	10 ♐ 18	28 ♎ 19	01 ♓ 29	06 ♉ 03	02 ♍ 57
Sep 14, 1993	12 ♈ 22	09 ♑ 38	05 ♏ 34	11 ♐ 19	13 ♐ 30	01 ♏ 37	29 ≈ 37	05 ♉ 30	07 ♍ 35
Sep 24, 1993	09 ♈ 43	11 ♑ 19	08 ♏ 46	14 ♐ 51	16 ♐ 59	05 ♏ 03	28 ≈ 07	04 ♉ 21	12 ♍ 15
Oct 4, 1993	06 ♈ 52	13 ♑ 30	12 ♏ 05	18 ♐ 39	20 ♐ 42	08 ♏ 36	27 ≈ 03	02 ♉ 38	16 ♍ 56

	ATROPOS	HEKATE	LILITH	MEDUSA	MOIRA	NEMESIS	PERSEPHONE	PROSERPINA	PYTHIA
Oct 14, 1993	04♈12	16♑05	15♏28	22♐43	24♐37	12♏14	26♒31	00♉31	21♍38
Oct 24, 1993	02♈03	19♑02	18♏57	26♐59	28♐41	15♏56	26♒32	28♈13	26♍19
Nov 3, 1993	00♈37	22♑17	22♏28	01♑26	02♑28	19♏42	27♒04	25♈59	00♎59
Nov 13, 1993	29♓59	25♑48	26♏01	06♑02	07♑11	23♏30	28♒05	24♈04	05♎37
Nov 23, 1993	00♈11	29♑32	29♏35	10♑46	11♑34	27♏20	29♒32	22♈39	10♎13
Dec 3, 1993	01♈06	03♒27	03♐10	15♑37	16♑01	01♐10	01♓22	21♈50	14♎43
Dec 13, 1993	02♈41	07♒31	06♐43	20♑35	20♑31	04♐60	03♓32	21♈39	19♎08
Dec 23, 1993	04♈49	11♒42	10♐15	25♑37	25♑02	08♐48	05♓59	22♈07	23♎25
Jan 2, 1994	07♈24	15♒60	13♐43	00♒44	29♑34	12♐34	08♓40	23♈08	27♎32
Jan 12, 1994	10♈23	20♒22	17♐07	05♒55	04♒07	16♐17	11♓34	24♈41	01♏27
Jan 22, 1994	13♈40	24♒47	20♐25	11♒08	08♒38	19♐54	14♓37	26♈40	05♏06
Feb 1, 1994	17♈12	29♒15	23♐36	16♒24	13♒08	23♐25	17♓49	29♈01	08♏25
Feb 11, 1994	20♈56	03♓44	26♐38	21♒41	17♒35	26♐48	21♓07	01♉42	11♏19
Feb 21, 1994	24♈51	08♓14	29♐29	26♒60	21♒59	00♑01	24♓30	04♉38	13♏44
Mar 3, 1994	28♈53	12♓43	02♑08	02♓19	26♒20	03♑03	27♓57	07♉47	15♏34
Mar 13, 1994	03♉01	17♓10	04♑30	07♓38	00♓35	05♑51	01♈27	11♉08	16♏42
Mar 23, 1994	07♉15	21♓36	06♑35	12♓57	04♓45	08♑22	04♈58	14♉37	17♏02
Apr 2, 1994	11♉31	25♓59	08♑19	18♓15	08♓48	10♑33	08♈29	18♉13	16♏31
Apr 12, 1994	15♉50	00♈17	09♑38	23♓32	12♓44	12♑21	12♈01	21♉55	15♏09
Apr 22, 1994	20♉11	04♈32	10♑30	28♓46	16♓31	13♑43	15♈30	25♉41	13♏07
May 2, 1994	24♉33	08♈40	10♑51	03♈59	20♈08	14♑34	18♈58	29♉31	10♏40
May 12, 1994	28♉54	12♈42	10♑39	09♈08	23♈34	14♑52	22♈22	03♊24	08♏11
May 22, 1994	03♊15	16♈37	09♑52	14♈13	26♈46	14♑33	25♈42	07♊18	06♏04
Jun 1, 1994	07♊35	20♈22	08♑33	19♈14	29♈44	13♑38	28♈56	11♊12	04♏38
Jun 11, 1994	11♊53	23♈58	06♑46	24♈09	02♉25	12♑10	02♉04	15♊08	04♏01
Jun 21, 1994	16♊08	27♈22	04♑39	28♈58	04♉45	10♑15	05♉03	19♊02	04♏18
Jul 1, 1994	20♊20	00♉32	02♑25	03♉39	06♉43	08♑06	07♉53	22♊55	05♏24
Jul 11, 1994	24♊29	03♉26	00♑17	08♉11	08♉14	05♑55	10♉31	26♊47	07♏14
Jul 21, 1994	28♊33	06♉02	28♐27	12♉37	09♉16	03♑58	12♉56	00♋36	09♏43
Jul 31, 1994	02♋32	08♉16	27♐27	16♉37	09♉45	02♑27	15♉04	04♋21	12♏45
Aug 10, 1994	06♋24	10♉06	26♐14	20♉26	09♉37	01♑30	16♉54	08♋01	16♏13
Aug 20, 1994	10♋09	11♉28	25♐60	23♉54	08♉53	01♑11	18♉21	11♋36	20♏05
Aug 30, 1994	13♋45	12♉18	26♐21	26♉58	07♉35	01♑30	19♉22	15♋04	24♏15
Sep 9, 1994	17♋10	12♉33	27♐15	29♉30	05♉46	02♑27	19♉55	18♋23	28♏41
Sep 19, 1994	20♋22	12♉12	28♐40	01♊26	03♉38	03♑56	19♉56	21♋32	03♐20

	ATROPOS	HEKATE	LILITH	MEDUSA	MOIRA	NEMESIS	PERSEPHONE	PROSERPINA	PYTHIA
Sep 29, 1994	23♋18	11♉15	00♑32	02♊38	01♈22	05♑56	19♉23	24♋28	08♐10
Oct 9, 1994	25♋57	09♉45	02♑47	02♊59	29♈13	08♑22	18♉17	27♋09	13♐10
Oct 19, 1994	28♋13	07♉52	05♑24	02♊26	27♓25	11♑11	16♉42	29♋11	18♐17
Oct 29, 1994	00♌04	05♉46	08♑18	00♊59	26♓05	14♑19	14♉45	01♌31	23♐31
Nov 8, 1994	01♌23	03♉42	11♑29	28♉47	25♓21	17♑45	12♉37	03♌05	28♐50
Nov 18, 1994	02♌07	01♉54	14♑53	26♉09	25♓13	21♑25	10♉32	04♌08	04♑13
Nov 28, 1994	02♌10	00♉31	18♑29	23♉30	25♓39	25♑18	08♉42	04♌36	09♑40
Dec 8, 1994	01♌29	29♈42	22♑15	21♉17	26♓38	29♑22	07♉17	04♌25	15♑09
Dec 18, 1994	00♌04	29♈28	26♑10	19♉48	28♓06	03♒35	06♉26	03♌35	20♑39
Dec 28, 1994	27♋60	29♈49	00♒12	19♉13	29♓59	07♒56	06♉10	02♌07	26♑11
Jan 7, 1995	25♋26	00♉42	04♒22	19♉34	02♈12	12♒23	06♉29	00♌08	01♒43
Jan 17, 1995	22♋38	02♉05	08♒36	20♉46	04♈44	16♒56	07♉22	27♋50	07♒14
Jan 27, 1995	19♋57	03♉53	12♒56	22♉44	07♈30	21♒33	08♉44	25♋29	12♒44
Feb 6, 1995	17♋39	06♉02	17♒19	25♉19	10♈29	26♒14	10♉33	23♋20	18♒12
Feb 16, 1995	15♋58	08♉30	21♒45	28♉25	13♈37	00♓58	12♉45	21♋40	23♒38
Feb 26, 1995	14♋58	11♉12	26♒13	01♊57	16♈54	05♓43	15♉16	20♋35	29♒00
Mar 8, 1995	14♋43	14♉06	00♓43	05♊49	20♈17	10♓30	18♉04	20♋11	04♓19
Mar 18, 1995	15♋09	17♉10	05♓13	09♊58	23♈44	15♓16	21♉05	20♋27	09♓34
Mar 28, 1995	16♋11	20♉22	09♓44	14♊20	27♈16	20♓02	24♉18	21♋21	14♓43
Apr 7, 1995	17♋46	23♉40	14♓14	18♊54	00♉49	24♓48	27♉40	22♋48	19♓47
Apr 17, 1995	19♋49	27♉03	18♓43	23♊35	04♉25	29♓31	01♊10	24♋45	24♓45
Apr 27, 1995	22♋14	00♊29	23♓10	28♊24	08♉00	04♈11	04♊47	27♋07	29♓35
May 7, 1995	24♋59	03♊57	27♓34	03♋18	11♉35	08♈48	08♊28	29♋50	04♈18
May 17, 1995	27♋59	07♊26	01♈54	08♋17	15♉09	13♈21	12♊14	02♌51	08♈51
May 27, 1995	01♌14	10♊56	06♈09	13♋18	18♉41	17♈48	16♊02	06♌08	13♈15
Jun 6, 1995	04♌40	14♊25	10♈18	18♋23	22♉10	22♈09	19♊53	09♌37	17♈27
Jun 16, 1995	08♌16	17♊52	14♈19	23♋29	25♉35	26♈22	23♊45	13♌18	21♈27
Jun 26, 1995	12♌00	21♊17	18♈11	28♋37	28♉55	00♉26	27♊38	17♌08	25♈11
Jul 6, 1995	15♌52	24♊38	21♈50	03♌46	02♊09	04♉19	01♋30	21♌07	28♈39
Jul 16, 1995	19♌50	27♊56	25♈15	08♌55	05♊15	07♉58	05♋21	25♌12	01♉46
Jul 26, 1995	23♌53	01♋08	28♈22	14♌04	08♊13	11♉22	09♋11	29♌23	04♉31
Aug 5, 1995	28♌01	04♋14	01♉06	19♌13	11♊01	14♉26	12♋58	03♍39	06♉48
Aug 15, 1995	02♍13	07♋13	03♉24	24♌22	13♊36	17♉08	16♋41	07♍59	08♉34
Aug 25, 1995	06♍13	10♋02	05♉09	29♌30	15♊57	19♉23	20♋20	12♍23	09♉44
Sep 4, 1995	10♍48	12♋41	06♉16	04♍36	17♊60	21♉07	23♋52	16♍51	10♉13

	ATROPOS	HEKATE	LILITH	MEDUSA	MOIRA	NEMESIS	PERSEPHONE	PROSERPINA	PYTHIA
Sep 14, 1995	15 ♍ 10	15 ♋ 07	06 ♉ 40	09 ♍ 41	19 ♊ 43	22 ♉ 14	27 ♋ 17	21 ♍ 20	09 ♉ 57
Sep 24, 1995	19 ♍ 34	17 ♋ 18	06 ♉ 17	14 ♍ 44	21 ♊ 02	22 ♉ 39	00 ♌ 33	25 ♍ 51	08 ♉ 55
Oct 4, 1995	24 ♍ 00	19 ♋ 11	05 ♉ 09	19 ♍ 41	21 ♊ 13	22 ♉ 21	03 ♌ 37	00 ♎ 24	07 ♉ 09
Oct 14, 1995	28 ♍ 27	20 ♋ 45	03 ♉ 22	24 ♍ 41	22 ♊ 13	21 ♉ 19	06 ♌ 28	04 ♎ 57	04 ♉ 50
Oct 24, 1995	02 ♎ 56	21 ♋ 55	01 ♉ 11	29 ♍ 34	21 ♊ 60	19 ♉ 38	09 ♌ 02	09 ♎ 29	02 ♉ 12
Nov 3, 1995	07 ♎ 24	22 ♋ 38	28 ♈ 56	04 ♎ 23	21 ♊ 11	17 ♉ 31	11 ♌ 16	14 ♎ 01	29 ♈ 34
Nov 13, 1995	11 ♎ 51	22 ♋ 52	27 ♈ 01	09 ♎ 06	19 ♊ 49	15 ♉ 13	13 ♌ 07	18 ♎ 30	27 ♈ 16
Nov 23, 1995	16 ♎ 18	22 ♋ 35	25 ♈ 42	13 ♎ 43	17 ♊ 58	13 ♉ 05	14 ♌ 30	22 ♎ 57	25 ♈ 31
Dec 3, 1995	20 ♎ 42	21 ♋ 47	25 ♈ 10	18 ♎ 11	15 ♊ 48	11 ♉ 24	15 ♌ 20	27 ♎ 19	24 ♈ 29
Dec 13, 1995	25 ♎ 02	20 ♋ 29	25 ♈ 29	22 ♎ 30	13 ♊ 31	10 ♉ 20	15 ♌ 36	01 ♏ 36	24 ♈ 11
Dec 23, 1995	29 ♎ 18	18 ♋ 48	26 ♈ 37	26 ♎ 38	11 ♊ 21	09 ♉ 60	15 ♌ 13	05 ♏ 47	24 ♈ 37
Jan 2, 1996	03 ♏ 27	16 ♋ 51	28 ♈ 28	00 ♏ 32	09 ♊ 31	10 ♉ 23	14 ♌ 12	09 ♏ 48	25 ♈ 40
Jan 12, 1996	07 ♏ 27	14 ♋ 48	00 ♉ 58	04 ♏ 09	08 ♊ 11	11 ♉ 28	12 ♌ 38	13 ♏ 39	27 ♈ 18
Jan 22, 1996	11 ♏ 17	12 ♋ 53	03 ♉ 59	07 ♏ 27	07 ♊ 26	13 ♉ 08	10 ♌ 38	17 ♏ 17	29 ♈ 24
Feb 1, 1996	14 ♏ 53	11 ♋ 14	07 ♉ 26	10 ♏ 22	07 ♊ 17	15 ♉ 20	08 ♌ 26	20 ♏ 39	01 ♉ 54
Feb 11, 1996	18 ♏ 12	09 ♋ 60	11 ♉ 15	12 ♏ 49	07 ♊ 44	17 ♉ 57	06 ♌ 18	23 ♏ 42	04 ♉ 43
Feb 21, 1996	21 ♏ 09	09 ♋ 15	15 ♉ 22	14 ♏ 43	08 ♊ 43	20 ♉ 56	04 ♌ 27	26 ♏ 22	07 ♉ 49
Mar 2, 1996	23 ♏ 38	09 ♋ 00	19 ♉ 43	15 ♏ 59	10 ♊ 11	24 ♉ 13	03 ♌ 06	28 ♏ 35	11 ♉ 08
Mar 12, 1996	25 ♏ 35	09 ♋ 16	24 ♉ 14	16 ♏ 31	12 ♊ 04	27 ♉ 44	02 ♌ 20	00 ♐ 16	14 ♉ 37
Mar 22, 1996	26 ♏ 52	09 ♋ 59	28 ♉ 55	16 ♏ 16	14 ♊ 18	01 ♊ 26	02 ♌ 12	01 ♐ 21	18 ♉ 16
Apr 1, 1996	27 ♏ 22	11 ♋ 08	03 ♊ 33	15 ♏ 12	16 ♊ 51	05 ♊ 18	02 ♌ 42	01 ♐ 46	22 ♉ 01
Apr 11, 1996	27 ♏ 00	12 ♋ 38	08 ♊ 35	13 ♏ 24	19 ♊ 39	09 ♊ 17	03 ♌ 45	01 ♐ 28	25 ♉ 51
Apr 21, 1996	25 ♏ 45	14 ♋ 27	13 ♊ 31	11 ♏ 01	22 ♊ 40	13 ♊ 22	05 ♌ 18	00 ♐ 27	29 ♉ 46
May 1, 1996	23 ♏ 42	16 ♋ 33	18 ♊ 31	08 ♏ 22	25 ♊ 53	17 ♊ 31	07 ♌ 18	28 ♏ 49	03 ♊ 45
May 11, 1996	21 ♏ 08	18 ♋ 52	23 ♊ 31	05 ♏ 46	29 ♊ 14	21 ♊ 43	09 ♌ 40	26 ♏ 46	07 ♊ 45
May 21, 1996	18 ♏ 26	21 ♋ 22	28 ♊ 33	03 ♏ 34	02 ♋ 44	25 ♊ 58	12 ♌ 21	24 ♏ 33	11 ♊ 47
May 31, 1996	16 ♏ 04	24 ♋ 02	03 ♋ 35	02 ♏ 01	06 ♋ 20	00 ♋ 14	15 ♌ 18	22 ♏ 27	15 ♊ 51
Jun 10, 1996	14 ♏ 23	26 ♋ 50	08 ♋ 36	01 ♏ 13	10 ♋ 02	04 ♋ 31	18 ♌ 28	20 ♏ 46	19 ♊ 54
Jun 20, 1996	13 ♏ 38	29 ♋ 44	13 ♋ 36	01 ♏ 13	13 ♋ 48	08 ♋ 48	21 ♌ 49	19 ♏ 41	23 ♊ 57
Jun 30, 1996	13 ♏ 52	02 ♌ 43	18 ♋ 35	01 ♏ 56	17 ♋ 38	13 ♋ 04	25 ♌ 20	19 ♏ 17	27 ♊ 60
Jul 10, 1996	15 ♏ 01	05 ♌ 46	23 ♋ 31	03 ♏ 20	21 ♋ 31	17 ♋ 19	28 ♌ 59	19 ♏ 35	02 ♋ 00
Jul 20, 1996	16 ♏ 60	08 ♌ 52	28 ♋ 26	05 ♏ 18	25 ♋ 26	21 ♋ 32	02 ♍ 45	20 ♏ 33	05 ♋ 59
Jul 30, 1996	19 ♏ 41	11 ♌ 60	03 ♌ 17	07 ♏ 46	29 ♋ 23	25 ♋ 43	06 ♍ 36	22 ♏ 07	09 ♋ 55
Aug 9, 1996	22 ♏ 58	15 ♌ 08	08 ♌ 05	10 ♏ 39	03 ♌ 21	29 ♋ 51	10 ♍ 32	24 ♏ 13	13 ♋ 48
Aug 19, 1996	26 ♏ 44	18 ♌ 17	12 ♌ 49	13 ♏ 53	07 ♌ 19	03 ♌ 55	14 ♍ 31	26 ♏ 45	17 ♋ 36

Date	ATROPOS	HEKATE	LILITH	MEDUSA	MOIRA	NEMESIS	PERSEPHONE	PROSERPINA	PYTHIA
Aug 29, 1996	00 ♐ 53	21 ♌ 24	17 ♌ 28	17 ♏ 25	11 ♌ 17	07 ♌ 54	18 ♍ 34	29 ♏ 41	21 ♋ 19
Sep 8, 1996	05 ♐ 22	24 ♌ 30	22 ♌ 02	21 ♏ 13	15 ♌ 14	11 ♌ 48	22 ♍ 38	02 ♐ 57	24 ♋ 54
Sep 18, 1996	10 ♐ 07	27 ♌ 32	26 ♌ 30	25 ♏ 14	19 ♌ 09	15 ♌ 35	26 ♍ 44	06 ♐ 29	28 ♋ 22
Sep 28, 1996	15 ♐ 03	00 ♍ 30	00 ♍ 52	29 ♏ 26	23 ♌ 00	19 ♌ 15	00 ♎ 50	10 ♐ 15	01 ♌ 40
Oct 8, 1996	19 ♐ 10	03 ♍ 22	05 ♍ 06	03 ♐ 48	26 ♌ 48	22 ♌ 45	04 ♎ 56	14 ♐ 12	04 ♌ 45
Oct 18, 1996	25 ♐ 24	06 ♍ 07	09 ♍ 10	08 ♐ 18	00 ♍ 29	26 ♌ 03	09 ♎ 01	18 ♐ 20	07 ♌ 35
Oct 28, 1996	00 ♑ 45	08 ♍ 43	13 ♍ 46	12 ♐ 55	04 ♍ 04	29 ♌ 09	13 ♎ 04	22 ♐ 36	10 ♌ 08
Nov 7, 1996	06 ♑ 10	11 ♍ 07	16 ♍ 46	17 ♐ 39	07 ♍ 29	01 ♍ 58	17 ♎ 04	26 ♐ 58	12 ♌ 18
Nov 17, 1996	11 ♑ 38	13 ♍ 18	20 ♍ 13	22 ♐ 29	10 ♍ 42	04 ♍ 29	20 ♎ 51	01 ♑ 26	14 ♌ 02
Nov 27, 1996	17 ♑ 08	15 ♍ 13	23 ♍ 23	27 ♐ 23	13 ♍ 40	06 ♍ 38	24 ♎ 51	05 ♑ 59	15 ♌ 14
Dec 7, 1996	22 ♑ 40	16 ♍ 04	26 ♍ 13	02 ♑ 21	16 ♍ 20	08 ♍ 21	28 ♎ 35	10 ♑ 34	15 ♌ 50
Dec 17, 1996	28 ♑ 12	18 ♍ 04	28 ♍ 40	07 ♑ 22	18 ♍ 39	09 ♍ 34	02 ♏ 11	15 ♑ 13	15 ♌ 44
Dec 27, 1996	03 ♒ 43	18 ♍ 53	00 ♎ 40	12 ♑ 26	20 ♍ 30	10 ♍ 13	05 ♏ 36	19 ♑ 53	14 ♌ 55
Jan 6, 1997	09 ♒ 14	19 ♍ 14	02 ♎ 08	17 ♑ 31	21 ♍ 51	10 ♍ 15	08 ♏ 50	24 ♑ 33	13 ♌ 22
Jan 16, 1997	14 ♒ 43	19 ♍ 04	03 ♎ 01	22 ♑ 39	22 ♍ 34	09 ♍ 39	11 ♏ 48	29 ♑ 14	11 ♌ 11
Jan 26, 1997	20 ♒ 11	18 ♍ 24	03 ♎ 15	27 ♑ 47	22 ♍ 37	08 ♍ 25	14 ♏ 29	03 ♒ 53	08 ♌ 36
Feb 5, 1997	25 ♒ 35	17 ♍ 14	02 ♎ 48	02 ♒ 55	21 ♍ 58	06 ♍ 39	16 ♏ 48	08 ♒ 31	05 ♌ 54
Feb 15, 1997	00 ♓ 57	15 ♍ 39	01 ♎ 40	08 ♒ 03	20 ♍ 36	04 ♍ 31	18 ♏ 44	13 ♒ 06	03 ♌ 25
Feb 25, 1997	06 ♓ 16	13 ♍ 46	29 ♍ 57	13 ♒ 10	18 ♍ 41	02 ♍ 14	20 ♏ 11	17 ♒ 38	01 ♌ 26
Mar 7, 1997	11 ♓ 31	11 ♍ 45	27 ♍ 47	18 ♒ 31	16 ♍ 25	00 ♍ 03	21 ♏ 06	22 ♒ 05	00 ♌ 07
Mar 17, 1997	16 ♓ 41	09 ♍ 48	25 ♍ 26	23 ♒ 19	14 ♍ 05	28 ♌ 12	21 ♏ 25	26 ♒ 28	29 ♋ 34
Mar 27, 1997	21 ♓ 48	08 ♍ 04	23 ♍ 08	28 ♒ 19	12 ♍ 01	26 ♌ 50	21 ♏ 08	00 ♓ 44	29 ♋ 47
Apr 6, 1997	26 ♓ 49	06 ♍ 43	21 ♍ 08	03 ♓ 17	10 ♍ 28	26 ♌ 02	20 ♏ 14	04 ♓ 54	00 ♌ 42
Apr 16, 1997	01 ♈ 45	05 ♍ 50	19 ♍ 38	08 ♓ 10	09 ♍ 35	25 ♌ 51	18 ♏ 47	08 ♓ 55	02 ♌ 15
Apr 26, 1997	06 ♈ 35	05 ♍ 28	18 ♍ 43	12 ♓ 57	09 ♍ 27	26 ♌ 15	16 ♏ 55	12 ♓ 48	04 ♌ 21
May 6, 1997	11 ♈ 18	05 ♍ 36	18 ♍ 25	17 ♓ 39	10 ♍ 03	27 ♌ 10	14 ♏ 50	16 ♓ 29	06 ♌ 54
May 16, 1997	15 ♈ 55	06 ♍ 13	18 ♍ 43	22 ♓ 13	11 ♍ 20	28 ♌ 34	12 ♏ 45	19 ♓ 58	09 ♌ 52
May 26, 1997	20 ♈ 23	07 ♍ 16	19 ♍ 34	26 ♓ 39	13 ♍ 13	00 ♍ 22	10 ♏ 56	23 ♓ 12	13 ♌ 09
Jun 5, 1997	24 ♈ 43	08 ♍ 43	20 ♍ 53	00 ♈ 54	15 ♍ 38	02 ♍ 31	09 ♏ 32	26 ♓ 09	16 ♌ 44
Jun 15, 1997	28 ♈ 53	10 ♍ 31	22 ♍ 38	04 ♈ 57	18 ♍ 29	04 ♍ 57	08 ♏ 40	28 ♓ 47	20 ♌ 34
Jun 25, 1997	02 ♉ 51	12 ♍ 37	24 ♍ 43	08 ♈ 44	21 ♍ 44	07 ♍ 39	08 ♏ 24	01 ♈ 03	24 ♌ 37
Jul 5, 1997	06 ♉ 36	14 ♍ 59	27 ♍ 07	12 ♈ 13	25 ♍ 18	10 ♍ 33	08 ♏ 44	02 ♈ 52	28 ♌ 51
Jul 15, 1997	10 ♉ 06	17 ♍ 35	29 ♍ 45	15 ♈ 19	29 ♍ 08	13 ♍ 37	09 ♏ 36	04 ♈ 11	03 ♍ 15
Jul 25, 1997	13 ♉ 18	20 ♍ 22	02 ♎ 36	17 ♈ 59	03 ♎ 13	16 ♍ 50	10 ♏ 58	04 ♈ 56	07 ♍ 47
Aug 4, 1997	16 ♉ 09	23 ♍ 19	05 ♎ 38	20 ♈ 06	07 ♎ 29	20 ♍ 11	12 ♏ 47	05 ♈ 04	12 ♍ 28

	ATROPOS	HEKATE	LILITH	MEDUSA	MOIRA	NEMESIS	PERSEPHONE	PROSERPINA	PYTHIA
Aug 14, 1997	18 ♉ 35	26 ♍ 25	08 ♎ 48	21 ♈ 35	11 ♎ 56	23 ♍ 37	14 ♏ 58	04 ♈ 33	17 ♍ 15
Aug 24, 1997	20 ♉ 32	29 ♍ 38	12 ♎ 06	22 ♈ 18	16 ♎ 31	27 ♍ 08	17 ♏ 29	03 ♈ 24	22 ♍ 09
Sep 3, 1997	21 ♉ 54	02 ♎ 57	15 ♎ 30	22 ♈ 11	21 ♎ 04	00 ♎ 44	20 ♏ 17	01 ♈ 41	27 ♍ 09
Sep 13, 1997	22 ♉ 36	06 ♎ 22	18 ♎ 58	21 ♈ 11	26 ♎ 04	04 ♎ 22	23 ♏ 19	29 ♓ 34	02 ♎ 14
Sep 23, 1997	22 ♉ 33	09 ♎ 50	22 ♎ 30	19 ♈ 24	00 ♏ 58	08 ♎ 02	26 ♏ 32	27 ♓ 17	07 ♎ 23
Oct 3, 1997	21 ♉ 42	13 ♎ 22	26 ♎ 05	17 ♈ 00	05 ♏ 57	11 ♎ 44	29 ♏ 56	25 ♓ 06	12 ♎ 37
Oct 13, 1997	20 ♉ 03	16 ♎ 56	29 ♎ 42	14 ♈ 52	10 ♏ 60	15 ♎ 26	03 ♐ 28	23 ♓ 14	17 ♎ 54
Oct 23, 1997	17 ♉ 45	20 ♎ 31	03 ♏ 19	11 ♈ 54	16 ♏ 05	19 ♎ 07	07 ♐ 07	21 ♓ 53	23 ♎ 14
Nov 2, 1997	15 ♉ 00	24 ♎ 06	06 ♏ 57	09 ♈ 59	21 ♏ 12	22 ♎ 47	10 ♐ 52	21 ♓ 09	28 ♎ 36
Nov 12, 1997	12 ♉ 09	27 ♎ 41	10 ♏ 33	08 ♈ 53	26 ♏ 21	26 ♎ 24	14 ♐ 41	21 ♓ 04	04 ♏ 01
Nov 22, 1997	09 ♉ 33	01 ♏ 14	14 ♏ 08	08 ♈ 41	01 ♐ 30	29 ♎ 58	18 ♐ 33	21 ♓ 37	09 ♏ 27
Dec 2, 1997	07 ♉ 30	04 ♏ 44	17 ♏ 08	09 ♈ 24	06 ♐ 39	03 ♏ 27	22 ♐ 28	22 ♓ 44	14 ♏ 54
Dec 12, 1997	06 ♉ 10	08 ♏ 09	21 ♏ 07	10 ♈ 56	11 ♐ 47	06 ♏ 49	26 ♐ 24	24 ♓ 22	20 ♏ 20
Dec 22, 1997	05 ♉ 38	11 ♏ 29	24 ♏ 29	13 ♈ 11	16 ♐ 53	10 ♏ 04	00 ♑ 20	26 ♓ 27	25 ♏ 45
Jan 1, 1998	05 ♉ 53	14 ♏ 41	27 ♏ 44	16 ♈ 01	21 ♐ 56	13 ♏ 09	04 ♑ 15	28 ♓ 54	01 ♐ 09
Jan 11, 1998	06 ♉ 49	17 ♏ 44	00 ♐ 56	19 ♈ 22	26 ♐ 56	16 ♏ 02	08 ♑ 08	01 ♈ 40	06 ♐ 30
Jan 21, 1998	08 ♉ 23	20 ♏ 35	03 ♐ 46	23 ♈ 07	01 ♑ 51	18 ♏ 41	11 ♑ 58	04 ♈ 41	11 ♐ 47
Jan 31, 1998	10 ♉ 27	23 ♏ 12	06 ♐ 30	27 ♈ 13	06 ♑ 41	21 ♏ 03	15 ♑ 44	07 ♈ 56	16 ♐ 59
Feb 10, 1998	12 ♉ 57	25 ♏ 31	08 ♐ 60	01 ♉ 35	11 ♑ 24	23 ♏ 06	19 ♑ 25	11 ♈ 21	22 ♐ 05
Feb 20, 1998	15 ♉ 49	27 ♏ 31	11 ♐ 12	06 ♉ 11	15 ♑ 60	24 ♏ 45	23 ♑ 00	14 ♈ 55	27 ♐ 02
Mar 2, 1998	18 ♉ 57	29 ♏ 07	13 ♐ 04	10 ♉ 57	20 ♑ 26	25 ♏ 57	26 ♑ 27	18 ♈ 36	01 ♑ 50
Mar 12, 1998	22 ♉ 20	00 ♐ 16	14 ♐ 32	15 ♉ 52	24 ♑ 42	26 ♏ 40	29 ♑ 44	22 ♈ 22	06 ♑ 26
Mar 22, 1998	25 ♉ 54	00 ♐ 54	15 ♐ 34	20 ♉ 54	28 ♑ 45	26 ♏ 49	02 ♒ 51	26 ♈ 12	10 ♑ 47
Apr 1, 1998	29 ♉ 37	00 ♐ 58	16 ♐ 07	26 ♉ 02	02 ♒ 35	26 ♏ 24	05 ♒ 45	00 ♉ 06	14 ♑ 52
Apr 11, 1998	03 ♊ 27	00 ♐ 28	16 ♐ 07	01 ♊ 14	06 ♒ 08	25 ♏ 24	08 ♒ 24	04 ♉ 01	18 ♑ 35
Apr 21, 1998	07 ♊ 23	29 ♏ 24	15 ♐ 34	06 ♊ 29	09 ♒ 22	23 ♏ 53	10 ♒ 46	07 ♉ 58	21 ♑ 54
May 1, 1998	11 ♊ 23	27 ♏ 51	14 ♐ 27	11 ♊ 48	12 ♒ 14	21 ♏ 57	12 ♒ 47	11 ♉ 55	24 ♑ 43
May 11, 1998	15 ♊ 27	25 ♏ 57	12 ♐ 51	17 ♊ 07	14 ♒ 40	19 ♏ 48	14 ♒ 26	15 ♉ 51	26 ♑ 56
May 21, 1998	19 ♊ 33	23 ♏ 55	10 ♐ 53	22 ♊ 28	16 ♒ 37	17 ♏ 38	15 ♒ 40	19 ♉ 47	28 ♑ 29
May 31, 1998	23 ♊ 40	21 ♏ 57	08 ♐ 42	27 ♊ 50	18 ♒ 01	15 ♏ 40	16 ♒ 24	23 ♉ 40	29 ♑ 14
Jun 10, 1998	27 ♊ 48	20 ♏ 17	06 ♐ 31	03 ♋ 12	18 ♒ 48	14 ♏ 06	16 ♒ 38	27 ♉ 31	29 ♑ 08
Jun 20, 1998	01 ♋ 56	19 ♏ 04	04 ♐ 33	08 ♋ 34	18 ♒ 55	13 ♏ 02	16 ♒ 18	01 ♊ 18	28 ♑ 11
Jun 30, 1998	06 ♋ 04	18 ♏ 24	02 ♐ 56	13 ♋ 56	18 ♒ 20	12 ♏ 32	15 ♒ 26	05 ♊ 01	26 ♑ 28
Jul 10, 1998	10 ♋ 11	18 ♏ 21	01 ♐ 50	19 ♋ 17	17 ♒ 05	12 ♏ 37	14 ♒ 05	08 ♊ 39	24 ♑ 13
Jul 20, 1998	14 ♋ 15	18 ♏ 53	01 ♐ 15	24 ♋ 36	15 ♒ 18	13 ♏ 15	12 ♒ 19	12 ♊ 10	21 ♑ 46

	ATROPOS	HEKATE	LILITH	MEDUSA	MOIRA	NEMESIS	PERSEPHONE	PROSERPINA	PYTHIA
Jul 30, 1998	18 ♋ 18	19 ♏ 58	01 ♐ 15	29 ♋ 54	13 ♒ 09	14 ♏ 24	10 ♒ 20	15 ♊ 34	19 ♑ 32
Aug 9, 1998	22 ♋ 17	21 ♏ 34	01 ♐ 46	05 ♌ 10	10 ♒ 55	15 ♏ 60	08 ♒ 17	18 ♊ 49	17 ♑ 50
Aug 19, 1998	26 ♋ 12	23 ♏ 37	02 ♐ 48	10 ♌ 24	08 ♒ 50	17 ♏ 60	06 ♒ 24	21 ♊ 53	16 ♑ 53
Aug 29, 1998	00 ♌ 03	26 ♏ 04	04 ♐ 15	15 ♌ 36	07 ♒ 09	20 ♏ 21	04 ♒ 50	24 ♊ 44	16 ♑ 46
Sep 8, 1998	03 ♌ 48	28 ♏ 51	06 ♐ 07	20 ♌ 44	06 ♒ 02	22 ♏ 60	03 ♒ 43	27 ♊ 19	17 ♑ 29
Sep 18, 1998	07 ♌ 25	01 ♐ 56	08 ♐ 19	25 ♌ 49	05 ♒ 33	25 ♏ 55	03 ♒ 07	29 ♊ 36	18 ♑ 56
Sep 28, 1998	10 ♌ 54	05 ♐ 17	10 ♐ 49	00 ♍ 49	05 ♒ 43	29 ♏ 04	03 ♒ 04	01 ♋ 31	21 ♑ 03
Oct 8, 1998	14 ♌ 12	08 ♐ 51	13 ♐ 35	05 ♍ 45	06 ♒ 30	02 ♐ 24	03 ♒ 33	02 ♋ 60	23 ♑ 42
Oct 18, 1998	17 ♌ 18	12 ♐ 36	16 ♐ 34	10 ♍ 34	07 ♒ 50	05 ♐ 55	04 ♒ 31	03 ♋ 59	26 ♑ 49
Oct 28, 1998	20 ♌ 08	16 ♐ 32	19 ♐ 45	15 ♍ 16	09 ♒ 40	09 ♐ 34	05 ♒ 55	04 ♋ 24	00 ♒ 18
Nov 7, 1998	22 ♌ 40	20 ♐ 36	23 ♐ 06	19 ♍ 49	11 ♒ 54	13 ♐ 21	07 ♒ 43	04 ♋ 12	04 ♒ 06
Nov 17, 1998	24 ♌ 49	24 ♐ 47	26 ♐ 35	24 ♍ 13	14 ♒ 29	17 ♐ 14	09 ♒ 51	03 ♋ 22	08 ♒ 10
Nov 27, 1998	26 ♌ 32	29 ♐ 05	00 ♑ 12	28 ♍ 24	17 ♒ 21	21 ♐ 13	12 ♒ 17	01 ♋ 54	12 ♒ 26
Dec 7, 1998	27 ♌ 43	03 ♑ 27	03 ♑ 54	02 ♎ 20	20 ♒ 29	25 ♐ 16	14 ♒ 57	29 ♊ 57	16 ♒ 51
Dec 17, 1998	28 ♌ 18	07 ♑ 53	07 ♑ 53	05 ♎ 59	23 ♒ 49	29 ♐ 22	17 ♒ 49	27 ♊ 41	21 ♒ 25
Dec 27, 1998	28 ♌ 12	12 ♑ 22	11 ♑ 33	09 ♎ 17	27 ♒ 18	03 ♑ 30	20 ♒ 52	25 ♊ 20	26 ♒ 05
Jan 6, 1999	27 ♌ 23	16 ♑ 54	15 ♑ 27	12 ♎ 10	00 ♓ 56	07 ♑ 41	24 ♒ 04	23 ♊ 11	00 ♓ 50
Jan 16, 1999	25 ♌ 49	21 ♑ 26	19 ♑ 24	14 ♎ 32	04 ♓ 39	11 ♑ 51	27 ♒ 22	21 ♊ 27	05 ♓ 38
Jan 26, 1999	23 ♌ 38	25 ♑ 59	23 ♑ 21	16 ♎ 19	08 ♓ 28	16 ♑ 02	00 ♓ 45	20 ♊ 18	10 ♓ 28
Feb 5, 1999	20 ♌ 60	00 ♒ 31	27 ♑ 19	17 ♎ 25	12 ♓ 20	20 ♑ 12	04 ♓ 12	19 ♊ 48	15 ♓ 20
Feb 15, 1999	18 ♌ 12	05 ♒ 02	01 ♒ 15	17 ♎ 44	16 ♓ 14	24 ♑ 19	07 ♓ 42	19 ♊ 57	20 ♓ 13
Feb 25, 1999	15 ♌ 34	09 ♒ 30	05 ♒ 11	17 ♎ 13	20 ♓ 10	28 ♑ 23	11 ♓ 14	20 ♊ 43	25 ♓ 05
Mar 7, 1999	13 ♌ 22	13 ♒ 54	09 ♒ 03	15 ♎ 51	24 ♓ 06	02 ♒ 24	14 ♓ 46	22 ♊ 02	29 ♓ 56
Mar 17, 1999	11 ♌ 48	18 ♒ 14	12 ♒ 52	13 ♎ 47	28 ♓ 11	06 ♒ 18	18 ♓ 18	23 ♊ 51	04 ♈ 45
Mar 27, 1999	10 ♌ 58	22 ♒ 29	16 ♒ 36	11 ♎ 12	01 ♈ 55	10 ♒ 06	21 ♓ 48	26 ♊ 04	09 ♈ 33
Apr 6, 1999	10 ♌ 53	26 ♒ 36	20 ♒ 14	08 ♎ 29	05 ♈ 46	13 ♒ 46	25 ♓ 15	28 ♊ 38	14 ♈ 17
Apr 16, 1999	11 ♌ 29	00 ♓ 36	23 ♒ 44	05 ♎ 59	09 ♈ 34	17 ♒ 16	28 ♓ 39	01 ♋ 30	18 ♈ 58
Apr 26, 1999	12 ♌ 42	04 ♓ 26	27 ♒ 05	04 ♎ 01	13 ♈ 18	20 ♒ 34	01 ♈ 58	04 ♋ 38	23 ♈ 35
May 6, 1999	14 ♌ 27	08 ♓ 04	00 ♓ 14	02 ♎ 47	16 ♈ 57	23 ♒ 38	05 ♈ 11	07 ♋ 58	28 ♈ 08
May 16, 1999	16 ♌ 40	11 ♓ 29	03 ♓ 11	02 ♎ 20	20 ♈ 30	26 ♒ 25	08 ♈ 18	11 ♋ 28	02 ♉ 35
May 26, 1999	19 ♌ 18	14 ♓ 39	05 ♓ 51	02 ♎ 41	23 ♈ 56	28 ♒ 51	11 ♈ 16	15 ♋ 08	06 ♉ 58
Jun 5, 1999	22 ♌ 15	17 ♓ 29	08 ♓ 11	03 ♎ 45	27 ♈ 14	00 ♓ 53	14 ♈ 04	18 ♋ 55	11 ♉ 13
Jun 15, 1999	25 ♌ 30	19 ♓ 08	10 ♓ 08	05 ♎ 25	00 ♉ 23	02 ♓ 28	16 ♈ 41	22 ♋ 48	15 ♉ 22
Jun 25, 1999	28 ♌ 60	22 ♓ 02	11 ♓ 38	07 ♎ 38	03 ♉ 20	03 ♓ 29	19 ♈ 04	26 ♋ 46	19 ♉ 22
Jul 5, 1999	02 ♍ 43	23 ♓ 37	12 ♓ 36	10 ♎ 18	06 ♉ 05	03 ♓ 54	21 ♈ 10	00 ♌ 49	23 ♉ 14

	ATROPOS	HEKATE	LILITH	MEDUSA	MOIRA	NEMESIS	PERSEPHONE	PROSERPINA	PYTHIA
Jul 15, 1999	06 ♍ 37	24 ♓ 39	12 ♓ 58	13 ♎ 21	08 ♉ 34	03 ♓ 40	22 ♈ 58	04 ♌ 56	26 ♌ 55
Jul 25, 1999	10 ♍ 42	25 ♓ 05	12 ♓ 40	16 ♎ 43	10 ♉ 46	02 ♓ 46	24 ♈ 24	09 ♌ 06	00 ♊ 24
Aug 4, 1999	14 ♍ 56	24 ♓ 52	11 ♓ 43	20 ♎ 20	12 ♉ 38	01 ♓ 16	25 ♈ 26	13 ♌ 18	03 ♊ 39
Aug 14, 1999	19 ♍ 19	24 ♓ 02	10 ♓ 07	24 ♎ 11	14 ♉ 06	29 ♒ 19	26 ♈ 60	17 ♌ 31	06 ♊ 37
Aug 24, 1999	23 ♍ 49	22 ♓ 37	08 ♓ 04	28 ♎ 14	15 ♉ 07	27 ♒ 07	26 ♈ 02	21 ♌ 46	09 ♊ 17
Sep 3, 1999	28 ♍ 26	20 ♓ 48	05 ♓ 45	02 ♏ 27	15 ♉ 38	24 ♒ 59	25 ♈ 33	26 ♌ 01	11 ♊ 34
Sep 13, 1999	03 ♎ 10	18 ♓ 46	03 ♓ 30	06 ♏ 47	15 ♉ 36	23 ♒ 11	24 ♈ 33	00 ♍ 16	13 ♊ 25
Sep 23, 1999	08 ♎ 01	16 ♓ 47	01 ♓ 35	11 ♏ 16	14 ♉ 59	21 ♒ 56	23 ♈ 03	04 ♍ 30	14 ♊ 45
Oct 3, 1999	12 ♎ 56	15 ♓ 06	00 ♓ 15	15 ♏ 50	13 ♉ 49	21 ♒ 21	21 ♈ 11	08 ♍ 42	15 ♊ 29
Oct 13, 1999	17 ♎ 58	13 ♓ 53	29 ♒ 38	20 ♏ 30	12 ♉ 08	21 ♒ 30	19 ♈ 07	12 ♍ 51	15 ♊ 35
Oct 23, 1999	23 ♎ 04	13 ♓ 17	29 ♒ 48	25 ♏ 15	10 ♉ 05	22 ♒ 21	17 ♈ 03	16 ♍ 57	14 ♊ 57
Nov 2, 1999	28 ♎ 15	13 ♓ 18	00 ♓ 42	00 ♐ 03	07 ♉ 51	23 ♒ 50	15 ♈ 11	20 ♍ 57	13 ♊ 38
Nov 12, 1999	03 ♏ 31	13 ♓ 57	02 ♓ 17	04 ♐ 55	05 ♉ 39	25 ♒ 54	13 ♈ 42	24 ♍ 51	11 ♊ 39
Nov 22, 1999	08 ♏ 50	15 ♓ 10	04 ♓ 30	09 ♐ 50	03 ♉ 42	28 ♒ 29	12 ♈ 42	28 ♍ 37	09 ♊ 13
Dec 2, 1999	14 ♏ 12	16 ♓ 53	07 ♓ 14	14 ♐ 46	02 ♉ 12	01 ♓ 28	12 ♈ 16	02 ♎ 12	06 ♊ 35
Dec 12, 1999	19 ♏ 37	19 ♓ 03	10 ♓ 27	19 ♐ 45	01 ♉ 13	04 ♓ 49	12 ♈ 24	05 ♎ 34	04 ♊ 01
Dec 22, 1999	25 ♏ 04	21 ♓ 36	14 ♓ 03	24 ♐ 44	00 ♉ 50	08 ♓ 29	13 ♈ 05	08 ♎ 40	01 ♊ 51
Jan 1, 2000	00 ♐ 32	24 ♓ 27	17 ♓ 58	29 ♐ 43	01 ♉ 01	12 ♓ 24	14 ♈ 15	11 ♎ 28	00 ♊ 14
Jan 11, 2000	06 ♐ 01	27 ♓ 34	22 ♓ 11	04 ♑ 42	01 ♉ 45	16 ♓ 32	15 ♈ 53	13 ♎ 52	29 ♉ 19
Jan 21, 2000	11 ♐ 28	00 ♈ 54	26 ♓ 39	09 ♑ 40	02 ♉ 59	20 ♓ 50	17 ♈ 53	15 ♎ 48	29 ♉ 07
Jan 31, 2000	16 ♐ 54	04 ♈ 24	01 ♈ 18	14 ♑ 37	04 ♉ 38	25 ♓ 17	20 ♈ 13	17 ♎ 13	29 ♊ 35
Feb 10, 2000	22 ♐ 16	08 ♈ 02	06 ♈ 08	19 ♑ 31	06 ♉ 40	29 ♓ 51	22 ♈ 51	17 ♎ 60	00 ♊ 40
Feb 20, 2000	27 ♐ 34	11 ♈ 47	11 ♈ 06	24 ♑ 22	08 ♉ 60	04 ♈ 30	25 ♈ 42	18 ♎ 06	02 ♊ 17
Mar 1, 2000	02 ♑ 44	15 ♈ 37	16 ♈ 12	29 ♑ 10	11 ♉ 36	09 ♈ 14	28 ♈ 45	17 ♎ 29	04 ♊ 21
Mar 11, 2000	07 ♑ 46	19 ♈ 30	21 ♈ 23	03 ♒ 52	14 ♉ 25	14 ♈ 01	01 ♉ 59	16 ♎ 11	06 ♊ 48
Mar 21, 2000	12 ♑ 36	23 ♈ 26	26 ♈ 38	08 ♒ 29	17 ♉ 25	18 ♈ 50	05 ♉ 20	14 ♎ 19	09 ♊ 34
Mar 31, 2000	17 ♑ 11	27 ♈ 23	01 ♉ 58	12 ♒ 59	20 ♉ 34	23 ♈ 41	08 ♉ 48	12 ♎ 05	12 ♊ 36
Apr 10, 2000	21 ♑ 28	01 ♉ 20	07 ♉ 20	17 ♒ 21	23 ♉ 50	28 ♈ 32	12 ♉ 21	09 ♎ 48	15 ♊ 51
Apr 20, 2000	25 ♑ 23	05 ♉ 17	12 ♉ 44	21 ♒ 34	27 ♉ 11	03 ♉ 23	15 ♉ 58	07 ♎ 45	19 ♊ 17
Apr 30, 2000	28 ♑ 50	09 ♉ 12	18 ♉ 09	25 ♒ 34	00 ♊ 38	08 ♉ 14	19 ♉ 38	06 ♎ 10	22 ♊ 52
May 10, 2000	01 ♒ 44	13 ♉ 05	23 ♉ 35	29 ♒ 21	04 ♊ 07	13 ♉ 03	23 ♉ 20	05 ♎ 14	26 ♋ 36
May 20, 2000	03 ♒ 57	16 ♉ 54	29 ♉ 01	02 ♓ 51	07 ♊ 39	17 ♉ 50	27 ♉ 03	05 ♎ 02	00 ♋ 25
May 30, 2000	05 ♒ 24	20 ♉ 40	04 ♊ 26	06 ♓ 02	11 ♊ 13	22 ♉ 34	00 ♊ 46	05 ♎ 31	04 ♋ 20
Jun 9, 2000	05 ♒ 56	24 ♉ 22	09 ♊ 49	08 ♓ 48	14 ♊ 47	27 ♉ 15	04 ♊ 29	06 ♎ 39	08 ♋ 19
Jun 19, 2000	05 ♒ 31	27 ♉ 58	15 ♊ 11	11 ♓ 06	18 ♊ 21	01 ♊ 52	08 ♊ 11	08 ♎ 23	12 ♋ 21

	ATROPOS	HEKATE	LILITH	MEDUSA	MOIRA	NEMESIS	PERSEPHONE	PROSERPINA	PYTHIA
Jun 29, 2000	04 ≈ 10	01 ♊ 27	20 ♊ 30	12 ♓ 50	21 ♊ 55	06 ♊ 24	11 ♊ 50	10 ♎ 37	16 ♋ 27
Jul 9, 2000	02 ≈ 02	04 ♊ 49	25 ♊ 46	13 ♓ 54	25 ♊ 27	10 ♊ 51	15 ♊ 26	13 ♎ 17	20 ♋ 35
Jul 19, 2000	29 ♑ 28	08 ♊ 02	00 ♋ 59	14 ♓ 13	28 ♊ 56	15 ♊ 12	18 ♊ 58	16 ♎ 41	24 ♋ 45
Jul 29, 2000	26 ♑ 52	11 ♊ 04	06 ♋ 07	13 ♓ 43	02 ♋ 21	19 ♊ 25	22 ♊ 25	19 ♎ 41	28 ♋ 56
Aug 8, 2000	24 ♑ 39	13 ♊ 54	11 ♋ 10	12 ♓ 24	05 ♋ 42	23 ♊ 30	25 ♊ 45	23 ♎ 18	03 ♌ 08
Aug 18, 2000	23 ♑ 09	16 ♊ 31	16 ♋ 06	10 ♓ 23	08 ♋ 57	27 ♊ 24	28 ♊ 57	27 ♎ 09	07 ♌ 20
Aug 28, 2000	22 ♑ 30	18 ♊ 51	20 ♋ 56	07 ♓ 53	12 ♋ 05	01 ♋ 06	01 ♋ 59	01 ♏ 11	11 ♌ 31
Sep 7, 2000	22 ♑ 44	20 ♊ 51	25 ♋ 37	05 ♓ 16	15 ♋ 04	04 ♋ 34	04 ♋ 49	05 ♏ 23	15 ♌ 42
Sep 17, 2000	23 ♑ 47	22 ♊ 30	00 ♌ 09	02 ♓ 57	17 ♋ 52	07 ♋ 46	07 ♋ 24	09 ♏ 43	19 ♌ 50
Sep 27, 2000	25 ♑ 32	23 ♊ 43	04 ♌ 29	01 ♓ 13	20 ♋ 27	10 ♋ 38	09 ♋ 42	14 ♏ 11	23 ♌ 56
Oct 7, 2000	27 ♑ 53	24 ♊ 28	08 ♌ 36	00 ♓ 17	22 ♋ 45	13 ♋ 06	11 ♋ 39	18 ♏ 44	27 ♌ 58
Oct 17, 2000	00 ≈ 44	24 ♊ 42	12 ♌ 27	00 ♓ 15	24 ♋ 45	15 ♋ 11	13 ♋ 11	23 ♏ 23	01 ♍ 55
Oct 27, 2000	03 ≈ 60	24 ♊ 23	16 ♌ 00	01 ♓ 03	26 ♋ 22	16 ♋ 36	14 ♋ 15	28 ♏ 05	05 ♍ 46
Nov 6, 2000	07 ≈ 35	23 ♊ 30	19 ♌ 10	02 ♓ 39	27 ♋ 31	17 ♋ 29	14 ♋ 47	02 ♐ 51	09 ♍ 28
Nov 16, 2000	11 ≈ 27	22 ♊ 07	21 ♌ 55	04 ♓ 55	28 ♋ 10	17 ♋ 41	14 ♋ 43	07 ♐ 40	13 ♍ 00
Nov 26, 2000	15 ≈ 33	20 ♊ 20	24 ♌ 08	07 ♓ 47	28 ♋ 14	17 ♋ 10	14 ♋ 02	12 ♐ 30	16 ♍ 19
Dec 6, 2000	19 ≈ 49	18 ♊ 18	25 ♌ 46	11 ♓ 07	27 ♋ 40	15 ♋ 57	12 ♋ 45	17 ♐ 21	19 ♍ 21
Dec 16, 2000	24 ≈ 14	16 ♊ 14	26 ♌ 43	14 ♓ 53	26 ♋ 30	14 ♋ 09	10 ♋ 59	22 ♐ 12	22 ♍ 04
Dec 26, 2000	28 ≈ 47	14 ♊ 19	26 ♌ 55	18 ♓ 58	26 ♋ 46	11 ♋ 56	08 ♋ 53	27 ♐ 02	24 ♍ 21
Jan 5, 2001	03 ♓ 24	12 ♊ 44	26 ♌ 19	23 ♓ 21	22 ♋ 37	09 ♋ 34	06 ♋ 40	01 ♑ 51	26 ♍ 08
Jan 15, 2001	08 ♓ 06	11 ♊ 38	24 ♌ 59	27 ♓ 58	20 ♋ 17	07 ♋ 22	04 ♋ 38	06 ♑ 38	27 ♍ 20
Jan 25, 2001	12 ♓ 52	11 ♊ 02	23 ♌ 01	02 ♈ 46	17 ♋ 60	05 ♋ 35	02 ♋ 57	11 ♑ 21	27 ♍ 49
Feb 4, 2001	17 ♓ 39	10 ♊ 60	20 ♌ 40	07 ♈ 44	16 ♋ 01	04 ♋ 23	01 ♋ 49	16 ♑ 01	27 ♍ 32
Feb 14, 2001	22 ♓ 28	11 ♊ 28	18 ♌ 14	12 ♈ 50	14 ♋ 33	03 ♋ 51	01 ♋ 17	20 ♑ 35	26 ♍ 27
Feb 24, 2001	27 ♓ 18	12 ♊ 24	16 ♌ 02	18 ♈ 03	13 ♋ 42	03 ♋ 59	01 ♋ 23	25 ♑ 03	24 ♍ 36
Mar 6, 2001	02 ♈ 08	13 ♊ 46	14 ♌ 20	23 ♈ 20	13 ♋ 30	04 ♋ 45	02 ♋ 05	29 ♑ 24	22 ♍ 11
Mar 16, 2001	06 ♈ 57	15 ♊ 29	13 ♌ 16	28 ♈ 42	13 ♋ 56	06 ♋ 05	03 ♋ 19	03 ≈ 37	19 ♍ 30
Mar 26, 2001	11 ♈ 45	17 ♊ 30	12 ♌ 54	04 ♉ 07	14 ♋ 58	07 ♋ 53	05 ♋ 02	07 ≈ 39	16 ♍ 54
Apr 5, 2001	16 ♈ 32	19 ♊ 47	13 ♌ 14	09 ♉ 35	16 ♋ 32	10 ♋ 06	07 ♋ 09	11 ≈ 30	14 ♍ 46
Apr 15, 2001	21 ♈ 16	22 ♊ 17	14 ♌ 11	15 ♉ 04	18 ♋ 34	12 ♋ 40	09 ♋ 38	15 ≈ 06	13 ♍ 19
Apr 25, 2001	25 ♈ 58	24 ♊ 57	15 ♌ 40	20 ♉ 35	20 ♋ 59	15 ♋ 30	12 ♋ 24	18 ≈ 28	12 ♍ 43
May 5, 2001	00 ♉ 37	27 ♊ 46	17 ♌ 37	26 ♉ 06	23 ♋ 46	18 ♋ 34	15 ♋ 25	21 ≈ 30	12 ♍ 58
May 15, 2001	05 ♉ 11	00 ♋ 42	19 ♌ 57	01 ♊ 38	26 ♋ 49	21 ♋ 49	18 ♋ 38	24 ≈ 11	14 ♍ 00
May 25, 2001	09 ♉ 42	03 ♋ 43	22 ♌ 36	07 ♊ 09	00 ♌ 08	25 ♋ 14	22 ♋ 02	26 ≈ 26	15 ♍ 45
Jun 4, 2001	14 ♉ 08	06 ♋ 49	25 ♌ 31	12 ♊ 40	03 ♌ 39	28 ♋ 46	25 ♋ 34	28 ≈ 13	18 ♍ 07

	ATROPOS	HEKATE	LILITH	MEDUSA	MOIRA	NEMESIS	PERSEPHONE	PROSERPINA	PYTHIA
Jun 14, 2001	18 ♉ 28	09 ♋ 57	28 ♌ 38	18 ♊ 10	07 ♌ 22	02 ♌ 24	29 ♋ 13	29 ♒ 27	20 ♍ 60
Jun 24, 2001	22 ♉ 41	13 ♋ 07	01 ♍ 56	23 ♊ 38	11 ♌ 14	06 ♌ 07	02 ♌ 58	00 ♓ 04	24 ♍ 20
Jul 4, 2001	26 ♉ 47	16 ♋ 19	05 ♍ 23	29 ♊ 05	15 ♌ 15	09 ♌ 54	06 ♌ 48	00 ♓ 01	28 ♍ 02
Jul 14, 2001	00 ♊ 45	19 ♋ 30	08 ♍ 56	04 ♋ 29	19 ♌ 23	13 ♌ 43	10 ♌ 42	29 ♒ 17	02 ♎ 03
Jul 24, 2001	04 ♊ 32	22 ♋ 41	12 ♍ 35	09 ♋ 51	23 ♌ 38	17 ♌ 34	14 ♌ 39	27 ♒ 55	06 ♎ 21
Aug 3, 2001	08 ♊ 08	25 ♋ 49	16 ♍ 19	15 ♋ 11	27 ♌ 58	21 ♌ 27	18 ♌ 38	26 ♒ 02	10 ♎ 52
Aug 13, 2001	11 ♊ 29	28 ♋ 55	20 ♍ 05	20 ♋ 26	02 ♍ 23	25 ♌ 19	22 ♌ 38	23 ♒ 51	15 ♎ 36
Aug 23, 2001	14 ♊ 34	01 ♌ 57	23 ♍ 55	25 ♋ 38	06 ♍ 53	29 ♌ 12	26 ♌ 39	21 ♒ 37	20 ♎ 30
Sep 2, 2001	17 ♊ 20	04 ♌ 54	27 ♍ 45	00 ♌ 45	11 ♍ 27	03 ♍ 03	00 ♍ 40	19 ♒ 36	25 ♎ 32
Sep 12, 2001	19 ♊ 42	07 ♌ 45	01 ♎ 37	05 ♌ 46	16 ♍ 03	06 ♍ 53	04 ♍ 41	18 ♒ 01	00 ♏ 43
Sep 22, 2001	21 ♊ 36	10 ♌ 27	05 ♎ 29	10 ♌ 41	20 ♍ 43	10 ♍ 40	08 ♍ 39	17 ♒ 02	06 ♏ 01
Oct 2, 2001	22 ♊ 58	13 ♌ 00	09 ♎ 20	15 ♌ 28	25 ♍ 25	14 ♍ 24	12 ♍ 36	16 ♒ 42	11 ♏ 24
Oct 12, 2001	23 ♊ 41	15 ♌ 22	13 ♎ 10	20 ♌ 06	00 ♎ 07	18 ♍ 03	16 ♍ 28	17 ♒ 02	16 ♏ 53
Oct 22, 2001	23 ♊ 42	17 ♌ 30	16 ♎ 57	24 ♌ 33	04 ♎ 51	21 ♍ 36	20 ♍ 17	17 ♒ 58	22 ♏ 26
Nov 1, 2001	22 ♊ 57	19 ♌ 22	20 ♎ 42	28 ♌ 47	09 ♎ 35	25 ♍ 02	23 ♍ 59	19 ♒ 28	28 ♏ 02
Nov 11, 2001	21 ♊ 25	20 ♌ 54	24 ♎ 22	02 ♍ 45	14 ♎ 18	28 ♍ 34	27 ♍ 34	21 ♒ 26	03 ♐ 42
Nov 21, 2001	19 ♊ 13	22 ♌ 05	27 ♎ 57	06 ♍ 24	18 ♎ 58	01 ♎ 27	00 ♎ 59	23 ♒ 50	09 ♐ 24
Dec 1, 2001	16 ♊ 33	22 ♌ 50	01 ♏ 25	09 ♍ 40	23 ♎ 36	04 ♎ 21	04 ♎ 13	26 ♒ 34	15 ♐ 07
Dec 11, 2001	13 ♊ 43	23 ♌ 08	04 ♏ 46	12 ♍ 28	28 ♎ 10	07 ♎ 00	07 ♎ 14	29 ♒ 36	20 ♐ 52
Dec 21, 2001	11 ♊ 03	22 ♌ 55	07 ♏ 57	14 ♍ 44	02 ♏ 38	09 ♎ 22	09 ♎ 58	02 ♓ 52	26 ♐ 37
Dec 31, 2001	08 ♊ 51	22 ♌ 12	10 ♏ 56	16 ♍ 20	06 ♏ 58	11 ♎ 22	12 ♎ 22	06 ♓ 21	02 ♑ 21
Jan 10, 2002	07 ♊ 20	21 ♌ 00	13 ♏ 42	17 ♍ 10	11 ♏ 08	12 ♎ 57	14 ♎ 23	09 ♓ 59	08 ♑ 05
Jan 20, 2002	06 ♊ 33	19 ♌ 24	16 ♏ 11	17 ♍ 10	15 ♏ 07	14 ♎ 05	15 ♎ 57	13 ♓ 46	13 ♑ 47
Jan 30, 2002	06 ♊ 33	17 ♌ 31	18 ♏ 22	16 ♍ 17	18 ♏ 51	14 ♎ 40	16 ♎ 59	17 ♓ 39	19 ♑ 27
Feb 9, 2002	07 ♊ 13	15 ♌ 30	20 ♏ 10	14 ♍ 33	22 ♏ 17	14 ♎ 41	17 ♎ 27	21 ♓ 36	25 ♑ 04
Feb 19, 2002	08 ♊ 31	13 ♌ 34	21 ♏ 34	12 ♍ 16	25 ♏ 21	14 ♎ 05	17 ♎ 17	25 ♓ 42	00 ♒ 36
Mar 1, 2002	10 ♊ 20	11 ♌ 51	22 ♏ 28	09 ♍ 26	27 ♏ 59	12 ♎ 55	16 ♎ 30	29 ♓ 42	06 ♒ 05
Mar 11, 2002	12 ♊ 35	10 ♌ 31	22 ♏ 51	06 ♍ 45	00 ♐ 06	11 ♎ 14	15 ♎ 08	03 ♈ 48	11 ♒ 27
Mar 21, 2002	15 ♊ 11	09 ♌ 38	22 ♏ 40	04 ♍ 29	01 ♐ 37	09 ♎ 11	13 ♎ 18	07 ♈ 54	16 ♒ 44
Mar 31, 2002	18 ♊ 06	09 ♌ 16	21 ♏ 54	02 ♍ 54	02 ♐ 26	06 ♎ 58	11 ♎ 12	11 ♈ 60	21 ♒ 53
Apr 10, 2002	21 ♊ 15	09 ♌ 22	20 ♏ 35	02 ♍ 08	02 ♐ 31	04 ♎ 49	09 ♎ 05	16 ♈ 05	26 ♒ 53
Apr 20, 2002	24 ♊ 36	09 ♌ 57	18 ♏ 48	02 ♍ 12	01 ♐ 51	02 ♎ 56	07 ♎ 10	20 ♈ 08	01 ♓ 44
Apr 30, 2002	28 ♊ 07	10 ♌ 51	16 ♏ 43	03 ♍ 02	01 ♐ 29	01 ♎ 29	05 ♎ 39	24 ♈ 09	06 ♓ 23
May 10, 2002	01 ♋ 45	12 ♌ 20	14 ♏ 30	04 ♍ 33	28 ♏ 35	00 ♎ 33	04 ♎ 42	28 ♈ 06	10 ♓ 50
May 20, 2002	05 ♋ 30	14 ♌ 03	12 ♏ 21	06 ♍ 38	26 ♏ 26	00 ♎ 13	04 ♎ 20	01 ♉ 59	15 ♓ 01

	ATROPOS	HEKATE	LILITH	MEDUSA	MOIRA	NEMESIS	PERSEPHONE	PROSERPINA	PYTHIA
May 30, 2002	09 ♋ 21	16 ♌ 03	10 ♏ 30	09 ♍ 13	24 ♏ 22	00 ♎ 26	04 ♎ 35	05 ♉ 48	18 ♓ 54
Jun 9, 2002	13 ♋ 15	18 ♌ 17	09 ♏ 05	12 ♍ 11	22 ♏ 39	01 ♎ 11	05 ♎ 24	09 ♉ 31	22 ♓ 27
Jun 19, 2002	17 ♋ 12	20 ♌ 45	08 ♏ 10	15 ♍ 29	21 ♏ 32	02 ♎ 24	06 ♎ 44	13 ♉ 06	25 ♓ 35
Jun 29, 2002	21 ♋ 12	23 ♌ 23	07 ♏ 49	19 ♍ 04	21 ♏ 07	04 ♎ 02	08 ♎ 32	16 ♉ 34	28 ♓ 15
Jul 9, 2002	25 ♋ 14	26 ♌ 09	08 ♏ 00	22 ♍ 53	21 ♏ 27	06 ♎ 02	10 ♎ 43	19 ♉ 52	00 ♈ 21
Jul 19, 2002	29 ♋ 17	29 ♌ 04	08 ♏ 42	26 ♍ 54	22 ♏ 27	08 ♎ 20	13 ♎ 14	22 ♉ 59	01 ♈ 48
Jul 29, 2002	03 ♌ 20	02 ♍ 04	09 ♏ 51	01 ♎ 04	24 ♏ 06	10 ♎ 55	16 ♎ 02	25 ♉ 53	02 ♈ 31
Aug 8, 2002	07 ♌ 23	05 ♍ 10	11 ♏ 25	05 ♎ 22	26 ♏ 17	13 ♎ 43	19 ♎ 06	28 ♉ 31	02 ♈ 25
Aug 18, 2002	11 ♌ 25	08 ♍ 20	13 ♏ 20	09 ♎ 47	28 ♏ 56	16 ♎ 43	22 ♎ 21	00 ♊ 51	01 ♈ 30
Aug 28, 2002	15 ♌ 26	11 ♍ 33	16 ♏ 34	14 ♎ 18	01 ♐ 58	19 ♎ 53	25 ♎ 47	02 ♊ 49	29 ♓ 48
Sep 7, 2002	19 ♌ 25	14 ♍ 47	18 ♏ 04	18 ♎ 55	05 ♐ 20	23 ♎ 11	29 ♎ 23	04 ♊ 22	27 ♓ 30
Sep 17, 2002	23 ♌ 21	18 ♍ 03	20 ♏ 47	23 ♎ 35	08 ♐ 58	26 ♎ 37	03 ♏ 05	05 ♊ 26	24 ♓ 53
Sep 27, 2002	27 ♌ 13	21 ♍ 19	23 ♏ 42	28 ♎ 20	12 ♐ 49	00 ♏ 09	06 ♏ 54	05 ♊ 58	22 ♓ 19
Oct 7, 2002	01 ♍ 01	24 ♍ 34	26 ♏ 48	03 ♏ 07	16 ♐ 52	03 ♏ 45	10 ♏ 48	05 ♊ 53	20 ♓ 09
Oct 17, 2002	04 ♍ 42	27 ♍ 47	00 ♐ 01	07 ♏ 57	21 ♐ 04	07 ♏ 25	14 ♏ 46	05 ♊ 10	18 ♓ 37
Oct 27, 2002	08 ♍ 16	00 ♎ 57	03 ♐ 22	12 ♏ 49	25 ♐ 23	11 ♏ 08	18 ♏ 47	03 ♊ 51	17 ♓ 50
Nov 6, 2002	11 ♍ 40	04 ♎ 03	06 ♐ 49	17 ♏ 42	29 ♐ 49	14 ♏ 54	22 ♏ 50	01 ♊ 60	17 ♓ 51
Nov 16, 2002	14 ♍ 53	07 ♎ 02	10 ♐ 21	22 ♏ 36	04 ♑ 19	18 ♏ 40	26 ♏ 54	29 ♉ 48	18 ♓ 37
Nov 26, 2002	17 ♍ 51	09 ♎ 53	13 ♐ 56	27 ♏ 31	08 ♑ 54	22 ♏ 27	00 ♐ 59	27 ♉ 28	20 ♓ 02
Dec 6, 2002	20 ♍ 32	12 ♎ 35	17 ♐ 34	02 ♐ 25	13 ♑ 30	26 ♏ 13	05 ♐ 02	25 ♉ 16	22 ♓ 01
Dec 16, 2002	22 ♍ 51	15 ♎ 05	21 ♐ 13	07 ♐ 19	18 ♑ 09	29 ♏ 56	09 ♐ 05	23 ♉ 26	24 ♓ 28
Dec 26, 2002	24 ♍ 45	17 ♎ 20	24 ♐ 54	12 ♐ 11	22 ♑ 48	03 ♐ 37	13 ♐ 04	22 ♉ 08	27 ♓ 19
Jan 5, 2003	26 ♍ 09	19 ♎ 18	28 ♐ 33	17 ♐ 01	27 ♑ 27	07 ♐ 14	16 ♐ 59	21 ♉ 28	00 ♈ 29
Jan 15, 2003	26 ♍ 55	20 ♎ 56	02 ♑ 12	21 ♐ 47	02 ♒ 06	10 ♐ 45	20 ♐ 50	21 ♉ 26	03 ♈ 54
Jan 25, 2003	27 ♍ 01	22 ♎ 10	05 ♑ 47	26 ♐ 30	06 ♒ 43	14 ♐ 09	24 ♐ 34	22 ♉ 01	07 ♈ 32
Feb 4, 2003	26 ♍ 22	22 ♎ 56	09 ♑ 20	01 ♑ 08	11 ♒ 17	17 ♐ 25	28 ♐ 10	23 ♉ 10	11 ♈ 21
Feb 14, 2003	24 ♍ 57	23 ♎ 13	12 ♑ 47	05 ♑ 41	15 ♒ 49	20 ♐ 30	01 ♑ 37	24 ♉ 49	15 ♈ 17
Feb 24, 2003	22 ♍ 50	22 ♎ 57	16 ♑ 07	10 ♑ 06	20 ♒ 16	23 ♐ 21	04 ♑ 53	26 ♉ 53	19 ♈ 20
Mar 6, 2003	20 ♍ 12	22 ♎ 09	19 ♑ 43	14 ♑ 22	24 ♒ 39	25 ♐ 58	07 ♑ 56	29 ♉ 19	23 ♈ 27
Mar 16, 2003	17 ♍ 22	20 ♎ 51	22 ♑ 23	18 ♑ 29	28 ♒ 56	28 ♐ 17	10 ♑ 43	02 ♊ 04	27 ♈ 38
Mar 26, 2003	14 ♍ 38	19 ♎ 08	25 ♑ 15	22 ♑ 23	03 ♓ 07	00 ♑ 14	13 ♑ 12	05 ♊ 03	01 ♉ 51
Apr 5, 2003	12 ♍ 22	17 ♎ 10	27 ♑ 53	26 ♑ 03	07 ♓ 11	01 ♑ 46	15 ♑ 20	08 ♊ 15	06 ♉ 06
Apr 15, 2003	10 ♍ 45	15 ♎ 07	00 ♒ 14	29 ♑ 26	11 ♓ 06	02 ♑ 50	17 ♑ 04	11 ♊ 38	10 ♉ 21
Apr 25, 2003	09 ♍ 56	13 ♎ 12	02 ♒ 16	02 ♒ 28	14 ♓ 51	03 ♑ 22	18 ♑ 20	15 ♊ 10	14 ♉ 37
May 5, 2003	09 ♍ 56	11 ♎ 35	03 ♒ 55	05 ♒ 07	18 ♓ 26	03 ♑ 20	19 ♑ 06	18 ♊ 49	18 ♉ 51

	ATROPOS	HEKATE	LILITH	MEDUSA	MOIRA	NEMESIS	PERSEPHONE	PROSERPINA	PYTHIA
May 15, 2003	10 ♍ 41	10 ♎ 25	05 ♒ 08	07 ♒ 16	21 ♓ 47	02 ♑ 41	19 ♑ 19	22 ♊ 34	23 ♉ 05
May 25, 2003	12 ♍ 07	09 ♎ 47	05 ♒ 51	08 ♒ 51	24 ♓ 45	01 ♑ 28	18 ♑ 58	26 ♊ 23	27 ♉ 16
Jun 4, 2003	14 ♍ 09	09 ♎ 42	06 ♒ 00	09 ♒ 47	27 ♓ 45	29 ♐ 45	18 ♑ 02	00 ♋ 17	01 ♊ 25
Jun 14, 2003	16 ♍ 42	10 ♎ 09	05 ♒ 34	09 ♒ 58	00 ♈ 16	27 ♐ 41	16 ♑ 36	04 ♋ 13	05 ♊ 31
Jun 24, 2003	19 ♍ 43	11 ♎ 07	04 ♒ 32	09 ♒ 22	02 ♈ 26	25 ♐ 29	14 ♑ 47	08 ♋ 12	09 ♊ 34
Jul 4, 2003	23 ♍ 06	12 ♎ 32	02 ♒ 57	07 ♒ 59	04 ♈ 10	23 ♐ 23	12 ♑ 45	12 ♋ 12	13 ♊ 32
Jul 14, 2003	26 ♍ 50	14 ♎ 21	00 ♒ 56	05 ♒ 55	05 ♈ 25	21 ♐ 37	10 ♑ 43	16 ♋ 14	17 ♊ 25
Jul 24, 2003	00 ♎ 52	16 ♎ 32	28 ♑ 41	03 ♒ 26	06 ♈ 07	20 ♐ 20	08 ♑ 53	20 ♋ 15	21 ♊ 12
Aug 3, 2003	05 ♎ 09	19 ♎ 02	26 ♑ 26	00 ♒ 49	06 ♈ 15	19 ♐ 39	07 ♑ 25	24 ♋ 16	24 ♊ 53
Aug 13, 2003	09 ♎ 41	21 ♎ 48	24 ♑ 25	28 ♑ 28	05 ♈ 45	19 ♐ 35	06 ♑ 27	28 ♋ 16	28 ♊ 25
Aug 23, 2003	14 ♎ 24	24 ♎ 48	22 ♑ 50	26 ♑ 41	04 ♈ 39	20 ♐ 08	06 ♑ 02	02 ♌ 14	01 ♋ 47
Sep 2, 2003	19 ♎ 19	28 ♎ 01	21 ♑ 51	25 ♑ 39	02 ♈ 57	21 ♐ 16	06 ♑ 10	06 ♌ 10	04 ♋ 57
Sep 12, 2003	24 ♎ 24	01 ♏ 25	21 ♑ 31	25 ♑ 27	00 ♈ 57	22 ♐ 55	06 ♑ 50	10 ♌ 01	07 ♋ 54
Sep 22, 2003	29 ♎ 39	04 ♏ 58	21 ♑ 50	26 ♑ 05	28 ♓ 42	25 ♐ 01	07 ♑ 59	13 ♌ 48	10 ♋ 34
Oct 2, 2003	05 ♏ 02	08 ♏ 39	22 ♑ 46	27 ♑ 27	26 ♓ 29	27 ♐ 32	09 ♑ 34	17 ♌ 28	12 ♋ 54
Oct 12, 2003	10 ♏ 33	12 ♏ 26	24 ♑ 18	29 ♑ 30	24 ♓ 01	00 ♑ 23	11 ♑ 32	21 ♌ 01	14 ♋ 51
Oct 22, 2003	16 ♏ 10	16 ♏ 20	26 ♑ 19	02 ♒ 08	23 ♓ 01	03 ♑ 33	13 ♑ 49	24 ♌ 24	16 ♋ 21
Nov 1, 2003	21 ♏ 54	20 ♏ 19	28 ♑ 48	05 ♒ 15	22 ♓ 05	06 ♑ 59	16 ♑ 23	27 ♌ 35	17 ♋ 17
Nov 11, 2003	27 ♏ 42	24 ♏ 22	01 ♒ 41	08 ♒ 46	21 ♓ 45	10 ♑ 38	19 ♑ 12	00 ♍ 32	17 ♋ 37
Nov 21, 2003	03 ♐ 35	28 ♏ 28	04 ♒ 54	12 ♒ 39	22 ♓ 00	14 ♑ 29	22 ♑ 12	03 ♍ 11	17 ♋ 16
Dec 1, 2003	09 ♐ 32	02 ♐ 36	08 ♒ 25	16 ♒ 50	22 ♓ 50	18 ♑ 30	25 ♑ 22	05 ♍ 28	16 ♋ 12
Dec 11, 2003	15 ♐ 30	06 ♐ 46	12 ♒ 11	21 ♒ 15	24 ♓ 09	22 ♑ 40	28 ♑ 41	07 ♍ 19	14 ♋ 28
Dec 21, 2003	21 ♐ 31	10 ♐ 56	16 ♒ 10	25 ♒ 54	25 ♓ 55	26 ♑ 57	02 ♒ 06	08 ♍ 40	12 ♋ 11
Dec 31, 2003	27 ♐ 32	15 ♐ 05	20 ♒ 22	00 ♓ 43	28 ♓ 03	01 ♒ 20	05 ♒ 36	09 ♍ 26	09 ♋ 35
Jan 10, 2004	03 ♑ 32	19 ♐ 13	24 ♒ 43	05 ♓ 41	00 ♈ 30	05 ♒ 49	09 ♒ 10	09 ♍ 32	06 ♋ 57
Jan 20, 2004	09 ♑ 32	23 ♐ 18	29 ♒ 13	10 ♓ 47	03 ♈ 12	10 ♒ 21	12 ♒ 47	08 ♍ 57	04 ♋ 34
Jan 30, 2004	15 ♑ 28	27 ♐ 19	03 ♓ 50	15 ♓ 59	06 ♈ 08	14 ♒ 58	16 ♒ 25	07 ♍ 42	02 ♋ 43
Feb 9, 2004	21 ♑ 21	01 ♑ 15	08 ♓ 34	21 ♓ 17	09 ♈ 15	19 ♒ 36	20 ♒ 03	06 ♍ 51	01 ♋ 31
Feb 19, 2004	27 ♑ 05	05 ♑ 05	13 ♓ 24	26 ♓ 39	12 ♈ 30	24 ♒ 16	23 ♒ 40	05 ♍ 37	01 ♋ 03
Feb 29, 2004	02 ♒ 52	08 ♑ 46	18 ♓ 18	02 ♈ 05	15 ♈ 52	28 ♒ 57	27 ♒ 16	03 ♍ 16	01 ♋ 17
Mar 10, 2004	08 ♒ 28	12 ♑ 17	23 ♓ 17	07 ♈ 33	19 ♈ 19	03 ♓ 38	00 ♓ 49	29 ♌ 04	02 ♋ 10
Mar 20, 2004	13 ♒ 56	15 ♑ 36	28 ♓ 18	13 ♈ 03	22 ♈ 50	08 ♓ 19	04 ♓ 19	27 ♌ 18	03 ♋ 38
Mar 30, 2004	19 ♒ 15	18 ♑ 40	03 ♈ 22	18 ♈ 35	26 ♈ 25	12 ♓ 58	07 ♓ 43	26 ♌ 09	05 ♋ 36
Apr 9, 2004	24 ♒ 23	21 ♑ 27	08 ♈ 28	24 ♈ 08	00 ♉ 00	17 ♓ 35	11 ♓ 01	25 ♌ 41	07 ♋ 59
Apr 19, 2004	29 ♒ 20	23 ♑ 53	13 ♈ 35	29 ♈ 41	03 ♉ 36	22 ♓ 09	14 ♓ 12	25 ♌ 55	10 ♋ 45

	ATROPOS	HEKATE	LILITH	MEDUSA	MOIRA	NEMESIS	PERSEPHONE	PROSERPINA	PYTHIA
Apr 29, 2004	04 ♓ 04	25 ♑ 55	18 ♈ 44	05 ♉ 14	07 ♉ 13	26 ♓ 39	17 ♓ 15	26 ♌ 48	13 ♋ 48
May 9, 2004	08 ♓ 32	27 ♑ 29	23 ♈ 52	10 ♉ 47	10 ♉ 48	01 ♈ 04	20 ♈ 07	28 ♌ 17	17 ♋ 07
May 19, 2004	12 ♓ 43	28 ♑ 31	29 ♈ 00	16 ♉ 19	14 ♉ 21	05 ♈ 23	22 ♈ 47	00 ♍ 18	20 ♋ 39
May 29, 2004	16 ♓ 34	28 ♑ 57	04 ♉ 07	21 ♉ 50	17 ♉ 51	09 ♈ 35	25 ♈ 13	02 ♍ 44	24 ♋ 23
Jun 8, 2004	20 ♓ 02	28 ♑ 46	09 ♉ 12	27 ♉ 19	21 ♉ 18	13 ♈ 38	27 ♈ 23	05 ♍ 34	28 ♋ 16
Jun 18, 2004	23 ♓ 03	27 ♑ 57	14 ♉ 15	02 ♊ 46	24 ♉ 40	17 ♈ 30	29 ♈ 14	08 ♍ 43	02 ♌ 17
Jun 28, 2004	25 ♓ 33	26 ♑ 35	19 ♉ 14	08 ♊ 11	27 ♉ 56	21 ♈ 10	00 ♈ 44	12 ♍ 09	06 ♌ 26
Jul 8, 2004	27 ♓ 26	24 ♑ 49	24 ♉ 09	13 ♊ 33	01 ♊ 06	24 ♈ 34	01 ♈ 49	15 ♍ 48	10 ♌ 42
Jul 18, 2004	28 ♓ 36	22 ♑ 50	28 ♉ 59	18 ♊ 51	04 ♊ 07	27 ♈ 40	02 ♈ 26	19 ♍ 39	15 ♌ 03
Jul 28, 2004	28 ♓ 59	20 ♑ 55	03 ♊ 41	24 ♊ 05	06 ♊ 59	00 ♉ 25	02 ♈ 34	23 ♍ 41	19 ♌ 29
Aug 7, 2004	28 ♓ 30	19 ♑ 17	08 ♊ 15	29 ♊ 13	09 ♊ 38	02 ♉ 44	02 ♈ 10	27 ♍ 51	23 ♌ 60
Aug 17, 2004	27 ♓ 10	18 ♑ 09	12 ♊ 38	04 ♋ 16	12 ♊ 05	04 ♉ 32	01 ♈ 14	02 ♎ 09	28 ♌ 34
Aug 27, 2004	25 ♓ 04	17 ♑ 37	16 ♊ 48	09 ♋ 12	14 ♊ 14	05 ♉ 44	29 ♈ 50	06 ♎ 34	03 ♍ 13
Sep 6, 2004	22 ♓ 27	17 ♑ 44	20 ♊ 42	13 ♋ 59	16 ♊ 05	06 ♉ 16	28 ♈ 03	11 ♎ 04	07 ♍ 54
Sep 16, 2004	19 ♓ 37	18 ♑ 29	24 ♊ 16	18 ♋ 36	17 ♊ 33	06 ♉ 05	26 ♈ 02	15 ♎ 39	12 ♍ 38
Sep 26, 2004	16 ♓ 59	19 ♑ 51	27 ♊ 27	23 ♋ 02	18 ♊ 34	05 ♉ 10	23 ♓ 59	20 ♎ 18	17 ♍ 25
Oct 6, 2004	14 ♓ 53	21 ♑ 43	00 ♋ 08	27 ♋ 12	19 ♊ 07	03 ♉ 36	22 ♓ 06	24 ♎ 60	22 ♍ 12
Oct 16, 2004	13 ♓ 31	24 ♑ 04	02 ♋ 15	01 ♌ 05	19 ♊ 06	01 ♉ 33	20 ♈ 32	29 ♎ 45	27 ♍ 01
Oct 26, 2004	12 ♓ 59	26 ♑ 49	03 ♋ 41	04 ♌ 36	18 ♊ 31	29 ♈ 18	19 ♈ 26	04 ♏ 31	01 ♎ 51
Nov 5, 2004	13 ♓ 16	29 ♑ 55	04 ♋ 21	07 ♌ 42	17 ♊ 22	27 ♈ 09	18 ♈ 51	09 ♏ 19	06 ♎ 40
Nov 15, 2004	14 ♓ 18	03 ♒ 18	04 ♋ 11	10 ♌ 16	15 ♊ 41	25 ♈ 25	18 ♈ 50	14 ♏ 08	11 ♎ 28
Nov 25, 2004	15 ♓ 59	06 ♒ 55	03 ♋ 10	12 ♌ 12	13 ♊ 38	24 ♈ 19	19 ♈ 21	18 ♏ 56	16 ♎ 14
Dec 5, 2004	18 ♓ 12	10 ♒ 45	01 ♋ 27	13 ♌ 24	11 ♊ 22	23 ♈ 56	20 ♈ 22	23 ♏ 43	20 ♎ 56
Dec 15, 2004	20 ♓ 54	14 ♒ 45	29 ♊ 14	13 ♌ 45	09 ♊ 08	24 ♈ 17	21 ♈ 49	28 ♏ 29	25 ♎ 34
Dec 25, 2004	23 ♓ 58	18 ♒ 53	26 ♊ 53	13 ♌ 12	07 ♊ 09	25 ♈ 20	23 ♈ 40	03 ♐ 12	00 ♏ 05
Jan 4, 2005	27 ♓ 21	23 ♒ 07	24 ♊ 47	11 ♌ 44	05 ♊ 36	27 ♈ 01	25 ♈ 51	07 ♐ 50	04 ♏ 29
Jan 14, 2005	00 ♈ 60	27 ♒ 27	23 ♊ 13	09 ♌ 31	04 ♊ 36	29 ♈ 14	28 ♈ 20	12 ♐ 24	08 ♏ 42
Jan 24, 2005	04 ♈ 51	01 ♓ 51	22 ♊ 25	06 ♌ 50	04 ♊ 12	01 ♉ 54	01 ♈ 04	16 ♐ 52	12 ♏ 42
Feb 3, 2005	08 ♈ 51	06 ♓ 18	22 ♊ 24	04 ♌ 05	04 ♊ 23	04 ♉ 56	03 ♈ 59	21 ♐ 12	16 ♏ 25
Feb 13, 2005	13 ♈ 00	10 ♓ 46	23 ♊ 10	01 ♌ 41	05 ♊ 08	08 ♉ 17	07 ♈ 05	25 ♐ 23	19 ♏ 48
Feb 23, 2005	17 ♈ 16	15 ♓ 15	24 ♊ 37	29 ♋ 58	06 ♊ 23	11 ♉ 53	10 ♈ 20	29 ♐ 23	22 ♏ 46
Mar 5, 2005	21 ♈ 35	19 ♓ 43	26 ♊ 40	29 ♋ 05	08 ♊ 05	15 ♉ 41	13 ♈ 41	03 ♑ 10	25 ♏ 15
Mar 15, 2005	25 ♈ 59	24 ♓ 11	29 ♊ 13	29 ♋ 05	10 ♊ 09	19 ♉ 39	17 ♈ 07	06 ♑ 41	27 ♏ 06
Mar 25, 2005	00 ♉ 26	28 ♓ 37	02 ♋ 26	29 ♋ 54	12 ♊ 33	23 ♉ 45	20 ♈ 37	09 ♑ 54	28 ♏ 15
Apr 4, 2005	04 ♉ 53	02 ♈ 59	05 ♋ 27	01 ♌ 26	15 ♊ 13	27 ♉ 57	24 ♈ 10	12 ♑ 45	28 ♏ 36

	ATROPOS	HEKATE	LILITH	MEDUSA	MOIRA	NEMESIS	PERSEPHONE	PROSERPINA	PYTHIA
Apr 14, 2005	09 ♉ 22	07 ♈ 19	08 ♋ 59	03 ♌ 35	18 ♊ 07	02 ♊ 13	27 ♈ 45	15 ♑ 10	28 ♏ 04
Apr 24, 2005	13 ♉ 51	11 ♈ 34	12 ♋ 44	06 ♌ 14	21 ♊ 13	06 ♊ 33	01 ♉ 21	17 ♑ 06	26 ♏ 43
May 4, 2005	18 ♉ 19	15 ♈ 44	16 ♋ 39	09 ♌ 18	24 ♊ 28	10 ♊ 56	04 ♉ 57	18 ♑ 28	24 ♏ 42
May 14, 2005	22 ♉ 47	19 ♈ 49	20 ♋ 42	12 ♌ 43	27 ♊ 52	15 ♊ 18	08 ♉ 32	19 ♑ 12	22 ♏ 16
May 24, 2005	27 ♉ 12	23 ♈ 46	24 ♋ 51	16 ♌ 25	01 ♋ 22	19 ♊ 44	12 ♉ 06	19 ♑ 14	19 ♏ 51
Jun 3, 2005	01 ♊ 35	27 ♈ 35	29 ♋ 05	20 ♌ 20	04 ♋ 59	24 ♊ 09	15 ♉ 36	18 ♑ 35	17 ♏ 48
Jun 13, 2005	05 ♊ 55	01 ♉ 15	03 ♌ 22	24 ♌ 27	08 ♋ 40	28 ♊ 33	19 ♉ 03	17 ♑ 15	16 ♏ 27
Jun 23, 2005	10 ♊ 12	04 ♉ 44	07 ♌ 42	28 ♌ 43	12 ♋ 25	02 ♋ 56	22 ♉ 25	15 ♑ 24	15 ♏ 56
Jul 3, 2005	14 ♊ 24	08 ♉ 01	12 ♌ 03	03 ♍ 07	16 ♋ 13	07 ♋ 17	25 ♉ 42	13 ♑ 15	16 ♏ 17
Jul 13, 2005	18 ♊ 31	11 ♉ 03	16 ♌ 25	07 ♍ 37	20 ♋ 04	11 ♋ 36	28 ♉ 51	11 ♑ 04	17 ♏ 28
Jul 23, 2005	22 ♊ 33	13 ♉ 49	20 ♌ 47	12 ♍ 12	23 ♋ 56	15 ♋ 52	01 ♊ 51	09 ♑ 07	19 ♏ 23
Aug 2, 2005	26 ♊ 27	16 ♉ 15	25 ♌ 09	16 ♍ 52	27 ♋ 49	20 ♋ 05	04 ♊ 41	07 ♑ 39	21 ♏ 55
Aug 12, 2005	00 ♋ 13	18 ♉ 19	29 ♌ 30	21 ♍ 36	01 ♌ 42	24 ♋ 13	07 ♊ 18	06 ♑ 49	24 ♏ 59
Aug 22, 2005	03 ♋ 49	19 ♉ 58	03 ♍ 49	26 ♍ 22	05 ♌ 35	28 ♋ 16	09 ♊ 40	06 ♑ 39	28 ♏ 30
Sep 1, 2005	07 ♋ 14	21 ♉ 07	08 ♍ 07	01 ♎ 12	09 ♌ 27	02 ♌ 13	11 ♊ 44	07 ♑ 09	02 ♐ 23
Sep 11, 2005	10 ♋ 25	21 ♉ 44	12 ♍ 22	06 ♎ 03	13 ♌ 17	06 ♌ 03	13 ♊ 27	08 ♑ 17	06 ♐ 34
Sep 21, 2005	13 ♋ 19	21 ♉ 45	16 ♍ 34	10 ♎ 56	17 ♌ 04	09 ♌ 45	14 ♊ 45	09 ♑ 58	11 ♐ 00
Oct 1, 2005	15 ♋ 54	21 ♉ 10	20 ♍ 42	15 ♎ 50	20 ♌ 46	13 ♌ 16	15 ♊ 35	12 ♑ 08	15 ♐ 40
Oct 11, 2005	18 ♋ 05	20 ♉ 01	24 ♍ 45	20 ♎ 45	24 ♌ 23	16 ♌ 36	15 ♊ 52	14 ♑ 43	20 ♐ 30
Oct 21, 2005	19 ♋ 49	18 ♉ 21	28 ♍ 42	25 ♎ 39	27 ♌ 52	19 ♌ 41	15 ♊ 35	17 ♑ 39	25 ♐ 29
Oct 31, 2005	20 ♋ 59	16 ♉ 22	02 ♎ 33	00 ♏ 34	01 ♍ 13	22 ♌ 30	14 ♊ 42	20 ♑ 53	00 ♑ 35
Nov 10, 2005	21 ♋ 32	14 ♉ 14	06 ♎ 16	05 ♏ 28	04 ♍ 21	24 ♌ 58	13 ♊ 17	24 ♑ 21	05 ♑ 47
Nov 20, 2005	21 ♋ 23	12 ♉ 13	09 ♎ 49	10 ♏ 20	07 ♍ 15	27 ♌ 04	11 ♊ 26	28 ♑ 02	11 ♑ 04
Nov 30, 2005	20 ♋ 29	10 ♉ 31	13 ♎ 12	15 ♏ 10	09 ♍ 52	28 ♌ 42	09 ♊ 18	01 ♒ 53	16 ♑ 24
Dec 10, 2005	18 ♋ 51	09 ♉ 17	16 ♎ 20	19 ♏ 58	12 ♍ 06	29 ♌ 49	07 ♊ 08	05 ♒ 53	21 ♑ 48
Dec 20, 2005	16 ♋ 36	08 ♉ 37	19 ♎ 14	24 ♏ 41	13 ♍ 55	00 ♍ 21	05 ♊ 11	09 ♒ 59	27 ♑ 13
Dec 30, 2005	13 ♋ 55	08 ♉ 32	21 ♎ 49	29 ♏ 20	15 ♍ 12	00 ♍ 15	03 ♊ 36	14 ♒ 10	02 ♒ 40
Jan 9, 2006	11 ♋ 07	09 ♉ 02	24 ♎ 03	03 ♐ 54	15 ♍ 54	29 ♌ 29	02 ♊ 35	18 ♒ 26	08 ♒ 07
Jan 19, 2006	08 ♋ 31	10 ♉ 02	25 ♎ 52	08 ♐ 21	15 ♍ 56	28 ♌ 06	02 ♊ 09	22 ♒ 45	13 ♒ 33
Jan 29, 2006	06 ♋ 23	11 ♉ 30	27 ♎ 13	12 ♐ 39	15 ♍ 13	26 ♌ 12	02 ♊ 21	27 ♒ 05	18 ♒ 58
Feb 8, 2006	04 ♋ 55	13 ♉ 21	28 ♎ 02	16 ♐ 48	13 ♍ 54	23 ♌ 59	03 ♊ 07	01 ♓ 27	24 ♒ 22
Feb 18, 2006	04 ♋ 11	15 ♉ 33	28 ♎ 15	20 ♐ 44	11 ♍ 58	21 ♌ 41	04 ♊ 25	05 ♓ 48	29 ♒ 43
Feb 28, 2006	04 ♋ 10	18 ♉ 01	27 ♎ 51	24 ♐ 27	09 ♍ 41	19 ♌ 33	06 ♊ 10	10 ♓ 09	05 ♓ 02
Mar 10, 2006	04 ♋ 49	20 ♉ 43	26 ♎ 51	27 ♐ 53	07 ♍ 20	17 ♌ 49	08 ♊ 19	14 ♓ 29	10 ♓ 17
Mar 20, 2006	06 ♋ 04	23 ♉ 36	25 ♎ 17	00 ♑ 60	05 ♍ 13	16 ♌ 37	10 ♊ 49	18 ♓ 46	15 ♓ 27

	ATROPOS	HEKATE	LILITH	MEDUSA	MOIRA	NEMESIS	PERSEPHONE	PROSERPINA	PYTHIA
Mar 30, 2006	07♋49	26♉39	23♎17	03♑42	03♍36	16♌01	13♊36	22♓60	20♓33
Apr 9, 2006	09♋60	29♉48	21♎02	05♑57	02♍29	16♌02	16♊37	27♈10	25♓34
Apr 19, 2006	12♋32	03♊03	18♎46	07♑39	02♍26	16♌38	19♊50	01♈16	00♈28
Apr 29, 2006	15♋22	06♊22	16♎43	08♑42	02♍56	17♌44	23♊13	05♈16	05♈16
May 9, 2006	18♋27	09♊44	15♎03	09♑03	04♍08	19♌18	26♊44	09♈10	09♈56
May 19, 2006	21♋45	13♊08	13♎54	08♑37	05♍56	21♌16	00♋22	12♈56	14♈28
May 29, 2006	25♋13	16♊33	13♎19	07♑24	08♍16	23♌33	04♋05	16♈33	18♈51
Jun 8, 2006	28♋49	19♊58	13♎18	05♑29	11♍04	26♌07	07♋53	20♈00	23♈03
Jun 18, 2006	02♌33	23♊22	13♎49	03♑04	14♍14	28♌54	11♋44	23♈16	27♈02
Jun 28, 2006	06♌23	26♊44	14♎49	00♑27	17♍44	01♍54	15♋38	26♈18	00♉49
Jul 8, 2006	10♌19	00♋03	16♎16	27♐58	21♍31	05♍03	19♋33	29♈04	04♉19
Jul 18, 2006	14♌18	03♋19	18♎04	25♐57	25♍33	08♍20	23♋29	01♉31	07♉31
Jul 28, 2006	18♌22	06♋30	20♎12	24♐36	29♍47	11♍44	27♋26	03♉37	10♉21
Aug 7, 2006	22♌29	09♋35	22♎37	24♐03	04♎11	15♍14	01♌22	05♉18	12♉47
Aug 17, 2006	26♌38	12♋34	25♎15	24♐18	08♎45	18♍47	05♌17	06♉30	14♉44
Aug 27, 2006	00♍49	15♋24	28♎05	25♐17	13♎26	22♍25	09♌10	07♉09	16♉07
Sep 6, 2006	05♍02	18♋04	01♏06	26♐58	18♎15	26♍05	12♌59	07♉11	16♉51
Sep 16, 2006	09♍16	20♋33	04♏14	29♐13	23♎09	29♍46	16♌45	06♉37	16♉53
Sep 26, 2006	13♍31	22♋47	07♏30	01♑09	28♎08	03♎28	20♌25	05♉24	16♉09
Oct 6, 2006	17♍45	24♋46	10♏52	05♑09	03♏17	07♎11	23♌59	03♉40	14♉41
Oct 16, 2006	21♍58	26♋25	14♏18	08♑42	08♏17	10♎52	27♌24	01♉32	12♉36
Oct 26, 2006	26♍10	27♋42	17♏47	12♑34	13♏26	14♎32	00♍39	29♈13	10♉04
Nov 5, 2006	00♎20	28♋34	21♏20	16♑41	18♏36	18♎08	03♍42	27♈00	07♉23
Nov 15, 2006	04♎26	28♋58	24♏53	21♑02	23♏48	21♎41	06♍29	25♈07	04♉54
Nov 25, 2006	08♎28	28♋52	28♏28	25♑35	28♏60	25♎09	08♍59	23♈43	02♉52
Dec 5, 2006	12♎23	28♋15	02♐02	00♒18	04♐11	28♎30	11♍07	22♈57	01♉29
Dec 15, 2006	16♎10	27♋08	05♐34	05♒09	09♐21	01♏42	12♍50	22♈49	00♉50
Dec 25, 2006	19♎47	25♋34	09♐04	10♒08	14♐29	04♏45	14♍03	23♈18	00♉54
Jan 4, 2007	23♎11	23♋42	12♐29	15♒13	19♐34	07♏35	14♍42	24♈22	01♉39
Jan 14, 2007	26♎19	21♋41	15♐50	20♒23	24♐34	10♏10	14♍45	25♈56	02♉59
Jan 24, 2007	29♎07	19♋42	19♐04	25♒38	29♐30	12♏28	14♍10	27♈56	04♉50
Feb 3, 2007	01♏30	17♋56	22♐10	00♓57	04♑20	14♏25	12♍58	00♉18	07♉07
Feb 13, 2007	03♏24	16♋31	25♐06	06♓18	09♑02	15♏58	11♍15	02♉60	09♉46
Feb 23, 2007	04♏42	15♋34	27♐50	11♓42	13♑36	17♏04	09♍11	05♉57	12♉42
Mar 5, 2007	05♏17	15♋07	00♑20	17♓08	17♑59	17♏38	07♍00	09♉07	15♉53

	ATROPOS	HEKATE	LILITH	MEDUSA	MOIRA	NEMESIS	PERSEPHONE	PROSERPINA	PYTHIA
Mar 15, 2007	05 ♏ 05	15 ♋ 10	02 ♑ 33	22 ♓ 34	22 ♑ 11	17 ♏ 39	04 ♍ 57	12 ♉ 28	19 ♉ 15
Mar 25, 2007	04 ♏ 01	15 ♋ 41	04 ♑ 26	28 ♓ 02	26 ♑ 09	17 ♏ 05	03 ♍ 16	15 ♉ 57	22 ♉ 48
Apr 4, 2007	02 ♏ 09	16 ♋ 39	05 ♑ 57	03 ♈ 29	29 ♑ 51	15 ♏ 57	02 ♍ 06	19 ♉ 34	26 ♉ 28
Apr 14, 2007	29 ♎ 39	17 ♋ 60	07 ♑ 01	08 ♈ 57	03 ♒ 15	14 ♏ 18	01 ♍ 32	23 ♉ 16	00 ♊ 14
Apr 24, 2007	26 ♎ 50	19 ♋ 40	07 ♑ 36	14 ♈ 24	06 ♒ 17	12 ♏ 18	01 ♍ 36	27 ♉ 03	04 ♊ 06
May 4, 2007	24 ♎ 06	21 ♋ 38	07 ♑ 39	19 ♈ 49	08 ♒ 54	10 ♏ 08	02 ♍ 15	00 ♊ 53	08 ♊ 01
May 14, 2007	21 ♎ 52	23 ♋ 50	07 ♑ 09	25 ♈ 13	11 ♒ 03	07 ♏ 59	03 ♍ 26	04 ♊ 45	11 ♊ 59
May 24, 2007	20 ♎ 24	26 ♋ 15	06 ♑ 04	00 ♉ 35	12 ♒ 39	06 ♏ 06	05 ♍ 06	08 ♊ 39	15 ♊ 60
Jun 3, 2007	19 ♎ 52	28 ♋ 50	04 ♑ 29	05 ♉ 54	13 ♒ 38	04 ♏ 38	07 ♍ 11	12 ♊ 34	20 ♊ 01
Jun 13, 2007	20 ♎ 15	01 ♌ 33	02 ♑ 31	11 ♉ 10	13 ♒ 56	03 ♏ 42	09 ♍ 37	16 ♊ 30	24 ♊ 04
Jun 23, 2007	21 ♎ 32	04 ♌ 24	00 ♑ 20	16 ♉ 22	13 ♒ 32	03 ♏ 19	12 ♍ 21	20 ♊ 25	28 ♊ 07
Jul 3, 2007	23 ♎ 35	07 ♌ 20	28 ♐ 08	21 ♉ 30	12 ♒ 27	03 ♏ 32	15 ♍ 20	24 ♊ 18	02 ♋ 10
Jul 13, 2007	26 ♎ 18	10 ♌ 20	26 ♐ 08	26 ♉ 32	10 ♒ 47	04 ♏ 16	18 ♍ 32	28 ♊ 10	06 ♋ 11
Jul 23, 2007	29 ♎ 36	13 ♌ 24	24 ♐ 31	01 ♊ 27	08 ♒ 42	05 ♏ 29	21 ♍ 56	01 ♋ 59	10 ♋ 11
Aug 2, 2007	03 ♏ 22	16 ♌ 30	23 ♐ 24	06 ♊ 14	06 ♒ 27	07 ♏ 09	25 ♍ 28	05 ♋ 44	14 ♋ 09
Aug 12, 2007	07 ♏ 32	19 ♌ 38	22 ♐ 52	10 ♊ 52	04 ♒ 19	09 ♏ 19	29 ♍ 09	09 ♋ 25	18 ♋ 04
Aug 22, 2007	12 ♏ 03	22 ♌ 46	22 ♐ 56	15 ♊ 18	02 ♒ 34	11 ♏ 35	02 ♎ 56	12 ♋ 60	21 ♋ 55
Sep 1, 2007	16 ♏ 51	25 ♌ 53	23 ♐ 33	19 ♊ 30	01 ♒ 21	14 ♏ 15	06 ♎ 49	16 ♋ 27	25 ♋ 41
Sep 11, 2007	21 ♏ 52	28 ♌ 59	24 ♐ 42	23 ♊ 25	00 ♒ 46	17 ♏ 10	10 ♎ 46	19 ♋ 47	29 ♋ 22
Sep 21, 2007	27 ♏ 05	02 ♍ 02	26 ♐ 19	26 ♊ 58	00 ♒ 51	20 ♏ 58	14 ♎ 47	22 ♋ 56	02 ♌ 55
Oct 1, 2007	02 ♐ 28	05 ♍ 02	28 ♐ 21	00 ♋ 06	01 ♒ 34	23 ♏ 36	18 ♎ 50	25 ♋ 51	06 ♌ 19
Oct 11, 2007	07 ♐ 59	07 ♍ 56	00 ♑ 45	02 ♋ 44	02 ♒ 50	27 ♏ 05	22 ♎ 55	28 ♋ 32	09 ♌ 32
Oct 21, 2007	13 ♐ 36	10 ♍ 43	03 ♑ 28	04 ♋ 43	04 ♒ 37	00 ♐ 42	27 ♎ 02	00 ♌ 54	12 ♌ 31
Oct 31, 2007	19 ♐ 17	13 ♍ 23	06 ♑ 28	05 ♋ 58	06 ♒ 50	04 ♐ 25	01 ♏ 08	02 ♌ 53	15 ♌ 13
Nov 10, 2007	25 ♐ 03	15 ♍ 51	09 ♑ 42	06 ♋ 22	09 ♒ 24	08 ♐ 15	05 ♏ 15	04 ♌ 26	17 ♌ 36
Nov 20, 2007	00 ♑ 50	18 ♍ 07	13 ♑ 09	05 ♋ 50	12 ♒ 17	12 ♐ 10	09 ♏ 19	05 ♌ 28	19 ♌ 34
Nov 30, 2007	06 ♑ 39	20 ♍ 08	16 ♑ 46	04 ♋ 24	15 ♒ 25	16 ♐ 08	13 ♏ 21	05 ♌ 55	21 ♌ 02
Dec 10, 2007	12 ♑ 28	21 ♍ 51	20 ♑ 33	02 ♋ 11	18 ♒ 46	20 ♐ 09	17 ♏ 19	05 ♌ 43	21 ♌ 56
Dec 20, 2007	18 ♑ 17	23 ♍ 13	24 ♑ 29	29 ♊ 11	22 ♒ 17	24 ♐ 12	21 ♏ 13	04 ♌ 51	22 ♌ 10
Dec 30, 2007	24 ♑ 05	24 ♍ 11	28 ♑ 30	26 ♊ 49	25 ♒ 56	28 ♐ 17	24 ♏ 60	03 ♌ 22	21 ♌ 40
Jan 9, 2008	29 ♑ 51	24 ♍ 42	02 ♒ 38	24 ♊ 30	29 ♒ 42	02 ♑ 21	28 ♏ 39	01 ♌ 21	20 ♌ 26
Jan 19, 2008	05 ♒ 35	24 ♍ 43	06 ♒ 51	22 ♊ 55	03 ♓ 33	06 ♑ 25	02 ♐ 09	29 ♋ 02	18 ♌ 30
Jan 29, 2008	11 ♒ 15	24 ♍ 13	11 ♒ 07	22 ♊ 13	07 ♓ 27	10 ♑ 27	05 ♐ 27	26 ♋ 41	16 ♌ 04
Feb 8, 2008	16 ♒ 52	23 ♍ 27	15 ♒ 27	22 ♊ 25	11 ♓ 24	14 ♑ 26	08 ♐ 31	24 ♋ 34	13 ♌ 21
Feb 18, 2008	22 ♒ 25	21 ♍ 45	19 ♒ 49	23 ♊ 29	15 ♓ 23	18 ♑ 22	11 ♐ 19	22 ♋ 55	10 ♌ 44

	ATROPOS	HEKATE	LILITH	MEDUSA	MOIRA	NEMESIS	PERSEPHONE	PROSERPINA	PYTHIA
Feb 28, 2008	27 ≈ 53	19 ♍ 57	24 ≈ 13	25 ♊ 17	19 ♓ 22	22 ♑ 12	13 ♐ 48	21 ♋ 53	08 ♌ 31
Mar 9, 2008	03 ♓ 16	17 ♍ 57	28 ≈ 37	27 ♊ 41	23 ♓ 21	25 ♑ 56	15 ♐ 55	21 ♋ 31	06 ♌ 55
Mar 19, 2008	08 ♓ 33	15 ♍ 57	03 ♓ 02	00 ♋ 37	27 ♓ 18	29 ♑ 32	17 ♐ 36	21 ♋ 50	06 ♌ 05
Mar 29, 2008	13 ♓ 45	14 ♍ 07	07 ♓ 26	03 ♋ 57	01 ♈ 13	02 ≈ 59	18 ♐ 48	22 ♋ 46	06 ♌ 01
Apr 8, 2008	18 ♓ 50	12 ♍ 38	11 ♓ 48	07 ♋ 38	05 ♈ 05	06 ≈ 14	19 ♐ 26	24 ♋ 16	06 ♌ 42
Apr 18, 2008	23 ♓ 48	11 ♍ 35	16 ♓ 09	11 ♋ 35	08 ♈ 53	09 ≈ 15	19 ♐ 30	26 ♋ 15	08 ♌ 04
Apr 28, 2008	28 ♓ 39	11 ♍ 02	20 ♓ 26	15 ♋ 45	12 ♈ 37	12 ≈ 00	18 ♐ 57	28 ♋ 39	10 ♌ 00
May 8, 2008	03 ♈ 21	11 ♍ 00	24 ♓ 40	20 ♋ 06	16 ♈ 14	14 ≈ 25	17 ♐ 49	01 ♌ 24	12 ♌ 27
May 18, 2008	07 ♈ 54	11 ♍ 28	28 ♓ 48	24 ♋ 36	19 ♈ 46	16 ≈ 28	16 ♐ 13	04 ♌ 27	15 ♌ 20
May 28, 2008	12 ♈ 16	12 ♍ 24	02 ♈ 50	29 ♋ 12	23 ♈ 09	18 ≈ 03	14 ♐ 16	07 ♌ 45	18 ♌ 34
Jun 7, 2008	16 ♈ 27	13 ♍ 44	06 ♈ 45	03 ♌ 54	26 ♈ 24	19 ≈ 07	12 ♐ 11	11 ♌ 16	22 ♌ 07
Jun 17, 2008	20 ♈ 25	15 ♍ 27	10 ♈ 29	08 ♌ 41	29 ♈ 28	19 ≈ 36	10 ♐ 12	14 ♌ 59	25 ♌ 57
Jun 27, 2008	24 ♈ 07	17 ♍ 29	14 ♈ 01	13 ♌ 32	02 ♉ 20	19 ≈ 27	08 ♐ 31	18 ♌ 50	29 ♌ 60
Jul 7, 2008	27 ♈ 32	19 ♍ 48	17 ♈ 19	18 ♌ 25	04 ♉ 57	18 ≈ 39	07 ♐ 18	22 ♌ 50	04 ♍ 15
Jul 17, 2008	00 ♉ 36	22 ♍ 21	20 ♈ 18	23 ♌ 21	07 ♉ 18	17 ≈ 15	06 ♐ 37	26 ♌ 57	08 ♍ 41
Jul 27, 2008	03 ♉ 17	25 ♍ 06	22 ♈ 55	28 ♌ 18	09 ♉ 21	15 ≈ 22	06 ♐ 31	01 ♍ 09	13 ♍ 16
Aug 6, 2008	05 ♉ 28	28 ♍ 03	25 ♈ 06	03 ♍ 17	11 ♉ 01	13 ≈ 13	06 ♐ 59	05 ♍ 27	17 ♍ 60
Aug 16, 2008	07 ♉ 07	01 ♎ 09	26 ♈ 44	08 ♍ 17	12 ♉ 15	11 ≈ 02	07 ♐ 59	09 ♍ 49	22 ♍ 51
Aug 26, 2008	08 ♉ 06	04 ♎ 22	27 ♈ 45	13 ♍ 18	13 ♉ 01	09 ≈ 08	09 ♐ 26	14 ♍ 14	27 ♍ 48
Sep 5, 2008	08 ♉ 22	07 ♎ 43	28 ♈ 03	18 ♍ 18	13 ♉ 14	07 ≈ 42	11 ♐ 18	18 ♍ 43	02 ♎ 52
Sep 15, 2008	07 ♉ 49	11 ♎ 09	27 ♈ 36	23 ♍ 19	12 ♉ 54	06 ≈ 54	13 ♐ 32	23 ♍ 14	08 ♎ 02
Sep 25, 2008	06 ♉ 28	14 ♎ 40	26 ♈ 24	28 ♍ 18	11 ♉ 59	06 ≈ 47	16 ♐ 04	27 ♍ 46	13 ♎ 16
Oct 5, 2008	04 ♉ 22	18 ♎ 14	24 ♈ 34	03 ♎ 17	10 ♉ 31	07 ≈ 22	18 ♐ 52	02 ♎ 20	18 ♎ 34
Oct 15, 2008	01 ♉ 45	21 ♎ 52	22 ♈ 22	08 ♎ 14	08 ♉ 37	08 ≈ 37	21 ♐ 53	06 ♎ 54	23 ♎ 56
Oct 25, 2008	28 ♈ 54	25 ♎ 31	20 ♈ 08	13 ♎ 10	06 ♉ 26	10 ≈ 27	25 ♐ 06	11 ♎ 28	29 ♎ 22
Nov 4, 2008	26 ♈ 10	29 ♎ 11	18 ♈ 12	18 ♎ 02	04 ♉ 11	12 ≈ 47	28 ♐ 27	16 ♎ 01	04 ♏ 50
Nov 14, 2008	23 ♈ 55	02 ♏ 52	16 ♈ 53	22 ♎ 51	02 ♉ 05	15 ≈ 35	01 ♑ 57	20 ♎ 32	10 ♏ 20
Nov 24, 2008	22 ♈ 22	06 ♏ 31	16 ♈ 20	27 ♎ 36	00 ♉ 22	18 ≈ 45	05 ♑ 32	24 ♎ 60	15 ♏ 52
Dec 4, 2008	21 ♈ 36	10 ♏ 08	16 ♈ 38	02 ♏ 16	29 ♈ 07	22 ≈ 14	09 ♑ 12	29 ♎ 24	21 ♏ 25
Dec 14, 2008	21 ♈ 39	13 ♏ 41	17 ♈ 45	06 ♏ 49	28 ♈ 28	26 ≈ 01	12 ♑ 56	03 ♏ 42	26 ♏ 57
Dec 24, 2008	22 ♈ 26	17 ♏ 10	19 ♈ 35	11 ♏ 15	28 ♈ 23	00 ♓ 01	16 ♑ 42	07 ♏ 54	02 ♐ 29
Jan 3, 2009	23 ♈ 52	20 ♏ 32	22 ♈ 04	15 ♏ 32	28 ♈ 53	04 ♓ 13	20 ♑ 30	11 ♏ 57	07 ♐ 60
Jan 13, 2009	25 ♈ 51	23 ♏ 46	25 ♈ 05	19 ♏ 38	29 ♈ 53	08 ♓ 34	24 ♑ 18	15 ♏ 49	13 ♐ 28
Jan 23, 2009	28 ♈ 18	26 ♏ 50	28 ♉ 32	23 ♏ 31	01 ♉ 21	13 ♓ 04	28 ♑ 05	19 ♏ 28	18 ♐ 52
Feb 2, 2009	01 ♉ 08	29 ♏ 41	02 ♉ 23	27 ♏ 09	03 ♉ 13	17 ♓ 40	01 ≈ 50	22 ♏ 52	24 ♐ 12

	ATROPOS	HEKATE	LILITH	MEDUSA	MOIRA	NEMESIS	PERSEPHONE	PROSERPINA	PYTHIA
Feb 12, 2009	04 ♉ 17	02 ♐ 17	06 ♉ 31	00 ♐ 28	05 ♉ 25	22 ♓ 22	05 ♒ 33	25 ♏ 56	29 ♐ 27
Feb 22, 2009	07 ♉ 40	04 ♐ 35	10 ♉ 53	03 ♐ 25	07 ♉ 54	27 ♓ 07	09 ♒ 11	28 ♏ 38	04 ♑ 35
Mar 4, 2009	11 ♉ 17	06 ♐ 31	15 ♉ 28	05 ♐ 56	10 ♉ 37	01 ♈ 47	12 ♒ 45	00 ♐ 53	09 ♑ 34
Mar 14, 2009	15 ♉ 03	08 ♐ 03	20 ♉ 12	07 ♐ 56	13 ♉ 32	06 ♈ 47	16 ♒ 12	02 ♐ 37	14 ♑ 22
Mar 24, 2009	18 ♉ 56	09 ♐ 05	25 ♉ 03	09 ♐ 21	16 ♉ 37	11 ♈ 39	19 ♒ 32	03 ♐ 44	18 ♑ 59
Apr 3, 2009	22 ♉ 57	09 ♐ 36	29 ♉ 60	10 ♐ 04	19 ♉ 50	16 ♈ 32	22 ♒ 43	04 ♐ 11	23 ♑ 21
Apr 13, 2009	27 ♉ 01	09 ♐ 32	05 ♊ 01	10 ♐ 01	23 ♉ 09	21 ♈ 24	25 ♒ 43	03 ♐ 56	27 ♑ 25
Apr 23, 2009	01 ♊ 09	08 ♐ 53	10 ♊ 05	09 ♐ 11	26 ♉ 33	26 ♈ 16	28 ♒ 31	02 ♐ 58	01 ♒ 08
May 3, 2009	05 ♊ 20	07 ♐ 40	15 ♊ 11	07 ♐ 35	00 ♊ 01	01 ♉ 06	01 ♓ 05	01 ♐ 22	04 ♒ 26
May 13, 2009	09 ♊ 33	06 ♐ 00	20 ♊ 19	05 ♐ 22	03 ♊ 32	05 ♉ 54	03 ♓ 22	29 ♏ 20	07 ♒ 13
May 23, 2009	13 ♊ 46	04 ♐ 02	25 ♊ 26	02 ♐ 47	07 ♊ 04	10 ♉ 39	05 ♓ 20	27 ♏ 07	09 ♒ 26
Jun 2, 2009	17 ♊ 59	01 ♐ 60	00 ♋ 34	00 ♐ 09	10 ♊ 38	15 ♉ 21	06 ♓ 57	25 ♏ 01	10 ♒ 57
Jun 12, 2009	22 ♊ 12	00 ♐ 07	05 ♋ 40	27 ♏ 51	14 ♊ 11	19 ♉ 59	08 ♓ 09	23 ♏ 18	11 ♒ 41
Jun 22, 2009	26 ♊ 24	28 ♏ 35	10 ♋ 45	26 ♏ 06	17 ♊ 44	24 ♉ 31	08 ♓ 53	22 ♏ 10	11 ♒ 34
Jul 2, 2009	00 ♋ 34	27 ♏ 34	15 ♋ 49	25 ♏ 05	21 ♊ 16	28 ♉ 58	09 ♓ 07	21 ♏ 43	10 ♒ 34
Jul 12, 2009	04 ♋ 42	27 ♏ 10	20 ♋ 50	24 ♏ 51	24 ♊ 45	03 ♊ 18	08 ♓ 49	21 ♏ 59	08 ♒ 50
Jul 22, 2009	08 ♋ 46	27 ♏ 22	25 ♋ 48	25 ♏ 23	28 ♊ 12	07 ♊ 30	07 ♓ 59	22 ♏ 54	06 ♒ 33
Aug 1, 2009	12 ♋ 47	28 ♏ 10	00 ♌ 42	26 ♏ 37	01 ♋ 34	11 ♊ 32	06 ♓ 40	24 ♏ 26	04 ♒ 05
Aug 11, 2009	16 ♋ 44	29 ♏ 31	05 ♌ 33	28 ♏ 28	04 ♋ 50	15 ♊ 23	04 ♓ 57	26 ♏ 30	01 ♒ 48
Aug 21, 2009	20 ♋ 35	01 ♐ 23	10 ♌ 20	00 ♐ 50	08 ♋ 00	19 ♊ 01	02 ♓ 59	29 ♏ 01	00 ♒ 04
Aug 31, 2009	24 ♋ 19	03 ♐ 40	15 ♌ 02	03 ♐ 40	11 ♋ 02	22 ♊ 23	00 ♓ 56	01 ♐ 55	29 ♑ 04
Sep 10, 2009	27 ♋ 55	06 ♐ 21	19 ♌ 38	06 ♐ 52	13 ♋ 53	25 ♊ 27	29 ♒ 01	05 ♐ 09	28 ♑ 54
Sep 20, 2009	01 ♌ 22	09 ♐ 21	24 ♌ 07	10 ♐ 24	16 ♋ 32	28 ♊ 09	27 ♒ 24	08 ♐ 39	29 ♑ 33
Sep 30, 2009	04 ♌ 37	12 ♐ 39	28 ♌ 29	14 ♐ 13	18 ♋ 57	00 ♋ 25	26 ♒ 13	12 ♐ 24	00 ♒ 57
Oct 10, 2009	07 ♌ 38	16 ♐ 11	02 ♍ 43	18 ♐ 16	21 ♋ 03	02 ♋ 10	25 ♒ 33	16 ♐ 20	02 ♒ 59
Oct 20, 2009	10 ♌ 23	19 ♐ 56	06 ♍ 46	22 ♐ 32	22 ♋ 48	03 ♋ 21	25 ♒ 26	20 ♐ 27	05 ♒ 34
Oct 30, 2009	12 ♌ 47	23 ♐ 53	10 ♍ 38	26 ♐ 58	24 ♋ 08	03 ♋ 52	25 ♒ 50	24 ♐ 41	08 ♒ 36
Nov 9, 2009	14 ♌ 48	27 ♐ 58	14 ♍ 16	01 ♑ 33	24 ♋ 59	03 ♋ 40	26 ♒ 44	29 ♐ 02	12 ♒ 00
Nov 19, 2009	16 ♌ 20	02 ♑ 12	17 ♍ 37	06 ♑ 16	25 ♋ 17	02 ♋ 45	28 ♒ 09	03 ♑ 29	15 ♒ 43
Nov 29, 2009	17 ♌ 19	06 ♑ 33	20 ♍ 41	11 ♑ 06	24 ♋ 58	01 ♋ 10	29 ♒ 50	08 ♑ 01	19 ♒ 41
Dec 9, 2009	17 ♌ 40	10 ♑ 58	23 ♍ 22	16 ♑ 02	24 ♋ 02	29 ♊ 06	01 ♓ 55	12 ♑ 35	23 ♒ 51
Dec 19, 2009	17 ♌ 19	15 ♑ 29	25 ♍ 37	21 ♑ 03	22 ♋ 31	26 ♊ 46	04 ♓ 18	17 ♑ 12	28 ♒ 11
Dec 29, 2009	16 ♌ 13	20 ♑ 03	27 ♍ 22	26 ♑ 09	20 ♋ 31	24 ♊ 29	06 ♓ 57	21 ♑ 51	02 ♓ 38
Jan 8, 2010	14 ♌ 26	24 ♑ 39	28 ♍ 33	01 ♒ 18	18 ♋ 14	22 ♊ 32	09 ♓ 47	26 ♑ 30	07 ♓ 11
Jan 18, 2010	12 ♌ 03	29 ♑ 17	29 ♍ 06	06 ♒ 30	15 ♋ 54	21 ♊ 08	12 ♓ 49	01 ♒ 09	11 ♓ 49

	ATROPOS	HEKATE	LILITH	MEDUSA	MOIRA	NEMESIS	PERSEPHONE	PROSERPINA	PYTHIA
Jan 28, 2010	09 ♌ 20	03 ♒ 56	28 ♍ 57	11 ♒ 44	13 ♋ 47	20 ♊ 23	15 ♓ 59	05 ♒ 48	16 ♈ 30
Feb 7, 2010	06 ♌ 34	08 ♒ 34	28 ♍ 07	16 ♒ 59	12 ♋ 05	20 ♊ 21	19 ♓ 15	10 ♒ 24	21 ♈ 14
Feb 17, 2010	04 ♌ 04	13 ♒ 12	26 ♍ 37	22 ♒ 16	10 ♋ 57	20 ♊ 58	22 ♓ 04	14 ♒ 58	25 ♈ 58
Feb 27, 2010	02 ♌ 05	17 ♒ 47	24 ♍ 36	27 ♒ 33	10 ♋ 28	22 ♊ 12	26 ♓ 04	19 ♒ 28	00 ♉ 43
Mar 9, 2010	00 ♌ 46	22 ♒ 19	22 ♍ 17	02 ♓ 51	10 ♋ 38	23 ♊ 56	29 ♓ 33	23 ♒ 55	05 ♉ 27
Mar 19, 2010	00 ♌ 10	26 ♒ 48	19 ♍ 55	08 ♓ 07	11 ♋ 25	26 ♊ 07	03 ♈ 04	28 ♒ 16	10 ♉ 10
Mar 29, 2010	00 ♌ 18	01 ♓ 12	17 ♍ 46	13 ♓ 23	12 ♋ 45	28 ♊ 39	06 ♈ 35	02 ♓ 31	14 ♉ 51
Apr 8, 2010	01 ♌ 05	05 ♓ 30	16 ♍ 03	18 ♓ 38	14 ♋ 34	01 ♋ 30	10 ♈ 06	06 ♓ 39	19 ♉ 30
Apr 18, 2010	02 ♌ 27	09 ♓ 40	14 ♍ 55	23 ♓ 50	16 ♋ 48	04 ♋ 36	13 ♈ 36	10 ♓ 40	24 ♉ 06
Apr 28, 2010	04 ♌ 19	13 ♓ 43	14 ♍ 24	28 ♓ 60	19 ♋ 24	07 ♋ 55	17 ♈ 04	14 ♓ 30	28 ♉ 39
May 8, 2010	06 ♌ 37	17 ♓ 36	14 ♍ 30	04 ♈ 06	22 ♋ 19	11 ♋ 22	20 ♈ 29	18 ♓ 10	03 ♊ 07
May 18, 2010	09 ♌ 16	21 ♓ 17	15 ♍ 11	09 ♈ 09	25 ♋ 29	14 ♋ 58	23 ♈ 49	21 ♓ 38	07 ♊ 32
May 28, 2010	12 ♌ 14	24 ♓ 44	16 ♍ 22	14 ♈ 06	28 ♋ 54	18 ♋ 41	27 ♈ 04	24 ♓ 50	11 ♊ 50
Jun 7, 2010	15 ♌ 27	27 ♓ 56	18 ♍ 00	18 ♈ 58	02 ♌ 30	22 ♋ 28	00 ♉ 13	27 ♓ 46	16 ♊ 04
Jun 17, 2010	18 ♌ 54	00 ♈ 49	20 ♍ 01	23 ♈ 43	06 ♌ 16	26 ♋ 20	03 ♉ 14	00 ♈ 23	20 ♊ 10
Jun 27, 2010	22 ♌ 32	03 ♈ 21	22 ♍ 21	28 ♈ 19	10 ♌ 11	00 ♌ 14	06 ♉ 06	02 ♈ 36	24 ♊ 10
Jul 7, 2010	26 ♌ 20	05 ♈ 28	24 ♍ 56	02 ♉ 46	14 ♌ 13	04 ♌ 10	08 ♉ 46	04 ♈ 24	28 ♊ 00
Jul 17, 2010	00 ♍ 18	07 ♈ 06	27 ♍ 45	07 ♉ 00	18 ♌ 23	08 ♌ 08	11 ♉ 13	05 ♈ 41	01 ♋ 42
Jul 27, 2010	04 ♍ 23	08 ♈ 11	00 ♎ 45	11 ♉ 00	22 ♌ 38	12 ♌ 06	13 ♉ 25	06 ♈ 24	05 ♋ 11
Aug 6, 2010	08 ♍ 36	08 ♈ 39	03 ♎ 55	14 ♉ 42	26 ♌ 58	16 ♌ 04	15 ♉ 18	06 ♈ 31	08 ♋ 28
Aug 16, 2010	12 ♍ 54	08 ♈ 30	07 ♎ 12	18 ♉ 02	01 ♍ 24	20 ♌ 01	16 ♉ 50	05 ♈ 58	11 ♋ 30
Aug 26, 2010	17 ♍ 19	07 ♈ 41	10 ♎ 36	20 ♉ 56	05 ♍ 53	23 ♌ 57	17 ♉ 58	04 ♈ 47	14 ♋ 14
Sep 5, 2010	21 ♍ 49	06 ♈ 19	14 ♎ 04	23 ♉ 17	10 ♍ 25	27 ♌ 50	18 ♉ 37	03 ♈ 03	16 ♋ 38
Sep 15, 2010	26 ♍ 24	04 ♈ 29	17 ♎ 37	24 ♉ 60	15 ♍ 00	01 ♍ 40	18 ♉ 45	00 ♈ 56	18 ♋ 36
Sep 25, 2010	01 ♎ 03	02 ♈ 26	21 ♎ 12	25 ♉ 57	19 ♍ 27	05 ♍ 27	18 ♉ 20	28 ♓ 39	20 ♋ 06
Oct 5, 2010	05 ♎ 47	00 ♈ 24	24 ♎ 50	26 ♉ 03	24 ♍ 16	09 ♍ 08	17 ♉ 22	26 ♓ 28	21 ♋ 02
Oct 15, 2010	10 ♎ 34	28 ♓ 39	28 ♎ 29	25 ♉ 13	28 ♍ 56	12 ♍ 43	15 ♉ 54	24 ♓ 37	21 ♋ 21
Oct 25, 2010	15 ♎ 25	27 ♓ 21	02 ♏ 08	23 ♉ 33	03 ♎ 37	16 ♍ 11	14 ♉ 02	23 ♓ 18	20 ♋ 58
Nov 4, 2010	20 ♎ 18	26 ♓ 38	05 ♏ 46	21 ♉ 12	08 ♎ 16	19 ♍ 37	11 ♉ 56	22 ♓ 35	19 ♋ 52
Nov 14, 2010	25 ♎ 15	26 ♓ 34	09 ♏ 24	18 ♉ 31	12 ♎ 54	22 ♍ 37	09 ♉ 49	22 ♓ 31	18 ♋ 07
Nov 24, 2010	00 ♏ 13	27 ♓ 06	12 ♏ 58	15 ♉ 58	17 ♎ 29	25 ♍ 31	07 ♉ 54	23 ♓ 05	15 ♋ 49
Dec 4, 2010	05 ♏ 12	28 ♓ 13	16 ♏ 29	13 ♉ 56	22 ♎ 01	28 ♍ 09	06 ♉ 23	24 ♓ 13	13 ♋ 13
Dec 14, 2010	10 ♏ 12	29 ♓ 51	19 ♏ 55	12 ♉ 42	26 ♎ 27	00 ♎ 29	05 ♉ 22	25 ♓ 52	10 ♋ 36
Dec 24, 2010	15 ♏ 12	01 ♈ 55	23 ♏ 14	12 ♉ 23	00 ♏ 46	02 ♎ 27	04 ♉ 56	27 ♓ 57	08 ♋ 15

Appendix C

Astro Communications Services Order Form

The following information can be used to order your birth chart, Lifetime Lunar Phase and Dark Goddess reports from ACS. You can write to them or better yet, call their toll free phone number for faster and more efficient service.

Dark Goddess Listing $5.00

Lifetime Lunar Phases Report $5.00
Shipping/Handling [per order](Can/Mex $3, Overseas $4) $3.00

Include birthplace, birth date, and birthtime

Astro Communications Services
5521 Ruffin Road, San Diego, CA 92123-1314
Call toll free nationwide
1-800-888-9983

Also by ACS Publications

All About Astrology Series of booklets
The American Atlas, Expanded Fifth Edition (Shanks)
The American Book of Tables (Michelsen)
The American Ephemeris Series 1901-2000
The American Ephemeris for the 20th Century [Noon or Midnight] 1900 to 2000,
    Rev. Fifth Edition
The American Ephemeris for the 21st Century 2001-2050, Rev. Second Edition
The American Heliocentric Ephemeris 1901-2000
The American Sidereal Ephemeris 1976-2000
Asteroid Goddesses (George & Bloch)
Astro-Alchemy (Negus)
Astro Essentials (Pottenger)
Astrological Games People Play (Ashman)
Astrological Insights into Personality (Lundsted)
Astrology for the Light Side of the Brain (Rogers-Gallagher)
Basic Astrology: A Guide for Teachers & Students (Negus)
Basic Astrology: A Workbook for Students (Negus)
The Book of Jupiter (Waram)
The Book of Neptune (Waram)
The Book of Pluto (Forrest)
The Changing Sky (Forrest)
Complete Horoscope Interpretation (Pottenger)
Cosmic Combinations (Negus)
Dial Detective (Simms)
Easy Tarot Guide (Masino)
Expanding Astrology's Universe (Dobyns)
Hands That Heal (Burns)
Healing with the Horoscope (Pottenger)
The Inner Sky (Forrest)
The International Atlas, Revised Third Edition (Shanks)
The Koch Book of Tables (Michelsen)
Midpoints (Munkasey)
New Insights into Astrology (Press)
The Night Speaks (Forrest)
The Only Way to... Learn Astrology, Vols. I-VI (March & McEvers)
    Volume I - Basic Principles
    Volume II - Math & Interpretation Techniques
    Volume III - Horoscope Analysis
    Volume IV- Learn About Tomorrow: Current Patterns
    Volume V - Learn About Relationships: Synastry Techniques
    Volume VI - Learn About Horary and Electional Astrology
Planetary Heredity (M. Gauquelin)
Planetary Planting (Riotte)
Planets in Solar Returns (Shea)
Planets in Work: (Binder)
Planets on the Move (Dobyns/Pottenger)
Psychology of the Planets (F. Gauquelin)
Roadmap to Your Future (Ashman)
Skymates (S. & J. Forrest)
Spirit Guides: We Are Not Alone (Belhayes)
Tables of Planetary Phenomena (Michelsen)
Twelve Wings of the Eagle (Simms)
Your Magical Child (Simms)
Your Starway to Love (Pottenger)